Jewel of Truth

Boundary's Fall

Jewel of Truth
Book Three of Boundary's Fall

by

Bret Funk

Tyrannosaurus Press LLC
Zachary, LA
www.TyrannosaurusPress.com

JEWEL OF TRUTH
Book Three of Boundary's Fall

First Printing 2006. All books for distribution in the United States were printed and bound in the U.S.A. All rights reserved. No part of this book may be reproduced in any form or by any means, electronic or mechanical—except by reviewers who may quote passages to be printed in magazines, newspapers, or on the web—without permission in writing from the author.

This book is printed on acid free paper.

ISBN-10: 0-9718819-2-8
ISBN-13: 978-0-9718819-2-1
LCCN: 2005928154

Cover art by Doug Roper

For Information Contact:

Tyrannosaurus Press
5624 Fairway Drive
Zachary, LA 70791
www.TyrannosaurusPress.com

To Danis

For morning coffee and all day tea.
For offering us a home when the waters came.
For reading my books before they're good enough to read.
For strength and dignity under incomprehensible circumstances.

This book is for you

What are critics saying about *Path of Glory*?

[*Path of Glory*] launches an epic fantasy that combines a vivid back-history with strong characterization to produce a memorable tale that belongs in most fantasy collections.

— Library Journal

Path of Glory is an entertaining epic and a deftly written saga of hope, determination, and courage.

— Midwest Book Review

If the following books keep the promise of [*Path of Glory*], then [Boundary's Fall] will certainly be a series to follow.

— Quantum Muse Magazine

Path of Glory marks a good start to what should be a great career.

— Scifantastic Magazine

Path of Glory is a captivating tale in which you follow Jeran and his close friends on their journey from boys, to men, and ultimately to leaders of men.

— SFRevu

Path of Glory makes the classic fantasy approachable for every reader, even those turned off by fantasy series in the past.

— Weedhopper Press

Path of Glory is epic fantasy in the tradition of *The Lord of the Rings* and the *Shannara* series.

— Baryon Magazine

Path of Glory is another wonderful story about three friends who have secret pasts and struggle against the evils in the world.

— Dark Moon Rising Magazine

Funk shines when it comes to characterization.

— The Harrow

What are critics saying about *Sword of Honor*?

Funk has shown his creativity in raising the standards and making this series stand apart and have a fresh appeal.

— Baryon Magazine

[Sword of Honor] continues an epic tale that should appeal to fans of high fantasy and multivolume series. A good choice for most libraries.

— Library Journal

Sword of Honor is a smoother and more consistent. The end is thrillingly dark, certain to leave the reader eager to pick up the next book of Boundary's Fall.

— The Harrow

[Sword of Honor] is a really entertaining story told through the eyes of genuine characters.

— SFRevu

[Sword of Honor] is populated with realistic characters who have human faults and foibles... The plot, told from various points of view, reads quickly and contains violence, intrigue, pathos, and much humor.

— School Library Journal

Sword of Honor combines myth and magic, good and evil, intrigue and even star-crossed interracial love stories – a real pleasure to read.

— Scifantastic Magazine

The overarching themes – overcoming differences, self-doubt, good versus evil – are universal. The storylines, while not overly simplistic, are simple enough to follow and should appeal to both young and more experienced readers.

—Curled Up With A Good Book

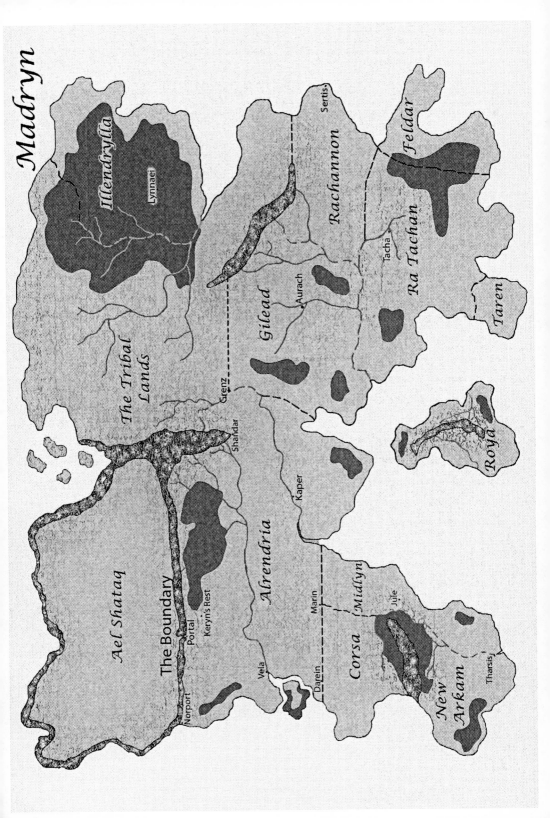

"Truth has many facets, and the Jewel of Truth is not an easy burden to bear. Calling something a treasure does not make it one, and seeing the truth is not always a gift. There are as many truths as there are people, and fewer lies than you might believe. Truthsense is more a curse than a blessing; only the Gods should see into the hearts of men."

— The Elder, Falkon

Remembrance

He galloped across the plains, his sandy blonde hair blowing in the wind. Guardsmen trailed behind him, sword or bow in hand, none sure what to expect. The hills whipped by, and the only sound other than the wind was the thunder of his horse's hooves, but he urged his mount for even greater speed. "Faster," he cried. "We must go faster!" The powerful horse snorted a cloud of steam, and they pulled ahead of the Guardsmen; the soldiers' mounts could not keep pace with his magnificent warhorse.

"Gods," Aryn prayed, "don't let me be too late. If you'll ever answer one of my prayers, answer this one!" Mindless of the rough terrain, the rider squeezed his eyes shut to force away tears. He trusted his mount completely. She had seen him through more dangers than he could count and into more battles than he had ever wanted to fight. She did not need him to guide her.

He rode for an eternity, until the Guardsmen were distant specks. Topping a hill, he brought his horse to a skidding stop. From his vantage point he surveyed the countryside. To the east a line of wagons burned. Lifeless shapes littered the ground around the caravan. "Maybe he saved her!" Hope surged, and the white mare bolted forward, flying down the hill as if she were fresh from the stable.

Even before reaching the caravan an evil pall enveloped Aryn, clinging thickly to the air. Uneasiness descended upon him, and he dropped from the saddle, sword in hand. He moved forward slowly, expecting an ambush at any moment.

Bodies littered the ground, many more than he had seen from the hilltop. A few wore the armor of the Guard, but most were clad in the dark grey of the Durange. Arrows riddled most corpses, but a few bore the grievous wounds of heated melee. A groan drew the rider's attention, and when he saw a Tachan roll over, he fought the urge to make the man suffer.

I won't torture him! No matter how much evil the Tachans bring to Madryn, I won't become like them! Aryn repeated this thought while he searched. He combed through the wreckage and despaired of ever finding what he sought. When a solitary moan drifted to his ears, he winced. The cry was full of anguish, but the voice was a familiar one. He sheathed his sword and hurried through the carnage, calling out her name.

He found her in the shadow of a wagon, beaten and broken. The blood staining her lips was the only color on her too-pale face. Her eyes were sunken and swollen, her lustrous hair matted and disheveled. A tattered dress barely covered a body blackened by dark bruises. Despite her wounds, she still had a radiance, a great beauty. The abuse suffered at the hands of the Durange had marred her body, but it had not despoiled her spirit. Tears filled Aryn's eyes at the sight of her. He thought her dead, and he cursed himself for being too slow.

"Tachan monsters! Of all your crimes, this is the worst! I'll see you dead for this. All of you! Dead!" He regretted the words instantly. She would have disapproved. She had always been the voice of peace, the voice of reason.

He reached out and touched her, and his tears—this time joyful—fell anew when her eyes fluttered open. "Aryn?" she whispered. Carefully, he picked her up and, shocked by her weightlessness, carried her away from the burning wagon.

He set her upon lush grass in a field of wildflowers, the last of the season, and unhooked a small flask from his belt. Falling to the ground beside her, he cradled her head in his lap and tenderly touched the flask to her lips. She responded to the touch, drinking deeply. Her eyes opened, and as Aryn gazed into those twin orbs of brilliant blue, so full of pain, a wave of grief washed over him. For her sake, he forced a smile. "Aryn," she whispered, her voice strained and hoarse. "Good… to see you."

"Peace, Illendre. Don't speak. You must save your strength. All will be well."

"The baby…"

Aryn touched Illendre's swollen abdomen. Almost immediately he felt movement. "The child is well, Illendre. Now rest. Help is on its way."

"No…" came Illendre's weak reply, "Aryn… the baby… comes. You must help—" A violent contraction cut off the rest. Her body spasmed and she groaned.

"Gods!" Aryn whispered fiercely. He removed his coat and tucked it beneath Illendre's head as a pillow. Then, he carefully worked himself out from under her and moved to her legs. He stared for a moment, and then frantically said, "I don't know what to do!"

A strange sound reached Aryn's ears, weak and lifeless, so unlike Illendre's musical laughter. "The baby is well," Illendre said, having regained some measure of strength. "You have but to catch him." She propped herself up, though it took much effort, and adjusted her makeshift pillow. "There's some time yet," she told him, patting the ground at her side. "Sit by me a moment. I'll tell you when the baby needs you."

Aryn obeyed, and he took Illendre's hand as he sat beside her, squeezing it gently. Some color returned to her face, and a measure of her beauty reappeared. She was still but a shadow of her self, and though Aryn refused to believe it, he saw death in her eyes. "Where's Alic?" he asked, hoping a change of subject would lessen the weight on his heart.

Illendre shook her head weakly. Another wave of pain rolled across her eyes. "He ambushed the Tachans before midday." Aryn looked at the sky; the sun stood well past its zenith. "They came as if from nowhere, howling like they, themselves, were wolves. I saw Alic several times during the battle. He was wild, almost unrecognizable."

"His love for you is strong," Aryn told her. "So strong it clouds his reason. When news of your capture came to us at Merriadoc, Alic begged King Faldar to release him from his oath so he could search for you." The memory was a painful one. "I think he would have come even if Faldar had refused."

A smile touched Illendre's lips, brightening her face. "Ever was Alic impetuous," she said, "and given to rash thought. Not like you, my sweet, sagacious Aryn."

Aryn stroked her cheek fondly. "But where's Alic?" he asked. "Surely he wouldn't abandon you after crossing half of Gilead!"

"I tried to escape in the"—another contraction wracked Illendre's body, and she clutched at Aryn, begging his indulgence—"in the confusion of the battle. But I was careless, and someone struck me from behind. When Alic came upon me, he found me motionless. I heard his words but could speak none of my own, nor could I reassure him that I lived." The admission pained Illendre, and Aryn could say nothing to ease her hurt.

"Rage overcame Alic's sense." At this, Illendre chuckled, though the laugh turned to a cough, and a thin stream of blood trickled from her mouth. "I always believed there to be a bit of Garun'ah in my beloved's veins." Aryn returned her smile, but his eyes drifted to the hilltop, and he willed help to arrive quickly.

"His rage overcame him," Illendre repeated, "and he swore to hunt down Tylor and exact his revenge." Aryn's heart ached at Illendre's suffering. He wanted to lessen her pain—he would have taken it if he had known how!—but all he could do was daub her brow with a moist strip of cloth torn from his shirt.

Illendre's smile faded. "What of my father? And the Magi?"

Aryn shook his head. "The Magi remain hidden. If they aid us, we have yet to see it. Nor has anyone seen Aemon." Illendre's eyes closed sadly, and Aryn hastily added, "But there's been evidence of his passage, if one knows what signs to look for. Your father may be keeping his whereabouts unknown, but he still fights for Alrendria."

With that news, Illendre breathed easier, and for a time she was silent except when the contractions wracked her body. Watching her, Aryn's hope began to wane, and as usual, Illendre saw into his heart. "Yes, my friend," she confessed, "my time grows short. Soon my son will be born, and then my purpose will be ended."

Aryn scrubbed at his eyes. "You can't leave me! You can't leave Alic! You're needed now more than ever."

"And yet my life is spent just the same." For an instant, the fire returned to her voice, and the power of the Gift made her eyes flare a brilliant blue. "The world existed long before my coming. It will survive my passing just as well."

"*I* will not," Aryn told her. "This world will be cold without the warmth of your smile, dark without the sparkle of your eyes." Illendre slumped, and for a moment, Aryn feared her dead. "Don't leave me, Illendre!" he cried, taking her hand. "I love you!"

Her eyes opened again, and a sad smile pulled at her lips. With a trembling hand, she caressed Aryn's cheek. "And I love you, Aryn. In many ways, you are dearer to me than Alic." Aryn turned away, and Illendre chided him for his guilt. "It is never a crime to love, and loving does not mean you have betrayed the trust of a friend. Or a brother. Alic and I share a heart, and my love for him will always be pure. But you and I share a soul, and my love for you is just as great."

Illendre turned paled, and she groaned. This time, the contraction lasted far longer. "It's time," she told Aryn. "This child will wait no longer." Aryn made to move, but Illendre held his arm, and the force of her grip surprised him. "You must promise me something." Aryn could tell that no refusal would be accepted.

"Anything! Should you wish it, I'll carry your body to Shandar and dig your grave with my own hands. Should you want the Darklord killed, I'll walk the blighted lands of *Ael Shataq* until Lorthas lies dead at my feet!"

"Dear Aryn," Illendre replied, and her laughter was a balm to his pain. "What I ask is far less dangerous, though no less important." Her eyes tightened as another contraction tore at her body, and she fought the urge to cry out. "I ask only that you care for my son, your nephew, as if he were your own."

"That… That is Alic's duty," he said, shaking his head.

Illendre nodded, though a shadow lay across her eyes. "And I would not take such a grand duty from him, but I'd rather my son become an artist and poet like you than a warrior like his father." Aryn tried to protest, but Illendre silenced him. "I know he'll have battles to fight, and his own burdens to bear. Much like you. But Alic is all warrior, more akin to Tylor Durange than he'd ever admit. He hasn't found the balance you have, and he would raise our son as he was raised."

"Your son will need such training," Aryn reminded her. "He'll be First of House Odara after Alic."

"And he'll receive training," Illendre assured him. "If not from Alic, then from you and Mathis. Or Gideon. Or Joam. Or even Iban, though I'd never have suspected such a tiger lurked beneath the dove's wings. There are thousands to teach my son how to command, but few who can teach him how to care.

"You have an understanding few outside the Magi ever attain," she added, "and even fewer truly appreciate. My son will be surrounded by teachers, and Alic will have him protected by a thousand swords, but there's only one guardian who I trust with such an important task."

A tense silence followed as Aryn warred with himself. "I swear on my life and House Odara to care for your son, to protect him from all harm, and to teach him all I can, meager knowledge though it may be."

"A poet to the last," Illendre chuckled. "I will take this memory of you to the Heavens and wait eagerly until we walk the Twilight World together." Illendre's eyes turned dim and distant; her voice grew strained. "Now quick! The baby comes!"

Despite the blood and the eternity of pained screams, it was over faster than Aryn expected, and before he knew it, he held a screaming child in his arms. He cut the lifecord and used what remained of his water to wipe the blood and birth from the newborn boy. He had eyes much like Illendre's and a shock of black hair upon his head. The nose was Alic's. As Aryn held the child, he felt an instant bond of love. "Look at your son, Illendre," he said, holding up the baby. "Never has a more beautiful creature been born in all of Madryn!"

He received no response, and when Aryn leaned to the side, he saw that lifeless eyes beheld the child. Drawing a shuddering breath, he willed his grief to leave until he found a better place to mourn.

With the child cradled against his chest, Aryn composed Illendre's corpse and closed her eyes. Then he took the coat from beneath her and swaddled the baby in it. Behind him, he heard the thunder of hooves as the Guard galloped down the hill. Torin, Aryn's subcommander, dropped from the saddle before his horse had fully stopped. "It was foolish to run so far ahead, Lord Odara."

Aryn laughed, though he felt no joy in it. "I follow my brother, Torin. We'll find no living Tachans within a league of his passage."

Torin nodded and noticed the bundle in Aryn's arms. His gaze quickly dropped to the ground, and a strangled cry escaped his lips. "We're too late!"

"I arrived with time enough to watch her die." Aryn looked for the last time upon the Lady Illendre. Black hair circled her head in a cloud, a warm smile was on her lips, and some small measure of color had returned to her cheeks. She looked to be asleep, and Aryn knew he could never bear to ruin this memory of her. "One duty remains to us. We must ride to my brother's aid, and lead him back to Alrendria. The Tachans are routed. The war is over."

"What of the child?" Torin asked. "Should I take him to Kaper?"

"The boy stays with me!" Aryn snapped. He regretted his anger, but he did not apologize for it. "He goes to meet his father." He gestured toward Illendre's body. "Select five of your most trusted men and have them take her to Shandar. She's to be buried beside her mother."

The baby shrieked, and Aryn glanced at the child squirming uncomfortably in its swaddling. "We passed a farm not many leagues back. Send a Guardsman to fetch some milk, or better yet, have him bring someone who knows about the raising of children. The rest of the Guard is to follow me!"

Jedelle came to Aryn's whistle, and he climbed into the saddle. Horse and rider were so well suited that Aryn rode at full gallop without fear of falling, even with the infant tucked awkwardly under one arm. They rode for leagues, to the south and east, until the sun hung low in the western sky. When they topped a rise overlooking a broad field and saw two armies facing each other, Aryn slowed. When he realized that the two forces faced each other without fighting, he stopped completely.

A lone rider broke away from the nearest host and hurried to Aryn's side. Aryn put his hand on his sword, ready to draw at the first sign of danger, but he relaxed when he recognized Larence, one of his brother's subcommanders. "Lord Odara!" Larence said, bowing from horseback. "Welcome to the battle. I urge you to hurry should you wish to see the end of this fight. They've battled half the day, and though no clear victor is in sight, mere men can't fight so fiercely forever."

Confused, Aryn cast his gaze into the valley. "I see no fight, only two armies staring at each other as if hard looks could cut like arrows."

"Then you don't look well enough, my Lord, for your brother has challenged Tylor the Bull to single combat. As we speak they wage a private war between the bounds of their armies.

A worried frown creased Aryn's brow. "Wait here, Larence. No, wait in the valley behind me. I lead a host of Guardsmen nearly equal in strength to my brother's. Intercept them before they're seen and bid them travel in secrecy to the far side of the valley."

"Lord Alic has promised freedom to the Tachans should he be the one to fall!"

"And should he fall," Aryn replied, "then they'll have it. Tell Torin to stay his attack until our armies are joined, but have him ready to fly at a moment's notice! I don't trust the Tachans. Treachery follows them close."

Larence saluted, fist-on-heart, and rode west to meet Aryn's Guardsmen. Aryn, in turn, rode into the valley, and before long he heard the clash of steel on steel, the angry taunts of Tylor Durange, and the stoic replies of his brother.

The Guard stepped aside at his approach, and Aryn rode through without comment, intent on reaching the front line. Joam Batai scrubbed a hand through his thick, curly brown hair and smiled when he saw Aryn. "Glad you could join us!" he laughed.

Aryn nodded but did not reply. He focused his attention on the battle. Alic stood near the Alrendrians. He had aged since Aryn had last seen him, though it had only been days. His sandy blonde hair, streaked with grey, was slick with sweat. New wrinkles cut deep rents across his once fair face, and his brow sagged as if drawn down by a heavy weight. The scowl he wore added winters to his life.

Alic saw his younger brother and ducked his head in grim greeting. Tylor noticed the movement and stepped back. At just over thirty winters, the Bull of Ra Tachan was nearly a score of winters Alic's junior. A mane of thick hair capped his arrogant face. He wore full armor but had cast aside the bull-headed helmet that gave him his name. Angry eyes glared at Aryn. "So, you decided to join the fight after all. Good! I'll deal with you after I finish with your brother. Then this feud will be ended!"

"So it will, Durange," Alic answered, his voice a booming baritone, "but long before you lay a hand on Aryn. And even should I fall, I'd be wary of challenging him. Small though he may be, he's still an Odaran wolf, and his bite stings as much as mine!" With that, Alic unleashed a volley of attacks.

Tylor retreated, but he quickly regained his footing, and his return attack was ferocious. Alic, a master of the blade, easily turned it aside, and the two combatants fell into a rhythm, much like a dance. It was a mesmerizing thing to watch.

The rider to Aryn's right leaned toward him. "How fares the war?"

Aryn risked a brief glance. "Gideon!" he called out joyfully, but his mood quickly sobered. "The war goes well. We won back Merriadoc, and the Tachans have been driven from Alrendria. The remnants of their army flee across Gilead, hoping to find shelter in Ra Tachan." He could not tell the good without the bad, and a pang of loss entered his voice. "But the victory is bittersweet. Faldar fell at Merriadoc. Mathis is king."

Joam let out a strangled cry, and Gideon's expression grew grim. "Bittersweet indeed, my friend. Faldar will be missed. But what is that in your arms? Do you desire a family so much you've taken to coddling your sword as you would a child? If so, perhaps a battlefield's no longer a site you should frequent."

Gideon's words brought a genuine smile to Aryn's lips. He held up the infant. "I hold Alic's son."

Dark brown eyes widened in shock. "Then she lives!" Gideon words carried the excitement of newfound hope. "Alic swore she was dead."

"She is," Aryn snapped. "Alic's rage blinded him to the truth, and this feud has cost him a wife who might have lived."

"If that's Alic's son," Joam said, "then Gideon's right. This is no place for you!" The two warriors urged Aryn to leave.

"I'll stay to show Alic his son," Aryn replied, turning his attention back to the duel. He refused to let their words sway him. "If battle is joined, I'll take the boy to safety."

The fighting had grown fiercer, as if the combatants grew less tired with the passage of time instead of more so. They exchanged blows constantly, though few hit armor; most were parried or dodged long before they struck. Alic and Tylor spun in a tight circle, neither able to get the upper hand, and both armies watched, awed by the display. Tylor taunted Alic, casting aspersions upon his House and Alrendria both. Alic ignored the jibes, except to laugh them off, and his indifference infuriated the Bull, driving Tylor to make even more cutting comments, to speak of things closer to Alic's heart.

"Your wife was sweet, Odara!" Tylor laughed when he saw his words strike home. "Did you truly think I had her all this time, drugged so her 'Gift' was useless, and did not avail myself of her?"

"She'd never have allowed it!" Alic snarled. "Drugged or no, she'd never have allowed it."

"Perhaps not," Tylor shrugged, swinging his sword in a vicious backhand. "But I held the life of her child forfeit, should she resist." His smile was cruel. "A beauty, Illendre was. Sweet as no other creature in all of Madryn."

Alic screamed, and Aryn's cry echoed it. Both Gideon and Joam had to restrain him. "It's single combat!" Joam cried. In his other ear, Gideon said, "The child! Don't forget the child!"

But Alic needed no help; Tylor's words were boon enough. He pounded the Bull with a series of mighty blows, bellowing with every strike. Tylor realized his mistake too late, and he retreated across the field, unable to do anything other than deflect Alic's onslaught.

With a triumphant shout, Alic slipped his blade through Tylor's guard and sliced a gash across the Bull's face. Tylor screamed and clapped a hand over his left eye. He raised his own sword for an answering blow, but Alic was faster. His blade clanged against Tylor's and the black sword shattered. It fell to the ground in pieces.

With his remaining eye, Tylor stared dumbly at the remnants of his sword. Blood gushed from beneath his hand, running in a river down his arm. He fell to his knees; the hilt of his sword dropped useless to the grass. "Mercy, Odara."

"Mercy?" Alic repeated. "What mercy did you show the Gileans? What mercy did you show Shandar or the Magi who dwelled there?" Alic's gaze turned hateful. "What mercy did you show Illendre?" He drew back his sword for the killing blow.

"Wait!" Tylor begged, and Alic stayed his hand. Weak laughter bubbled from the Bull's throat. "You claim to be so much better than me, yet in the end, I discover we're the same. Hatred burns in you as hotly as it does in me. You're no nobler than I. Just luckier!"

Alic hesitated. Slowly, he lowered his blade. "I'm not like you, Durange!"

A shadow burst from among the Tachan soldiers, and Aryn realized what was happening too late. "Alic!" he yelled as Salos stepped forward. "Betrayal!"

Alic moved, but not fast enough. The dagger, thrown from an impossible distance, drove through Alic's armor with a sickening screech. Alic's eyes widened in surprise and then closed. His blade fell to the ground beside Tylor's.

Gideon drew his sword. "Betrayal!" he shouted. "For Alrendria and Alic Odara!" The Guardsmen rushed forward, surprising the Tachans with the speed of their attack. The army that appeared on the hill behind them surprised them even more.

Alic fell to his knees opposite Tylor. Only a few hands separated him from the Bull of Ra Tachan. "Ironic," Tylor chuckled. "It looks like you'll beat me to the Twilight World after all, if only by a few moments!" Aryn rushed to Alic's side and drove a fist into Tylor's temple on the way. The Bull crumpled, and with a satisfied grunt, Aryn turned to face his brother.

Though many winters separated their births, they were as close as brothers could be, and Aryn felt the weight on his shoulders grow heavier when he saw Alic's expression. He had seen the same look in Illendre's eyes. "Don't you leave me too!" His voice brought Alic back from the brink.

"Aryn." Alic opened his eyes, and a warm smile replaced his frown, exposing teeth stained red with blood. "I don't have much choice. Shouldn't have trusted the Tachans. But I had to avenge Illendre."

"It was the Scorpion," Aryn explained, easing Alic into a seated position.

Alic nodded knowingly, but shook his head when Aryn reached for the blade. "Leave it," he commanded. "Pulling it will do no good, and leaving it will prolong my time with you, if only for a moment." He looked at the bundle in Aryn's arms. "What's that you bring? My Naming Day's a few days off, and I'm unaccustomed to getting presents in the field."

Aryn cleared the covers from the infant's face and held the child out. "It's your son!" he announced.

"My son?" Alic blinked in confusion. "Then she lives?" Hope and regret tinged his words.

"No longer," Aryn told him, and though the heat of his anger had departed, he added, "Yet she lived when you came upon her, you fool!"

"My son," Alic repeated, cocking his head to the side. "She is there!" he said after a moment. "I can see her in his eyes!" He reached out a hand, then withdrew it. "May I hold him?" he asked, as if he had no right to his own child.

Aryn gave the boy to his father but stayed close, lest Alic's strength fail. Around them, the Guardsmen drove the Tachans from the field. Some small pockets resisted, groups of desperate men who feared to face justice for their crimes, but the Alrendrians would not let their betrayal go unpunished. "I can see both of you in him," Aryn assured his brother. "He'll make you proud."

"Jeran," Alic said, clutching the child to his chest. "Call him Jeran." He held the infant a moment longer, and then handed the bundle back to Aryn. "Best you hold him. I don't know how much life remains within me. My legs grow numb."

A strained silence followed. "How fares the war?" Alic asked, but when Aryn tried to tell him, he raised a hand. "No, there's less time than I thought. Soon I'll join Illendre in the Heavens, and then I'll learn all I need to know." Alic's skin grew pale, and the fire in his eyes died. "You must promise me something, little brother," he said, his voice growing weak.

Aryn fought to hold his tears in check. "You'll be First after me," Alic told him, and something in his brother's voice told Aryn that this was not the promise. "That much I discussed with Faldar, and he agreed. But now an even greater duty falls to you. You must raise Jeran in my stead, as both father and mother. You must teach him how to be a warrior, how to lead men so he can take the title of First when you are finished with it."

Aryn started to shake his head, but Alic grabbed his arm. "There are few in this world I love, little brother, and none but you to whom I'd entrust my son."

"I swear to do what you ask of me, Alic, to the best of my abilities. But I've already sworn a promise to another, and doing both may prove impossible."

The smile on Alic's face grew broader. "She got to you before me, eh?" he asked, and laughed weakly when Aryn nodded. "I accept your promise, Aryn, though it's not the one I wished for. Train my Jeran how to lead and I'll be happy, but train him first how to love, for I'm sure such was the oath you swore to Illendre."

Alic swayed, and Aryn guided his brother to the ground. "I can see them!" Alic said, awed. "Paeya and Yurien, and a stranger who beckons for me to join them. And there's Faldar! You beat me there, you old devil! And..." Alic's voice faded, but his empty face suddenly came alive. "There she is! Can you see her, Aryn? She's as beautiful as ever, with her hair blowing in the wind and such a sweet smile on her face! She's waiting for me."

Struggling for breath, the great warrior slowly raised his hands to his throat and, with great difficulty, removed the wolf's-head medallion and offered it to Aryn. "For Jeran. When the time's right." Aryn, his hand trembling, took the necklace, and Alic's eyes closed to near slits.

Tears stained Aryn's cheeks, but he made no move to wipe them away. Alic's eyes cleared one last time. "You always were a crier!" he laughed before growing still.

"And you, Alic, were always a hero," Aryn replied, reaching out to close his brother's eyes.

He sat there until the battle was over, with Jeran cradled in one arm and Alic's head in the other. When Gideon returned, he led a long line of Tachan prisoners, the Scorpion among them. "What should we do with them?" Gideon asked. "Kill them here?"

Aryn shook his head. "Take them to Kaper. Their fate is King Mathis' decision." As he stood, Aryn looked at the trampled field and the weary faces of his men. "Dress Tylor's wounds," he ordered. "Bind him and the Scorpion tightly, and keep both under constant guard. If any of their wagons remain unburned, we'll give them a taste of their own tender care." He looked down at Alic. "Five Guardsmen ride to Shandar bearing the body of the Lady Illendre. Alic would want to be near his wife."

The Guardsmen hurried to carry out Aryn's orders, and after pausing to lay a comforting hand on Aryn's shoulder, Gideon led the prisoners from the field. Aryn looked at the child in his arms, all that remained of his family. "Ready, Jeran?" he asked, and it seemed as if the boy smiled at him. "We have a long ride ahead of us."

Chapter 1

The setting sun cast crisp, white rays upon Kaper, and the snow-capped buildings amplified the light until the city burned brighter than the sun. The ancient estates of the old city lay silent and empty. Many of the noblemen had left to bring their Families news of the war; most of the remainder had fled, certain the Durange would strike at the heart of the Alrendria.

Beyond Old Kaper, beyond the magic-wrought Wall circling the heart of a city, the new city teemed with life. Columns of smoke rose from the chimneys like a multitude of fingers stretching toward the heavens, and the sound of singing drifted through the streets when the wind caught it. A handful of indistinct forms, heads ducked low and cloaks drawn tight to brace themselves against the bitter wind, hurried down the avenues. The cold air burned the lungs, and the stronger gusts threw bits of ice with enough strength to drive all but the heartiest to their homes.

Prince Martyn stood at the summit of the castle's highest tower, staring north. He shivered, but not from cold. His right hand gripped the hilt of his sword, and the press of metal against his flesh comforted him. With his left hand, he scrubbed at the icy tracks running the length of his cheeks.

At his right stood Treloran, Prince of Illendrylla and heir to the Aelvin Empire. A thick, fur-lined coat hung around the Elf's shoulders, but Treloran was not troubled by the cold either. He, too, stared north, but his pale green eyes were drawn farther east than Martyn's. The Aelvin Prince appeared as if from the legends: tall and proud, with slanted eyes, pointed ears, and more than a share of arrogance and condescension. Yet Martyn had discovered far more beneath Treloran's icy exterior than haughtiness and disdain for the frivolity of man; he had found a brother, a man who shared his fears and hopes. He had found a friend.

Howling winds whipped around the tower, drowning out most sound and driving the cold to the bone. Yet the frigid air could not match the chill in Martyn's heart. No wind, no matter how violent, could match his fury.

A carelessly-placed footfall broke the thin layer of ice on the tower's stones with an audible crack, but the two princes barely reacted. Treloran casually glanced over his shoulder; Martyn did not move. "War is coming," King Mathis said as he took a place at Martyn's side. "You should be more wary."

"You're the only one who uses this tower, Father," Martyn replied, his words measured.

"All the more reason to be careful," Mathis said, trying to hide his frustration. "The place where you feel safest is the best place for an assassin to attack."

The King's warning had little impact. "I defeated the *Noedra Synissti* before."

"Don't confuse good fortune with good ability," Mathis snapped, but he then drew a steadying breath and placed a hand on Martyn's shoulder. When

19

Martyn recoiled from the touch, Mathis sighed, but he made no further attempt to reassure his son. "And don't let pride open you to danger."

"I don't want a lecture. Not now."

Mathis frowned, but he went to the edge of the tower and leaned out over the cold stone. Silence swallowed them, and each man was left to his own thoughts. After a while, the King said, "A messenger arrived from Portal."

Martyn came to life immediately. "Why didn't you tell me? What did he say?" Something in his father's gaze, or the way the King hesitated, made Martyn guess the truth before Mathis voiced it. "Lord Talbot's found no sign of Tylor," Martyn said, his teeth grinding together.

"No." Mathis shook his head. "Nor does he have any idea where the breach in the Boundary is."

"He's been looking for both for more than seven winters!" Martyn's scowl deepened. "You'd think the old fool would have found something." Under his breath, he muttered, "I could almost suspect him of aiding the Durange."

Mathis rounded on his son, grabbed Martyn by the shoulders, and squeezed him with enough force to make the prince wince. "You go too far! Gideon Talbot's loyalty is unquestionable! There are few in this kingdom I trust more than him. I've suffered your brooding, your foul moods and unpredictable rages, but I won't allow you to denounce a good man because you disagree with my decision to keep you in Kaper."

Martyn returned his father's glare. "I'm sorry," he said, struggling to control his anger. "I meant no disrespect."

The King let go slowly. "I know, Martyn. I know."

Their eyes remained locked for a moment; it was Martyn who turned away first. "You're going to tell him to continue the search, right? If he needs more men, we can send more Guardsmen to Portal."

"I've ordered Talbot to return to Portal. Any Guardsmen he doesn't require for defense are being sent to the Corsan border."

"I can't believe you'd abandon him," Martyn said, his voice cold. "After all he did for Alrendria."

"Once Portal's ready for war—"

Martyn cut his father off with a gesture. "I thought Portal was *always* ready for war." He knew instantly that he had pushed too hard. His father's whole demeanor changed. Though he refused to turn around, Martyn sensed the fury boiling beneath the King's stern glare.

"Once Portal's ready for war," Mathis repeated, his voice the forced calm of a sea awaiting a storm, "Lord Talbot will expand along the Boundary, fortifying watch stations and guard posts. Even if Tylor has hidden his encampments with magic, he must move supplies through the mountains. Given enough time, we will flush the Durange—"

"Enough time! Jeran's been a prisoner for two seasons! That's time enough, if you ask me! If we send a strong enough force, Lord Talbot could search the whole Boundary before the end of spring."

"And where will these Guardsmen come from?" Mathis demanded. "Our eastern border, or our southern one?"

Both fronts had seen some fighting, and all indications were that the skirmishes would escalate as soon as the snows melted. The Guard was spread out, its ranks thinned by winters of peace. Sending more men north was not an option. Martyn knew that, but he ignored the whispering voice in the back of his mind that echoed his father's words. "Who knows how long they'll keep Jeran alive!"

"He may already be dead!" Mathis shouted. "If he is, then we waste time and Guardsmen searching for him. We have neither in abundance." Mathis saw his son's pain and made an effort to calm himself. "I want Jeran back too. But we can't put Alrendria at risk for one man. Not even Jeran Odara."

Martyn's gaze returned to the north. "He wouldn't abandon me."

"*He* is not the Prince of Alrendria."

A strained silence descended over them. Martyn's obligations as Prince of Alrendria had become a common topic, and Martyn hated listening to his father's lectures as much as Mathis hated giving them. He wanted to argue. Imagining Jeran in the clutches of Tylor Durange sickened him. But as usual, Martyn knew he was wrong. Alrendria's enemies would not wait for him to ease his conscience.

In the east, Ryan Durange had reunited most of the Tachan Empire. Only Rachannon remained outside the union, and King Vestlin had no desire to lose the throne he had gained at the end of the Tachan War. He claimed he would bow to no man, not even the Bull, but more than a few Rachannen were ready to cast their lot with the Durange. Vestlin had already put down several bloody rebellions and massed soldiers along the border with Ra Tachan, but the Rachannen had also moved troops to the Gilean border, making it impossible to tell on which side Vestlin meant to fight.

In the west, Corsan incursions into Alrendria had grown more frequent. Reports came daily of villages sacked and peasants murdered. King Murdir had fortified the border as if preparing for an even greater conflict, and Corsan Raiders sailed the waters of the Western Sea in unprecedented numbers. The Black Fleet, the Darklord's navy, posed an even greater threat. They appeared as if from nowhere, sometimes sailing against the wind. The Black Fleet attacked any ship they happened upon and destroyed villages all along the coast. Few lived to tell of the horror of the fleet's passing, and even fewer were willing to return and reclaim their lives.

Midlyn had closed its borders. No one knew which side of the conflict King Hasna meant to join. Mathis expected him to fight alongside Alrendria, but Martyn feared the worst. In his heart, he thought his father did as well. The Elves, who had so readily agreed to reestablish trade with Alrendria, were not as eager for a military alliance. Only a handful supported aiding Alrendria against the Darklord, even though both the Emperor and his granddaughter, Princess Charylla, had offered their support. It would take many seasons to convince *Ael Alluya* to join the war.

But at least they're willing to talk, Martyn thought. *It may not be much, but it's a start*. They had two people to thank for that start: Lord Geffram Iban and Jeran Odara. Iban was dead, and Jeran... Sometimes Martyn hoped Jeran was dead, too. It would be better for him if he were.

Mathis saw Martyn's pensive face and once again guessed his thoughts. "I want Jeran and Dahr back as much as you do," he said. "But if we risk Alrendria just to lessen our guilt, we cheapen their sacrifice." It was not easy for Martyn to abandon his friends; he owed them too much. The Garun'ah could be counted among Alrendria's allies because of Jeran and Dahr. The Tribesmen were fierce and loyal, honorable and brave. In the little time Martyn had spent with them, he had seen the strength needed to survive this war.

Martyn studied his father. The King looked haggard, the weight of command hung heavily around his shoulders. Not for the first time, Martyn saw doubt in his father's eyes, doubt that weakened his resolve. Mathis turned away and drew his cloak tight about his shoulder before starting toward the stairs. Martyn stopped him.

"Let me go north," he pleaded. "Lord Talbot and I might be able to track Tylor to his lair."

"I won't risk you needlessly," Mathis said with a stern shake of his head. "And you'd be little help tracking the Bull. Lord Talbot knows those lands. If Jeran can be found, Gideon will find him." Martyn protested, but Mathis silenced him. "Don't worry, Martyn. You'll have your chance for revenge. Before this war is over, you'll have more blood on your hands than you can imagine."

The King walked away. "Oh, I almost forgot!" he called back, a sly smile on his face. Martyn faced his father stoically, ready for another lecture. His anger simmered beneath the surface, but for now, he had a rein on his temper. "A messenger arrived not long ago. The Aelvin Ambassador will reach Kaper by sunset." Martyn's eyes lit up, and for the first time, the hint of a smile ghosted across his face. "Go and see her," Mathis said.

"I thought you disapproved!"

"I do," Mathis answered slowly. "This bonding can only cause problems. The Emperor should never have forced it on you, especially without consulting with me first. But what's done is done, and I can afford to offend the Elves no more than I can the Gileans. We need both if we are to win this war. Go!" Mathis repeated. "You two will have little enough time to explore your love. You might as well enjoy it while you can."

"How… How do you know I love Kaeille? I never said a word!"

Mathis could not contain his laughter. "Do you really think me a fool, Martyn? What little I couldn't figure out for myself I had only to ask about. You're not as discreet as you think. Just remember, for Alrendria's sake, that you took this Elf as a mistress only because the Emperor demanded it. I don't want our alliance with Gilead threatened by your… exuberance."

Martyn nodded, and Mathis turned to leave. "We'll find Jeran," the King called back as he descended the stairs. "The Five Gods willing, we'll find him unharmed. And if they're not willing, we'll make the Durange pay for it."

"Thank you, Father," Martyn said, and then softer, he added, "And… I'm sorry." As soon as the King's footfalls faded, a broad smile spread across Martyn's face. "Did you hear that, Treloran? The Elves are coming."

"I am frozen, not deaf." Martyn ignored the Aelvin Prince's jest. "It will be nice to have someone to talk to other than Humans."

"You're free to leave any time, Elf! Your presence here is barely tolerated as is." Laughing, he waved for Treloran to follow. "Come! Let's meet them at the gate."

Martyn hurried through the twisting corridors of the castle. He paused to greet the Guardsmen and servants he passed. His earlier sadness had disappeared; thoughts of Kaeille had driven them away.

"Lady Liseyl!" Martyn called as he turned a corner. Liseyl turned away from her charges, two young maids new to the castle. Seeing the prince, she shooed them away and offered a deep curtsy. Martyn inclined his head politely. Liseyl was one of the slaves Jeran had freed in the Tribal Lands; since arriving in Kaper, she had risen quickly through the ranks of servants. "My father says the castle has never run more smoothly than under your care."

"I'm honored, my Prince." Liseyl's cheeks flushed the faintest shade of red. "I do the best I can."

"You had better watch out, though," Martyn warned. "If you do much better, my father may make you responsible for all of Kaper." He winked before hurrying on down the hall, leaving Liseyl staring after him.

A short time later, Martyn skidded to a stop when confronted with his aged, but still imposing, greatmother. "There you are, little Marti," Sionel said, beckoning. Martyn went to her obediently, and she patted his cheek. "Your father was looking for you."

Martyn nodded. "He found me, Greatmother."

"Did he tell you the Elves were coming?"

"Yes, Greatmother."

"Hmmm. Did he tell you we received a message from Lord Talbot?"

"Yes, Greatmother."

"Hmmm," she repeated. This time, she sounded vexed. "Won't Mathis let me tell anyone anything?" she snapped. Her blue-gray eyes narrowed to slits. "Did he tell you that Princess Miriam and a party of Gileans will arrive tomorrow?"

"What?" Martyn exclaimed. "Father said it wouldn't be long, but he didn't say Miriam would be here tomorrow!" He paced the hall, and Treloran wisely stepped out of his way. "I can't believe this!" Martyn shouted, and he mumbled a string of curses harsh enough to make a Corsan raider blanch.

Sionel frowned. After a moment, she said, "Maybe Mathis had a reason for not telling you. You do seem to be in a foul mood."

"Perhaps it would be better if we continued to the gates," Treloran said softly, placing a hand on Martyn's shoulder. "If you are allowed only one day of reunion, you had best not waste it here."

Martyn stopped in midstride and met the Aelvin Prince's gaze. "You're right! We've no time to waste!" He started forward, but Sionel intercepted him.

"Did Mathis tell you we received a communication from Lady Jessandra?"

After failing to find Jeran in the Tribal Lands, Jes had returned to Vela, where she had resumed her duties as First Seat of House Velan. Since then, her communication with Kaper had been infrequent. Nevertheless, Martyn hoped to hear that she and the Magi had rescued Jeran, or at the very least located him.

"She says the Corsan raids are growing more frequent. The Guardsmen we've sent are barely enough to control the fighting, and her people are afraid. She suggests we send reinforcements, and asks that your father grant her the ability to recruit people into the Guard."

"Is that all?" Martyn demanded.

Sionel's eyes widened. She sniffed indignantly. "She also said their best commander fell in a raid. She has a few Guardsmen capable of command, but she wonders if your father has anyone he'd like to put in charge of the Corsan front."

Sionel tapped her lip thoughtfully, and Martyn waited, but when she pushed past him to examine a nearby tapestry, he grew impatient. "Any news of Jeran?"

The old woman frowned thoughtfully. "Only that his loss grieves her deeply, and she hopes you and your father find him unharmed." Sionel's eyes grew distant. "A nice girl, that Jessandra. She'd make Jeran a fine wife." Martyn smirked at the thought. *She's older than the Boundary!*

Sionel scanned the hall as if no longer certain where she was. "Where is Jeran?" she asked. "Has he gotten himself lost again? You'd think after all this time he'd know his way around. Well, don't you worry, Marti. I know every corner of this place. I'll find him."

Smiling, Martyn kissed Sionel on the forehead, then continued down the hall. Behind him, his greatmother walked slowly in the other direction, yelling, "Jeran! Where have your hidden yourself this time? Don't worry. Sionel will find you!"

Martyn and Treloran entered a small courtyard filled with recruits. The young men stood in a loose circle. Within the ring, two swordsmen barely old enough to be considered men sparred. Joam Batai watched from the sidelines, a deep scowl painted on his face. Puffs of white smoke punctuated his every breath, and his head glowed red with cold. "Prince Martyn," Joam called out when he saw the princes. "Prince Treloran. Are you here to practice?"

"Not today, Joam," Martyn answered quickly. Ornate benches and hand-carved statues had been moved aside to clear room for the recruits. The trainees fought atop a meticulously planned flowerbed, their heavy boots packing the fallow soil. "Tired of the practice yards on the other side of the castle?"

"The practice rings are all in use," Joam replied, running a hand along his smooth pate. "Your father ordered all able-bodied men to submit themselves for militia training." He smirked. "Unless they want to join the Guard, that is."

"Militia training," Martyn repeated. "Doesn't he think the Guard will be sufficient?"

Joam shrugged. "Better safe than sorry, lad." He studied the young men before him, all dressed in the grey uniforms of the Alrendrian Guard. The expression he wore was not a happy one. "Kaper could use a well-trained militia. Most of these boys will be sent to the front." One of the combatants jumped back, rubbing vigorously at his thigh. "As soon as they learn enough not to chop off their own legs! For the Gods' sake, Etai, be careful! You know the sides of those things are sharp, don't you?"

"If the bulk of your Guardsmen are sent to the borders," Treloran said, "the interior of Alrendria will be defenseless."

"Not quite defenseless," Joam replied. A gust of wind shook the branches, knocking snow upon his shoulders. Joam shrugged to brush it off. "But not as well protected as I'd like. The borders'll hold, though. We've got nothing to worry about."

Martyn studied the Guard Commander. "Will you be staying in Kaper, or going to fight?"

"My duty is to protect the king," Joam replied gruffly. The expression he wore hinted that this was a touchy subject. "I go where he goes."

"Then the safest place in Madryn will be at my father's side," Martyn laughed, clapping Joam on the shoulder. "I hope I have as good a protector when I go to war."

"Don't count on any fighting, my Prince," Joam told him. "If I have my way, you'll stay safe in Kaper until this business is over."

Martyn's good humor abruptly soured. "You wouldn't dare!"

"I thought it was a bad idea when Mathis went to fight the Tachan War," Joam replied, "and I was far more impetuous in my youth. With the wisdom of age, I certainly think it's a bad idea, and I intend to make sure your father feels the same way."

His hands tightened into fists, and Martyn struggled to maintain his composure. "When the time comes," he said through clenched teeth, "I *will* go to war. I'll make the Durange pay for what they've done. No one will stop me. Not my father. And certainly not you."

Joam laughed off Martyn's temper. "That's what I told my father, long ago. Wish I'd listened to him now. He wasn't as daft as I thought." Without waiting for Martyn's response, Joam turned back to his recruits and barked out a new set of orders. Martyn stomped through the snow-covered courtyard.

"He has your best interests in mind," Treloran said. "Astalian often says the same to me."

"Perhaps," Martyn grumbled, "but Astalian knows that you're a warrior. He wouldn't stop you from fighting, only caution you against it." Practice rings were set up everywhere, and soldiers ranging from raw recruits to long-time veterans fought within them. The clash of steel on steel filled the courtyards and cul-de-sacs despite the fading light. The sight made Martyn proud, but it also filled him with sadness. Not too long ago, these small alcoves and quiet gardens had been the hideaways of lovers, not soldiers.

They left the courtyards behind and found their way to the main avenue, the broad paved thoroughfare leading to the old city. Heavily-laden wagons passed them periodically, hauling their loads toward the castle. Treloran eyed the wagons curiously. "What do they hold?"

"Grain and other foodstuffs," guessed Martyn. "Ore for our blacksmiths and weapons bought from the city's craftsmen. My father's preparing for a siege, though many don't understand why. Kaper hasn't faced an attack in centuries."

"That is what was said in Lynnaei," Treloran reminded Martyn, "until the MageWar."

As they approached the gate to the old city, a Guardsman stepped out of the shadows, blocking their way. Though the gates stood open and the King had insisted that the public's access to the castle grounds not be restricted, Joam demanded increased security, and as a result, few visited the grounds without need.

The Guardsman recognized Martyn and saluted. "Greetings, my Prince. Are you here to welcome the Elves?" Martyn nodded, and the Guardsman smiled. "Word arrived from the bridge not moments ago. The Aelvin delegation should arrive after sunset." The guard gauged the position of the sun. "Still a while, my Lord. Will you wait here? I'll have food and drink brought."

"No thank you," Martyn said hastily, waving away the courtesy. "Treloran and I will walk the parapet." The Guardsman resumed his post, and the two princes entered a stairway carved into the wall's white stone.

The castle wall rose nearly a hundred hands above the palace grounds. It had one gate, the only entrance to the castle. The ramparts were wide enough for two men abreast and protected by crenellations half again as high as a man. The snow white stone stood in stark contrast to the more foreboding Wall, visible in the distance, the mage-created fortification separating the old city from the new. The portcullis and grates covering the arrow slits were gilded bronze instead of solid iron. It galled Martyn that Kaper's last line of defense was more aesthetic than functional.

On the far side of the wall, a deep pit cut a V-shape around the hill. Teams of craftsmen walked the perimeter, clearing debris from the pit and seeking imperfections in the construction. They would find few; the castle's defenses had been strengthened with magic after their construction. It would stand against all but the most determined assaults.

A chill ran down Martyn's spine. His father was putting great effort into shoring up the castle's defenses. Kaper's real defense lay in the Wall. Raised with magic instead of simply fortified with it, the Wall was twice as high as the castle's wall and more than three times as thick. If an attacker breached the Wall, the castle's defenses would be no great obstacle.

Two silhouetted forms, one large and one small, appeared in the distance. The two men stood still as statues, staring north. Martyn went to join them. "Guardsman Bystral! Mika! Good to see you."

They turned at his call, but neither showed much reaction. Bystral, tall and broad-shouldered, the son of a blacksmith, saluted. His massive arms were bare, but he showed no discomfort. His sandy blonde hair was pulled back in a ponytail, and he wore a thick beard. His dark eyes met Martyn's. "Welcome, my Prince."

Mika saluted in the manner of the Guardsmen too. Martyn smiled and returned the salute. Mika had proved to be an exceptional young man. Though only fourteen winters old, Mika's bearing hinted at the man he would become. He wore his hair short, in imitation of Jeran's style, and his clothes bore a resemblance in color and cut to a Guardsman's uniform. A wooden sword hung on his left hip, and on his right he wore a *dolchek*, the curved, serrated blade of the Garun'ah.

Mika's appearance might have been comical but for his expression. His blue-green eyes, which should have been wide with innocence, were dark and hard. Here was a boy grown old before his time, forced to endure hardships no man of any age should have to suffer. "Are you here to meet the Elves?" Martyn asked.

Surprise flicked across Mika's face. "Elves?" He schooled his features, drew a deep breath, and in more solemn tone, said, "No, Prince Martyn. Guardsman Bystral and I are watching for Jeran."

"Watching for Jeran?" Martyn frowned in confusion.

"I figure he'll be back any day now. He'll probably have that traitor's head with him, too. Or maybe even Tylor's."

Martyn cringed at the calmly-spoken words. He turned to Bystral. "You encourage this?"

"No, my Prince," Bystral answered. "But he stands here regardless of whether or not I stand with him. I figured the company might do some good." At the prince's probing glare, the Guardsman shrugged. "If anyone could escape the Bull of Ra Tachan, it's Lord Odara."

Martyn rolled his eyes and turned to Mika. "I, too, want to see Katya Durange punished. And no one wants Jeran back more than I. Not even you, my friend. But don't deceive yourself. There's little chance that Jeran will escape. Even if Tylor kept him alive, he'll be guarded at all times."

"It doesn't matter," Mika said. Martyn found the boy's conviction comforting. "The Darklord could order his entire army to watch Lord Jeran. He'd still find a way to escape!"

"If what you say is true," Martyn said, "then I hope he escapes soon! We could use a warrior of his prowess!"

Mika smiled, but his expression quickly grew serious. "Prince Martyn, I want to join the Alrendrian Guard. I want to help defend this land."

"You're still too young," Martyn answered. "You can't join the Guard until your fifteenth winter is past."

"The Garun'ah begin training their children to fight as soon as they can hold a *dolchek*," Mika replied, clutching the weapon at his waist.

"We are not Garun'ah," Martyn reminded him, and the boy's eyes narrowed angrily.

"There may come a time when you'll wish you had trained me. I've watched the new Guardsmen in the practice yards. I'm already better than them!"

Martyn laughed. It rolled up from his gut, his first real laugh in a long time. "You know, you remind me of Jeran sometimes." Mika beamed at the compliment, and the prince turned to Bystral. "Your duties seem lax enough to allow for standing on walls. Would you be willing to use your time more constructively, Guardsman?"

"I will serve Alrendria in whatever manner you desire, my Prince."

"Then I request you assist our eager young warrior here. Give him the training he desires." Mika nodded as if he had expected nothing less. "Make no mistake," Martyn said, wagging a finger at the boy. "You'll be trained in all matters important to a Guardsman. Sword and bow skill are fine, but until you're disciplined, you'll never be a true Guardsman."

Mika saluted again. "I won't disappoint you, my Prince."

"See that you don't."

The four watched the sun sink in the western sky. After the last rays of light disappeared, a shrill note echoed up from Old Kaper, the ululating tone of an Aelvin horn. Drawing his cloak about his shoulders, Martyn waved for his companions to follow. "Come. Let's greet our Aelvin guests."

Chapter 2

They arrived ahead of the Aelvin delegation. The young Guardsman was gone; an older soldier named Farid had taken his place. Twenty more Guardsmen, in full armor and white cloaks emblazoned with the Rising Sun of Alrendria, stood at attention, ten on each side of the gate. The flickering torches illuminated their faces and flashed off their pristine armaments. "Prince Martyn," Farid greeted him with a salute. "The Elves should arrive momentarily."

"We figured as much," Martyn replied, but he smiled before the Guardsman could respond. "How goes the watch?"

"Quietly," Farid replied. "Hard to believe a war's brewing."

"Believe it. Alrendria will be at war by summer. I'd bet my life on it."

Bystral bent down and whispered in Mika's ear, and the boy laughed. Under Martyn's stare, the Guardsman grew uncomfortable. "I was just counseling the boy on the folly of wagering one's life on peace." Martyn rolled his eyes, and Mika laughed again. Even Treloran had trouble keeping a straight face.

Another trumpet blast echoed up the dark avenues of Old Kaper. Two horses came into view, a white stallion with a black streak splitting its head, and a roan mare. Shadows hid the riders' faces, and they wore long cloaks drawn tight around their bodies. The Guardsmen grew wary, and Farid stepped between the strangers and the prince. "Halt," he called, holding his torch forward. "What is your purpose here?"

The horses stopped at Farid's command, but neither rider spoke. Martyn stepped forward, squinting into the darkness, and Bystral placed himself between the prince and the strangers. When the burly Guardsman moved, one of the riders leaned forward. Expecting an attack, the Guardsmen drew their weapons; the rasp of steel sliding against leather filled the night.

The mare's rider, a tower of shadow, whispered to his companion in a low rumble. "Yes," a familiar voice answered. "I think that's Prince Martyn."

"Vyrina?" Martyn called, pushing past Bystral. Farid hurried toward him, but Martyn shrugged off the watch captain's attempt to keep him safe. "Can't you recognize a Guardsman when you see one?" he demanded. "Vyrina, is it really you?"

The stallion's rider threw back her hood, exposing her face to the light. Deeply sunken eyes stared out from a wan face, but she called out warm greetings. "It's good to see you, my Prince." She slipped as she stepped down from her saddle and had to steady herself. "We only recently learned that you survived."

"Who's with you?" Martyn asked eagerly. He did not believe it, but he prayed it was Jeran. When the figure half-fell from his horse and stepped into the light, Martyn's hope died. Dark, almond-shaped eyes regarded the prince dispassionately. "Well met, Frodel *uvan* Merck," Martyn said, and the Tribesman ducked his head in greeting. Martyn turned to Vyrina. "Are the others with you?"

She shook her head. "We're the only ones who escaped." Though the Guardswoman had spoken no accusation, guilt assaulted Martyn. He struggled to hide it. *I didn't ask them to sacrifice themselves! That was Jeran's doing.* The thought brought little comfort, and keeping his eyes on Vyrina's pallid features became increasingly difficult.

"What happened?" Mika asked as Bystral demanded, "Where have you been?"

"One question at a time," Martyn ordered, raising a hand to silence them. "And as prince, I get to ask them!" He winked at Vyrina and flashed one of his best smiles. "After we escaped the valley, we rode north. Mika's army met us."

When death at Tylor's hand had seemed likely, Jeran had ordered Mika to leave their party to seek help. The young man had raced across the Tribal Lands with neither food nor rest, and after he reached Kohr's Heart and told the *Kranora* what had happened, he demanded his right to lead the attack. When Martyn and his party came upon the Tribesmen, Mika rode at their front, urging them to run faster. "We searched the valley," Martyn added, "but saw nothing save the scars of battle. What happened? Where are the others?"

"The fighting was fierce," Vyrina told him. Her face paled at the memory, but she forced herself to continue. "The Bull's soldiers were everywhere! If not for those columns of fire and the aid we received from the creatures of the forest, we wouldn't have stood a chance. I..." Memories overwhelmed her, and Vyrina choked on her words.

"Even still, fight difficult." Frodel continued, and the Guardswoman touched his arm fondly. "Smoke everywhere. Enemy everywhere. We kill and hide and kill again, but still enemy come. Twice almost I struck down by bolt, and twice more Dahr nearly kill me."

"You should have seen him," Vyrina interrupted. "He looked like an animal himself! His eyes were fire and he howled like a beast. He cut through the Bull's soldiers like a farmer scything wheat."

"Never I see Blood Rage possess man so," Frodel murmured.

"Once we knew you were safe," Vyrina continued, "we hid, hoping we wouldn't be discovered. The Gods were on our side, and Tylor's men passed without spotting us. But they had prisoners. Jeran. Wardel too. Maybe others."

A fit of coughing doubled Vyrina in half, and Frodel looked at her nervously. One of the guards broke rank and ran to the guardroom. He returned with a flask and offered it to Vyrina. She drank thirstily, and then passed the flask to Frodel. The Tribesman sipped the water, and bowed his head in thanks.

"We decided to follow," Vyrina continued, her voice weak, "hoping for a chance to free them. We tracked the Bull south, around the city of Shandar, and north again along the Anvil. We thought our presence remained a secret, but the Bull was smarter than we credited him."

"Never I see better tracker than Bull of Ra Tachan," Frodel said. "We follow like mice in field. Left trail only best *Dar'Tacha* could follow, and still he knew we there. We walk into trap like cubs on first hunt."

"I'm not sure how we survived, and I can't get Frodel to speak of it." Vyrina offered the Tribesman a weak smile, and Frodel put his arm around her, drawing her close. "I took two arrows at the start of the ambush and lost consciousness.

When I woke, I was in a cave, and Frodel was tending my wounds. He was bruised and bleeding from a thousand cuts, but would do nothing for himself until certain I would recover."

Vyrina smiled, and Martyn saw love in the gaze they shared. "Winter came quick, but it was a long time before either of us was strong enough to travel. When we were ready, we started south, but we were forced to hide our identities to escape attack."

"Attack by Alrendrians?" Martyn asked, shocked. Vyrina nodded.

"Many rumors are circulating through the villages of the north," she told him. "Some claim that Tylor killed you, others that the Tribesmen ended your life. But no matter the story, no matter whether you live or who is to blame for your death, there's little trust of the Garun'ah."

"My father must be told," Martyn said. "The Garun'ah are our allies, and we can't allow them to be attacked by our own people."

"We would have returned quicker," Vyrina added, "but for fear of causing greater injury. Neither of us has completely healed."

"Late is better than never, Guardsman. I, for one, am glad to have you back." He waved to Farid. "Frodel is to have full access to the castle. Be sure the Guard knows it." The watch commander relayed the order to one of his men, who disappeared in the direction of the barracks. "Do you need anything?" Martyn asked.

Frodel shook his head, and Vyrina smiled. "Just a hot meal and a hotter bath."

"We await the arrival of the first Aelvin delegation," Martyn told her. "Will you wait with us?"

Vyrina glanced at Frodel, who suddenly appeared uneasy. He shifted uncomfortably from foot to foot, and his eyes flicked first to Treloran, then to the road behind him. "With your permission, Prince Martyn," Vyrina answered, "we'll press on. It's been a long journey."

"As you will, Guardsman. Once you've cleaned and eaten, seek me out. You should tell your story to my father."

"I will, my Prince. Thank you." Vyrina led her horse through the gate. Frodel followed a step behind.

"I told you he was alive!" Mika said triumphantly as soon as the two were gone.

Treloran looked at the boy. "Just because Jeran Odara lived at the end of the battle does not mean he lives now."

Mika cast a dark glare at the Aelvin Prince but said nothing. Laughing, Martyn clapped Mika on the shoulder. "I never doubted it," he said, turning to face the road again. Another long note drifted through the brisk winter air. Far down the broad avenue a light appeared, and several more quickly came into view.

The Guardsmen resumed their posts and stood at attention, their hands on their weapons. Two soldiers in carrying halberds took positions on opposite sides of the road. They crossed their polearms to block entry to the castle grounds.

An ornate carriage appeared, drawn by two identical white horses. A light-haired, green-eyed Elf sat in the driver's seat, his expression fixed. Dozens more carriages followed, and behind them, scores of wagons. A few wagons held brown-robed *Ael Namisa* huddled together for warmth, the rest overflowed with goods.

Ael Chatorra walked in formation alongside the procession. A few carried swords; the rest held bows strung and ready to draw. No wide-eyed recruits walked among the ranks, only hardened veterans, and they marched with blank expressions, their eyes fixed on the road. If the sights of Kaper awed them, they showed no sign of it.

A stone clattered in the distance, and fixed expressions wavered nervously. Eyes narrowed, flitting back and forth, almost panicked. The Aelvin soldiers suddenly looked uncomfortable and afraid; the illusion of control was gone. Martyn suspected that many would have handed over their bows immediately if it gained them the protection of a single tree.

The procession halted two dozen hands from the prince, and the door to the front carriage opened. A tall Elf with slanted, grey-green eyes stepped lightly from the carriage and walked forward. Pale hair, too light to be called blonde framed a narrow face slightly lined by age. *Ael Chatorra* watched closely as the Elf approached the Alrendrians, and two guards followed on his heels. The Elf's gaze drifted over the faces of his welcoming party with confidence. When he met Martyn's eyes, a tight smile spread across thin lips.

"I am Jaenaryn *el'e* Healira," the Elf said without the slightest hint of accent, "*Ael Alluya* and representative of Emperor Alwellyn the Eternal, who speaks for the Goddess Valia." He delivered his greeting in a powerful tenor that belied his thin frame. "I come to reopen *Ael Shende Ruhl*, the Path of Riches. I am to be chief ambassador in Kaper and will speak with the Emperor's voice in all matters pertaining to the Empire."

With his left hand, Jaenaryn gestured to the procession behind him. "With me travel many of my people, our representatives to your lands. Servants and merchants, warriors and craftsmen, we come to learn your ways and teach you ours." Jaenaryn bowed low, and all around him, *Ael Chatorra* lowered their weapons. "We request entry to your home, Prince Martyn of Alrendria."

Martyn returned the bow, but he remembered the lessons learned during his time in Illendrylla and kept his eyes locked with Jaenaryn's. To do otherwise would imply that Martyn considered himself inferior. "You are well come to Kaper, Jaenaryn *el'e* Healira. We have anticipated the arrival of our cousins from the Eternal Forest and look forward to this opportunity to renew our friendship."

Martyn's hand swept out to encompass the city. "We are preparing a section of Old Kaper for your people. I apologize that it's not yet completed, but winter has slowed our progress. Until your new homes are ready, you will be given quarters in the castle, where you will be denied no luxury." Jaenaryn bowed in acknowledgement. "Several markets in New Kaper have been cleared for your merchants," Martyn continued, "and the eastern side of Makan's Market, the market at the foot of the Great Bridge, has been set aside for you as well."

"Your hospitality and consideration are greatly appreciated," Jaenaryn replied. White puffs of steam issued from his mouth with every breath, and the Elf suddenly shivered.

"My hospitality is poor indeed," Martyn laughed, "since I force you to suffer in the cold. Come, Jaenaryn, and join us at a feast in honor of your arrival. My father has requested that your party, from *Ael Namisa* to *Ael Alluya*, dine with us tonight so that he may meet you all."

"It will be as you request," Jaenaryn responded.

"Open the gates for the friends of Alrendria!" Martyn called, turning to Farid. "Let all in Kaper know the Elves are our guests, and instruct them to welcome our cousins with open arms."

The halberdiers stepped aside, and the Aelvin procession started forward. Jaenaryn declined the offer to ride; he stepped in beside the princes and followed Martyn up the broad avenue. "You fare well, my Prince?" he asked Treloran.

"The Humans have treated me well," Treloran nodded, "and I have learned much since leaving Illendrylla."

"Do you not miss your home?" the old Elf asked.

"There are times," Treloran admitted, "when I yearn for the comforts of Lynnaei. The trees here are thin and the skies too open, but I have many winters before me and would not waste this opportunity to learn of our younger cousins."

"Wisely spoken," Jaenaryn said, and he turned away, as if finished. After a thoughtful pause, he asked, "Have these Humans taught you such a civil tongue, my Prince, or have you finally grown past childhood?"

Treloran's eyes narrowed, and sensing the tension, Martyn hastened to intervene. "I doubt Treloran learned a civil tongue from anyone here," he said, forcing a laugh. "The noblemen of Alrendria are more hot-blooded than the Garun'ah."

The Aelvin Prince's eyes snapped to Martyn, but he said nothing. Jaenaryn turned toward Martyn too, but his gaze carried far less heat. "You do yourself a disservice, Prince Martyn. Among my people, it is considered a grave dishonor to be compared with the Wildmen."

"In Alrendria," Martyn countered, "we consider all men, and all races, equal in the eyes of the Gods."

"Ah, yes," Jaenaryn replied, "Alrendrian open-mindedness. I had forgotten." The Elf's eyes drifted around the darkened gardens. "The last time I walked Kaper's streets, I could not turn a corner without seeing a Mage. I wonder where the Gifted hide tonight."

An uncomfortable silence followed, and Martyn changed the subject to dispel the awkwardness of the moment. "Is Kaeille with you? I did not see her among *Ael Chatorra*."

Jaenaryn's condescending smile infuriated Martyn, but he maintained his composure. "Your *advoutre* is among my company, Prince Martyn, but she may not resume her rank until after the bonding. Even then, with her loyalties divided, her time as *Ael Chatorra* will be short."

One word caught Martyn's ears; he missed much of what Jaenaryn said. "Bonding?"

"I forget that you are unaccustomed to our ways. *Advoutre* bond themselves to the person whose life they will share. It is similar to marriage but not as restrictive. At least, not to you. Kaeille *el'e* Cemarilia must renounce her right to wed and swear an oath of loyalty. The details were explained in my dispatches to the King."

"An oath?" Martyn repeated. "What oath must I swear?"

Jaenaryn cocked his head to the side, and Treloran barely hid his smile. "You swear no oath," the Elf answered. "Kaeille *el'e* Cemarilia is your *advoutre*, not the other way around."

They continued on in silence, the barren trees and empty gardens gliding past as they walked across the castle grounds. Suddenly, something else Jaenaryn said registered to Martyn. "You mean I can't see Kaeille until we're bonded?"

"Once the intention to bond is announced," Jaenaryn explained, "the *advoutre* is not permitted to see her consort until the ceremony. This is to prevent any accusations of impropriety."

"When will the ceremony take place?" Martyn asked through teeth clenched in the semblance of a smile.

"If it pleases you," Jaenaryn answered, "we will hold the ceremony tomorrow. Around midday? Any sooner would be inappropriate."

Martyn turned to Bystral, who walked a half dozen steps behind the princes. "When does the party from Gilead arrive?"

Bystral scratched his beard thoughtfully. Mika tugged on the Guardsman's sleeve, and when the larger man looked down, he whispered something. "I believe the Gilean's arrive around midday," Bystral said suddenly. Mika smirked.

Martyn spent the remainder of the march in brooding silence. An army of servants greeted them at the castle, eager to escort the Elves to their quarters and arrange for the storage of the Aelvin wares. The courtyard quickly emptied, leaving Martyn alone with Treloran and Jaenaryn. He led them toward the castle, and King Mathis met them on the steps. Dark circles ringed the King's eyes, but he smiled warmly as Martyn introduced the Aelvin Ambassador.

"It is an honor, King of Alrendria," Jaenaryn said, bowing low at the waist. Martyn noted that the Elf dropped his eyes to the ground. *He didn't show me that much respect!*

"The honor is mine," Mathis said, urging the Elf to rise. "The children of Valia have not walked the halls of my castle in a long time. I bid you join me in celebrating your arrival. A feast has been prepared."

"We would be honored," Jaenaryn replied formally. "I request only time enough to clean the dust from my body."

"We will await your arrival in the dining hall." Mathis waved, and a servant hurried to his side. "Take the Aelvin Ambassador to his rooms," the King ordered. "Make sure he wants for nothing." Bowing, first to the King and then to Jaenaryn, the servant bid the Elf follow him.

"You need not stay with us," Mathis said to Treloran. "I'm sure you're eager for news of your family."

"I thank you, King Mathis, but there is no need." Martyn knew better; Treloran desperately wanted to hear about Illendrylla, but impatience was a Human trait the Aelvin Prince often complained about. He would not give Martyn the opportunity to tease him. "My people will return shortly. What news they have will not be forgotten in so short a time."

"It's easy to be patient when you live longer than stone!" Martyn grumbled, but he returned the Elf's smirk. "But some stones lead more exciting lives than you Elves."

They followed the King to the dining hall, a long chamber with high walls and arched ceilings of grey stone. Sconces dotted the walls, and the light from their flickering flames cast long shadows across the twin rows of tables running the length of the room. At the far end of the hall, the King's table lay perpendicular to the others. Behind the King's table, a fire crackled in a hearth nearly twenty hands across.

Martyn scanned the room. Representatives from all six Great Houses were in attendance, and many of the Families had sent their own envoys. The King had made it known that he wanted the Elves to feel welcome in Kaper, and for once, the nobility did not intend to argue. Small pockets of men and women carried on casual conversations, but a tense buzz filled the hall as the attendees awaited the Elves' arrival. In one corner, Hoster Manel talked in low tones with Lady Estel Pryn. When a servant walked up with wine, they both fell silent. In another corner, Vito Menglor stared cold daggers at his political rival Joahr Phizan, who pretended not to notice.

A parade of lesser nobles trailed Utari Hahna through the chamber, seeking her favor. Utari, who would soon leave for Lynnaei as the Alrendrian Ambassador, looked regal in a shimmering gown. Her ebony skin glowed in the light reflecting off the multitude of gold necklaces she wore. Martyn called out greetings, and Utari responded with a slight inclination of her head.

The princes barely made it three steps before Alynna Morrena spotted them. Dressed in a sheer blue gown that showed little flesh yet still managed to border on scandalous, Alynna walked with a confident sway that only the most stouthearted could ignore. Calculating eyes swept past Martyn indifferently, but when her gaze fell on Treloran, red lips parted in a hungry smile. Like a shark that has tasted blood, she darted toward her prey. Treloran had no chance of escape.

Alynna's uncle, Brell Morrena, followed his niece. The Second of Morrena wore fine black clothes emblazoned with the Tiger of his House. His black hair and goatee were neatly trimmed and oiled, his dark eyes cold. "My Liege," he said, taking Mathis by the arm. "There's a matter of some urgency we must discuss."

Mathis allowed Brell to draw him aside, and Alynna wrapped herself around Treloran. She stood on tiptoe to whisper in the Aelvin Prince's ear, and he blushed dark red before she dragged him away. Left alone, Martyn started toward the King's table, but a hand pulled him back.

"My Prince, forgive me." A small man bowed low, and an obsequious smile spread across his face. "I want to apologize for the delay in answering your summons. I was visiting family in the Kaldescon, a circumstance which I now most sincerely regret. I returned as quickly as I could, but the weather across House Menglor was terrible."

Martyn frowned, confused, and the expression seemed to upset the man. "Zarin Mahl?" he said at last, half in question.

The small man bobbed his head, and his smile grew even broader. "Your summons pleased me, my Prince. I am not often invited to an audience with the royal family. It's more honor than a humble servant like myself deserves."

"Iban warned me of you," Martyn said carefully.

Zarin's eyes widened. "Geffram and I were friends for many winters. It pains me to hear that he thought so ill of me."

"I don't doubt your friendship, Master Mahl, but Iban was no fool. He knew which wolves bite and which disguise themselves as sheep."

"Geffram was a wise man." Zarin's expression grew sad. "He'll be sorely missed in the dark times ahead."

Thoughts of Iban's sacrifice sent a pang of guilt through Martyn. "Before his death," Martyn said, "Lord Iban suggested that I seek you out."

"There's little I could do for one such as you," Zarin said, "but I'd be happy to serve in whatever manner you desire, meager though my skills may be."

Martyn's expression hardened. "I require neither flattery nor humility, Master Mahl."

Zarin's gaze turned serious. "What *do* you desire, my Prince?"

"Your eyes. And your honesty. It's hard to know who to trust."

"My eyes aren't what they used to be," Zarin laughed, "and honesty isn't always a pleasant gift."

The prince's calculating gaze matched Zarin's. "I want them nonetheless."

For a moment, silence reigned. "Then they are yours," Zarin said, bowing low. "If you'll excuse me, my Prince, it seems the Elves are arriving. It's time we sought our places."

Elves filed into the hall in small groups, and Martyn hurried to his place at the King's Table. To his right, *Ael Chatorra* shared tables with Guardsmen and *Ael Pieroci* with merchants and lesser nobles; to his left, *Ael Namisa* and a handful of Aelvin craftsmen sat with their counterparts in Alrendrian society. Jaenaryn and his highest ranking subordinates sat at the King's table with Brell and the representatives of the Great Houses, Martyn, and the King.

Martyn smiled to himself. He had told his father of the Emperor's feasts. It seemed the King had taken to the idea.

Once the room was full, Mathis stood, and the room fell silent. "Tonight, we welcome our cousins from the Eternal Forest, the first of many who will come now that the Path of Riches is restored. Let us not waste the opportunity presented here! Reestablishing trade is not about acquiring wealth, no matter what our merchants may claim." A murmur of laughter rumbled through the chamber. "Reopening the Path of Riches is about bringing together two great Races and forging the first links in a lasting alliance."

Applause exploded throughout the room, and Mathis offered a toast, first to Illendrylla, then to Alrendria. After they drank, Mathis sat, and the low murmur of conversation filled the chamber. The King introduced the Aelvin delegates to the Alrendrian nobility, but an uncomfortable silence quickly descended upon the King's table and spread through the chamber. The Elves stared warily at the Humans, and the Alrendrians casually ignored the Elves. The air in the dining hall grew uncomfortable.

Sensing trouble, Mathis called for the food, and a steady stream of servants appeared carrying platters piled high with Alrendrian delicacies and exotic Aelvin dishes. The food, especially the Aelvin food, broke the tension, but it was wine and *brandei* drunk in excessive amounts that loosened tongues. The buzz of conversation filled the hall as friendships made during the visit to Lynnaei were renewed.

A dark figure drew Martyn's gaze. Konasi, the dark-haired, narrow-eyed representative of the Magi paced the edge of the room, his gaze shifting suspiciously from one Elf to the next, a deep frown on his face. Martyn waved, and the Mage approached reluctantly.

"What's the matter?" Martyn demanded.

"There are Gifted among the Elves," the Mage replied.

"The Elves brought no *Ael Maulle* with this delegation."

"There are Gifted among the Elves," Konasi repeated. "Perhaps many. I find it difficult to determine."

Treloran laughed aloud. "Most Elves are Gifted, Mage," he whispered, and Konasi jumped. His eyes narrowed as he stared at the Aelvin Prince. That Konasi was a Mage was a secret. "Do not worry, Mage, no one has betrayed you; you can hide from the Gifted no better than the Gifted can hide from you. And an Elf's hearing is more acute than a man's, so you had best keep your voice down if you do not want my people to hear you."

Konasi sputtered, and his eyes flicked around the room. "All Elves with strength in the Gift are trained as *Ael Maulle*," Treloran explained. "None here save I have enough talent to uncover your secret, and I will not insult my hosts by betraying that which they wish to remain hidden."

"I don't trust them, Prince Martyn," Konasi said darkly.

"You don't trust anyone," Martyn laughed. "And I don't trust you." The sour glare he received made him laugh even harder. "Return to your quarters. I'll not have you mar this celebration with unfounded suspicions." Konasi stormed out of the chamber.

The remainder of the meal passed without incident, and as the night grew later and the casks emptier, the celebration grew in intensity. Mathis asked the Elves an endless string of questions. Martyn had seen his father like this before, carefully weighing each answer, siphoning every response for useful information. Treloran and Jaenaryn talked amongst themselves, sharing information of home. Martyn heard only snippets of their conversation. For the most part, he ate in silence. His thoughts wandered continuously to Kaeille, almost within his grasp yet still out of reach.

He set down his goblet; the wine suddenly tasted sour. *One more day and I'll be able to see her whenever I want!* It seemed like an eternity.

Slowly, the guests sought their beds, until only Martyn, Treloran, Jaenaryn, and the King remained. Jaenaryn stood. "I thank you for this fine welcome, King Mathis, but I must request your permission to leave. The road was long, and I am weary."

"Go with my best wishes. I hope your stay in Kaper is enjoyable." The Elf departed, and Mathis yawned. "I think I'll retire as well. It's been a long day, and tomorrow's likely to be longer."

Martyn and Treloran sat for a while more, and Treloran shared news of Illendrylla. Finally, barely able to keep his eyes open, the Aelvin Prince excused himself, leaving Martyn alone in the dining hall. After a while, servants appeared to clear away the mess.

Stretching, Martyn returned to his chambers. He threw open the door and walked blindly through the room. "I thought you would never come!" a familiar voice said from the other side of the bed.

Martyn jumped and had a flame burning in an instant. Kaeille sprawled across the bed in a diaphanous gown only a shade lighter than her pure, unblemished skin. Her black hair was longer than Martyn remembered, just short of the shoulder. Her eyes were like emeralds, sparkling and warm. "You look beautiful," he said breathlessly, and Kaeille smiled. "What are you doing here? I thought we weren't supposed to see each other before the bonding."

"Technically, that is correct." Kaeille stood slowly. Only a couple of hands separated them, and Martyn felt waves of heat rolling from her. Her gown clung to her lithe, athletic frame. She dropped the strap from her left shoulder enticingly, exposing more flesh. "But the truth is that we must not be caught together before the bonding."

She reached for the other strap, then hesitated. "But if you would prefer to wait..."

Smiling, Martyn blew out the candle.

Chapter 3

"What do I have to do?" Martyn asked as he fumbled with the laces to his shirt.

"How many times must I tell you?" With exasperation, Treloran shook his head. "You need to do nothing. Kaeille will swear her oath and she will be bonded to you."

Martyn smoothed the wrinkles from his shirt and grabbed his finest cloak. The golden sun emblazoned on it sparkled in the firelight as he fastened it about his neck. "If that's all, then why the ceremony?"

"Long ago, my people forgot their honor and the pledges they made to each other. For centuries, Aelvin society declined and my people grew more uninhibited, until we were little better than…" Treloran trailed off, and his cheeks flared red.

"Until you were little better than Humans?" Martyn rolled his eyes.

Treloran nodded. "When things were their bleakest, when it seemed we would never recover, Lothlarin the Pious, prophet of the Goddess Valia, arrived. Through his teachings, the Elves rediscovered their morality—"

"They repressed themselves," Martyn interrupted.

"—and restored the Empire. Lothlarin established the Feast Days, like *Ael chatel e Valia* and originated the bonding ceremony."

"But *why*?" Martyn asked again. He started for the door and waved for Treloran to follow. "If he intended to restore Aelvin morality, why allow consorts at all?"

"Five centuries is a long time to spend with one person," Treloran said, and Martyn laughed, "even for an Elf. The bonding allows two individuals to share themselves without risking the decline of society."

"You mean it ensures the poor can't take advantage of the rich, and that the powerless can't worm their way into positions of authority." Martyn's laughter turned bitter. "Human nobles have ways of retaining power too; at least we don't pretend they benefit everyone."

"It is more than that!" Treloran said defensively. "An *advoutre* is an advisor, a counselor, and a friend. By removing any opportunity for advancement, it ensures that an *advoutre*'s advice is always in the best interest of the one they bond. In many Aelvin households, *advoutre* are respected members of the family. There is no animosity between married and mistress."

"If only that were to be true for me!" Martyn lamented. He cast his eyes toward the ceiling as if bidding the Gods to take heed. With a snort, he continued down corridors all but empty of people. Only a few servants walked the halls, and they moved quickly out of the prince's way. "Are only women *advoutre*?"

"*Advoutre* are often women," Treloran answered, "but it is not uncommon for men to bond someone they love but cannot marry."

"And there's no stigma attached?"

Treloran frowned thoughtfully, and finally shook his head. "Not like in your land. Consorts are not hated or feared, nor are they considered a threat. The bonding ensures as much. To some, though," Treloran added after a long pause, "it is considered an admission of inferiority."

"You mean those who bond do so because they're incapable of improving their own station?"

"Only a few believe this," the Aelvin Prince added hastily. "Most Elves believe it is a great sacrifice. To give up everything for love."

"And what will Miriam think? Will she think me a martyr or a monster?"

"She is Human," Treloran replied matter-of-factly. "She will not understand, nor will she welcome Kaeille. Grandfather did you no favor when he forced this upon you."

"How reassuring," Martyn mumbled. He fell silent, brooding, and Treloran did not pursue conversation.

The chamber where the bonding would take place was small, spartan, and long unused. A handful of chairs, unused, lay scattered about the room, and a raised dais stood against one wall. Jaenaryn stood on the platform. He wore dark robes, and in his hand he held a gnarled staff.

Guardsmen Bystral and Lisandaer stood at attention before the Elf. Both offered Martyn a smile as he approached. "Welcome," Jaenaryn said formally, bowing low. "The bonding may now begin."

Martyn stopped at the base of the dais and looked up expectantly. In slow and measured tones, Jaenaryn said, "There is one who will be bonded to you. Will you hear her oath?"

"I will." Martyn cast his eyes about the room nervously and murmured, "I thought my father would be here."

"The King didn't want to call attention to the ceremony," Bystral whispered. "He sends his regrets, but he thought it wise to keep his distance." Martyn understood, but he wondered how much of his father's displeasure was feigned.

Jaenaryn tapped his staff against the floor twice, and the double doors at the rear of the hall opened. Kaeille entered, wearing a gown of pale green. A thin, gauzy veil covered her face, but her green eyes gleamed. She crossed the room with stately, measured steps. It took all of Martyn's willpower not to run to her.

Kaeille stopped several hands away, and Treloran took his place at her side. Jaenaryn studied her for a moment, and then drew a slow breath. "You wish—"

The door flew open, and a Guardsman ran in. "My Prince," he said breathlessly. "The King sent me to tell you that the Gileans approach."

"Wonderful," Martyn muttered. He looked at Jaenaryn. "We must hurry."

"The rules of the bonding are quite specific," Jaenaryn replied, but in response to Martyn's frantic expression, he relented. "But I will do what I can."

The Guardsman took a position at the rear of the hall. Martyn drew a deep, steadying breath and looked at Kaeille. She smiled, and that simple gesture sent his pulse racing. Thoughts of the night before filled his mind. Sweat beaded his brow and slicked his palms.

Jaenaryn tapped his staff again. "Do you wish—"

The door flew open again and Liseyl entered. She looked at Martyn and curtsied. "Lady Sionel sent me to tell you that the Gileans have arrived."

Bystral chuckled, and Martyn glared at the Guardsman. "Your warning is noted," Martyn replied wryly, "though late." Liseyl curtsied again and walked to the side of the room. As she studied Kaeille, her lips pressed into a thin line.

Martyn, with an apologetic shrug, nodded to Jaenaryn, and the Elf slammed his staff against the floor. "Do you—"

"My Prince!" Jolina called out as she burst into the room. Martyn cupped a hand over his eyes. "The Gileans are—"

"Enough!" Martyn shouted. Jolina jumped back. "Guardsman Jolina, prevent anyone else from entering this chamber. Guardsman Mendorin. Liseyl. Help her. We are not to be disturbed."

A deep frown drew at Jaenaryn's lips. "Does this woman wish to be *advoutre* to this man? Does she understand the significance of this bonding?"

"Kaeille *el'e* Cemarilia desires this bonding," Treloran, as Kaeille's advocate, said. "She is ready to give her oath."

Jaenaryn turned toward Kaeille. "Then step forward and speak."

Kaeille took one step toward Martyn and looked into his eyes. She was nervous; her hands trembled. "I give the oath of *Ael Chatorra*." Her voice carried no hint of her anxiety. "My mind is yours, to offer counsel in times of need. My heart is yours, to be cherished or spurned. My soul is yours, from now until the Goddess calls me home. My body will be sword and shield to you, and I place your life above all save the Emperor's. Our lives will become as one. Your last breath will preface my own. All this I give out of love." A single tear traced a path down her cheek. "By this oath, which I swear on the honor of my family and before the eyes of the Goddess, I will abide until the end of my days."

A silence fell over the room. After a pause, Jaenaryn's staff cracked against the dais. "The oath has been given," Jaenaryn said to Martyn. "Should you wish to refuse, now is the time. Once complete, there is no reversing this bonding."

"The oath is accepted," Martyn replied, surprised that he had voice enough for those few words.

"The oath has been given and accepted. Has this been witnessed?" Treloran named himself as a witness, and the two Guardsmen hastened to do the same. "Have all the forms been followed?"

"None may dispute this bond," Treloran said, and the Guardsmen echoed him.

"As the voice of the Emperor, who speaks in the stead of the Goddess, I recognize this bonding. Lift the veil, Prince of Alrendria, and gaze into the eyes of your *advoutre*."

Hesitantly, Martyn lifted Kaeille's veil, surprised by the trembling of his own hands. Kaeille laughed at him. "I will not bite, beloved," she whispered. "Not here."

Martyn's cheeks burned, and noticing the eyes upon her, Kaeille's expression soon matched the prince's. They embraced. "That's all?" Martyn asked. "The ceremony's over?"

"I could ask Jaenaryn to recite some of the Goddess' teachings," Treloran said, "if you feel the ceremony ended too quickly."

"No!" Martyn cried, waving his arms in an exaggerated manner. "I wouldn't want to inconvenience the ambassador."

With the ceremony finished, they started toward the main hall. Bystral and Lisandaer congratulated the couple as they passed, and Liseyl met them at the door. "My dear, that gown looks lovely! You should wear dresses more often." The compliment sparked a chorus of agreement from the Guardsmen.

Kaeille's cheeks turned dark red. She suddenly looked uncomfortable. "If you will excuse me." She bowed to Martyn.

"You needn't be so formal," Martyn chuckled, grabbing her arm. "Where are you going?"

The gentle sound of Kaeille's laughter was music to Martyn. "I would exchange this"—she touched the form-fitting gown—"for something more comfortable. Like armor."

"But you look beautiful!" Martyn protested.

"Perhaps I will wear it again later," Kaeille replied, smiling, as she started toward the door.

Martyn and Treloran followed a few steps behind Kaeille. "I'm glad that's over with!" Martyn said. "Thank the Gods we finished before Miriam arrived."

"Finished what before I arrived?"

Martyn stopped immediately but still collided with Kaeille. His *advoutre* faced a woman Martyn had never seen before, but he would have known her even if her statement had not given away her identity. Miriam wore a dress of white, long-sleeved and high-necked, that hinted at beauty without revealing it. She stood several fingers taller than Martyn but was slim, and she had a youthful, innocent face with pronounced cheeks framing a narrow nose. Blonde hair hung to her waist in a braid. Ice blue eyes, carrying all the arrogance of nobility, fastened on Martyn, but a polite smile pulled at her full red lips. "You are indeed most handsome, Prince Martyn. Even more so than I imagined."

Martyn straightened and returned the smile. "The tales I've heard pale in comparison to your true beauty, Princess. You are well come to Kaper. I trust you've been treated well."

"Your father's hospitality has been more than satisfactory," Miriam replied coolly. Her eyes flitted around the chamber, but Martyn noted that they kept returning to Kaeille. "Your castle and city are spectacular. Not as lovely as my father's, of course, but I could see this place becoming a home to me, should I decide to stay."

Martyn frowned at the last but chose not to comment. Miriam shifted her gaze to Kaeille. "This must be the Aelvin tart," she said excitedly. Her gaze grew sharper. "A pleasure to meet you, my dear."

Treloran stiffened, but Kaeille did not react to the insult. "Kaeille is my *advoutre*," Martyn said hastily, trying to prevent the situation from becoming worse. "At the Emperor's insistence, to show our good faith to the Elves, I accepted her as a confidante."

"And a companion?" It was not quite a question.

Kaeille raised her chin. "I am pledged to aid Prince Martyn in whatever manner best serves him and Alrendria."

Miriam's cold gaze slid over Kaeille's slender figure. "I'm sure he's found many uses for your... talents."

Struggling to maintain her composure—though her expression never changed, it was a struggle Martyn knew Kaeille was losing—the Aelvin woman said, "I am *Ael Chatorra*, a member of the Emperor's elite archer regiment." Her voice matched Miriam's in iciness.

"I did not address you, Elf," Miriam snapped. "Do not speak unless spoken to."

"She is *not* a servant," Martyn said, a bit too harshly. He took a deep breath, fighting to keep calm. "An *advoutre* is a position of great honor. Kaeille will be given the same courtesy and respect due any other noblewoman."

Miriam's eyes returned to Martyn. After a thoughtful pause, she said, "Of course, Martyn. I didn't mean to offend." Miriam inclined her head to Kaeille. "I apologize, Lady…"

"Kaeille," supplied Martyn.

"When dealing with other Races," Kaeille said, "one must often utilize patience and tolerance. It is fortunate the Goddess granted her people both in abundance."

A wry smile twisted Miriam's lips. "She's well spoken, at least."

Seeking to change the subject, Martyn introduced Treloran. The Aelvin Prince received a more pleasant greeting, though the princess remained aloof. "Your father wanted you to join us," she told Martyn. "He was going to send a Guardsman, but I insisted on seeking you out myself." Her eyes gleamed. "I just couldn't wait to meet my future husband."

"How flattering," Martyn said wryly. With an apologetic smile to Kaeille, he offered his arm to the Princess of Gilead. "You honor me, Princess."

"Please, Martyn, call me Miriam. If our fathers have their way, we'll soon be wed. Such formality between us seems… inappropriate."

They left the chamber and strode arm in arm through the halls. Guardsmen and servants paused to watch them pass, saluting or cheering in greeting. Martyn wore a broad smile the entire time, but he felt no joy. Out of the corner of his eye he watched Miriam, but her expression remained inscrutable.

Joam met them at the entrance to the main hall. "Your father bid me bring you to him, my Prince. Please follow me." Joam led them to one of the King's audience chambers, a warmly furnished room with a bright fire burning in the hearth. Cushioned chairs circled a low table, and colorful tapestries hung from the walls. The King stood on the far side of the room, his back to the door.

Mathis turned when they entered, and he smiled. "Martyn. Miriam. Come! Join us." Mathis dismissed the servants in attendance; they set their trays and pitchers on the table and hurriedly left. Once they were gone, Mathis gestured to the man at his side. "This is Tarien, King of Gilead. Tarien, my son, Martyn Batai."

Tarien inclined his head formally, his eyes appraising, and Martyn studied the King of Gilead with a similar probing gaze. Tarien was shorter than his daughter and thin, with a sharp nose and small, dark eyes. His hair was black, and a small beard circled his mouth, coming to a sharp point at the chin. He wore a tunic of dark blue, and a grey cape hung from his throat, clasped in front with an ornate golden pendant. "Prince Martyn," he said in a powerful voice. "It's a pleasure to finally meet you."

Martyn bowed deeply. "I'm honored, King Tarien."

Tarien's eyes shifted to his daughter, and he smiled at the sight of her. "I see you've met my daughter." His voice hardened. "Has she informed you of her decision?"

"Decision?" Martyn prompted.

Tarien sighed. "Miriam has invoked an antiquated law."

"It's my right!" Miriam replied defiantly. "The law was created to protect the nobility in situations just like this."

"I've tried to explain the advantages of this union to Miriam," Tarien said, restraining his temper, "but she's inclined to think only of herself and not the good of Gilead."

Martyn licked his lips nervously. "What do you mean? What law is this?"

"The Emperor's request that you take a mistress angered my daughter," Tarien explained. "She doesn't like the idea of sharing you. I can't say it appeals to me either, but I understand that these things happen, especially to princes. Miriam, however, won't listen to reason. She's invoked the Protectorate."

"The Protectorate?"

"An ancient law. One that has outlived its usefulness. Miriam will live here for a four-season, learning about you and your people. At the end of that time, she will choose whether or not to take you as husband."

"I won't give my life to someone who doesn't love me," Miriam snapped. "I won't leave my home to be queen of a lecher's realm, no matter how polite or attractive he may be."

"Prince Martyn took the Elf as his consort because the Emperor demanded it!" Tarien yelled. It had the sound of an old argument.

"I saw them together, Father! There's more than duty in their eyes when they gaze upon each other."

"What effect will this have on our alliance?" Martyn interjected, hoping to stop the two Gileans before their argument escalated.

Tarien calmed himself. "Our plans for alliance will continue; we can thank the Tachans for that. But if Miriam decides against marriage, support will dwindle. My daughter is popular among my countrymen. Without her, there's little chance of this alliance lasting beyond the war."

A tense silence filled the chamber. "It's easy to see that Miriam is not only beautiful, but wise." Martyn offered the princess his best smile. "Thus I'll not attempt to deceive her. It's true that I have feelings for Kaeille. But if not for the Emperor's insistence, I would not have taken her as *advoutre*." The half-truth stung at his honor, but Martyn kept up the charade. "You are to be my wife, Miriam. My queen. I will put you second to none." He lifted her hand and kissed it gently. "I accept your challenge. Within a four-season I will convince you of my sincerity."

Miriam's cheeks flushed slightly. "Your reputation is well deserved." She turned to her father, her gaze victorious. "I told you my decision wouldn't jeopardize the alliance."

His daughter's smugness did nothing to appease Tarien's temper. "You fail to see how much we need Alrendria. Without their support, the Tachans will sleep in Aurach by next winter."

Another silence descended upon the room. This time, Mathis broke it. "My friend, perhaps you don't realize how much Alrendria needs you. I observed you and your people carefully during my time in Gilead. I believe you to be a man of honor."

"I thank you," Tarien said, but a hint of suspicion had entered his voice.

"There's something I must tell you, and I warn you, it will test your faith." Martyn's eyes widened; they had not planned on warning Tarien about the weakening Boundary until after the alliance was formalized. He started to protest, but Mathis guessed his intention and signaled him to silence. "I would tell you what I know, the whole of it, if you're willing to listen."

Tarien pulled a hand along his pointed beard. Finally, he nodded. "Leave us," he told Miriam.

"Father! I have as much right to be here as—"

"Leave!" Tarien snapped. His tone brooked no argument. "When I'm convinced you'll put the needs of Gilead ahead of your own, you'll be invited to attend these audiences. Until then, you'll learn only what I decide to share with you."

The princess' face remained calm, but her eyes burned with anger. She spun on her heels and stormed from the room. Joam followed her and closed the door behind him, ordering men to guard the princess. A thud echoed through the room as Joam settled against the door to guard them from eavesdroppers.

"You might want to sit," Mathis said, gesturing at the chairs. He offered his fellow king an apologetic smile. Tarien remained standing, and Mathis drew a deep breath. "You know that the Durange have risen in the south. You also know that Alrendria faces trouble in the west and that Lord Geffram Iban, High Commander of the Guard, fell in battle on his return from Lynnaei. What you do not know," Mathis added, raising a hand to forestall his fellow king's unspoken comment, "is that Iban was not killed by brigands. Tylor Durange killed him."

"Tylor…" Tarien stammered. "The Bull of Ra Tachan?" Against his will, Tarien fell into a chair. "But… But…"

"The Boundary has been breached; the magic is weakening. The Darklord's armies have returned, and Lorthas himself seeks a way to bring down the barrier altogether. The MageWar has begun anew."

Tarien started to speak, but Mathis did not give him the opportunity. "There is more, my friend." The King of Gilead listened in stunned silence as Mathis told him of the Black Fleet ravaging the coast under the Darklord's sigil, the Drekka host forming the north, and the alliance of the *Kohr'adjin* and *Kohrnoedra* meant to foment war between the Elves and Garun'ah. Mention of Salos the Scorpion and his ShadowMagi brought a numbing pall upon the room, and the admission that the Magi had offered little in the way of help did little to lift it.

When he had finished, Tarien downed the wine he held in shaking hands and looked for the pitcher to refill it. "This is unbelievable."

"Agreed," Mathis replied. Martyn saw doubt on his father's face, but he saw relief too, as if a great weight had been lifted from his shoulders.

"With our alliance…" With shaking hands, Tarien poured another glass of wine and set the pitcher down. "I had hoped for support against the Tachans, but you are surrounded by enemies." The Gilean King squeezed his temples. "Gilead stands little chance, especially if the Rachannen join the war."

"I'll send every man who can be spared," Mathis assured his fellow King. "Troops and supplies, weapons and horses. Lord Fayrd commands a strong garrison in Western Grenz. With your permission, I'll instruct him to aid in the defense of the entire city."

Tarien smiled weakly. "Yes. With the Elves reopening the Path of Riches, I can see why you'd want to keep Grenz secure."

"Protecting the Aelvin merchants is one concern," Mathis admitted. "But Grenz offers the best crossing of the Celaan from here to the Anvil. If we hold both sides of the city, Alrendria's eastern border will be protected, true, but we'll also have an area for launching our own attacks, should the Tachan advance prove unstoppable."

"Without support," Tarien admitted, "my warriors won't be able to hold the south. I can't defend Gilead from both Ra Tachan and Rachannon."

"We're in this together, Tarien. For good or ill." His words did little to comfort the Gilean King. "I've begun training militia, so much of the Guard can be sent to defend key locations in Gilead. We can win this! I know we can."

Muted voices drifted through the door, indistinguishable but rising volume. "What of Roya?" Tarien asked, glancing at the door. "What aid can we expect?"

"The Royan fleet is the strongest in Madryn," Mathis said, "but Tobin must patrol the seas. Even with my Rakers aiding him, the Black Fleet has landed in both our lands. The Darklord's ships leave nothing but destruction in their wake."

"New Arkam is the worst attacked," Martyn added. "We can expect no aid from them."

"What of troops?" Tarien asked, dismissing the Arkamians with a wave. "Will Tobin send his army?"

"Roya's strength is in its navy," Martyn answered. "Tobin may spare a few squads, but he needs his forces to protect his own cities."

"Then we're doomed," Tarien said with a shake of his head. "Even without the threat to the north."

"Not so!" Mathis insisted. "The Alrendrian Guard is the finest fighting force on Madryn. They—"

"They *were* the finest," Tarien interjected, "but there've been few wars for them these last winters. Many claim the Guard has lost its edge."

"Even if what you say is true," Mathis said defensively, "it will take but a few battles to sharpen it again."

"You've already lost Iban, your greatest commander."

"Iban will be missed," Mathis admitted, "but Alrendria has others to take his place." Tarien opened his mouth again, but Mathis forestalled him. "Lord Gideon Talbot guards the Boundary, and he's a commander to rival Iban. Lord Fayrd protects Grenz, and with it, our eastern border. Our border with Corsa is well defended"—the lie grated in Martyn's ears, but he kept his expression even—"and I am sending a new commander there today. I have given the Firsts of each Great House the power to recruit into the Guard, and to conscript, if necessary."

"But the Boundary!"

"It is weakening, but the Boundary still stands, and Lorthas remains trapped. Whatever pass the Bull has found must spend most of each four-season blocked by snow and ice. I—"

The door to the chamber opened, and Joam entered, followed by a broad, barrel-chested man with a thick, dark beard and piercing black eyes. Numerous scars lined the stranger's face, and more half-healed wounds poked out from beneath the ragged sleeves of his thin, brown coat. He wore a chainmail shirt under the coat and a battered sheath at his hip. The sheath was empty, but even weaponless, he seemed a formidable man.

Mathis and Tarien eyed the newcomer suspiciously. He ducked his head and smiled, but the expression did little to improve his appearance. "I am Bantor, of the Krellian clan. I come from Vestlin of Rachannon."

Tarien stiffened, but Mathis interposed himself between the Gilean and the Rachannan. "What does King Vestlin want?" Mathis demanded, studying Bantor with cold eyes.

"My king wishes to discuss alliance." The grin disappeared when he looked at Tarien, and a sneer twisted Bantor's lips. "I suppose he offers succor to the Gileans too. Don't know why; a few winters under Tachan rule might stiffen their backs."

Tarien's hands clenched, and he started toward the Rachannan. Mathis shot him a beseeching glance, and the Gilean King stopped. "Why ally with us?" Mathis asked. "Rachannon is a Tachan land."

"Vestlin has little love for the Durange," Bantor replied.

"Vestlin doesn't want to lose his throne to his little cousin," Tarien spat.

A sly smile touched Bantor's lips, and he looked at the Gilean King. "There is that," he admitted. "One rarely loses a throne without losing a life. Pasil of Taren and Corand of Feldar can attest to that. Or they could have." Bantor turned to Mathis. "I come with Vestlin's terms. Will you hear them?"

"You?" Tarien sneered at the slovenly warrior. "A diplomat?"

"We Rachannen prefer to negotiate at sword point," Bantor responded, his temper flaring. "Not through false words and womanly cowering!" He feinted toward Tarien, and the Gilean King flinched. Joam shoved Bantor against the wall, but the Rachannan made no further move. At Mathis' signal, Joam released him. Bantor's guttural laughter echoed through the room.

Before Mathis could attempt to salvage the situation, the door to the chamber slammed open and Kal strode in with Jasova at his side. As soon as he saw the Tribesman, Bantor slipped past Joam and lunged to the attack. Kal reacted quickly, dodging the Rachannan's wild swing and slamming the man into the wall. The two grappled for a moment, and it took both Joam and Jasova to pull them apart.

"When seeking alliance," the King said, his voice as sharp, "it is not wise to attack one's allies."

"Allies?" Bantor repeated. He stared at Kal in disbelief. "Then the rumors are true? Alrendria deals not only with the Elves and Gileans, but with the Wildmen of the North?" Kal and Bantor glared at each other for a long moment, then Bantor shrugged off Joam's restraining hand and offered a stiff bow. "Forgive me, Tribesman. I thought you meant to harm my host."

Kal's eyes sparkled, and when he spoke, a slow breath punctuated each word. "I will forgive your insult, Human," he growled. Martyn could only guess how much effort it took the Tribesman to control his Blood Rage. "But lay hands on me again, and you will regret it."

"Enough of this!" Mathis snapped. "The Garun'ah are our friends. And Kal, the Rachannen have as much right to this alliance as any. If we're to have a hope of winning, we can't be selective in our choice of allies."

"If we're to win," Tarien added, "We must be allies in action, and not merely in word."

Bantor's harsh gaze swept over the room slowly, pausing on both Kal and Tarien. "Agreed. I'd rather be a friend of Gilead than a slave of the Durange." His expression hinted that the decision was a close one.

At Mathis' call, two Guardsmen appeared at the door's entrance. "Find quarters for the Rachannen Ambassador. Make sure he's given every comfort." To Bantor, he added, "I'll make myself available to you tomorrow." Bantor left under the watchful eyes of his escort. Once he was gone, Mathis turned to Kal. "Now, what's so important, *Kranach* of the Tacha, that you felt the need to burst in uninvited?"

Kal stepped forward until only a few hands separated him from the two kings. "I come bearing warning," he said calmly, staring at Mathis as an equal. "The Drekka have left the north. They attack the Tribes at every opportunity, and the *Kohr'adjin* use the confusion to their advantage. Most of the Tribes are unifying against the threat, but..." Kal trailed off, unwilling to say more.

Mathis swallowed nervously. "The Garun'ah will not send aid?"

Kal's eyes lowered to the ground. "The Tacha still send Hunters, as do the Channa, but fewer can be spared."

"What of the Afelda?" Martyn asked. "The Sahna? The other tribes?"

Kal shook his head. "The Afelda pledged to follow Jeran. With him gone, they vow only to avenge his death. The Sahna will send no aid south but promise that no enemy who enters their lands will leave alive. The smaller Tribes need their Hunters to defend themselves."

Tarien's face fell, and Mathis' shoulders slumped. "Are we destined to lose?" Martyn asked. "Do the Gods truly stand against us?" He paced the room, his frustration growing with every step. "At every turn we are struck blows. Lord Iban is taken. Jeran and Dahr are lost to us. Tylor's army grows stronger by the day, and we can barely stand in the same room without drawing blades!"

Mathis put a comforting hand on Martyn's shoulder. "Kal's news is unfortunate, but all is not lost. We've found an ally in Rachannon where we thought to find only enemies. The Drekka's return may limit our aid from the Garun'ah, but battling the Drekka may unify the Tribes against the Darklord."

"I bear further good tidings, Prince of Alrendria," Kal told Martyn. "My people have opened talks with the *Aelva*, the first in more than five hundred winters. The war which the *Kohr'adjin* nearly began upset the *Kranora*. They do not wish ignorance to blind them to the truth again. Even now, representatives meet with Nebari *el'e* Salerian on the edge of the Great Forest. Given time, and much help from Garun and Valia, our two Races may learn to understand each other."

Sighing, Mathis took a seat and waved for the others to sit as well. "That *is* good news," he admitted. "Maybe enough to counter the bad." Tarien and Martyn sat, but Kal remained standing. Jasova started for the door. "Guardsman," Mathis called. "I desire a word with you."

Jasova turned to face the king. "My son tells me you distinguished yourself in the Border Wars."

"I did my duty," Jasova answered, "nothing more."

Mathis laughed, and the sound of honest laughter was refreshing. It brought a smile to Tarien's face, and even Martyn felt emboldened by it. "You did well enough to catch Iban's eye," the King said, "and that old wolf didn't give praise lightly."

"Lord Iban was a great man," Jasova said. "I'm honored that my service pleased him."

"Your service has pleased me as well," Mathis replied. "Hopefully it will continue to do so." The King paused for a moment to examine the Guardsman. "I'm giving you command of our western campaign. Select a company of two hundred Guardsmen. You are to escort Brell Morrena on his return to Marin. Once he's safely home, you'll continue to Vela to lead our struggle against the Corsans."

Jasova eyes widened, but no hint of his surprise entered his voice. "As you command, King Mathis. I won't disappoint you. With your leave?" After waiting for Mathis' dismissal, he saluted fist-on-heart and quickly left.

"A wise choice," Joam said. "I've heard good things about that one."

"I'm not done yet," Mathis said. "The Guard needs a new High Commander. I've chosen you."

"My place is at your side," Joam replied, his eyes wary.

"And for a time, that's where you'll stay," Mathis assured him. "But once we've prepared our forces, you'll travel east to aid Tarien against the Tachans."

"My place is at your side," Joam repeated.

"Your place is where you're most needed, and you're needed in Gilead." Mathis crossed the room and clapped Joam's shoulder fondly. "I promise not to leave Kaper while you're gone, and I won't put myself into danger without your permission."

"I don't like this," Joam said flatly.

"You don't have to," Mathis laughed. "You just have to do it."

Mathis called for more food and drink and then resumed his place in the center of the room. "Come, my friends. We've talked about the past. We know of the threat posed by Tylor and the Darklord." The King's eyes darkened, and grim determination fixed itself on his face. "Now let's discuss what we're going to do about it."

Chapter 4

The rhythmic clang of hammers rang through the dark caverns. Men and women clad in rags and drenched in sweat plodded along to the distant beat, oblivious to their surroundings. The dark no longer bothered them, exhaustion and hunger had become close companions, and the heat was preferable to the bone-numbing cold outside. A few cringed whenever grey-armored guards walked past, but most paid the soldiers no more attention than they paid to anything else.

A pickaxe hit the wall with a dull thud, slipping into the crack between two stones and digging deep into the cavern wall. The discordant sound broke the workers' rhythm, and they paused to look. When the hunched slave wrenched the pickaxe free, the tunnel groaned and the crack widened. A few slaves backed away, but not many; death was no stranger to the mines of Dranakohr. For some, he was a welcome visitor.

The wall gave way, burying the man, and the falling stone drowned out his cry for help. When the dust cleared, a mound of dirt and rock ten hands high marked his tomb. The other slaves watched silently, unable or unwilling to help. One woman fell weeping against the wall. Another threw down her shovel and stepped toward the mound but froze after a step. With a shake of her head, she turned away. Most simply started working again.

Only one slave threw himself against the pile, desperately throwing handfuls of dirt and rock over his shoulder. "Quick," Jeran cried, "We need to get him out!" Few responded to his pleas, half-heartedly picking at the pile. Jeran begged the others to help, but his efforts were in vain.

One hand moved to his throat, to the cold metal collar. The dark iron band weighed him down, taunting him. Locked behind that magic-wrought band lay the solution to all his problems. Not for the first time, Jeran wished he could use magic. He would not have known what to do if he could, but he would have had a chance.

The irony was not lost on him. For winters he had prayed to be normal, to be free of magic. Now that his wish had been granted, he wanted access to his Gift. Magic filled him, but he could not use it; the collar prevented it. A dark chuckle rolled up from his gut, but it turned into a frustrated growl. He cursed his fellow slaves and redoubled his efforts, taking double handfuls of dirt, searching for some sign of life, a scrap of rag or the hint of flesh.

A loud crack echoed in Jeran's ear. The people at his side backed off immediately, but Jeran ignored the warning. Gritting his teeth, he continued to dig. The second swing sliced through his shirt and cut a line of fire across his back. Several more lashes followed in quick succession. Each blow was an agony, but Jeran emptied his mind and opened himself to magic. Calm suffused him, and the pain lessened. But the relief was bittersweet; magic danced before him, beckoning, but he could not touch it. It almost made him wish for the sting of the lash.

When the whip had no effect, the guard cuffed Jeran with a vicious backhand. The blow sent Jeran to the ground, burying his face in the rubble. He pushed himself to hands and knees, spat a mouthful of dirt and blood, and resumed digging.

The guard stepped back and, laughing cruelly, planted a solid kick in Jeran's gut. The force of the kick flipped Jeran over and drove the breath from his lungs. He lay there, gasping for air, his hands protecting his face.

"I can do this all day," the guard laughed as Jeran rolled to his hands and knees. He brought his whip down with a vengeance. Tears stung at Jeran's eyes, but he did not cry out. Weakly, he pulled at the mound.

"Not a fast learner, are ya?" The guard grabbed a handful of Jeran's hair and hauled him to his feet. His other fist was drawn back to strike, but when he saw Jeran's icy blue eyes, he stopped. Recognition flitted across his face, and fear quickly followed. Licking his lips, the guard released Jeran. "What are ya doing?" he demanded, but the joy had gone from his voice.

"Man... buried..." Jeran said between gasps. "Must help..."

The guard looked at the pile of loose stone. "He's dead. Give it up." Jeran glowered before throwing himself back on the mound. The guard turned away. "Do as ya like," he said, waving his hand in frustration. "The rest of ya, back to work! Ya'll not return to your barrows till ya've mined your quota."

The slaves fled, and after a final, scathing look at Jeran, the guard pressed on. Jeran's wounds throbbed, and his rags, heavy with blood and sweat, weighed him down. Small stones clattered down the tunnel, and Jeran threw handfuls of dirt behind him, but for all his work, the pile grew no smaller, and Jeran found no sign of the buried man.

He stopped long enough to catch his breath and saw a broken shovel poking out from the shadow of a nearby wall. When he bent to lift it, the skin over his wounds pulled tight, and Jeran almost collapsed. With the shovel, he managed to work the mound more quickly, but every impact sent another jolt through his body. Twice the cavern spun around him, forcing him to stop and catch his breath.

A gnarled hand, stained nearly black, broke free of the mound. Jeran pulled at the rubble with his hands, and once the man's arm was free, Jeran grabbed it. Bracing his feet against the mound, he heaved with all his might.

The man slid out far easier than Jeran expected, and he lost his balance. He screamed aloud when his back slammed into the cold stone of the tunnel. When the old man landed on top of him, driving the sharp edge of a stone into Jeran's back, he screamed again.

He lay there for some time, gasping. As his pain faded, his thoughts once again turned to the man he had saved. Rolling the body off him, Jeran sat up and checked for signs of life. The man's chest rose and fell, if only barely.

Sighing heavily, Jeran went in search of water. He found a collector, a large iron cauldron sitting beneath a stalactite, and looked inside. A thin layer of water with black flakes of iron and gritty debris coated the bottom. He took the wooden cup beside the cauldron and examined the thin trickle running down the stalactite, wondering how long it would take it to fill the cup.

"Too long," he muttered, bracing his feet against the cauldron's clawed feet. He drew several deep breaths to ready himself, then grabbed the cauldron with one hand and leaned back. Pain exploded through his body, but the heavy vat tilted up on its edge. Groping blindly with the cup, Jeran scraped the bottom.

Without warning, Jeran's strength gave out. He stumbled backward, fighting to maintain his balance, as the cauldron slammed down with a crash. It rocked back and forth before settling upright.

Exhausted, Jeran fell against the wall. Spots of color danced across his vision when his back scraped rough stone, and he almost lost his grip on the quarter full cup. He considered drinking the water himself and leaving the old man on his own, but his conscience eventually won and Jeran stumbled back to the site of the cave-in.

Kneeling beside the stranger, Jeran cradled the man's head. The stranger's eyes shot open. "Who are you?" His voice echoed hollowly through the cavern, and Jeran scrabbled backward. "You can't have my things! I'm not dead yet."

"I'm not here to rob you," Jeran said. "I saved you!"

"Took your time about it!"

Jeran shoved away his anger. "I did the best I could."

The old man snorted and eyed the cup. "You gonna offer me that or just taunt me with it?"

Jeran held out the cup, and the man snatched it out of his hand. He looked inside suspiciously, and his lips pressed into a narrow line. "This is all you could get? Did you drink it?" Jeran stared at the floor, concentrating on maintaining his focus, so that his pain would remain a dim buzz. The old man took a sip of water and handed the rest to Jeran. "Take it! It's only fair. You did the hard work. All I did was lay under the rocks."

A smile pulled at Jeran's lips, but he quickly wiped it away. "Thank you." He accepted the cup and downed its contents.

"No, thank you." As the man sat up and fussed with his clothes, Jeran studied him. Deep creases crossed the man's brow, and dark spots marred his flesh. Thick, white hair and a bushy beard hid his face, but two lively brown eyes meticulously examined the tattered, blackened rags he wore. The man's hands darted over his garments, plucking out bits of debris and brushing off dirt. After a time, the man nodded and turned his gaze on Jeran.

A thick band of iron circled the man's throat. "You're a Mage?" Jeran asked.

"Used to be," the stranger said, extending a hand. "My name's Yassik." Jeran stared dumbfounded, and Yassik cocked his head to the side. "Like this," he said, grasping Jeran's forearm. "It's an old custom." His unkempt beard split to show a bright, toothy grin. Silence filled the cave. "This is the part where you tell me your name."

"Yassik?" Jeran repeated, still shocked.

"No, Yassik's my name. What's yours?"

"The Mage historian? The one who wrote *Twilight Over Illendrylla*?"

"You've read my work?" Yassik beamed. "Marvelous! Literacy doesn't seem to be in fashion these days. Not like it used to be. You'll have to tell me which books you've read. And which you liked. It's been a long time since—" The Mage cut off abruptly, and his eyes narrowed. "No changing the subject. Your name!"

"Jeran. Jeran Odara."

"I knew I recognized you." Yassik grabbed Jeran's chin and tilted his head back and forth. "Shave off that beard—which is quite unflattering, I must say—and color your hair blonde, and you're the spitting image of your father."

Pulling away, Jeran self-consciously ran a hand down his chin. Since being taken prisoner, he had not been allowed access to anything he could use as a weapon, not even a razor. "You knew my father?"

"It was not hard to. Alic Odara seemed to be everywhere. Quite a man." Yassik looked around and cupped a hand behind his ear. "Don't hear anyone. How long was I out?"

"I'm not sure, but the workday was almost over."

Groaning, Yassik climbed to his feet. "I guess we'd better find our way back then. I'd hate to be down here when the ShadowMagi turn off the lights." He glanced at the faintly-glowing orbs casting a dim, yellow light down the tunnel.

Yassik offered Jeran a hand, and Jeran winced as the Mage pulled him to his feet. "How do they make those?" Jeran asked, gesturing toward the lights with his chin. "I thought magic didn't work near the Boundary."

"Magic can't cross it," Yassik explained, "and the Boundary perverts any flows used around it, causing unexpected results, but the distance has lessened over the winters." Yassik's eyes grew far away. "We had a lot of accidents in the beginning. No one anticipated the Boundary's effects on magic, and more than a few Magi lost their lives trying to understand the new rules. In the end, the Assembly decided it wasn't worth the risk."

Yassik started down the dimly lit corridor, and Jeran hastened to follow. "Lorthas kept trying?" Jeran asked.

"Not personally, but he insisted that his ShadowMagi, those who displeased him, at least, continue the research." Yassik stumbled, and Jeran reach out to steady the old man's steps. "Thank you. It seems the Darklord's perseverance paid off; his ShadowMagi have learned to do things here we thought impossible." Yassik touched his collar. "Not the least of which is how to construct these... things." His eyes grew distant again, introspective. "Who'd have thought it possible to amplify the Boundary's effects? I mean, it's a remarkable feat of magic. The mechanics behind it alone are worthy of study. I'd be impressed if I weren't so disgusted."

They shuffled through the corridors until the tunnel branched. Jeran started toward the left passage, tugging his rags close about his body. "I'm not looking forward to facing the cold."

A gnarled hand grabbed his arm. "Then why face it?" Yassik asked, glancing at his tattered clothes. "I'm not exactly dressed for an evening in the Boundary. Let's go the long way."

The Mage started toward the right shaft, and Jeran hurried to stop him. "That tunnel's empty," Jeran said. "The others told me it led to a dead end."

"Of course they did. That's what they were told, and they beat anyone who tries to prove otherwise." He stared at Jeran curiously for a moment. "Haven't you ever wondered why the guards don't walk you back to the Barrows? You think they want to tidy things up after the slaves go home?"

Yassik resumed his shuffling walk and Jeran kept close by his side. The ShadowMagi's lights faded, and darkness slowly descended, a black so deep that even with his mind focused Jeran could see nothing. Yassik grabbed his arm, pulling him forward. "Where would we go?" Jeran asked. "It would be suicide to hide in the mountains."

The faintest hint of light appeared, and a knot of tension loosened in Jeran's shoulders. The light intensified, and Jeran scanned the tunnel for the source. Faint patches of pale green clung to the moist rock, pulsing weakly. He touched one patch, and it flaked away, falling to the floor of the tunnel. Its light quickly died.

"A reasonable answer," Yassik snorted. "But it doesn't strike you odd that the guards' uniforms are never spotted with snow? Or that they never complain of the cold?"

Jeran frowned. "I guess I never thought about it."

"Hah!" barked Yassik. "Better get used to thinking. There's not much else to do here besides work and think."

The tunnel twisted and turned, and numerous side passages broke off from the main path, but Yassik continued on, choosing tunnels seemingly at random. After a time, Jeran grew suspicious. "If this route is for the guards, how do you know about it?"

"It's a little late for concern, isn't it?" Yassik chuckled. "But it's good to see you won't just blindly follow someone forever. A bit of caution would serve you well." Jeran's suspicions grew. He slowed, looking uncertainly over his shoulder at the dim passage behind him. "You might as well keep following," Yassik said, not looking back. "You'll never find your way back, and you could lose yourself in here for days if you don't know where you're going."

"How do you know so much about the tunnels?" Jeran demanded.

"I'm a scholar!" Yassik said as if that were answer enough, but when Jeran stopped dead, the old man laughed again. "I've been here a long time, and one old man is hardly worth noticing. I once disappeared for four days and no one realized it! When I stumbled out of the tunnels half-dead and covered in this glowing stuff, the guards thought I was a ghost."

Yassik urged Jeran forward and soon, the tunnel started sloping upward. "If you want, I can teach you the tunnels. Once you know your way around, you can show the others."

"Why haven't you shown them already?"

"Lorthas and I were never on good terms," Yassik replied. "I'm still not sure why he didn't just kill me. Maybe it amuses him to think of me as his prisoner. In any case, I've been reluctant to call attention to myself. If I remind him that I'm here, he might change his mind."

Yassik raised his hand for silence and peeked around the corner. He waved and disappeared around the bend. Jeran hurried to keep up. He suddenly found himself in familiar territory: the broad, brightly-lit caverns of Dranakohr.

Dranakohr, Kohr's Hammer in the lost language of the Orog, guarded the Darklord's pass through the Boundary. An ominous structure carved into a mountain at the top of a narrow and treacherous ascent, Dranakohr had been built by ShadowMagi to mimic the appearance of a castle, but its dark spires and forbidding parapets were formed of unbroken stone.

Jeran memories contained one view of the fortress from outside, an image blurred by the drugs used to block his Gift. He had walked the interior several times, but Tylor had surrounded him with guards on each trip, making it all but impossible to see anything other than grey armor and sneering faces. They were below the castle now, in a maze of crisscrossing tunnels larger than most cities. Those tunnels were divided into two zones: the Barrows, where the slaves lived, and the *ghrat*, an area off limits.

Jeran and Yassik emerged on the edge of the Barrows, not far from the passage to the castle proper. Anger pulsed against the calm of Jeran's focused mind. "I don't believe it!" Thoughts of the bitter cold flitted through his mind. Even during Harvest, a hand or two of snow often lay outside; now that winter had come in earnest, the drifts stood taller than a man. More than a few slaves had died from exposure. "There's a path! All this time... Why...?"

"They use the cold to cull the weak," Yassik explained, his voice soft, his eyes studying Jeran. "Besides, if a slave dies outside, it's one less body to deal with." Yassik glanced up and down the tunnel, then grabbed Jeran's sleeve and pulled him forward. "Hurry! It's best if they don't see us loitering here."

Yassik hurried through the passages, and Jeran labored to follow. His back still ached from the lashing, and his muscles burned, making even walking an effort. Soon, other shuffling forms came into view, men and women of all ages and from all lands, entire families spirited away in the dead of night or captured by the crews of Lorthas' black warships and brought in secret to Dranakohr.

Many of the huddled forms recognized Jeran, and most shrank away. A few stared with unhidden anger. Jeran met their stares, fighting the urge to hide from their cold, accusing eyes. He wanted to reassure them, but when he opened his mouth, no words would come. Ashamed, he pressed on; now he preceded Yassik through the tunnels, urging the Mage to go faster.

"They don't hate you," Yassik said once they reached an empty stretch of tunnel. His words offered little comfort. "They hate what your presence means for them. The Darklord protects you, and it chafes Tylor to have you here and be unable to torment you. He takes his frustrations out on them."

"I didn't ask for leniency," Jeran replied. "I'd gladly take whatever punishment Tylor decided to serve if it would spare those people suffering."

Yassik considered Jeran's words, his eyes probing, boring into Jeran in the manner of the Magi. "You would," he said with an approving nod. "Perhaps not gladly, but I believe you *would* suffer in their stead. You have a lot of your father in you, and your uncle as well." The compliment did little to lighten Jeran's mood, and as they continued through the Barrows, Jeran did his best to ignore the stares.

Few guards patrolled the Barrows. The slaves had nowhere to go, no possibility of escape. A full unit guarded the entrance to the castle above, and a squad watched each entrance to the *ghrat*. A handful of grey-armored men usually stood at the mouth of the tunnel to the outside, but it was more a punishment for them than a deterrent to the slaves. The guards rarely stopped anyone from passing; only a fool would brave the Boundary in winter.

Even during the Boundary's short growing season, no guards blocked the entrance to the fields. Tylor allowed the slaves free access to the valley as reward for their service. Each spring, he burned a semi-circle into the ground around the mouth of the pass. Any slave who crossed the charred grass was killed instantly. Jeran had heard that the guards often forced slaves to cross the line, and then ordered them killed as escapees.

Someone grabbed Jeran's shoulders and spun him around. Angry brown eyes stared at him for a moment. "It *is* you!"

"Malkin?" Jeran asked. Malkin had been a smith in Keryn's Rest. Jeran had seen others from the village here since his capture, but he had never had the courage to approach them. Jeran had never liked Malkin, but he was glad to see the smith alive.

"You remember me, Odara?" Malkin asked, and his plain hatred startled Jeran. "Good. Because I remember you and that lying uncle of yours!"

Jeran stiffened. "Don't speak of—"

"Don't order me, boy!" Malkin hissed. "Your uncle told us we had days before Tylor arrived. He told us everything would be alright, so long as we abandoned our homes." Malkin spat on the ground. "That coward. If not for him, none of this would have happened."

Jeran's hands clenched into fists, and his glare matched Malkin's. The smith was still an imposing figure, but he was not nearly as menacing as Jeran remembered. "My uncle did all he could for Keryn's Rest! He tried to lead Tylor away when he could have run and hid, and he paid the price for it too!" Jeran's eyes narrowed to slits. "And you had no intention of abandoning Keryn's Rest! You wanted to fight. I see you did a good job of it."

Malkin slammed Jeran against the wall, driving fresh spikes of pain through his body. "You and that Gods-cursed uncle cost us everything!" Malkin whispered. "The village in flames! Innocents slaughtered! Women and children used and taken as slaves! All this is your fault, Odara. The Bull wanted you. Not us."

Jeran could no longer control himself. With a snarl, he kicked off of the wall, ramming Malkin against the far side of the tunnel. Stunned, the smith released his grip, and with two well-placed blows, Jeran dropped the larger man to his knees. "Hate me if you will," Jeran said slowly. "Blame me for your own inaction, or for the will of the Gods. But never lay your hands on me again, or I'll remove them from your arms."

Malkin's eyes widened, and the sincerity of the threat even took Jeran by surprise. Ashamed, Jeran stepped back, and in a calmer tone, he said, "It pains me that my friends and neighbors have suffered here, but Dranakohr is not my doing, nor my uncle's. If you must lay blame, lay it on the Durange." Jeran walked away stiffly, trying to hide the pain that Malkin's accusation had brought. Trying to hide the fact that he agreed with the smith.

Yassik hurried to catch up. "You were rather rough on him."

Stunned, Jeran turned toward the Mage. "*I* was rough on *him*?"

"You did a little better at the end," Yassik admitted, "but you really must learn control." Jeran shook off the Mage's words, but Yassik grabbed Jeran's sleeve and pulled him to a stop. "With that collar on, losing your temper has no effect on your Gift, but outside Dranakohr, away from the Boundary, such a loss of focus could prove disastrous."

Jeran guessed where the conversation was headed. "I don't know what you're talking about."

"An unexpected loss of focus almost always gives the Gift the upper hand. A Mage could burn himself to a crisp or cause unspeakable damage if he allowed his emotions to rule. Maintaining focus is not merely a matter of holding magic; if you intend to master your Gift, you need to learn how to control the—"

When he saw the look on Jeran's face, Yassik broke into loud laughter. "Don't let my appearance mislead you, boy. I may look crazy, but I've been using magic for a long time, certainly long enough to tell when someone's focusing." He wagged a finger in Jeran's face. "It has something to do with the eyes, I think."

Jeran swallowed nervously, and Yassik guessed his thoughts. "Now, no need to worry. One would have to use magic for a long time to know what I know. As long as you don't try to focus around Lorthas, the fact that you are learning to focus magic should remain secret." Yassik frowned. "You might not want to practice around the Scorpion either, but he doesn't come into the Barrows without a good reason, so that shouldn't be much of a problem."

They continued walking in silence. Eventually, Yassik stopped beside a small hole cut into the wall. Similar holes, each about half the height of a man, dotted both sides of the tunnel. "Home, sweet home!" Yassik said, patting the wall fondly. "I'd invite you in, but the place is a mess."

Jeran almost smiled, but he quickly schooled his features. "It's not a crime to laugh," Yassik told him.

Jeran's stone-faced composure had returned in full. "What's there to laugh about?"

"Little enough," Yassik replied. "That's why you have to take advantage of every opportunity!" The Mage extended his hand, and this time Jeran took it without prompting. "Thanks again. Come by tomorrow, and I'll take you through the tunnels again." Without waiting for Jeran to reply, Yassik ducked down and disappeared into the hole.

Jeran hurried to his own barrow, doing his best to avoid the eyes of the other slaves walking the tunnels. He had to duck to fit through the low entrance, and when he did, his wounds reopened. Stifling a groan, he scurried down the shaft. After a few dozen hands, the tunnel widened, opening into a broad chamber. The roof was low, just high enough for Jeran to stand straight-backed, and the chamber spartan, devoid of decoration. A tiny ball hovered in the center of the room, its light yellowish and weak. A few crudely-drawn pictures graced one side of the chamber. One depicted a sunrise over a blue ocean, another, the city of Kaper from a distance.

A small pit, filled with dark ashes, commanded the center of the room, but they had used their last bit of fuel days ago. Even now, cold permeated the chamber; by midnight, with the winds howling through the corridors, temperatures would drop dangerously, driving the chill to the bone.

Four holes, even smaller than the entrance, jutted off from the main room at various angles. Wardel crawled out of one as Jeran entered the barrow. The Guardsman took one look at him and laughed. "And I thought *I* was dirty!"

Jeran looked at his tattered garments, smeared with dirt, and a small smile touched his lips. "There was a cave-in."

"Again?" Wardel sighed. "Keep this up, and there won't be any caves left."

Wardel's grin astounded Jeran. "How can you do that? How can you stay so cheerful?"

The smile disappeared. "If I weren't cheerful," Wardel answered, "I'd be miserable." After a moment of uncomfortable silence, the Guardsman reached into the sack at his side and withdrew a white stone. He studied it for a moment, and then nodded. Walking over to the seascape, he drew a flock of small, white birds above the crashing waves.

Long brown hair, flaked with dirt and hanging in stringy clumps, framed Wardel's wan face. A scraggy beard covered his jaw. His once well-maintained uniform was tattered, the Alrendrian Sun faded. Despite this and the haunted look that entered his eyes from time to time, Wardel weathered his enslavement well. The long periods of moody silence that marked the first few ten-days in the mines disappeared once he discovered a use for the soft, colored stones littering the mineshafts. Now he spent most evenings working on his murals or scouring the tunnels for the right shade of rock.

"So, you finally returned," Quellas said, crawling from his den. "I was starting to worry about you." Despite his words, no hint of concern entered the Guardsman's voice. Quellas was thin, almost gaunt, his face pinched and hard. Harsh blue eyes stared accusingly across the barrow.   "I was detained," Jeran said. He had no time for Quellas' games. "Where's Reanna?"

Quellas threw himself to the floor, digging through his meager supply of rations. "She's in her den," Wardel answered, his eyes never leaving his work. He had a brown stone out now and was trying to outline the hull of a Raker with it.

Jeran crawled through the tunnel into Reanna's den. "Reanna?" he called out softly, scanning the dimly lit chamber for signs of the Tribeswoman. She crouched in the corner, her back to the wall, her knees drawn up to her chest. She trembled uncontrollably with her arms wrapped tightly around her legs. Twin trails traced paths down her cheeks, the skin washed clean by tears.

Their capture had affected Reanna worse than it had the others. Her once-vibrant eyes were sunken and dull; her hair hung limp around her shoulders. She mumbled in Garu, the words low and incomprehensible.

Jeran hurried to her, and at his touch, Reanna jumped. Her eyes struggled to focus, but she did not recognize him immediately. "Jeran," she whispered, the word a half-question. Her voice trembled when she said it.

"Are you cold?" Jeran asked, shrugging off the topmost layer of his dirt-covered rags. Reanna shook her head, but she did not stop him from wrapping the coat around her shoulders.

"In my soul," she replied, the words flat and lifeless. She looked up, and her eyes seemed to peer through the stone. "I cannot live like this. No child of Garun can live like this! This is worse than death, Jeran."

Jeran wrapped an arm around Reanna. With his free hand he stroked her hair, offering what small comfort he could. "I have no soul," Reanna lamented, almost wailing, and she collapsed into his embrace. Her sobs echoed through the den, and Jeran clutched the frightened Tribeswoman to his chest, not knowing what else to do.

Reanna wrapped her arms around him, and Jeran hissed, trying to hide the pain her embrace caused. When her fingers ran over one of his lash marks, Reanna jerked upright and she muffled her sobs. "Blood!" she said, sniffing her hand. "You are wounded?"

Jeran shook his head. "It's nothing. Just some trouble with a guard. I'll be fine."

"I have some water." Reanna pushed Jeran away. "We must clean your wounds before they grow poisoned." She grabbed a flask tucked into the corner of the chamber and the cleanest rag she could find.

"Water's too precious," Jeran said stubbornly, trying to stop her. "We can't waste it."

"Precious?" Reanna repeated. "There is a field of water as twenty hands tall outside. All we have to do is thaw it." She forced Jeran onto his stomach; he could do nothing to resist. "If we run out, I will get more."

Reanna used any excuse to go outside. No matter how cold, no matter whether she walked through blinding sun or blackest night, she relished every moment in the real world. It was almost as if, staring at the crisp blue sky or countless stars, she could forget for a moment that she was a slave of the Darklord.

Again, Jeran tried to protest, but Reanna would not listen. She pulled the rags from his wounds and daubed Jeran's back with a rag soaked in half-frozen water. Jeran jumped at her every touch, and when she finished, Jeran hurriedly climbed into some cleaner rags. "I thought the guards had orders not to touch you," Reanna said.

"They do, but I'm not as easy to recognize as I once was. Sometimes they make mistakes."

"You should report the guard. He should be punished."

"To what end? If the guard is punished, he'll take it out on others. These people already live in fear of Tylor, and the Bull torments them because he can't touch me." Jeran shook his head. "I'd rather the whip than their hatred."

There was a long silence, and Reanna stared into his eyes. "How do you maintain your balance in this place?" she asked, a note of awe in her voice. "I barely have strength to crawl from the barrow each morning. My own honor deserts me. The other day I considered fleeing the mines to seek my death in the Boundary."

Jeran grabbed Reanna by the shoulders. "You will not! Don't even think such a thing! We must be patient, Reanna. A chance for escape will come. We must wait for it."

"I do not have the strength," she said, on the verge of sobbing. "Without my soul, I am nothing."

"You are *still* a child of Garun," Jeran assured her. "You are Reanna *uvan* Isbek, Snow Rabbit, *Dahrina* of the Tacha. Your soul is still within you; you just can't see it."

Another silence filled the chamber. "I am afraid," she admitted, a tremble in her voice.

Jeran's hand sought hers. "So am I," he told her. "So am I."

They sat in silence for a long time, gaining comfort from the other's presence. As night fell, so did the temperature, and Jeran knew it was growing late. "I should go to my own den," he said, starting to pull away.

Reanna's hand tightened on his arm. "Please," she whispered. "Do not go. It is in the dark of night when my strength is weakest." She went to the corner, where a small pile of hides sat on the floor. "The night will not be as cold if we share our bodies' warmth."

Jeran joined her on the pallet. After piling the hides atop them, he wrapped his arms around Reanna, taking comfort in the press of her body against his. In a few moments her breathing was slow and even, but Jeran did not fall asleep until much later.

Chapter 5

Jeran woke long before dawn, though in Dranakohr, dawn could only be detected by a slight warming of the air and the calls of the guards ordering them back to work. He sat in silence, his legs folded beneath him, his eyes closed. He emptied his mind and tried to seize magic, but the flows remained elusive. Since his capture, holding magic had proved difficult; simply sensing it was often a struggle. Even when the gossamer strands of light and color surrounded him, it took most of Jeran's willpower to take one. Once he held the tiniest flow, though, he was usually able to gather more.

Keeping the magic controlled proved even more difficult. It fought with a life of its own, struggling to free itself, struggling to fill him, to use him as a conduit. Jeran battled the magic as long as he was able, but in the end, the power of nature overwhelmed him, leaving him breathless and empty. It was a frustrating process made no more palatable by the knowledge that he had worked at it tirelessly since his capture. Despite days of seizing magic and releasing it, drawing as much as he could and waiting for it to run wild, he had little more control than when he had started. Other Gifted might fear the consequences of such reckless practice, but Jeran had no concerns. His collar, his curse, protected him.

When his attempt to hold magic failed, the den turned dark, the heightened senses of the focused Mage abandoning him. Sighing heavily, Jeran touched the dark band circling this throat. The collar symbolized his confinement, but it was also the source of his salvation. It prevented him from using his Gift against his captors, but it provided him with the ability to train without endangering those around him.

Jeran tried to seize magic again, but the flows of energy, each a different shade of color, shied away from his attempt to control them. The failure infuriated Jeran. Before being captured, he had been able to seize magic at will; now most of his efforts were in vain. *Is it the Boundary? Or am I doing something wrong? I wish Tanar were here.*

Without warning, the flows rushed toward him, and he felt a surge of energy. The victory was bittersweet; power coursed through him, but something was different. Where once Jeran had felt like a river, channeling magic where he needed it, he now felt like a pond. Magic filled him, but it had nowhere to go.

The feeling made him uncomfortable, but Jeran ignored it as he gathered more strands of power. He made no attempt to use the magic, nor did he try to extend his perceptions—his one attempt to do so had rendered him unconscious and left him nauseated for days. Bit by bit he brought magic under his control, until he held every flow in the room. The magic fought him, struggling to free itself, but Jeran kept his mind focused. More magic came, drawn to his call, and for a moment, Jeran felt a rush, the sweet feeling of life, of freedom.

Before long, sweat beaded his forehead, and his breathing quickened. The magic surged, first once, then a second time. Jeran stopped drawing magic and concentrated instead on holding what he had. Jeran trembled with the effort of containing the flows until, with a final surge, the magic won, leaving the room dark and Jeran panting. He had no idea how long the struggle had lasted but was certain it was longer than the time before. His lips twisted up in a triumphant grin, and he readied himself to try again.

"How can you sweat in this cold?" Reanna asked, stretching her arms above her head. "It is cold even for me, yet you sit bare-chested, dripping water like it is summer in the Tribal Lands."

Jeran smiled but did not speak. His mind was focused; he was trying to figure out what he had done differently. Reanna saw the look in his eyes. "Are you in *mahk'tarin*?" she asked. "Do you commune with the Gods?"

Jeran laughed, but the sound carried little mirth. "I doubt the Gods would offer me much comfort, and I'm certain they don't want to hear what I have to say to them."

"One should not mock the Gods." Reanna shrugged off the hides and moved toward him. Using the cleanest rag she could find, she wiped the sweat from his body and examined his wounds, then wrapped his tattered shirt over his shoulders. "If you are not careful," she chided, "the cold will be your death."

"Of all the things that could kill me, I worry about cold least."

A tense silence followed. "Is there any hope?" Reanna whispered.

Jeran heard desperation in her voice, and he smiled as he traced a hand tenderly down the line of Reanna's chin. "There's always hope," he told her, but a harsh laugh bubbled up from his gut. "Just not a lot." Closing his eyes, Jeran listened to the sounds outside the barrow. "It'll be morning soon. You'd better get ready for the mines."

Reanna looked at her ragged clothes. "I am ready," she told him, crossing to the far side of the den. "I have food. Would you like some?"

Jeran shook his head. "Later," he said as he crawled from Reanna's den.

Quellas and Wardel sat around the ashes of the firepit. Wardel glanced up from his coloring stones and offered Jeran a friendly nod. Quellas grinned mischievously. "Enjoy yourself, Lord Odara?"

Jeran crossed the room in an instant, grabbed Quellas by the throat, and shoved him backward. The Guardsman's head slammed into the floor, and Quellas grunted in pain. Anger surged through Jeran, and his hand tightened. "My patience grows thin, Guardsman," Jeran hissed. "You had best remember your manners."

Quellas struggled, but his efforts were for naught, and his movement grew more panicked. "Didn't we talk about your temper yesterday?" a voice called from the barrow's entrance.

Jeran jumped back and released his hold on the Guardsman. Gasping for air, Quellas rolled to his feet, but instead of rounding on Jeran, he turned to face the newcomer, tensed for action. "Yassik!" Wardel called out jovially, stepping between Quellas and the Mage. "Welcome! You already seem to know Jeran, but the fellow behind me—the one holding that rock like it's a dagger!—that's Quellas. We served together."

Yassik ducked his head in greeting, but his eyes remained on Jeran. "Guardsman Wardel and I have spoken of you," he admitted. "I've heard endless accounts of your tolerance and patience. To be honest, I haven't seen much in the way of either."

"Perhaps captivity changes a man," Jeran muttered. *I almost killed him! I wanted to kill him! What's happening to me?*

"Perhaps," Yassik agreed. "Or perhaps you're pushing yourself too hard. Learning control offers many dangers, and not all of them are physical ones. The first sign of overextension is a loss of self-control."

Jeran's temper flared. "Who are you to lecture me?"

"Me?" laughed Yassik. "I'm just a slave, and a poor excuse for one. But answer this: What good is increasing your strength if the first time you lose your temper, your Gift runs wild? Continue down the path you've chosen, and it will be your downfall."

Jeran laughed, cold and hard. "And what would you have me do, Mage? Follow the path you choose? Dance for the Magi and bow to the Assembly?" He shook his head forcefully and pointed a warning finger at Yassik. "The Mage Assembly wants to control everyone with the Gift. Why should I exchange one enslavement for another?"

"The Assembly has fallen far," Yassik admitted, "but they're not as bad as the Darklord. There's a lot they could teach you, if you'd give them the chance."

"I've witnessed the Assembly's compassion firsthand. One of your *enlightened* Magi tried to tie a leash to me once, and I had to teach him a lesson." Jeran tried unsuccessfully to calm himself. "I like you, Yassik. Don't make me teach you the same lesson."

"You walk a thin line," Yassik said, ignoring Jeran's threat. "I don't fault you for wanting to strengthen your Gift. I don't even fault you for your anger. You've suffered a lot, and only a fool would think your suffering was finished. But power without control leads to destruction. Even Lorthas knows this! If you don't restore your inner balance, you will fail. We will fail." Yassik's gaze bored into Jeran. "If you're not even willing to try, you might as well swear fealty to Lorthas now."

"Jeran has not lost his balance!" Reanna cried as she crawled from her den.

"Hasn't he?" Yassik asked, regarding the Tribeswoman for a moment before turning back to face Jeran. "You may cling to the vestiges of equanimity, but your center crumbles. Where once compassion dominated, now hatred rules. You have confused anger with honor, vengeance with justice."

"How dare you?" Reanna interposed herself between Jeran and Yassik. She towered over the Mage; at full height, her head brushed the ceiling of the barrow. "You speak—"

"*Shtal!*" Yassik snapped, his voice reverberating through the barrow. "*Yahn Jeran sin tsalla Drakmor varlorn!*"

Reanna's eyes widened. "*Tsha'ma,*" she whispered, backing away.

"I'm honored, *Dahrina,* but I'm only a lowly Mage, not one of Garun's Chosen." To Jeran, he said, "You may listen to my words or ignore them; the choice is yours. I won't bind you to the Assembly nor lead you down any one path. I only want to make sure that you survive."

Emotions warred within Jeran. "I apologize," he said, though he had to wrench the words from his mouth. As if the words were a balm, Jeran's anger evaporated. "Really, Yassik, I'm sorry."

A calm quiet descended on the barrow. Even Quellas relaxed enough to drop his stone dagger and finish his meal before returning to his den. Yassik and Wardel discussed the Guardsman's drawings. Jeran and Reanna ate in silence, but the Tribeswoman studied him whenever she thought Jeran was not looking.

Before long, a harsh voice echoed down the hall, ordering the slaves to the mines. Reanna and the Guardsmen donned their hides and started for the entrance. When Jeran made no move to follow, Reanna turned. "Go," he told her, forcing a smile. "They don't care if *I* work." Reluctantly, she disappeared into the dark. Once he and Yassik were alone, Jeran turned to the Mage. "You might want to go."

"They might withhold my rations, but like as not they won't miss one old man for a while. Tylor has thousands of slaves in these mines, and the guards couldn't care less about their duties in the Barrows." Yassik ran a hand through his bushy white beard and studied Jeran. "That collar you wear offers us a unique opportunity for training, and we'd be fools not to take advantage of it. But you don't know your limits. Magic drains the spirit more quickly than it does the body. By the time you're physically exhausted, you've already gone too far."

"I must learn as quickly as I can! It takes you Magi winters to learn control. I must learn it before I escape."

"That's one thing, at least," Yassik smiled. "As long as you believe you'll escape, we still have a chance!" His eyes grew serious. "But learning to focus magic will do you no good if you kill yourself in the process or turn yourself into another Darklord. You should keep practicing. You *must* keep practicing. But you must learn to control yourself before you learn to control magic." Yassik eyed him up and down again. "Halve your practice."

"Halve!" Jeran repeated, shocked.

"For now. We'll increase it when you're ready." He turned to crawl out of the barrow, but at the entrance, he craned his neck around. "Continue your meditations though. And don't worry, I'll provide you with different exercises, ones that will make you yearn for the simplicity of holding magic."

Jeran followed Yassik out of the barrow and through the tunnels, but as they neared the secret passage to the mines, one of Tylor's guards confronted them. "Where do you think you're going?"

"To the mines," Jeran answered. "But my friend forgot his coat. I told him I'd accompany him."

"Not today," the guard countered. "You'll have to find your own way, old man. The Master wants a word with your young friend."

"The Master!" Yassik said, assuming the role of a half-crazed old man. He bowed and cringed as if the guard himself were Lorthas. "Blessings to the Master! Take young Jeran. If the Master wants his company, who am I to argue?"

The guard pushed Yassik aside. "This way," he said, shoving Jeran forward. Jeran stumbled but caught himself before he fell and preceded the guard through the twisting passages.

At the entrance to Dranakohr, the intersection of a dozen different passages with a raised stone enclosure in its center, a dark-armored warrior looked up. "Where are you going with that thing?"

"The Master wants to see him," Jeran's guard replied.

"Hmm. Probably gonna use his magic to tear him apart," the man said. "Or maybe he'll roast him alive. I saw him do that once—"

"The Boundary separates Lorthas from me," Jeran interrupted. He grabbed the band at his throat and shook it roughly. "And I wear this, so I can't cross over to him. Lorthas' magic frightens me only slightly more than you do."

The guard stiffened. He left the enclosure and approached Jeran, his fist drawn back to strike. "I wouldn't," Jeran's guard said. "This is the Odara."

The man checked his swing. Jeran laughed at the man as he was pushed past the guardpost and toward the only tunnel with an iron gate protecting it. "Hurry back, Irit! Zhakar's bringing some of the slaves today!"

The gate stood open, and Jeran saw rust on the hinges as he passed. Once through, the tunnel climbed sharply, and the rough walls smoothed, opening wider and growing more regular in size. The gentle twists and turns became sharp angles, and the walls became etched to look like stacked stone. Even the floors gave the illusion of tiles, though Jeran knew the shades and patterns were the work of Magi, not masons.

Wooden doors, solid and sturdy, appeared at regular intervals. Tapestries depicting scenes of Tylor's triumphs or landscapes of Ra Tachan spotted the walls, and statues of stone and bronze accentuated every intersection. No torches or sconces lighted the way; the stone itself glowed with an unnatural radiance.

They climbed for an eternity, and the immensity of Tylor's stronghold amazed Jeran; not even the King's palace in Kaper with its catacombs below matched Dranakohr in size. Jeran stopped at the first window they passed. In the east, the sun had just crested the mountains, and the sight of it stole Jeran's breath. He had seen neither sunlight nor blue skies since his capture; the slaves went to the mines before dawn and returned well after nightfall.

The guard shoved him, forcing Jeran down the hall. His collar grew colder with every step they drew nearer to the Boundary; it would feel like ice by the time he stood in the large chamber where Lorthas held his audiences. Jeran had spent a great deal of time in that room, but little of it in the real world.

A second set of footfalls echoed on the stone behind them. "Halt," called a familiar voice. The guard pulled Jeran to a stop. "Leave. I'll escort him from here."

"Of course, Commander." The guard's hand disappeared from Jeran's shoulder, and his footsteps receded down the hall. A gauntleted hand pushed Jeran forward. "You look terrible."

"The service isn't as good as in Kaper..." Jeran admitted, scrubbing at his beard, "but it seems to suit you, Katya." He craned his head around to look at her. Tight red curls fell past her shoulders, covering dark armor. A cloak of black, trimmed in gold and with the Darklord's insignia pinned to the breast, covered the form-fitting leather mail. Hard green eyes stared at Jeran, but sadness lurked behind Katya's cold gaze.

"I don't blame you for hating me," Katya whispered.

"I don't hate you," Jeran replied.

"After what I did—"

"You saved Martyn and Treloran. Do you have any idea what their deaths would have started?" Jeran stopped dead and turned to face Katya. "You did your duty as a Guardsman and sacrificed a great deal to do it." He forced a smile. "I just wish you hadn't hit me so hard."

Katya laughed, but the sound was as devoid of emotion. "If not for that, my uncle would have killed you. You owe me your life, Odara."

Jeran looked down pointedly at his ragged clothes. "My life…" Another strained silence descended, and Katya urged Jeran forward. After a time, with the bleak and barren halls passing them by in silence, Jeran asked, "Why are you here?"

"The Master requested your presence. I'm—"

"No," Jeran interrupted. "Why are you still *here*?"

For a moment, he did not think Katya would answer. "Where else would I go? You may not hate me, but the rest of Alrendria does. There's no place in Madryn where I'd be safe."

"So you stay here?"

Katya's lip quivered slightly. "They are my family."

"Your family?" Jeran glared at her. "You're better than this, Katya Durange! You're better than *them*."

"This is my home," Katya replied, her voice regaining strength. "This is the only place I'm wanted. My uncle has his faults, but he's not the monster you believe him to be!" Jeran's eyes betrayed doubt, and Katya grew defensive. "Would you abandon your uncle if our positions were reversed?"

"And Salos?" Jeran asked coldly. "Lorthas?"

Katya sighed. "What would you have me do? Where would you have me go? Out there I'm the walking dead. Here, I can live. Maybe I can even temper what is to come." Her eyes begged for Jeran's understanding. "They are my family."

"Your family is out there," Jeran said, pointing south. "Your family is despairing because he thinks he's been betrayed. Salos, and even Tylor—no matter how honest your feelings for him—may be blood, but they are no more your family than the Darklord!"

There was a long, pained silence. "He would kill me, if he had the chance." Katya avoided his name as if it might invoke his presence. And his wrath.

"You don't know Dahr as well as you think. He couldn't kill you if he wanted to. Not even if you planned to drive a blade into his own heart."

"The mere sight of me would break his heart again." Katya blinked away tears. "I did that once, and it was more than I could bear. It's best if he forgets me." Her expression hardened. "And we had best keep moving. The Master doesn't like to wait."

She pushed Jeran forward, and they continued down the passageway. "Do you know what happened to the others?" Jeran asked.

"As far as I know," Katya said, "everyone survived. The princes returned to Kaper. Frodel and Vyrina followed us, probably hoping to free you and the others. My uncle discovered them and set an ambush." Her tone grew flat. "They fell into it."

Jeran's eyes fell to the stones at his feet. "Did he kill them, or are they slaves too?"

"No. They're free."

Jeran stared at Katya quizzically, and after checking the hall to make sure they were alone, Katya elaborated. "Vyrina fell instantly, but Frodel evaded my uncle's archers. He could have escaped, but he refused to leave without Vyrina, and my uncle's men subdued him. They were to be brought to Dranakohr with you for questioning."

Katya glanced around nervously, and her voice lowered so much that Jeran could barely hear her. "That night, I slipped from our encampment and incapacitated the guards. I cut Frodel's bonds and revived him, gave him a supply of food, and told him to take Vyrina into the mountains.

"The fool of a Tribesman nearly strangled me!" she added, a hint of anger tingeing her voice. "He let go just before I lost consciousness, mumbled something about a blood debt, and disappeared. My uncle was furious, but getting you back to Dranakohr was more important than finding the two of them."

"And Dahr?" Jeran asked. "Where is he?"

"There's been no word," Katya said, and Jeran heard concern in her voice. "He wasn't captured, but he hasn't returned to Kaper. It's like he just disappeared!" Katya licked her lips nervously.

"If you're worried about him, you could go look for him."

Katya did not respond, and she stopped in front of an elaborate oak door, its hinges and latch gilded, an intricate pattern worked into the wood. "The Master said you were to enter alone," she said, her voice now calm and controlled. "I wish you well, Odara." She spun on her heels and marched down the hall.

Jeran pushed open the door and stepped inside. It swung closed behind him, enveloping him in darkness. A fire crackled on the far side of the chamber, casting a weak light that barely reached across the room. Jeran waited a moment, but when nothing happened, he started forward.

The Darklord's Hall was decorated differently than the first time Jeran had been brought here. It reminded him more of his memories from the Twilight World. Tapestries lined the walls, depicting ancient battles from before the MageWar, and a long red carpet ran the length of the chamber. A fine chair with plush red cushions sat beside the fire, and not far from it, separated by a low table was a cruder, wooden seat. A bottle, two glasses, and several trays sat on the table.

Lorthas sat in the chair, a glass of wine held in one skeletal, bone-white hand. "Jeran!" the Darklord called jovially, waving him forward with his free hand. "Please, join me. I've had wine and food brought." Jeran shuffled forward, scanning the room for observers. Lorthas noticed but chose not to comment, though his thin lips drew up in a knowing smile. "I must apologize for neglecting you. Things have been hectic in *Ael Shataq*, and Tylor demands much of the time I can spare on the rest of Madryn."

Lorthas wore the robes he favored, a thin material slightly lighter than his pale skin. Bleached white hair hung loose about his shoulders. When Jeran stepped into the light, the Darklord's grin turned into a frown. Fiery red eyes flared with the power of the Gift, and he stiffened in his seat. "You have looked better," he said, his voice cool and even.

"Slaves are not given much opportunity to bathe," Jeran replied. He ran a hand the length of his chin. "Nor is it wise to provide slaves with razors. For some reason, the guards think they might be used as weapons."

Lorthas set his wine on the table and leaned forward, resting his chin in his hands to hide his scowl. "And your clothes?"

"You're not impressed?" Jeran asked, feigning disappointment. "I wore my best for you."

"Am I to believe that all of my workers are in a similar... state?"

"Most of your *slaves* are in significantly worse condition."

Lorthas eyed Jeran for a long time. "Tylor and I have discussed this," he said with the kind of exasperation reserved for willful children. "That man can be infuriating."

The Darklord gestured for Jeran to sit, and Jeran did as he was told. "A drink?" Lorthas reached for the bottle, but Jeran declined. Lorthas poured him a glass anyway. He used a metal rod with a hook at one end to push it across the table. "The Boundary can be inconvenient at times," Lorthas chuckled, moving the rod to a platter of food. "You look hungry."

The aromas wafting from the platter made Jeran's mouth water. "You waste your time," Jeran said flatly. "I will never serve you."

Lorthas sighed. "What must I do to convince you of my good intentions? We want the same things: peace and trust among all the peoples of Madryn." A silence fell between them, and Jeran tried to ignore the food, though he could not hide the complaints from his stomach. "You won't serve me," Lorthas said suddenly, a victorious smile spreading across his face, "but perhaps you'll serve your countrymen. Perhaps we can strike a bargain? If you keep me apprized of the condition of my workers, I will, in return, temper Tylor's treatment of them."

If I can help them, it might be worth it. Jeran's eyes narrowed suspiciously, and he struggled with the decision. "How do I know I can trust you?"

"Why, you have only to use your eyes!" Lorthas smiled, showing a set of perfect white teeth. He looked as if he had just won a great battle, and the sight made Jeran nauseous. "If our meetings don't improve conditions in the Barrows, then you'll know I'm a lying monster, just like everyone thinks. Conversely, when you see your suggestions acted upon and Tylor punished for his mistreatment, you'll have proof of my good faith. Perhaps you'll even begin to trust me."

"I will never serve you, Darklord."

Lorthas' smile broadened. "Of course not. But meeting with me is not the same as serving me, is it? And if it can benefit so many..." Lorthas raised his glass. "Do we have an agreement?"

Jeran hesitated, but in the end, he saw no better option. No one would thank him for leaving their pallets cold and their bellies empty. He had a duty to protect his people; if meeting with Lorthas kept them alive and healthy, he had no choice. Slowly, he raised his own glass to toast the bargain.

"Now," Lorthas said after they had finished their drink, "let's talk particulars." Red eyes surveyed Jeran. "Select a score of people you can trust. At the conclusion of every work day, they will be provided razors." Lorthas wagged a finger at Jeran. "A careful tally will be kept, and the instruments will be collected each night, so choose carefully. The first time a razor is used as a weapon will be the last. I'm willing to be conciliatory, but I have no intention of letting my workers use my generosity against me."

Lorthas ran a hand along his bony chin. "A number of hot springs flow beneath the Boundary. I'll have my Magi determine which ones flow near the Barrows and divert them to bathing chambers." Lorthas' eyes sparkled slyly. "I'd welcome your aid in this task. Simply swear not to use your Gift against my servants, and I'll gladly remove that—"

"I'll swear no oath to you," Jeran said, his voice the cold crackle of ice in midwinter.

"A pity," Lorthas replied. He tapped a finger against his cheek. "How else can I make your lives more enjoyable?"

"You could set us free," Jeran suggested.

Lorthas' surprised laugh caught Jeran off guard. For a moment, the Darklord sounded Human. "Allow me to rephrase. How can I make your stay more bearable?"

"The Barrows are cold," Jeran said. "The piles of worn hides we have are unacceptable. Blankets would be a blessing, and fuel for the fire pits. Something that doesn't smoke much."

"Fuel is hard to come by," Lorthas told him. "The Boundary makes winters in *Ael Shataq* harsher than anything you have experienced."

"Perhaps the ShadowMagi can make it warmer. Like they make the lights."

"That's not possible. We've learned how to do a great many things near the Boundary, but creating fire is not one of them. All attempts so far have been... disastrous." Lorthas tapped his lower lip. "Blankets I can find, and new clothes as well. I will have them brought immediately." The Darklord shook his head ruefully. "It's quite embarrassing, I must admit. Had I known that Tylor allowed conditions to degenerate so much, I'd have taken matters into my own hands long ago."

"Food is scarce," Jeran said, ignoring the Darklord's comment.

"Food is scarce everywhere, but I'll see what can be done." Lorthas settled back in his chair. "Anything else?"

"The guards use their whips freely, and Tylor thinks his order to spare me gives him the right to punish others in my place."

The Darklord's face tightened; the vein at his temple throbbed. "I'll discuss Tylor's behavior and impress upon him that discipline and trust is more effective a motivator than fear." Lorthas stood. "Perhaps we should conclude this meeting. I'll have the razors brought tonight. Remember to impress upon the workers the need for proper conduct."

Lorthas looked at Jeran again, and his lips curled up in pity. He picked up a brass bell beside his chair and rang it. "We will meet again in five days to discuss our progress."

A servant rushed into the hall behind Jeran. "Our guest requires a bath before returning to the Barrows. Provide him with a razor and some soap; though be sure to collect both before he returns to the tunnels." The servant started to lead Jeran toward the chamber's entrance, but Lorthas raised his hand. "Give him clean clothes, enough for him and those who share his barrow. And have Tylor brought to me."

The servant escorted Jeran to a bathing chamber. He sealed Jeran inside, allowing him to bathe in private. Jeran cleaned himself quickly, trying not to enjoy the luxury of a hot tub too much. He trimmed his hair and shaved, then dressed in the fresh clothes waiting for him beside the tub. The new outfit felt far better than the filthy rags he had worn all winter, but when he saw the Darklord's insignia embroidered on the breast, he nearly changed back into his old clothes. He sliced the stitching with his razor and ripped the sigil from the shirt.

The servant and a guard waited outside. Jeran traded his razor for three more outfits and allowed the guard to lead him back to the Barrows. Once back in his barrow, Jeran placed an outfit in front of each den, then sat near the firepit, cleared his mind, and practiced his meditations. He took Yassik's advice and refrained from seizing magic; instead, he studied the flows around him, trying to see where they came from and where they went. After a while, he noticed a pulsation within the bands that matched the beating of his heart.

The temptation to reach for the magic grew, but Jeran resisted. He left the barrow and walked the tunnels aimlessly. At the entrance to the *ghrat*, he saw a lone guard leaning against the dark stone, snoring. Jeran considered stealing the man's dagger, but he decided against it and continued on.

He made it only a handful of steps before his eyes were drawn back to the dark passageway. No one knew what lay beyond that tunnel; the slaves were forbidden entry. Jeran wondered what Lorthas was hiding, and more importantly, his meeting with the Darklord weighed heavily on his mind. Jeran felt like a traitor, and he yearned to do something to provoke his captors, something to evoke Tylor's rage.

Smiling, Jeran slipped past the guard and entered the tunnel to the *ghrat*.

Chapter 6

Jeran sprinted down the tunnel to put some distance between himself and the guard. The light faded, but Jeran slowed only when his foot caught a rock and he fell. He rolled to his feet and hunched over, gasping for air. Peering into the gloom, he tried to guess how far the tunnel went, how deep beneath the mountain he would have to travel before reaching the *ghrat*.

Once he caught his breath, Jeran started forward, but after a dozen steps the tunnel turned, plunging him into complete darkness. He reached out to his Gift and opened himself to magic, but even with his senses enhanced he saw nothing. After a few more steps, Jeran tripped again, falling to his knees. Sharp rocks tore at his flesh and debris clattered down the tunnel. Jeran gritted his teeth and knelt for a time, ears straining for the sound of approaching footsteps. Once certain no one had heard him fall, he pulled himself to his feet. The dank, stale air burned his lungs, but he forced himself to continue.

This time, he was more careful. He moved at a snail's pace, with one hand pressed firmly against the wall and the other outstretched, feeling blindly for obstructions. The stone around him absorbed sound; before long, even the few noises drifting from the Barrows faded, leaving Jeran floating in a world of nothingness. He could not see, not even his own hand held a finger's width from his face; he heard nothing other than his own footfalls and the pounding of his heart.

He walked for an eternity, testing the ground before every step. Spots of colors began to flash before his eyes, reds and blues and purples so vibrant Jeran at first thought he was looking at magic. When he reached out to them, they disappeared, and Jeran lost his concentration. He tried to refocus, but he could not.

Something skittered over Jeran's hand, its many legs tickling his flesh, and he barely stopped from crying out. His reflexive movement sent the creature flying, and it hit the wall of the tunnel with a clack. Jeran heard it run away. *Is it fleeing or looking for friends?* Jeran wondered, his pulse racing.

With his hand placed firmly against the wall but ready to pull away in an instant, Jeran continued on. He moved quickly, desperate to find his way back to the light. He strained to hear some sound, a noise from the *ghrat* or even a patrol pursuing him from the Barrows.

Fear took root. The tunnel pressed in from all sides, and Jeran imagined himself encased in stone. The weight of the mountain pressed down on him, making it hard to draw breath. His steps quickened, and he leaned heavily on the wall, using the cold stone to support his weight. When the wall dropped away, Jeran pitched sideways. He lay on the tunnel floor for a time, his arms wrapped around his knees, drawing slow, deep breaths. He considered turning back, but the path behind was as dark and empty as the path before him. *What if the ghrat's just ahead? It's a long way back to the Barrows.*

From somewhere deep inside, he found enough confidence to press on. He explored the opening in the tunnel with his hand, and was relieved to find that it was a cul-de-sac and not a second passage. He tugged at his collar. *Some light. I just need some light!* It was no use; Jeran could not remove the collar, nor could he use his Gift. Tylor had taken it from him.

If I pretend to go along with Lorthas, he'll remove the collar. Then I could make light.

Jeran banished the thought. Lorthas was no fool; he'd see through any deception. And even if his gambit succeeded and they removed his collar, Jeran knew he would be under constant scrutiny. With his Gift, the Darklord would consider Jeran a threat; without it, he was just another common.

He left the cul-de-sac and continued on, vacillating between caution and extreme foolishness. For a time, he walked slowly, feeling out each step, his free hand waving frantically for obstructions. When panic set in, he hurried forward, trusting to fate and luck, praying that the gaps he felt in the tunnel wall lead to dead ends and not more tunnels. He hummed, listening to the echoes, and twice, when the pitch suddenly changed, he predicted the presence of an alcove.

Nothing dispelled his dread. Each step took Jeran farther from the Barrows, and the farther he went, the harder it became to continue. More than once, Jeran turned around, ready to give up, but each time, the thought of slinking back to the Barrows in defeat hardened his resolve.

When his outstretched hand touched smooth, cold rock, Jeran jerked it back. Despair rushed through him. *All this way and there's nothing here!* Jeran felt along the side of the tunnel; the same cold stone confronted him to his left as to his front, but when he stepped to the right, his hand plunged into the darkness. With realization came embarrassment, and Jeran turned the corner.

To his relief, the tunnel opened up and the grade grew more even; the jagged outcroppings and loose stones that had littered the previous section disappeared. The less treacherous path restored Jeran's confidence, and he moved more quickly. A dim light appeared in the distance, beyond another twist in the passageway, and Jeran hurried toward it. He heard the voices just before he reached the corner.

"—have to do this?" someone grumbled.

"Because the Master told us to," replied a second. Jeran froze, swallowing nervously. He stepped back, scanning the tunnel in the growing light, looking for a place to hide. There was nothing, not so much as a crack in the smooth stone.

"Baths!" the first voice spat. "Why do slaves need baths?"

"Have you smelled them?" the second man asked, chuckling softly. "If we're going to work down here, I'd rather not be able to smell the commons from more than twenty hands away. Besides, with proper grooming, a few of them might even look… presentable." The words carried a certain hunger, and Jeran's gut clenched. Before he realized it, he had started forward, his hands tightened into fists.

He stopped himself and stumbled backward, not sure what to do. A full-speed flight would probably kill him, especially when he reached the more treacherous parts of the tunnel, but staying still meant capture in an area off limits to prisoners.

When the glowing sphere of light rounded the corner, Jeran panicked. He jogged backward, afraid to turn around, afraid to turn away from the light and return to darkness. He hit the wall with a thud and fell, stunned. Far ahead, two men turned the corner, following a few paces behind the ball of light. "I guess you have a point, Castor," the first said. "But I still think digging baths for commons is a waste of our Gift."

The second ShadowMage, Castor, made a tisking sound. "Any excuse to use magic, remember? It was but yesterday you said that to me." There was a brief silence. "What difference does it make if we use our Gift to melt snow or dig tunnels? The thrill is still the same! The power!"

Jeran scrabbled around the corner, hoping he remained unnoticed long enough to escape. Once safely out of sight, he stood and ran, but he had not gone a dozen steps when his shoulder slammed into an outcropping. He dropped to the ground hard, driving the air from his lungs. The sphere of light rounded the bend, and Jeran knew he would never make it back to the Barrows without being caught.

As the light approached, Jeran saw a shadow deepening on the far wall. He dove into the hollow, hurrying to the farthest depths, and wedged himself into a crack. He pulled his shirt up to hide his pale face.

When the ShadowMagi drew near, Jeran held his breath, afraid that the sound of his breathing would betray him. He prayed that they could not hear the thundering of his heart despite their magic-enhanced senses. One black-robed man stopped at the mouth of the alcove and peered into the darkness. The ball of light floated backward and moved a few hands closer to Jeran.

"What are you stopping for, Tibek?" Castor asked, turning to face his companion.

Tibek shrugged. "Might as well do another Delving."

"If you insist," Castor sighed, folding his arms across his chest. Tibek drew several deep breaths, and Jeran tensed. He pressed deeper into the rocks, ignoring the jabbing pain and the pressure on his chest, and watched the ShadowMagi from beneath the edge of his coat.

Tibek's aura flared to life; Jeran saw the colors dance around the Mage's body, a subtle interplay of orange and red around a core of black. The aura flickered, the colors faded and blurred, but just seeing magic being used was a painful reminder of what Jeran had lost. The urge to seize magic overwhelmed him, and Jeran opened himself to the flows. He savored the rush even though he was denied the sweet release.

Jeran studied how Tibek wove the flows to search for water and failed to notice Castor take a sudden interest in the alcove. By the time he realized the second ShadowMage had moved, the man stood but a few steps away. Jeran's hold on magic slipped, and the sudden release made his head swim. He tensed, ready to fight, knowing that he stood little chance against two Gifted.

"Nothing," Tibek said, letting out a satisfied sigh. "The water's too deep, and we're still too close to the Boundary. There'll be better places in the Barrows."

"Very well," Castor replied. He stood silently for a moment, and Jeran thought for sure that he had been seen. "I was hoping we wouldn't have to go there. The stench is overpowering." He laughed, cruel and low, and turned back to his companion. "I guess that's why the Master wants to clean up the commons."

The ShadowMagi continued down the passage, but Jeran waited for a count of a hundred before moving. He crept from the alcove, half expecting Castor and Tibek to be waiting in the tunnel. The passage was empty, though, and the floating light gone. Jeran was left in darkness again. Fear returned, and with it a growing need to escape. Returning to the Barrows was impossible; he had no choice but to go to the *ghrat*.

Jeran found his way back to the first turn without incident, and as soon as the tunnel widened, he increased his speed. Soon, he reached the second corner and poked his head around just far enough to see. In the distance, a tiny pinprick of light shone through the darkness. Jeran hurried toward it.

As the end of the tunnel drew near, Jeran slowed, realizing for the first time that guards were likely posted on this side of the tunnel too. He dropped to his knees and crawled forward on all fours. He strained to hear voices or footfalls, but only silence greeted his approach. At the mouth of the tunnel, he waited for a time, but saw no movement and heard nothing.

Risking discovery, Jeran poked his head into the light and was confronted with an empty chamber. No guards patrolled the elliptical hall or the numerous passages that entered it, nor did Jeran see any indication of a guardpost. Two magic-wrought spheres hovered at the ceiling, casting a warm light across the chamber.

Standing, Jeran turned toward the nearest tunnel and started down it, relieved to be in the light again. The hall he chose was well lit, with a steep downward grade. Numerous openings, round and about eights hands high, lined the tunnel.

Before long, Jeran came to a branching. He took the left tunnel and found more empty chambers. When he reached another intersection, he turned left again, and the same scene confronted him. A vast catacomb wove beneath the mountains, a catacomb of nothing. Jeran wondered why the slaves were denied access; it was warmer here, and the accommodations were far more appealing than the Barrows.

Confused, Jeran explored some of the rooms. Though most were empty, a few held simple furnishings—a chair carved from stone, a couple of faded tapestries, or a threadbare pallet rolled in the corner. All of the chambers, even those completely empty, felt used, and Jeran felt a familiar sensation in the back of his mind. *A Reading? Here?* The tingling he felt signified an event of such emotional significance that it had impressed itself into the very land. A quirk of magic had left Jeran with a talent for Reading, the ability to view those events, but he had not dared to open himself to the Readings he had sensed in the Barrows. In Dranakohr, the emotions linked to a Reading were not likely to be pleasant; and with his Gift warped by the Boundary and the Darklord's collar, Jeran had no idea how viewing a Reading would affect him.

He dismissed this reading as well, and as he continued his exploration, the number of magical spheres increased until the hall was lit as bright as day. Confronted with another set of crossing passages, Jeran stopped. He considered turning back, but finding his way out of the *ghrat* would take some time, and in truth, he did not relish the thought of crossing through the tunnel to the Barrows again.

Turning left, he moved quickly, his footfalls echoing on the stone. But the sound of marching feet soon drowned out his own steps, and Jeran froze. The patrol was coming toward him, and the echoes made it impossible to tell how close it was. Jeran dove into the nearest chamber and scrambled to the corner, where he pressed himself flat against the wall.

As the footfalls grew near, Jeran edged forward so he could peer out through the room's opening. A squad of soldiers appeared, marching in sloppy formation. At a command from their leader, the soldiers stopped in the hall outside Jeran's hiding place. The commander walked up and down the line, studying his men, and Jeran heard several make crude comments under their breath. Harsh chuckles followed the leader down the line.

His face flushed with anger, the leader called out three names, and the most vocal of the soldiers stepped out from the group. The squad continued on, and the three guards stood at attention until the other soldiers disappeared.

"Guard duty!" a scarred soldier snarled. "What did we do to deserve guard duty?"

"What did we do?" replied a dark-skinned woman with hawkish eyes. "*We* did nothing! You, on the other hand, felt the need to mock the Commander."

"All I did was repeat the rumor about her and the Wildman!"

"You repeated it where she could hear," snapped the final soldier, a burly figure with a sharply hooked nose. Scar-face spat on the floor. "You're lucky you got guard duty. The last soldier who joked about the Commander's tryst had his jaw broken."

"She's a fiery one, eh?" Scar-face smiled, but it quickly turned to a grimace, and he rubbed a hand across his bruised and blood-caked chin.

"You'd better learn to watch your tongue," hawk-eyes said. "Next time, you'll find yourself guarding one of the watch towers. And if you get me stationed out there, you'll not survive the first night."

The guards paced the hall, and coming to the *ghrat* no longer seemed such a good idea to Jeran. It was only a matter of time before he was discovered here or missed in the Barrows. Either way meant trouble. The soldiers stopped in the passage just outside Jeran's hideaway and sat against the far wall. "I hate guard duty," scar-face said.

"It's better than shoveling snow," hawk-eyes replied. "That's what most of the men are doing, you know."

"Another avalanche?"

"Not again!"

"Seems like it happens every other day. As soon as the ShadowMagi open the pass, another storm comes through, and we have to start digging all over again." Scar-face cupped his hands behind his head. "You were at the pass the last few days, weren't you, Oram? Any news?"

"Not much. Winter has everything bogged down. But it sounds like the war will start for real once spring arrives."

"It's about time! We've been freezing here for winters. I'm ready for a good fight."

Cruel laughter echoed in Jeran's ears. "You'll change your mind quick enough once you fight a battle or two," Oram said. Of the three guards, he looked like the only one to have ever used his weapon.

Scar-face sneered at his companions. "I've heard that the Garun'ah have joined the Alrendrians." After a pointed pause, he said, "*All* the Garun'ah."

"You mean the Drekka?" More laughter greeted the man's nod. "You're a fool, Pyk. The Drekka have been fighting the other tribes since Aemon's Revolt. They're not gonna switch sides now."

"That's not what I heard," Pyk said defensively, nervously wiping his brow. "I also heard that two patrols disappeared. Just gone! No one knows what happened."

"Probably got lost in the mountains," Oram said. "Or ran into some Garun'ah."

"Or maybe the ghosts found them!"

"Ghosts! Do you believe everything you hear?" Oram and hawk-eyes shared another laugh, and Pyk's face grew redder. "Next you'll be telling us about monsters in the Darkwood."

"Men have been disappearing there!" Pyk said. "Entire convoys lost!"

"Deserters," spat hawk-eyes. "Or maybe they ran into Talbot. That old wolf knows what he's doing." She chuckled again. "Monsters in the Darkwood. If children's tales like those frighten you, Pyk, you'd better hope you never see battle."

The sound of marching steps returned. Oram stood and offered an arm to hawk-eyes. "Come on! We don't want them to find us loafing." His eyes smoldering with embarrassment, Pyk stood and the three men started down the passageway.

Jeran sighed once the guards were gone. A deep voice behind him said, "I thought they'd never leave." Jeran jumped and whirled around, reaching unconsciously for the sword he no longer carried. He saw nothing and edged toward the opening, his eyes scanning the room for something to use as a weapon. In the far corner, the wall itself seemed to move, and Jeran saw two slitted eyes staring at him.

"Who are you?" Jeran demanded. A man stepped forward, but like no man Jeran had ever seen. He stood shorter than Jeran by more than two hands but half again as broad. Powerful muscles covered his body; his arms were thicker than Jeran's thighs, his legs as broad as tree trunks, and his shirt stretched tightly over his broad chest. Leathery grey skin spotted with bristly hair covered his body. Golden eyes studied Jeran through slitted lids, and a broad, flat nose dominated his face. Slightly-pointed ears framed a smooth head. In the shadows, the man had all but blended into the rock.

Jeran backed toward the opening. "Wait!" the stranger called, and Jeran paused, held by the pleading quality of the words. The stranger pressed his palms together and bowed formally. "I am Grendor," he said in a voice that boomed through the chamber even though he spoke in a whisper. "*Choupik* of the Vassta. I am here to serve."

Jeran licked his lips. "You're an Orog?" Though Jeran had never really seen an Orog—no one living save the Magi had—he knew the answer. He had viewed Readings from before the raising of the Boundary, when Orog still walked among men.

"I am, Honored One," Grendor replied, bowing again. "And you are a Human from beyond the tunnels?"

Jeran nodded. "A prisoner of the Darklord."

"As are we all, friend Human." Grendor's mouth split open in a broad grin. "Even those who think they serve willingly would discover themselves slaves, should they go against the wishes of the Lost One."

"What is this place?" Jeran asked, scanning the chamber. "Where am I?"

"You are in the *ghrat*," Grendor replied. "And this is my *lientou*. It shames me that I offer such poor hospitality, but what I have is yours." Grendor walked to the far wall and unrolled a thin pallet. He waved to Jeran. "You look unwell, friend Human. Please, sit. I offer no harm."

Jeran went to the pallet while Grendor crossed to the far side of the *lientou* and withdrew a clay pitcher from a crook in the wall. Two clay cups followed, and Grendor poured them each some water. Jeran took the cup and forced a smile. "My apologies," he said, sipping gingerly. "It's just that I've never seen an Orog before. Meeting you was a surprise."

"Never seen an Orog?" Grendor repeated. "Do my brethren seclude themselves from the eyes of man?" A whimsical smile touched his lips. "The younger Races, moving as if a fire burns beneath their feet, have always seemed excitable to us Orog. I can understand why my people would hide."

"You don't understand," Jeran said. "There are no Orog south of the Boundary, nor have there been for many centuries."

"No... Orog?" A sharp edge entered Grendor's voice. His lips trembled, and the color drained from his face.

"Few survived the MageWar," Jeran explained. He wished he could take back his words, but saw no option other than to continue. "Those who did couldn't bear the isolation. No one has seen an Orog in nearly seven hundred winters."

Grendor closed his eyes, and his head fell. He looked to be on the verge of collapse, so Jeran hurried to his side and led him to the pallet. "You bring grave news, friend Human."

"Please, call me Jeran."

Grendor studied Jeran's face, and he dipped his head in acknowledgment of the request. "Grave news indeed, friend Jeran. My people have borne their suffering, have toiled for centuries in the Darklord's service because, in our hearts, we believed that our sacrifice guaranteed freedom for our brethren."

Jeran offered to refill Grendor's cup, but the Orog waved him away. "The Elders discourage us from speaking of our brethren, especially around Humans. They demanded that we stay away from your caves. I had thought them overly protective. Now I understand their wisdom." A tear traced a track down Grendor's cheek. "There is a saying among my people, friend Jeran. 'He who doubts the Elders watches the sun rise in the west.' "

"I did not mean to cause pain," Jeran said. "I only wanted to see what was in the *ghrat*."

"Sorrow," Grendor replied. "Sorrow and suffering fill the *ghrat*. Not just for me, but for all my people. No, friend Jeran, do not look ashamed. You could not know what effect your words would have, and you were right to tell me. The

Elders were wise to hide the truth too; their misdirection gave my people strength to live when all hope was gone. But in the end, all truths must be known. Only through truth can the path of the Mother be clearly seen."

Grendor's smile returned, though weaker than before. "And the Elders also say that one should not blame the messenger for the message."

"Why are you here?" Jeran asked, seeking to change the subject.

Grendor looked confused. "I am a slave."

"No," Jeran laughed. "I mean, where is everyone else? Why are you the only one here?"

"The others work the mines and tunnels below. The luckiest shape the stone above and see the light of day. Today, the morning fever held me, and the Elders told me to rest."

Footsteps approached, and Jeran pressed himself into the corner. Grendor hid as well, moving back into the shadows, standing so still he all but disappeared. If Jeran took his eyes off the Orog for even an instant, he had trouble spotting him again.

A column of soldiers marched past, oblivious to their surroundings. Nevertheless, Jeran remained frozen until the last echo disappeared. "Do they always patrol down here?" Few soldiers guarded the Barrows.

"Only those who have earned the Darklord's displeasure. Duty in the *ghrat* is monotonous, and when the earth-fires flare, the temperature grows unbearable."

"I know some people who'd love it here." Jeran told Grendor about the Barrows, and how the Humans feared freezing to death above all else.

"They would like it here for only a while, friend Jeran," Grendor's replied. "A night or two of the fires, and your people would pray for cold."

"I must return," Jeran said, starting for the entrance. "If I'm discovered here, my people will suffer."

"If you came through the guarded tunnel, you will not be able to return," Grendor warned. "The patrol came from that direction, and they would not have gone to the tunnel except to post a watch."

"My absence will be noticed soon," Jeran said, his shoulders slumping. He had made a great discovery, but he doubted the slaves punished for his action would think it worthwhile. "If it hasn't been already."

"There is another tunnel," Grendor said, starting for the door. "I will take you to it, should you wish it."

Hope blossomed in Jeran's heart, but suspicion quickly followed. "Why isn't it guarded?"

"Because only I know of it, friend Jeran." Grendor beckoned for Jeran to follow. "We must hurry, before all the guards have been posted."

Jeran followed warily, his ears straining for any sound. "How do you know about this tunnel?"

"I have always been fascinated by your Race," Grendor explained. "I did not believe the Darklord's soldiers to be fair representatives of all Humans, so I sought a passage to your tunnels." Grendor's cheeks turned dark grey. "The Elders say I risk punishment unnecessarily. But I had no choice; I need to know the truth." A grin split Grendor's face. "If not for my explorations, you would not have a means to return home. So perhaps my foolishness served a purpose."

The walls of the *ghrat* slid past, and Jeran quickly lost his way. He was forced to rely on Grendor. When the Orog raised a hand, Jeran froze, and they waited for what seemed a long time. "Are we lost?" he whispered, but Grendor clapped a hand over Jeran's mouth the moment he spoke.

The low murmur of voices came to Jeran's ears. Footsteps soon followed, and a party of guards hurried through the intersection ahead. After the sound of their passage faded, Grendor started moving again, with Jeran a step behind. Grendor stopped several more times, and Jeran quickly learned to trust the Orog's senses. Two more parties passed them, the second less than twenty hands distant, and Jeran heard a third group discussing their duty in a nearby chamber.

When the Mage-created lights faded and the tunnels filled with shadows, Jeran knew they were getting close. The dying light made it hard to see, but Grendor continued on without slowing. He eventually stopped at the mouth of a dark tunnel. "This ends behind a large rock not far from where your smiths work. The crevasse at the end is a tight fit for me, but you should have no difficulty slipping through. It is a straight tunnel, so do not fear losing your way."

Grendor reached into his shirt and withdrew two long sticks. He pressed one into Jeran's hand. Save for a three-finger width at the bottom, the shafts were stained a dark color; a ball of yellow-orange powder capped the tops.

"These will light your way," Grendor said, striking one stick against the wall. A bright flash erupted from the end, and a hissing sound filled the tunnel. The top of the stick burned with a slow, steady light. "There is a sharp bend at the exit. Extinguish the flame there, friend Jeran, and it will not be seen. The second stick is for your return."

Jeran slipped the unused stick into his coat. "Thank you. It was an honor to meet you, Grendor."

"The honor was mine, friend Jeran," Grendor replied. "You will return?"

"I... I'm not sure."

Grendor nodded. "You do not wish harm for your people." A broad smile brightened the Orog's face. "I was right; our guards are not good examples of your Race." His expression grew serious, and he nodded to himself as if coming to a tough decision. "I will not tell the Elders they were wrong, though. Even I am not that foolish!" The Orog grasped Jeran's forearm warmly. "Each night, after I return from my duties, I will wait here. There is much I can learn from you, friend Jeran."

"There's much we can learn from each other," Jeran replied.

Chapter 7

Jeran sat in the center of the barrow with his eyes closed and his legs crossed beneath him. He breathed slowly and allowed the flows to dance at the edge of his reach. Even with his eyes closed he saw the vibrant strands, and he yearned to fill himself with their power. He confined himself to studying the flows, though, seeking a better understanding of what they were and where they came from.

His magic-enhanced hearing detected the faintest noise at the entrance to the barrow, and a familiar aroma reached his nose. "Good morning, Yassik. Where did you get almonds?"

"I'm already teaching you the subtle arts of the Magi," the old man replied. "You don't expect me to give away all of my secrets, do you?"

Smiling, Jeran opened his eyes. Yassik looked a different man. His wild hair and bushy beard had been washed and groomed, and he wore new clothes, sturdy breeches, and a thick wool shirt. The hollowness of his cheeks had disappeared and his skin had lost its pallid complexion.

In the days since Jeran's meeting with the Darklord, most of the slaves had been given new clothes and warm blankets. Meals, though meager, were of better fare, and punishments had been less severe. The entire atmosphere in the Barrows had changed. Where once despair reigned, hope had returned, and with it a measure of happiness.

The slaves' good fortune had not improved their behavior toward Jeran. With every gift, with every act of kindness, the guards reminded them that they owed Jeran for their good fortune. Few thanked him for his sacrifice; most kept their distance, afraid they might say the wrong thing and suffer the Darklord's wrath. Some considered him a traitor, though none objected to the hot baths or fresh clothes Jeran's betrayal bought them. Their hateful stares haunted him every night.

"The baths must be ready," Jeran said, sniffing the air. "You used to have a far more distinctive smell."

"The ShadowMagi opened the first this morning," Yassik replied. "I'd forgotten how relaxing a dip in hot water could be." Yassik's eyes grew serious, and his lips compressed into a narrow line. He hesitated before saying, "You're playing a dangerous game."

"The results justify the risk," Jeran said, his tone flat.

"I don't disagree. I just want to emphasize the danger. Lorthas is no fool."

"Your concern is appreciated," Jeran said dryly.

"You've a better rein on your temper, at least." Yassik joined Jeran at the firepit. "Not many days past you would have lashed out at such a warning."

"I listened to your advice. It made a big difference." Jeran grasped Yassik's shoulder fondly. "I never properly thanked you."

"Let's say we're even. Without you, I'd still be buried in the mines." Yassik turned to admire Wardel's newest creation, a drawing of a giant bull being coaxed to his destruction by a sword-wielding warrior who looked a lot like King Mathis. "How go your studies?"

"Not well," Jeran admitted. "I'm examining the flows as you suggested, but so far, I haven't been able to circumvent the collar's magic."

"It's not likely you will," Yassik chuckled. "I've been working on the problem for winters, and, no offense, I have a little more expertise." The old Mage withdrew a long, two-finger wide stick from the firepit. "The purpose of the exercise is to teach control. There are times—whether you talk of muscles or magic—when brute force is the best course." Yassik gripped the stick in both hands and tried to break it, but the stout wood barely bent. "But many situations require a finer touch. If you desire mastery of your Gift, you must learn finesse." With that, he wedged one end of the stick under an outcropping of rock, levered its middle on a stone, and with a quick snap of his hand, broke the wood in two.

"I understand," Jeran replied. "I'll continue to practice."

A long silence ensued. "You were gone again last night," Yassik said, his words probing. "Where do you go?"

Jeran was not quick to answer. Yassik had earned his trust, but Jeran was not sure he was ready to share his secret. The consequences of defying Tylor's demand to stay out of the *ghrat* might make the Bull's harsh reprisals over the luxuries Jeran had earned for the slaves seem trivial in comparison. Yet the need to tell was overwhelming, and after checking to make sure they were alone, he leaned in close and whispered, "To the *ghrat*."

A hungry smile spread across Yassik's face. "The *ghrat*." Wringing his hands together eagerly, he met Jeran's gaze. "And what did you find there, my young friend?"

"A miracle." When Yassik's eyes narrowed, Jeran added, "Orog."

"Orog!" Yassik's mouth fell open. "The Gods be praised!" Excitement quickly faded, and Yassik's questioning nature took over. "You're certain they're Orog? How would you know? The Orog have been gone since the Raising."

"I've seen them in my Readings," Jeran said, offering Yassik another of his secrets.

"A Reader too, eh?" Yassik's grin returned, broader than before. "Aren't we full of surprises today?" He could not keep the grin from his face. "You have no idea how wondrous this news is. Never in our wildest dreams did we think Lorthas would allow the Orog to live. He always feared them, as did all the Darklords. To know they survived, even under these conditions, will bring the Assembly some peace."

He leaned forward and grabbed Jeran's shoulders, his eyes burning with excitement. "Tell me everything you know! How do you get there? How many Orog are there? Have you spoken with an Elder?"

Jeran did his best, but for every answer he gave, Yassik asked two questions. "Enough! It's simpler just to take you there. You can ask the Orog yourself."

"Orog?" Wardel repeated as he ducked into the barrow. Jeran winced. *So much for secrets*, he said, cursing himself. "Is that what Tylor's hiding in the *ghrat*?"

Clean-shaven and dressed in fresh clothes, Wardel looked like a new man. He nodded to Jeran, and seeing Yassik, he smiled and reached into the bag tied to his waist. "I found a violet one!" he told Yassik cheerfully, holding up the stone triumphantly.

"Don't speak of the Orog," Jeran said. "I want to keep them a secret."

Wardel ducked his head in acknowledgment, but his eyes never left the mural as he crossed the chamber. With the purple stone, he added highlights to the sunrise over Kaper. "I wouldn't dream of it, but I can't be too sure about him." He gestured to the right.

Jeran followed Wardel's finger, and for the first time noticed two eyes staring at him from the darkness. "Guardsman! Out here now!" Quellas emerged from his den slowly, and Jeran fixed a menacing glare on him. "How long have you been eavesdropping?"

"We're not Guardsmen anymore," Quellas mumbled. "We're slaves."

"How long!"

"Long enough to know you're going to get us killed! Do you think Tylor will let this go unpunished? The *ghrat* is off limits!"

"Tylor won't know I'm going to the *ghrat* if the four of us keep our mouths shut," Jeran replied, forcing the edge from his voice. "Can I count on you, Quellas?"

They stared at each other for a long time. Finally, the Guardsman nodded, and the defiance drained from his shoulders. "Of course, Lord Odara."

"Good. Why don't you join us?" Jeran asked, forcing a smile. "There's room enough."

"I'd prefer to rest," Quellas said. "Some of us had to work the mines."

"As you wish." Quellas retreated into his den, and Jeran signaled to Wardel to watch for the other man's return. Wardel moved so that he could better see into Quellas' barrow.

"You handled that better than last time," Yassik mused.

"I still want to strangle him," Jeran stated. Wardel laughed.

Reanna crawled through the entrance with a bucket of half-melted snow clutched in her trembling fingers. She shivered uncontrollably, and her lips had taken on a blue tinge. Jeran and Wardel moved to intercept her; the Guardsman took the bucket from Reanna's stiff fingers and Jeran led her to the firepit. Her skin felt colder than the water, and flakes of ice crusted her long, straight hair. Jeran wrapped a blanket around the Tribeswoman's shoulders, rubbing her vigorously. "How long were you outside?" Jeran demanded.

"Not... long..." Reanna gasped, her teeth chattering.

"Too long," Jeran admonished. "You'll freeze to death if you're not careful."

"Freeze..." Reanna repeated. "Better... End suffering."

Wardel and Yassik exchanged a glance, but Jeran grabbed Reanna's chin and forced her to look him in the eye. "Don't say that!" Anxiety heated his voice, and Reanna flinched. "We'll find a way out of here! I swear it. But you mustn't give up hope."

Frozen tracks ran the length of the Tribeswoman's cheeks. Jeran brushed them away. "I have no hope," she whispered, her voice lifeless. "My soul is gone. I live only for you."

"Come on." Jeran pulled Reanna toward her den. "You're exhausted." She allowed him to lead her away. He laid her on her pallet, newly stuffed with fresh straw, and covered her with thick blankets. When he stood, Reanna reached out plaintively. "Do not go!" she begged, and her desperation kept Jeran from leaving. "I do not want to be alone."

Jeran lay beside her and wrapped his arms around the Tribeswoman's icy skin. Reanna's breathing slowed, and with Jeran near, she relaxed. Jeran stroked her hair and rubbed a hand down her side. She turned toward him, burying her face in his neck. The press of her body, the way she drew him closer with every indrawn breath, quickened Jeran's heartbeat. The barrow soon grew uncomfortable.

Jeran stayed until certain Reanna slept. Carefully, so as not to wake her, he pulled away. She startled him by saying, "I am so cold."

"You shouldn't stay outside so long."

"On the inside, Jeran. I am cold on the inside."

He gently kissed her forehead. "All will be well, Snow Rabbit," he said. "We won't have to endure this forever. But you must not despair."

A smile touched her lips. "For you, *bahlova*, I will find new hope." Within moments, she slept soundly, and Jeran crept from the den. Wardel was gone, but Yassik remained. He sat peacefully in the center of the chamber, his legs crossed beneath him.

The Mage's eyes snapped open when Jeran entered. "She's not well," the old man said matter-of-factly. "The children of Garun have never borne captivity well."

"She'll survive," Jeran said, his voice ringing with conviction.

"Perhaps," Yassik said, eyeing him curiously. "Perhaps she will at that."

"It's late enough," Jeran said to change the subject. "The guards in the *ghrat* will be shirking their duties by now. If you wish to meet Grendor, now's the time."

Yassik climbed to his feet, groaning with the effort, and followed Jeran out of the den. They crept through the tunnels. Few people passed them—no one without a reason wandered the Barrows at night—and those they did see paid them little mind. One man, recognizing Jeran, scampered away, begging forgiveness.

"I bet he was up to no good," Yassik murmured. "It's a good thing the Darklord's Pet stopped him from making a grave mistake." Yassik's jest earned a harsh glare from Jeran, but the Mage did not seem to notice.

The sound of clanging hammers echoed down the dimly-lit tunnel. "Do they work all night?" Jeran asked, surprised as always to find the smiths still at their craft.

"Sometimes," Yassik answered. "An army always needs something forged or repaired. And slaves don't have the luxury of refusing to work."

Anger surged through Jeran. "How can they serve so blindly? Don't they know these weapons will be used against Alrendria? Against our people?"

"Of course they do," Yassik replied. "But what choice do they have? They either work or suffer." Jeran started to protest, but Yassik interrupted. "They are no guiltier than those who work the mines. Without ore, the blacksmiths would have nothing to forge. And you"—Yassik forestalled Jeran's attempt to speak with a wave—"with your casual disregard for Alrendria, improved the health of Tylor's slaves. The more dead slaves, the less work Tylor gets done."

Jeran sighed. "I guess you're right."

"They do what they can. What they have to, and they try not to bring harm to those around them." He patted Jeran on the shoulder. "If it makes you feel better, boy, I've never seen smiths work so slow in my life."

Jeran offered the old man a tight smile as they entered the smithy. Three rows of forges, each separated by small mountains of coal, charcoal, and ore ran the length of the vast chamber. Only a handful of the forges were in use. The smiths, their bodies smeared with soot, their heads over their work, hammered relentlessly, oblivious to their surroundings. The swirling smoke rose in tendrils to the chamber's ceiling, where it disappeared into a hole bored through the rock.

After checking to see if anyone was watching, Jeran stepped from the shadows and hurried toward the hidden entrance to the *ghrat*. One smith caught the movement out of the corner of his eye. "Is that you, Odara?" Seeing no way to hide his presence, Jeran stepped forward. "What are you doing here?" Malkin growled.

"Our business is none of your concern," Jeran said tersely.

Malkin dropped him hammer and stomped toward them. He stared at Jeran suspiciously. "Are you spying on us? Don't we work fast enough for your master?"

"*My* master?" Jeran repeated.

"We know you spend time with the Darklord." Malkin's eyes bored into Jeran. "We know about the extra food the guards bring you. Is betraying Alrendria not enough, Odara? Do you have to betray us too? Well, you'll find nothing to complain about here, so you'd best run back to your barrow."

Jeran stiffened, and Yassik put a restraining hand on his shoulder. "Let him go, old man," Malkin taunted. "He won't catch me by surprise this time!"

"Enough!" a new voice called out, and Malkin frowned. Another man, a leather apron tied around his waist and a heavy hammer resting on his shoulder, stood several steps away. Jeran knew him too.

Dralin was much as Jeran remembered, broad and muscular with deep set, dark blue eyes and light brown hair. Grey spotted his head, and his skin bore the remnants of old wounds, but Keryn's Rest's other smith had changed little over the winters.

Malkin opened his mouth, but Dralin cut him off with a wave of his hammer. "We've talked about this before," the smith said, his voice a low rumble. "Return to your barrow. Now. If I see you in the smithy before morning, you'll regret it."

Malkin's hands tightened into fists, but he did not countermand the order. He stormed off, casting menacing glares over his shoulder. Dralin watched until Malkin had gone, then he turned an appraising eye on Jeran. "You've grown."

Jeran eyed the smith warily. Of all the slaves in Dranakohr, those captured from Keryn's Rest had been the cruelest; their accusing eyes haunted Jeran most of all. Dralin had always been kind, but he had not been a slave the last time Jeran had seen him. Jeran offered his hand. "It's been many seasons."

Dralin gripped Jeran's arm at the elbow, squeezing tightly. "You wear them well, lad." With his chin, he pointed to the tunnel down which Malkin had fled. "I apologize for that. I'll talk to him tomorrow. If he troubles you again, I'll have him work double shifts for a ten-day."

"You're in charge here?"

"Since Breckt died," Dralin nodded, "about two winters past." A sad smile ghosted across the smith's face. "Can't say there's nowhere I'd rather be, but the smiths have it better than most, and the head smith best of all."

Jeran looked at Dralin but could not find the right words. "Dralin... I... Uncle Aryn and I never meant..." He broke off.

"Not all of us feel as Malkin does," the smith said. "Your uncle did what he could. He was a good man, Jeran, and so are you. Whatever bargain the Darklord forced on you, things are better in the Barrows than before. That's what's important."

"The line between savior and traitor is very thin," Jeran said, turning away. "Sometimes I think Malkin's right. That I am a traitor."

"I walk the same line," Dralin assured him. "Most of us do. How quickly should we forge weapons? Too slow and the guards grow suspicious, too fast and we aid our enemies. How many blades can be flawed before the guards notice?" At Jeran's surprised look, Dralin smiled. "We all fight as we can, lad. So, ignore Malkin." Dralin clapped Jeran on the shoulder. "He's a fool. We know which side you fight for."

Dipping his head respectfully, Dralin returned to his forge, and Jeran and Yassik slipped into the shadows. They waited until certain no one was watching, then crawled through the crack behind two outcroppings of rock. Jeran took Yassik's arm and pulled him down the tunnel until the light from the smithy faded. After thirty steps, they reached a turn, and once safely behind it, Jeran withdrew one of Grendor's firesticks from his shirt.

With a hiss, the stick flared to life. Yassik leaned in close and examined the slow-burning torch. "Interesting," he murmured. His eyes flicked to Jeran, and he looked to be on the verge of asking a question, but Jeran turned away before the Mage could speak. With the firestick to light the way, they moved quickly. Before long, a pinprick of light appeared in the distance. "That's the *ghrat*," Jeran whispered, dropping the stick and stepping on it to extinguish the flame.

When they reached the end of the tunnel, Jeran signaled for Yassik to halt. He crept forward and peeked around the corner. When he saw Grendor, a smile split his face, and he stepped into the lighted tunnel, waving for Yassik to follow.

Jeran greeted the Orog warmly, but Grendor's return smile was forced, and Jeran saw fear dance across his friend's face. "What's wrong?" he asked nervously. His eyes flicked from one side of the tunnel to the other. "Did the guards learn of our meetings?"

"I wish it were so, friend Jeran," Grendor replied somberly. "I would rather face the Darklord than the Elders." Mentioning the Elders stole what little strength Grendor had left; his shoulders slumped, and he looked as if he were about to collapse. "They insist on meeting you."

Yassik stepped from the shadows and Grendor stumbled backward. "It's all right!" Jeran said, reaching out to the Orog. "This is my friend, Yassik. He was... He *is* a Mage, and he knew Orog in the winters before the MageWar. When I told him your people lived, he wanted to meet you."

If anything, Grendor looked more frightened. "A... Mage?"

"Yassik." Jeran waved the Mage forward. "This is Grendor."

Grendor bowed formally. "Greetings, Honored One. I am here to serve."

"Your service is welcome, Stonefinder," Yassik replied, returning the bow. "It warms my heart to see Shael's children again."

"We must hurry," Grendor said with a nervous look. "The Elders do not like to wait." The Orog led them quickly through the *ghrat*, stopping only once to hide from guards. He refused to answer Jeran's questions and spoke only to urge them to hurry.

The temperature rose as they descended, and the air grew stifling. Before long, sweat soaked Jeran's clothes, and Yassik wiped his brow constantly. "I think I prefer the cold," Jeran muttered, gasping for air.

"I warned you, friend Jeran."

"How can it be so hot?" Yassik asked, stopping to touch the smooth walls.

"The earth-fires burn not far from here," Grendor explained, "and the heat moves through the stone. Deeper in the caverns, I have seen lakes of liquid rock and stones hot enough to melt steel with a touch." Grendor stopped before an open archway. "This is where the Elders meet."

The chamber appeared no different than any other in the *ghrat*. Few ornaments adorned the wall, and a few rolled-up pallets sat on the floor. Jeran and Yassik entered first, with Grendor a few steps behind. On the far side of the hall, nine Orog, five women and four men, sat in a semicircle, their hands folded in their laps. They studied the Humans through slitted, yellow-brown eyes.

Jeran approached, bowing low. "Greetings, Honored—" The Elder nearest Jeran raised a finger to her lips, and Jeran fell silent. The Elders studied him silently, and Jeran endured their inspection with all the confidence he could muster. Eight of the Orog were ancient, their slate grey skin heavily wrinkled and splotched with lighter flecks, their backs hunched as if burdened by great weights. Long, pointed ears framed weathered faces like wilted flowers. All wore robes a shade darker than their skin, and if not for their hair—four had thin white hair hanging loose and four were hairless save for small tufts of coarse bristles—Jeran would not have been able to tell man from woman.

The ninth Elder was younger than her companions, but her eyes carried seasons of knowledge and her bearing was that of one used to command. Few lines marred her smooth, unblemished skin, and light brown hair hung to her shoulders. She sat with her back straight, and her piercing gaze bored into Jeran, making him uncomfortable.

Jeran returned the Elders' stare, but Yassik paid them little attention. His eyes roved the room, and a slight smile painted his lips. Grendor's breathing grew more rapid as the silence continued, and his skin turned almost as pale as Jeran's.

"You are Magi," the youngest Elder said at last.

Jeran turned to Yassik, but the old man seemed not have heard the question; he hummed to himself while studying the chamber's sloped ceiling. "My companion is a Mage," Jeran said, clearing his throat. "I have the Gift."

The Elder's lips pressed together thoughtfully. "Our memories tell us that the Magi train all who have the Gift." She looked Jeran up and down. "But our memories claim many things which no longer seem true."

"A great deal has changed since the Orog sacrificed themselves," Jeran replied. "Some for the better, some for the worse. The Magi are not as they once were. Many Gifted go their entire lives ignorant of their abilities."

"You are not ignorant of your Gift," one man said, his voice raspy and weak. "Why, then, did you not seek training?"

Jeran considered his answer carefully. "In Alrendria, a Mage cannot rule, and I am the leader of House Odara, one of the six Great Houses."

"He speaks truth," a woman announced, "but not complete truth." The other Elders nodded. Nine pairs of eyes fastened on Jeran, boring deep into his soul.

"For a long time, I feared my Gift," Jeran added hastily. "And I don't trust the Magi. Not all of them, at least." He offered Yassik an apologetic glance.

The silence returned, and Jeran licked his lips nervously. He wanted the Elders to speak, even to chastise him; he could not bear their soundless scrutiny. "His words are true," and youngest Elder announced eventually, and the others agreed. "It is refreshing to see that honesty lives among some of Balan's children." Her eyes flicked to Grendor. "Perhaps the *Choupik* is right when he says honor lives among them as well."

One of the Elders hobbled toward Jeran. Though she barely reached his midriff, she seemed to tower over him. "You said six Great Houses? Our memories say there are more."

"Once there were," Jeran explained, "but the winters have seen many die, and the smaller houses were swallowed by larger. Now, only six remain."

"That is the way of things," the Elder said sadly. "What was once many becomes few, and then none."

The other Elders stood, and the younger one approached Jeran with a graceful stride. Just shorter than Grendor, Jeran towered over her, but powerful muscles covered her body. She touched his finely-woven clothes and stood on tiptoe to sniff the air around his head. "You have stood with the Darklord."

Jeran saw no way to hide the truth; the Orog knew things they should not. "I have."

She looked into his eyes. "Why?" Jeran sensed that he was being tested again.

"I barter for the well-being of my people."

The Elder snorted. "You deal with the Dark One!"

"I protect my own!" Jeran snapped. "The Darklord wants something from me. So long as he thinks he might get it, he treats my people better."

"And if he finds out you are misleading him?"

Jeran raised his chin. "Then I will suffer for it."

"Compassion," the Elder said, and an excited murmur went up among the Orog. The Elder turned away, and her gaze finally fell on Yassik. "What is your companion called?"

"His name is Yassik."

Another excited murmur rippled through the Elders. A broad-shouldered man strode forward, his powerful strides belying his withered frame. "Our memories tell of a great Mage named Yassik. A writer of words."

"Your memory does not serve you well," Yassik said modestly. "I am a writer of words, but a Mage of only middling ability."

"Why are you here?" the young woman asked Jeran, cutting off the other Elder's next question with an exasperated look.

"At first, I just wanted to see what was in the *ghrat*. Now I come to learn about your people. Grendor has taught me much about the Orog and the sacrifice you made for Madryn. It pains me to see your noble deeds rewarded with slavery and suffering." Jeran raised himself to full height. "I swear this before the Gods; when the time comes, and we Humans free ourselves from the shackles of the Darklord's servitude, we will bring you with us. As slaves or as free men, we will endure together."

The reaction was not what he anticipated. The Elders converged in the center of the chamber to talk in hushed whispers. For debated for quite a while, their words indecipherable. Finally, the younger woman approached Jeran again. "You may continue to learn of us," she told him, as if that had been in question. "We have long hidden the truth from our people, but the time for deception is past. Perhaps it is time for our Races to renew their friendship."

Jeran started to smile, but the woman's next statement stunned him. "But we will not aid you in your attempts to escape. We Orog have suffered greatly, but we have not yet atoned for our sins. We earned the chains we wear, and with each passing winter, we deserve them more. Until Shael removes the fetters from our souls, we shall not remove them from our bodies."

"You need not fear, friend Human," another Elder rasped. "No Orog will betray your trust. Continue your struggle, and know that our blessings go with you."

"I am Lorana," the woman told Jeran. "May you find peace in the halls of the *ghrat*, friend Jeran." Her eyes shifted to Grendor. "You have done well, my son. I see the honor in this Human." Grendor's cheeks flushed dark gray. Embarrassed, he turned away from his mother's approving stare.

"Leave us now," Lorana added, and her tone left no doubt that she spoke to Jeran as well as her son. "The Honored Yassik wishes to speak with us. I will return him to the Barrows when we have finished our talk." Waving for Yassik to join her, Lorana rejoined the circle of Elders. As soon as the Mage stood in their midst, the low rumble or voices echoed through the chamber.

Jeran watched until Grendor forcibly pulled him from the room. "Only the deaf stay when the Elders tell them to go," the Orog chided. They walked side by side through the halls, and for the first time, Grendor made no effort to hide. Jeran wondered how much of their skulking in shadow had been to hide from the guards, and how much to hide from other Orog.

Most Orog ignored his passage, but the few who realized that Jeran was not a guard stared with curiosity. "Why won't the Elders help us escape?" Jeran asked suddenly.

Grendor's eyes dropped to hide his shame. "Because of our sin."

"Sin? What sin?"

For a time, Grendor said nothing. "When the MageWar began, my people swore an oath to the Great Aemon to fight the Darklord until his defeat. But after the Boundary was raised and we were trapped inside *Ael Shataq*, the Elders realized that victory was not an option. Unable to accept their defeat, the Elders broke their promise and fled to the mountains, hoping that fear of the Boundary would keep the Darklord away."

Grendor shivered, and for a moment, Jeran thought he would not continue. "They were wrong. Lorthas sent his armies and, in time, they found us. Nowhere was safe; Orog were hunted across the length and breadth of *Ael Shataq*. Thousands died from hunger, thousands more in battle, and most of the rest were captured and turned into slaves.

"Because the Boundary does not affect us, the Darklord demanded that we search the mountains for a passage to Madryn. At first, the Elders refused. Knowing that our brethren lived beyond the Boundary gave the Elders strength; so long as the Orog endured, it did not matter what happened to those in *Ael Shataq*.

"When Lorthas told the Elders that the Orog in Madryn were gone, they knew he spoke the truth. He promised to let us live, and to keep the knowledge of our brothers secret, if we agreed to serve him.

"The Elders were conflicted. Many wanted to fight, and my people would have done so gladly even though it meant our demise, but the Goddess Shael came to the Elders in their dreams and told them that the Orog still had a purpose. She asked them to ensure the survival of our people, no matter the cost." Grendor's turned away from Jeran. "So for centuries we have dug the tunnels through the Boundary. We have cleared the passes through which his troops march. We have worked the mines that supply his troops with steel and gold."

"But that doesn't explain anything!" Jeran exclaimed. "If anything, the Elders should be excited by the opportunity to free your people."

Grendor tilted his head as if Jeran's words made no sense. "We broke our oath to Aemon. Not only did we stop fighting the Darklord, we now serve him. If we break our oath to Lorthas, too, we compound our sin. My people have lost their honor, and honor is the greatest of virtues." Grendor squeezed his eyes shut. "We are condemned to serve Lorthas until our souls are cleansed."

"But... doesn't serving your enemy increase your dishonor? Doesn't working the Darklord's mines worsen your sin? To honor your vow to Aemon, you must escape!"

A sad smile spread across Grendor's face, and he nodded. "I knew you would understand. But if we escape, we break our vow to Lorthas. We have damned ourselves, friend Jeran. Ours is a fitting punishment for those without honor."

"That's ridiculous! The Orog are the most honorable of the Races. Even Emperor Alwellyn thinks so. You have deceived—"

Jeran turned a corner and came face to face with Tylor Durange, the Bull of Ra Tachan. Small wrinkles lined the Bull's face, and streaks of grey ran the length of his temples, but he appeared a man in his prime, with few signs of his advancing winters. A patch covered his left eye, but his right glared at Jeran. He seemed angry but not surprised.

"I knew I'd find you here eventually, Odara," Tylor growled. At his signal, two guards stepped forward. "The *ghrat* is off limits to Humans."

"Is it?" Jeran asked, trying to sound surprised. "I apologize if I've broken the rules. I was never told—"

Jeran reeled from the Bull's backhanded blow. He staggered, fighting to maintain his balance. "I don't have time for games," Tylor snarled. "We've worked hard to ensure that the slaves never learned of the Orog. Lorthas will not be pleased."

"I'll be sure to mention it at our next meeting," Jeran said, bracing himself. "If only I had known—"

This time, Tylor's blow knocked him to the floor, but Jeran struggled to his feet and wiped the blood from his mouth. "You know that Lorthas doesn't like it when you... discipline... me."

Tylor's hands clenched. "You're right," he murmured, and a sly smile parted his lips. "Take the Orog. Punish *him*."

"No!" Jeran's voice rang out with such command that the guards hesitated. "Leave him alone."

Tylor laughed, and the sound echoed down hall. The other Orog had disappeared into the *lientou*. "Who do you think you are? You are the slave here, Odara, remember?" At his gesture, the guards grabbed Grendor.

"If you harm him," Jeran said between clenched teeth, "I'll accept Lorthas' offer."

Tylor's eyes narrowed. "Never," he said, though Jeran saw a modicum of doubt. "You Odaras are too predictable. You'd never give Lorthas what he wants."

"Try me, Durange," Jeran taunted, but even he heard the lie in his tone. "When I command Dranakohr, you'll find me a kinder master that I've found you."

"Take him away," Tylor told the guards. Grendor did not struggle as the guards led him down the tunnel.

"Coward!" Jeran yelled at Tylor's retreating back, and the Bull whirled to face him. Jeran forced a laugh. "You're a coward, Durange! I'm the one you hate! I'm the one who killed your sons! If someone must be punished, then punish me! Or do you truly fear Lorthas' wrath? If so, then go! Return to Dranakohr to lick your Master's boots."

The next thing Jeran knew, he was lying on the floor, the metallic taste of blood in his mouth and bright lights flashing before his eyes. "Release the Orog," Tylor commanded. "Take Odara to the trophy room. I'll deal with him later."

Staggering, dazed and dizzy, the soldiers half-dragged, half-carried Jeran through the caverns. He tried to pay attention to their route but soon lost his way in the twisting maze of tunnels. By the time the guards shoved him toward a black iron door, all Jeran knew was that he was far from both the Barrows and the *ghrat*.

The door swung open on silent hinges, and one of the soldiers shoved Jeran inside. With a loud clang, the door slammed shut, and the lockbar rasped into place. Bright light suffused the room, and Jeran winced from the sudden change in illumination. His eyes tearing, he shaded his head with one hand until his vision adjusted.

He stood in a huge chamber, more than a hundred hands across and twice as long, with its ceiling lost in darkness far above. A table covered in rags sat in the center of the room, and dozens of spheres hovered over Jeran's head, pulsing with their magical light. Ornate tapestries covered the walls, some little more than tattered rags, relics of battles long past, others more recent weavings depicting Tylor's own triumphs.

Between each pair of tapestries hung a portrait. The likenesses of battle-scarred warriors and liveried noblemen stared down at Jeran, and above each, a weapon or some other trinket had been fastened to the wall.

The display disgusted Jeran, but his eyes were drawn to each of the macabre mementos. When he saw Iban's grim visage glaring down at him, and the Guard Commander's sword hanging above it, Jeran's anger rose; but when his eyes fell on the display at the far end of the hall, his strength left him.

Two life-sized pictures dominated the far wall, one of a beautiful, dark-haired woman, the other of a proud older man. At the first sight of his parents, Jeran's stomach heaved, and he clapped a hand to his mouth to keep from vomiting. Trembling, he stepped forward to get a clearer view, and when the rags on the table moved, he jumped in surprise.

"Hello?" Jeran called out tentatively, but he received no response. A chair faced the table, and Jeran pulled it out, intending to sit, but when he moved it, the prisoner jerked upright.

"Have you come back so soon, Tylor?" the prisoner whispered in a hoarse and tortured voice. The man wore tattered rags, and the way he sat his chair spoke of aching muscles and bruised bone. A thick beard hid the man's face, and long sandy-blonde hair hung in a tangle about his head. When he looked up, Jeran's knees gave out. He stared into the man's blue eyes, eyes hauntingly familiar and yet completely alien.

"Uncle Aryn?" Jeran whispered.

Chapter 8

The air quivered with tension. Cold eyes stared across the table, but other than the occasional clink of silver on porcelain, no sound could be heard. Martyn was afraid to speak; he feared saying the wrong thing and pushing Miriam into a rage. The strained silence added its own pressure to the situation and made it more difficult to keep the peace.

"Are you enjoying your meal?" Martyn asked when Miriam's slender white hand reached for her wine glass. He smiled, but it was forced.

The princess dabbed her mouth daintily with a napkin. "It's excellent, Martyn. Once again, your chef has outdone himself."

The silence returned, and Martyn sighed heavily. He stabbed at his venison passionately. As had become their custom, the prince and princess dined in one of the small antechambers near Miriam's quarters. Not for the first time, Martyn regretted suggesting the idea.

He glanced at his almost-empty plate and sighed again, this time in relief. *At least we didn't fight tonight.* Cold glares and heated words accompanied most dinners, but on more than one occasion, their arguments had grown more animated. More than a few dishes had been broken during their discussions.

Martyn thought of Kaeille. Images of the Aelvin woman soothed his nerves and brought a smile to his face. Her gentle touch had kept him sane during his incarceration in Kaper. If not for her, Miriam would have driven him mad days ago. *I'll even forgive her for making me ask Miriam to dine with me in the first place.* He stabbed at his plate again.

Miriam sipped her wine. As if sensing Martyn's thoughts, she asked, "Will you be seeing that... Will you be seeing *her* tonight?" Martyn froze with his fork halfway to his mouth. "You are! You're going to see her!" Miriam's voice rose in pitch and volume. "You probably can't wait to be free of me."

"As a matter of fact," Martyn said, setting his fork on the table, "I do have plans to see Kaeille. She'll be advising me on Aelvin law and suggesting how I might convince Jaenaryn to supply Alrendria with more Aelvin-made weapons." Martyn had hoped for a more intimate meeting, but duty came first. "You're more than welcome to attend."

"How kind." Miriam's face resumed its calm facade, but her eyes smoldered. "Tell me, Martyn, is her company so much more enjoyable? Do you truly prefer your whore's... your *advoutre's* company to mine?"

Martyn raised his glass to hide a scowl. He struggled to keep his voice amicable. "At least she can go an entire night without starting a fight."

"I have no wish to fight," Miriam said, blinking innocently. "I just want to understand what you find so enticing about her. She seems no different than any other warrior woman. Hard muscle and small wits."

"If you understood why I love Kaeille," Martyn growled through clenched teeth, "then perhaps I'd love you instead." He regretted the words instantly but could not take them back, and he braced himself for Miriam's reaction.

The princess' lips quivered, and she gripped the tablecloth so tightly her knuckles turned bone white. "How dare you!" she said, her voice rising. "What happened to my prince's honeyed tongue?"

Once again, Martyn's mouth betrayed him. "Perhaps your prince decided that flowery words would never melt your frigid heart."

Mouth agape and working soundlessly, Miriam rose slowly. The glare she offered could have pierced armor. "Of all the cruel things you have said, this... this..." She trailed off, and Martyn saw her eyes flick toward the table. With a lightning-fast motion, Miriam snatched her wine glass and drew it back to throw. Drops of red sprayed across the chamber's fine rug.

"Wait!" Martyn yelled, cringing and covering his eyes. He tensed, but when glass did not shatter against his flesh, he risked a look. Miriam stood transfixed, the wineglass still in hand and ready to throw. "Why do we do this, Miriam? I have no wish to goad you, yet every night ends the same." He gestured toward her chair. "Please, sit with me. Please?"

At first, Miriam refused to move, and for a time Martyn thought he had ruined everything. Eventually, the princess exhaled sharply, smoothed her dress, and sat. She set her glass down carefully, as if she had never intended to use it as a weapon. "This," Martyn waved a hand between the two of them, "is about more than just us. We have a responsibility, a duty to our lands and to our peoples. To defeat the Darklord, Alrendria and Gilead must work together. How can we expect them to do that when we can't go an entire meal without trying to kill each other?"

Another strained silence fell, and Martyn stared anxiously across the table. "You're right, Martyn," Miriam said coolly. "It was foolish to think our nations could work together."

Defeated, Martyn's slumped in his chair. In the back of his mind, he heard his father's voice. "You *must* win her over. Victory depends on alliance with Gilead. Remember, Tylor has the might of *Ael Shataq* behind him. How long before the Boundary falls or an army slips through? When the time comes, we will need Gilead!"

Martyn walked around the table and knelt at Miriam's side. He took her hand, and when she did not draw away, a smile played across his lips. "I don't want to hurt you, Miriam. I don't enjoy watching you suffer. Help me find a way for this to work!"

Tears glistened in the princess' eyes, but she fought them. "This is not how I envisioned our future." She turned away, groping blindly on the table.

"Nor I," Martyn said, pressing a napkin into her hand. Miriam lifted it to her face in a trembling hand and wiped her eyes. "In a perfect world, we'd be free to wed for love. I knew that was not to be, but I always hoped the Gods would let me love the woman duty required me to marry."

Martyn put a hand on Miriam's cheek and turned her face so she looked into his eyes. "I didn't want to love another," he told her, hoping she could sense his sincerity. "But I have no control over my heart."

"You ask me to share you," Miriam replied between sniffles, "but you don't want to share. You never even gave me a chance! You attend me only as duty requires, and as soon as you feel your obligation is satisfied, you run to… her."

"What alternative do you offer?" Martyn asked, his voice growing heated. "Cold, angry stares and sharp words? Why should I spend my time with you rather than with someone who loves me?"

"Because I'm to be your wife!" Miriam yelled. "Your queen! When you enter a room, will your eyes seek me or her? When the weight of command falls heavy on your shoulders, who will you go to for comfort?" Tears streamed down Miriam's cheeks, leaving watery tracks on her pale skin. "On our wedding night, whose face will you see beside you?"

For the first time, Martyn truly understood Miriam's pain, and his own role in it disgusted him. "I'm sorry," he whispered, squeezing her hand. "I spend so much time thinking about how unfair this is for me that I sometimes forget I'm not the only one suffering."

Taking the napkin from the princess' hand, Martyn wiped away her tears. "I'll try harder," he promised. "I'll do whatever I can to make your life better, but you must help me, Miriam. For the sake of our lands. For the sake of Madryn. Will you help me?"

Miriam, her lips pressed tightly together to keep from sobbing, nodded, and Martyn smiled. He rang a small bell on the table, and a servant entered. "Find Lady Kaeille and inform her that I must cancel our meeting."

Bowing deeply, the servant hurried off. Martyn offered Miriam his arm. "My Lady," he said, inclining his head formally. "Come with me. There's something I'd like you to see."

Miriam took Martyn's arm and allowed him to lead her through the palace. They climbed to the towers, where they braved the winter cold and walked the icy ramparts. Above, thousands of stars shone through the crisp air, and below, the lights of Kaper flickered back in answer.

"Before my mother died, she and my father came up here when they needed to be alone." Miriam shivered despite the heavily-lined coat she wore, and Martyn wrapped his arm around her. "I remember thinking how different they looked up here, how happy. In the castle, they were King and Queen, but up here, they were just a man and his wife. They loved looking at the city."

"It's beautiful," Miriam whispered.

"You've never come up here before?"

Miriam fixed Martyn with a pointed look. "I have done very little since my arrival."

"You should see the city at sunrise," Martyn said, hiding his embarrassment. "Perhaps you'll join me some morning?"

"I would like that," Miriam replied, and Martyn wondered if she were being sincere or merely diplomatic. They stood for some time in silence, sharing each other's company, until the chill of night drove them back inside.

As the days crawled by, Martyn resolved to ingratiate himself to the princess. With Liseyl's help, he arranged numerous chance encounters, and when he appeared to accidentally happen upon Miriam, he always took a moment to talk to her or invite her to accompany him on some errand. He soon learned that there was far more to the Gilean princess than a pretty face, and he came to look forward to their time together. Those few times when Miriam was unable to join him, he felt her absence.

Martyn tried to show Miriam something new each day. Kaper had millennia of history, and each chamber in the castle, every relic on display, had a story behind it. Miriam seemed awed with each discovery, and Martyn wracked his brain for other wonders to show her.

One night, Martyn took Miriam into the catacombs. They walked through the narrow, twisting corridors, their footsteps echoing hollowly on the cold stone. Sounds came out of the darkness, the skittering of tiny feet and the rhythmic dripping of water. When something darted across the tunnel at the edge of the lantern's light, Miriam squeaked and grabbed Martyn's arm tightly. Surprised by her sudden movement, he nearly dropped the lantern. "This place frightens me," Miriam whispered, a quaver in her voice.

"There's nothing to fear," Martyn assured her. "We use the catacombs for storage. There are vast storehouses down here, cold and dry, with enough supplies for a long siege." They pressed on for a time, but with every step, Miriam grew more uneasy. "Perhaps this was not the best place to visit," Martyn said. As he led her back to the palace, Martyn told tales of the many afternoons he, Jeran and Dahr had spent exploring and playing in the catacombs.

Miriam laughed at the stories, but when Martyn finished, her face grew grave. "Jeran and Dahr. You speak of them often and fondly, yet there's always sadness in your voice when you do. Why?"

"They were my friends," Martyn answered, his smile fading. "Men of honor and valor." He took a steadying breath but could not keep the anger from his voice. "They were betrayed by the woman Dahr loved, another friend. The last time I saw them, they fought against an enemy a hundred times our strength, all to ensure my escape. The Bull of Ra Tachan captured Jeran; no one has seen or heard from Dahr since the battle."

A rafter creaked and Miriam jumped. She pressed against Martyn, gripping him with surprising strength. "It must be very hard," she whispered, "to lose two friends at once and know you're the reason they're gone."

Martyn glared, and Miriam recoiled. Mortified by his reaction, Martyn begged Miriam's forgiveness. "You see things clearly. Losing them pains me greatly, but not as much as knowing that, if not for me, they'd still be among us." He paused thoughtfully. "But to be honest, it's confinement in Kaper that angers me the most."

"You mean being forced to be near me?" Miriam asked, but from the mischievous glint in her eye, Martyn knew she teased.

"Not at all." With Miriam peering so deeply into his eyes, he could not lie. "A little, perhaps. At first. But you're not bad company, Princess, now that you've stopped throwing crockery."

Miriam lowered her eyes to the floor, and the faintest hint of red touched her cheeks. "Alrendria fights a war," Martyn continued, "perhaps the greatest since the MageWar, and I'm not allowed to take part. I should be in Gilead or along the Corsan border, inspiring men and leading battles. Instead, I'm trapped in Kaper, coddled like a toothless infant."

"A living king is better than a dead warrior," Miriam reminded him, and she sounded so much like Joam that Martyn pushed away from her.

"A king only has power so long as his people believe in him. What will Alrendria think if I hide in Kaper while my Guardsmen do the killing—and the dying!—in my stead?" Martyn frowned, his eyes distant. "I should be with them."

They stopped in front of the door to the castle. "Perhaps you should say these things to your father," Miriam suggested. "You'd have more success convincing him you're not a child if you spent less time brooding atop the towers and more time acting like a prince."

Miriam's words stung, and a scathing retort came to Martyn's lips, but he considered what she had said before lashing out. "Maybe you're right." He looked into her eyes. "Sometimes, you seem to know me better than I know myself."

"You flatter me," Miriam replied. She looked at Martyn and swallowed nervously. Unable to control himself, Martyn leaned in and brushed his lips to hers. He started to withdraw, but the princess pressed against him with far more passion than he expected.

When they parted, Martyn's heart pounded in his chest and Miriam seemed unable to speak. "We should get back," Martyn murmured. He opened the door to the castle to find Zarin Mahl staring at him. Miriam shrieked at the man's sudden appearance, and she nearly pulled Martyn off balance when she jumped. Her grip on his arm was tight enough to make him wince.

"Ah, there you are," Zarin said amicably. He smiled and bowed to Miriam, as if he had not noticed the princess' terror. "I've been looking for you."

"How... How long were you out there?" Martyn asked.

"Not long, my Prince," Zarin replied. "Certainly not long enough for it to matter. Do you have a moment?"

"Why?" Martyn asked, instantly alert. "What's happened?"

"Oh nothing serious," Zarin said with a casual wave. "Just a few matters I wanted to bring to your attention." Zarin's eyes flicked toward Miriam, but the ingratiating smile never left his face.

"Miriam is to be my wife," Martyn said after weighing his options. "And your queen. Anything you need to say to me can be said to her." He fixed a steady stare on Zarin and hoped the diminutive man understood: he wanted Miriam to trust him completely, but he was not yet sure how far she could be trusted.

"Very well," Zarin said. He pulled a small kerchief from his pocket and coughed into it. "Shall we walk a bit?" He moved away from the door. "The stench from the catacombs causes me no end of suffering."

Zarin led them through the halls slowly, seeming to choose direction at random, turning first this way and then that. Martyn and Miriam followed in silence, and just as Martyn was starting to grow impatient, Zarin murmured, "I've received reports of dissent."

"Rebellion?" Martyn asked. "In Alrendria? Are they supporters of the—" He stopped suddenly and looked around. News of Tylor's return had spread, but that the Boundary was weakening remained a closely kept secret.

"Oh my! Nothing so dire as rebellion." Zarin knew everything; Martyn had taken him into his confidence as soon as Zarin agreed to act as his eyes and ears. Even he had been distressed by the news of the Boundary, though he had seemed more upset that he had no inkling of the truth than by the news itself.

"If not rebellion, then what?"

"Well, even in the best of times there are a few unhappy people grumbling about poor roadways, high taxes, or misbehaving Guardsmen. The complaints I hear these days are slightly—only slightly, mind you!—more severe, but it's not so much the tales as what happens to the tellers that concerns me."

"Zarin, you're trying my patience. If there are no problems, then why—?"

"I hear of dark taverns where those with a grudge against Alrendria go to drown their miseries and share their tales."

"Half the taverns in New Kaper fit that description!" Martyn snorted "You're jumping at shadows, Zarin! It's not a crime to be angry and drunk."

"Perhaps not, my Prince. But I've instructed my… friends… to keep an eye on anyone suspicious, and those who speak out against the crown have developed the habit of disappearing. My friends are skilled at what they do; for them to lose a mark is not impossible, but it's also not likely. Given the number of incidents, I begin to doubt coincidence."

The implication worried Martyn. "You think Tylor is recruiting Alrendrians?"

"Not just Alrendrians, Prince Martyn. The Bull has agents in every land, searching for anyone with a hatred of Alrendria or a hunger for power. But it's not greedy Gileans or Rachannen slavers you need to worry about; if Tylor's agents seduce the right man, our enemy may gain a distinct advantage."

"What could the Durange learn from agitated farmers and disgruntled craftsmen?" Martyn said, waving dismissively. "If some backwards commoners wish to offer their services to the Bull, let them. It would cost too much in time and effort to root them out."

"That may be true, Martyn," Miriam interjected, "But I don't believe Master Mahl speaks of village inns. I suspect the problem is far closer to home."

"Your Highness is quite perceptive," Zarin said. "The taverns I speak of— with one or two exceptions—are all in Kaper, some even in the old city. One tavern in particular may interest you: The Blacksmith's Beard."

"Guardsmen frequent that tavern!" Thoughts of Katya drifted through Martyn's head. "If the Bull places more spies among our Guardsmen…"

"Precisely. This is an area where I feel your father has been quite lax, especially in light of what we've learned. An agent positioned high enough in the Guard might gain knowledge of great value to our enemies."

"This can't be allowed! I'll have the Guard raid those taverns and flush out the traitors. We must ensure that Tylor doesn't—"

"There may be a better solution," Miriam said. Annoyed by the interruption, Martyn almost lashed out, but Miriam waited until she had his full attention before continuing. "If you destroy the taverns, the traitors will find new places to meet, and you'll no longer know where to find them."

"What do you suggest?" Martyn asked. Zarin studied the princess in his calculating manner while he waited for her to speak.

"Why not place our own agents in the taverns?" Miriam suggested. "Have them report on any suspicious people and activities. If they can find out who Tylor's agents are, we can deal with them directly or slip our own men among them."

"Your princess has a cunning mind, Prince Martyn," Zarin said, and Miriam smiled at the praise. "That is precisely what I would suggest. You'd do well to heed her advice in this matter."

"Who am I to argue?" Martyn laughed. "I assume you have men in mind for this duty?" Zarin nodded. "Then I'll leave it in your capable hands, Master Mahl. Report to me regularly. Was there anything else?"

"Nothing of consequence," Zarin said, but he frowned and tapped his lips thoughtfully. "I did see that sour-faced footman snooping around the King's study the other day."

"Konasi?" Martyn asked. "I take it you don't trust him?"

"Most people are curious, and it's a rare fellow who won't take a peek at anything he thinks he isn't supposed to, but I get the distinct impression that that man's loyalties are divided. I would keep a close eye on that one, were I you."

"Believe me; my father already has two eyes on that one." Few in the palace knew that Konasi was a Mage, and the King wanted to keep it that way. That Zarin had not puzzled out the truth was a testament to their success.

"As you say." They reached an intersection and Zarin stopped. "That's all for now, my Prince. Perhaps I'll have more to tell you tomorrow." He turned toward Miriam, but before he could bid his farewell, a shrill cry echoed through the hall.

"Alarm! Alarm! Rouse the Guard!"

"Mika?" Martyn called. He started forward, but a shadowy form brandishing a long dagger darted across the hall ahead of them. The man moved fast, too fast for Martyn to identify; all he saw was a flash of dark blue from the man's flapping cloak.

Martyn drew his dagger and started forward. "Take the princess to her quarters," he told Zarin. "Keep her safe."

"I'll protect her as best I can." Zarin took Miriam's arm and tried to lead her away. She resisted.

"I'm not a child either, Martyn," she told him haughtily. "I need coddling no more than you do."

"Of course you don't," Martyn replied as he stalked down the hall. "But until we're wed, you're a guest in Kaper. This is not your problem yet, and I couldn't bear it if anything unfortunate were to happen to you." Miriam scowled but did not struggle when Zarin again tried to pull her down the hall.

With the princess cared for, Martyn ran after the stranger. At the intersection, he almost collided with Mika. "Hold!" Martyn cried out, dancing away from the boy's darting blade. "Attack your enemies, Mika, not your friends!"

"Prince Martyn!" Mika exclaimed, sounding relieved. "I thought you were the assassin." His eyes narrowed. "There's been a murder! The killer ran this way. I was chasing him, and when you appeared, I... I..."

"You thought I was him," Martyn finished. A Guardsman appeared, and Martyn waved for him to hurry. "It's alright." He looked at the rip Mika's dagger had made in his tunic. "I'm just glad you weren't any faster."

The Guardsman stopped beside him and looked from the prince to Mika questioningly. "Mika witnessed a murder," Martyn explained. He pointed in the direction the assassin had run. "The killer went that way. Has the Guard been roused?"

"Master Mahl raised the alarm," the Guardsman answered. "I was patrolling a nearby passage, but a squad will be here in moments."

"When they arrive, send a detachment to look for the killer. I want him alive." Martyn doubted they would find anything; by now, the assassin had had ample opportunity to disappear. "Post a guard outside Princess Miriam's chambers and send for my father and Joam."

Taking Mika's arm, Martyn turned the boy back the way he had come. "The killer went the other way!" Mika protested.

"I know," Martyn said. "But chasing assassins is a job best left to Guardsmen. Take me to the body, Mika, and tell me what you saw."

"Prince Martyn," the Guardsman called out, "you must not go alone."

Martyn fought the frustration he felt at the Guardsman's tone. "The assassin went in the opposite direction. He has to pass this way to get to me. So long as you don't leave your post, we'll be safe." The sound of running feet echoed in the distance. "When the Guard arrives, send a detachment to protect me."

"Yes, my Prince," the Guardsman answered, saluting fist-on-heart.

Mika preceded the prince down the corridor and described what he had seen while they walked. "I was on my way to meet Bystral and heard two voices arguing. I stopped so they couldn't see me, and..."

"Tried to eavesdrop?" Martyn asked with a smile. When Mika did not answer, he prompted, "What did you hear?"

"Nothing," Mika answered guiltily. "They were talking too low. But they didn't sound happy! The one kept trying to get away, I think, but the other wouldn't let him."

They reached a corner and Mika paused. He looked both ways and then turned left, beckoning for Martyn to follow. "I peeked around the corner just in time to see one man drive his dagger into the other man's chest. I must have made a noise, because the killer stiffened and ran. That's when I cried out the alarm."

On the floor lay a crumpled form. "I stopped to help," Mika added, "but he was already dead, so I drew my *dolchek* and started after the assassin."

"That was foolish. What would you have done if the killer turned to fight?"

Mika's eyes hardened. "Whatever I had to."

"You know," Martyn laughed, kneeling beside the corpse, "I believe you would have at that. You'll make a great Guardsman one day!"

The victim wore violet robes, thick and heavy. Blood stained the material dark. A hood half-covered the victim's head, and long dark hair spread across the floor, hiding the man's features. A small, ornamental dagger lay not far from his outstretched hand.

Pounding feet approached, but Martyn did not wait for the Guardsmen. Grabbing the corpse by the shoulder, he flipped the body and gasped. Behind him, Mika mimicked the sound.

"Send for Jaenaryn," Martyn told the Guardsman who entered the hall. He ran a finger along the victim's pointed ear. "And Prince Treloran. An Elf has been murdered." One Guardsman left to carry out the prince's orders and two others positioned themselves next to Martyn, one on either side.

"Who killed the Elf?" Martyn muttered, not expecting an answer.

"Maybe it was one of those Aelvin assassins," Mika volunteered. "Or maybe they have agents in the castle. Or maybe the Elf was a traitor, and his own people killed him. Or—"

"A more important question," said a stern, feminine voice, "is what was the Elf doing down here in the first place?"

Startled, everyone whirled to face the speaker. She was tall, reed thin, and dressed in a gown of white with a dark grey cape draped over her narrow shoulders. Her features were pinched but commanding, her skin flawless, unmarred by blemish or wrinkle. Sharp cheekbones framed a long, narrow nose, and dark brown eyes observed the scene with casual interest. Auburn hair sat atop her head in an elaborate bun, save for two curling strands that dangled to either side of her face. In her left hand she held an oak staff; in her right, she carried a small book bound with black cord.

The Guardsmen drew their weapons fluidly, but the woman paid them no heed. When they advanced, she offered them a small, distasteful frown. "That's a good question," Martyn admitted, signaling for the Guardsmen to lower their swords. "But I have a better one. Who are you, and what are you doing here?"

The woman's lips twisted up. "Such fine manners, Prince Martyn. There was a time when I would have received a far grander welcome in Kaper." She started forward, and the Guardsmen moved to intercept her.

The woman ignored them, and the soldiers stopped, allowing her to pass. Mika drew his *dolchek* and lunged at the woman, but froze less than a hand from her. He struggled against unseen bonds, his face constricted in a snarl. The two Guardsmen fought against air as well.

The woman's smile broadened, and she patted Mika on the head as she passed him. Stopping in front of Martyn, she inclined her head politely. "I am Lelani Iosa," she said in a calm, commanding voice. "High Wizard of the Magi."

Chapter 9

"You walk a dangerous line, King Mathis, and play games with dangerous opponents." The High Wizard stared at the King, her expression unreadable, and folded her hands on the edge of the table. The air of the chamber crackled with tension. "The Assembly is concerned."

"Concerned?" Mathis laughed harshly. "You haven't acted concerned. As far as I can tell, the Mage Assembly has abandoned Madryn. Where were you when Tylor killed Iban, or when Jeran and Dahr sacrificed themselves?"

"Mind your tone," Lelani said as if addressing a child. "I'm no lordling for you to intimidate." Mathis' face reddened, but from anger or embarrassment, Martyn could not tell. "You presume much, and your ignorance makes our actions no less real. We neither require your blessing nor desire your approval."

Martyn leaned back and put a hand over his mouth to keep from saying something he might regret. They sat in a small chamber, a dining hall converted to a war room. The High Wizard sat at one end of a long table; the book she had carried since her arrival sat in front of her. The King, his crown resting heavily atop his head, sat at the other end. They stared at each other so intently no one else dared speak.

Joam sat to Martyn's left. The new tassels naming him High Commander of the Alrendrian Guard hung limply on his shoulder. Anger flushed his face, and his lips pressed into a narrow line. He drummed the fingers of one hand against the table; the other hand tugged at his mustache.

"Then tell me, High Wizard," Mathis asked, schooling his features, "what *actions* have the Magi taken?"

A hoarse chuckle came from Joam's left. "Yes, Mage." Bantor glowered. "Tell us what you Magi have done to help us poor mortals."

Lelani's lips parted in a thin smile, but she did not so much as glance at the Rachannan. "The Assembly's plans don't concern you, King Mathis. Rest assured; you'll be told all you need to know."

Bantor opened his mouth, but Bystral and Lisandaer, who flanked the Rachannan like guard dogs, gave him scathing looks. Bantor shrugged off their glares but said nothing. He took a long draught from his mug, gripping the handle so tight his hand shook from the effort.

Guardsman Bystral had taken over as commander of the city garrison, and Lisandaer had been given command of the castle's defense. Both wore their new rank proudly, and both turned cold gazes on Lelani. Martyn understood; he did not like hearing someone speak to his father with disrespect either.

Konasi sat beside Lisandaer. He, too, stared at the High Wizard, but adoration filled his gaze. His smug smile infuriated Martyn more than Lelani's condescension, and he wished his father had not decided to include the Mage in this meeting. Not that the King had had much choice; Lelani had all but insisted. "What Konasi has told me is most troubling," she had said, chiding the King publicly. "Your advisor from the Assembly deserves better treatment than that of a scullion." Rather than argue, Mathis had simply.

Martyn knew his father's patience was wearing thin, but the King's voice betrayed no frustration. "The Assembly has been less than forthcoming," he said. "The Magi have not been the allies I expected."

"It seems," Lelani said, casting a sidelong glance at Bantor, "that Alrendria is not as discerning in its choice of allies as it once was. You should be grateful for whatever aid you receive from us."

Bantor's face contorted, but King Mathis cut the Rachannan off before his rough tongue caused even more problems. "The Rachannen approached us," he snapped. "So far, they've given us no cause to doubt their intentions. I won't turn away a potential ally solely on the basis of prejudice."

"Prejudice," Lelani repeated. "The same prejudice that saw my people massacred twenty winters ago? The same prejudice that started the Tachan Purge?"

"The Rachannen want to fight the Tachans!" Mathis yelled.

"The Rachannen *are* Tachan," Lelani retorted, her tone icy.

Mathis sat back and spread his arms wide. "What would you have me do?" he demanded, an edge to his voice. "Turn down every ally whose ideology differs from mine? Ignore the pleas of any man whose ancestors slighted the Magi?" The King snorted. "It would be easier to go to Portal and offer Lorthas my crown! Why wait for the Boundary to collapse?"

Across the table, Jaenaryn's lips drew down in a frown. Treloran glanced at Martyn, but the Aelvin Prince showed no other reaction. Though Martyn had never told the Elf outright, he knew Treloran had long suspected the truth about the Boundary. In her seat beside the Elves, Miriam paled when the King spoke of the Boundary's fall, and every mention of Lorthas' name made her shiver.

Fire lit Lelani's eyes, but her expression did not change. "I thought you wished to keep the truth about the Boundary secret, Highness. Perhaps you should keep a tighter rein on your tongue."

"*I* will decide which of my secrets will be kept and which will be shared." Mathis said, and Martyn's winced. His father's temper was hard to rouse, but once awakened, it was fierce. That temper now threatened Alrendria's alliance with the Magi.

From the chair to Lelani's right, Kal chuckled. "You have the courage of a *tyrgran*, King Mathis. Even *Tsha'ma* walk soft around Magi." Martyn did not know what a *tyrgran* was, but he thought the words a compliment.

"And to think, the *Tsha'ma* are known for their wisdom," Konasi whispered, but not quietly enough.

Mathis shot a glare at the Mage, but he drew a deep breath and calmed himself. "It doesn't matter anymore," he said with a dismissive wave. "News of Tylor's escape has spread. Before long, people will realize what it means."

"The Boundary... is falling?" Miriam whispered.

"That the Boundary will fall is not news, child," Lelani lectured. "The Magi have known since the Raising that this time would come."

"The Boundary is forever," Bantor said. "You Magi made it that way."

"The Boundary goes against nature," Lelani replied, and the cold certainty of her words left little room for doubt. "There is no force on Madryn more powerful than nature."

"If you knew this," the Rachannan growled, "why have you never warned anyone?"

Konasi stared at the Rachannan in disgust. "You have no right to question the wisdom of the Assembly, Rachannan, and we do not need to justify our decisions to you!"

"It is a legitimate question," Treloran said. "If you knew this all along, then why have we not spent the last eight centuries preparing for Lorthas' return?"

"After the MageWar, the Assembly decided that the Races deserved peace." Lelani spoke slowly, as if the admission were being forced from her. "It was a decision the Assembly did not make lightly or alone. The Tsha'ma agreed, as did Ael Alluya. We knew only that the Boundary would eventually fall, not when. Only over the last few winters did we learn how extensive the degradation was."

"What was decided in the past is irrelevant," Jaenaryn said, speaking for the first time since the meeting began. "What matters now is how long we have before Lorthas is free."

"It's difficult to say," Lelani replied. "We know the Darklord's minions have found a path through the mountains, but the Boundary itself, the barrier that blocks magic, remains intact. But for how long, I cannot say. It could fall in a few seasons or it could stand another millennium."

"A millennium?" Bantor shouted, sputtering ale across the table. "You talk of a thousand winters as if they are a season! The troubles of the future are not ours. Let those who come after us deal with their own problems."

"That," Lelani turned a pointed glare on the Rachannan, "is what they said after the Raising. And here we sit, eight hundred winters later, no closer to a solution."

Bantor shook his head, but Lelani forestalled any additional comments. "Silence," she ordered, "and I'll tell you of a day long past, when the earth still trembled from the Raising."

Bystral shut his mouth, and the Guardsman turned his full attention on the High Wizard. The others, all save Bantor, leaned in to hear Lelani's story. The Rachannan muttered darkly, but seeing that he had no supporters, he settled back and drank deeply.

"In the days following the Raising, the heroes of Madryn celebrated like nothing you have ever seen. The Four Races sang and danced as one, and they toasted the beginning of a new era. But in the shadow of the Boundary, with the grim reminders of death all around, the celebration could not last. The Drekka and Arkam Imperium remained, as did elements of the Darklord's vast army, and these groups had to be defeated before the war would truly end.

"As the days passed, the alliance began to dissolve. Homesickness crept into the hearts of our men. Some whispered of leaving, of returning to friends and family, home and hearth. Before long, those whispers grew louder and more frequent.

"The Elves petitioned to return to Illendrylla. They tired of war and wanted to return to the safety of their forest. The Garun'ah wanted to go east too, to join their brethren hunting down the remnants of the Drekka. And the few Orog who survived the war wanted to find a sanctuary, some place away from the other Races where they could mourn the death of their people.

"Even the Alrendrians, on whose land the Boundary stood, saw no need to keep the alliance together. Pockets of resistance existed throughout Alrendria, and the Darklord had allies in almost every land. Lord Cramdyne Durange, a commander in the Alrendrian Guard second only to Commander Keryn, was the most adamant about ignoring the Boundary and eliminating the remaining threat so that life could return to normal."

A silence descended. Everyone waited for the High Wizard to continue, but she seemed conflicted. "We Magi should have stopped them. We should have insisted that the alliance remain firm. But we were overly confident." She whispered the last, and it seemed to take all her will to admit the mistake. "Some in the Assembly, in their pride, thought the Boundary would last forever; others simply longed to live in a peaceful world again. When the Races began to fragment, we did nothing.

"Only a few realized the danger. High Wizard Aemon, Emperor Alwellyn, and Lord Vaso Keryn made impassioned pleas to the Four Races. They warned us of the Boundary's collapse and insisted that if we let the alliance dissolve, we would lose our greatest advantage against the Darklord.

"No one listened. Even the Magi, myself included, thought their words the ravings of paranoid old men." Her eyes, which had softened during the story, regained their edge. "I have lived a great many winters, and I regret few things. But I regret that I did not heed Aemon that day."

Lelani sipped her wine and set her glass delicately upon the table. "It happened just as they predicted. The Races split, and though the bonds between them remained strong for seasons, they eventually faded. The Elves retreated to their forest, shutting off contact with the outside world. Lord Cramdyne Durange and King Jorain's long-standing rivalry ended with Lord Durange exiled from Alrendria. He carved out his own empire in the east, driving the Garun'ah from their ancestral home."

Kal grunted, and Frodel, who sat beside the *Kranach*, echoed the sound. Martyn had once made the mistake of mentioning Cramdyne Durange before the Tribesmen; it was not a mistake he would ever repeat. "By the time the Assembly realized their mistake, the damage had been done, and the alliance could not be restored. We hoped that, when the day of the Boundary's fall arrived, the Races would again be united against the Darklord.

"It was a vain hope. Instead of a daunting foe, Lorthas will find Madryn a land of petty nations, its inhabitants barely able to keep from killing each other."

"That's not true, High Wizard," Martyn exclaimed. "Are we not proof to the contrary? Alrendria, Gilead, and Rachannon—not to mention Roya!—stand united against the Darklord. At this table sit representatives from the three surviving Races, both mortal and Mage. Our alliance is as strong today as it ever was!"

"Is it?" Lelani fastened her gaze on the prince. A thin smile touched her lips. "Your naivety is refreshing, child. That this collection of…"—she tapped a finger to her lips thoughtfully—"dignitaries… can sit here without weapons drawn is a feat of no small measure, I grant you, but it is a far cry from the alliance of old."

The High Wizard surveyed the group. "This is no alliance. This isn't even a gathering of friends. Over there we have the Elves, aloof as always, willing to reopen *trade* after centuries of isolation. When the war begins," Lelani said to Mathis, "see how quickly your Aelvin allies rush to your aid. The Emperor's words don't carry as much weight with *Ael Alluya* as they once did. Lorthas will walk the streets of Kaper long before *Ael Chatorra* fights at your side."

The High Wizard's hand moved to encompass the Tribesmen. "And here we have the Garun'ah. Warlike and honorable, they would make excellent allies, except that their hatred of the Elves nearly rivals their hatred of the Drekka. If, by some miracle, Illendrylla does join your cause, watch how quickly the Tribesmen slip away."

Kal rose, and Frodel growled, a deep, guttural sound that reverberated through the room. "Now, now, boys," Lelani chided, "no need to get angry. Your *Kranora* mean well, but they can't expect the Hunters to cast aside generations of blood feuds." Kal hesitated; uncertainty entered his eyes. A pleading look from the King made him resume his seat.

"And the Human nations," Lelani laughed, turning away from the Tribesmen, "are a joke. You can barely keep from fighting yourselves. Corsa and Ra Tachan would side against Alrendria regardless of Tylor's fate. The Royan fleet is impressive, but even it has proved no match for the Black Fleet. And the Gilean forces won't be able to stand up to Rachannon's pitiful excuse for an army."

Both Miriam and Bantor stood, outraged, and Lelani covered her mouth in feigned embarrassment. "My apologies," she said, inclining her head to Bantor. "I keep forgetting that the Rachannen butchers are now our allies." Bantor fumed, but he maintained a grim silence.

"Even the Alrendria Guard," Lelani continued in a voice laced with acid, "is a shadow of its former self. There was a time when no force in Madryn could stand against the Guard, but long winters of peace, broken by wars we wouldn't have considered battles during the MageWar, have weakened it. When Lorthas breaches the Boundary, I doubt Alrendria will survive a season."

Bystral slammed his fist against the table. "You go too far, Mage! The Guard is as disciplined as ever! The Darklord's forces don't stand a chance!"

"Is that what you tell the Corsans raiding your borders?" Bantor chuckled. He downed the last few dregs of ale and threw his mug. "Does it make them quake in their boots, Guardsman?"

Bystral glowered, but it was Lisandaer spoke. "You'll be begging for the Guard when the Tachans attack your lands, Dog!"

"The Tachans don't worry us!"

"Why come to Kaper then?" Miriam asked, her musical laughter filling the room. "A casual visit? Just wanted to chat with old friends?" The princess' eyes hardened. "You need Alrendria, and you know it."

Bantor returned Miriam's glare in kind, and his lips twisted up in a cruel smile. "At least my father didn't have to sell me to Alrendria to gain its protection!"

"How dare you!" Miriam said, her voice rising in volume. She glanced at Martyn, and her face flushed bright red. "I... You..." Mortified, she choked on her own response.

Treloran came to her defense. "You should watch your tongue, Human. You speak to a princess."

"I will speak as I please, Elf!" Bantor shot back, sneering the last word. "I don't fear the likes of you."

"And me?" Kal asked, rising to his feet. He towered over the Rachannan. "Do you fear me, little man? I have no tolerance for Soul-Stealers and those who allow their kind to thrive."

"Poor Human," Jaenaryn added, his eyes on Bantor. "Even the Wildmen are better behaved than you."

Kal growled, and his grip on the table turned his knuckles white. "You press your luck, *Aelva*."

"I meant no offense, Tribesman."

"You offer it nonetheless."

The Elf sighed heavily. "This is why dealing with Wildmen is more trouble than its worth," he said under his breath. "They are little more than undisciplined children."

"Do not speak as if I cannot hear you!" Frodel growled. His chair slid away from the table, and the Tribesman stood, his hand reaching for his blade.

"Primitive Savage!"

"Honorless Dog!"

The table erupted in a cacophony of yells. Miriam screamed across the table at Bantor, and Bantor snapped back a harsh reply. Lisandaer and Konasi stood hands apart, yelling at each other at the top of their lungs. Bystral shouted his approval to Lisandaer, and Joam, from his position by the doorway, bellowed for the Guardsmen to be silent. Kal and Frodel exchanged insults with the Elves, who parried each of the Tribesmen's snarled threats quietly, if in haughty, condescending tones.

Martyn watched in horror as Alrendria's allies fought like bitter enemies. He wanted to say something but did not know what words to use. He looked around the room, wondering if he should call for the Guard before blows were exchanged.

Only High Wizard Lelani and the King remained unaffected. Mathis stared across the table, his chin resting on folded hands, seemingly oblivious to the yelling. The High Wizard settled back in her chair with a satisfied smile.

Martyn's own anger surfaced. "You did this!" he said. "You... bewitched them."

Lelani rolled her eyes. "Why do the ungifted believe a Mage can accomplish nothing without magic? I did do this, Prince Martyn, but only with well-chosen words." She surveyed the chamber smugly. "What do you think of your alliance now, child?"

Martyn's jaw tightened. "What right have you to—?"

"Enough!" King Mathis' voice cut through the chamber like a knife. All eyes turned toward him. "This display is an embarrassment." The King spoke barely above a whisper. His eyes scanned the table, but none save Martyn and Lelani dared meet his gaze. "It shames me to consider you my allies."

The ensuing silence carried more of a threat than the arguments preceding it. "The High Wizard is right," Mathis told them. "If this is the best we can do, we have no chance of victory. If our alliance is nothing more than a suppression of hatred, we might as well surrender now." He took the crown from his head and hurled it across the room. It crashed against the wall and fell to the floor with a loud clatter.

"But I believe our alliance can be more. I believe the Three Races can form a bond stronger than the one forged during the MageWar. I believe the nations of man can set aside their differences to face a common enemy." Mathis' lips twisted upward, and he leaned over the table with a look fierce enough that even Lelani took note. "If you don't share my beliefs, High Wizard, then leave. The Magi have been hiding for a long time. You won't be missed."

Konasi sputtered, but Lelani silenced any retort with a gesture. "You'll feel differently when Lorthas unleashes his ShadowMagi upon you."

"Perhaps," Mathis admitted. "But I welcome no one to this alliance who doesn't believe in it wholly. To fight at our side, I need not prove our worth to you; you must prove yours to me." The King's eyes roved the table. "Your presence in Kaper bought you admittance to this council. If anyone here doesn't want to fight alongside Alrendria, they may leave. If anyone here can't set aside their differences for the greater good, they may leave. But if you leave, the rest of us will abandon you to your fate. When the Darklord returns, we will turn a deaf ear to your pleas."

Lelani smiled. "You bluff with confidence, King Mathis."

"If you think my threat idle," Mathis replied, his expression blank, "then test it."

The High Wizard ran a hand along her chin, then settled back in her chair. "One day, perhaps, I will. But not today."

Everyone resumed their seats, and a few mumbled apologies were exchanged. "The news I have isn't good," Mathis began. "In the east, the Tachan army plans to march, but whether toward Gilead or Rachannon, we don't know." He looked at Bantor, then at Miriam. "Both nations have fortified the Tachan border, but both are wasting nearly as many troops on their shared one.

"Tomorrow, High Commander Joam will lead the Guard south, where a Royan fleet waits to transport them to Gilead." Mathis turned to Bantor. "I would have you go as well with dispatches for your king. Rachannon must withdraw from the Gilean border. If we're to stand against the Tachans, we must be allies in more than name. King Vestlin must be made to understand that."

Bantor mumbled under his breath about distrustful Gileans, but Miriam either did not hear or chose not to respond. "To foster a true alliance," Mathis continued, "we must protect each other. Alrendrians guarding Rachannon. Rachannen guarding Gilead. Only through trust do we have a chance of winning."

"I don't like the idea of Gilean pigs guarding my home," Bantor replied, and Miriam's lips pressed into a line. "But working with Gileans is better than living beneath the Durange's boots."

Mathis ignored the Rachannan. "The Drekka threaten the Tribal Lands, but we still need the Garun'ah at our side. I discussed this with Kal, and we have reached a decision." The King turned to Vyrina, who sat silently between Frodel and Jaenaryn. "I'm sending you and Frodel north. Six squads of Guardsmen await your command in Grenz. You're to lead them into the Tribal Lands and aid our allies in fighting the Drekka. In exchange, the Tacha will send Hunters south to join our cause. It's not much, but simply announcing our alliance with the Garun'ah might give our enemies cause for thought."

"I will serve Alrendria to the best of my abilities," the Guardswoman said. At her side, Frodel beamed.

Mathis tossed a satchel to the Guardswoman. "These dispatches are for the Emperor. Lady Utari prepares to depart for Illendrylla. Deliver them to her, and she will make sure they reach Lynnaei." Vyrina took the satchel and saluted fist-on-heart.

"We fare even worse in the west," Mathis admitted. "With every passing day, the Corsans raid deeper onto Alrendrian soil. So far, losses have been light, but Commander Jasova has had no luck driving the enemy back. His troops are spread thin, and the raiding parties have little difficulty slipping past our patrols. To make matters worse, Midlyn has closed its borders and refuses all requests for aid. I can only assume they mean to side against us."

A chorus of dark muttering erupted. "Morale is low everywhere, and even in Vela, which has stood untouched since the MageWar, the First believes a Corsan assault would be disastrous. Lady Jessandra tells me the people need a hero, a symbol, someone to remind them of their duty and inspire them to meet it."

The King wrung his hands together. "Martyn will travel west with the troops bound for Vela," he said at last. Martyn smiled, but many in the room did not seem as happy. Joam, in particular, wore a dark scowl. "My son will join Commander Jasova and lead the fight against the Corsans."

Martyn's smile broadened, and he closed his eyes, envisioning the adventure to come. "He will do this after escorting Princess Miriam to Vela."

"What?" Martyn demanded, and a chorus of gasps followed the prince's declaration. "She won't be safe!"

"Vela is as safe as Kaper," Mathis replied, and Miriam smiled coldly. "Perhaps safer." When his words had no effect, the King sighed. "Miriam has yet to decide whether she will be Queen of Alrendria. I believe that if she sees this great land and learned a little of its people, it would make her decision an easy one."

"Don't worry, my Prince," Miriam said, her expression turning stony. "I wouldn't dream of separating you from your... advisor. Your Elf may join my entourage."

Martyn wanted to explain that his outburst had nothing to do with Kaeille, but Mathis waved for him to be silent. "I've made my decision, Martyn. You'll escort Miriam to Vela and make sure no harm befalls her. Once there, you'll coordinate with Jasova."

Martyn licked his lips. "I won't let you down, Father."

"Kal will accompany you," Mathis added, with a nod to the Tribesman, "as a representative of the Tribes."

"And I will go too," Treloran announced.

This caught even Mathis by surprise; the King turned a startled gaze on the Aelvin Prince. "Absolutely not!" Jaenaryn said, shaking his head. "This is a Human war, and I will not allow you to involve yourself in it."

"Remember to whom you speak. I am Treloran el'e Kelemeilion, grandson of Alwellyn the Eternal. You have no right to tell me where I will or will not go."

"This is a Human war," Jaenaryn repeated, "and *Ael Alluya* have yet to decide whether or not to cast our lot with the Humans. It would be irresponsible—"

"*I am Ael Alluya*," Treloran reminded him, "and *Ael Chatorra*. As heir to the Empire, I may decide which side of the conflict I stand on; as an Aelvin warrior, only the *Hohe Chatorra* may command me." Treloran gaze was sharp enough to cut. "Unless Astalian or the Emperor himself orders me back to Illendrylla, I will go where I choose."

"My Prince, I—"

Treloran's patience ran out. "It was the Emperor who bade me join the Humans. It was He who wanted me to learn their ways, to foster an understanding between our peoples. You have defied me since your arrival, but will you defy your Emperor? Here, in front of all these witnesses?"

Jaenaryn lowered his gaze, and Treloran returned his attention to King Mathis. "I would accompany your son, unless you have an objection."

After a stunned silence, Mathis shook his head. "Your presence will be welcome," he assured the Aelvin Prince. "Martyn values your counsel." To Jaenaryn, he added, "Prince Treloran will be guarded as I guard my own son." Jaenaryn nodded curtly but said nothing.

The meeting concluded to allow the parties time to prepare for their departures. As Martyn hurried from the chamber, he spotted Zarin surreptitiously studying a tapestry. He walked over and offered greetings. "Your men are in place?"

"They are. And I found a suitable candidate for that other matter we discussed."

"He's willing?"

Zarin nodded. "Betraying his king, even to aid Alrendria, is not something that appeals to him, but he's willing."

"I'll leave the matter in your capable hands," Martyn told Zarin. "I'm leaving for Vela in the morning."

"Yes, yes," Zarin replied, waving his hand absently, as if the news were commonplace. "Best of luck to you, my Prince." He bowed and walked off.

Martyn turned, eager to pack, but he faced one final obstacle. Mika stood before him, an eager glint in his eye. "You're going to Vela?" the boy asked, and when Martyn nodded, Mika smiled. "Can I go with you?"

Martyn moved so that he and Mika stood eye-to-eye. "I'd be honored, but it cannot be. You've a much greater duty to perform." Mika's disappointment quickly turned to curiosity. "With Joam leaving Kaper, no one will remain to protect my father. No one I trust, at any rate." A smile spread across Martyn's face. "No one except you, that is."

Mika's expression grew grimly serious. "No harm will befall the King in your absence, my Prince." He saluted. "I promise you."

"With a Guardsman like you at his side?" Martyn replied. "I should think not." Mika bid the prince farewell and hurried away to prepare for his new duty. Martyn headed toward his own chambers, equally anxious to begin his adventure.

Chapter 10

Jeran stared in stunned silence; joy and horror passed through him, warring for control. He wept at the sight of his uncle, then laughed until the tears returned. During the long winters, only he had held to the belief that Aryn lived. Even King Mathis had long since given up hope. Seeing his uncle alive was far different than believing he lived, though.

Long, frayed hair and a bushy, unkempt beard hid most of Aryn's face. Thick smudges of dirt blackened what little skin showed. Bony arms, not the powerful arms Jeran remembered, the ones that had plowed fields all day and still had strength enough to play in the evening, protruded from beneath tattered rags. Once broad and powerful hands curled into half-claws; a long, yellowed nail curled from the end of each finger. Only the eyes bore a resemblance to the man Jeran had known. Though dull and listless, they held a remnant of Aryn Odara.

Long-healed scars criss-crossed Aryn's chest; other, more jagged marks lined his arms. Guilt washed over Jeran, and a Reading tickled at the edge of his awareness. Jeran forced it away. He had no desire to relive Aryn's torture first hand. He reached out slowly, his hand trembling, and took his uncle's hand. "Uncle Aryn?"

Blinking repeatedly, Aryn tried to focus. His expression remained blank, and the lack of recognition rent Jeran's heart. "You're not Tylor," Aryn said, his brow furrowed. Suspicion entered his eyes, and he tried to pull away, but Jeran had no trouble keeping his grip. Defeated, Aryn slumped forward, but his eyes remained locked on Jeran. "You're not Tylor."

"No, Uncle Aryn. It's me. It's Jeran."

Jeran hoped the name would bring a smile to Aryn's lips, or at least a hint of recognition. Instead, what little life Aryn had shown vanished. Tears ran down his cheek, and he made no effort to wipe them away. The Reading surged, and it took all of Jeran's will to hold the vision at bay. Panic surged—he had not had trouble controlling his Readings since beginning his training with the Emperor—and he released Aryn's hand. As soon as they broke contact, the tingling vanished. "Uncle Aryn," Jeran pleaded. "It's me!"

"Jeran." The word was little more than a croak. "I had a nephew named Jeran. He was a good boy." The hint of a smile forced its way onto Jeran's face, but it faded when Aryn added, "He died long ago. I killed him."

"No!" Jeran took his uncle's shoulders and shook him, trying to wake him from his stupor. "Uncle Aryn. I'm here. I'm alive!"

"I sent him to his death," Aryn said. "And that's just as good, isn't it? I failed him. I failed them both."

Jeran's life, eight winters in Kaper, living in comfort and safety while his uncle suffered, now seemed a cruel joke. Tylor's joke, and this reunion the punch line. Anger threatened to overwhelm him. Anger at Tylor, who had done this to his uncle, and at King Mathis for not rescuing his long-time friend. Mostly, though, Jeran was angry with himself for not convincing anyone that Aryn lived.

Aryn jerked away, and his eyes narrowed to slits. "You're not Tylor," he snapped. "Why are you here?"

"Uncle Aryn, it's—" The words caught; Jeran could not bring himself to say them again. "Tylor brought me here."

Aryn reached for one of the ornate goblets resting on the table. Jeran noticed them for the first time, the expensive platters and bejeweled chalices surrounding Aryn. "Another trophy?" Aryn asked, running his hand down the side of the goblet. "Tylor likes his trophies."

"Yes," Jeran muttered. "I'm just another trophy."

"You're not the first," Aryn said knowingly. "You'll not be the last either. I've been here..." The silence that filled the room pressed in on Jeran. "...forever." Aryn stood and hobbled around the table, favoring one leg. "Stand still," he snapped when Jeran tried to back away. "Not too battered," Aryn said as he circled Jeran slowly. "Tylor's trophies usually arrive in worse shape."

"I've been in the Barrows for over a season. It gave me a chance to heal."

"The Barrows?" Aryn asked, suspicion returning to his voice. He laughed, and the sound, half chuckle, half cackle, sent a chill down Jeran's spine. "Tylor doesn't collect trophies from the Barrows."

"I'm someone he's wanted for a long time. I've been his prisoner since Harvest, but he hasn't been able to touch me. Today, I angered him, and..."

"And he brought you here." When Jeran nodded, Aryn glared daggers at him. "I am not a fool." He spat at Jeran's feet and paced the room, his eyes full of rage. Without warning, he ran to the door. "Your tricks will not work again, Tylor!" Aryn shouted, pounding on the oak with his fists. "I won't believe this creature's lies!"

Jeran stared wide-eyed, and when Aryn whirled to face him again, he backed away. "I have ears! I am not a fool, and I have ears. My life in his room... it's better than most who live under Tylor's boot. If what you say is true, if you've lived in the Barrows, what possible pain could bringing you here cause?"

A tear fell unchecked down Jeran's cheek. "You have no idea."

Aryn grunted then stomped away, muttering to himself. He paced beneath the portraits of Alic and Illendre, and from time to time, he paused to glare at Jeran. After a while, he returned to the table, poured them each a goblet of wine, and smiled. "Tell me, stranger," he said, motioning for Jeran to sit. "What was your crime against the Durange?"

Jeran swallowed nervously. Despite his uncle's tone, he felt as if he were on trial. "I killed two of his sons."

"A grave mistake," Aryn said, and he chuckled. "Luckily, the Bull has sons enough to go around. I doubt he even knows all their names." Aryn kicked his feet and the chair opposite him skidded backward. He gestured again, and this time Jeran sat. "Now," Aryn asked, "why are you really here? What did Tylor promise you?"

"I told you; I'm here because Tylor wants to punish me."

"Hmmm." Aryn leaned forward and pressed his mouth against his folded hands. "You're a liar, boy, and not a good one."

Jeran tried to speak, but Aryn laughed it off. "Why deny it?" His anger returned. "The only thing I don't understand is why? After all these winters, does Tylor really think I know anything about life in Alrendria?"

"I'm not here to get information from you!"

"Good! Because you won't. If seasons at the hands of the Purifiers couldn't loosen my tongue, chatting with an insufferable child won't."

Aryn's words hurt, mostly because they meant he did not know who he was talking to. "Nothing to say?" Aryn asked. "No quick response or preplanned excuse? The war must fare badly for the Durange. In the past, Tylor sent far more convincing agents."

The silence stretched out for a long time, and Jeran shifted uncomfortably in his seat. "All right, stranger, let's pretend I believe you're not Tylor's man. What's your name? I can't call you stranger forever."

Gone were the hunched shoulders and shifting eyes; Aryn now sat proud and straight-backed, with the calm air of command Jeran remembered. Even his voice had changed, becoming deeper and more powerful. "Uncle Aryn!" Jeran exclaimed, relieved to see his uncle returning to normal. *It must have been an act for Tylor's benefit.* "Thank the Gods! You had me worried."

Jeran took Aryn's hand. Aryn did not pull away, but he eyed Jeran oddly. "It's me…" Jeran said. "It's Jeran."

At the mention of Jeran's name, the strength faded from Aryn again. His shoulders collapsed, dropping as if a great weight had suddenly settled upon them. His face lost all color, and his eyes grew listless. "Jeran," he murmured, his voice held but a shadow of its strength from the moment before. "I had a nephew named Jeran."

Aryn mumbled beneath his breath, and coarse, cruel laughter filled the chamber. "This is even sweeter than I imagined," Tylor said, pushing the door open.

"Why do you insist on sending these children?" Aryn yelled, bolting to his feet. "This one doesn't even look like Jeran!"

"Ahhh," Tylor said with a smile. "He's in one of his talkative moods. How fortunate." The ice in the Bull's voice did not match the friendly smile he wore. "I'll scrape every bit of information out of you, Odara!" he roared. "If it takes me the rest of my life, I will!

"To be honest," Tylor said to Jeran in a calmer voice. "I've not sent anyone to interrogate him for more than three winters. We learned all we could from him long ago." The Bull chuckled. "I do this to humor him. It makes him feel better to think he held on to some secrets."

Jeran's hand clenched, but he kept himself rooted in the chair. "Your uncle held out far longer than I anticipated," Tylor admitted. "It took Salos and his Purifiers seasons to extract the information we needed." The Bull turned his gaze on Aryn's shrunken form, and his grin doubled in size. "What we learned was worth the wait. For a farmer, your uncle kept himself well informed."

"Why do you do this, Tylor?" Aryn asked, and the pleading sound sickened Jeran. "Why do you keep me here? You claim to be a man of honor! Prove it. End my suffering!"

Tylor laughed. "Aryn... How many times must I tell you? You're my guest here, not my prisoner. A very special guest. I'd as soon lose my good eye as send you away." Under his breath, so that only Jeran could hear, Tylor whispered, "Sometimes he begs me to take his life. Other times he taunts me. Visiting your uncle is always an adventure. Without him to entertain me, I'd have never survived my time in Dranakohr."

"Why did you send him here?" Aryn asked, pointing at Jeran. "Just because he claims to be my nephew doesn't mean I'll share my secrets!"

"You're far too crafty for me, Aryn," Tylor replied. "He truly doesn't recognize you? The Purifiers must have damaged him more than I thought. I'll have to commend—"

With a snarl, Jeran lunged from his chair, reaching out for Tylor's throat. The Bull's first blow staggered him; the second sent him crashing against the wall. He fell to the floor, where he lay stunned and desperately trying to draw breath.

"I told you you'd fail!" Aryn jeered, hopping up and down in his seat and pointing at Jeran. "I told you Tylor would be displeased!" Aryn's mad cackle hurt more than Tylor's blows. "Punish him!" Aryn scream. "Punish him like you punished the others!"

"Get up," Tylor commanded, a grin on his face. "The Darklord wants to see you." Jeran climbed to his feet slowly. The room spun, but Jeran fought to maintain his balance, determined to give Tylor no more reasons to gloat.

Once they were in the tunnels, Tylor's mood darkened. "Now you know the way of things, Odara. From now on, remember that I may not be able to harm you, but Aryn is mine to do with as I please."

Jeran peered into the Trophy Room as Tylor closed the door. The last he saw, Aryn cowered on the mound of rags in the back of the room with his arms wrapped around his knees. "If I agree to do as Lorthas wants, he'd grant me Aryn's life in exchange."

"Perhaps," Tylor replied, but the smile never left his face. "But Lorthas is trapped behind the Boundary, and I am not. Ally yourself with him, and Aryn will disappear. Test me if you will, but you'll find that my soldiers are far more loyal to me than to the Darklord."

Jeran opened his mouth, but Tylor waved his hand dismissively. "The Darklord would be angry, of course," Tylor added. "He'd rant and rave; he might even punish me. But in the end, Lorthas needs me more than he needs your uncle." Jeran glared daggers at the Bull, but Tylor shoved him forward. "Move," he growled. "Lorthas doesn't like to wait."

Jeran followed Tylor through the halls, plagued by the memory of his uncle's troubled eyes and Tylor's threat. At first, the tunnels were filled with flickering lanterns, but as they drew closer to the castle, dimly pulsing spheres replaced the oil lamps. The magical spheres brightened at the approach and dimmed after they passed, cloaking the passages in shadow. The rough stone of the deep caverns gave way to finely-carved halls, and soldiers wandered the passages and stood guard at the intersections. Most laughed or drank, and few paid attention to their duties. Many were a rough-looking sort, men with cruel smiles and a hungry gleam in their eyes, but seasons inside Dranakohr had dulled more than their discipline. Soft flesh had replaced hard muscle, and most had dispensed with uniforms entirely. They wore clothes only slightly less ragged than the slaves in the Barrows or patchwork outfits strung together from their conquests.

As Tylor approached, all conversation stopped and each group went to rigid attention. As soon as the Bull's back was to them, they resumed their bawdy talk. By the time they passed the fifth guardpost, Tylor wore a scowl deep enough that Jeran dared not speak, lest his words provoke the Bull's anger. "You!" Tylor snarled at one slovenly man whose paunch rolled out from beneath an unlaced leather jerkin. "Your name, soldier?"

The guard whirled to face the Bull. "Gryzbik, my Lord!"

"Explain yourself."

The soldier's eyes went wide. His mouth worked nervously, but all he could manage was, "My Lord?"

"You're a disgrace." Tylor spat at Gryzbik's feet and glared at his companions. "All of you." Quick as a viper, Tylor's hand darted out. He grabbed Gryzbik around the throat and slammed him against the wall. Drawing his dagger, he leaned in close and pressed the tip of the blade against the man's gut. "Are you a soldier or a pig?"

"A…" Gryzbik swallowed his fear. "A soldier, my Lord!"

"Then act like one!" Tylor snapped. "In two days time, I will return. If any man in your squad is not presentable, I'll gut you." Tylor released the terrified man, who slumped against the cavern wall. Without warning, Tylor lashed out, slicing a deep gash across Gryzbik's face. "So I'll remember you," he said as Gryzbik cried out piteously.

"You're to work double shifts in the *ghrat* until further notice," Tylor told the others. "Remember that you're soldiers in the Darklord's army. If you can't remember, I can arrange for you to become slaves." The guards flashed hasty salutes and hurried away, dragging Gryzbik after them. Tylor shoved Jeran forward.

Once they entered the castle proper, the halls bustled with activity. Servants hurried from place to place, bowing deeply to Tylor as they passed. Squads of soldiers more deadly looking than the men guarding the caverns below marched the halls, and black-robed ShadowMagi glided down the corridors.

Jeran pretended to ignore them, but he took in everything, memorized every detail, studied every face. He was so intent on his task that he did not notice when Tylor stopped. A hard blow to the back of the head brought him back to reality.

"Your mission?" Tylor asked a dark haired, stony-eyed man in his mid-twenties who stood before them.

"A success, my Lord," the soldier replied. He took a goblet from a waiting servant and downed its contents, then tossed the cup back onto the tray. "We raided twoscore isolated villages, destroyed their stores, and captured many prisoners. Our soldiers wore the uniforms of the Guard, and those who fled are already spreading the rumors."

"Well done, Keldon," Tylor said, clapping the man on the shoulder. The Bull saw something, though, and he frowned. "What is it? What are you hiding?"

Keldon's lips pressed into a thin line. "We were ambushed on our return."

"Talbot?" Tylor asked. "Has that insufferable fool finally found us?"

"No," Keldon replied. "Not Talbot. We were set upon by monsters in the Darkwood. They appeared without warning, stepping out of the night like ghosts, running through our camp, terrorizing the horses, slaughtering men like cattle. A quarter of the unit was dead before the alarm sounded. I've never seen such butchery—"

"How many?" Tylor interrupted.

"Six score," Keldon replied. He turned his back on Tylor. "Over half my men."

"And what happened to these monsters?" Tylor's voice carried an edge. "Did you kill them? Drive them off? Did you at least bring back a trophy?"

"They disappeared without a trace," Keldon answered. "When dawn broke, we searched the area but found nothing. Rather than risk another attack, I ordered the men to break camp."

Tylor scratched his chin thoughtfully. "It was Talbot," he said at last. "That old fox is a cunning foe." For a time, Tylor was quiet, his eyes distant. "We've been too lax. It was only a matter of time before someone stumbled upon our supply lines. Come to my chambers tonight and we'll discuss the situation."

"Yes, Father," Keldon said with a salute. After sneering at Jeran, the soldier continued down the hall. Tylor shoved Jeran forward again, and they did not stop until they reached Lorthas' chamber.

The Darklord waited, a glass of red wine in his hand and a tight smile on his face. "Ah, Jeran," he said, gesturing to the chair across from him. "Sit." When Jeran started forward, Tylor turned to leave. "Wait there, Tylor. We have a few matters to discuss." Tylor scowled, but he leaned against the wall and waited, his arms folded across his chest.

Jeran stared defiantly at the Darklord, and he refused the drink he was offered. Lorthas studied him for a moment, then shook his head and made a tisking sound with his tongue. "What am I to do with you? I've gone to great effort to keep the Orog and my Human servants separate, to keep them from even learning of each other. With one rash action, you destroyed countless seasons of toil."

Lorthas folded his hands in his lap and waited, as if expecting a response. Jeran remained silent, and he met the Darklord's gaze without flinching. Inside he squirmed under Lorthas' intense scrutiny. "You cause me no end of trouble," Lorthas chuckled. "Sometimes I wonder if I've made the right decision regarding you."

Behind Jeran, Tylor grunted, and Lorthas' eyes swung to the Bull of Ra Tachan. "If it were up to him," Lorthas said, "you'd be long dead. Isn't that right, Tylor?" Tylor refused to answer, but Jeran felt the Bull's eyes stabbing into his back. "Luckily, I'm not as short-sighted."

Lorthas sipped his wine, and he gestured again at the glass in front of Jeran. When Jeran did not take it, the Darklord sighed. "You are brash, independent and impetuous, with a strong sense of honor and misguided loyalties." A broad smile spread across Lorthas' face, a genuine smile, one that made the Darklord look human. "In my youth, I was much like you. But these qualities you exhibit so casually can be dangerous. If you aren't careful, they may bring you great misfortune."

The Darklord studied Jeran; his finger idly tapped his lower lip. "What Tylor sees as a liability, I see as strength. Once I make you see the truth, once you realize that I'm right, that those like you and I must take control to save Madryn from itself, you will make a formidable ally."

Suddenly, Lorthas' eyes hardened "But I can't reward you for disobeying my commands, even if I applaud your determination. Even you are not exempt from the rules, Jeran. You must remember that." Lorthas settled back in his chair and stroked his chin. "I will strike another bargain with you, and this will be the last. If you disobey me again, I'll loosen my hold on Tylor. I trust we agree that giving him greater control over the Barrows is not in the best interest of your people?" After a moment, Jeran nodded, and Lorthas' smile returned.

"My secret is out, and we can do nothing to change it," Lorthas said to Tylor. "There's no point in separating our servants anymore. Open the *ghrat*. Give the humans free rein." Tylor scowled but said nothing.

"I understand that you've been reunited with your uncle," Lorthas said after casting a sharp look at Tylor. "I would have told you, but I knew you wouldn't react well. Tylor and Salos were... overzealous... in their methods. I have no Healers among my Magi, nor skill in that discipline, else I would have had your uncle brought across the Boundary."

Jeran struggled to keep his expression even, to hide how much thoughts of his uncle hurt. "If you promise to obey those few rules you haven't yet broken," Lorthas said after a long pause, "I'll turn your uncle over to you. Perhaps—"

"No!" Tylor shouted. "Aryn Odara is mine! You have no right—"

"Remember who is master here!" Lorthas roared. His voice thundered through the chamber, and Jeran cringed. He had never seen Lorthas' anger fully realized; he hoped he never saw it again. "You rule Dranakohr by my whim. If you insist on defying me, you'll regret it."

Tension pulsed through the chamber, but Tylor backed down, his eyes smoldering, and Lorthas turned back to Jeran. "As I was saying, if you abide by my rules, I'll give you access to your uncle. Perhaps, under your care, he'll regain what Salos and the Purifiers took from him. Once you agree to serve me fully, we can discuss freeing him. Until then, he'll remain under Tylor's watchful eye." Lorthas' blood red eyes flicked toward Tylor, daring him to argue. "Do we have a deal?"

What choice do I have? If Lorthas gives Tylor free reign over the Barrows, how many innocents will suffer because of the Bull's hatred for me? And Uncle Aryn, hasn't he already suffered enough? "We do," Jeran spoke barely above a whisper; he could manage nothing louder. "I won't disobey you again."

Lorthas nodded as if he had already known the answer. "Excellent. I know I can trust you, Jeran. You Odaras are nothing if not honorable." The Darklord signaled for Jeran to leave. "I'll send for you in a few days so we can discuss conditions in the Barrows."

As the doors closed behind him, Jeran heard Lorthas lash out at Tylor, but the words were indistinct. Jeran no longer cared. A guard waited for him, and Jeran followed his escort in a daze, fighting bouts of nausea. His promise disgusted him. Before, he had been a prisoner struggling against evil; now he was a collaborator, and both his promise and the knowledge of what would happen if he broke his pledge would prevent him from fighting.

The Darklord has too many strings tied to me. Aryn... Reanna... My countrymen... Each slave was a thread connecting him to the Darklord, and Lorthas knew it. He would do nothing to Jeran, but by threatening those around him, Lorthas could make him dance however he chose. *I'm a traitor. I've betrayed King Mathis. I've betrayed Alrendria.*

Jeran lost himself in dark thoughts, and before he knew it, he was in the Barrows. The guard shoved him, and Jeran fell. The jarring impact sent spikes of pain through the bruises he had received at Tylor's hand, and when he wiped a hand across his face, it came away red.

Forcing himself to his knees, and then to his feet, Jeran hobbled through the caverns. Many who he passed looked frightened, but a few, like Malkin, took joy in Jeran's pain. "Did you displease your master?" the smith laughed.

Yassik appeared, a worried look on his face. "By the Five Gods! What did they do to you?"

The Mage reached out, but Jeran slapped the hand away. "You knew." Yassik backed away. "You knew about my uncle."

Yassik lowered his eyes guiltily. "I would have told you, but what good would knowing have done? There's nothing you can do for him here." Jeran tried to leave, but Yassik would not let him. "Your uncle is a great man. He deserves better."

Jeran fought off Yassik's restraining hands and stormed away. The Mage called after him, but Jeran ignored him. He ran through the tunnels and ducked into his barrow. At first he thought it empty, but Reanna crawled out of her den when she heard him enter.

"There you are," she called out. "I was wondering—" When she saw him, she gasped. "What did they do to you?"

Jeran laughed bitterly. "They stole my soul," he said, crawling into his den. Reanna followed, and though Jeran tried to make her leave, she refused. Kneeling at his side, she cleaned his wounds with a rag dipped in half-frozen water. At first, Jeran fought off her ministrations, but the Tribeswoman was relentless. Jeran eventually gave up. "They have my uncle," he said, the words choking in his throat. He told Reanna of Aryn and his sacrifice, and of the tortures he had suffered ever since.

"I can't do this anymore," Jeran said. "Everything I do hurts someone else. Every time I fight, innocents suffer. If I weren't here, things would be better for everyone."

Reanna's slap stunned him, and her one blow hurt more than all of Tylor's. "How dare you!" she snarled. "When my world went dark, you would not allow me Garun's embrace, but now that *you* suffer, you seek release without a thought for anyone but yourself!"

Tears filled her eyes, and she clutched Jeran's shoulders desperately. "You are all I live for, Jeran Odara. You are my sun, the only light that shines in a world of darkness. Without you, I am nothing." Their eyes locked, and Reanna lunged for him.

Their kiss was long and passionate. When they parted, sweat beaded Jeran's brow and his heart pounded in his chest. Stunned, he fought to find the right words. "Reanna..." The Tribeswoman's breathing was quick and shallow, and her chest heaved with every intake of air. She eyed him hungrily. "Reanna..."

"Now," she interrupted, "is *not* the time for talk."

Their need drew them together, and for a time they forgot the terrors of Dranakohr.

Chapter 11

"You!" yelled a black-cloaked soldier. "Get back to work!" He turned away, pulling his cloak tight about his shoulders, without waiting to see if the slaves listened. In a few quick steps he had disappeared into the shelter where his companions huddled around a small fire.

Jeran glared at the guardhouse, and he imagined storming the hill, killing the guards, and escaping. With a wistful sigh, he hefted his shovel and returned to work. Even if he succeeded in slipping past the guards posted along the trail to Dranakohr, Tylor would take his anger out on the other slaves, and Jeran could not bear the thought of innocents suffering on his behalf. Hunched over to ward off the wind, he hobbled to his crew and resumed digging.

Teams of slaves worked doggedly all around him, driven by the threats and lashes of their overseers. A line of black cut across the white landscape outside Dranakohr: the foundation of a wall to guard the approach to Tylor's fortress. The foreboding structure, raised by hand and strengthened by magic, would add an extra layer of defense to the already unassailable keep.

High in the mountains, teams of starved and exhausted slaves quarried stone. Scores of wagons, visible as tiny black specks, hauled the stone through the Boundary's narrow, twisting passes to where more slaves waited to place the blocks. Black-robed Magi were everywhere, pacing incessantly through the deep drifts and cursing the circumstances that put them in contact with so many commons.

The days passed slowly, and more than a few slaves lost their lives. Rock slides and avalanches killed nearly as many as did the bitter cold. Wagon teams slipped from icy ledges and hungry beasts prowled the outskirts of the slave camps. As spring drew closer, a few bold souls tried to escape, but all were cut down by Tylor's soldiers or battered to death by the Boundary's remorseless weather. Others—mostly women—disappeared without a trace, and though Tylor's soldiers eagerly searched for the lost, more often than not they returned with apologetic shrugs and satisfied smiles.

The luckiest slaves were assigned the task of keeping the work area clear of snow. This was an endless chore—hardly a day went by when less than a finger's width of powder did not fall—but deaths among those working the construction site were far fewer than anywhere else. By pure chance or Lorthas' manipulations, Jeran, his barrow-mates, and Yassik all found themselves working the shovels. They rose well before dawn each morning, bundled up in their warmest clothes, and trudged to the construction site, where they shoveled until long past sunset.

A cry drew Jeran's attention, and he turned to see a wall of snow collapse across one of the larger trails, blocking access to the wall. A line of wagons had just entered the valley; if the path was not clear when they arrived, the ShadowMagi would be displeased. Jeran ran through the knee-deep snow, watching for signs of a sinkhole or snowdrift. He had seen several slaves swallowed whole, disappearing in a puff of white mist without even time enough to cry out. Teamwork and luck had saved a few, but most were never seen again.

Quellas appeared at Jeran's side, shovel at the ready. Only his nose and eyes were visible through the furs he had wrapped around his face. "Got caught resting again, eh?" the Guardsman asked jovially, gesturing toward the guards' shelter. "You're lazy, Odara!"

Jeran returned the Guardsman's smile. "Maybe so." As the winter wore on, Quellas' attitude had improved. Gone were his angry tantrums and dour glares, and his wry sense of humor had returned. Where he once had worked half-heartedly in the mines, he now shared in all duties, not quite eagerly, but with the grim determination of an Alrendrian Guardsman.

They reached the snowslide and began digging furiously. A handful of other slaves joined them, but they were not fast enough. "Dig faster, vermin!" a ShadowMage sneered. "How do you expect us to finish this wall if you can't keep the walkways clear?" A ball of fire danced above the Mage's head, casting just enough warmth to ward off the chill.

Part of Jeran yearned to warm himself beneath the Mage's flame, but he shoved off the desire and increased the distance between himself and the black-robed man. He redoubled his efforts, and the other slaves followed his lead, but the ShadowMage was not satisfied. "Filthy commons! Out of my way!" Without waiting, he released his magic.

A wall of heat enveloped Jeran. He threw himself to the ground, dragging Quellas with him, as flames roared over their heads. Screams cut through the crisp air as slaves dove for cover; one man, the left side of his body ablaze, dove into a snowdrift. The snow hissed and boiled as the ShadowMage carved a path through it. Jeran felt himself sinking, and then water, first a trickle but soon a stream, ran beneath him. He opened his eyes in time to see the ShadowMage stride forward, the snow melting away in front of him.

Water soaked his furs, and as Jeran stood, he wondered what would happen as his clothes refroze. Offering a hand to Quellas, he pulled the Guardsman to his feet, and both hurried to the wounded slave. The man lay in a curled-up ball, weeping, but his burns were not severe. Jeran helped him to his feet and told him to return to the Barrows. Once the man was on his way, Jeran surveyed the path.

The ShadowMage had cut a channel ten hands across through the snow. Brown grass that had not seen sunlight in over a season stood exposed, the tips of each blade singed black. The refreezing walls, in some places twice as tall as a man, stood sheer and stark. Streams of water ran down the sides of the newly-formed trail, cutting niches and cracks in the snow.

Panicked shouts erupted all around them as the ShadowMage's impatience weakened the hard-packed snow. "How do we get out of here?" Quellas asked, looking at the cliff-like walls. Jeran saw a channel cut by the melting water, but before he could point it out to the Guardsman, a loud cracking drew his attention.

A jagged line spread along the sides of the path; the icy walls strained under the changes in temperature. "Diggers!" Jeran yelled. "We need to brace this drift!" He threw himself against the wall, grabbing handfuls of snow and packing it into the widening crack. He prayed to the Five Gods that the wall would refreeze before the drift collapsed. Quellas climbed to the top and began digging a new trench to take the weight off of the weakened wall. He threw the snow down to Jeran, who used it to shore up the sides.

Other slaves came to their aid, but it a long and exhausting job. When the wall was finally secured, the slaves collapsed where they stood. Jeran welcomed the snow that fell inside his furs; the cold tingle felt refreshing on his overworked muscles. "I think I'd prefer death to another workday like this," a haggard young man lying beside Jeran said. He hugged his shovel tightly to his chest.

"Careful what you wish for, Ehvan," Quellas warned. "Death is no stranger here, and once he comes, you might find that digging snow isn't as bad as you thought!"

"If death comes, I hope he brings a bottle of wine. I haven't tasted wine in seasons." The speaker, a stocky middle-aged woman named Iyrene, squeezed her shoulders and neck with one hand, grimacing as she worked at the knotted muscle. "Do you think it's warm? Where death takes you?"

Several of the diggers shrugged noncommittally, and a few offered opinions, but most of the slaves had little energy for talk. "The Elves believe that worthy souls go to the Heavens," Jeran said, hooking his hands behind his head and settling into the snow, "where they walk with the Five Gods in paradise for eternity."

"That sounds nice," Iyrene laughed. "What about the unworthy souls?"

"An unworthy soul returns to the Nothing. I don't know much about the Nothing, but it doesn't sound warm."

"In that case," Iyrene said, rising to her feet, "I'd better get back to work. I'm not sure how the Five Gods decide worthiness, but as far as slaves and diggers go, I'm not good at being either." Amidst a sea of groans and muttered curses, the others set back to work.

"Coming, Jeran?" Quellas asked, offering his hand. Jeran waved for him to go on.

"I'll be there shortly. I need a moment or two more." Quellas nodded and walked away, leaving Jeran alone on the cold, snow-covered ground. He settled back and let his gaze roam over the valley.

The stark, black mountains rose to his left; jagged cliffs and rugged peaks filled the sky from horizon to horizon. The Boundary formed a wall impassable even during the height of summer, but in winter, snowdrifts more than twenty hands deep could swallow a man without warning and glassy sheets of ice offered treacherous footing. The Boundary all but guaranteed death.

A brilliant blue sky, unbroken by clouds, allowed the sun to unleash its full fury. Many had taken to wrapping strips of cloth over their eyes to dim the glare, yet the sun's warmth was absent. Even at midday temperatures stayed well below freezing, and the chill wind whipping down from the mountains drove straight to the bone.

Jeran cleared his mind. Yassik had told him to start focusing his will as far from the Boundary as possible. The Mage believed the collar's power was related to its proximity to the Boundary; by focusing where the collars were at their weakest, Yassik hoped to discover a way to remove them.

Focus came easy, but the heightened senses were no boon. In an instant, the light became unbearable, forcing Jeran to squint. Sounds from far below—orders barked by frustrated soldiers, the quiet rasp of shovels in snow, the constant plinks and thunks of hammers striking stone—echoed loudly to his ears.

Jeran took a deep breath and pushed the sounds away, relishing the crisp feel of the mountain air. He scanned the horizon, and now he could discern the distant shapes of wagons creeping down the trails. As he watched, one fell, tumbling end over end down the mountainside and disappearing in a puff of white. Jeran offered a quick prayer that no one had fallen with it.

He turned his gaze to Dranakohr. The castle stared down from its perch on the nearest mountain. A single path, barely wide enough for a wagon, snaked up from the floor of the valley, switching back repeatedly before ending a hundred hands from the castle in a steep cliff. A wooden bridge suspended from huge chains arced the gap.

Ominous towers climbed the mountainside. Their walls were smooth, carved out of the mountain by ShadowMagi and strengthened with their magic. Covered walkways and open balconies connected the towers. Countless arrow slits riddled the towers, the holes only a shade darker than the black rock of the mountains, and small catapults had been mounted atop every turret.

No guards walked the parapets; no warriors manned the towers. Dranakohr's location remained secret, and with only one entrance to the valley, Tylor had ample time to prepare a defense if an army found him. Even without the new wall, attacking the stronghold would be a folly; with it, an attack would be suicide. The rugged terrain and soldiers lying in ambush at every switchback made approaching Dranakohr deadly. Once in the valley, a direct assault on the castle would prove fruitless. No force in Madryn, not even the entire Alrendrian Guard, could conquer Dranakohr directly.

Jeran knew a wise commander would besiege the castle rather than waste men in a direct assault. In most cases, such a tactic would be effective, especially in an isolated location like the Boundary. But the tunnels crossed the mountains, so Dranakohr had all the resources of *Ael Shataq* at its disposal. Any army trying to starve Tylor's troops would find itself battered and broken by the Boundary's harsh winter.

The ShadowMagi were an even better defense than the weather. Even with the limitations put on their Gift by the Boundary, ShadowMagi could rain fire upon an enemy or fill the valley with snow and rock. A mere thought could collapse a tunnel, burying any enemy lucky enough to penetrate Dranakohr's outer defenses.

Tylor had a small army of ShadowMagi at his disposal. Many were poorly trained, lacking the strength and finesse common among *Ael Maulle* and *Tsha'ma*, but those Jeran had come into contact with were not likely the best Tylor had at his disposal. The more powerful Magi had more important duties to attend to.

Jeran was glad King Mathis had yet to discover Tylor's hideout. No doubt the King would attack, or at the very least attempt a rescue, if he knew where Tylor held Jeran and his uncle. Such a move would be foolish, and it would condemn many good Guardsmen to death.

Thoughts of home made Jeran's focus waver, so Jeran turned away from Dranakohr and took several deep breaths. He lost himself in meditation, and his eyes roved over the construction site and beyond, to where valley funneled together to form a narrow crevasse. A herd of goats balanced precariously on the rise, hopping deftly from one rocky outcropping to the next, and above, several hawks circled, scanning the ground for prey.

The path out of Dranakohr descended into the crevasse, disappearing for a time and then rising again in the distance. It hugged the mountains, winding back and forth for as far as the eye could see. Jeran followed the path until it disappeared in the south, and as he looked toward Alrendria, a feeling of homesickness overwhelmed him.

He extended his perceptions, bracing himself for the nausea caused by the collar. To his surprise, he felt only a minor discomfort, and he sent his perceptions south, absently following the trail. He traveled through the crevasse and up the distant mountains. Rounding a switchback, Jeran came face to face with a large bear. He flinched and started to retreat, then remembered he was only there in spirit and continued onward.

Jeran climbed to the top of the highest mountain and looked south. The rolling plains of Alrendria, covered white in snow, spread out below him. From the peak, he commanded a remarkable view. Several villages, little more than dark specks, dotted the horizon. Tiny plumes of smoke rose from the chimneys.

The desire to escape welled up in Jeran. He rushed forward, seeking freedom, but something tugged at him, and Jeran felt a stretching sensation. Against his will, he slowed. Summoning his willpower, he pushed ahead with redoubled effort but could not send himself any farther. The land blurred, and then all but disappeared, and Jeran cried out. He drew back his perceptions, and the world returned to focus.

Perched on the mountaintop again, Jeran stared one more time at Alrendria, but the sight no longer held power over him. The peace it had offered was no more real than his flight through the mountains had been. Anger raged through him, and Jeran fought to maintain his focus. He returned to his body and prepared to face grim reality.

He felt her behind him and schooled his features, afraid to show her weakness. "When I look down there, I see the life stolen from me." Reanna placed a hand on Jeran's shoulder. A hint of despair entered the Tribeswoman's voice. "My soul dances on that mountain, just out of sight. If I run fast enough, I know I could reach it. I could be whole again."

Reanna's pain stabbed at Jeran. His heart ached, and he did not know how to comfort her. He was determined to save her, to save all of the slaves. *If it takes me the rest of my life, I'll restore their freedom.*

"You stare so intently," Reanna said, squeezing Jeran's shoulder fondly. "What do you see?"

"Hope," Jeran replied, and his conviction surprised even him. He gazed into Reanna's almond-shaped eyes. "I see hope."

She smiled and opened her mouth, but a sound from below distracted her. Jeran turned in time to see a wagon slip on a sheet of ice and tip over. Huge stones landed on the snow-covered slope and tumbled toward the construction site, gathering speed and dislodging debris. Shouts echoed up the hillside as slaves and warriors alike dove for cover.

The avalanche hit the wall with a resounding crash, and the ground trembled with the force of the impact. Reanna staggered, and her grip on Jeran's shoulder tightened as she struggled to keep herself steady.

Below, chaos reigned. Pained and frightened screams echoed up the hill. Those fortunate enough to escape the avalanche either fled or probed desperately in the snow for survivors. Guards ran toward the commotion, and the ShadowMagi rushed toward the weakened wall, using their Gift to keep the fortification from collapsing.

"Jeran, look!" Reanna shouted, an excited gleam in her eyes. In the confusion, Tylor's soldiers had abandoned their posts on the far end of the wall. A large gap lay open, offering passage out of Dranakohr. Escape beckoned. "We are free!" Reanna took a lurching step forward.

Jeran reached out to stop her, but she was already gone. "Reanna, wait!"

"Hurry," Reanna called as she raced down the hillside. "Before they notice."

Jeran was on his feet in an instant, chasing her. She saw him coming, and a wild smile spread across her face. She quickened her pace, running effortlessly through the snow. Jeran did his best to follow but was no match for the Tribeswoman's sure-footed step. Reanna pulled farther ahead.

"Reanna!" Jeran called desperately. He slipped on a patch of ice and tumbled down the steep incline end over end. As he gained speed, his vision blurred, and he found it increasingly difficult to draw breath without sucking in a mouthful of snow.

A sudden impact jarred him, and he lay on the ground panting. When he tried to rise, dizziness overwhelmed him. Reanna lay unmoving beside him. "Are you all right?" he asked, and Reanna groaned.

"The Afelda will never call you Jeran Fleet-foot," Reanna answered, rubbing her hip.

They lay less than two hundred hands from the construction. The way before them stood open; no soldiers were near enough to stop them. Seeing freedom so close, the fervor in Reanna's eyes grew. She lurched to her feet and started forward, but Jeran tackled her. "What are you doing?" Reanna struggled to pull away, but Jeran held on tightly. "We can be free!"

"We'd never make it out of the mountains," Jeran said. "Tylor has guards stationed all along the pass. And think of the others! Wardel... Yassik... All of the slaves! If we're caught, Tylor will punish them, and if we did manage to escape, Tylor would make them suffer even more."

"We can be free!" Reanna insisted. "The others will understand. In our place, they would leave our fate in Garun's hands!" She fought like a wild animal, but Jeran held her to the ground.

"I need my soul!" she snarled, the Blood Rage taking over. It was all Jeran could do to hold on. "We need to breathe free!" She raged in *Garu*, the words harsh and guttural. Jeran was glad he could not understand them.

Reanna thrashed about, flailing wildly. She gripped Jeran's hair with one hand, hauling him backward; with the other, she beat at his face and torso. A jolt of pain accompanied each blow and one forceful elbow made his vision spin, but Jeran refused to let go and he refused to fight back. "I don't want to hurt you, Reanna. I want to save you!"

Reanna's struggles slowed, then ceased altogether. Tears streaked her face, tracks that quickly froze in the bitter wind. "Why?" The accusation hurt more than all of her blows combined.

He wiped away her tears. "We would never have escaped."

"He's right," said a new voice. A shadow fell over them. Jeran turned to face the speaker, not sure whether or not he should expect a fight. "My uncle has troops hidden along the path to Alrendria," Katya said. "Seasoned troops, not the fools he has guarding the Barrows."

"I am Reanna Snow Rabbit of the Afelda," Reanna snarled, a hint of her anger returning. "I am more than a match for any Human."

Katya pursed her lips and studied Reanna. "In open country, I'd give you odds against a whole company of my uncle's men. But here, there are only a few navigable passes, and our troops are already hidden along them."

Reanna glared at Katya, but she no longer looked ready to fight. Jeran released his grip on the Tribeswoman and climbed to his feet. "You look well, Katya."

A cloak of black, open in front and with the Darklord's standard emblazoned on the back, wrapped around Katya's shoulders. Beneath the fur-lined cloak she wore dark leather armor, cleaned and polished until it gleamed. Her sword swung at her side. She he did not look as if she intended to draw it, but Jeran knew she could be ready to fight in an instant.

Coppery hair, blown by the gusting mountain wind, fell in tight rings around her shoulders. Katya smiled, but the expression held more sadness than mirth. "I've been treated well," she replied. "You, on the other hand, have looked better."

Jeran laughed harshly. "Digging snow from dawn till dusk wears on a man."

"Then you're in luck. The accident has caused quite a commotion. My uncle has given you prisoners the rest of the day off. Work will resume tomorrow."

Jeran helped Reanna to her feet, and they began the long walk back to the Barrows. "You're lucky I was the one who came across you," Katya added. "Few would have been so... forgiving."

"Yes," Reanna replied darkly. "You are a blessing from Garun. Your *bavahnda* would be proud."

Katya winced, and Jeran glared at Reanna, urging her to remain quiet. They continued on in silence, while dark clouds, heavy with snow, rolled in from the west. "I can see how unhappy you are here, Katya," Jeran said. The statement caught Katya by surprise, and she whirled to face him. "There's a place for you in Alrendria. That's where you belong. That's where we both belong."

For an instant, moisture glistened in Katya's eyes. But only for an instant. "The only thing waiting for me in Alrendria is the executioner's axe. I sealed my fate when I betrayed Prince Martyn."

"You *saved* Martyn," Jeran reminded her. "You're a hero and an Alrendrian Guardsman."

"Few would agree," Katya snapped. "Even my father is proud of me!" She laughed; it was a cold sound. "Do you know how many winters I yearned for his praise? How many nights I cried because he barely acknowledged my existence?" Her lips drew down in a frown. "Now I have what I always wanted."

"You did what you had to do," Jeran insisted. "What was best for Alrendria."

"Did I?" Katya shook her head. "Or did I do what was easiest. I'm not sure."

A line of weary prisoners waited at the entrance to the Barrows. Katya handed Jeran and Reanna over to the guards before striding toward a group of dark-armored soldiers who jumped to attention at her approach. She frowned at them and yelled out a string of harsh criticisms. The soldiers blanched under Katya's tirade, and when she ordered them to attend to the wounded, they hurried to obey.

While they waited their turn to enter the Barrows, Reanna refused to speak to Jeran or even meet his eyes. Once within the dark confines of the tunnels, she pushed ahead of him and kept her distance; when Jeran increased his pace to walk at her side, she moved even faster. Eventually, Jeran resigned himself to walking a half dozen steps behind her.

They reached a fork in the tunnel, and most of the slaves shambled down the leftmost passage, but when Reanna went to follow, Jeran grabbed her arm. "This way. There's someone I want you to meet." Reanna glared at him, but Jeran tightened his grip when she tried to shake him off. "Please," he whispered.

Reanna allowed Jeran to lead her through the twisting tunnels to Tylor's Trophy Room. Jeran knocked lightly before opening the door. "Uncle Aryn. I brought someone to meet you."

They stepped inside, but Aryn did not greet them. He huddled in the back of the chamber, his arms wrapped tightly around his knees. The once-proud Guard Commander rocked back and forth slowly, tears streaming down his face.

"Uncle Aryn!" Jeran exclaimed. He hurried to his uncle's side, kneeling in the dirty rags of the pallet. Aryn did not respond to Jeran's touch; he continued to mutter, the words low and indistinguishable. A Reading danced at the edge of Jeran's awareness, as one often did in his uncle's presence, but Jeran forced it away.

"Uncle Aryn," Jeran said again, his voice catching. "I brought Reanna. She's the one I told you about."

Aryn stopped mumbling. His eyes searched the room, but he continued to shake. Jeran wiped away his uncle's tears. The long beard and wild hair were gone; with Lorthas' permission, Jeran had shaved and groomed his uncle. Aryn wore fresh clothes as well, not the rags Tylor had kept him in. He looked much as Jeran remembered, except for the haunted look in his eyes.

"Reanna," Jeran beckoned to the Tribeswoman. "This is my Uncle Aryn."

Reanna knelt at Jeran's side. "He has suffered greatly."

"Suffered?" Aryn repeated, his voice wild. "Oh, I've suffered... but not like Jeran. That poor boy..." Aryn's sobs echoed through the room. "He was just a boy! A boy! I should have protected him. I broke my oath to both of them!"

"He's usually not this bad," Jeran said. "I had hoped..."

"What have I done?" Aryn lamented, and his trembling grew worse. "What did *he* do? Nothing! Neither of us deserved this." Reanna placed her hand on Jeran's cheek. Tears glistened in her eyes; her anger had evaporated.

"Just a boy..." Aryn murmured. "Dead... Dead... I should have saved him."

"He loved me so much." Jeran buried his head in Reanna's midriff and sought comfort in her embrace. "Like I was his own son. I can't begin to understand how he's suffered."

"Perhaps you soon will." The silence that followed was pronounced. Jeran pulled back and looked into Reanna's eyes. The Tribeswoman smiled weakly. "I carry your child, Jeran Odara."

Jeran hit the wall with a jarring thud. He heard a mad cackle and did not know if it came from his uncle or from himself.

Chapter 12

"*Travak turon evaren,*" Jeran said, smiling as he set the handleless cup down. "How was that?"

"Good," Grendor replied, nodding slowly. "You learn quick study, friend Jeran. Before long, you will speak Ourok as well as I."

Jeran leaned against the wall of Grendor's *lientou* and closed his eyes. Aside from low table and a small pallet crammed into the far corner, the room was empty. One wall held a half-drawn mountainscape with bright blue skies and a golden sun; a drawing the Orog started after meeting Wardel. Though he lacked the Guardsman's finesse, Grendor's passion made up for his lack of skill.

Compared to the other *lientou*, Grendor's chamber was extravagant. Most Orog were content with thread-bare cushions and a hard pallet, and some had no pallet at all. Their simple ways impressed Jeran, and he asked Grendor why his people did not want more.

"Why do we need more?" Grendor replied. "This pallet serves me. To ask for a better one would be frivolous. To acquire fancy things would only hide what I truly am." Grendor's eyes grew distant. "I am a slave. We are all slaves. To pretend otherwise would make atonement all the more difficult."

Grendor stood and walked to his drawing. "Self-deception is one of the great evils, friend Jeran. We must always remember what we are." He stared at the picture for a long time, and then reached out to wipe away the chalk.

Jeran leapt up and grabbed Grendor's arm. "That is as much a part of you as your captivity," he said. "Deny it, and you deny yourself."

Grendor considered Jeran's words and stepped backed. "You speak the truth, friend Jeran. I will make an Orog of you yet." A broad smile split Grendor's face, and he picked up a blue stone and began to work on the skyline.

At first, only Jeran and Yassik had ventured into the *ghrat* after it was opened, but as the days passed, curiosity overcame fear and more Humans ventured into the Orog's caves. Initially, the Elders were cautious, strictly monitoring contact between the two races, but once they realized that the Human slaves were not like the Darklord's soldiers, they relaxed their rules.

Jeran spent much of his time in the *ghrat*. He wanted to learn all he could about the Lost Race, but there was another reason he preferred the Orogs' company. The stares that plagued him in the Barrows did not follow him into the *ghrat*. He had hoped that, with time, the others would stop blaming him, but as winter passed and the days grew longer, the hatred he felt from his fellow captives only grew.

Some despised him because they believed he dealt with the Darklord only to protect himself and his friends. To them, Jeran was a traitor, and they refused to acknowledge that his sacrifice had benefited all the slaves. Others hated him for *not* betraying Alrendria. The Darklord's offer had become common knowledge in the Barrows, and some believed that Jeran should have accepted Lorthas' proposal. They believed that, with him in charge of the Barrows, they would be treated far better than they were under Tylor's command.

No matter what he did, he could not please anyone, and the silent torture had driven Jeran to the *ghrat*.

Outside, winter neared its end, though the snows around Dranakohr would remain well into summer, and tension permeated the mountain citadel. Each day, more troops crossed the Boundary from *Ael Shataq*, swelling Tylor's army. Jeran tried to keep track of their numbers, but it proved too difficult. Some days, only a handful crossed the Boundary; on others, hundreds crossed. Eventually, he gave up trying. Tylor's forces already outnumbered the local garrisons. By the time the passes opened, all of House Odara would be at risk.

Even worse, nothing Jeran could do would stop it, and that knowledge grated on his soul more than any other. He had done his best to uncover Tylor's plan, to find out where the Bull intended to lead his army. He listened at every opportunity, eavesdropped on guards and ShadowMagi, but so far had learned nothing of consequence. Even if he did learn something, he had no way to get the information out of Dranakohr, no way to warn Lord Talbot or the King. *Some hero I am.*

Now Jeran had a new concern, a concern far more important than the opinions of slaves or the destination of Tylor's army. More important than even his uncle's condition. He cursed himself, as he often did when he thought of the child Reanna carried. He did not want his child raised a slave, tortured by the Durange or used as another chain to bind him to the Darklord. But he had no choice. Escape was impossible.

After Tylor marched, they might have a better chance, but by then, Reanna would be in no condition to travel. And if Tylor discovered that Reanna was pregnant, he would guard her day and night. Jeran's child would be too great a prize for Tylor to lose.

"Where are you, friend Jeran?" Grendor asked softly, and Jeran opened his eyes. The Orog's slit-like eyes showed concern. "Your thoughts were dark, your mind distant. What troubles you?"

"I was thinking of my friends," Jeran replied with a wan smile. "Of my lost freedom." His mind drifted back to his unborn child, and his stomach clenched. "How can you stand it? How can the Orog so calmly surrender their freedom?"

"It is part of our atonement," Grendor replied. "Part of the price we must pay for our—"

A gravelly voice from the entrance to the *lientou* cut off Grendor's statement. "*Kurana, Grendor. Esta teym ocha an Devuhg. Hie! Hie!*"

An elderly Orog woman, hunched at the shoulders and supporting herself on a gnarled staff, stood at the entrance of the *lientou*. Dark splotches spotted her gray skin and deep lines creased her face. The flesh hung loose on her arms, but the hint of once-powerful muscle remained. She stood hands shorter than Jeran, shorter even than Grendor, but she was half again as broad. She glared at Jeran before hobbling inside. Her steps barely covered a hand's width each.

"*Kurana, Tana,*" Grendor said, a broad smile splitting his face. He went to the old woman, wrapping his arms around her in a gentle embrace. She patted Grendor's back with her free hand. "*Tana,*" Grendor said, turning the old woman to face Jeran, "*est yander miena Hyumehn torvahn, Jeran Odara.*" Jeran stood and bowed, and Grendor continued, "Jeran, this is my grandmother, Zehna."

"*Kurana,* Zehna," Jeran said. "It's a pleasure to meet you."

Zehna studied him, her eyes squinted almost shut. "For such tiny creatures," she said, "you are very loud." After a moment more, she turned back to Grendor. "It is time for the Telling," she said, wagging a finger in Grendor's face. "You will not miss it again. Bring your friend if you must, but tell him to keep quiet."

She turned and hobbled away, and Grendor sighed. He waved for Jeran to follow. "The Telling?" Jeran asked as they followed the old woman through the tunnels.

"A story," Grendor explained. "Part of our history. Every three days, the Elders gather our people to share stories of our history so that all will remember how the Orog came to be here, and why we suffer as slaves. There was once a time when I would never have missed a Telling."

"What happened?"

"Your Human curiosity poisoned Grendor," Zehna said with a derisive sniff. "My grandson distrusts the words of his Elders."

Grendor sighed. "Since learning the truth about the Orog on your side of the Boundary, I have wondered what other secrets the Elders may have kept from us." Zehna harrumphed, and Grendor's cheeks darkened. He was careful to keep his eyes away from his grandmother. "My questions have not been well received."

"He who questions the Elders," Zehna muttered, "fights with the hilt of his blade."

Zehna led them into a vast semicircular cavern. Three other tunnels emptied into the chamber, and Orog poured through each, talking amongst themselves and meandering among those already seated on the cold, stone floors. Jeran followed Zehna down the gently-sloping incline to an open spot near the platform dominating the front of the hall.

A number of Humans dotted the assemblage, sitting in tight clusters among the Orog. Their presence surprised Jeran, and he did not hide his shock well. "*Some* of your people," Zehna said when she saw the look on his face, "are wise enough to listen to the Elders. They know when to accept their fate and when to fight it." The old woman's harsh glare returned to Grendor. "Perhaps my grandson would be wiser to share his time with them."

"The easy path leads to comfort," Grendor replied, "the difficult path to salvation."

Zehna's eyes narrowed dangerously. "The moth that flies to the brightest flame burns the fastest."

"Open eyes see the truth, closed eyes only darkness."

"A wise man listens to advice; a fool heeds only his own counsel."

"A wise man learns from others," Grendor said, trying to hide a smug smile, "but he seeks his own truth."

Before Zehna could reply, someone appeared on the platform, and a hush fell over the room. "We will continue this discussion later," the old woman warned.

An ancient Orog stood atop the platform, leaning heavily on a short staff. A hint of strength remained in the old man's bearing, but time had taken its toll. The Elder's flesh hung loose, his shoulder slumped, and deep creases cut across a face plagued by a lifetime of memories. Sightless white eyes stared unblinkingly at the assemblage.

"*Kurana, Ourok.*" The cavern amplified the sound, carrying the words throughout the chamber. In the Human tongue, the old Orog said, "And greetings to you, friend Humans. It gladdens me—it gladdens all the Elders!—to have you join our Tellings. Perhaps as you learn of our past, we will learn more of each other."

A murmur went up among the Orog, and the Elder raised his hand for silence. "Today, I tell a story of a hero, of a man willing to defy evil and embrace honor, no matter the cost. Today, I will speak of the Great One, Aemon the Wise, Savior of our Race."

It took some time to quiet the assembly. The mere mention of Aemon's name whipped the Orog into a frenzy. A thousand voices offered prayers in Aemon's behalf, and several groups began to chant his name. The Humans stared wide-eyed; it was rare to see anything evoke such a response from the Orog.

"Who is that?" Jeran whispered.

"Craj," Grendor replied. "The Eldest."

"Long ago," Craj began, and the room fell silent when he spoke, "before the Boundary, before the MageWar, long before Lorthas was born, the Four Races lived in peace. Following the Great Rebellion, Madryn was divided among the Races, and all were content. The Garun'ah controlled the east, preserving the Balance and keeping a watchful eye on their Aelvin cousins, but the Elves had withdrawn to their forest and posed no threat. The death of Emperor Llwellyn had soured their taste for conquest. We Orog returned to our mountains, and the Humans took control of the lands west of the Anvil.

"For many winters, we lived among the Humans. We helped build their cities and raised our homes beside theirs. We taught them many things, and they taught us as well. Our Races were as one.

"Back then, Magi ruled Alrendria, and in the seasons following the Great Rebellion, they governed justly, honoring their pledge to protect those not given the gift of magic and holding true to the ideals with which they had founded Alrendria. But as the winters passed, ambition entered the hearts of the Magi. Their promises to the Gods forgotten, they sought to control all Madryn, and with every passing winter, the Magi divided Alrendria between fewer of their number, until only the most powerful ruled. These Magi scoured their lands for those with the Gift, training armies loyal only to them. On the surface, they pretended to work toward common goals, but in secret they plotted and schemed against their brothers in the hopes of gaining complete control over Alrendria.

"In time these Magi made the whole of humanity their slaves. Under them, Humans suffered worse than they ever had under the Elves, but none dared resist the might of the Magi, who became known as Darklords. And the Humans were not the only ones to suffer. The Darklords feared us too—they could not sense us, nor could they affect us with their Gift—and we Orog paid for their fear.

"First they restricted our presence in Alrendria, banishing us from their cities and keeping watch on all Orog who passed through their lands. Our ancestors did not protest. Alrendria belonged to the Humans, and we did not want strife between our Races. We left willingly, hoping our show of good faith would assuage their fears.

"It did not, and the Darklords' fear soon turned to hatred. We Orog were forbidden from entering Human lands, and those who did were threatened with death. Again our people honored the Darklords' demands. We isolated ourselves, leaving behind our friends and homes.

"Our efforts only slowed the Darklords' growing distrust. They believed our immunity to magic made us a threat, that we conspired to take Alrendria for ourselves. In an uncharacteristic moment of concord, the Darklords decided to deal with the threat we posed to them.

"Darklord Balthamel, who ruled the city now known as Grenz, was the most ardently opposed to our existence. His lands bordered ours, and he lived in constant fear of an Orog invasion. Balthamel raised an army in secret and called upon his most gifted apprentice, a young Mage named Aemon, to lead the attack. He told Aemon that the Orog were ready to move against the Magi, that we were massing our forces in the city of Ul Soalan, a city on the tip of the Anvil.

"But Aemon, wise beyond his winters, was troubled by the Darklord's demand. He requested time to prepare, and when Balthamel agreed, Aemon traveled to Ul Soalan. He asked our Elders about the history of Madryn, for even in those dark times our Tellings were sought by men of wisdom, and the Elders were happy to indulge the young Mage's curiosity. What they did not know was that Aemon studied them more than their words. He sought to understand his master's hated, to see if the Darklords' war against our people was justified.

"When Aemon returned to Balthamel's keep, he refused to lead the attack. When Balthamel threatened to kill his apprentice, the young Mage remained steadfast. 'I serve truth,' Aemon told the Darklord, 'but you live a lie. By your orders, we have enslaved a land of freedom; at your whim, we have persecuted a race of noble beings. You justify your actions by claiming they serve the greater good, but the only thing you serve is yourself.'

"With that, Aemon ripped Balthamel's insignia from his robe and threw it to the floor. 'I will not serve you. I will never serve another Darklord.' Aemon turned to leave, and Balthamel attacked. None could be allowed to oppose the will of the Darklords, not even one of their own.

"Though young, Aemon was greatly gifted. He and Balthamel battled for a day and a night without rest, using magics powerful enough to level a city. When at last their struggle ended, Balthamel lay dead, his castle in ruins, and Aemon was a changed man. He realized that refusing to serve was not enough; to absolve himself of guilt, he had to stop the Darklords.

"There, on the ruins of his master's castle, he declared war. Many in Alrendria, man and Mage alike, heard Aemon's call to arms, and they flocked to his banner, ready to oppose the Darklords. For the first time in their long reign, the Darklords were afraid. They allied themselves and sought to destroy Aemon before his revolt gained strength.

"But Aemon disappeared, and the Darklords raged. How, they wondered, could an apprentice hide from their powers, a feat not even they themselves could manage? Suspicious, they turned on one another; each Darklord accused the others of hiding Aemon, of planning to use him to further their own ends. Their alliance shattered, and the Darklords returned to their castles to prepare their individual defenses.

"Meanwhile, Aemon traveled the whole of Madryn, from the heart of the Great Forest to the center of the Darklords' realms, and everywhere he went, he gathered support. Men of all four Races came to his call, but we Orog were his staunchest allies. We were the ones who hid him from the Darklords." The Eldest's voice rang through the cavern. "We were the ones who saw through the lies of those who wished him harm. We protected him from the magic of his enemies!

"When we suffered, only Aemon the Noble heard our pleas. In our time of pain, only Aemon the Just came to our aid. Since Aemon's Revolt, he has been a friend to our people, our dearest supporter among the Assembly and in the lands of man." The Eldest's sightless eyes fell toward the floor. "And that makes our betrayal worse. Our sin all the greater."

A stunned silence filled the chamber. "My grandfather did all that?" Jeran whispered, but the chamber amplified his words, sending them echoing. A startled silence spread out from him in a wave, and thousands of eyes swiveled toward him.

"What did you say?" Zehna croaked. Jeran tried to back away, but the old woman's hands shot out as fast as lightning, and she took a hold of his head. She leaned in close, so close that Jeran could feel her breath on his cheek. "What did you say?" the old woman repeated, her eyes boring into Jeran's.

"I asked if my grandfather really did all that," Jeran replied breathlessly.

"You claim to be the grandson of the Great Aemon?"

Zehna's suspicion angered Jeran. "I am Jeran Odara, son of Alic and Illendre. Illendre was Aemon's daughter."

Zehna stared into Jeran's eyes for a long time, searching for something. With a gasp, she released Jeran and fell backward, wobbling unsteadily. Grendor grabbed her and steadied her. "He speaks the truth," she whispered. "He is descended from the Great One."

A roar filled the cave, and a thousand voices called out, a thousand hands reached toward Jeran. "How could such as you come from the Great Aemon?" Zehna asked, her voice barely audible.

Zehna's venomous glare cut through Jeran's calm facade. His mouth dried, and his hands began to shake. The pleading voices and outstretched hands made him uneasy. "Let's go!" he pleaded, and Grendor followed him mutely through the throng.

Once free of the cavern, Jeran rounded on the Orog. "What was all that?" he demanded, and Grendor started to stammer an answer, but he was unable to meet Jeran's eyes. Jeran grabbed the Orog's chin and forced his gaze up. "I'm no different now than I was this morning! Tell me what's happening!"

Grendor drew in a shuddering breath. "By the time an Orog can speak, he knows two things: that Aemon saved us from the Darklords, and that we broke our promise to him. You are Aemon's kin." Grendor stopped, as if that were answer enough, and he looked away nervously. "Had we known, we would have shown you greater respect."

"You've shown me nothing but kindness," Jeran assured him.

"We broke our oath! We subjugated ourselves to the Darklord. How could Aemon forgive that? Can you even begin to understand?"

"I do understand." Jeran answered slowly. "I've done no better. I enslaved myself to the Darklord to protect my people, just as your Elders did to protect yours." He put a hand on Grendor's shoulder. "Sacrificing yourself to save others is noble. Guilt should not come from that. But by giving up, we have made our earlier actions count for nothing."

"How can we fight?" Grendor demanded. "Anything we do will bring more suffering."

"I don't know." For the first time in a season, Jeran's destination was clear, but the path remained clouded. "I only know that we must find a way, or in the end we will serve the Darklord in more than name."

They shared a look, and Jeran saw his determination reflected in Grendor's eyes. "When the time comes, friend Jeran, I will fight with you."

"And risk the anger of the Elders?"

"The Elders cannot be much more angered with me," Grendor said, offering Jeran a toothy smile. "They already believe I watch the sun rise in the west."

"What an inspiring scene," came a sibilant whisper. "It's good to see the Races coming together. The Master was right, much that the Four Races found impossible to do on their own can be accomplished under his watchful eye."

The sound sent a chill down Jeran's spine and a spike of fear through his heart, but he struggled to hide both. "Salos," he snarled, his voice dripping with venom. Grendor's face drained of color at the Scorpion's appearance, and the Orog pressed against the wall.

"You remember me?" Salos asked, gliding down the hall. He sounded pleased. The Scorpion looked much like Jeran remembered. His robes, darker than the black of night, hung loose on a narrow frame; his bones were pronounced and his skin pale. As he studied Jeran, bloodless lips twisted up in the semblance of a smile, pulling the skin of his face taut and giving him a skeletal appearance. Dark eyes burned with the fire of the Gifted. "I remember you."

The Scorpion circled Jeran slowly. Jeran wanted to run, but he forced himself to remain calm, drawing on his training to keep his fear in check. "You're no longer the terrified boy I met in the Darkwood, are you?" He reached out to touch Jeran's arm, an arm hardened by seasons of work in Dranakohr.

Jeran flinched at the touch, and Salos' smile broadened. "But you're still afraid, aren't you?" He did not wait for an answer. "I'm flattered. We only met briefly; it generally takes time for me to leave such a lasting impression." A few slaves stepped into the light, carrying tools for the smithy. Seeing the Scorpion, they ran, nearly trampling each other in their haste to escape. The tools clattered to the floor forgotten.

Jeran summoned his courage and laughed. "Why should I fear you? You're allowed to touch me no more than your brother is. If anything were to happen to me, Lorthas would not look on it kindly."

Salos' gaze hardened, but the cold smirk remained. "You hide behind the Master's protection?" He ran a bony finger along Jeran's cheek. "Then maybe he's right. Perhaps you're closer to joining us than I believed." The Scorpion's words stabbed like a blade, but before Jeran could protest, Salos cut him off. "Don't make the mistake of thinking yourself indispensable. Should I wish you dead, Lorthas could do nothing to gainsay me."

"I defeated you eight winters ago," Jeran said, but the words echoed hollowly in his ears. "I was little more than a child then. You—"

"—had a friend in hiding," Salos reminded him. He looked around the tunnel. "But where is your pet Tribesman now?" Cruel pleasure danced across the Scorpion's eyes, the first real enjoyment Jeran had ever seen there. "He's not in Kaper, or Grenz, or any other part of Madryn. Nor is he among the Garun'ah. If he were, my agents would have told me."

The Scorpion leaned in so close that the tip of his hooked nose brushed Jeran's skin. "Are you certain he even survived that valley?" Jeran tried to answer, but no words would come, and Salos took the silence for surrender. "Don't cross me, child. The Master likes you; I would hate to deprive him of his favorite toy."

A gust of wind suddenly howled through the tunnel, stirring the hem of Salos' robes and pinning Jeran and Grendor against opposite walls. Jeran struggled against the Scorpion's magic, but it was only after Salos disappeared that the wind died and he could move again.

He fell to the ground with a thud, wincing as sharp stones dug into the tender flesh below his knee. Strong hands grabbed his shoulders and helped him stand. Groaning, Jeran looked at Grendor's eyes. "How could he do that? How could he hold you against your will?"

"He is a ShadowMage," Grendor replied, confused. "Did you hurt your head when you fell, friend Jeran?"

"That's not what I meant!" Jeran said. "I thought Orog were immune to magic. How could he use his Gift against you?"

"A stone thrown by magic is just as deadly as a stone thrown by hand," Grendor explained. "Magic does not affect us, but we cannot negate its effects on the world around us. Had I touched the flows used to make the wind, it would have ceased, but the wind is just wind."

Jeran considered Grendor's words as they walked. Their footfalls echoed in the otherwise silent halls, but Jeran's run-in with the Scorpion had left its mark; he could not shake the feeling of being watched. Twice he turned, convinced he heard someone following, and he even took a few random turns, hoping to confuse his pursuers and force them into revealing themselves. His efforts were in vain; the only thing he managed to do was earn a dozen or so worried looks from Grendor.

When Jeran stopped to get his bearings, he realized that his twisting path had taken them close to the Trophy Room. He decided to introduce Grendor to his uncle, but before they reached the chamber, a desperate wail reverberated through the caverns. "No!" a woman begged in the distance. "Please, no!"

Jeran moved forward cautiously, but when a loud slap turned the woman's next scream into pained sobs, he ran toward the sound. "I told you to be quiet!" a gravelly voice said as a second blow echoed down the tunnel. Cruel laughter replaced the sobbing.

Waving for Grendor to stay back, Jeran poked his head around a bend in the tunnel. In the hollow of a dark recess, two dark-armored soldiers flanked a crumpled form. The woman cowered against wall, trembling uncontrollably. Blood trickled from the hand she had clamped over her mouth. Her clothes were tattered, her legs bare to just below the waist, and one pale breast lay exposed. The woman made no attempt to cover herself; she simply stared at her attackers in wide-eyed horror.

"Good choice, Grasta," one soldier said, leering. "This one's got some life in her. Better than that last one!" The soldier reached for the laces of his leather jerkin.

"What do ya think yer doin'?" Grasta asked, grabbing his companion's hand. "I found her."

"But, last time—"

"I found the last one too!" Grasta shoved the second soldier against the wall. "Keep watch. I'll let you know when I'm done."

Sneering, the second soldier backed toward the mouth of the alcove. "No one ever walks these tunnels," he grumbled. "What am I supposed to watch for?"

"Me," Jeran said, directing a lightning-fast swing at the soldier's jaw. The man stumbled backward, crashing into Grasta. "Back away from her," Jeran ordered. "Both of you."

Grasta pressed a hand to the bloody gash running the length of his forehead. "This doesn't concern you, slave," he snarled. The woman reached out toward Jeran, whimpering piteously. "Leave now, and you won't suffer for this foolishness!"

Jeran's hands clenched, and an icy rage danced at the back of his mind, but he kept it under tight control. Calm suffused him, a calm unlike anything he had felt since entering Dranakohr. Without trying to, he focused his will and flows of magic appeared all around him; strands of light and color danced through the caverns. He filled himself with magic, and the collar grew cold as he did so. Power suffused him, and Jeran wished he could unleash it on the men before him.

"You will not get a second chance to leave here," he said, stepping forward.

Fear danced across the unnamed soldier's eyes, but Grasta drew his sword. "*You* are the slave," he reminded Jeran. At a nudge from Grasta, the second soldier drew his weapon. Side by side, they advanced.

With a sigh, Jeran let his shoulders slump. When he heard Grasta chuckle, a smile touched his lips and he charged. As he passed between them, Jeran grabbed Grasta's sword arm and twisted. Pivoting, he launched a kick at the second soldier. The man flew backward, hit the wall, and fell to the floor stunned.

Grasta grappled with Jeran, but a well-placed blow knocked the blade from his hand and sent it skittering across the floor. Grasta fell back, but Jeran did not give him time to recover. He leapt to the attack, driving the man into the alcove. At first Grasta fought back, but Jeran had the advantage, and his opponent soon found himself on the defensive, pinned against the wall, barely able to block the blows raining down upon him.

A cry from behind warned Jeran of the second soldier's return. He stepped aside at the last instant and watched as the second soldier's blade drove deep into Grasta's chest. Grasta howled, and the second man froze.

The hesitation was more than Jeran needed. He grabbed the hilt of the blade and pulled, driving it into the soldier's gut. The man doubled over, losing his grip on the sword. A smile pulled at Jeran's lips as he wrenched the blade free from Grasta's gut and drove it into the second soldier's heart.

An eerie silence filled the tunnel in the aftermath of the battle. Jeran, breathing heavily and splattered with the blood of his opponents, turned toward the woman. "You're free to go," he said, his voice calm. "Don't travel the tunnels alone."

The woman ignored him. She sat wide-eyed and trembling, her eyes locked on something over Jeran's shoulder. Before he could turn, hands grabbed Jeran and slammed him into the wall. He grunted as the breath was driven from his body and the sword he held clattered to the floor of the cave. "This time," Tylor growled, "you've gone too far. You think you can murder—"

"If you're going to kill me, just do it." Jeran ignored the blood trickling down his cheek. "I'd rather a blade in my side than another of your speeches."

Tylor shoved Jeran into the wall again. This time Jeran heard a crack and felt a stabbing pain at the base of his nose. He fell to the ground, the cavern spinning around him and bright lights flashing in front of his eyes. He reached for the sword, but Tylor stomped on the blade, clamping it to the rocky ground. Smiling, the Bull drew back his own sword to strike.

"You claim to be a man of honor," Jeran said, laughing weakly. "Yet you allow things like this?" He turned his gaze on battered woman cowering in the corner. "If not for me…" Tylor's eye followed Jeran's, and a measure of sympathy entered the Bull's face when he looked on the woman.

"Lord Iban always said a commander's honor is reflected in the actions of his troops," Jeran added, looking at the bodies of Grasta and his nameless companion. "How sad, that this is the best you have to offer."

Tylor stared at the woman for a long time, then signaled to the soldiers who guarded the passage behind him. "Take her to the ShadowMagi and have her wounds healed." One of the soldiers leered as he stepped forward and mumbled something that Jeran could not hear. Tylor heard it, though, and he caught the soldier by the scruff of the neck. "She is not to be harmed."

Tylor pointed to the bodies. "Strip them of their gear and toss them to the wolves. They deserve no better." He grabbed a fistful of Jeran's hair and hauled Jeran to his feet. "As for you, if you ever lift a blade again, you will lose your hand."

"I grow tired of your threats, Durange," Jeran laughed. "You're far more likely to take your other eye than my hand. You boast often, but we both know you're not really willing to risk Lorthas' anger." Tylor's jaw clenched, and he slammed Jeran's head into the wall a third time before storming away. Jeran sat dazed long after Tylor's footfalls faded in the distance.

Once the Bull was gone, Grendor appeared. He used a rag torn from his shirt to wipe the blood from Jeran's face. "A brave man will face a rabid dog," he said, "but only a fool pulls its tail. You should not risk your life so casually."

Footfalls approached, and Jeran tensed. His eyes scanned the ground for something to use as a weapon, but not so much as a pebble presented itself. With his magic enhanced hearing, he caught a few snippets of an argument.

"…told you he's our best bet."

"…crazy? He's… Darklord's tool!"

"…to both the Bull of Ra Tachan and the High Inquisitor, didn't he? Know anyone else who would have survived either encounter, let alone both?"

"It's only because he has the Darklord's blessing! This is a mistake!"

Two men rounded the corner and approached cautiously. Jeran recognized Ehvan, the young man who had worked with him as a digger. "Are you all right, Lord Odara?" Ehvan asked, stooping at Jeran's side.

Jeran tried to answer, but his words were slurred. He nodded, but the motion made the tunnel spin twice as fast, and he fought a sudden wave of nausea. With both Ehvan and Grendor helping him, Jeran regained his feet. Every indrawn breath brought a fresh stab of pain to his ribs, and he clamped a hand to his side, relying on his companions to keep him standing.

Ehvan stared at his companion for a moment. "Well?"

The stranger frowned, but finally nodded. "If you think it for the best."

Smiling triumphantly, Ehvan faced Jeran again. "We need you to help us, Lord Odara."

"Help?" Jeran asked, spitting blood. "How?"

"We need you to lead us."

"Lead you? Where?"

"To victory," Ehvan answered, an eager glint in his eye. "We want to fight the Darklord."

Chapter 13

Rolling plains, broken by small stands of trees and the occasional small village, surrounded them. A cool breeze blew through the early spring air, pushing large white clouds lazily across the bright sky. The wind brought a mélange of scents to Martyn's nose, and he inhaled deeply, relishing the moist, earthy smell of the land, the odor of woodsmoke, and a hint of the season's first wildflowers. The sun beamed down, and he closed his eyes, enjoying the warmth on his face.

Miriam, resplendent in a dress cut for riding, rode on Martyn's left. Her golden hair had been woven in an elaborate bun that swayed precariously with her horse's every step. Unconsciously, the princess reached up to steady her hair and caught Martyn's eyes on her. Spots of color bloomed on her cheeks, but she smiled, and he returned the gesture in kind. Embarrassed, she turned away, but Martyn kept his eyes on her a moment longer.

The princess still looked uncomfortable—she had been more than upset upon learning she would have no carriage!—but she had adjusted quickly to the saddle, and to her credit, had only complained once, and even then in private, so that only Martyn would know. He was flattered she felt she could confide in him.

They had grown closer during the long winter in Kaper, and while their arguments had lessened in neither number nor intensity, something had changed. It was not that Martyn looked forward to the fights, exactly, but he did not try to avoid them either. He was willing to risk the princess' icy rage if he could see her warm smile from time to time.

On Martyn's right, Kaeille wore the dark green leathers of *Ael Chatorra*. An Aelvin bow hung from her saddle, and she carried a short blade at her hip. Kaeille looked no more comfortable on horseback now than she had the first time Martyn had seen her ride, but she suffered in stoic silence, and whenever Martyn asked about it, she denied any discomfort.

The two women tried to ignore each other assiduously. If their eyes met, even if by accident, they were like as not to flinch as if stung. Their behavior worried Martyn; he understood, but he worried nonetheless. Alrendria's alliances with Illendrylla and Gilead, perhaps even victory against the Darklord, revolved around his ability to make these two stubborn women get along. Martyn was not sure he was up to the task.

Treloran and Kal, stone-faced and silent, flanked the prince. They were little better than Miriam and Kaeille, but they, at least, had an excuse: an ancient hatred between their peoples and sporadic fighting along their border. Both had friends who had died in that fighting, and neither was the type to let such a thing go unavenged. Suspicion filled the sidelong glares they cast at each other, and Martyn had yet to decide if the two insisted on riding together because they did not trust each other or to prove that they did.

The Aelvin Prince and the *Kranach* had yet to come to blows, though a couple times Martyn had thought fighting inevitable. He had once made the mistake of complimenting the scenery, and his offhand remark had sparked a debate on nature. A prayer muttered by a Guardsman had started another argument, and had Miriam not been standing between them, weapons would have been drawn. Since then, Martyn kept several Guardsmen nearby with orders to intervene if they even suspected the two might try to kill each other.

As the days passed and Kaper drew farther behind them, the arguments stopped, and on several occasions, Martyn had even seen Kal and Treloran talking quietly. Whenever they saw the prince's eyes on them, they stopped immediately.

The bulk of the Guardsmen rode behind Kal and Treloran. Martyn led nearly a thousand men to Vela's defense, most of them taken from the garrison at Kaper. An equal number rode east with Joam, leaving Kaper defended by green recruits and hastily-trained volunteers. Martyn understood the plan, he even understood the necessity of gutting Kaper's defenses, but leaving his father unprotected made him uneasy.

Behind the Guard, a long line of supply wagons trundled along the trampled path. Laden with supplies for the garrison in Vela and the army along the Corsan border, they were of even more importance than the Guardsmen. Two full squads protected the wagons at all times, and though they had encountered no trouble, Martyn wondered if he should add more soldiers to the patrol.

A second army walked behind the supply wagons, an army of Martyn's own creation. The prince had ordered his column to stop in every village they passed. Many were empty, the occupants having fled in advance of Martyn's army, but in every place he found people, Martyn warned the villagers of the Bull's escape and asked that those willing to serve Alrendria volunteer for service.

The response had not been as overwhelming as Martyn had hoped; few jumped at the chance to defend their nation, and some went so far as to laugh at the suggestion. But a handful from every village agreed, children and stooped-shouldered men, boys tired of life on a farm and retired Guardsmen who saw defending Alrendria as their duty. It was not the vast warhost he had hoped to raise, but Martyn remembered Lord Iban's many lectures and tried to turn his defeat into a victory.

"Many of you can do more good here than on the front lines," he told those who refused to enlist. "Craftsmen—blacksmiths and fletchers in particular—are in great demand. Your wares are more valuable to us than your presence in the field. I beg you to guard your land and ensure that our armies remain well supplied. For what good is winning a battle if we leave our lands defenseless? The Alrendrian Guard, whose duty in times of peace is to protect your homes from brigands and thieves, is needed elsewhere. Thus their duty now falls to you." In each town, he formed a watch, and put a retired Guardsman or village leader in command. He charged these groups to protect themselves and their neighbors.

As his party grew closer to Vela, his army of commoners grew. A few score men even rode up on their own; word of Martyn's call to arms had reached them from neighboring villages. Martyn accepted every pledge, and his army swelled until he had more than twice as many militiamen as fully-trained Guardsmen. He even sent a small detachment back to Kaper to bolster the city's defenses.

"It's a beautiful day, is it not?" Miriam suddenly asked, turning to Martyn. The way the sun framed her face made the prince's pulse race.

Martyn responded with a warm smile and watched as the anger in Miriam's gaze softened. "It is," he agreed. "And I can think of few things more pleasant than sharing it with you."

"Wait until tonight," Kaeille whispered, leaning in close. "I will show you things far more pleasant."

Blushing, Martyn gently pushed Kaeille away and glanced sidelong at Miriam, praying that the princess had not heard. "We should arrive in Vela before sunset tomorrow. From what I hear, it's a beautiful city."

"You've never seen it?" Miriam asked.

"Until my journey to Illendrylla, I'd barely been more than a day from Kaper. My father was... concerned... for my safety."

Miriam laughed, and it was a genuine, musical sound, far different from the forced laughter Martyn often endured when his princess and his *advoutre* shared company. "My father was overprotective too," she assured him. "I couldn't play in the courtyard without a half score of guards hovering over my shoulder. He even had a few soldiers, all women of course!"—Miriam's cheek turned dark red—"specially trained to guard me when I bathed."

Against her will, Miriam smiled, and she shook her head nostalgically. "Honestly, Martyn," she laughed, "in my private bathing chamber, and with guards already posted outside my rooms! How much danger could I possibly have faced?"

"Perhaps," Martyn said, a mischievous gleam in his eye, "it wasn't assassins your father wanted to protect you from." Miriam's brow drew down, and Martyn laughed heartily. "I can think of any number of men who'd risk their lives to see your beauty." The princess put a hand over her mouth as if affronted, but from the way she looked at him, Martyn knew he had earned her favor. "In fact," he added, pressing his advantage "if you think it wise, I could assign a Guardsman to—"

"That won't be—"

"Perhaps you'd feel more comfortable if I volunteered for the duty?"

Scandalized, Miriam flushed even more. "Martyn!" she exclaimed, her eyes shifting back and forth quickly to make sure no one else had heard. "We are to be married!"

Martyn nodded sagely. "Then who better to guard your bath?"

The princess turned away, but before her features were completely hidden, Martyn saw her beaming ear to ear. Satisfied, he turned toward Kaeille and found the Aelvin woman sitting rigidly in the saddle, glaring daggers. The words froze on his tongue, and for a time Martyn sat there shocked, his mouth half open. Kaeille said nothing, but her eyes never shifted, and they never softened. Slowly, Martyn dropped back to ride between Treloran and Kal.

"You play a dangerous game," the Aelvin Price said, shooting a glance at the two women. With Martyn gone, Miriam and Kaeille glared at each other openly, though the smiles they wore would make a stranger think them old friends.

"He is training," Kal explained, his booming voice full of mirth. "Prince Martyn expects a war to east and west. He uses his women to understand what it will be like."

Treloran tried to hide a smile, and Martyn glowered at his companions. "If I wanted abuse, I would have stayed with the women. From my friends, I had hoped for support." Neither looked chagrined, and Martyn drew a deep breath. "What am I to do?"

"Your duty," Treloran replied sullenly. "You can do nothing more."

"Among the Blood," Kal added, "sharing a mate is common." He waited until he had Martyn's full attention before continuing. "Before the wasting sickness came, my father had two wives, and long ago I loved Jielan *uvan* Grast, a *Dahrina* of great skill and greater beauty. I wanted to be her *bavahnda*, but her heart was divided, and she asked me to share her with Auticha *uvan* Risstyk. A good Hunter, but easy to anger. We were often at odds.

"I went to my father. 'It is not easy to share love,' he told me. 'Only with Garun's blessing can such a union survive. I cannot tell you what to do in this. Only you know your heart; only you can decide if your love is strong enough to share.'

"I saw fear in his eyes, though, and knew he thought I would choose poorly. I went to my mother, and the look she gave me made my father's seem encouraging. 'Be certain,' she told me. 'Sharing love is not a simple thing. Mieshan and I were *chanda* long before we met your father, and even still we fought for his attention. If you cannot share your heart fully, do not share it. If you cannot love both, you will bring pain to all.' "

Kal frowned and looked at Treloran as if just remembering the Elf was present. "You have made your choice, so my father's advice will serve you little, but if you want your life to have more than sorrow, you must make your women like each other."

"Or at least not hate each other," Treloran muttered.

Martyn spared another glance ahead. Miriam and Kaeille sat straight-backed, ignoring each other as heatedly as they had stared at each other a moment before. "And how do I do that?"

Kal shrugged. "I chose not to share my love, so I cannot help you. Jielan took another mate a few winters past, a warrior Auticha did not care for. Perhaps you should ask him."

"The next time I see him," Martyn replied with a sarcastic smile, "I'll be sure to bring it up." Kal's expression was blank, but his eyes danced. This time, Treloran made no effort to hide his grin.

Martyn had hoped talking to Kal and Treloran would cheer him up; so far, it had worsened his mood. "What did you think of Marin?" he asked to change the subject.

Their journey had taken them through House Morrena, and as a courtesy to Jysin, First of the House, Martyn had stopped in the city of Marin. As the only city along Alrendria's border with Corsa, and the only major source of water for leagues, Marin had become a center of trade nearly as prominent as Grenz. In size it dwarfed even Kaper, sprawling across the countryside as far as the eye could see, its red brick buildings and stone-lined plazas standing in stark contrast to the low-lying grass. A thousand market squares dotted the city, each built around an ornate fountain. Some believed the Magi had brought water to Marin long ago; others claimed that it was a natural feature. Whatever its source, the fountains were the lifeblood of Marin. Without it, the city would wither.

Marin sprawled around a tall, flat-topped hill. A fortress of dark stone and hard angles surrounded by a dozen towers linked with crenellated parapets stared down from the hilltop, and a single gate on the northern face allowed access to the castle. The city itself was built on a series of hills ringing the castle, five circles in all, and atop each a wall of thick, dark stone with three heavily-guarded gates. The gates on the outermost ringwall faced north, southeast, and southwest. At the next, they opened to the east, west, and south. With each successive ringwall, the gates continued to shift, and the roads between fortifications twisted and curved without pattern.

At first, the configuration had confused Martyn, and Kal had looked even more troubled by the labyrinthine streets. Treloran understood immediately. "An ingenious design."

"Ingenious?" Martyn scoffed. "Irritating you mean."

"I'm sure anyone attacking Marin would feel the same way," Miriam had said, riding up to join them. "Have you never learned Marin's history, Martyn?" Martyn had—as a child, Joam had lectured him tirelessly on the strengths and weaknesses of all Alrendria's great cities—and the prince struggled to dredge up some memory from those lessons.

Marin had survived many attacks. It was one of the few cities able to stand against Lord Peitr Arkam during the Secession, and though it had changed hands many times during the MageWar, neither side had been willing to destroy it completely. The Corsans had coveted Marin for some time, but they had never been able to conquer it.

"Imagine attacking here," Miriam lectured, sounding smug. "Even if you breached the outer wall, you'd have to fight through streets so narrow they make using siege weapons all but impossible. Look there"—she pointed to a crowded intersection barely wide enough for a cart to pass through—"and there. Barricading those spots would be a simple task, and a handful of well-trained soldiers could hold them against an army. If you made it to the second wall, you'd have to do the same thing three more times before reaching the castle."

Miriam's casual understanding of what had so easily escaped his notice embarrassed Martyn. "Joam would have welcomed you as a student," he said gruffly.

For some reason, his words had made Miriam blush. "It disappointed my father that he had no sons." The hint of a smile had touched the princess' lips, but Brell Morrena appeared before Martyn could further flatter his betrothed. Brell invited them to join Jysin at the castle for a feast, and Martyn accepted the invitation.

The feast was a lavish event, with all the prominent noblemen of House Morrena in attendance. Jysin was the epitome of hospitality. Tall and thin-faced, with shoulder-length hair and a well-oiled, neatly-trimmed black beard, he showed Martyn every courtesy. In the three days they stayed in Marin, Martyn wanted for nothing, and Jysin himself accompanied Martyn to the Corsan border so he could see the patrols guarding Alrendria's border.

The visit went so smoothly that Martyn should have expected trouble. "You are a credit to your House, Lord Morrena," Martyn had said on the last day of his visit. "I've been most impressed. My father will be happy to know the border is in good hands."

"No Corsan dogs will get past my men," Jysin replied, a broad smile on his face. "And I could defend this city with half the Guardsmen I have under my command. You may assure your father of that."

"Your confidence is a great relief," Martyn replied, handing the First of Morrena a letter sealed with the King's sigil. "My father instructed me to give you this if convinced of Marin's—and your—safety."

Jysin took the letter and scanned it suspiciously, his eyes narrowing to slits. "Do you have any idea what this says?" he asked, his voice one of barely-restrained anger.

"The King has ordered you to reassign six columns of Guardsmen. Three are to accompany me, one is to return to Kaper, and two will join High Commander Batai on the eastern front."

"My Prince, I must protest! Six columns is nearly a third of my Guard! What of the safety of my people?"

"You just said you could defend Marin with half the number of soldiers," Martyn replied. "I am leaving you with two thirds. Is there a problem, Lord Morrena?"

"Of course not! It's just that—"

"Then it's settled. Please have the columns ready to march when my party leaves." Jysin had fumed, but he did not argue, and when Martyn left Marin, three columns followed him. They were far from Jysin's best—one column had only a handful of men older than twenty-five winters, and none had seen combat—but all carried themselves as Alrendrian Guardsmen, and that fact alone comforted Martyn.

The remainder of their journey through Houses Morrena and Vela had been uneventful. Martyn did not know whether to be glad or frustrated that his visit with the First of Morrena had been the most exciting part of his adventure. "Well? What did you think? We never had the opportunity to discuss it."

"It was a fine city," Treloran said after a thoughtful pause. "Your enemies would be foolish to attack there."

"Too many walls," Kal growled. "I will never understand how you Humans can live inside so many walls."

"The walls are welcomed when an army approaches," Martyn laughed. "Several solid spans of stone separating you from your enemies increase your chances of survival quite a bit."

"That is another thing I will never understand about Humans," Kal said with a shake of his head. "The way you fight is… barbaric! You cower behind walls. Refuse to meet in honest battle unless forced. Slaughter children and those who have not taken up a blade…" His words trailed off, and his eyes grew distant. "It is not our way."

Martyn did not appreciate the *Kranach's* tone. "To Humans, war is not a matter of honor. It's a matter of survival."

"Perhaps if Humans did not fight so often," Treloran interrupted, "you would not need to worry so much about survival." Kal grunted a laugh, but he cut it off abruptly, and his expression grew stony. He glared at Treloran as if the Elf had tricked him into laughing.

"*We* fight too much?" Martyn exclaimed. "You and the Garun'ah have been warring for centuries. You barely stopped long enough to fight the MageWar!"

Both Kal and Treloran stared at Martyn as if he spoke gibberish. "The Tribesmen refuse to see the true balance of nature," Treloran replied. "In their ignorance, they are willing to fight us. But they do not fight amongst themselves, other than isolated skirmishes in which few are killed."

"The *Aelva* force nature into their own pattern, violating the Balance," Kal added. "Our Races have clashed many times over such matters. But rarely have I heard of Elves fighting each other. Only Humans war against their own kind."

"What of the Drekka?" Martyn demanded. "The *Noedra Shamallyn*?"

Kal looked aghast, but it was Treloran who answered. "Illendrylla shares a border with the Drekka. They act like no other Tribesmen. They are cruel and violent. My people have clashed with the Tribes throughout the ages, but the Drekka do not conduct themselves as do the other Wild... Tribesmen. I would hardly consider them the same."

Kal eyed Treloran, and his expression grew thoughtful. "The *Aelva* are deadly enemies, cunning and stealthy, but never have I seen one betray his own Race. In many battles, I have watched them perform great feats to protect their brothers."

Martyn squeezed his temples to fight a burgeoning headache. "You make it sound as if fighting one's Race is wrong, but fighting between Races is fine."

"Peace is always preferred," Treloran said, "but the differences between Races are great at times. We were each raised by a different God, each given different instructions. It is only natural that we come to blows from time to time. But to fight one's own?" The Aelvin Prince looked ill at the thought. "It *has* happened, but no Elf who respected the teachings of Valia would harm another of our kind unless forced. To do so would violate Valia's first law: Love thy brother as you love thyself.

Kal nodded in agreement. "The Tribes often fight... For land... For food... For Garun's favor. But our battles rarely end in death, and when they do, both tribes send the fallen to join Garun in the Twilight World. In times of need, all of the Tribes come together to help each other, as during *Cha'khun*. We are all the Blood of Garun."

"I give up," Martyn said, throwing up his hands in mock defeat. "Any argument that gets an Elf and a Tribesman to defend each other is one I can't hope to win." He backed away slowly, smiling when he saw the suspicious stares Treloran and Kal directed at each other.

Martyn circled wide around his army, then spurred his horse to a fast trot and made his way to the front of the column, where he signaled a halt. The mighty River Alren glittered in the light of the evening sun, its westward-flowing waters drawing fishing boats and barges toward Vela. To Martyn's right, the land was open; vast, rolling hills stretched from horizon to horizon.

"Company, dismount!" Martyn called out, his voice carrying in the dry spring air. "We will camp here. Tomorrow, we reach Vela." The prince stared at the sky for a moment and thoughtfully stroked his chin, as he remembered Lord Iban so often doing. The commanders and subcommanders formed rank around him, waiting for their orders.

"Minimal defenses," Martyn announced, and he saw relief blossom in his men's eyes. "Post sentries every six hundred hands, two roving patrols, and have a full column guard the supplies. Tambron! Pylias!" Two men, lanky and unassuming, stepped out from the line. "Assemble your scouts. See if there are any villages in the vicinity, and keep your eyes open for Commander Jasova's outriders. I want to find them before they find us!"

"Leeta! Asmerald!" As Martyn doled out the assignments, he studied his officers. For most, this was their first command, and he wondered how they would bear up when the fighting started. He wondered about himself, too; planned warfare was different from the brawls and skirmishes he had faced in the past. *When the time comes, will I prove myself to be as brave as Jeran or as fearless as Dahr?* Martyn doubted it, but he tried not to let his doubt show.

For a time, Martyn watched his men hurrying about their tasks, but he quickly grew bored. Dismounting, he handed his reins to a waiting servant and worked his way through the camp. Guardsmen Hassan and Jhorval flanked him, never more than five paces away. Martyn thought it foolish to be guarded in his own camp, but the King had chosen Martyn's bodyguards himself, and Martyn had neither the authority nor the patience to convince the grim-faced men to leave him be.

A sea of white canvas already covered the grassy plains. In the distance, bare-chested soldiers toiled under the setting sun, digging latrine pits, picketing the horses, and erecting the encampment's defenses. Other men, those lucky enough to be spared duty, lounged on the soft grass outside their tents or crowded around the cookfires.

Beyond the tents, the supply wagons were packed in tight clusters. A squad of Guardsmen protected them, and additional sentries patrolled the area. Theft had been a problem. Some of the volunteers had been disappointed with their allotments and had taken it upon themselves to increase their rations.

Trailed by his shadows, Martyn moved quietly among the wagons, wondering how long it would take someone to notice his presence. The first time, he had gone completely unnoticed, but today he barely made it past the second wagon before a tall, wiry woman stepped out in front of him, saluting fist-on-heart. "Kohl told me you had come to inspect the wagons again, my Liege. I'm happy to report that there've been no thefts since your last visit."

"Very good, Evana," Martyn said, offering the woman a smile. Evana had brought the pilferage to Martyn's attention after single-handedly stopping four men from stealing food. Those four had been punished severely before being sent home in disgrace. Afterward, Martyn had put the Guardswoman in charge of the wagons and gave her free rein in their protection. Since then, hardly a grain of rice had gone unaccounted for.

Evana led the prince around, pointing out the changes she had made in the last few days. Satisfied with the arrangements, Martyn left the wagons and entered the area where the recruits were stationed.

The militia's tents had neither the uniformity nor the regularity of the Guardsmen's. They were arranged haphazardly, thrown up wherever space could be found and secured poorly, so poorly that Martyn watched one snap its final line and blow away in the stiff breeze. Two dirty, thin-faced boys took off after it.

Guardsmen moved among the trainees, calling out orders and arranging the recruits into groups. Scores of practice rings had been drawn between tents. A Guardsman waited in each for a volunteer. Hundreds of bleary-eyed young men, exhausted from a long day in the saddle, surrounded the rings, but few entered.

"How do you fools expect to become Guardsmen if you won't even lift a sword?" demanded Larence, a Guardsman from House Aurelle. He leveled his practice blade at the chest of one recruit. "You. Enter the ring. Now!"

"My great-mother can hold a sword better than that!" chided Kartoc, disarming his competitor. When the young man stooped to retrieve the weapon, Kartoc hit him across the back. The boy fell to the ground, whimpering. "If you lose your blade in the field, you die. Now pick it up and try again!"

It was the same in every ring, frustrated Guardsmen berating unskilled children. Martyn sighed. "Not much of an army, is it?"

"Takes a while to rub the edges off," Hassan replied. "Most of those boys never held a weapon before you convinced them to fight. Give 'em time. They'll do all right."

"I hope you're right," Martyn said. Beyond the practice rings, the remainder of the recruits had been divided into three groups. One set, under the stern eye of Guardsman Olivia, practiced with bows. A handful of targets lined the top of a nearby hill, but few of the trainees fired at them. Most stood with arrow notched and drawn, waiting for the Guardswoman to approve their stance and form. Olivia walked the line behind her charges, snapping orders.

The second group had been ordered to help the Guardsman carry out the duties of the camp. Some dug privy pits, others relayed messages between officers. One company, despite Martyn's order, constructed an observation tower from bits of wood and stone. A grey-haired Guardsman yelled at them to work faster.

The third and final group was comprised of the volunteers who did not meet the Guardsman's rigorous standards. They were neither given chores nor expected to study swordskill or bowmanship. Instead, they carried heavy weights from one side of the camp to the other or ran in armor until exhausted. Ikabhod and Nevarrah, two iron-muscled Guardsmen from Hrisbard, in House Morrena, prodded them with acerbic comments and threats of reduced rations.

A heavy-set young man carrying a rock the size of Martyn's head grumbled as he passed the prince. "Why do we have to carry these Gods-forsaken stones?" Sweat drenched his body, slicking the rolls of fat on his arms and belly and dripping onto the dry soil at his feet. "It's pointless. They just want us to quit!"

"Maybe we should," said a wan, sickly-looking boy. "We'll probably just get killed anyway. Why work so hard just to get killed?"

"Battle is exhausting," Martyn said sharply. The young men jerked to attention when they noticed the prince, and the fat one dropped his stone in surprise. It missed his foot by half a hand. "You never know how long it will last, and even if it ends quickly, you'll want nothing more than to seek your bedrolls when it's done. In the thick of it, with sword in hand and armor on your back, you'll wish the weight you carry was as light as that stone."

The boys blanched, but Martyn did not let their chagrin soften his anger. "This is a war," he told them, "not a game. You're learning how to be Alrendrian

Guardsmen, not village thugs. If the training is too tough, if you can't understand why you must be fit in both body and mind, then return to your homes. There's no dishonor in not wanting to fight. If you don't have the heart, go now, and you'll not be punished. Once you've taken the Guardsman's Oath, it's too late."

Martyn's expression grew grim. "I'd rather have a score of loyal men at my side than a hundred-thousand whose heart isn't in the fight." The recruits could only stare at first, but finally, the fat one saluted, hefted his stone off the ground with a grunt, and took off at a run, huffing and puffing with each step. His companions tried to keep up.

"Well said, Prince—" A shrill note interrupted Hassan, and Martyn sprinted to the front of the column. Breathing heavily, he stopped beside Miriam, who was talking to Pylias, Martyn's Master of Scouts, amidst a group of ten subcommanders. "What's going on?" Martyn gasped. *Maybe, after this, I should go back and run with the recruits for a while.*

"Riders approaching from the west," Pylias replied. "About five score."

Martyn followed the Guardsman's finger to where a small cloud of dust rose on the horizon. "Friend or foe?"

A tiny, thin-faced warrior answered. "They wear Alrendrian armor, and their leader was a hawk-faced man with a black beard."

"It's Jasova!" Martyn smiled ruefully. "He found us first. Now I owe him a cask of Odaran Ale." He started forward to meet the commander, and to his surprise, Miriam stayed at his side. She even smiled when she caught him staring at her. Martyn offered the princess his arm, and together, they strode to the front of the camp with a small contingent of Guardsmen.

Martyn watched the Alrendrian party approach. They thundered across the plains at full speed, raising a cloud of thick dust. The Golden Sun flashed off their breastplates, and even from this distance, Martyn heard them shouting his name.

Suddenly, Martyn frowned, and he squinted to see better through the gathering dust. "That's not Jasova!" he shouted, grabbing Miriam's arm and pulling the princess back. "Ambush! Guardsmen, we're under attack!"

The soldiers nearest Martyn drew their blades, and behind them, a wall of hardened Guardsmen appeared as if from nowhere, coming to their prince's call. Horn blasts filled the air, calling out a warning, but it was too late. The riders had crossed into bow range, and the first volley of arrows fell from the sky like rain.

Chapter 14

Martyn threw Miriam to the ground, shielding her with his body, and they tumbled down a hill through tall, browning grass. The sound of flying arrows, followed by solid thuds and the screams of men, filled the air. A lance of pain shot through Martyn's arm, and Miriam cried out. She clung to Martyn desperately. A spot of red blossomed on her dress, but with the Guardsmen advancing and enemy riders bearing down on them, Martyn could not stop to tend to her wound. He grabbed her tightly around the shoulders and rolled them beneath the frame of a wagon.

"Miriam?" When the princess did not answer, Martyn rolled off her. After sparing a quick glance at his own arm—his injury was little more than a scratch— he tore at the bloody tear in Miriam's dress.

The arrow had lodged in the crease where chest met arm, and the red stain was rapidly spreading. The shaft was broken, lost in the fall or in Martyn's attempt to protect them. "Miriam?" Martyn called again. Nervously, he touched the princess' brow, and when he saw her breathing was even and her pulse strong, he sighed in relief.

Miriam's eyes fluttered open at Martyn's touch, and the ghost of a smile touched her lips. "You saved me," she whispered. Her eyes flicked toward her wound, but as soon as they saw the blood soaking her dress, her face paled and her eyes rolled upward. Martyn grabbed Miriam's chin and forced her to look into his eyes.

"You didn't think I'd let my queen be killed before our wedding, did you?"

Miriam chuckled weakly. "It would have solved a few problems."

"And caused a thousand more," Martyn added. "The arrow hasn't gone deep," he told her, "but removing it will hurt. And I'll need something to stop the bleeding."

"Use my dress," Miriam whispered. "Not the whole of it, mind you," she added wryly. "But a bit could be spared."

As Martyn tore a strip from the hem of Miriam's dress, his hand touched the smooth, pale skin of her leg. His heart quickened at that touch, and a mixture of excitement, guilt, and embarrassment filled him. *What are you doing? There's a battle going on out there!* He hurriedly ripped a bandage. "This will hurt," he warned, bracing the wound with one hand and grabbing the broken shaft with the other. With a swift motion, he pulled the arrow free.

Miriam clapped a hand over her mouth, and Martyn tied the bandage around the wound tightly. They crawled to the rear of the wagon, and after making sure that no enemies were near, Martyn crawled into the open and waved to a group of Guardsmen. The soldiers hurried toward them.

"Thank the Gods!" A stream of blood ran down the Guardsman's face, but he smiled at the prince. "No one knew where you were, my Prince!" The young man's face was pale, and his eyes had a manic gleam. "There must be thousands of them! They're everywhere, killing anyone they find. There's no pattern to the attack, no order! We don't stand a chance!"

"There are no more than ten score!" Martyn replied. The others looked nervous, and with their squad commander shouting about how quickly they were going to die, Martyn did not expect morale to improve. "And they're likely more interested in the supply carts than us."

The supplies in the wagons were needed on the front. If even one was lost, it would be a setback. "We need to rally the Guard and protect the wagons! You!" Martyn pointed to the squad commander. "Take the Rising Sun banner and head toward the wagons. Gather as many soldiers as you can. You three, you're with me. The rest of you, protect the princess. If anything happens to her, I'll hold you responsible."

For the first time, Martyn wished for his bodyguards—*Even one seasoned Guardsman would be an improvement over these baby-faced recruits!*—but they had been separated at the start of the ambush. The squad broke up, and Miriam was shuttled away in a tight knot. Martyn's eyes shifted to the three young men at his side. "Let's go!" he told them, drawing his sword.

The three Guardsmen followed Martyn into chaos. Horses, their tether lines cut, galloped freely through the camp. The once-ordered rows of tents lay scattered, the canvas torn and flapping free in the breeze. Bodies littered the ground, their pained moans audible over the sounds of battle. The odor of smoke reached Martyn's nose, and he winced. In the distance, three thin tendrils of black stretched toward the sky.

The clang of swords came sporadically from every direction, and armored forms ran and galloped past haphazardly. All the combatants wore Guardsmen's uniforms, making it difficult to tell friend from foe. A shout drew Martyn's eyes, and he saw Pylias locked in combat with another soldier in Alrendrian armor.

"Prince Martyn!" a voice called out, and Martyn turned to see a Guardsman running toward him. "Thank the Gods! We thought you were—"

An arrow sprouted from the soldier's chest and he fell to the ground with a strangled cry. "Trust no one you don't recognize on sight, my Prince," Jhorval said, stepping out from behind a nearby tent. A bloody gash ran the length of the Guardsman's face, and he had a number of bandages slung over his shoulder. He went to the body and removed a small dagger from the dead man's hand. "I think this was meant for you," he told Martyn while handing several bandages to each man in Martyn's company. "Tie one on your right arm, and give one to any man you know."

"Where's Hassan?" Martyn asked, but a frightened scream made him turn away before Jhorval could answer. Not far off, a ring of recruits stood clustered on a hill. A handful of horsemen galloped in circles around them, darting in to strike and fleeing before the young men could counter attack.

Martyn sprinted to their aid, ignoring Jhorval's shouted warning. He stooped to heft a fist-sized stone and hurled it toward the riders. He had hoped to distract one of them, but the rock hit one rider squarely in the head, knocking him from his horse. He fell at an odd angle and lay unmoving.

A second horse reared when it reached the fallen rider, and the recruits struck out. They pulled the soldier from his saddle and set upon him. Two of the riders broke away and turned toward Martyn; the others cut a swath through the recruits. Martyn watched at least five young men, boys barely old enough to enlist, cut down. Guilt surged through him, but he forced it away and focused on the riders racing toward him.

The riders expected Martyn to be easy prey, but the prince was ready for them. As they passed, he ducked beneath one blow and parried the other. Swords met, and fire laced up Martyn's wounded arm. He turned to face the return charge, but the three young Guardsmen surrounded one of the riders, jumping around his frightened horse and waving their swords threateningly.

Martyn raced forward, grabbed the rear of the man's saddle, and vaulted onto the horse's back. His sword hit the rider's leg on the way up, and the blade clattered to the ground. Weaponless, Martyn clung to the saddle as the rider galloped away.

The rider swung wildly, trying to knock Martyn from the saddle, and the prince took several solid blows to the head and an elbow to the chin that made the countryside spin. The horse, frightened by its riders' erratic movement, twisted and reared, forcing Martyn to hold tight to his enemy to stay mounted. *And I though this was a good idea?*

Out of the corner of his eye, Martyn saw another rider hurtling toward him. Tensed, he watched the soldier approach, watched his arm draw back, watched him aim a killing blow. At the last instant, Martyn hurled himself from the horse and heard the satisfying sound of a sword slicing through armor. The enemy rider screamed as Martyn tumbled across the ground.

The dead rider landed near Martyn, the other man's sword still buried in his chest. The second rider fled; Martyn saw the trail of dust left by his passage. Groaning, the prince climbed to his feet and wrenched the blade from the soldier's back. Free of its fighting riders, the warhorse had calmed, and it grazed not too far off. Martyn climbed into the saddle, and turned the horse toward the beleaguered recruits. Jhorval knelt in the grass ahead of him, taking aim with his bow.

More than half a score had fallen to the riders, but the others had tightened their circle around their fallen comrades and fought desperately. The riders attacked recklessly, ignoring their flank, and Martyn caught his first target completely unaware. His blow drove deep into the man's chest. The horseman did not even scream; drooling blood, he fell from his saddle.

Jhorval dispatched another rider with a well-aimed shaft, and the others broke off their attack to advance on Martyn. He met the charge, trading blows with one rider and then turning around for another pass. He kept a wary eye on the two horsemen trying to flank him.

The rider in front of him suddenly vanished, and then a second fell. The recruits rallied to their prince, attacking the riders with a vengeance, pulling them down with their bare hands and hacking mercilessly with sword or dagger. Martyn's triumphant smile faded when he saw the final rider galloping toward him. The prince had no time to raise his blade, and he tried to maneuver away, but the horse shied away from the screaming recruits.

Out of nowhere, an arrow caught the rider in the throat, and he tumbled backward out of the saddle. Martyn saw Kaeille in the distance. The Aelvin warrior lowered her bow and raised a hand, then drew another shaft from her quiver and scanned the field.

Martyn fought the urge to run to the Aelvin woman's side. He turned to the twenty or so recruits still standing. "Form rank behind me. Groups of four. Watch all directions and call a warning if anyone approaches." Jhorval joined them, and Martyn ordered the Guardsman to hand out bandages to the recruits.

"What are these for?" one boy asked.

"To tell friend from foe." While the recruits tied the strips to their arms and gathered their weapons, Martyn scanned the camp. More fires blazed among the tents. Riders darted in and out of the swirling dust, appearing and disappearing as they criss-crossed the camp. The supply wagons appeared intact, but every passing moment brought them closer to destruction. Martyn's horse stomped impatiently.

"Rally to me!" Martyn yelled, drawing the attention of the nearest Guardsmen. "Form up around the wagons and we'll drive these brigands back to Corsa!" A cheer went up among the recruits, and they followed Martyn through the camp, calling out to every party they passed. Men ran toward them, drawn by the sound of the prince's voice and the growing cries of 'For Martyn and Alrendria!' By the time they reached the wagons, Martyn's party had grown to eight score, nearly half of them true Guardsmen.

More than three times that number already guarded the wagons. A young man stood between two of the nearest, waving the Rising Sun banner and bellowing at the top of his lungs. "Rally to the standard! Protect the wagons!" When he saw Martyn, his cry changed. "Rally to your Prince! Rally to Prince Martyn!"

Evana raced over. Dirt smeared the woman's face, and the bandage tied to her arm was caked with blood. "The wagons are secure, my Prince, and with only minor damage, but the Corsans have ravaged the other sections of the camp. Casualties are high. Most of my guards raced ahead when they heard the alarm. Then the riders appeared wearing Alrendrian armor. We didn't know it was an attack until they started firing."

"None of us knew, Guardsman. It's not your fault." The sounds of battle came from beyond a hill to the northeast. Martyn tapped his lip. "Round up as many Guardsmen as you can spare and lead them east around that hill. Jhorval and I will take our men west. If we're lucky, we'll be able to trap the Corsans between us."

"And if we're not lucky?"

"Then run," Martyn replied. "These boys are no match for mounted riders. Retreat back here. I doubt the Corsans number more than several hundred; they might be willing to pick us off individually, but I doubt they're willing to face any organized resistance."

Martyn moved his men around the hill, making enough noise to warn the Corsans of his approach, flushing them out and driving them before him. Kal rose out of the grass and loped toward them, his *dolchek* red with blood. "You make more noise than a cub on his first hunt."

The prince laughed. "I'm pushing the Corsans ahead of me. We'll trap them on the far side of that hill."

"Clever," Kal said, "but you ignore the enemy beyond that rise." The *Kranach* pointed to a steep fold in the land to their south. "Go much farther, and you are trapped."

Martyn eyed the Tribesman suspiciously. "How do you know? And even if there are riders, how can you be sure they're not our men?"

Kal fixed Martyn with an odd look. "Can't you smell them?" He sniffed the air. Without waiting for a reply, he started toward the hill, crouching low and moving quickly through the tall grass. Signaling for silence, Martyn dropped from his saddle and joined the Tribesman. At the top of the rise, he crouched and crawled forward.

Half a hundred riders hid in the valley, grouped behind a man in dark armor. For the moment, the riders seemed unaware that they had been discovered. On hands and knees, Martyn scrambled down the slope. Drawing his sword, he ordered the charge, and the Alrendrians topped the rise and descended the hill at a dead run, screaming a battlecry.

On foot, Kal kept pace with Martyn's horse, and the *Kranach* was the first to enter the fray. His feral growls and slashing *dolchek* frightened more than the Corsan raiders. Their horses began to kick and buck; several tossed their riders and galloped away.

The ferocity of the attack startled the Corsans, and a number of them fled southward with no thought of their companions. The leader, all but his eyes hidden by the dark metal of his helmet, wheeled his mount around and shouted for his men to rally. When he saw Martyn, his eyes narrowed to slits, and he charged.

Martyn lost himself in the fray. Horses pressed in from every side, jostling and vying for position. The prince swung savagely at any Corsan who entered his reach; in the heat of battle, with bodies pressed close, telling friend from foe became an easy task. With Jhorval on one side and Kal on the other, Martyn cut a path through the raiders.

The Corsans yielded easily, and before long, they raced south with the Alrendrians in full pursuit. "Something's wrong!" Jhorval yelled. "I've fought the Corsans before. They don't run so easily."

As if to confirm the Guardsman's suspicions, a low thunder rumbled through the air. Kal sniffed the air tentatively, but with the wind at his back, Martyn doubted the *Kranach* would smell anything other than his allies. "There," Jhorval yelled, pointing to a cloud of dust on the western horizon. A group of riders crested a neighboring hill and charged the Alrendrians. The fleeing Corsans turned when they saw their reinforcements.

"Ambush!" Martyn yelled, but once again, his warning came too late. "Fall back!" The Alrendrian horsemen skidded to stop, but the Corsans approached quickly. Small groups broke off from the main force, circling the valley and trapping Martyn's men.

"We'll never get out in time," Martyn said, his expression grim. He scanned the line and saw a spot where the enemy lines were thin. A determined look spread across his face. "Guardsmen!" he yelled. "Charge!"

The Guardsmen drove like a wedge into the heart of the Corsan forces. The Corsan line bent and broke, giving them the chance to escape. Martyn rode at the front, hacking at anything that moved. The dark-armored Corsan commander reared up in front of the prince, deflecting Martyn's awkward attack and making one of his own. He rammed his mount into Martyn's, driving the prince backward.

The Alrendrian retreat stalled. The Guardsmen formed into clusters, trying vainly to reach their prince before the full might of the Corsan host reached them. Martyn and his opponent circled each other, guiding their mounts with their knees. They exchanged a series of blows, neither getting the upper hand, but then a lucky strike glanced off the Corsan's armor. Martyn's sword clanged hollowly against the rider's shoulder plate. Snarling, the Corsan brought his blade around for a blow that Martyn barely dodged.

Another rumble drowned out the sounds of battle, and Martyn groaned. *This is it. Whatever chance we had is lost. But the Gods be damned if they think I'm dying before him!* He drove his horse forward, and the Corsan commander fell back.

A horn sounded to the east, and Evana led a hundred Guardsmen over the hill. Martyn's new standard bearer rode at her side, waving the Rising Sun high over his head and shouting for the Alrendrians to protect its prince. A second horn sounded to the west, and another column appeared with Jasova at its head.

The Corsan met the Martyn's attack, and they danced in a circle, their mounts stamping and snorting. Martyn had the advantage until a strike caught the hilt of his sword, sending the blade clattering to the ground. The Corsan drew his weapon back, but as the blade soared toward Martyn's head, something hit him, driving him off his horse. He landed atop his blade, the pommel pressing painfully into his gut. Somewhere above, he heard the clang of blades meeting.

When his vision cleared, Martyn stared up into the eyes of a Guardsman. The soldier wore Alrendrian plate, minus the helmet, and over it a tunic of white with the Rising Sun of Alrendria embroidered on its front. Pale blue eyes regarded Martyn with concern, and the Guardsman's lips pressed into a narrow line.

The Guardsman's sword was locked with the Corsan's, and his free hand gripped the Corsan's throat tightly. The Corsan struggled, but the Guardsman seemed not to notice. "Are you injured, my Prince?" he asked. "I only intended to knock you aside, not unhorse you."

Martyn did the best to hide the throbbing pain he felt as he stood. "I'm fine," he replied, retrieving his sword. The ease with which the Guardsman held the Corsan awed him. "Keep him alive," the prince ordered. "He has a lot to answer for."

"As you command," The Guardsman's grip tightened on the Corsan's throat, and Martyn took a half step forward, his arm raised in protest. Before he could intervene, the Corsan's eyes rolled up into his head, and he slumped. With a casual flick of his wrist, the Guardsman tossed the Corsan aside, and he smiled while he watched the man fall. "He won't trouble anyone for a while, my Prince."

The Guardsman's gaze hardened, and he scanned the battlefield. He started forward, then paused and turned back to Martyn. "Unless you need me, my Prince, I will go on. There are still Corsans to kill."

Martyn could not suppress his laughter. "Go, Guardsman! With my blessing!" He watched the warrior ride into the fray before regaining his own saddle and assessing the battle for himself.

The Corsans had been routed; they fled in every direction, chased by bands of Guardsmen. The few remaining pockets of resistance were contained, and Martyn saw no need to remain in harm's way. He started toward the camp, calling to a group of recruits and ordering them to follow him with the Corsan prisoner.

Jasova galloped over, a grin on his face. "It's good to see you alive and well, Prince Martyn. One of my scouts saw smoke. We feared the worst."

"Your fears were almost justified," Martyn said, trying to keep his voice light. "I fell into their trap like a raw recruit." Bodies littered the ground in and around the tents. Many of the fallen cried out, begging for help; others moaned incoherently. The pleas of his countrymen rent Martyn's heart, but their cries did not hurt him as much as the silent, unmoving forms staring toward the heavens. Most of the dead were children, boys Martyn himself had convinced to leave home and fight for Alrendria. *They never even had a chance to learn how to defend themselves!*

"This was your first battle," Jasova reminded him. "Unless you count the valley." Something dark crossed the Guardsman's eyes. "Pray that it's your last."

"I won't waste prayers on pointless wishes," Martyn snapped, his mood turning sour. He told Jhorval to secure the camp and increase the patrols around the perimeter. The recruits he ordered to tend to the wounded and gather the dead. They hurried to comply, and once they were alone, Martyn rounded on Jasova. "How could Corsans get so far into Alrendrian without being detected?"

"They cross the borders in small numbers and regroup inside Alrendria to raid villages and farms." Jasova frowned. "We don't have enough men to patrol the border, let alone the interior. Even if we did, we'd be hard pressed to stop all of them."

Martyn understood the tactic. "How many men have you withdrawn from the border?"

"Nearly half," Jasova admitted. In the distance, Treloran and Kal carried a wounded Guardsman to a group of undamaged tents marked as an infirmary. "I had to or risk both attack from our flank and rebellion among our people. The townsfolk are frightened, Martyn. They don't believe the Guard is strong enough to protect them." Jasova's frown deepened. "I'm not sure I disagree."

Martyn did not like hearing that from a Guard Commander, but he knew Jasova would not say such a thing lightly. If Jasova doubted their ability to win, then Martyn had cause enough to worry. "What measures have you taken?"

"I've increased patrols along the major trade routes and garrisoned all large towns with Guardsmen. Patrols rove the countryside, but they rarely find a raiding party before it's attacked somewhere. The borders are our weakest point, but so far, Murdir has not attacked directly. It's only a matter of time, though."

"What of the armor?" Martyn asked. "I've never heard of raiders disguising themselves as Alrendrians before. The Corsans have too much pride to resort to such tactics."

Jasova ran a hand through his goatee. "Murdir is too arrogant to resort to such trickery, but we already suspected that Corsa has ties to the Darklord. Perhaps Lorthas pulls the strings. Regardless, it's causing no end of trouble. Not only is it difficult to tell friend from foe until you're face to face, but my patrols have encountered resistance in a number of villages. The Corsans have convinced many that the Guard's behind the attacks."

"I'd heard rumors," Martyn admitted, "but I didn't know it was this bad. I may have a solution, though, one that will allow us to send men back to the border." He told Jasova about the militias he had established in the villages he had passed through, and of his plan to do the same south of Vela.

Jasova nodded his approval. "Scores of aging Guardsmen wait in Vela, most of them desperate to serve. All but a few are toothless old men, but each and every one has seen his fair share of battle. They'd make excellent commanders for—"

"Well," said a disapproving voice. "It looks like we arrived just in time." Martyn and Jasova turned toward the sound. A short woman with pale blonde hair pulled back in a ponytail and light blue eyes regarded the prince scornfully, her thin lips turned down in a scowl. High cheekbones and a pronounced chin framed a sharp nose, and she stopped glaring at Martyn only long enough to survey the battlefield. Her skin was milk white in complexion, untouched by sun and unmarked by age or blight. She wore a long dress of dark blue trimmed in white. No stains or frayed threads, not even a wrinkle marred the outfit, and around her neck hung a chain of finely-wrought gold with a heart-shaped ruby dangling against the pale flesh of her throat.

Several more people stood behind, each dressed in blue and each with a matching necklace. All looked young, none of them past their prime, and the speaker could have easily passed for twenty-five winters. But something in her eyes, or in the way they looked at everyone around them, made Martyn suspect the truth. "Greetings, honored Magi. If any of you have skill at healing, then I humbly request your help. Many of my men have been gravely wounded."

"You act as if you've never seen a Healer before," the woman sniffed. "Skill at Healing! For such an affront—" The Mage fell silent, and she peered deep into Martyn's eyes. "Things are worse than I expected if the Prince of Alrendria can't recognize one of our Order."

Martyn forced a broad smile. "Mage…?"

"Sheriza."

"Mage Sheriza, a winter ago, I wouldn't have realized you were a Mage."

Sheriza's eyes glittered dangerously. "We can forgo the pleasantries," she said icily, though so far, Martyn had found little pleasant in their conversation. "There are wounded to heal."

"My men are taking the wounded to those tents," Martyn said, pointing to the makeshift infirmary. "I will have—"

"You," Sheriza said, pointing to a passing Guardsman. "Show us to the wounded, and tell the other… soldiers"—she spoke the word as if the sound alone pained her—"to bring the most grievously injured to us." As the Magi departed, Martyn heard one whisper, "I haven't seen common 'healers' and their toys since I was a child. This will be interesting."

"The more Magi I get to know," Martyn growled, "the more I understand why people can't stand them."

Jasova smirked. "Better be careful how loud you talk, Prince Martyn. One never knows when a Mage might be listening."

Martyn signaled for Jasova to follow. He surveyed the carnage and hated himself for thinking that things would be much worse if the wagons had been destroyed. As they walked, Martyn called out encouragement to the wounded and terrified recruits, telling them that they had served Alrendria well, that this was the first step to becoming Guardsmen. Some appeared heartened by his words, but many ignored him, and Martyn wondered how many would be missing come morning.

"You two!" Martyn called to a pair of young men sitting back to back, staring dumbly at the camp. "Recruits!" he called again when they did not respond, and the boys jumped at his whip-like tone. "Find Prince Treloran and *Kranach Kal*," he told one. "Have them meet me at the supply wagons." He turned to the second man. "I left Princess Miriam under guard near the front of our procession. Find her and bring her to me."

At the wagons, a semblance of order had been restored. Evana stood atop one wagon, organizing their defense and calling out a string of orders to the Guardsmen and recruits toiling below. To one side, Pylias crouched in the center of a mass of Guardsmen, drawing in the sandy soil. The men leaned in close, listening as the Master of Scouts outlined a plan to sweep the countryside for any remaining Corsans. Subcommanders Tomei and Nevarrah rounded up all the recruits they could find and assigned most to sentry duty or to rounding up the wounded. A handful were charged with gathering the dead.

"Reclaim their gear?" Martyn heard one boy say, his face turning pale.

"You heard me!" Nevarrah shouted, his patience at an end. "You think armor grows on trees? To win this war, we'll need every blade we can get, and taking one from someone as won't need it is far easier than forgin' a new one every time a friend takes a dagger in his gut. Being a Guardsman isn't all glorious battles and hero-like stories. Sometimes we have to do things... things we don't like. Now get about your duty!"

"And build a pyre to the south of the camp," Martyn added softly, testing the wind with his finger. "Burn the Corsans. The Alrendrians we'll give to the ground."

"Yes, Sir!" the boys said, hurrying away. They tried to show confidence, but Martyn saw the terror in their eyes. He turned to Nevarrah. "You were a bit harsh. They're just children."

"They want to be Guardsmen," Nevarrah said coldly. "Best they learn what that means before they take the Oath."

Martyn nodded, but he saw something in Nevarrah's eyes he had never before seen. Fear. "Where's Ikabhod? He's usually the gruff one."

"He took an arrow," Nevarrah answered, his lips compressing in a thin line. "He'll not survive the night."

Cursing himself for being a fool, Martyn tried to reassure the Guardsman. "A number of Magi skilled in Healing arrived not long past. They can work miracles, the Magi. Ikabhod will be fine." From the corner of his eye, Martyn saw Kal and Treloran walking toward him. They were covered in dirt and blood, but neither appeared injured. The relief he felt at seeing his friends faded when his thoughts turned to Kaeille. He wondered where she was, and why she had yet to seek him out.

"Are you well?" Martyn asked as the Elf and Tribesman drew close.

They shrugged off Martyn's concerns. "These Corsans risked much," Treloran said as his eyes roved over the battlefield. "Their leaders will be disappointed."

"Disappointed?" Martyn repeated. "That they didn't manage to kill all of us?"

"This was not a defeat," the Aelvin Prince replied calmly. "The supplies destined for Vela are intact, casualties were not as severe as they could have been, and this tactic will never work again. They wasted their surprise, and for little gain."

"A lot of good people died today, many of them children!"

"They died with honor," Kal said, "defending their homeland and their prince. They walk the Twilight World with the Gods. Among the Blood, some would say they are the lucky ones, and that we had yet to prove our worthiness."

"I wish I had your faith," Martyn said, but the Tribesman's words did little to lessen the guilt weighing on his heart. He started to say something, but the appearance of a wounded Guardsmen, his hand clamped tightly over his bleeding belly, froze the words in his mouth. Martyn rushed to the man's side. "What happened?" he demanded, easing the soldier to the ground.

"Attacked..." the Guardsman answered. "Eldon and Sami... dead." The Guardsman went wild, and he gripped Martyn's shirt tightly. "They took her!" he yelled. "I couldn't stop them!" He slumped, and in a quiet murmur kept repeating, "They took her. They took her."

"Dear Gods!" Martyn whispered.

"When I found him," the boy Martyn had sent in search of Miriam said, "he was making more sense. He said someone was already chasing the Corsans."

"Who?" Martyn demanded. "Did he say who was chasing them?"

"The Elf woman," the boy replied nervously. "And some Guardsman."

Oh Gods! No! Martyn drew a steadying breath. "Take this man to the Healers, and tell Mage Sheriza to join me here immediately." With Martyn's help, the boy lifted the Guardsman and started him hobbling toward the infirmary.

"Jhorval!" he yelled, and the Guardsman raced toward him.

"Yes, my Prince?"

"Fetch my horse!" Martyn commanded. "The princess has been kidnapped."

Chapter 15

Majestic hills dominated the countryside, towering green domes offering sweeping views of the lush plains. Wildflowers of every imaginable hue covered the hills in patches thick enough to hide the grass, making one appear red, another blue, and others any of a thousand shades. Sometimes, the winds made the flowers ripple like waves on the ocean. Few streams ran through this part of Alrendria, but where water flowed, it was clear as crystal. Small lakes lined the bowls of some valleys, and small stands of thin, white-barked trees grew on the banks of the lakes. Large beasts, broader than oxen and with long, curving horns roamed the grasslands in herds so great they sometimes spread from horizon to horizon, blocking passage to all but the most determined traveler. Wild horses, silhouetted in the bright sunlight, galloped past at near-impossible speeds.

These things made the plains of House Velan a spectacular sight, but Martyn saw none of them. The hills passed in a blur, the wildflowers unnoticed. The forests he avoided at all costs, except when tracking the Corsans necessitated entry. The lakes and streams, impossible to bypass, barely registered, though he noted absently that they rarely grew too deep to ford and that, despite the nearness of summer, the water remained bitter cold. The beasts and other wildlife proved more an annoyance than anything else. Songbirds and chittering squirrels kept him from hearing riders; the countless delays avoiding the herds caused him no end of frustration. Even the wild horses, who kept their distance, angered him. He saw the ease with which they traveled the steep slopes and wished his own mount could move so effortlessly.

Martyn leaned low in his saddle, urging every ounce of strength from his mount. An open stretch of grassland spread out before him, and he had no intention of stopping until he crossed it. Behind him, his companions struggled to keep up; only Kal managed to stay ahead. From time to time, the *Kranach* left a sign, an arrow drawn in the loose soil or fashioned from small stones, showing them which way to go. The prince would have given his right arm to know how the Tribesman could move so quickly on foot.

Above, the sun neared its zenith. *Two days. Are we already too late?* He ran his hand along his mount's lathered neck and lost himself in dark thoughts. Some time later, with the sun noticeably lower, he became aware of a presence at his side. Sheriza, her once pristine dress stained with dirt and sweat, rode up on his right. The Mage clung to her saddle awkwardly, and she stared at Martyn with barely-contained rage. "Prince Martyn, unless you intend to run that poor beast to death, you had better stop this foolishness. Now!"

Reluctantly, Martyn slowed his horse to a trot, then to a walk. Behind him, some distance back, the others dismounted and walked in his direction. As Martyn stepped out of his saddle, he looked expectantly at Sheriza. She sat rigidly, her eyes blank and distant. When she did not immediately explain the delay, annoyance began to gnaw at Martyn's patience.

It took some time for Sheriza to rouse herself. "There's a small stream beyond that hill," she told him, pointing southwest. "We will set up camp there."

"Must I remind you that Princess Miriam's life is at stake?" Martyn glowered.

The haughty tone that worked so well on members of the court had no effect on the Mage. "Must I remind *you*," Sheriza replied in a way that made Martyn's question seem friendly, "that it will be harder to catch your betrothed's abductors if we must do so on foot?" The Healer dropped to the ground and smoothed the wrinkles from her dress. She looked at Martyn with exasperation, as one would stare at a child who refused to listen to reason. "There was a time, not so long ago, when even the Kings and Queens of Alrendria heeded the words of the Magi."

"Not so long ago," Martyn countered, "the Magi cared about the world and those who live in it."

"The Magi respect all life, Prince Martyn," Sheriza said, her eyes widening, "and we Healers respect it even more. To imply that..." The Mage took several slow breaths and calmed herself. "You are young," she said at last, "and concerned, though whether for your future queen or current mistress, I'm not sure. In either case, I'll forgive your rash words, but if you don't learn to watch your tongue, I'll teach you manners myself."

Though Sheriza stood more than a hand shorter than him, she somehow seemed to tower over Martyn. He bowed low, struggling to hide the anger seething inside. "My apologies, honored Mage. I meant no offense."

"You may call me Sheriza, young one," the woman replied. "Titles and feigned deference do not impress me."

"Then we're even," Martyn replied, infuriated by the Healer's condescension. "I'm not impressed with those who believe their 'gifts' make them better than others."

Thwack! The backhanded slap came out of nowhere. Martyn's head snapped to the left, and he felt warmth trickling down his lip. He spat blood and rubbed his jaw. "I would have expected something more... original... from a Mage."

When he looked at Sheriza, he found the Mage doubled over, breathing hard and clutching her face as if it had been Martyn who struck her. She slowly straightened and took Martyn's chin, inspecting the wound. "I owe you an apology, Prince Martyn." For once, Martyn could not detect a hint of derision. "You're not the only one with a temper, though mine comes with a price." She squeezed his chin gently, and Martyn fought the urge to pull away. "I would heal this for you, but I'll need my Gift for the horses. They're closer to death than you know."

"All tempers come with a price, Mage Sheriza." Martyn shoved the anger and anxiety he felt into the recesses of his mind and tried to remember the things his father and Lord Iban had taught him. "I fear that we have started off badly. Fear for the safety of my queen may fuel my actions, but it does not excuse them."

A slight smile touched Sheriza's lips. Her eyes flicked to their companions. "I told them all you needed was a good slap in the face to see reason." Martyn forced a smile, but he saw nothing amusing in the Mage's words.

Sheriza insisted on tending the horses before they continued. She moved among the mounts, pausing beside each and laying her hands on their heads. When she stepped away from the last, she looked at Martyn and said, "They're no longer in immediate danger, but they're still weak. We must not travel any more tonight."

Her tone had a pleading quality that Martyn could not ignore. "Very well. We'll resume our chase at first light." The Mage nodded gratefully, but when she stepped away from the horse, she swayed, and Martyn rushed to catch her before she fell.

"Forgive me," Sheriza said, wiping her brow with a kerchief taken from a pocket concealed in the folds of her dress. "Horses are much larger than humans, and the cost of healing depends as much on the size of the patient as on the extent of the injuries."

"Jhorval, help the Mage." Martyn ordered, and he handed Sheriza to the Guardsman before leading his party into the sheltered glade Sheriza had told him about. As he walked, he noted the sweat lathering his horse's back and the way its head hung low. He thanked the Gods that Dahr had not seen how cruelly he had treated his mount.

The last two days had been a nightmare of frantic runs and short, sleepless rests, and the effort had taken its toll. Dark rings circled Treloran's eyes, though the Elf walked straight-backed beside his horse, and he gripped the pommel of the saddle for support. Jhorval, with his arm wrapped around Sheriza, stumbled as he walked, and for a moment, it was hard to tell who was helping whom. Pylias all but hung from the reins of his and Sheriza's horses, but his hawk-like eyes remained alert.

Cresting the hill, Martyn saw Kal sitting cross-legged on the shores of a small stream. The Tribesman was bare-chested and dripping from a swim in the cold water, but he smiled when Martyn approached and showed no sign of fatigue. "How did you know we'd stop here?" Martyn asked.

"The Mage sent a message," Kal replied. He leaned low and splashed several more handfuls of water against his face, letting the cold water trickle down his body. The *Kranach* closed his eyes and drew a deep breath as the wind dried the water from his body.

"Have you seen any sign of them?" Martyn asked, desperate for some news. Kal shook his head.

"Avoiding the last herd of *bau'vahla* cost us the trail, but you have pushed us hard. Even the Blood would have trouble keeping pace with you, Prince of Alrendria. My instincts tell me we have circled around our prey. Now they will come to us."

"Are you sure?" Martyn asked. "How can you be sure?"

Kal cocked his head to the side as if confused. "How does the *sahlm*, the river racer, find its way home each summer? How does a hound know its master, even if a score of seasons have separated them?" The Tribesman looked pointedly at Martyn. "How do you know your arrow will hit its target, even when the winds are wild?" Shrugging, the *Kranach* closed his eyes again and let the wind wash away his fatigue. "I am a Hunter. I know."

Farid gathered the horses, but Martyn took the reins from the Guardsman. "I'll do it," he said, leading the mounts to a cluster of gnarled trees at the stream's edge. After tying the horses so that they could reach both the water and the lush grasses beyond the grove, Martyn removed the packs and saddles from their backs and gave each horse a lengthy curry. He lost himself in the rhythmic strokes.

"You treat them well," Sheriza said, startling Martyn from thoughts of Kaeille and Miriam. "Far better than I'd have thought, considering your earlier behavior."

Tending the animals had benefited Martyn as much as the horses; his earlier anger had evaporated. "I learned from the best. Dahr cared for my father's animals more than he cared for most people. No one could match his devotion to them." Thoughts of Dahr darkened Martyn's mood. "Everything I know, I learned from him."

"I've heard of this Dahr," Sheriza said, a mysterious smile on her face. "Some among the Assembly claim he's *Tier'sorahn*, that he can speak with animals."

Tier'sorahn. The word was foreign to Martyn, and he did not try to hide the fact. "Dahr has a gift with bird and beast, but talk to them…? Never in my presence. Not so that I believed they talked back, at least." The price shook and his head and pointed to Kal's distant silhouette. "Perhaps you should talk to him. Dahr spent some time among the Garun'ah, and Kal would know more about *Tier…sorahn* than I."

Sheriza pursed her lips thoughtfully. "Perhaps I will, Prince Martyn. Perhaps I will." The Mage inclined her head politely and departed, leaving Martyn to wonder about her rapidly changing moods.

By the time he finished with the horses, the camp had been set. The tents were arranged in a semicircle around a small fire. A pallet of leaves and moss, Kal's only accommodation unless the weather grew stormy, lay some distance off. A pot of stew bubbled over the firepit.

A strange sound came from behind one tent, and curious, Martyn went to investigate. He found Treloran standing bare-chested in the knee-high grass, moving through a series of odd stances. His motions were quick and graceful, but the awkward positions left Martyn wondering how the Aelvin Prince managed to keep his balance. "What are you doing?" Martyn asked.

Treloran stopped in mid-stance, pressed his fingertips together in front of his face, and bowed his head. Only then did he turn to Martyn. "*Chiumatai*," he answered, his breathing slow and even. "I have ignored my practice far too long."

Martyn's eyebrow arced. "It's a dance?"

"It is combat," Treloran said, "and a meditation practiced by my people since before the time of the Sub-Aelvin…" Treloran's face turned bright red, and he averted his eyes. "Since before the Great Rebellion."

Martyn smiled wryly and ignored the Elf's slip. "Will you teach me? I could use something to take my mind off Miriam and Kaeille."

"*Chiumatai* takes great patience. I am—"

"If you don't think I can do it, that's fine," Martyn said with a shrug. He turned his back and started to walk away.

"Wait!" Treloran called desperately. Fighting a smile, Martyn turned to find the Aelvin Prince hurrying toward him, chagrin painted across his features. "That is not what I meant! It is just that *chiumatai* is not easy to learn. None have become *sinsanae*, a master, in less than a hundred winters."

"Seeing as I don't have a hundred winters," Martyn laughed, "perhaps you should stop wasting my time and begin my instruction."

"I am hardly the one to teach you, but as there are no *sinsanae* around..." Treloran showed Martyn the first stance, a placement of feet and hands that looked simple enough until the prince tried to emulate it. His first few attempts sent him sprawling to the ground. Treloran's countless suggestions, from the way he hold his arms to the speed at which he drew breath, was a constant irritation, but Martyn was determined not to lose his temper. By the time the sun touched the horizon, Martyn's muscles ached from exertion and sweat slicked his body in an oily coat.

"Do not look so frustrated," Treloran told him. "You held the first five stances. That is good for a first lesson." Martyn did not feel like he had attained any great victory; he may have stood without the Aelvin Prince's aid, but he had never felt anything other than awkward. He felt better, though, and he agreed to work with Treloran the next time they made camp.

The two princes returned to the camp to find Sheriza stooped over the fire, stirring the pot. "What are you staring at?" the Mage asked in response to Martyn's slack-jawed expression. "Magi have to eat too." Her eyes narrowed, and she cocked her head to the side. "Or did you expect me to use my Gift to stir the stew?"

"No. It's not that," Martyn said. "It's just—"

"No matter," Sheriza said, waving her hand dismissively. She took a few steps toward Martyn, eyed him up and down, and wrinkled her nose. Behind her, the spoon continued to circle the pot. "I've never known a nobleman to be so slack in matters of hygiene," she told him, "and that's more of an insult to you than you might believe. Cleanliness is not the priority among your class that you pretend it to be."

Martyn stared at Sheriza until the Mage sighed heavily. "Perhaps I wasn't direct enough. You need a bath." At a loss, Martyn hurried downstream, past where the horses grazed. Diving into the icy water, he scrubbed himself clean with coarse sand from the riverbed.

Some time later, he returned to the camp dressed and clean-shaven. "My, my," Sheriza said when he appeared. "There *was* a man beneath that grime, and a fairly striking one at that. You should bathe more than once a moon, Prince Martyn. It suits you."

Ignoring the Mage, Martyn ladled himself a healthy serving of stew from the bubbling pot. As the food settled in his stomach, exhaustion caught up with him, and Martyn yawned. He intended to retire to his tent, but Pylias and Kal's return delayed his slumber.

"We've found them!" Pylias said triumphantly. "There's a camp to the northeast."

"Ready the horses!" Martyn announced excitedly. "We can surprise them while they sleep."

"A herd of *bau'vahla* lies between us and our prey," Kal told him. "By the time we circle it, our quarry will be gone."

"If we stay here," Pylias added, seeing the frustration on Martyn's face, "The Corsans will pass close by. We can set an ambush. They're expecting us from the behind; if we attack from the front, they'll never know what hit them."

"Sitting here while my queen remains in the hands of those Corsan dogs doesn't appeal to me," Martyn said, "but it seems we have no choice. If we can do nothing until morning, then I intend to get some rest. I suggest you do the same."

* * * * * * * * * * * * * * * * * *

"Do you see them?" Martyn asked for the tenth time. He lifted his head so that his eyes barely topped the tall grass and scanned the horizon, squinting to ward off the bright sunlight. "We should be able to see them."

From his place beside the prince, Kal growled. "I must remember to apologize to Dahr."

"Apologize?" Martyn repeated, confused. "For what?"

"I accused him of being too impatient," the *Kranach* explained. "Now I understand what he suffered." Treloran, perched precariously in the branches of a nearby tree, chuckled, and Martyn glared at the Aelvin Prince. "Our prey will come," Kal assured Martyn. "But in its own time. Trust in the Gods, Prince Martyn, and if you must ask someone for haste, ask them. But do so silently."

Treloran chuckled again, and Martyn dropped back to his belly and tried to relax. Kal's comment brought memories of Dahr, and thoughts of Jeran soon followed. *Are they alive? Are they free?* Martyn doubted the latter; if either had escaped, he would have returned to Kaper.

Katya. She's to blame for this! Thoughts of the traitor made Martyn's gut clench. His lips drew down in a scowl, and his hands trembled with rage.

"You are ready to hunt," Kal whispered. "I can see it in your eyes. Good. The waiting is over. Our prey approaches." Martyn raised himself up to get a better look. In the distance, a small party approached. Though the riders were too far away for Martyn to see them clearly, excitement welled up in the prince.

"I see the princess," Treloran called to them in hushed tones. Balanced on two narrow branches and standing amidst the thick green leaves, the Aelvin Prince all but disappeared into the foliage.

"I see her too," Kal agreed. "You have good eyes, Elf."

Martyn crawled to where Pylias, Jhorval, and Sheriza waited. "They're coming," Martyn told the Guardsmen. "You know what to do." Jhorval moved off, and Martyn turned to Sheriza. "You're certain you can do nothing to aid us?"

"I told you that I can not use my Gift to cause harm," Sheriza answered with an exasperated sniff. "No Healer can. The mere thought that my actions might cause pain..." Shivering violently, Sheriza raised a hand to her mouth, but when Martyn went to her, she waved him away. "I will be at your side, Prince Martyn, and I'll do what I can. If your queen or any of your party needs healing, they will receive it. But I cannot use my Gift to hurt."

"The Healer is in your care," Martyn said, turning to Pylias. "Make sure no harm befalls her." Pylias saluted fist-on-heart and drew his sword. Sheriza flinched when the blade left its scabbard, but she took her place beside the Guardsman without comment.

Returning to his position, Martyn met resistance from the one place he did not expect it. "It is not my place to tell a man when to hunt," Kal said, "but are you certain you wish to lead our attack? Losing the princess to these *tralkta* is bad enough, but if you fell into their hands as well…"

"Was it wise to bring the Prince of Illendrylla and the *Kranach* of the Tacha, Alrendria's only representative from the Tribes, with me?" Martyn countered. "In the heat of the moment, I chose those I knew I could trust, and right or wrong, we are here. Now, with our enemy racing toward us and no help in sight, is not the time to discuss the wisdom of my choices. We are Miriam's only hope."

"Spoken like one of the Blood," Kal laughed, clapping Martyn on the shoulder. "I was wrong to question your place. I hope you will not take insult." The *Kranach* waited for Martyn's nod before drawing his *dolchek*. His eyes narrowed to slits, and he fastened them on the approaching riders, seeking his first target.

"We have a problem," Treloran called down urgently.

Panic surged through the prince. "Have they seen us?"

"No," Treloran said, but he pointed toward the eastern horizon, "But those riders will reach the Corsans before the Corsans reach us." Cursing, Martyn stood and stared to the east. Two figures on horseback were bearing down on the Corsans at a full gallop. One wore shining armor and tunic of an Alrendrian Guardsman, the other the dark green leathers of *Ael Chatorra*.

"It's Kaeille!" Martyn said, casting his eyes toward the Heavens accusingly. The Corsans had spotted the riders and turned to intercept them. "Mount up and charge!" Martyn called, sprinting to his own mount and vaulting into the saddle. He launched himself down the hill, steering the beast with his knees as he fumbled to free his sword from its scabbard.

Kal ran at Martyn's side, the Tribesman's long strides keeping pace with Martyn's horse, and Treloran jumped from his perch, landed lightly on the ground, and ran toward his own mount. The Aelvin Prince had an arrow notched as soon as he was in the saddle, and he scanned the field for a target.

Martyn approached the riders quickly, and though their attention was focused on Kaeille and her companion, Martyn could not help but wonder if he had made a mistake rushing into the fray. *Now's not the time to doubt yourself.* Aiming for the nearest rider, he shouted, "For Alrendria!"

An arrow whizzed past Martyn's ear, taking one of the Corsans in the throat. The man fell, and the frightened animal careened into the rider beside it. An eager smile worked its way onto Martyn's face, and he drove his horse forward, raising his sword to meet the attack of his first opponent.

Swords met in a flash of sparks, and a jolt of pain shot down Martyn's arm. Their blades locked, Martyn and the Corsan spun in a tight circle, their horses pressed against each other. As he struggled to wrench his blade back for a second swing, Martyn saw his opponent smile, and the man's free arm drew back to strike. Twisting at the last instant, Martyn barely avoided the Corsan's dagger, and the dark blade nicked his thigh before slicing a deep rent across his saddle. Instinctively, Martyn brought his elbow down on the Corsan's wrist. He heard the satisfying snap of bone, and the man cried out as he pulled his hand away.

Martyn's joy was short lived. The two horses collided, pinning Martyn's leg between them. A fresh wave of pain exploded through the prince's knee, and his leg throbbed. He jerked on the reins, but his horse refused to obey. Eyes watering, he batted at the Corsan with his sword, hammering the man relentlessly. His opponent fought back, matching Martyn swing for swing, but when he brought his blade around in a high arc, Martyn ducked the blow and brought his own sword in low. It caught the Corsan in the gut, driving through armor and into the soft flesh beneath. Gasping, the man tumbled to the ground.

With the Corsan down, the horses separated, and with the release of the pressure came more pain than Martyn had ever felt before. His entire leg was on fire, tingling and burning at the same time, and it was all he could do to stay in the saddle. Turning his horse, he saw a young Corsan with a panicked look in his eyes wheeling his mount from left to right. Martyn heeled his horse forward, but before he could attack, Kal barreled past him, his *dolchek* at the ready.

As he approached the rider, Kal lowered his shoulder and ducked low, ramming the horse at full speed and knocking both beast and rider to the ground. The Tribesman vaulted over the fallen animal and landed on the Corsan, his *dolchek* falling with a single, killing blow. When he rose, a streak of blood across his face and more dripping from his blade, he howled in triumph, and his eyes glittered wildly as he searched for more enemies.

Out of the corner of his eye, Martyn saw three shapes pass in a blur, pursued by a fourth. The prince tracked the riders; two Corsans in front flanked the third, and the flash of cornsilk blonde hair could only belong to Miriam. The unknown Guardsman chased them, his silver plate flashing in the sunlight.

"Miriam!" Martyn shouted, urging his horse to a gallop and angling his charge to cut off the Corsans. The Guardsman, seeing Martyn approach, guided his horse to the left, and in a flash of understanding, Martyn kept his mount to the right. The knee-high grass hid rocks and pitfalls, but the Corsans rode at a reckless pace, forcing Martyn to do the same if he were to have any chance of catching them.

As he neared his target, Martyn swung his sword, but the awkward angle and the frantic pace made it impossible to land a blow. Sheathing his blade, he reached out and tried to grab the Corsan's clothes, reins, or anything he could use to unhorse the man, but he could not get a solid grip. Frustrated, he stood in his saddle, crouching low, with one hand wrapped firmly around the pommel and the other gripping the back of the saddle. He timed his jump carefully, waiting until their horses ran down the breadth of a straight valley, but his leg gave out when he leapt. He caught hold of the Corsan's waist, but his momentum nearly pulled them both down; only the Corsan's firm grip on Miriam's reins kept them from falling.

The princess squeaked when Martyn's head slammed against her shoulder, but with her hands bound to the saddle and a strip of heavy canvas wrapped around her eyes, she had no way of knowing he was there. The Corsan flailed wildly, but there was little the man could do to knock Martyn free. Martyn drew his belt knife and stabbed; he felt a grim satisfaction when the Corsan stiffened. Pulling his blade free, Martyn shoved the Corsan from the saddle and grabbed the reins to Miriam's horse. He brought both mounts to a stop.

Dismounting, Martyn cut the bonds that held Miriam and gently lowered the princess to the ground. He removed the thick canvas straps covering her mouth and eyes. Free, Miriam fell into his arms, sobbing. "Oh, Martyn, I knew you would come." Martyn could do nothing but stand there and hold her.

Pounding hooves approached, and Martyn tensed, but it was only the Guardsman, a tall broad form in shining Alrendrian plate. He dropped to the ground at the prince's side and pulled the helmet from his head. Locks of golden-brown fell around a chiseled face with strong, proud features. "You!" Martyn exclaimed, recognizing the man who had saved him from the Corsan commander. "It seems I'm now twice in your debt."

Piercing, dark brown eyes regarded Martyn and the princess calmly. "I merely did my duty, Prince Martyn," the man replied humbly. "If anyone deserves thanks, it is the Elf. Without her, I would never have been able to track these mongrels."

"Nevertheless, Guardsman..." Martyn paused.

"I am Dayfid, your Highness."

"Nevertheless, Dayfid, I'm in your debt. You have served your King and country well this day." The Guardsman beamed with pride. "Come," Martyn said, "Let's rejoin the others. I'm sure they're worried about us." He turned to Miriam. "Are you fit to ride?"

"So long as I can share your horse," she nodded. "I don't want to be alone again." Smiling, Martyn lifted Miriam onto horseback and climbed into the saddle behind her. They returned to the site of the battle, where Pylias and Jhorval were building a pyre on which to dispose of the Corsans' bodies. Kal and Sheriza were nowhere to be seen, but Treloran squatted beside Kaeille's unconscious form. Blood-soaked bandages covered the Aelvin woman's arm and torso, and she lay unmoving while Treloran daubed her head with a moist rag.

When Martyn saw her, his heart fluttered. "Oh, Gods," he whispered. He shot a nervous glance at Miriam, but his eyes instantly returned to Kaeille.

"Go to her," Miriam whispered. "It's all right."

"Not until you're cared for," Martyn insisted with a firm shake of his head. He scanned the camp for Sheriza, and when he found her crouching at the side of a fallen Corsan, one hand cupped to either side of the man's head and the wounded soldier weeping in pain, anger surged through the prince. He galloped over to her, skidding to a stop hands away from the Healer, and leapt from the saddle.

As they approached, the Corsan shuddered and went still; the pain left his eyes, and he wore an expression of calm contentment. Only when the man lay quiet did Sheriza look up. Her gaze danced over Martyn and settled on the princess. "Oh my," the Healer murmured when she saw Miriam. "You poor thing! What a nightmare you must have endured. Come here, my dear. Come here!"

Miriam did as she was told, casting one last, languishing glance at Martyn before approaching the Mage. Sheriza moved away from the Corsan and stopped before the princess. Her hands glided over Miriam's body, never touching but never more than a finger's width away. Martyn seethed throughout the examination, and when Sheriza sat cross-legged in the grass, bidding Miriam to do the same, he could no longer control his tongue. He gestured angrily toward Kaeille's prone form. "Kaeille—"

"Has already been attended to," Sheriza replied, not bothering to look up. Her hands hovered beside the princess' temples. "She will be fine."

The Healer's words disarmed Martyn. "Good," he muttered, and he started to turn away. When his eyes fell on the Corsan's slumbering form, his anger surged anew. "Then perhaps you could explain why you were wasting time healing our enemy when—"

Sheriza's eyes snapped open, and she fixed a glare cold enough to freeze water on Martyn. "Do not presume to counsel me on the use of my Gift," the Healer snapped. "And do not accuse an ally of treachery until you know the facts. I did not heal that man, though by the rules of my Order I should have. You would not begrudge anyone, not even your enemies, a peaceful passage, would you, Prince Martyn?"

Martyn looked at the Corsan again and noticed the man's motionless chest and bloodless complexion. Embarrassed, he glared at Sheriza, but the Healer ignored him. "Just relax, dear," Sheriza told Miriam in the sweetest of voices as she placed her hands on the princess' cheeks. "This may tingle, but it won't hurt, and I promise you'll feel much better when I'm done."

Miriam gasped, and her whole body went rigid, but when Sheriza took her hands away, the princess smiled contentedly before slumping into the Mage's arms. Sheriza lowered her to the ground and glanced up at Martyn. "She will need to sleep. Then we can start back."

His anger held in check by the barest of threads, Martyn nodded. He went to Kaeille, and the Aelvin woman smiled at his approach. "It's good to see you," she said. She sounded weak and tired, but Martyn saw that the bandages had been applied some time ago, and when one slipped down, it exposed only healthy flesh.

Kneeling beside her, Martyn took Kaeille's head in his hands and placed a forceful kiss on her lips. "I was so worried!" he told her. "Promise me you'll never do anything like this again! I was almost as worried for you as I was for..." Common sense returned at the last instant, and Martyn reconsidered what he had been about to say. "I was worried."

"I am your *advoutre*," Kaeille countered, her expression determined, "and *Ael Chatorra*. The princess' safety is more important than mine. Do not ask me to value my life above hers; to do so would violate everything I believe in, everything I promised you when we were bonded."

Emotions warred inside of Martyn. He worried about Kaeille, but he worried about Miriam as well. He loved Kaeille, he had loved her since the first time he saw her, but he cared for Miriam too, and the more time he spent with the princess, the more she worked her way into his thoughts. *How can I love two women? How could they both love me?*

"If you will not ignore her, then protect her," Martyn said. "We can't let anything like this happen again. Miriam needs someone to guard her, someone who can be with her at all times. I can think of no one better suited to the task."

Pride filled Kaeille's eyes. "She will never know harm while I watch over her."

"We must go," Kal said, appearing out of the tall grasses to the south. "There are more riders in the distance, and we are in no condition for another fight."

"Ready the horses!" Martyn ordered. He helped Kaeille to her feet. "We were supposed to be in Vela two days ago, and it's not polite to keep the First waiting."

Chapter 16

"There it is!" Martyn exclaimed, stopping his horse as he crested a hilltop. He stood in the saddle, a broad smile on his face. The others drew rein beside him and stared. Miriam gasped, and even Kal looked impressed.

The silhouettes of distant villages punctuated the plains below. Herds of horses roamed the countryside, and scores of wagons trundled down the three hard-packed roads leading to the river. The mighty river Alren cut a line of dark blue from east to west, widening as it neared the shore until the far bank was only an indistinct blur. A thousand vessels sailed the calm waters of Velani Bay. Small fishing boats and pleasure craft bobbed in the tranquil waters while Alrendrian Rakers, Royan Warships, and large ocean transports waited for berths in the city's harbor. Smaller transports and large, flat barges traveled the river, transporting goods from the interior of Houses Velan and Odara to the rest of Alrendria.

A black, crag-covered cliff dominated the far side of the bay, and at its summit, overlooking the harbor and the Western Ocean, stood a castle of pristine white, its tall spires and curving minarets a stark contrast to the dark, rugged landscape. Along the base of the cliff, innumerable docks stretched into the harbor like grasping fingers. Most of the docks held damaged vessels; blackened hulls, broken masts, and tattered sails lined the cliff face from one end to the other. Many floated limply, but the most seriously damaged had been hauled up on shore, where teams of shipwrights surrounded them, assessing the damage and affecting repairs.

What happened here? Has Vela seen battle? Anxiety spoiled Martyn's awe, and he wondered if bringing Miriam here had been a wise idea.

"We should keep moving, Your Highness," Dayfid said, interrupting the prince's dark thoughts. "Commander Jasova will be waiting, and none too patiently." The Guardsman's eyes flicked southward. "And the Corsans have been known to raid even this close to the city from time to time. I wouldn't want you and the princess caught in another battle."

"You worry more than Joam!" Martyn made a grandiose gesture that took in the entire countryside. "Do you see any Corsan raiders? Do you see *anyone*? A moment or two to enjoy the view will not prove disastrous." A sudden thought entered Martyn's mind, and he laughed out loud. "We're returning victorious from battle. Why should we sneak into the city like thieves when we should be hailed as heroes?"

"Arrogance and pride," Sheriza whispered. The Healer's eyes were on the ocean, and her words were quiet, as if she had not intended them to be heard. When Martyn asked her to repeat herself, the Mage did not hesitate. "More than one Alrendrian King has lost his life to pride. One would think they'd eventually learn their lesson."

Martyn glowered, and his hands clenched on his reins, but he managed to ignore the comment. He looked pointedly at Dayfid. "Let's not flaunt our presence, Guardsman, but let's not hide it, either."

Dayfid saluted and took his place at the front of the procession, his sword drawn, ready to defend his prince in an instant. "Miriam?" Martyn called, extending his hand. "Would you ride beside me? Word of your capture has certainly preceded us, and I'm sure the Velani are eager to see you safe." The princess took Martyn's hand, squeezing it once for comfort. Her attitude had changed dramatically since her rescue.

"Treloran? Kal? I want you at my side as well. I think it's important that we demonstrate our alliance." The Aelvin Prince and the Tacha's *Kranach* stared at each other for a moment, but they both stepped forward to flank the prince. With a smile, Martyn signaled his retinue to proceed. Sheriza and Kaeille fell toward the back of the procession with the Guardsmen.

No trumpeting fanfare announced their approach, and no one lined the streets to watch them pass. Of them all, Kal drew the most attention. It was not unheard of to see Garun'ah in Alrendria, but a few merchants recognized Kal as a Tribesman and were quick to point him out to their friends. One excited child pointed at Treloran and began jumping up and down, screaming 'Elf!' until the woman at his side forced him to be quiet and ushered him away, apologizing to Treloran for the insult. Even Dayfid drew a few eyes. Atop his snow-white horse, with his silvery armor glittering in the sunlight, he was the image of a knight, a picture torn straight from the pages of a children's tale.

Martyn and Miriam occasioned no comment, and they traveled through the villages without so much as raising an eyebrow. "It seems I'm not so well known in these parts," Martyn laughed, hiding his disappointment.

Sheriza sniffed. "One must travel one's land in order to be recognized."

"Lady Mage," Martyn replied, refusing to be goaded, "I assure you that my incarceration in Kaper was never my own choosing. Had my father allowed it, I'd have traveled the length and breadth of Alrendria these last few winters."

"Don't worry, Martyn," Miriam told him, stroking his arm. "In a few days there won't be a peasant within a hundred leagues who doesn't know you're here, and every one of them will swear they saw you ride through."

Martyn laughed at the princess' words and lost himself in her eyes. Only when they approached the docks did he return his attention to the road. Unlike Kaper and Grenz, no Mage-created bridges spanned Velani Bay, not even in the east where the river narrowed; the only way to cross the harbor was by boat. Martyn shivered at the thought—his last experience on a boat, the trip up the Celaan on the *River Falcon*, had not been pleasant—but he masked his discomfiture behind a facade of confidence.

A long, flat boat with low sides bobbed in the water. Though large enough to accommodate the entire party, water lapped at the sides of the vessel, sending salty spray into the air and slicking the deck. Martyn went to dismount, but the ferry master waved him forward hurriedly. "No need for that, m'Lord," the man said, bowing hastily. "Not unless you want ta." Nodding, Martyn urged his horse forward. The ferry master took hold of the reins and led Martyn's mount to the front of the barge.

"Oulian! Dinmar!" the lanky man shouted when Martyn's horse was tied to the rail. Two darkly-tanned and disheveled men appeared at his side. "Get the rowers ready, and make sure they look lively!" The two men raced along the sides of the ferry, calling out orders to the broad, bare-chested oarsmen. Out of the corner of his eye, Martyn saw Kaeille admiring the well-muscled workers, and he scowled.

"Ya'll be wanting ta go ta the main gates, m'Lord?" the ferry master asked.

"With all haste. My arrival was delayed, and matters require my immediate attention."

"Ya heard the man," the ferry master bellowed. "Snap to it, boys, and row like the Father of Storms is at your back!" The ferry lurched, and Martyn's stomach lurched with it. Grimacing, he closed his eyes, his hand clamped tightly on the pommel of his saddle. He considered dismounting, but a quick look down showed the rickety planks bowing under the weight and water seeping through the cracks. Martyn prayed the crossing would be quick.

Treloran looked almost as uncomfortable as Martyn, but no one else seemed troubled by the swaying deck. Kal strode boldly to the front of the ferry and leaned out over the rail to stare at the dark clouds hovering on the horizon. Sheriza and Dayfid argued over a wound the Guardsman refused to let the Mage heal. Kaeille stood in the stern, her eyes fastened on Martyn. The few glances he stole told him much. She longed to be at his side, and at least part of her resented that she was not, but she knew her place. Their eyes met for a moment, and a smile touched the Aelvin woman's lips. The sight of it made Martyn's heart skip a beat.

"Isn't this wonderful?" Miriam asked suddenly.

Startled, Martyn turned to face her, and the sight of the bay—the water lapping against the sides of the ferry, the much-too-distant shore—nauseated him. He swayed in the saddle, struggling to keep his breakfast. "Isn't what wonderful?" he managed through clenched teeth.

"Sailing!" Miriam exclaimed, throwing her arms out in an expansive gesture that Martyn was certain would toss her into the dark waters. "I mean, this is nothing like a true sailboat, but it's still a joy." The princess beamed, and Martyn could do nothing but stare slack-jawed. "Once we're married, we'll get ourselves a fine vessel and sail the coast of Alrendria—"

Miriam stopped in midsentence, and the smile faded from her face. She assumed a haughty air. "If I marry you, that is. I have yet to make my decision."

"I look forward to... sailing with you." Martyn hoped his smile looked genuine. The princess turned away stiffly, and Martyn stared at her, confused. Miriam's mood had been tempestuous of late, changing dramatically and without warning, but Martyn did not think she was angry with him. He sighed and decided not to approach her until she did not look capable of shoving him overboard.

They made the remainder of the passage in silence. Martyn's good humor slowly returned, not because he had finally reached Vela, but because land drew nearer with every stroke of the oars. When the ferry bumped against the dock, Martyn fought the urge to vault over the railing. He waited for the ferry master to drop the gate and handed the man a gold coin as he passed. "For you," Martyn said, laying the coin in the man's hand, "for such a quick and safe passage." The ferry master protested as he slipped the coin into his pocket, but Martyn waved him to silence and handed him a second. "For the crew. You've served your prince well."

"Prince?" the man repeated, his eyes going wide. "Aye, they have served well, your Highness." He bowed again before making room for the others to pass. Martyn led his party onto the road snaking along the base of the black cliff. They passed dozens of wagons laden with grains and other wares on the way to the city gates. A contingent of Guardsmen marched by in the opposite direction, patrolling the docks.

After a time, the road turned sharply, cutting between twin towers of dark stone and climbing into the city. Dayfid pushed to the front of the procession. "All hail Martyn Batai," he yelled. "All hail the Prince of Alrendria!" A Guardsman appeared as if from nowhere, holding the Rising Sun banner. The ivory standard snapped in the wind. The streets, which a moment ago had buzzed with conversation, became eerily quiet.

"Long live Prince Martyn!" one man cried, and the silence was broken as quickly as it had formed. A hundred times a hundred voices shouted in chorus. "Martyn! Martyn! Martyn!"

A column of armored Guardsman descended the hill. Jes rode at the front beside Jasova, carrying herself straight-backed and proud, her midnight black hair falling in tiny spirals around her shoulders. She bowed her head politely. "Prince Martyn, you honor this House with your visit. Vela is yours to command."

"Lady Jessandra," Martyn replied, taking Jes' hand and touching it to his lips, "This visit is long overdue. All my life I've heard tales of your city, but I can see they did not do Vela justice." A sly smile worked its way onto the Martyn's face. "I apologize for the delay, but Princess Miriam felt obligated to attempt negotiations with the Corsans." Miriam flushed and glared at Martyn.

Jes smiled at the princess. "Did she convince them of their foolishness?"

"No member of her escort will raise a hand against Alrendria again." The Guardsmen cheered, and Miriam looked even more embarrassed.

"You are well come to Vela, Princess Miriam," Jes said, greeting the princess as an equal. "We hope your journey was not too... exciting. Prince Treloran. Kal *uvan* Arik"—Jes bowed to each as she called out their names—"We welcome you to Vela also, and hope this will be the first of many visits by your Races." Martyn introduced the remainder of his party, and Jes greeted them warmly.

With the formalities complete, Jes bid Martyn to follow her into the city. They traveled the main avenue, a broad road that made a line as it climbed the steep hill of the promontory. Narrower streets, many barely wide enough for two carts abreast, branched off the main thoroughfare, winding between houses and shops of coarse black stone. A small fountain graced every intersection, and a stream of cold, fresh water spouted from the mouths of statues. Merchants and traders circled each fountain, their wares displayed in brightly-colored wagons. Innumerable parks with beds of multi-hued flowers and immaculately-trimmed shrubs dotted the city. Despite all the color, Vela had a stark, unnatural feel to it.

The people were as severe as their city. Most dressed plainly in sturdy outfits with little or no ornamentation. Their expressions were for the most part calm and unaffected, and they treated each other with a sort of subdued congeniality. The Velani had neither the grim determination found in Marin nor the fiery passion of Kaper. Martyn felt as if he were in a different land; Vela was as strange to him as Illendrylla.

Martyn's thoughts drifted to the extensive fortifications he had grown accustomed to in cities like Kaper, Grenz, and Marin. "Do you not worry for your safety, Jes? Your city seems open to attack."

"We have adequate defenses, I assure you." Jes waved her hand in a semi-circle that took in much of the city. "The ocean protects us on three sides, with cliffs steep enough to discourage climbing and high enough to render siege weapons ineffective. With House Odara and the Boundary to our north, we need only fear attack from the south, and the Alren has few crossings, all easily defended."

Jes pointed to where the road cut between two houses. The buildings were stout and unadorned, with solid oak doors and narrow, iron-barred windows all closed despite the heat of the day. The avenue narrowed as it neared the buildings, and an archway decorated with ornate stone carvings spanned the distance between the structures. A line of tightly-packed houses and shops stretched out to either side.

"Do you see?" Jes asked. "We've passed two other arches like this one, and there are more ahead. The walls of these buildings are thicker than most, and the facades that flank the road only appear to be stone." Martyn saw the hidden hinges as they passed underneath the archway, the thick gates coated with a layer of rock to disguise their purpose. "The buildings themselves are barracks, and each holds two squads of Guardsmen."

"An ingenious disguise," Martyn said, admiring the construction. "But what's to stop an enemy from bypassing the gates and using the alleys between buildings?"

"Nothing," Jes admitted. "Which is why those alleys lead to dead ends where archers can fire from protected positions."

Martyn laughed aloud, and even Kal seemed impressed by the subtlety of Vela's defenses. Martyn caught the *Kranach* examining the buildings closely as he passed them. "My regards to your architects," Martyn said. "The Velani are clever craftsmen."

"The Velani cannot take credit for the design," Jes replied. "Vela was built by the Darklord Bolshevan." The mere mention of Darklords cast a pall over the procession, and they continued on in silence. A few more questions came to mind, but Jes' brooding expression forced the prince to keep his thoughts to himself.

Eventually, they reached a solid wall of dark stone fifty hands high. Guardsmen patrolled the top in great numbers, and the gates were closed and barred. Behind the wall, the palace's towers stared down at them, gleaming white in the sun. The rearing stallion of House Velan flapped atop the highest tower, and the Rising Sun of Alrendria waved beside it.

"This palace is not the original," Jes told them after ordering the Guardsmen to open the gate. "Bolshevan's castle was torn down during Aemon's Revolt, the black stone and blacker memories destroyed by those he had oppressed. The Mage Assembly created this castle some winters later, perhaps to show the people the difference between the Assembly and the Darklords, perhaps because they, too, wanted to be reminded of beauty when they stood here."

As the gates opened, near-blinding light assaulted them. It took a moment for Martyn's eyes to adjust to the glare, and a moment more to realize the light came from the castle. The palace was immense, a collection of structures connected by covered walkways. The ivory white stone, smoothed and polished, stood in stark contrast to the dark rock around it, demanding attention. Flowering vines hung in tendrils from latticed balconies and beds of flowers grew beneath every window. Even the towers, one at each corner of the palace, appeared more aesthetic than functional. This was not the fortified keeps of Marin or Kaper, and Martyn wondered how well the castle would withstand an attack.

Gardens covered the majority of the grounds. A small vineyard stretched along one section of wall, the vines snaking up the stonework. Small orchards, the trees planted in precise arrangement, dotted the courtyards. Flowers and shrubs of all sizes and types lined the white-stoned walkways. "It's beautiful," Miriam whispered.

"As lovely as Lynnaei," added Treloran.

The others voiced their own approval, and Jes smiled politely, but Martyn thought he caught a hint of pride in the Mage's often inscrutable expression. "I know you're eager to hear reports of the war, my Prince," Jes said, "but there's one more thing I wish to show you." She led them around the palace, through open fields, around bushes trimmed into the shapes of man and beast, and past vast flower beds grown into scenes as detailed as any painting.

Martyn stared at the smooth rock of the promontory. As if reading his mind, Jes said, "It took centuries to make this ground fertile. Wagonloads of silt from the Alren are carted up to the palace each winter. Other gardens are scattered throughout the city. They were originally created to supply Vela during siege, but most have been converted to parks."

Behind the castle, an open courtyard converged to a sharp point as it neared the cliff edge. A low wall, no more than eight hands high, separated the courtyard from the edge of the cliff. When Jes pointed toward the Western Ocean, Martyn hurried to the wall to take a look, pulling a reluctant Miriam behind him.

When he reached the wall, Martyn leaned over the edge, and Miriam gasped as the prince stretched out over the steep drop. The palace stood more than a thousand hands above the surface of the sea. Sea birds nested on the craggy outcroppings of volcanic rock below. Several hovered beside the cliff with wings outstretched, using the strong updrafts to hold them aloft. Martyn called for Miriam to look, but the princess refused to get near the edge.

A stiff breeze gusted against Martyn's face, forcing him to squint. The harbor was to his left, where the broad, fast-flowing Alren opened into the placid waters of Velani Bay. The vessels, which had looked so large from below, now flitted across the waters like toys, leaving tiny streaks of white wake behind them. Stark cliffs wrapped along the coastline to Martyn's right. Villages identifiable only by the thin streams of smoke rising from chimneys dotted the shoreline, and others sat atop the cliffs. Narrow trails traversed the cliffs, connecting the two strings of villages to each other and to Vela.

The Western Ocean filled the horizon, uninterrupted except by a hazy line to the southwest. Martyn sucked in a breath. "Atol Domiar," he whispered.

"The cursed isle?" Miriam asked, swallowing nervously. Martyn nodded, but did not speak, and Miriam drew close to him. She trembled against him, and he put his arm around her for comfort.

"I know not of this place," Kal said, joining them along the wall. The *Kranach* stood with arms folded and stared boldly across the water, his eyes on the distant island. "Why do you speak of it with fear?"

"It is a haunted place," Martyn said.

"Raising the Boundary changed the weather throughout Madryn," Sheriza explained, filling the silence that followed Martyn's words. "We Magi had anticipated changes, but not the extent of them, especially not in this part of Madryn." The Mage's eyes glistened, and Martyn found himself pitying the Healer and her centuries-long memory.

"When the rains started, no one gave them a second thought. The Boundary required most of our attention, and though Lorthas had been imprisoned, a number of his ShadowMagi, as well as the Drekka and the Arkam Imperium, remained free. The Assembly focused their efforts on ending the war. We believed we could deal with the weather at our leisure.

"But a season passed, and then a second, and the rains did not let up. Water rolled over plains that a winter earlier had been dry and dusty. New streams formed and then flowed together, forming the Alren." Sheriza pointed to the river behind them, a monstrous blue snake empting into the bay below.

"This area was not always on the coast." Sheriza made a sweeping gesture that encompassed the Western Ocean. "Before the Raising, Vela overlooked broad valleys and fertile fields. The craggy cliffs around us were hidden beneath eons of soil, and Vela itself rose only half as high as it now does.

"Two great cities stood in the valley beyond. One had been ravaged by the MageWar, changing hands many times during the course of the war, but the other... Somehow, the other city—Paelin, I believe it was called—had survived intact, its buildings unmarked and its residents unharmed. And, at the edge of vision, dominating the horizon stood Atol Domiar, a majestic mountain covered in forest.

"A third season of rain came, and then a fourth, and the waters rose. Vela remained safe, preserved by fate and by virtue of the ancient stone beneath it, but the water claimed most of this region, cutting deep channels through the loose soil, carving new rivers and forming lakes in lands that had before known only drought."

Sheriza drew a deep breath, and it was a moment before she could continue. "The commons struggled day and night to stop the waters, to hold them back until we Magi came to deal with the problem. But we never came, and when the dams burst, water flooded the valley, carving out the cliffs you see today and burying the cities beneath sea.

"Many fled to Atol Domiar, and most made it there safely, but the mountain that was now an island had neither food nor shelter for the tens of thousands who sought refuge on it. The land was chaos, the ports washed away and all but a handful of sailing vessels destroyed in the storms that raged incessantly. By the time we Magi came to aid those stranded on Atol Domiar, less than a thousand survived."

"They starved?" Miriam gasped, her hand going to her mouth. "How horrible! Surely it couldn't have taken so long to mount a rescue!"

"It took longer than you might think, my dear," Sheriza answered sadly, "but you're right. The people on Atol Domiar did not die of hunger. With food and water scarce, and with no idea when help might arrive, they turned upon themselves."

Sheriza said no more, but her story left a pall over the party. "A sad tale," Martyn said at last, "and a valuable lesson. In these desperate times, when victory seems so out of reach, we must remember to stay united against our enemies. The day we turn upon ourselves is the day we lose this war." He turned to Jes. "Thank you for this. I have always wanted to lay eyes on Atol Domiar."

"It was not the view I wanted you to see," Jes admitted, pointing west. Martyn followed her finger but had to squint to see the small dots moving along the horizon. "Ships?"

Jes nodded. "They've been there for seasons, watching us and destroying any vessel that leaves the harbor unescorted."

"Are they Corsan?" Martyn asked.

Jasova shook his head. "Not like any Corsan ship I've ever seen."

"Then it's the others. The Black Fleet." Martyn eyed the vessels with a newfound curiosity. And fear. "If we could take one, it would answer a lot of questions."

Jes glared at Martyn. "The thought did occur to us," she said wryly. "Our attack resulted in the score of half-destroyed ships you saw in the harbor below. Six others were lost completely."

"More than a score of Rakers lost?" Martyn exclaimed. "How...?"

"Magi." Jasova spat. "Those ships have Magi on them. They rained fire and lightning upon us, made the waters rise and the winds howl." The Guard Commander's tone and the way he tensed every time he looked at the black ships made it obvious that he had witnessed the battle firsthand.

"Lorthas' minions, no doubt," Sheriza sniffed when Martyn turned his gaze on her. "The Assembly would never stoop to such meaningless violence."

"Maybe they should," Martyn said, and Sheriza's eyes widened. "If the Assembly won't send us help, Magi able to use their powers to kill, we'll be at a disadvantage against the Black Fleet." Martyn's expression darkened. "We can put this off no longer. Lady Jessandra, would you lead us to the council chamber?"

With a nod, Jes started toward the palace, and the others, save Sheriza, followed. Seeing the Mage walking away, Martyn moved to intercept her. "You will not join us?"

"You go to a war council," the Healer replied. Her nose wrinkled when she said 'war', as if the word itself was enough to nauseate her. "I will have nothing to contribute."

"Nevertheless," Martyn said, clearing his throat, "your presence would be appreciated. I value your insight. I don't want to waste lives unnecessarily, and I know the safety of my soldiers is your greatest concern." Seeing doubt linger in the Mage's eyes, Martyn extended his hand. "Please?"

After a long, thoughtful pause, Sheriza nodded. "Very well, Prince Martyn. If you think it necessary."

They followed Jes to a chamber deep within the palace. Maps, some ancient and tattered, others newly-drawn, lined the wall, and small tables piled high with books, charts, and more maps lay crammed against the walls. A large round table surrounded by a number of high-backed chairs dominated the room, and atop it, held down at the corners by daggers driven into the wood, was a giant map of House Velan and northern Corsa. Settlements and trails were clearly marked with fresh ink from a pot teetering on the edge of the table. A series of blue markers indicated Alrendrian garrisons and Guard patrols; red markers showed the position of Corsan units. The red vastly outnumbered the blue.

Only Martyn remained standing. He circled the table like a hawk, studying his companions as much as he did the map. "The Corsans are pushing deeper into our territory," he began, looking at the dozen or so red markers standing far beyond the Alrendrian border, "and their raiding parties travel even farther, wreaking havoc among our villages and instilling fear in our people. This has to stop!"

"Those monsters have more men than they should," Jasova said, his mouth turned down in a frown. "Murdir shouldn't be able to field an army this large, not without ignoring his other borders! The man is no fool; he must be getting help! But from where? The Royan fleet patrols the southern sea, and any reinforcements he receives by land must cross Alrendria first. Unless Midlyn has sided against us..."

For a moment, no one spoke. "Do you think our enemy comes from behind the Boundary?" Miriam asked. "That this Black Fleet is ferrying men to Corsa from *Ael Shataq*?"

"From there or Ra Tachan," Jasova said with a resigned shrug. "For all I know, they could be coming from here! Murdir is not selective of his allies; he'll take any man who can swing a sword, no matter their grudge against Alrendria." The Guard Commander's hands tightened into fists, and his expression turned grim. "I don't know where Murdir gets his reinforcements, but this I *can* tell you. Our lines are thin and getting thinner. Unless something changes soon, we're going to find Corsans camped across the Alren."

Martyn circled the table, his eyes on the map. "Nykeal commands the front?"

"Her and Subcommander Tieral."

"These are all villages?" Martyn asked, pointing to a series of black dots on the map. When Jasova nodded, the prince tapped a finger to his lips thoughtfully. "How many retired Guardsmen do we have available? Those too old to fight but not so old that they've grown weak-minded."

"Six score. Maybe seven."

"If we're to stop the Corsans, we need to devote our Guardsmen to the front and leave the villages to deal with any raiders that make it through. As we travel south, we'll assign an old Guardsman and a handful of recruits to each village. The old men can coordinate with each other and teach the villagers how to defend themselves. The young men can relay messages to the front. It will be a good way for them to gain experience without forcing us to put untried men on the line.

"You and I will visit as many villages as we can on our way south," Martyn told Jasova. "We'll recruit for the Guard, establish the militia, and ask the villagers to contact their nearest neighbors. If the villages stand together, the raiders will not find them such easy targets."

Martyn continued to circle the table until he stood behind Kal. Putting one hand on the side of the Tribesman's chair, he leaned in and studied the map. "Alrendrian scouts are good, but I've never seen anyone track like the *Kranach* of the Tacha. What I wouldn't give for a few score of your Hunters." The prince's eyes gleamed as he turned to face Kal. "I know your people face attack from the Drekka, but would they be willing—"

"The *Dar'Tacha* go where their *Kranor* commands," Kal replied, "and Arik *uvan* Hruta listens to his *Kranach*. I will send a message immediately, and you will have several hundred of our by best trackers. But it will take a season for a messenger to cross Madryn."

Martyn turned his gaze on Sheriza. The Healer pretended to ignore the stare at first, but she eventually relented. "I can arrange to have the messenger deposited somewhere in the Tachan Tribal lands tonight."

A broad smile split Martyn's face, and he inclined his head politely. "How long will it take your Hunters to get here?" he asked Kal.

The Tribesman frowned. "If my *Kranor* receives the message quickly, they will be here in a moon."

"That fast!" Miriam exclaimed. "The Tribal Lands are across Madryn!"

Kal flashed a toothy smile. "I will ask them to hurry."

"Excellent," Martyn said, wondering if his companions shared his excitement. For the first time, circumstances seemed to favor them. He moved to where Sheriza stared uncomfortably at the map. "How many Healers can you send south?"

The Mage's eyes grew distant and introspective. "I *can* send them all. I *will* send a dozen." Martyn opened his mouth, but Sheriza did not let him speak. "Before you argue, Prince Martyn, know that a dozen is not an insignificant number. It takes great discipline and sacrifice to be a Healer, and few among the Gifted choose this path."

Martyn raised his hands in surrender. "I was only going to thank you," he said with a broad grin. He started to turn away, but paused. "Do you think any other Magi would be willing to join us? Magi who can take a more... active... role in the fight. The ShadowMagi will tear my men apart if not."

Sheriza seemed poised to argue. Her eyes narrowed and her lips twitched, but she held her temper. "I will inquire, Prince Martyn. I can promise no more. The Assembly is against involvement."

"Again, you have my thanks." Martyn finally sat. He stared long and hard at the map. "We are in a desperate position," he said, trying to hide his fear. "Every day brings the raiders deeper into Alrendria, and every day sees Corsa claim more of our land. Our numbers are few, and our soldiers spread thin. We cannot hope to hold the line."

A grumble went up among the table; no one liked talk of defeat. "I have a plan," Martyn told them. "One that might tip the balance in our favor. But ideas are all I have. My experience is limited. That's why I've asked you here. I need your help, your advice, that we may drive the Corsans back to their homes and secure our southern border for the war ahead."

They talked late into the night, with Martyn first outlining his plan, and then the others sharing their insights. When they were finished, what remained was little like what Martyn had envisioned, but he knew it was far better. *I just hope it's good enough!*

"Select six hundred recruits," Martyn told Dayfid, "the best of them, and give them the Guardsman's Oath. Make sure they're properly outfitted and have them ready to march south in three days time."

"Yes, my Prince!" Dayfid said sharply, saluting fist-on-heart. He stood to leave, but stopped and stared at Martyn, waiting until the prince nodded before he spoke. "I want to accompany you south, my Prince. I want to prove myself in battle, not chase brigands through the fields of Alrendria."

"You *shall* accompany us," Martyn replied. "Your service has not been forgotten." Martyn turned to Jasova. "I want Guardsman Evana to join us as well. I believe I've a command suited to her particular talents."

"Treloran," Martyn said, turning toward the Aelvin Prince. "I've grown accustomed to having you at my side, but a more important task requires you to remain in Vela, if you'll take it." The Elf straightened, and green eyes met blue. "If we fail and Vela is attacked, our numbers are too few to survive a pitched battle. If Vela is to survive, we will need archers to man her walls. I have never seen anyone wield a bow like you; the best marksmen in Alrendria cannot match your skill. If you're willing, I'd like you to take command of the City Guard and the recruits' training. Prepare this city for a siege."

Dayfid whirled to face the prince. "You'd give control of our defenses... to an *Elf*?"

"This *Elf*," Martyn replied coolly, "is my friend and our ally. He is also *Ael Chatorra*, a warrior trained by the great Astalian. You will watch your tongue, Guardsman, and remember your place."

"My apologies," Dayfid said as he shrank away from Martyn's cold stare. "I was taken by surprise. My words were not meant as insult." Martyn dismissed the Guardsman with a wave, and Dayfid hurried from the room. Once he was gone, Martyn turned back to Treloran.

"It would be an honor," the Aelvin Prince said. "I will not fail you, Martyn."

"Then it's settled," Miriam said excitedly. "When do we leave?"

"*We* do not," Martyn replied. "You will remain under Lady Jessandra's care. She will teach you of Vela and Alrendria, and hopefully convince you of the benefits to be gained by our marriage."

"A task only slightly harder than defeating the Corsans," Jes whispered under her breath.

Miriam looked stricken. "But, I—"

"I will not risk you so casually," Martyn replied. "Your well being is too important to me."

At first, Miriam smiled, but suspicion quickly took hold and her eyes sought Kaeille. "She will not be going either," Martyn said, earning himself a cold stare from the Aelvin woman. "Kaeille will remain in Vela to aid Treloran and protect you."

The two women shared a look, then both faced the prince, each preparing an argument. "Enough!" Martyn snapped. "This is not a matter for discussion. I cannot do what I must if I'm constantly worried about you two." Chastened, the women settled in their chairs, not knowing whether to glower at Martyn or each other.

"That's it, then," Martyn said, standing. "We'll meet tomorrow to make preparations." Dismissed, the others stood and started toward the exit. "Jasova," Martyn called, waving the commander back. "We have a few things to discuss. And Kal, what I have to say concerns you as well."

Chapter 17

Quellas peered around the corner, his body pressed to the wall. For ten heartbeats, the Guardsman remained frozen. "Clear," he whispered before darting into the shadows. Jeran hesitated an instant before following, but he felt Yassik right behind him when he dove into the hole hidden on the far wall of the tunnel.

The trio crawled on hands and knees, their ears straining for sounds of pursuit, their hands feeling the way through the pitch black tunnel. When the tunnel widened enough that they could stand, all three sighed in relief, but Quellas urged them to move quickly. "Hurry!" he called through clenched teeth. "We're already—" The Guardsman's foot caught on a jagged stone, and he fell. His head hit the ground hard, but he gritted his teeth and kept from crying out.

A loud flash accompanied by a loud hiss brightened the tunnel for a moment before fading to a dull and steady glow. Jeran held the firestick high, careful to keep his eyes averted from the flame, and scanned the floor. "You won't get there at all if you're not more careful," he said, offering Quellas a hand.

They moved quickly until the firestick burned out and then were forced to continue in darkness, finding their way by memory and feel. They had traveled this path before, but with each branching of the tunnel Jeran grew less certain. He wanted just a glimmer of light, but even focusing his Gift could not dispel the gloom, and the darkness pressed in upon them.

Each time the tunnel narrowed, Quellas' breathing grew labored and his voice panicked. Soon, he could barely control his nerves even when the passage was broad enough for the three of them to walk side by side. "I felt another tremor last night," he said nervously. "What if the rock loosened?"

"This is a mountain, boy." Yassik gave the Guardsman a gentle nudge. "That tiny vibration you felt barely stirred the air."

"If you say so," Quellas replied with an anxious laugh. "You know more about this sort of thing than I do. I still wish we were meeting outside!"

"You're not alone in that," Jeran called over his shoulder. The wall on his left suddenly disappeared, and Jeran paused before turning down the new passage. "But if you're wishing, why not wish to meet in Portal... or Kaper?"

The banter helped, but eventually fear wormed its way back into Quellas' heart. "Why do we have to meet so deep in these Gods-forsaken tunnels anyway!" he demanded, nearly shouting. "There are plenty of places in the Barrows, or even in the *ghrat* where we—"

Yassik sighed heavily. "Must we do this every meeting?"

"Tylor's soldiers don't use these tunnels," Jeran said, trying to remain patient. "They may not even know they exist." He had made this same speech a dozen times, and it always reassured the Guardsman. Just not for long. "There are too many eyes and ears in the Barrows, too many people we can't trust. We—" A stone clattered, and Jeran fell silent. In the quietest of whispers, he urged his companions to hide. His own hand tightened around the makeshift cudgel he carried, and he crouched low, tensed for action.

"Lord Odara?" called a familiar voice. "Is that you?" Before Jeran could answer, a glimmer of light appeared, growing steadily brighter. Jeran kept a firm grip on his cudgel until Ehvan stepped from the shadows. "Thanks the Gods!" he said, smiling broadly and hurrying to join them. "I promised them you'd come, but after what happened last time, even I wasn't sure."

The smile Jeran wore faded. "That fool's idea is ridiculous." Even now, five days later, the memory was enough to make him seethe. "Attack the ShadowMagi? If we're to win our freedom, we can't throw away our lives in a pointless attack!"

"Grissam's just eager for the fighting to begin," Ehvan said. "Hiding and stealing bread isn't exactly what we had in mind when we talked of rebellion."

"I've known a few rebels in my day," Yassik said, "and the only ones who survived were the patient ones." The Mage made no attempt to hide his scowl. He thought this uprising was even more foolish than Jeran did, and he had no qualms about sharing his opinion. "If you want to be anything more than an irritating memory, you had best choose your targets with care."

Ehvan bowed his head politely, as he always did when Yassik spoke against the rebellion. "We should hurry. The others are already there." He started back the way he had come at a fast walk, quickly pulling ahead of Jeran and his companions. The flicker of the torch guided them, making the journey easier, and before long the tunnel opened into a large chamber.

The light from hundreds of stolen torches brightened the cavern like day, but the flickering lights could not penetrate far enough to illuminate the ceiling. Out of the darkness, stalactites appeared, hanging like giant fangs over the heads of the rebels. A small stream trickled from the wall and down a narrow channel to a pool at the center of the chamber. The babbling water echoed off the walls, filling the air with strange sounds.

Over a hundred people crowded the chamber, most of them hauling sacks stolen from the Barrows to one of the many piles spread throughout the cavern. The muted buzz of conversation stopped when Jeran entered, and dozens of weary eyes turned toward him. "I told you he'd come back!" Ehvan proclaimed proudly, preceding Jeran. "Lord Odara would never abandon us."

"Better for us if he had," grumbled a thin-faced man named Sorvan. A long, barely-healed scar ran down the man's face. "I'm tired of running every time someone sneezes. Grissam's right. It's time to take the battle to the Bull!" The murmuring returned, growing in volume until it roared through the cavern.

"Enough!" Jeran shouted, and the word fell like a hammer blow. "Do you not remember where we are? Have you forgotten that an enemy surrounds us, an enemy who would gladly see you dead?" He started toward the open area where they held their meetings, trying to keep in mind that these were villagers and craftsmen before him, not soldiers. It did no good; Jeran could think of only Reanna and his son, and what Tylor would do to them if he discovered Jeran's role in this rebellion.

Jeran sat on a crudely-fashioned chair and signaled for the others to join him. Quellas stood to his right, Yassik to his left. "I didn't seek you out," he reminded them. "You asked me to lead you. Remember that, and follow my orders, or I'll leave you to your fates." Nearly six score crowded around him, and not just those Jeran had selected for the rebellion. New faces, ones he did not recognize. Their presence concerned him.

"Another forty are interested in joining," Ehvan announced. "They are good and honest people, all of them, and we think—"

"Forty?" Jeran repeated. His scowl wiped every hint of smile off Ehvan's face and left the young man shifting nervously from foot to foot. "Do you not understand what's at stake here?" he asked, his eyes roving over the rebels. "One traitor, one thing said at the wrong time or to the wrong person will bring Tylor down on us. All of us and everyone we care about will suffer for what we're doing.

"Secrecy is our best weapon! Those of you who still work the mines must not talk about the rebellion. Our numbers must grow at a trickle, not a flood, or we'll draw the eyes of the Darklord." Jeran drew a deep, calming breath and turned to Ehvan. "Select the ten you believe to be the most trustworthy and assign them a task. Something that tests their loyalty and nothing that betrays us."

"Only ten?" Ehvan sounded disappointed. "What of the others?"

"Ignore them," Jeran answered. "If the slaves are talking about us, then so are the guards. Tylor's no fool; he must suspect what we're doing and he'll be looking for some way to infiltrate our numbers. If they're still interested after the next meeting, we'll consider approaching them."

Jeran let his gaze roam the chamber. A woman near the back of the group cringed when his stony glare passed over her, and she tried to hide behind those beside her. Jeran stared at her for a moment, and his frown deepened. "Thirteen deaths have been reported since our last meeting, and yet I see one of the dead in front of me. I wonder how many others might have survived."

"Eight," Orphain called out proudly.

"Is that all?" Jeran called back harshly. Yassik shook his head slowly. Jeran shared the Mage's frustration, but not his composure. "You couldn't save more? Why not arrange an accident for the entire Barrows? I doubt anyone would notice." This time, apologies followed Jeran's rebuke. "This must stop. No more 'accidents'! Do you understand?"

A mumbled agreement returned, and Jeran took it as assent. Ehvan handed over a parchment which Jeran inspected carefully. The map was crude, but an area of fresh ink on the right side drew Jeran's notice. "We've found no new passages to the surface," Ehvan told him, "but two that may cross the Boundary."

Jeran looked at Yassik. "I'll check them," the Mage said, unconsciously touching his collar. A broad grin worked its way onto his face. "Quellas can come with me!" The Guardsman cast a dark look at the Mage, but Yassik only laughed louder. "Look at the map, boy," he said, jabbing a finger at the parchment. "Those tunnels are big. We'll have a great time."

Ehvan cleared his throat, and Yassik quieted. "We've also found two more caverns with water sources."

"What about the three you've already found?" Jeran asked.

"We have cells stationed in each," answered a gaunt woman with stringy, close-cropped hair and tired eyes. Smears of dirt covered her face, and her clothes were little better than rags. She was one of the few brave enough to crawl through the unexplored tunnels. Jeran thought her name was Abiwan. "And enough supplies to last a ten day."

"It's not enough," Jeran told her. "We need half a season's supply in each, a whole season if we can manage it. And in these two caverns as well." He pointed to the spots on the map.

The grumbling started again, but Jeran silenced it. "Eventually, we will be discovered and forced into hiding. How long will we last without food? How easy will navigating the tunnels be without light? Stealing supplies helps us and hurts the Darklord far more than killing the pathetic fools forced to guard the Barrows."

Jeran turned to the map again. After a while, he ran a finger along a dark line cutting across several tunnels. "If this is the Boundary, "then this cavern should be very close to it. If it is, move our headquarters there." Ehvan nodded and took the map, and Jeran saw a woman he remembered from Keryn's Rest raise her hand to speak. Time had not treated her well; the warmth Jeran remembered was long gone, but at least when she looked at him, Jeran did not feel hated.

Before he could call on her, a man stepped into the light dragging a stooped figure. The prisoner's arms were bound by thick cord, and a smear of blood ran from his mouth. Jeran's frown deepened. "What's this, Makenna?"

With a strong shove, the prisoner tumbled to the ground and rolled to a stop in front of Jeran. "A traitor, Lord Odara." Makenna, a native of House Odara, ran goods from Norport to Portal until stumbled upon one of Tylor's patrols. Jeran had expected trouble from the former smuggler, but the brawny man was one of the few who agreed with his suggestions. "He was going to talk to the guards. I stopped him."

Whimpering, the prisoner crawled forward. "Please, Lord Odara! My wife is sick, deadly sick. I wouldn't have told them anything. I just wanted some medicine."

The man's desperation knifed at Jeran's heart, but he refused to be swayed by the words or by the terror in the man's eyes. That he had grown up with the man, that he had been friends with his brother, made what he had to do even harder. "We can't risk discovery, Frey, not for any reason. We can't allow our own desires to jeopardize everyone's lives."

Jeran closed his eyes for a moment, and when he opened them again, his gaze was cold and hard. "You did the right thing, Makenna. You know what has to be done now."

Frey's eyes widened. "Jeran! Please!" he cried out frantically. "Remember all the times you and Dominik took cakes from my mother's bakery? When we used to play Seeker in the woods by your uncle's farm?" He lunged forward and wrapped his arms around Jeran's legs. "I just wanted to protect my family! Please!"

Makenna cuffed Frey on the back of the head, and he fell heavily to the floor. Ehvan dragged him away from Jeran, and Makenna drew his fist back for another blow. "No!" Jeran called, rising to his feet. "We're not Tylor's soldiers, and I won't let you act like them. Frey made a mistake, and he must pay for it, but there's no need for cruelty. His actions were treacherous, but his intentions were not." Jeran met Makenna's glare. "Make it quick."

"NO!" Frey howled, and Ehvan clamped a hand over his mouth until someone ran forward with a gag. As Makenna led Frey away, Jeran turned to the others. "Tell Frey's wife that he died in a cave-in. I don't want this spoken of." He started to turn away, then paused. "Is anything we can do about her illness...?"

An old woman, one Jeran did not recognize, said, "I know where to find her. I'll see that she's cared for."

Nodding, Jeran faced Ehvan. "Makenna needs a new companion." Companions were Ehvan's idea, and one that had impressed Jeran enough to earn the young man a place high in the rebellion. Companions watched each other, kept each other from making mistakes, and reported mistakes when they were made. With few exceptions, Companions could not be friends, nor could they come from the same village or even the same Family; this ensured that the only bond they shared was to the rebellion and that any indiscretion would be instantly reported.

"I'll find one immediately," Ehvan replied. "We should keep an eye on him for a few days."

Jeran open the meeting to discussion, but most of the suggestions amounted to little more than complaints, and Jeran was forced to listen time and again to someone tell him how they needed to take more action against the Bull. Some advocated sabotage, collapsing mineshafts or destroying the forges, and a few wanted to do more, something that would strike fear into the heart of Tylor's men, something that would make them feel like heroes instead of thieves.

Grissam was the worst. He wanted to launch an assault against Dranakohr, and every day's delay made him more impatient. A dark-skinned, dark-haired man with a rough nature and cruel disposition, Grissam wore the brand of a Rachannen slave on his shoulder, though he had earned his freedom some winters ago by saving his master from thieves. He had repaid his former master by murdering him in his sleep and selling his family into slavery.

When Jeran counseled the rebels to remain hidden, Grissam pushed his way to the front of the assembly. "Now's not the time to cower like children; now's the time to take back our lives!" He wore all black, his clothing scavenged from the bodies of the dead. Even in the flickering light it was difficult to see him, he blended in so well with the shadows.

Grissam's words struck a cord among the rebels, and the man gained confidence from the support. He stepped to within an arm's length of Jeran. "The guards are undisciplined children. We're strong enough in numbers and spirit to kill them all, yet you bide your time. Look at them!" Grissam hooked his thumb toward the men and women behind him. "How much longer do you think they have? Unless that's been your plan all along. To make us rot in these caves so your master doesn't have to deal with us."

Jeran gripped the arms of his chair, struggling to maintain his composure. Yassik leaned in close and whispered, "A Mage's strength comes from his ability to harness his emotions." Jeran stood slowly, but before he could answer Grissam's accusations, another figure entered the cavern, making enough noise to alert anyone within a thousand hands.

"I did it!" the boy cried, smiling when his eyes found Jeran. Jeran had seen him before: Travor, a young man from one of the villages along the Boundary. He had been one of the first captured by the Bull and had all but grown up in the Barrows. Laughing, Travor threw something that hit the stone with a thud and rolled across the floor. It stopped at Jeran's feet. "I did it, Lord Odara!"

Lifeless eyes stared up at Jeran. Revulsion welled up in him like a tide, but anger quickly replaced it, a cold anger that seethed beneath the surface. Blood pounded against his temples. "What have you done?"

Travor smiled. "I saw him hiding in a tunnel, looking at something he had stolen"—Travor patted his pocket—"so I snuck up on him from behind. I threw his body into a chasm, but I thought I'd bring you his head as a trophy!" He raised his arms above his head and spun around, as if expecting cheers. None greeted him; only nervous stares and the sounds of retching.

"What happens when the other guards go looking for him?" Jeran growled. "Do you think they'll believe he ran away? You know how the Bull deals with deserters."

"It could have been an accident," one voice from the back of the assembly called. "Accidents happen all the time."

"To us," Jeran replied, "but how many of Tylor's guards have died? None since I've been here, except by the Bull's own hand." No one dared speak; unconsciously, Jeran seized his Gift, and though he could not use the magic, he felt it pulse within him. His eyes glowed with power. "Tylor wants an excuse to punish us. At the first hint of a rebellion he'll send his soldiers to kill us. His real soldiers, not the thugs guarding the Barrows!"

Travor shrank back. He licked his lips nervously and tried to stammer a reply. "But... But... But they'll never find him. I made sure of it."

"Leave the lad alone, Odara," Grissam said, clapping Travor on the shoulder. "I wish we had a hundred like him for every coward like you. I say we follow the lad's example and start killing these mongrels when we have a chance!"

No longer able to control himself, Jeran grabbed his chair and threw it. It hit the floor and shattered into a thousand splinters. "I wanted no part of this rebellion. You asked me to lead you, and I came. I did it to save lives. Yours. Mine. As many as I can. But I won't lead if you refuse to follow."

Ehvan opened his mouth to offer his allegiance, as did several others, but Jeran waved them to silence. "Discuss it after I'm gone. You can tell me what you've decided at the next meeting." Jeran stormed toward the passage to the Barrows. "Yassik, find out if those caverns are near the Boundary. I'll meet with you in the morning."

Jeran moved quickly through the darkness. Even with his magic-enhanced senses he could barely see, but he heard the steady dripping of water, the distant trembling of the ground, the high-pitched screeches of cave bats. These sounds reached Jeran's ears, and they made the caverns feel less desolate.

He longed to embrace his Gift fully, to feel the magic coursing through him, filling him with energy and life, and finally releasing with an explosion of power. Jeran laughed, though in truth he felt as if a cloud hung over his heart. *How long did I want to be normal? How many nights did I pray for my Gift to leave me?* Now that it was gone, Jeran wanted nothing more than to have it back, and the irony of that realization brought a rueful smile to his lips.

He heard the footfalls long before he saw the flicker of torchlight. Jeran stopped and waited for Ehvan to catch up to him. "How...?" The young man doubled over, drawing deep breaths and trying to find his wind. "How can you move so fast? I got lost twice trying to catch you, and I have a torch and a map!"

"What do you want?" Jeran asked harshly.

"We have chosen," Ehvan replied, saluting fist-on-heart. "We will follow you."

"I meant what I said," Jeran warned. "If anyone disobeys—"

"They will not, Lord Odara," Ehvan cut him off. "I'll make sure of it."

"Then listen closely. No one is to attack a guard except in defense of their life or the life of another. If anyone does, they will be dealt with severely."

"Yes, Lord Odara."

"I'm leaving you in charge, Ehvan. Make sure my orders are followed." Ehvan tried to refuse, but Jeran insisted. "This is not an honor, Ehvan, and it's not a favor. By the end of this rebellion, you'll curse me for doing this to you." Jeran offered the young man a thin smile. "But you're one of the few I trust, and I need someone who will keep the men in line when I can't be here. Use Makenna; he's a rough sort, but he's got a good head on his shoulders."

Trying to hide his pride, Ehvan saluted again. "I liked the idea of sabotage," Jeran added. "If ways can be found to disrupt mining without endangering the lives of our own people, have it done. In the meantime, continue to gather supplies and explore the tunnels. If we're lucky, we'll find another way out of the mountains. If we're not, we'll at least have hiding spots to run to when the fighting starts."

Ehvan's eyes flashed excitedly. "Will there be fighting, Lord Odara?"

Jeran sighed, wishing that at least one of the rebels was not eager to go to war. "More than you can bear," he answered. "More than you'll ever want to see again." He continued down the tunnel, and as he walked, he felt something, a nervousness, a fear that was not his own, and it both confused and frightened him. "The only question remaining, is how long until it starts." He thought of the ragtag group of farmers and crafters huddled deep within the mountains, quietly preparing for war. "If I were you, I'd pray it doesn't start any time soon."

Jeran hurried to his barrow, where he found Reanna laying upon his pallet. The Tribeswoman's eyes were open, and she had her hands pressed against her belly. "How are you feeling today?" Jeran asked, smiling when she looked up at him.

"Much better," she replied, patting her stomach. "Our little Hunter is in a good mood." Motherhood had erased Reanna's desperation. Jeran no longer worried about her taking her life. She stood, groaning as she did so. "I will not outrun Eirha Fleet-Foot for a few seasons," the Tribeswoman lamented. "If Sadarak Cat's Claw could see me now, he would change my—" Reanna's eyes widened in sudden surprise. "He moves! Come, Jeran, feel your son's strength!"

Jeran was at her side in an instant, pressing his hands against her abdomen. He waited for what seemed an eternity, and then he felt it, a pressure against his hands, gone as quickly as it appeared. He laughed aloud. "You keep saying 'he'. How can you know?"

Reanna eyed Jeran strangely. "I am his mother," she said by way of answer.

"You're starting to sound like a *Tsha'ma*," Jeran chuckled.

"What's all the laughing about?" Wardel asked, poking his head into the barrow. "Did you forget we were slaves again?"

"It's my son!" Jeran said proudly, half-pulling the Guardsman into the cramped chamber and shoving his hands against Reanna's stomach.

"By the Five Gods!" Wardel said when he felt a kick. His smile matched Jeran's. "I'm surprised you're not bruised!"

"He has Garun's strength," Reanna agreed.

"What will you call him?"

"Alic *uvan* Jeran," Reanna replied.

"If it's a boy," Jeran added.

Reanna cast another odd look at Jeran, then shrugged off the hands and donned her fur jacket. "These will not hide our son much longer," she said with a worried look at her stomach. "And if the weather warms much more, the guards will wonder why I wear them."

If Tylor finds out that Reanna is with child... Dark thoughts robbed Jeran of joy. Tylor would delight in making any child of Jeran's suffer, but if it were a son... The Bull blamed Jeran for the death of two sons; he would consider taking one from him justice. "We'll think of something," he promised, forcing his fears away. "With summer approaching, Tylor has been preparing for war. Perhaps he'll be gone before he learns about... about our son. If not, we can take you to live with the rebels."

"We have spoken of this, Jeran Odara." Reanna's voice held an edge Jeran had not heard for a long time. "Our son will be born free, under the stars, not buried in the bowels of this mountain."

Jeran sighed, but decided against another argument. "We'll think of something," he said again, patting Reanna's arm comfortingly. "I'm going to check on Uncle Aryn, but I'll be back before too long." To Wardel, he whispered, "Keep an eye on her?"

"Of course."

"I am not a child," Reanna snapped, "nor a smooth-palmed Human. I can care for myself."

Jeran backed out of harm's way. "But you have to protect our son," he smiled, "so there's no one to protect you!" He dove through the barrow entrance before Reanna could retaliate.

Jeran went to the Trophy Room, eager to tell Aryn about his son. When he got there, he found his uncle lying across the table, his face a mass of bruises. A trickle of blood ran from his lip and pooled on the dark oak. Jeran hurried to Aryn's side and was relieved to find his uncle breathing.

Using the pitcher sitting undisturbed on the edge of the table and a rag ripped from his own shirt, Jeran mopped the blood from his uncle's face. He carried Aryn to his pallet and cradled his uncle's head until Aryn's eyes fluttered open. "What happened?" Jeran asked.

Aryn pushed away and rolled to his feet. He stood in a half-crouch, his eyes scanning the floor for something to use as a weapon. He mumbled to himself, and tensed every time Jeran so much as shifted his position. "Tylor sent you."

"What happened, Uncle Aryn!" Jeran repeated desperately.

"As if you didn't know!" Aryn laughed. "But I'll humor you this time... *Jeran.*" He spat the name like it was a curse. "Tylor thinks you're up to something. When I wouldn't tell him what it was, he tried to beat it out of me. And when that didn't work, he sent you in to comfort me."

Quick as lightning, Aryn grabbed Jeran by the shirt. "I told you before; you'll get nothing out of me! Nothing!" He laughed, and Jeran flinched from the mad cackling. A Reading tried to force itself upon him, but Jeran forced it away. He had no desire to see what grim memories plagued his uncle.

"I only want to help," he whispered.

Before Aryn could reply, the door opened and an armored guard stepped inside. "Lord Odara," he said, bowing slightly. "The Master has sent for you."

Snarling, Aryn pushed Jeran away and started toward the guard. "Not you," the soldier said, pushing Aryn aside. "I said Lord Odara." When Aryn lunged forward, the guard cuffed him across the face, knocking him to the ground, then drew back his foot to kick.

Jeran pinned the soldier against the wall. "Lay a hand on him again, and I'll... I'll..." Jeran wanted nothing more than to kill the man, to tighten his hands around the soldier's throat and watch him writhe in pain as the life slowly choked out of him. *I'm no better than Tylor,* Jeran thought, and the realization disgusted him.

"The Master has requested your presence, Lord Odara," the soldier gasped.

Aryn's eyes bored into Jeran's back. "Now I know you're not my nephew," he yelled as Jeran left the room. "Jeran would never serve the Darklord!"

Those words cut deeper than any knife, and they followed Jeran up the long climb to Dranakohr.

Chapter 18

Doubts plagued Jeran as he walked the halls of Dranakohr. His meeting with Lorthas had not been pleasant. The Darklord had made no accusations, but something had danced beneath the surface of his fiery eyes, something that hinted at hidden knowledge. No matter which direction Jeran steered the conversation, the Darklord returned to the Barrows. His inquiries were casual, almost friendly, but Jeran suspected that Lorthas knew about the rebellion.

If Lorthas knows... Tylor suspected, and the Bull fueled Lorthas' misgivings, but even Tylor's suspicions were based on guesswork. *If Lorthas knew, I'd have worse than questions to face.*

His footfalls echoed hollowly in the empty hall. For a time, Jeran debated which upset him more, that Lorthas suspected the rebellion and his role in it or that the Darklord trusted him enough to let him wander Dranakohr unguarded. The irony did not escape him, and he laughed darkly.

With the onset of spring, Tylor's soldiers were growing restless, eager to leave this snow-covered tomb. The slaves jumped at every shifting shadow and stared as suspiciously at old friends as they did at the guards. Even the Orog were nervous. From the way the Elders watched him when he visited Grendor, Jeran thought they expected him to be the cause of any trouble.

He heard footsteps ahead and Jeran ducked into a side passage, trying to keep from sight. Two guards appeared, leading Ehvan between them. The young man walked with his head low and his eyes on the ground. Concerned, Jeran stepped from the shadows. "Where are you taking... him?"

The guards stopped. "To the Master, Lord Odara."

"The Master wants to make sure that conditions in the Barrows have improved," the second soldier said, glaring at Ehvan. When he turned away, Ehvan met Jeran's eyes and nodded slightly to let Jeran know he was well. "Don't know why it matters if slaves are happy, though."

"You'd best be on your way then," Jeran said, pressing his lips into a thin line. "Lorthas doesn't like to be kept waiting."

"Yes, Lord Odara!" They continued on, shoving Ehvan ahead of them.

As Jeran watched them go, he ignored the bile rising in his throat. *What have I become? They call me Lord Odara and follow my orders without question! Am I already the Darklord's creature? Do I serve Lorthas without even knowing it?*

"I tire of your excuses!" someone shouted. Jeran recognized the voice: Keldon, one of Tylor's commanders and another of the Bull's sons. "This makes the third caravan you've lost!"

Down the hall, Jeran found a door ajar and peered through the crack. Keldon sat at a desk, one hand on a mug, the other playing with a dagger. He glared stony-eyed at a fully armored but nervous soldier. "We were attacked!" the soldier said desperately. His eyes kept dropping to the dagger, and every time they did, Keldon's smile grew broader. "They came out of nowhere! Half of my men were dead before we could sound the alarm! The rest fled, but it's impossible to move quickly through the Darkwood with wagons. We *had* to abandon them, or none of us would have made it out alive!"

Keldon leaned forward, drawing the soldier's eyes. Whatever the man saw in that gaze, it frightened him more than the blade on the table. "I warned you about traveling through the Darkwood at night."

"It was midday!"

"And you still saw nothing?" Keldon's voice softened, grew more sympathetic, and the soldier seemed to think the change in tone did not bode well. He pressed back in his chair, swallowing nervously.

"The creatures moved like lightning! I saw nothing but glowing yellow eyes and moving shadows, heard nothing but the screams of my men. The men... They weren't just killed. They were savaged. You've never heard anything like it, my Lord. The ghosts—"

"Ghosts and monsters!" Keldon yelled, slamming his fist against the desk. "Is that your only explanation?"

"But, my Lord," the soldier said, his voice quavering, "you saw them too!"

"What I saw were Guardsmen from Portal, under the command of Lord Gideon Talbot." The soldier opened his mouth again, but Keldon raised a gauntleted hand. "I know what you think you saw, which is why I've been so lenient." As soon as the soldier relaxed, Keldon's lips twisted in a cruel grin. "But you push the bounds of my patience. You let Talbot slaughter your men like cattle and abandoned our supplies without so much as killing a single Guardsman."

Keldon's fingers drummed the desk. "You will gather more supplies and take them through the Darkwood. Leave tonight, and choose your escort from those who guard the Barrows. If the *monsters* attack again, we don't want to lose valuable troops." The soldier drew a shuddering breath, but he stood and saluted. "And Norvil," Keldon added before dismissing the soldier, "if the supplies don't make it out of the Darkwood, make sure you don't either."

Jeran put some distance between himself and the doorway, but he slowed when the soldier turned in the opposite direction and all but ran away. After that, Jeran moved randomly through the corridors, lost in thought. When he regained his senses, he found himself on a balcony overlooking the valley.

With the help of the ShadowMagi, Tylor's fortification had grown at an incredible pace, and Jeran marveled at the curved wall blocking the entrance to Dranakohr. Wagons passed beneath the stone arch of the completed gatehouse, their axles bent under heavy loads, and armed men patrolled the parapets. Only a few sections of wall remained incomplete, the stone supported by a skeleton of scaffolding. The fortification should be finished by midsummer, and any chance of escape would die with its completion.

The clang of metal drew Jeran's attention. His jaw fell open when he saw Tylor's army in the field, standards raised and ready to march. Row upon row of mounted men marked the front ranks, their polished armor catching the morning sun and reflecting it back toward the heavens. Giant horses wearing armor stomped the ground restlessly, snorting clouds of steam. Behind the cavalry, following the curve of the mountain, stood legions of infantry, rank upon rank in rigid formation, pikes brandished with casual ease, swords sheathed at the hip or bow slung over the shoulder.

In each squad stood at least one dark-robed figure. But where the soldiers' armor amplified the light, the ShadowMagi's robes absorbed it. They stood in tiny circles of darkness, and even their own troops kept distant. To Jeran, every one of them was more frightening than ten thousand armed warriors.

A horn's shrill note cut through the air, and with a cheer that thundered up the mountain and shook the walls of Dranakohr, Tylor began his march. The squads navigated around each other with practiced ease, and a chill entered Jeran's heart when he saw their well-disciplined maneuvering. "It's begun," he whispered, though he realized that this day was no true beginning. This was just the MageWar reborn, the end of a centuries-long ceasefire. "I wonder where they're going."

"Such matters shouldn't concern a slave," Katya said, stepping up on Jeran's right. The wind tossed her red-gold curls. "But you never really were a slave, were you?" She smiled, but the expression held no humor. "Sometimes I wonder if you planned on being captured all along."

"If you think imprisonment in Dranakohr was the best plan I could devise," Jeran replied, "I'm insulted."

For a time they stood in silence, watching the army pass beneath them. "It's an impressive sight, isn't it?" Katya asked, glancing at Jeran. "Even when it's an enemy army."

Jeran raised an eyebrow. "Enemy army?"

"Your enemy."

"Ours. Whether you believe it or not."

Katya turned south, to where the peaks of the Boundary jutted like white-tipped daggers into the cold blue sky. "Do you think he's all right?"

Jeran frowned. It was a long time before he spoke. "I think he's alive. But all right? I doubt he's been all right since the valley."

Katya pressed her fingertips against her temples. "He was magnificent," she said. "The way he charged down the hill, his hair blowing wild in the wind, that uncontrollable look in his eyes. I'd never seen anything like it." The silence that stretched between them held a sharp edge to it. "If only I hadn't been the cause," she added in a whisper.

Jeran gestured toward the troops below. "You're not going with them?"

"My uncle wanted me too," Katya answered, her tone flat. "He wanted me to lead the army, but Salos thought it wiser to keep me from the fighting. He thinks me poisoned by my time in Alrendria."

"And so you're to remain here?" Jeran shook his head and made a tisking sound with his tongue. "That must gall you."

"It's not the insult you might think. At my uncle's urging, I've been given command of Dranakohr in his absence."

"A great honor," Jeran said wryly, and Katya scowled. "But where would *you* rather be, Katya Durange? Here in Dranakohr, or marching with the army?"

"I... I'm not sure," she answered, a quaver to her voice. For a while longer, they watched the procession, neither willing to speak. "Whatever you're planning," Katya finally said, "you'd better do it soon."

Jeran's head whipped around, and his surprise must have shown because Katya laughed at him. This time, the laughter was genuine. "Now who's being insulting? Dranakohr seethes with tension; even those fools my uncle has guarding the workers can see it. Today, our army marches south, and in a few days, my uncle will follow to lead the attack against Alrendria. You don't think he'd leave you free, do you?"

"Why would he fear me?" Jeran shrugged, feigning indifference. "I'm his prisoner."

Katya rolled her eyes. "There's no benefit in letting you live. If you side with the Darklord, you will be placed above Tylor; if you remain loyal to Alrendria, my Uncle risks the whole of Dranakohr by leaving you alive. Either way, your being free, if you'll forgive the term, threatens him. He's looking for an excuse, *any* excuse, to remove that threat."

"Why does he need an excuse?" Jeran snorted. "If he wants me dead, he could just kill me. The Bull's killed before, and with far less justification."

"You do him an injustice," Katya snapped, her jaw clenching. "My uncle's not the tyrant Alrendria paints him to be. He's a man of honor! He—"

"—is a murderer and a coward," Jeran interrupted. "Hundreds have died by his whim, thousands at his command. He kidnapped and murdered my mother, razed an entire city of Magi for no other reason than they were Magi, and let Salos—"

The backhanded slap caught Jeran off guard. He reeled from the blow, but refused to give Katya the satisfaction of acknowledging it. Katya glared at him, her chest heaving with each indrawn breath and her eyes burning. "When the Scorpion murdered my mother, it was Tylor who comforted me. When my father realized I possessed only the tiniest hint of the Gift and abandoned me to the Boundary's merciless winter, it was Tylor who rescued me. He nursed me back to health, cared for me as his own!

"Is your soul clean, Jeran?" Katya demanded, pacing the balcony. "How many lives have been condemned because of your orders? My uncle's made mistakes, but he's not evil. He's passionate and—"

"Your uncle is a slave to his passions," Jeran said, struggling to keep his voice calm. Rage, his rage at Tylor, his rage at the world, threatened to overwhelm him, but Katya did not deserve to bear the brunt of it. She was as much a victim as he was. "When he's angry, he kills. When he's wronged, he seeks satisfaction through revenge. He behaves with honor and compassion only when the mood strikes him."

Katya tried to turn away, but Jeran grabbed her and forced her to look at him. "The true measure of honor is not how we behave when events suit us. It's not how we act when others are watching. True honor comes from within, and it dictates our actions even when the entire world has turned against us and no one will know that we've done wrong."

Jeran released Katya and she stepped back. "There's a difference between passion and obsession," he told her, letting his gaze return to the valley. "A difference between a virtuous act and a virtuous person. Don't confuse the two." The last of the cavalry passed through the gate, and the first ranks of infantry lined up to march. "Your uncle leaves Dranakohr all but undefended."

"Such matters should not concern a slave," Katya repeated, her voice cold and hard. Jeran sighed and turned to leave, but he made it only a step before she added, "But it might concern the leader of a rebel army."

Jeran turned around slowly. Katya's face remained inscrutable, and Jeran tried to make his own match hers. *She's only guessing*, he thought, he prayed, but something told him differently. "This morning," she told him, "A guard caught a scrawny fellow trying to steal a cartload of swords and took him to a secluded spot for questioning. I was drawn by the screams, and by the time I found them, the guard had coaxed most of the information out of the boy. All except your name; no matter how much he had been made to suffer, the boy refused to name their leader."

Jeran licked his lips nervously. "Tylor knows?"

"He suspects. But he doesn't know."

"But if the boy confessed—?"

"There was an accident," Katya said. "After the guard told me what he'd learned, the boy went berserk. He grabbed a knife. The two of them grappled... I'm not sure what happened, exactly, the room was very dark, but when the dust settled, both were dead."

They stood there, eyes locked, for a long time. "I have to go," Jeran said at last.

"Just remember what I said, Odara," Katya called to him. "Your time's running out."

Jeran ran through the halls, anxiety building with every step. If Tylor suspected, then Katya was right; the Bull would never leave him alive. The Barrows were no longer safe, for him or those who followed him. *I have to send the rebels into hiding!* Deep in the unexplored tunnels, they would be safe from Tylor's rage. Jeran had hoped—he had prayed!—that the fight for Dranakohr could be postponed, delayed until the rebels understood what was at stake, but time had always been against him, and his luck had run out.

Reanna will have to go too. Convincing the Tribeswoman would be difficult—Reanna feared the tunnels more than she feared the Darklord—but Jeran knew he would have to make her see reason. With her safe, he could do what he had to do.

Jeran turned a corner and almost ran into Quellas. The Guardsman, wide-eyed, jumped back a step. "Jeran!"

"Quellas?" Jeran looked up and down the hall, but the two of them were alone. "What are you doing here?" Ehvan's tired form, hunched between two guards, came to mind. "Did the Darklord summon you for questioning?"

Quellas licked his lips nervously and nodded. His eyes darted up and down the hall. Drawing Quellas close, Jeran whispered, "Tylor knows about the rebellion." The color drained from the Guardsman's face, and as Jeran related what he had learned, Quellas' skin grew paler.

"Stay calm," Jeran said when he had finished, squeezing the Guardsman's shoulder reassuringly. "Tylor only suspects. As long as we are careful—"

"I understand," Quellas said, pulling away. "I'd better go."

"Yes," Jeran agreed. "It's never a good idea to keep the Darklord waiting. I'll see you tonight in the barrow." Quellas left without another word, his steps quick and his eyes haunted. Jeran sympathized; meeting the Darklord was not a pleasant experience.

Jeran entered the uppermost level of the Barrows. No guards watched the intersection of tunnels; no voices drifted out of the darkness, no sounds at all, not even the constant clanging from the forges. A spike of fear entered Jeran's heart, and he could not shake it. He hastened his steps. Convincing Reanna to go into hiding seemed even more important than before.

A hand darted out of the shadows, clamping down over Jeran's mouth and pulling him into a hidden alcove. He started to struggle, but a familiar voice whispered, "I must speak with you." Grendor's slit-thin eyes were as wide as saucers, and smears of dirt covered his face.

"Now isn't the best time," Jeran replied, pulling free of the Orog's grasp. "Can't it wait?"

"I am afraid not, friend Jeran," Grendor replied sadly. "We must discuss this now."

Jeran frowned. "Is it the Elders again? I really don't have—"

"Not here," Grendor said. "We cannot discuss it here. Follow me." Grendor started down a tunnel that led to the *ghrat*. Jeran hesitated. He considered ignoring the request, but a single, desperate look from Grendor changed his mind. Sighing heavily, he followed, and the tunnels quickly grew black as pitch, the magical orbs and flickering torches dark. Jeran's fear returned. He seized his Gift, but even with his mind focused he could barely make out Grendor, a moving shadow in a sea of shadows. He relied on the Orog's vision to navigate them through the caves.

When they reached the *ghrat*, Grendor led him straight to the Elder's hall. More than three score Elders waited for him, sitting silently in a semi-circle. At Jeran's entrance, they turned as one to regard him, and he shrank back from the mixture of sympathy and anger that greeted him. "The Dark One's ears will not hear us here," Grendor said, stepping back so Jeran had the floor to himself.

Jeran bowed to the Elders. "I'm honored that you wish to speak with me," he said, hoping his voice did not betray impatience, "but we must make this brief. I don't have much time."

"You don't have any time," Zehna scowled. Despite himself, Jeran swallowed nervously. "You squandered the time the Gods gave you, and now you have brought Their wrath down upon us all. My only hope is that your transgressions do not send my people screaming into the Nothing."

"Tana!" Grendor exclaimed, returning to Jeran's side. "You promised no accusations! The enemy of our enemy is our friend, and no one is more the Dark One's enemy than Aemon and his kin."

"You should choose your companions more wisely," the aged Orog countered. "You seek honey where only wasps fly."

"Enough!" Jeran thundered. Grendor jumped, but Zehna simply turned her disapproving glare from her grandson to Jeran. "I don't have time to listen to this. If you have something to tell me, do so!"

"The Dark One's second, the Bull, has been amassing troops all day."

"I saw them," Jeran nodded, his patience at an end. "They marched this morning. The war has begun."

"No!" Grendor said desperately, grabbing Jeran's shoulders. Jeran winced; he felt as if the Orog might crush him. "The Bull has been amassing troops in the *ghrat*!"

Jeran felt his strength ebb. Grendor's grip was the only thing that kept him standing. His mouth worked, but no words came out. "The man you call the Bull has learned of a rebellion," Lorana said, approaching Jeran. "Swordsmen have been filtering into the *ghrat* all day, in small numbers so as not to arouse suspicion. We were confined to our *lientous*, told not to step outside on penalty of death." Her eyes darted toward Grendor, and the young Orog shrank away from Lorana's glare. "But Grendor listens to our captors almost as well as he listens to his Elders."

Grendor's cheeks darkened, but he said nothing. Jeran tried to pull away. "I... I..." He struggled to find the words, any words, but his mind felt sluggish, and the world seemed to move too slowly. "I have to go," he managed. "I have to warn the others."

"Be quick, friend Human," Lorana counseled. "The men below grow restless. They will move before much more time has passed."

"If the Orog suffer from your foolishness," Zehna added in a hoarse croak, "you had better hope the Bull-man finds you before I do."

"Enough, Zehna," Craj, the Eldest, said. "The young man has enough to burden his soul without adding the threats of an old woman." The withered Orog turned his sightless eyes on Jeran. "Go, friend. May the peace of the Mother shelter you."

Jeran ran blindly through the tunnels, relying as much on memory as on his magic-enhanced senses. When the first screams echoed in his ears, he knew he was too late, but the fate of his countrymen no longer mattered. He heard a piteous cry to his left, a woman's voice begging for mercy, but he ignored it. Only two lives mattered to him: Reanna's and his son's.

Two shapes lurched out of the shadows, running toward the screams, and Jeran, his hands clenched into fists, turned to attack. "Jeran!" Wardel cried out. The Guardsman raised his hands, palms forward, and backed away. Yassik showed less of a reaction, but the Mage saw something in Jeran's eyes that worried him. "Is it a quake?" Wardel asked.

"Tylor knows," Jeran whispered, his voice hoarse. Wardel's face paled, and Yassik mouthed a prayer. "Yassik, hurry to the Barrows and tell everyone to stay in their chambers. The Darklord needs slaves to keep these mines operational. The soldiers won't kill anyone who doesn't put up a fight."

Yassik ducked his head and ran off, his ragged, dirt-smeared robes flapping behind him. Jeran turned to Wardel. "Find Ehvan and tell him to take the rebels into the tunnels, as deep as they can go and as close to the Boundary as they can manage. If we fight now, all is lost. We must go into hiding; that's our best chance for victory."

"What about you?" Wardel asked. "What are you going to do?" The screams were growing louder and more numerous, and now the clanging of sword and the harsh laughter of the Bull's soldiers mixed in to the melee.

"I'm going to get Reanna. We'll meet you in the tunnels." Wardel saluted and ran down the tunnel. Jeran resumed his frantic run to the barrow, where he prayed Reanna would be waiting.

A woman appeared before him, running blindly, arms outstretched and her head craned over her shoulder. She hit Jeran with a thud, screaming as she fell. Huddled on the floor, she wept, refusing to look at him. A dark-armored soldier followed a few steps behind, a sword in one hand and a sputtering torch in the other. Seeing Jeran, the man charged.

At the last instant, Jeran twisted. He felt the blade slip past him, scoring a scratch across his midriff. Grabbing the soldier's arm, Jeran continued to turn, using his momentum to send the soldier crashing into the wall. The man fell beside the crying woman, and Jeran stooped to retrieve his sword. He looked at the fallen soldier for a moment, then his jaw tightened and he drove the blade into the man's chest. The soldier shuddered, then went still.

Jeran pulled the woman to her feet. "Return to your barrow. Do not fight. If you do what they say, I doubt they'll hurt you. Understand?" The woman did not respond, not so much as a nod, and Jeran gave her a shove. "Go!"

The woman lurched to a run, but Jeran did not wait to see if she followed his instructions. He resumed his own run, stopping only to cut down any soldiers who happened across his path. He heard voices in nearby tunnels, men and women fighting Tylor's troops or fleeing and begging for their lives. He ignored them; even those slaves who crossed his path he barely acknowledged, yelling for them to return to their barrows as he shouldered past.

The flickering light of a torch greeted him at his barrow, and Jeran dove inside. "Reanna!" The common room was empty, but their items were undisturbed and there was no sign of a struggle. "Reanna!" Jeran called again, dropping to his hands and knees so that he could crawl into their sleeping area. "We have to go!"

To his relief, Reanna slept soundly on her bedroll. He scrambled to her side and caressed her cheek. "Reanna?"

"Wha–?" Reanna stirred, and when her eyes opened, she jumped. "You startled me, *bahlova*. I did not expect you back so soon." Her cheeks turned red. "I am shamed. You should never have gotten this close without me knowing. This son of yours does the strangest things to me."

"We must hurry," Jeran urged, pulling her from the pallet.

Her smile disappeared. "What is wrong?"

"Tylor knows of the rebellion. His troops are scouring the Barrows, attacking anyone who resists. If we don't flee, I'm certain we'll meet with some accident by morning."

Reanna frowned. "You want to take me into the tunnels."

"That is the only place where you'll be safe. Our people know them much better than Tylor's. We can hide for seasons without being found. We may even be able to find another path to the surface." Reanna's expression grew dark, and she opened her mouth to protest, but Jeran would not allow it. "No!" he snapped. "No more arguments. We must go. For our son."

Though the look she gave him would have killed most men, Reanna nodded submissively. "For our son," she whispered. Jeran crawled to the common area first and then turned back to help Reanna. In her condition, navigating the narrow passage was difficult; she was forced to back out on her hands and knees.

Once she was out, he helped her to her feet. "You are well?" he asked, noting Reanna's pained expression.

Reanna waved away Jeran's offer of help. "Alic does not like this commotion. He was happier napping." One hand went to her stomach, and she closed her eyes, drawing slow, deep breaths.

"Are you ready?" Jeran asked, an edge of desperation in his voice.

"Let us go, *bahlova*," Reanna said, "before I change my mind." They turned to leave, and found themselves face to face with Tylor Durange.

The Bull looked surprised. "How fortunate," he said. "Now I don't have to waste time hunting you down." The Bull moved forward slowly, as if stalking prey. A number of guards crowded the entrance to the barrow behind him. A smile spread across Tylor's face, pulling at the scar that ran out from beneath his eye patch. "Jeran, you have no idea how long I've waited for this."

To his guards, he said, "Take them. Alive."

Chapter 19

"There's no need for this," Jeran said, lowering his sword. Reanna tried to push past him, but Jeran pinned her to the wall. He kept his body between her swelling abdomen and Tylor's line of sight. "We will go peacefully."

Tylor leaned back and folded his arms across his chest. In his ebony armor, the Bull all but faded into the shadows. He watched Jeran with a casual, unconcerned air. "You must think me a fool, if you believe I'd waste this opportunity."

"Lorthas will not—"

"Lorthas grows tired of your games," Tylor snapped. The corners of his lips pulled up in a grin. "Besides, the Darklord is trapped behind the Boundary. I am not." The Bull signaled, and his guards began to crawl into the chamber. "You have a great deal to pay for, Odara, and I have come to collect."

"Lorthas has allies on this side of the Boundary," Jeran replied. He heard desperation in his voice. "If you think you can kill me without facing his wrath, then—"

"Kill you?" Tylor repeated, confused. "Who said anything about killing *you*?"

Jeran glanced nervously over his shoulder. Reanna quivered against the wall, but not in fear. Her eyes burned with the fire of the Blood Rage. "I will not be soulless anymore," she spat, her muscles tensed for action.

Jeran held her, though it took most of his strength to do so. "For Alic," he whispered, careful to keep his words low. "Remember Alic."

"Sadly," Tylor said, drawing Jeran's attention, "I can't afford much delay. I won't get to enjoy this as much as I hoped." He signaled again, and a black-robed form stepped into the barrow. "Dolbaer, the tunnels." The ShadowMage's eyes went black for a moment, and then a rumbling filled the barrow. In a shower of stone and debris, the tunnels to the sleeping chambers collapsed.

"Seize them," Tylor commanded, and his soldiers surged forward. "Try not to kill the Tribeswoman," he added offhandedly, "if it can be avoided."

Jeran threw himself forward, but Reanna was faster. She drew a small knife from her clothes and fell upon the nearest guard. A wild growl escaped her lips as she sliced the man's throat, and the other soldiers backed away. Jeran took advantage of their hesitation and drove forward, his blade a whirlwind that pushed the soldiers back even faster. *If I can get us into the tunnels, Reanna might be able to get away.* Saving her and Alic were all that mattered; if he had to die, Jeran considered the price well worth it.

The ShadowMage pointed at Jeran, but Tylor waved for him to stop. "That won't be necessary," the Bull said. "The situation is under control. You may return to Dranakohr." The black-robed Mage had trouble hiding his surprise, but he bowed stiffly and left, pushing through the guards crowding the entryway.

Half a dozen men were in the barrow and more waited in the tunnels outside. Reanna grappled with two. With every swing of his sword, the certainty that escape was impossible grew, and Jeran felt the cold hand of defeat squeeze his heart. His eyes, narrowed to razor-thin slits, fastened onto Tylor. *If he dies, Reanna will be safe. And if I die, Tylor will have no further grudge against them.*

Jeran drove the soldiers toward the tunnels while Tylor watched from his place against the wall, unprotected, seemingly unconcerned. When he was close enough, Jeran pivoted and lunged for the Bull. "Durange!" he yelled, his sword swinging for Tylor's chest.

The blade hit with a thud, and a numbing pain reverberated up Jeran's arm. His blow struck just below Tylor's ribcage, and the force of it made the Bull grunt, but the blade did not so much as scratch the black mail. "An ingenious ploy," Tylor said, wresting the blade from Jeran's grasp. "You're an exceptional swordsman, Odara. Maybe even better than your father." The Bull ran a finger down the side of his armor, inspecting it carefully. His grin returned. "Forged by my MageSmith. It's more artwork than armor, and far more uncomfortable than I like, but it does have its advantages."

Jeran made no effort to fight as Tylor's soldiers surged into the barrow. He did not see Tylor's back-handed blow until it was too late. The steel gauntlet hit just beneath his jaw, launching Jeran from his feet. His head slammed against the floor with a jarring impact, and the world spun.

When Jeran woke, he found himself bound hand and foot beside the barrow's exit. Only two soldiers remained, one standing to either side of him, their swords drawn and their eyes focused on him as if he still posed a threat. Across the room, Tylor sat on a chair brought down from Dranakohr, slowly and methodically sharpening a dagger. He no longer wore the cumbersome black armor. In fact, he looked like a different man. Gone were the dark and brooding expressions; he wore a light smile and his eye danced with newfound exuberance.

Reanna lay stretched across a table inclined so that her feet were nearer the floor than her head. Thick chains bound her hands and feet, and twin straps wrapped across her middle, holding her in place. "Tylor," Jeran croaked. "Tylor, please don't do this."

"Jeran," the Bull greeted him warmly. He lifted his dagger and inspected it closely, twisting it back and forth so it would catch the light. "I was worried you'd sleep through the interrogation."

Bile rose in Jeran's throat, and his chest constricted painfully. Every movement sent spikes of pain through his head and chest. "She's done you no wrong," he said, his voice pleading for compassion. "You're a better man than this, Tylor. Don't exact your revenge on the innocent; it's me you really want."

The Bull set the dagger down and stood. He paced the chamber slowly. "You think this pleases me? I get no pleasure from torture, especially not from torturing women! This is Salos' passion, not mine, but I have no choice." The smile disappeared as Tylor stooped to retrieve the dagger.

"You don't have to do this!" Jeran shouted desperately. "I'll tell you what you want to know! I'll do whatever you want! I swear it!"

Tylor ran a hand along his chin. "If only I believed you." He knelt beside Jeran so they could see each other eye to eye. He remained that way for some time, silent, eyes locked. For a moment, Jeran felt hope surge. Then it faded. Tylor leaned in close. "I know about the baby. I know about your son."

Jeran drew in a ragged breath. "Have mercy!" he begged. "Do what you want to me, to Aryn, to anyone who's wronged you. But leave the child alone. He's innocent!" A tear traced a path down Jeran's dirt-smeared cheek. At that moment, he would have done anything, promised anything, to save Reanna and his son.

Tylor's face hardened. "What mercy did you show Batra?" he demanded, contempt in his eye. "What mercy did you show Grysbin?"

"I had no grudge against them," Jeran said. "Their deaths were accidental. I didn't even know they were your sons!"

"They are dead!" Tylor returned. "And their deaths must be avenged. An eye for an eye, Odara." He started toward Reanna, who stirred. Halfway to her, Tylor paused. His eyes tilted toward the roof of the barrow, and the Bull appeared to consider something. "This will end the feud, Odara. Your son's sacrifice will cleanse the bad blood between our families. You are not wholly evil; in time, I think we could even learn to respect each other."

Tylor watched Jeran, waiting for him to agree, to willingly give over the life of his child for a feud he had not started. Rage welled up from deep within, and in a cold, harsh whisper, Jeran said, "If you hurt them, you will die by my hand, and the pain you suffer before that will make an eternity in the Nothing seem like bliss."

"Now who's being unreasonable?" Tylor asked with a heavy sigh.

Jeran struggled against his bonds, but the sturdy cord held him tight. "Send in the traitor," the Bull called out. Footsteps echoed down the silent tunnel. Outside the barrow, they paused, and irritation flashed across the Bull's features before the steps resumed and Jeran heard the sounds of someone crawling into the barrow.

"Quellas?" Jeran asked when the Guardsman appeared. Quellas could barely look at him; he kept his eyes carefully averted from both Jeran and Reanna. *Quellas? He's a friend!* Then, a darker thought occurred. *He knew about the rebels. He knew about my son!* They had been betrayed, completely and utterly, and Jeran blamed himself for not seeing it.

"I'm sorry," Quellas whispered, his voice trembling. "If I thought we had a chance, I'd have led the fight to take Dranakohr. I don't want to be the Bull's slave." Quellas' face paled, as if he had just remembered that Tylor was present, but if Tylor had heard, he paid it no heed.

"The first cut is yours, traitor," Tylor said, holding out the dagger. Quellas' eyes widened. "It's your final test. Pass it, and you can join my ranks as a commander."

Quellas stepped back, and Tylor forced the blade into his hands. The one-time Guardsman's eyes fell to the dagger, then shifted to Reanna, and finally fell on Jeran. "I can't," he said, his voice trembling.

"You will," Tylor told him, his voice hard, "or you will join her on the table."

"Touch her," Jeran said in a voice to match the Bull's, "and you will beg for Tylor to be the one to kill you."

Quellas hesitated, but a Jeran bound and helpless could not compete with the Bull of Ra Tachan armed before him. He approached Reanna, and as he did, the Tribeswoman's eyes fluttered open. When she saw Quellas, a smile momentarily brightened her face, but then she realized she was bound and saw Tylor looming over Quellas' shoulder. "*Onahrre!*" she spat. "How can you betray your friends? How can you betray your people?"

"I'm sorry," Quellas replied. Reanna thrashed on the table, but the chains held her securely, and she could do little more than shift her position a finger's breadth. Kneeling at her side, Quellas extended the blade in a quivering hand. "I'm sorry..." he repeated. "I'm sorry." He sliced a shallow gash across her arm, and when blood oozed from the wound, Quellas blanched. He turned to Tylor.

"You are pathetic," Tylor said, snatching the blade away. "Return to Dranakohr. Your rooms await you." With one final, apologetic glance at Jeran, Quellas darted from the barrow.

Tylor glanced at the blade, now red with blood, and then reached into his shirt to withdraw a vile of thick, pungent liquid. "This is something of my brother's," he told Jeran, turning the bottle over in his hand. "It makes the tiniest cut feel like the most grievous of injuries." He uncorked the vial and a strong, acrid scent filled the room.

Jeran struggled so much that the guard to his right hit him several times to subdue him. Jeran ignored the blows; at the moment, only Tylor had the means to harm him. Without warning, his Gift rushed into him, heightening not only his senses, but his emotions as well. Guilt... desperation... regret... those and a hundred other feelings flooded Jeran, but anger eclipsed them all, exploding from him in a violent frenzy. He pulled against the cords that bound him until his wrists and ankles bled; he tried repeatedly to harness his Gift, to use magic to stop Tylor, but his collar thwarted each attempt to use the flows of energy around him. Failure increased his frustration until Jeran writhed on the ground like a wild beast.

Leaning over Reanna, Tylor cut a small gash on the Tribeswoman's other arm. Snarling, she spat at him, clawed at him, her teeth gnashing. "Your torture will not break me. I am Reanna *uvan* Isbek, Snow Rabbit of the Afelda! You will be long in your crypt before I give you the satisfaction of—"

Reanna's speech cut off abruptly, and her eyes widened in pain. Frothy spittle foamed at the corners of her mouth, and she trembled. Tylor seemed impressed. "Salos told me it was potent, but I never expected this." He watched Reanna's reaction. She did not scream, and in a couple of moments, her breathing calmed and the fire had returned to her eyes. "Ah well," Tylor sighed as he extended the blade, "as a commander, one must learn patience."

"Tylor!" Jeran begged. "End this now!"

"End it?" the Bull repeated, a broad smile spreading across his face. "Why, Jeran, we've only just begun."

Tylor was slow, even tentative at first. He placed every cut with precision. After every touch of the dagger he waited to see Reanna's reaction, to watch the noble Tribeswoman thrash and writhe as Salos' poison did its work. The two guards beside Jeran grew nauseated by the proceedings. One turned away, retching loudly, and refused to look in Reanna's direction. The other kept his head down and his eyes on the floor. Even Tylor sometimes looked troubled. From time to time he looked at the dagger in his hands with disgust, but whenever doubt returned, he had but to look at Jeran to renew his determination.

Throughout it all, Reanna did not cry out. Drawing on every ounce of will, she endured the pain. Each cut paled her flesh and brought tears to her eyes, and she gritted her teeth and growled as the poison burned through her body, but she refused to scream, depriving Tylor of his greatest satisfaction.

Jeran screamed enough for the both of them. He screamed until his throat was raw and bloody. His cries echoed through the Barrows, and those who heard them buried themselves in their pallets, hoping to block the tortured sound with the thick fur of their bedrolls. The sound even reached the *ghrat*, where the Orog hung their heads and prayed for the soul of Aemon's kin.

Through a haze, Jeran watched Tylor torture his lover and the son he had never known. He felt every wound as if they had been placed upon his own flesh, felt the burning agony of the poison as if it worked through his own veins. He wanted to help them but could do nothing except beg for forgiveness. As he watched the life ebb from Reanna's body, Jeran felt an emptiness build in his heart, a hollow pit of failure and regret.

Once, he saw Reanna staring at him with pity, her own pain forgotten. She, with her clothes blood-soaked and tattered, with her once sun-bronzed skin pale and savaged with a criss-crossing of inflamed wounds, stared at him as if his suffering was worse than her own. Seeing that, Jeran's self-loathing grew until he could no longer bear it.

"Stop!" Jeran said in a croaking whimper, his hand stretched out imploringly. "I'll do anything! Swear anything! But I beg of you, stop this now."

Tylor paused, the tip of his blade hovering over Reanna's chest, and he tapped his lips. The Bull savored the moment, relishing the sight of a vanquished foe begging for mercy.

"Do not do this!" Reanna shouted, and her voice carried such ferocity that it stunned Jeran. "I am not—"

"I will do whatever it takes to end this," Jeran said flatly, cutting Reanna off. Tylor turned to face him. "I will swear myself to the Darklord," Jeran told him, "or to you. I will be your slave, will serve however you desire. *Do* whatever you desire."

"NO!" The scream Tylor could not force from the Tribeswoman with a night of torture Jeran had drawn forth with a handful of words. "Do not give up your soul for me! For us!"

Jeran turned tear-filled eyes on Reanna. "I have no soul. I would rather live as a slave in a world with you than as a king in a world where I had killed you."

"Your pain speaks, *bahlova*, not your heart. I know that." Reanna reached toward him, her arm straining against the cold iron bonds. "By serving this *dra'kalath*, by serving evil of any kind, you betray yourself, me, and your son. I cannot allow you to make such a mistake."

Jeran refused to listen. Again he begged Tylor to take him as a slave, but his eyes remained on Reanna, begging her to understand. Using what little strength remained, she turned away from him. As her eyes passed the entrance to the barrow, Jeran saw something cross her face. Her pain melted away and she smiled a toothy, happy smile. The smile Jeran adored.

Reanna fixed him with a look so loving it made the pain he felt retreat to the farthest recesses of his body. "I love you, Jeran *uvan* Alic," Reanna said in a voice filled with the strength of her Race. "You are the greatest of men. We will wait for you in the Twilight World." Her eyes returned to the door, and she nodded, a single dip of the head.

When the quarrel exploded through her chest, Jeran screamed, a scream Tylor echoed an instant later. "What have you done?" the Bull demanded, grabbing Katya and slamming her against the wall. The crossbow she had used to kill Reanna clattered to the barrow floor. "He was ready to swear himself to me! I had won!"

Katya's backhand rang out through the chamber. Tylor stared daggers at his niece as he wiped the trickle of blood from his mouth. "What have *you* done, Uncle?" Katya replied, her voice matching Tylor's in intensity. "Where is the man who raised me, the noble prince fighting to regain what was wrongfully taken from him?" Her voice cracked with emotion, but Katya forced herself to continue. "Where is the man I love like a father?"

She gestured at Reanna's broken, lifeless body. "Is this your legacy? Does victory for us mean a lifetime of tortured souls? Of broken lives? I would have followed you anywhere, Uncle. I would have fought King Mathis or the Darklord himself for you. But this—" She shook her head, and the gaze she leveled at Tylor transcended disappointment. "This disgusts me."

"Rrraahhh!" Tylor hurled Katya across the room. She hit the far wall with a crash and collapsed atop Reanna. With his back to Jeran, the Bull drew slow, deep breaths, but it was only when Katya stirred that Tylor regained a measure of composure. "Take him to the Trophy Room," he ordered, "and take the body to the grave pit." With that, the Bull ducked low and darted out of the barrow.

The two guards hauled Jeran to his feet and started shoving him toward the tunnel entrance. "Leave him," Katya ordered, brushing the dust from her clothes. "Return to Dranakohr." The soldiers hesitated, and Katya glowered. "He is bound. Do you think me incapable of escorting him myself?" Fearing her wrath, the guards fled.

Katya knelt at Reanna's side and withdrew the quarrel from the Tribeswoman's chest. Tenderly, she closed Reanna's eyes, and her mouth worked silently as if in prayer. Then she grabbed a blanket crumpled on the floor and draped it over the body. For a time, she remained kneeling beside the body, her head bowed and her eyes closed. Then she crossed the room to Jeran. "If I cut these bonds, can I trust you?"

Jeran met her gaze. "Can either of us ever trust again?"

"I had no choice," Katya said, sawing at the cords around Jeran's wrists. "My uncle would not have let her live, and she would not have survived her wounds in any event. All I could do was spare her pain."

"I know," Jeran said, sobs wracking his body. "Dear Gods, I know. And it's all my fault." He buried his head against Katya's shoulder and cried. Katya held him close, awkwardly comforting him.

After a moment, she sliced the ropes that bound his ankles. "We should go."

"Reanna was with child," Jeran murmured. He went to the Tribeswoman's side and touched his hand to her brow. Slowly, he moved his hand down to her abdomen and closed his eyes to fight back tears. "Tylor knew. He knew! This... This was retribution for a son I killed by accident, a son I killed to save my uncle's life."

"Jeran, I..." Ashamed, Katya hung her head. "The Garun'ah prefer pyres to graves. I'll make sure she's has that much, at least." She wiped the tears from his cheeks. "I'll even sing for her. I think I remember the song."

Katya pulled Jeran to his feet and led him through the Barrows. The tunnels were silent; no guards patrolled the passages, and even the ever-present clanging from the forges had stilled. Jeran walked in a haze, his mind numb, his body sluggish, and he was startled when he found himself before the door to the Trophy Room. It swung open with a creak, and Jeran stepped inside. When he turned, he saw tears heavy in Katya's eyes. "Jeran, I—" Unable to finish, Katya swung the heavy door shut. Only after the lock clicked did Jeran turn around.

Aryn slept at the table, his head cradled in his folded arms. He mumbled incoherently, occasionally shouting out something that made no sense. The tingle of a Reading danced around Jeran when he looked at his uncle, but he ignored it. Something had changed. Something was different.

On the far side of the chamber, beneath the portraits of his parents, the wall had been rearranged, and a new trophy occupied the place of honor. Two blades framed a large portrait, the largest and most elaborate display in the entire chamber. To the left of the oaken frame hung a *dolchek*, the blade more than two hands long, slightly curved and wickedly serrated. To the right, a longsword inscribed with Aelvin runes glimmered when it caught the light from the magical spheres hovering above.

The figure in the portrait mocked Jeran. Black hair cut short framed pronounced cheeks and a strong jaw. Blue eyes, proud and fierce, flashed with an internal fire. A cloak of Odaran blue was fastened around the figure's neck, and at his throat hung a wolf's head medallion.

Jeran touched his own throat but felt only the cold iron of his collar. The portrait captivated him; he could not take his eyes from it. He stared into his own eyes, though prouder. He looked at his own face, though stronger. He studied the man before him, familiar yet completely alien. And as he stared, his anger returned.

The man in that portrait is a leader, Jeran thought, approaching the painting. *He would have led the rebels.* Jeran slammed his fist into the wall. *That man would have seen through Quellas' treachery!* He hit the wall again. *He would have saved Reanna! He would have done something to protect his son!* Jeran screamed, and he rained blow after blow against the cold, unforgiving stone. Blinded by tears, Jeran tore the painting from the wall and tore it to pieces, stomping on the splintered frame. He screamed incoherently, and not even he was certain what words were said.

A hand grabbed his shoulder, spinning him around. For a moment, Jeran stared into his uncle's eyes, eyes full of sympathy and concern. Then a single, well-placed blow sent Jeran reeling into unconsciousness.

Chapter 20

Nightmares plagued Jeran's sleep, falling upon him so quickly he could barely tell where one ended and another began. He raced through the Barrows, cutting down anyone in his way; friend and foe alike fell to his savage swings. Their deaths were annoyances, evoking little more than frustration. All that mattered was saving Reanna and his son.

Sometimes he reached her only to be captured or killed in the escape, but mostly he arrived too late and Reanna writhed on the stone table, bleeding from a thousand cuts. The face of her tormentor changed; sometimes Tylor wielded the blade, sometimes another—Quellas, Salos, or some nameless soldier. In one dream Wardel tortured Reanna, and the thought of another friend betraying him made that nightmare all the more disturbing to Jeran. In the worst, he arrived to find Reanna laying on the barrow's floor with Tylor kneeling over her. As the Bull lowered his blade, Reanna saw him standing in the doorway. Tears flowing from her eyes, she begged for help, but Jeran ignored her. "I'm sorry, *bahlova*, but this is necessary." Beside him, Jeran saw the shadow of the Darklord, and he felt a bony, claw-like hand fondly grasp his shoulder.

In a never-ending onslaught, Jeran's worst fears were realized, his gravest mistakes revisited in excruciating detail. He knew he dreamed, and he tried to claw his way back to consciousness. Trapped, he could do nothing but ride the whirlwind and pray that the nightmares stopped before he lost all hope.

…His uncle knelt before Tylor in a field outside Keryn's Rest, but this time, Jeran's arrow flew wide and the Bull ended Aryn's life with a single blow…

…Martyn in a stone box with enemies on all sides and a dagger at his back…

…The Great Forest burned, and Elves fought in the streets of Lynnaei…

…Tylor stood on a bloody field, surrounded by the bodies of Guardsmen. Howling in triumph, the Bull raised his newest trophy, the head of King Mathis…

…Two Dahrs in a practice ring, eyeing each other with contempt…

…A blood-covered infant, the blank stare of death in its eyes…

…Magi sitting on the walls of Kaper, watching as the city crumbled…

…Two giant, blood-red eyes hovering above a range of black mountains…

Waking was a relief unto itself, but for a long time, Jeran refused to open his eyes. He lay in a tight ball, his breathing quick and shallow, his heart pounding in his chest. He prayed for the memories to fade, but he did not believe they ever would.

A sense of danger filled him, and Jeran sat up, tensed for action. He looked for something to use as a weapon, and for a moment, confusion froze him in place. Gone were the stone walls of the Trophy Room, the portraits, and tokens taken from Tylor's conquests. Aryn was nowhere to be seen. Bright sunshine fell across Jeran's face, and he breathed deeply, drinking in the scent of fresh air and new growth. Thick white clouds drifted through an azure sky, and birds wheeled in lazy circles on currents of warm air. Rolling hills spread out around him, broken by patches of thick vegetation.

I'm free! The thought renewed Jeran. He spun in a slow circle, his arms outstretched. *Reanna would love it here! How did I—*

Jeran's elation fled as quickly as it came, leaving him empty. The paradise was an illusion, fate's cruel joke. He had seen this place before, but never awake. He spun again, this time eyeing the land suspiciously. The feeling of danger had not lessened, and Jeran grew worried. He had been told by many that the Twilight World was full of danger, but in this part of it, he had always felt at peace.

Crouched low, Jeran moved forward, making sure to keep hidden in the tall grass. His eyes swept the landscape, watching for unexpected movement. He crept as if hunting game, using all the skills learned from his uncle. Except this time, Jeran knew he was the prey.

Whoosh. Jeran dropped to the ground as a ball of light soared past his head, missing him by less than a hand. Burrowing beneath the grass, Jeran followed the object's flight. The sphere darted over the field before turning around and climbing. It hovered high above the plains, a glowing ball of white light streaked with bands of red, gold, and black.

The sphere orbited the field in ever-widening circles. A trail of darkness, more a dimming of color than the absence of light, marked its passage. Occasionally, the sphere plummeted toward the ground, stopping a few hands above the surface and wobbling back and forth. When it did not find what it was looking for, it returned to the sky and resumed circling.

Jeran pressed himself even deeper into the grass. During his time in Illendrylla, he had often sought it out that sphere, calling to it through the vast reaches of the Twilight World. Just as no two people were identical, so too were the lights of each man's soul unique in the Twilight World. The sphere was Lorthas'; the Darklord hunted him.

The Darklord climbed higher, then moved toward Jeran's position. On his belly, Jeran edged toward the stream, hoping he could lose Lorthas in the swiftly-moving current. A black boot appeared in the grass before him, blocking his way. Jeran squeezed his eyes shut and waited to hear the cold rasp of Lorthas' voice.

"What's this?" asked a familiar voice, but not the Darklord's. "We can't have you disturbing all the dreamers." Jeran opened his eyes in time to see Lorthas' sphere explode, showering the field with a thousand glittering embers. "He'll be surprised by that, I'll wager," the man chuckled, offering Jeran his hand. "And the headache will make him think twice about returning."

Jeran knew the man. He had seen him in the Twilight World before, and he claimed to be a friend. "I'm not accustomed to seeing you cower in the dirt," the Guide said. "In the past, courage generally overruled your common sense. Wisdom or fear? Which did you learn in Dranakohr, I wonder."

Jeran ignored the Guide's hand and stood, brushing the dust from his clothes. "Guilt," he replied. "Guilt and hatred are the only things I learned in Dranakohr."

"The only things?" The man cocked his head to the side. "You must have learned control of your Gift—marginal control, at least—or Lorthas would have found you long before I did. You allowed him to put his mark on you, and that makes you easier to track." Waving for Jeran to follow, the man headed for the shade of a large oak. "As for the other things," he said, not looking to see if Jeran followed, "if they are all you learned, then you wasted your time."

"Wasted my time!" Jeran yelled. He hastened his steps so he could walk beside his strange companion. "What noble quests should I have undertaken while imprisoned in the mines? What grand truth was I to learn as the Darklord's slave? Perhaps if I'd tried a little harder, I could have gotten a few more friends killed!"

"Self pity is a waste of energy," the man said, wagging a finger. "I'd rather you focus on rage. Though not my favorite emotion, anger can be harnessed under the proper circumstances." He shook his head sadly. "Perhaps I didn't guide you as well as I should have."

"Guide?" Jeran's laugh was cold, his spirit colder. "Where were you a season ago, when your counsel might have made a difference? Why did you withhold your sage advice when I needed it most?"

The man did not answer. Jeran followed, but when he opened his mouth to speak, the man raised his hand for silence. Anger seethed within him, but Jeran held his tongue, and with each silent step, his anger grew, building as the Guide reached the tree and studied it with a hand cupped thoughtfully under his chin. After a drawn out pause, he nodded and sat between the outstretched arms of two broad roots. Leaning back, he sighed contentedly and looked at Jeran. "You would not have listened before."

Jeran's frown deepened. "And you think I'll listen now?"

A wry smile pulled at the man's lips. "Let's say I'm no longer convinced you'll ignore me."

Jeran sat on a broad, flat rock. "Then tell me," he demanded, leaning forward with feigned interest. "What counsel do you offer?"

The man's smile broadened, as if he were glad Jeran had finally summoned enough courage, or manners, to ask. "It's not your fault."

The words hit like a hammer blow, and Jeran turned away. "That's it?" Tears stung at his eyes, but Jeran forced them away. Thoughts of Reanna filled his mind, thoughts of the slaves fleeing Tylor's wrath. "That's all you have to say?"

The Guide's casual shrug infuriated him, as did his answer. "I could embellish it a little, if you'd like, add a few cryptic flourishes, but in essence, yes, that's all. You can't blame yourself for decisions made by someone else, and you shouldn't condemn yourself for events over which you had no control. Your intentions were honorable, and that—"

"You presume a lot!" Jeran jumped to his feet. "If I'd acted differently, if I'd made different choices, none of this would have happened."

An ages-old weariness entered the man's eyes, and his smile faded. "The same is true of anyone," he said, his tone lecturing but sympathetic. "If Lorthas had chosen differently, the world would be a much different place. If Tiam Durange had borne no sons or your parents had chosen not to wed, things would not be the same. If King Mathis had decided against taking in two young wards, if Lord Iban had remained true to his peace-loving nature, or if Alwen had not cured the fever that plagued your third Naming Day, you would likely not be here today."

"How… How do you know these things?" Jeran stammered.

"Had you not pretended to love the Tribeswoman"—Jeran stiffened, but he could not deny it—"she would not have died by Tylor's hand, but by her own. Would that death have been preferable to the one she suffered?" White-hot rage flared up in Jeran, but the Guide paid it no heed. His next words sounded rote, as if they had been said countless times. "Every man's decisions, if changed, would create a different world. Time is an elusory path; once traveled, you cannot retrace your steps. Regretting your choices instead of trying to fix them wastes time. I—"

"Enough!" Jeran stormed away through the knee-high grass. "I could get better advice from the Bull of Ra Tachan. Do me a favor—"

"You were never this rude before." The interruption caught Jeran off-guard, but the statement that followed left him speechless. "Your uncle would be disappointed." Jeran fixed a cold gaze on the Guide, and the man's smile returned. "Do you think you're the only one I share my time with? He doesn't remember our conversations, but I've seen a great deal of Aryn these past few winters."

Jeran licked his lips, and his hands trembled with anxiety and excitement. For the first time since discovering his uncle's condition, hope entered his heart. The Guide knew so much; surely he could help. "Can you heal him? Can you make him the way he was before?"

"No man is ever the same from one moment to the next," the Guide said, stroking his chin with his thumb and forefinger. "Time changes us immutably. But can he be healed? Can he recover much of what he's lost? Yes." The smile that blossomed on Jeran's face died when the Guide added, "But not by me. And not by you either. At least, not the way you are now. And certainly not in Dranakohr."

Jeran had the decency to look embarrassed. He opened his mouth, but the Guide raised a hand and shook his head, letting Jeran know that no apology was necessary. Jeran asked another question that had plagued him for some time. "The Garun'ah and the Elves believe that the honorable come here, to the Twilight World, when they die. Is it true? Do the dead live on after life?"

In answer, the man turned toward the stream. Jeran followed the Guide's gaze, and when he saw Reanna standing on the far bank, an infant clasped tightly to her chest, tears came unbidden to his eyes. The Tribeswoman looked more beautiful than Jeran remembered. Her flesh was unmarked by Tylor's cruel treatment, her eyes bright and happy. Though her form was indistinct, she saw Jeran, and as he watched, she held up a child for him to see. His heart pounding, Jeran started toward them, but the Guide restrained him. "You can't."

Besieged by memories, buffeted by waves of regret and self-doubt, Jeran's strength deserted him, and he sank back to his knees. "Are they real," he asked, dreading the answer, "or just my imagination?"

"They're as real as I am," the man replied. Jeran dared not admit aloud that he sometimes doubted his guide's existence. He stared silently at Reanna and his son. "When you die, you will learn the truth. Until then, faith will have to suffice."

Jeran took a step toward the bank, and the Guide made no move to stop him. He stood there, staring at Reanna and his son. Reanna smiled at him, and she held the infant forward as if she wanted Jeran to take him. He started forward, but something stopped him when his feet touched the cold water of the stream. His heart aching, he stepped back, and Reanna smiled sadly. Slowly, she and the baby faded from sight. "Faith is not an easy thing to keep," Jeran said, fighting back tears.

A comforting hand touched his cheek, and the Guide's gentle voice echoed in his mind. "This is enough for today, my friend. It's time for you to wake."

Jeran's eyes snapped open, and it took a moment for him to realize that the hand he felt cradling his head was not the Guide's. "There, there, boy," Aryn whispered. "Everything will be all right." Aryn's lips were drawn down in a frown, and he watched his nephew with the strong, vibrant eyes of the old Aryn, the Aryn that Jeran had known as a child.

"They're gone, Uncle Aryn," Jeran whispered, forcing the words out. Sensing Jeran's pain, Aryn drew him into an embrace and rocked him back and forth. "Tylor took them."

"Shhh. Everything will be fine, Jeran. Everything will be just fine. I'll never let anything happen to you. I swear it! I promised them!" The Reading that perpetually accompanied his uncle surged up unexpectedly, and Jeran fought against it; he had no desire to experience his uncle's suffering. In his weakened state he was no match for the power of the Reading, and it encompassed him, drawing him into the past...

The walls of the Trophy Room faded and were replaced by even more familiar surroundings. Jeran found himself in the living room of the Odara farmhouse, where he had lived with Aryn all those winters ago. It was much as he remembered, though less cluttered. Fewer pictures lined the walls, and the room had an unlived-in feel, but a warm fire burned in the hearth and Aryn's warm laughter drew Jeran's attention.

Aryn, looking much the same, but without the hint of gray gracing his temples, knelt on the divan, its plush cushions thick and unworn, its wooden frame unmarked and polished until it gleamed. He had his back to Jeran and he leaned over the back of the seat, looking at something on the floor.

His curiosity piqued, Jeran hurried to join his uncle. Leaning over the back of the divan, he came face to face with himself.

An infant, less than two winters old sat on the floor. As Jeran watched, his younger self reached out a pudgy hand and grasped the back of the divan. With a look of intense concentration, the toddler pulled himself to his feet, and then with a shuddering, stiff-legged gait, stepped away from the couch.

Aryn erupted with laughter. "There you go, Jeran!" he called out, clapping his hands joyously. "I knew you'd walk today. I just knew it! Aleesa will be furious. She and Gideon are arriving tomorrow, you know."

The infant Jeran looked up at the proud, beaming face of his uncle. "Gidden?" he asked, his eyes lighting up.

"That's right," Aryn said, vaulting over the couch. "Gideon's coming tomorrow." He scooped Jeran up and clutched the boy to his chest. "Oh, we're going to have a lot of fun. Why..."

The scene shifted, and the sudden change startled Jeran; he had never moved directly from one Reading to another before and the effect was disorienting. When his vision cleared, he found himself still in the farmhouse, but upstairs in his old room. Little Jeran, now four winters old, slept soundly beneath his blankets. Aryn hovered over the bed, a broad smile on his face, and Tanar stood at his side. The Mage, his white hair and beard streaked with the last remnants of brown, looked just as happy as Aryn. "He looks just like his father," Tanar said, laughing quietly. "Proud and strong."

"*His father?*" *Aryn shook his head.* "*There's so much of Illendre in him, how can you see Alic at all?*" *Laughing quietly, Aryn put his arm around Tanar and led him from the room.* "*He'll be so excited when he finds you here tomorrow. You know how much he loves—*"

The room blurred again, and Jeran stood outside. Aryn stood beside an eight-winter-old Jeran. This Jeran held an axe in his hand and was cautiously eyeing a section of log set up on the splitting block.

"*Just remember what I told you,*" *Aryn said, clapping Jeran on the shoulder.* "*Use your whole body, not just your arms. You can do it, boy.*" *Aryn moved away, and the young Jeran set his grip. Jeran winced at his own memory of this event and stepped back.*

Using all his strength, the young Jeran raised the axe and brought it crashing down. His aim was off, and he missed the center of the log. A small chunk of wood, nearly a hand in width, split off and smashed into his face. He crumpled to the ground, crying. Aryn was at his side in an instant, cradling Jeran in his arms. "*There, there, boy, it'll be all right. As long as I'm around, I'll never let anything hurt you...*"

Another Aryn, wearing the armor of a Guard Commander, sat on Jedelle. In his arms he held an infant. Around them was nothing but empty grasslands and small trees. To the north, the land rose in a low, grass-covered plateau. "*What do you think, Jeran?*" *Aryn asked the child, his gaze roaming over the countryside.* "*Does this look like a good place for a home...?*"

Jeran saw himself battling a young, bare-chested Dahr with wooden swords. "*You need to bring them to Portal,*" *Lord Talbot said as he and Aryn watched from the porch of the farmhouse.* "*They have a lot to learn, and it's time Jeran knew the truth. You can't hide him here forever.*"

"*One more winter, Gideon!*" *Aryn said, almost begging.* "*Let me protect him for one more winter. Next spring, before the planting, I'll bring them to Portal. I promise...!*"

The scene shifted again, and a dozen more times after that. "He's still here, the Aryn you knew," *Jeran heard the Guide's voice echo in the recesses of his mind,* "but each day Dranakohr takes a little more of him away. Each day it becomes a little harder to bring him back." *Fresh tears came to Jeran's eyes, but these were tears of joy. Gathering his strength, he removed himself from the Reading...*

...and returned to Dranakohr and his uncle's loving embrace. "There, there, Jeran. Everything will be fine now. We're together again."

Jeran sat up and grabbed his uncle's shoulders. "You called me Jeran!" he said, almost shouting. "Do you really believe it, Uncle Aryn?"

The question caught Aryn off guard, and he tried to pull away. "Sometimes..." he whispered, a tremor in his voice. "I want to believe it, boy, but you don't know how many times Tylor brought me someone who looked like you, just to taunt me. And now..." Aryn wiped a hand across his eyes. "Now you're a man. Nothing like the boy I remembered. If it is you, I missed so much. I missed..."

Jeran climbed to his feet and extended a hand. After pulling Aryn to his feet, Jeran looked through the splintered remains of Tylor's trophies. With a smile, he scooped up his two blades. The *dolchek* he tucked into his belt, but the Aelvin sword he held high, studying the finely-wrought metal.

A memory from the Great Forest came to him, and a smile ghosted across his face. Closing his eyes, Jeran gripped the hilt in both hands and held the blade in front of his face. He took several slow, calming breaths and then began moving through the stances he had learned from Joam and Lord Iban.

Aryn grabbed Jeran's shoulder. "What are you doing?"

Jeran's eyes snapped open. "Escaping. Want to come?" Aryn's smile was a match for Jeran's, and the older man stepped back while Jeran continued his exercise. Moving ever faster, Jeran closed the distance between himself and the thick oaken door. With a cry of rage, he swung his magic-wrought blade and a hand's length of silvery steel shattered the lock and sent splinters flying across the tunnel.

Shoving the door open with his shoulder, Jeran darted into the tunnel, sword at the ready. Movement drew his eyes to the left, and he pivoted lightly, his sword swinging in a wide arc. At the last instant he recognized Wardel crouched over the body of an unconscious soldier. The Guardsman stared at the approaching blade with horror.

Jeran checked his swing, stopping his sword less than a finger from Wardel's throat. The Guardsman swallowed nervously. "Well," Wardel said, forcing a weak laugh, "Looks like we got here just in time."

"What are you doing?" Jeran asked.

"Rescuing you," Wardel replied. His eyes moved from the unconscious guard to the shattered door of the Trophy Room. "Looks like we did a good job."

"I told you we had to hurry if we wanted to save Jeran," Yassik said, stepping from the shadows. Dirt covered the Mage's clothes, and streaks of black darkened his skin and peppered his white hair. A ring of keys jingled in one of the Mage's hands. In the other, he held a cudgel, its end glistening in the torchlight. Yassik looked from the keys to the ruined door. With a sigh, he tossed the ring to the ground.

"I thought you meant he was in danger!" Wardel said bitterly. "Not that he'd meet us for supper if we took too long."

Yassik embraced Jeran. "It's good to see you, boy. We thought you were done for."

"Not me," Jeran said. "Reanna paid that price in my stead."

The Mage's eyes darkened, and he nodded sadly. Wardel clamped a comforting hand on Jeran's shoulder. "She died an honorable death, Jeran, the way she would have wanted. We can't bring her back, but we can give her sacrifice meaning. I think it's time to leave Dranakohr. I can think of no more fitting a memorial than for us to breathe free tonight."

The Guardsman's words encouraged Jeran, and a determined glint entered his eyes. "There's one thing I have to do first."

"Killing Tylor's not an option." Wardel shook his head vigorously. "I know how you feel, Jeran, but—"

"I'm not going to kill Tylor," Jeran interrupted, and both Yassik and Wardel relaxed. Both tensed again, though, when a shadow darkened the tunnel. Wardel reached for his sword, but Jeran stayed his arm. "Wait! Wardel, this is my uncle, Aryn Odara."

Aryn had scavenged bits of armor from Tylor's collection. He wore a well-oiled leather breastplate; thick, sturdy gauntlets; and well-made boots, none of which matched. Three daggers hung from a belt at his hip, and in his hand he held Lord Iban's sword. "Guardsman," he said, ducking his head in greeting.

Wardel stared wide-eyed. He saluted fist-on-heart, showing more formality to Aryn than he ever had to Jeran. "Lord Odara," he said breathlessly. "It's an honor." He turned to Jeran, and in a nervous, almost conspiratorial whisper, he said, "I thought you said he was weak-minded."

Aryn laughed, and the sound brightened the tunnel. "I'm having a good day, Guardsman," Aryn answered. "Don't worry. I'm sure I'll be more entertaining before too long." Without waiting for Wardel's hastily-stammered apology, Aryn turned to Yassik. "I believe we met before, Mage Yassik, a long time ago."

"Not so long ago to my reckoning," Yassik replied, gripping Aryn's arm warmly. "But I have a few more winters in the accounting." The Mage eyed Aryn up and down. "You look well… considering."

"I've been better," Aryn assured him. He turned toward Jeran. "You were planning an escape, right?"

"We have a stop to make first." Jeran looked at the Trophy Room's shattered door and the body of the guard on the tunnel floor. "And we'd better hurry. There's no telling how long before our absence is noted."

Jeran removed several lanterns from their places on the tunnel wall and handed them to his companions. He signaled the others to step back, and once they were clear, he threw his own into the Trophy Room. Flames engulfed one of Tylor's prized tapestries and quickly spread, destroying the Bull's collection.

"Strip them," Aryn said, kneeling beside one of the dead guards. "If we put the bodies in there, it might buy us a little more time." They did as Aryn instructed, and once the guards had been deposited in the Trophy Room, Wardel shouldered the remains of the door closed.

"Come on!" Jeran said, urging the others to follow him. "We have a war to fight."

Chapter 21

Keeping to the shadows, Jeran stared at the entrance to the *ghrat*. A lone guard blocked the passage. Yassik stood across the tunnel, pressed deep into a hollow. Even in the dim light, Jeran saw the disapproving expression on the Mage's face. Yassik had no qualms about telling Jeran he was a fool; though the Mage did not know what Jeran planned, he was already convinced he would not like it.

Wardel had taken to the tunnels, scouting for open passages and noting the positions of Tylor's soldiers. Jeran had intended to do the same, but his uncle insisted on going. "If I can't be trusted with such a simple task," Aryn had said in response to Jeran's protest, "I might as well go back to the Trophy Room."

Killing the soldier posed a problem; every dead body increased their risk of discovery. If someone noticed their escape before they were away, a single ShadowMage would be enough to stop them. But leaving the man alive posed its own risks. Jeran raised his sword, careful to keep the Aelvin blade out of the light, and prepared to attack.

The sound of approaching footsteps froze him in place, and Jeran pressed deeper into the shadows. The soldier jumped to attention, and he reached for his sword. The guard was not supposed to change until dawn. *If Tylor already knows, we don't have a chance!*

Wardel appeared, strolling casually down the tunnel. "That fool!" Yassik hissed. "What's he doing?"

The guard strode toward Wardel with arrogant superiority. "What are you doing, slave?" When he saw the sword at Wardel's side, he stumbled, and his confidence waned. "Where'd you get that?"

"This?" Wardel looked at the blade. "Oh! He gave it to me." He pointed past the guard. Before the soldier could turn, Aryn's dagger plunged into his back. Cupping a hand over the soldier's mouth, Aryn lowered the man to the cold stone, pulled his dagger free, and neatly sliced his throat. The thrashing stopped almost instantly. Aryn wiped the blade on the soldier's shirt before tucking it away again.

"What were you thinking?" Jeran demanded, stepping out from concealment. "You could have gotten yourself killed!"

Aryn said nothing. "This was the easiest way into the *ghrat*," Wardel said in their defense. He handed Jeran a map of the tunnels marked with the positions of the guards he had found. "You did want to go to the *ghrat*, didn't you?"

"What about the body? The guards will be suspicious!"

"It's been taken care of," Aryn said. Wardel dragged the soldier back the way he had come. "There's a pit not far from here, narrow but deep. We will use it to hide any bodies we... find."

Jeran wanted to argue, but instead he dropped to a crouch and spread the yellowed map on the tunnel floor. Aryn crouched beside him and unrolled an identical map with marked with the guards he had found. They studied the maps carefully, and when Wardel returned, Jeran knew he had to make a decision. A deep frown worked across his face, and his finger traced a path. "We should use this tunnel to escape. It's longer than the others, and it exits the Barrows right beneath the castle, but it's the least guarded. Once outside, we can hug the mountains and hope the guards outside are as incompetent as those down here."

Jeran tapped a finger against his lip. "The wall will be our biggest problem. I saw it from Dranakohr the other day and it's almost complete. We're going to have a tough time getting past it without being spotted, but I can't see any way around that." He looked at his companions, hoping for suggestions. None were forthcoming.

Aryn patted his shoulder. "No point in planning too much, boy. Even the best plans don't count for much after the battle begins. Might as well get on with it and worry about any obstacles after they appear." A warm smile flitted across Aryn's face. "Unless you think staying here is a better option."

Jeran rolled up the maps. "Let's go. They should be getting ready to start." Sharing puzzled looks, Aryn and the others followed Jeran into the *ghrat*.

The tunnels were empty. Nothing, neither guard nor prisoner, roamed the halls; not the faintest whisper of sound reached their ears. Jeran strode forward boldly, moving with determination and purpose, turning corners and crossing through intersections without looking for sentries. The others moved more cautiously, hugging the walls and darting from passage to passage, straining to hear approaching footfalls or a shouted alarm. After a time, Aryn began muttering to himself, his words low and unintelligible. Yassik watched the elder Odara closely, and the Mage's lips drew down in a frown.

A low murmur rose in the distance, the sound of many voices engaged in conversation. Jeran quickened his pace, stepping from the shadowy corridor into a large, brightly-lit chamber. Yassik and Wardel had to pull Aryn between them; he fought every step, shying away from the bright lights and cacophony of voices.

Hundreds of Orog sat cross-legged on the floor or lay upon ragged, dust-covered furs. A few Humans were present despite Tylor's new edict. Most sat in tight clusters, others alone, but everyone whispered anxiously to their nearest neighbor, and the sound filled the cave with a thunderous roar.

Seeing the Humans, a near fervent look entered Yassik's eyes, and the Mage looked like he would gladly trade the shortsword he held for pen and paper. At Wardel's questioning glance, the Mage waved dismissively. "It's nothing, my boy. I've just been a philosopher too long. Can't stop thinking sometimes." He started forward again, dragging a glassy-eyed Aryn behind him.

The Elders stood at the front of the chamber on a shelf of raised stone. More than three dozen figures, more women than men and all bowed with age, faced the assembly, and at their center, standing beside a low pedestal, was an Orog who made the others look young. Pale grey skin, spotted black, hung loose on the Eldest's bones, and his eyes were fogged and sightless. He hunched nearly in two despite the gnarled staff he used to support his weight. When he crossed behind the podium, only the top of his head and a few wisps of translucent hair could be seen.

As if he could see as well as any, the Eldest turned his head at Jeran's arrival. "He comes," Craj said in a voice that reverberated through the chamber. A hush fell over the assembled Orog and Humans, spreading out from the Elders in a wave.

"Jeran!" Grendor cried out, jumping to his feet. The name thundered through the suddenly-silent chamber. "Jeran, you're alive!" Sprinting up the narrow aisle, Grendor enveloped Jeran in a great hug, lifting him off the ground easily despite being more than a hand shorter. Finally, after Jeran thought he would never breathe again, Grendor let him go. "It is not safe for you here," the Orog warned. "If you are free, then you must run."

"With him here," Zehna yelled from the front of the hall, "it is not safe for any of us. For once, my grandson speaks wisely. You should leave. Now."

Jeran bowed politely to the Elders. "I do not wish your people harm," he said slowly, making sure his words carried through the cavern, "but I must be allowed to speak. I have learned something of great importance."

"This is the Telling," Zehna shot back angrily, thumping a fist against her thigh. "This is no place for gossip and intrigue!"

"Then I will tell a story," Jeran replied confidently, stopping a handful of steps from the raised platform.

"Have you not suffered enough?" Zehna yelled, and those in the room cringed. Jeran remained resolute; the concern in the old woman's voice upset him far more than the scorn. "Have you not made my people—and yours!—suffer enough? What do you hope to gain—?"

A loud crack exploded through the room, and all eyes shifted toward the sound. Craj slammed the gilded end of his staff into the stone a second time and turned his sightless gaze on Zehna. The old woman fell silent, and her cheeks turned a dark shade of grey.

"Do we now silence those voices that speak of unpleasant things?" the withered old man asked, and Zehna hung her head. "We Elders cannot guide the Orog without knowledge, and a sightless rabbit walks boldly into the wolf's mouth." Craj turned toward Jeran, and the skin on the back of Jeran's neck prickled as the Eldest considered his request. "Today was my day to Tell," the ancient Orog announced, "but I will stand aside to hear this Human's tale." Craj stepped back from the podium, his staff clicking on the stone as he felt out a path.

Jeran jumped up on the platform and turned to address the assembly. When he did, Aryn laughed aloud. "That young man looks like my nephew," he told Wardel, clapping the Guardsman on the back. "Spitting image! I haven't seen Jeran in winters, though..."

Wardel hushed Aryn and guided the older man to the ground, where space was hastily made for them and Yassik. Once one the floor, Aryn wrapped his arms around his knees and curled up in a tight ball. Wardel watched the former Guard Commander with a mixture of sympathy and sorrow.

"I've come to share a story," Jeran called out loudly, hoping his anxiety did not show. His heart pounded in his chest and sweat beaded his forehead, but he did not want the Orog to know he was nervous. "It's a story I've heard many times, but one I never truly understood."

To his right, Zehna harrumphed, but the Elder made no comment. "I will tell you of the Jewel of Truth," Jeran said, tearing his gaze from the Elders and directing it across the cavern. At his side, Craj nodded, as if he had expected the tale.

"Long ago, in the winters following Aemon's Revolt, before Lorthas resurrected the title of Darklord, Madryn experienced a period of unity, a time when the races welcomed each other as friends and embarked upon their greatest work, *Ael Shende Ruhl*.

"It was a time of great change. The ancestral lands of the Drekka had been ceded to the Humans and the nation of Gilead was forming. The Great Houses of Alrendria had splintered a dozen times, and thieves and glory-hunters scoured the ruins of the Darklords' keeps, seeking treasure. In a world suddenly free of Darklords, all Four Races vied for power, but quietly and without raising arms against each other.

"During this time, a Human named Ryk lived on a farm in the shadow of the Anvil. He was an honest man, a man of few needs and fewer desires. Though all around him the world changed, for Ryk and his family, life remained much the same. Through merciless summers and bone-numbing winters, Ryk toiled beside his brothers. When droughts cracked the land, he carted water for leagues to nourish his crops and the crops of his neighbors. When floods destroyed his harvest and plagues decimated his herds, he saved what he could and continued on with his life.

"But the winters passed one by one, and Ryk's brothers left to seek a better life. Each departure made maintaining the farm more difficult, but Ryk endured without complaint. He had only two goals: to please his father and to please the Gods. So long as both were satisfied, then so was he. Until he met Jarille Desalle.

"Jarille and her family had been ousted from their home in the aftermath of Aemon's Revolt, and the Desalle Family settled near the Anvil, where they hoped to restore their Family and reclaim their fortunes. Ryk was overwhelmed the moment they met, but Jarille did not return his affection. Her family had fallen far, and in the haughty noblewoman's mind, loving a commoner would have been admitting her disgrace.

"Yet Ryk was adamant, and Jarille did not have the courage to rebuff him, so she set him an impossible task. 'Long ago,' she told him, 'Kohr offered the gift of magic to the Four Races, but the Goddess Shael, in her pride, defied her husband, and her insolence cost the Orog that Gift. Ashamed, the Goddess wept, and her tears hardened into a gem of unsurpassed beauty. Shael blessed this gemstone and named it the Jewel of Truth. Whoever held it, she promised, would see into the hearts of men and know when they lied. She gave the jewel to the Orog as payment for the gift they were denied.' As she said this, Jarille smiled, and Ryk's heart melted at the sight. 'Were a man to bring me this jewel, I would deny him nothing.' "

" 'Where is the Jewel of Truth?' Ryk demanded. 'If it exists, I will find it!'

" 'Legend says it was lost in the Anvil many winters ago.' Jarille leaned in close and peered deep into Ryk's eyes. 'You would really find me the Jewel?' she whispered.

" 'I will have it in less than a winter,' Ryk assured her, surprised by his own confidence. 'When I return, we will wed.' He left, stopping only to bid farewell to his aging father."

The hall was still; not the hint of a whisper rose to combat Jeran's voice. The Orog watched transfixed, as if they actually saw the story unfolding. "Not sure where to begin," Jeran continued, "Ryk traveled to the Orog city of Osar Mienos. The Elders there counseled him to seek Ecri, a disciple of Shael living deep in the mountains of the Anvil, and despite the approaching winter, Ryk left immediately. He searched for the reclusive hermit through howling winds and blinding snows until, starving and half-frozen, he reached Ecri's cave. Crawling inside, he saw a Human woman stirring a pot over a small fire.

" 'I have come to see the Elder Ecri,' Ryk called out weakly, and the woman turned toward him. Golden curls framed a milk white face, and two depthless blue eyes regarded him with a curious expression. Red lips parted in a welcoming smile, but Ryk, overcome by the rigors of his journey, collapsed at the mouth of the cave before she could speak.

"When Ryk woke, he lay before the fire, wrapped in a soft fur blanket. The woman sat beside him, and seeing him stir, she offered him a warm bowl. 'I am Ryk,' he said, taking the stew and drinking hungrily. 'Ryk Menglor. I have come a long way to seek the Elder Ecri.'

" 'And you have found me,' the woman said with a smile, 'though I don't enjoy being called an Elder by someone who has seen more winters than I.'

" 'You're Ecri?' Ryk asked, shocked. 'The priest?'

" 'Priestess,' Ecri corrected. She laughed at Ryk's confusion. "Can only men serve the Gods? Can only Orog honor the Mother?' Ryk stammered an apology, and Ecri patted his hand. 'Eat,' she told him. 'Then we will talk about what has brought you to my mountain.'

"Once Ryk had sated himself, he told Ecri of his quest. 'The Jewel of Truth,' she murmured, tapping her lip thoughtfully. 'Many believe it to be a myth. But...' She fell silent, then abruptly stood and disappeared into the dark recesses of her cave. Ryk followed her through the twisting, dark tunnels, finally emerging in a vast cavern. An ethereal glow illuminated the room, forcing Ryk to squint until his eyes adjusted. When they did, he found himself in a library. Shelves, filled with yellowed scrolls and time-worn books and stretching so high that their tops disappeared in the shadows above, ran the length of the cavern.

"Ecri went to a thick tome sitting alone in the center of the chamber and flipped through the pages. 'I was right!' she exclaimed after a long search. 'I've already archived some notes on the Jewel. Perhaps they'll lead us to other volumes.' She started eagerly across the cavern, then stopped. 'This will not be an easy task or a quick one,' she warned, fixing Ryk with a warning gaze. 'I have cataloged only a fraction of the works in this place. Is this a task you truly wish to undertake, my friend?'

" 'With all my heart,' Ryk answered. 'I will do whatever it takes to prove my love to Jarille.' Ryk looked around the cavern, and his excitement waned. 'Where do we begin?'

" 'We will need help if we are to find the Jewel. Only so much knowledge is stored in books.' With her eyes distant, Ecri ran a hand through her golden hair, and Ryk could not help but admire the priestess. Suddenly, Ecri nodded. 'He's the one!' Ecri ran toward the mouth of the cave. 'If the Jewel exists, he'll know where to find it.'

"Ecri scrawled a note on a scrap of parchment and tied it to the leg of a snowy white owl. She carried the bird outside and whispered in its ear. It immediately took to wing, made two graceful circles above Ecri's head, and flew northwest.

"Ecri saw Ryk's confusion and laughed. 'Falkon is the wisest of the Elders. He will help us find the Jewel. Hurry!' she called, racing back into the cave. 'We have much to do before he arrives!'

"Ryk and Ecri worked side by side the winter through, searching crumbling volumes and reading faded scrolls. By day, they shared delight at every new find, and at night, when the winds howled and the storms raged, Ryk spoke of his life on the farm. Ecri told a far more tragic story.

" 'You need not cry for me,' Ecri told Ryk when she finished her tale, and she wiped the tears from his cheek. 'The Orog saved me, and they brought me to Shael. If my suffering was the price I had to pay to find the Mother, I'd gladly pay it again. Besides, had my life been different, we would not be here now, would we?' Ecri's courage impressed Ryk, as did her willingness to help him. As the days passed, a strong bond grew between them.

"The long winter gave way to spring, and the snows receded. Spring warmed into summer, and Ryk's patience grew thin. He pressed for their search to begin in earnest, but Ecri insisted on more study; she seemed certain they would find the Jewel's exact location among the countless tomes if they only took enough time to study them. Ryk reluctantly agreed, mostly because the few hints they had found gave him no idea where to begin his search.

"One day, the two friends heard a loud noise from the mouth of the cave. 'He's here!' Ecri said excitedly, though Ryk thought he detected a hint of disappointment. They hurried to the cave's mouth and found two Tribesmen dressed in furs and covered in quickly-melting snow. Ecri's face showed a mixture of surprise, relief, and confusion. 'What do you want here, Children of Garun?'

" 'We seek truth,' one said, bowing low. 'I Prak *uvan* Yorch.'

" 'I Rassi *uvan* Nomakai,' said the other. 'We Sahna. We wish be *Kranor*, but we *chanda* and not fight for right. *Tsha'ma* tell us come to mountain. Seek truth.'

"Ryk's eyes brightened. 'It's too odd to be coincidence,' he announced, earning a dark glare from Ecri. 'We, too, seek truth, the Jewel of Truth, a relic of the Goddess Shael.' He shared his story with the Tribesmen, telling them what they had learned of the Jewel and its whereabouts.

"The Tribesmen listened with growing interest. 'Tsha'ma wise,' Rassi said, and Prak nodded. 'Jewel tell who lead Sahna.' He ducked his head and opened his arms, palms up, toward Ryk. 'We join quest, if you allow. Gift of Shael be what we seek.'

" 'The Jewel of Truth was not Shael's gift,' a new voice announced. All eyes turned toward the speaker: an Orog, stoop-shouldered and frail, his skin spotted dark and eyes clouded with age. Though as broad as the Tribesmen, he was only half their height, and he walked with the aid of a gnarled staff. An Elf, a boy even by Human standards, dark haired and green eyed, stood at his side. The Elf wore a heavy pack, and in his hands he carried a bow.

The Tribesmen tensed, and they eyed the Elf warily. The Aelvin boy tightened his grip on the bow, but the old Orog stepped between them before fighting could erupt. 'The Jewel was not Shael's gift,' he repeated. 'The Truthsense, the ability to see through deception, was her apology to us. The Gifted created the Jewel, and bestowed upon it a similar power, the power to see truth.

" 'Falkon!' Ecri exclaimed, catching the old Orog up in a tight hug. 'My message arrived safely?'

" 'It did, my dear, and your owl is fine. Sorcia cares for him even now. I would have returned him, but if you intend to seek the Jewel, there would be none here to care for him.'

" 'Why Gifted make Jewel?' Prak asked suspiciously.

"Falkon studied the Tribesman before answering. 'Despite their powers, the Gifted are men like any other; they cannot abide knowing that someone can do something they cannot. Once they learned of the Truthsense, Gifted from all three Races studied my people. Some believed our gift was even greater than theirs.'

" 'They succeeded?' Ecri asked.'

" 'They did, my dear, but then they discovered that knowing the truth is not the treasure they believed it to be. That is why they hid the Jewel. That is why the knowledge of how to create it was lost long ago.'

" 'But you know where it is?' Ryk asked eagerly. 'You know where we can find the Jewel of Truth?'

" 'The Jewel has been lost for ages,' Falkon replied, ' but I believe I know its whereabouts.' He hobbled forward and looked into Ryk's eyes. 'Are you sure you want it, though? Truth has many facets, and the Jewel is not an easy burden. Calling something a treasure does not make it one"—Falkon cast a sidelong glance at his Aelvin companion—"and seeing truth is not always a gift. There are as many truths as there are people, and fewer lies than you might believe. The Truthsense is more a curse than a blessing; only the Gods should see into the hearts of men.'

" 'I need the Jewel to win Jarille's heart,' Ryk told Falkon. 'I will do what I must to obtain it.'

" 'Then tell your stories,' Falkon said, 'and I will judge your worthiness.' He stared into their eyes while they told their tales, and when the last finished, Falkon nodded. 'You all speak the truth—the truth as you see it, in any case—and your goals are noble. I will lead you to the Jewel, so that you may find the answers you seek. You may even take it,' he told Ryk. 'I have seen into your heart and judge you worthy. But none outside this cave must ever know the Jewel's secret, and once you have finished with it, you must return it to its proper place.'

"Ryk swore to do as Falkon asked, and the Orog told them to prepare for a long journey. To Ryk's surprise, Ecri began to pack. 'You're coming with us?'

"She looked hurt. 'You don't want me to?'

" 'No, it's not that!' Ryk said hastily. 'I'd welcome your company. I just thought… That is… What about your books?'

" 'You've become my dearest friend, Ryk. I want to see your quest completed and your prize won. I want to see you happy.' Knowing that Ecri would be with him, a great weight lifted from Ryk's heart, and he drew the priestess into a tight embrace. In doing so, he missed the tears that stained the pale flesh of her cheek.

"The way through the mountains was dangerous, and the six companions relied on each other for survival. Once, Ryk was separated from the others and would have been lost forever if not for Falkon and the old Orog's keen hearing. When a mountain cat surprised the party and pinned Prak beneath its sharp claws, Rassi threw himself at the beast, killing it with his bare hands and saving his *chanda's* life. Before they reached the Jewel, each owed his life to the others many times over, and a strong bond grew among the party.

"When the heat of midsummer burned all trace of water from the earth and the faith of even the stoic Tribesmen began to flag, Falkon stopped and pointed to a narrow path winding up the side of a long and treacherous cliff. 'At the top of that path lies the Jewel of Truth.'

" 'How you know, old one?' Prak demanded.

" 'I do not, my friend,' Falkon replied. 'But I believe. If that is not enough for you, then wait here. None among us will fault you for it.' With as much speed as he could muster, Falkon hobbled up the incline. The others wearily followed, and they made the climb without incident until, within sight of their goal, Rassi slipped.

"Ecri reached for him, but too slowly, and Rassi disappeared in a shower of stone. A numbness crept through the party. To have endured so much only to lose a companion so close to their goal...

"They heard Rassi's frantic cries and crawled to the edge of the cliff. Not far below, the Tribesman clung to a ledge, his feet dangling. Rassi screamed to Prak to help him, but Prak lay frozen in terror, staring blankly at the dizzying heights.

"Norvel, the Aelvin boy, grabbed a rope, and with Ryk supporting one end, scrambled down the cliff. After securing the Tribesman, Ryk and Ecri hauled Rassi up to the ledge. Prak embraced his *chanda*, and tears flowed freely down the Tribesman's face, but he could not bring himself to look into Rassi's eyes.

" 'Come, my friends," Falkon urged once they were safely reunited. 'Let us behold this ancient wonder.' They followed the Orog into the cave, and what they saw stole their breath. Resting upon a pedestal in the center of a rounded chamber was a diamond the size of a fist. The jewel sparkled with its own light, sending flashes of color throughout the cave. Peace and tranquility permeated the cavern, and no one could hide his awe.

" 'Who will be the first to hold it?' Falkon whispered. 'Who will be the first to seek truth?'

"Ecri stepped away from the gem and looked at Ryk, who stood transfixed, his eyes fastened on the Jewel. 'I know enough truth. Beholding this wonder is more than I deserve.'

" 'I not need hold stone,' Prak answered, his head bowed in shame. 'I find *Kranor*. When snowcat attack, Rassi kill beast. Save life. But fear hold me when he in danger. *Tsha'ma* right. In mountains I find truth.'

" 'We are *chanda*,' Rassi said, taking Prak by the shoulders. 'You save my life hundred times. One moment fear not destroy life of honor.' Rassi lifted the Jewel from its pedestal and turned to his companion. 'I see in you only honor. Only goodness.' A smile touched the Tribesman's lips. 'Now I know Jewel work.'

"Norvel took the stone from Rassi's hand. He studied it for a moment, then a frown contorted his face. 'It is only glass!' he cried. 'Not a gem at all!' Tears filled the Elf's eyes, and his breath came in sobbing gasps. 'I had hoped... My family has displeased the Emperor's son and now faces hard times.' He looked guiltily at his companions. 'I planned to steal the Jewel, hoping that if I presented it to the Emperor, he would restore my family's honor.' Norvel shook his head. 'I am a fool. Even if the Jewel of Truth were a gemstone, how could I regain honor by stealing it? I do not deserve forgiveness.'

" 'But you have it, my young friend,' Falkon told him. 'All here save Ryk, to whom the Jewel has been promised, have thought of taking it. I do not need Truthsense to see that.' The Orog turned to Ecri. 'That is why you refused to touch it, is it not, my dear?'

"Lowered eyes and embarrassed expressions were the only answer Falkon received, but it was admission enough. 'You have proven yourself honorable on this journey, my friend. If your Emperor and his kin cannot see you for what you are, perhaps they are the ones who have betrayed you.'

"Trembling, Norvel handed the Jewel to Falkon, who caressed the stone lovingly, as if it were alive. 'What do you see when you hold it, Falkon?' Ecri asked.

" 'I see nothing, my dear,' Falkon answered. 'The Jewel is a thing of magic, so to me, it is nothing more than a trinket. But the quest to find it, and the companions I shared this adventure with… Sometimes, the seeking of a thing is greater than the finding.' Falkon handed the Jewel to Ryk. When he took it, his eyes widened.

" 'Is this… Is this how all Orog see the world?' Ryk asked, his body tingling with magic. Colors and light danced around his companions, and he understood things in a way he never had before.

" 'Like all gifts,' Falkon explained, 'Truthsense is stronger in some than others. And it can also be deceptive. The Jewel reveals deception, not truth; and it does not have the power to overcome the beliefs of its bearer. If you believe a thing, the Jewel will not tell you differently. It is an empty gift, like Fool's Gold. For it to provide an understanding of others, it requires a deeper understanding of self.'

"Silence filled the chamber, and no one was eager to break it. Finally, Ryk turned to Ecri. 'I must return to Alrendria to wed my one true love. You said you wanted to see my quest fulfilled. Will you still accompany me?' Hiding a broken heart, Ecri agreed to return to Alrendria with Ryk. Amidst pledges of lifelong friendship and promises of a reunion, the six companions parted company, and Ryk returned to the home of Jarille.

"When she saw Ryk, Jarille was amazed. The simple farmer had returned a hero, and he held in his hand a treasure of immeasurable value. She embraced him warmly and welcomed him into her home, and when she looked upon him, she saw a man she could love.

" 'I have completed your quest,' Ryk told her, 'and I have come to deliver this Jewel to the woman I love.' With visions of power and fortune dancing in her eyes, Jarille held out her hand. Ryk gave the Jewel to Ecri.

" 'Jarille loves only power,' he said, looking into Ecri's tear-filled eyes. 'The truth was there all along, but not even the Jewel could have helped me see it. I was trapped in a cage of my own creation, prisoner of a truth I made myself believe. Come with me,' he offered Ecri his hand. 'I have not seen my father in nearly a winter. I know he will be eager to meet my wife.' "

Jeran stepped back, his story done, a murmur grew among the Orog. The murmur quickly became a roar of conversation, and it took several raps from Craj's staff to quiet them again. "Like Ryk," Jeran said, "I trapped myself in a prison of truth. I was not alone. I shared that prison with you, with all the Orog."

The roar returned, this time angrier, and Craj's staff slammed down, demanding silence. Once. Twice. A third time. When the room quieted, Jeran continued. "I believed that by serving the Darklord, I could protect my friends. I believed that the actions of one man were inconsequential, that simple concessions could do little harm. I believed that the price of my betrayal would be limited to my own, personal disgrace."

Jeran let his gaze roam the assembly. "I was wrong, and it cost me someone very dear to me and a son I will never know. The price is one I can hardly bear, but it was what I needed to free me of my prison. It opened my eyes to the truth!" This time, no voice raised to fill the silence.

"I was wrong," Jeran repeated. "By serving evil, no matter our intentions, we only strengthen it. I would save you from making the same mistake as I! You think you have betrayed your oath to Aemon. You believe this"—he waved a hand in a gesture that encompassed the *ghrat*—"is punishment for that betrayal, and that once you're punished for your sins you'll be freed. You believe *you* have become evil, and that belief has enslaved you."

A quiet murmur started among the Orog, and this time, Jeran made no attempt to quiet it. "The Orog have long since atoned for whatever sins burden your souls, and the time of your salvation is at hand. I am leaving Dranakohr tonight, and I will take any Orog who will join me."

Only one stepped forward, and a frantic cry followed him. "NO!" Zehna screamed when Grendor leapt onto the platform. The old woman ran forward, tears in her eyes, her hand outstretched.

"Jeran is right, *Tana*," Grendor said, tears stinging his own eyes. "It is time we fulfill our vow to the Great Aemon." Turning to Jeran, the young Orog smiled. "I would join you, friend Jeran, if you will have me."

"I wouldn't have left without you," Jeran answered, clapping Grendor on the shoulder. He faced the assembly one last time. "No others? I understand. You need time to think on my words. But this I vow, as the grandson of Aemon, High Wizard of the Magi: I will return. I will set you free." He signaled to Wardel and Yassik, and the two men stood, hauling Aryn to his feet between them.

Jeran turned to go, but Lorana blocked his way. Though the woman was more than two hands shorter than he, he felt as if she loomed over him. "I knew this day would come," she said quietly, "All the Elders did. I had hoped... Care for him. He knows nothing of the world."

"I will," Jeran replied, bowing his head respectfully. "Like a brother." To Grendor, he said, "Make your farewells quick. We've already stayed too long."

Grendor said goodbye to his family and the five companions pushed their way through the crowd. Jeran reached the tunnel entrance first and darted through, desperate to get away from the hands trying to stop him and the voices demanding answers he did not know. He nearly walked into a guard.

"What...? You!" The guard's eyes narrowed and he reached for his sword. Before Jeran could react, a dagger exploded through the man's throat.

"We'd better hurry." Aryn said, pulling his blade free and wiping it on the dead man's sleeve. Aryn reached for the body.

"Go," commanded a deep voice. "We will deal with this." A powerfully-built Orog stood behind Aryn, and a few younger ones behind him. All had the bearing of warriors, and Jeran recognized the leader, Drogon. "Some among us are not deaf to your words, friend Human," Drogon said, gripping Jeran's arm in parting. "The *Choupik* await your return."

Jeran led his friends into the tunnels, but their chosen path took them deep into a dark stretch of tunnel. Even holding his Gift, Jeran saw nothing, and his confidence began to flag. Unable to feel rock in any direction, he grew confused. He could not shake the thought that he had led his friends to their death.

"Take my hand," Grendor said, pushing to the front. "I will lead the way." Jeran sheathed his sword through a loop in his belt and gripped the Orog's hand; when he did so, a chill rushed through his body. Aryn squeezed Jeran's other hand and they moved on, trusting to Grendor's eyes and Jeran's memory.

"There should be a tunnel on our right up ahead," Jeran whispered. "It will lead us outside."

"Watch out," Grendor said suddenly, "there's a loose—"

The stone beneath Jeran's foot shifted, and he lost his balance. He pitched sideways and tensed, expecting to hit the wall. He met resistance as he fell, and time itself seemed to slow. Pain flared through his body, an agony that drove all thought from his head and left him gasping for air. He felt something tug at his arm before he lost consciousness.

When he came to his senses, he was lying on the tunnel floor, gasping for air. Sweat soaked his clothes. "What happened?" he asked through clenched teeth.

"You fell into the Boundary," Yassik said, and Jeran felt someone dabbing his head with a cloth. "You didn't seem to like it either."

Jeran tried to stand, and every muscle in his body protested. It took both Grendor's and Wardel's help for him to regain his feet. He moved slowly at first, shuffling down the tunnel with each step placed carefully in front of the last. His head pounded against his skull, and bright spots of color danced in front of his eyes, but Jeran did his best to ignore it.

After a while, the tunnel began to brighten, and voices drifted to their ears. "—stop complaining! Would you rather be sent to the Darkwood? Or to Portal? At least down here you have a chance of surviving this war."

"I want out of these caves!" A second voice demanded. "I've been trapped down here for seasons. The ShadowMagi promised me glory and power, and all I've seen so far is dirt and snow!"

"Both of you, shut up! I'm tired of hearing your voices."

Wardel dropped to his knees and crept forward. Moving slowly, he peered around the corner and raised four fingers. A hacking cough echoed through the tunnels and the Guardsman uncurled his thumb. Jeran drew his sword and started forward, but when Grendor moved to join him, he pushed the Orog back. "Let me get you out of Dranakohr before I get you killed."

"I am a *Choupik*," Grendor said harshly. "I am not afraid to fight."

"But you are unarmed," Jeran said, "and untrained. We... We need someone to watch the tunnel. Make sure no one follows us." Grendor frowned, but he obeyed.

The fight was over quickly. Wardel had one soldier down before Jeran even turned the corner. Aryn dove past him, his sword swinging viciously. Jeran almost smiled at the sight of his uncle, dressed in mismatched armor and driving two soldiers back with a series of powerful swings, but there was something disturbing about Aryn's intensity, something in his eyes that Jeran had never before seen.

Once it was over, Grendor entered the chamber and stooped to retrieve a sword from one of the fallen guards. "Now I am only untrained, friend Jeran," he said, and Jeran knew he would not be able to convince the Orog to avoid any more fighting.

The smell of fresh air and midsummer flowers beckoned, and Jeran led his companions into a cloudless, starlit night. A thin sliver of moon shone down from above, but after the deep darkness of the tunnels, it seemed as bright as midday. They stood at the base of Dranakohr, breathing deeply, enjoying the illusion of freedom. But they were not free yet. The shadow of the wall spread out before them, blocking the entrance to the valley. A few guards could be seen in the flickering light of torches, their silhouettes pacing the parapets.

Jeran clung to the cliff face. The going was slow, but no guards shouted warning and no alarms echoed down from the castle. Once they crouched at the base of the wall, their need for haste increased. Dawn was not long from breaking, and if they were caught in the open when daylight hit, there would be no escape.

They raced along the wall, stopping at the broad gate. Only one soldier guarded the gate, and he slept soundly. Aryn dispatched him quietly, but the gate was barred and no simple mechanism existed to unlock it. "There's an unfinished section toward the far end," Jeran said. "We can cross there."

"It's risky," Aryn said, his lips drawn down in a frown. "We've been lucky to get this far." He studied the gate. "But if we open this monstrosity, all of Dranakohr will know it. Lead on, Jeran."

Running in short bursts, they crossed the remainder of the wall. Every moving shadow or sudden noise had them diving for the ground, certain they had been discovered. By the time they reached the scaffolding, all five were gasping for air and slicked in sweat. They huddled together to catch their breath, and Jeran seized his Gift. With his senses enhanced by magic, he scanned for signs of pursuit. Once convinced that they were not being followed, he started up the steps.

A shadowy figure waited for them atop the scaffolding. "I was wondering how long it would take you to get here," Katya said, stepping into the light. She held a sword at her side, but she did not raise it when Jeran appeared. "I saw you staring at the wall when we spoke."

"I'm leaving," Jeran said simply. The grip he held on his blade tightened. He had no wish to fight Katya, but he would not return to the tunnels.

"I was starting to doubt you'd ever do it." Katya looked east, to where the tiniest hint of light touched the sky. "Too much longer, and someone would have noticed that you killed all the sentries." She laughed at Jeran's confused expression and made a tisking sound. "You didn't think you'd be able to escape without killing them, did you? You've been in the caves too long, Odara. Why I should—"

A noise drew Katya's attention to the castle. "You'd better hurry. You'll want to be gone before the guards notice your absence. My uncle will tear the Boundary apart looking for you." A shout echoed down from above, and then a bell began to toll. "In any case," Katya said with a sigh, "you'll want to be gone before they get down here."

"Come with us," Jeran said, grabbing Katya's arm.

"We've had this conversation," Katya replied, her eyes sparking. "There's nothing for me out there."

"There's nothing for you here!" Jeran insisted.

"Argue about it much longer," Yassik interjected, "and it won't matter."

Frowning, Jeran sheathed his sword. "You're a good friend, Katya Durange."

"Then you'll do me one last favor?"

Jeran nodded. "Anything."

"Hit me."

Jeran stepped back, surprised. "What?"

"If they find me uninjured, my father will know the truth. In your haste to escape, you might not take the time to kill me, but you certainly wouldn't leave me to raise an alarm."

"I won't..." Jeran shook his head. "I can't—"

From out of nowhere, a fist appeared. Katya fell to the ground heavily, blood running from her lip. Jeran turned to Wardel, who shrugged. "She wanted us to do it," the Guardsman said. "Besides, she might have asked you, but no one asked *me* if I wanted to become the Darklord's slave." Without waiting for a response, the Guardsman crossed over the wall and started down the other side of the scaffold.

With freedom at hand, Jeran and the others sprinted down the mountain at a reckless speed, sending showers of loose stone ahead of them. Above, they heard Dranakohr awaken and knew pursuit would not be far behind.

By the time the sun cleared the mountains, they had reached the base of the valley. Calling for them to follow, Yassik led them off the trail, through a stand of trees, and into an open field. Small patches of snow still clung to the shadows, and a small stream babbled down the center of the valley.

"We did it!" Wardel said. "We're free!"

"We're not free yet," Yassik told him. "But I think..." The Mage's face contorted. After a moment, a loud click echoed through the still, morning air, and the old man's mouth split open in a broad smile. Reaching up, he removed the collar from his throat.

Laughing aloud, Yassik hurried to Jeran. "To feel magic again... The way it's supposed to feel!" the old man murmured as he grabbed Jeran's collar. A second click rang out, and Jeran felt a great weight lift from his shoulders. Magic rushed into him in a torrent, filling him, and he gasped. He focused his will, and a ball of light appeared above his head. The sensation was invigorating, like nothing he remembered. For a time, he stood there, reveling in the feeling. Then, with a scream of rage, he threw the collar into the distant trees.

Yassik moved to throw his collar as well but stopped himself. "We might need this," he said, tucking the iron band into his robes. He closed his eyes again and took several deep breaths. "I don't know this area well, and we're too close to the Boundary for me to even guess where this will take us"—the air in front of them bent in upon itself and then exploded outward, revealing a different grass-covered plain, one without mountains—"but wherever it is will certainly be safer than here."

Without waiting, Yassik stepped through the Gate. Once through, he turned to his companions. "Are you coming? I can't hold this thing open forever." As if Yassik's words had released their muscles, the others hurried forward, racing to be the first to join the Mage in freedom.

Interim

The hot summer sun blazed, scorching anyone foolish enough to venture outside. Not so much as a whisper of wind stirred the air, and no clouds hovered in the dark blue skies, yet a haze covered Kaper like a shroud. The air, heavy with moisture, clung to everything until even drawing breath seemed a chore.

The sound of clanging metal rose from the courtyard, where a squad of militia trained. No one wore armor; even the leather shirts used to soften the bite of the practice swords had been discarded. Sweat-soaked men circled each other in pairs, cautiously trading blows. Bystral circled them all, watching. Dark rings circled the Guardsman's eyes, and the slump of his shoulders spoke of near exhaustion.

One trainee lunged in a sudden attack, but when his opponent dodged, he lost his balance, and his opponent's answering blow caught him squarely in the back. With a grunt, the trainee fell, landing atop his own blade. His scream pierced the afternoon air. From his vantage point, King Mathis winced.

"By the Gods, men!" Bystral thundered, calling a stop to the sparring and hurrying to the injured man. "These aren't toys; they're real blades! How many times do you have to be told that?" The Guardsman tore a strip of cloth from the man's breeches and tied it around his wound, but by the time he had pulled the boy to his feet, dark blood had already soaked the cloth.

"Off to the healer with you," Bystral ordered, and he told two other trainees to escort the man. "The rest of you, gather around. We've talked about the importance of balance before. If you don't..."

Mathis watched the wounded man hobble off. *He'll need stitches for that.* He had heard of a thousand such injuries, and he wondered how many more had not been reported. *If only we had a few of those Mage Healers! In exchange for miracles, I'd gladly sacrifice some pride!* The reports he received from Martyn were remarkable: bones mended in an instant, life-threatening injuries healed with a touch. Martyn also said the Healers were arrogant to a fault, but in Mathis' experience, that was not a peculiar trait among Magi.

Thoughts of his son organizing the defenses along the Corsan border made Mathis worry. Martyn had grown in the last few seasons; he had become a man. Knowing that his son was responsible for rallying the villages of southern Alrendria to repel the Corsan invaders filled him with pride, yet Mathis could not help but see the boy he had once bounced on his knee.

In a way, Mathis envied Martyn. He no longer had the luxury of racing to face danger. As king, duty demanded that he think of Alrendria first, that he live to inspire his people, not die to defend them. It was a lesson his father had taught him, though the learning had been painful. The one time King Faldar had ignored his own advice, on the eve of the final battle against the Durange, it had made Mathis king.

Shaking off his dark thoughts, Mathis left Bystral to his task. The Guardsman had taken his new post as commander of the city garrison seriously—Martyn had been wise to suggest him for the command—but he still had much work to do before the trainees were ready for battle. With Kaper all but bereft of true Guardsmen, Mathis needed those young men. He just hoped Bystral could make them into soldiers.

Once inside, breathing air untouched by the merciless sun, the King's mood improved. The halls were empty. Only those forced to wander the halls did so; the remainder hid in their quarters or swam in the castle's spring-fed pools. A few braver souls had even taken to the catacombs, where temperatures remained comfortable in even the hottest weather.

Mathis heard something behind him and stopped. His hand dropped to the sword at his hip, but the hall behind him was empty. The only thing moving was a time-worn tapestry, its edge fluttering in an unfelt breeze. Mathis frowned, and he stared intently down the hall but saw nothing out of the ordinary.

Nerves, he thought, though he had good reason to be nervous. Two more murders had taken place since Martyn left for Vela. That both victims had been Elves did little to assuage Mathis' fear; his enemies would gladly kill him if given the chance.

Then why do I refuse a guard? Mathis knew the answer. He refused to be afraid in his own home, refused to be escorted from one room to another in the place where he had grown up, the place where he had raised his own family.

"My Liege?" a voice called, and Mathis jumped. The Guardsman—one of the new recruits, judging by his boyish face and the way he looked uncomfortable in his armor—fell backward at the King's sudden movement. Mathis did not know which of them look the more startled, but he remembered something else his father had said: *A man looking over his shoulder will walk right into his enemy's blade.*

The Guardsman, mistaking the King's dark expression for anger, backed up another step and saluted fist-on-heart. "My Liege?" he repeated, this time on the verge of panic.

"Yes, Guardsman?"

"Dispatches, my King." He thrust a stack of papers forward in a trembling hand. "And a message from Master Caleb."

Caleb had been working night and day to meet Mathis' demand for arms and armor. "From Caleb?" Mathis repeated. "What's his message?"

"He wanted me to tell you that a number of weapons have disappeared."

Mathis' frown returned, and he stroked his grey-streaked beard. "Have Master Caleb send me a list. Double the guard on the armory and station a Guardsman at every forge." The Guardsman ducked his head and turned to leave, but Mathis stopped him. "Station a guard at the bowsmith and the fletchery as well, and ask Master Windel to check his stocks."

The Guardsman hurried to obey, and Mathis started walking again. He made only a handful of steps before he stopped again. Sighing, he turned around. "You might as well come out," he announced. "You're not bad, but I'm neither blind nor deaf, and I was trained by the best."

Mathis waited, his sword half drawn. When the tapestry moved again, the hint of a smile ghosted across his face. He drew a breath to call an alarm. He was ready for anything, except for what confronted him. A boy of fourteen winters wearing patchwork armor: bits of discarded chain and plate hand-sewn into a stout leather top, mismatched leather gauntlets too big for his hands, and padded leggings. On his left hip hung a sheathed shortsword, and in his right hand he held a curved, serrated blade.

Another old saying came to mind, this one from Mathis' grandmother Sionel: *In all the world, only three types of people are accomplished sneaks: thieves, assassins, and children, and I've yet to meet a child that's been pickpocketed.*

"Come here, boy," Mathis called, and the young man saluted. Something about the child stood out, and Mathis felt that he knew the boy. "Now, lad, and don't be frightened,"—the boy looked anything buy frightened—"who are you, and why are you following me?"

"My name is Mika Alkhael, King Mathis," the boy answered crisply, ducking his head low. "I'm here to protect you."

"Alkhael," Mathis repeated, and recognition came like a thunderbolt. "Liseyl's son? She's told me about you. And so has Martyn. Why, I've—" The rest of what the boy said sank in, and Mathis found himself at a loss for words. "You... You're here to... *protect* me?"

Mika nodded. "At Prince Martyn's command. I wanted to go with him, but he said that with the Guard fighting the war there'd be no one here he could trust. So—" Mika whirled around suddenly, raising his *dolchek*. Mathis stared, confused, until a servant appeared at the far end of the hall. One convinced the King was not in danger, Mika resheathed his blade and turned back around. "So I volunteered," he continued.

"I see," Mathis said, hiding a smile. "I hate to disappoint you, lad, but I have an entire garrison protecting me. I have no need of you, though I appreciate your loyalty." Mathis eyed the blade at the boy's hip. "Tell me, Mika, where did you get that sword?"

Mika's grip tightened on the blade. "Guardsman Bystral had it made for me," he said defensively. "Prince Martyn ordered him to train me to be a Guardsman. I'm too young to join now," Mika said, holding his head high, "but as soon as I'm of age, I'm going to join the Guard."

"And a fine Guardsman you'll make," Mathis said. The child had provided him with some much needed amusement, but he had a stack of reports to read and a thousand other duties to attend to. "But I don't need protection, especially not from a child, so you had best be on your way." Mika frowned, as if unsure of what he should do, but a stern glare from the King sent him sulking down the hall.

Mathis headed in the direction of his quarters, the dispatches tucked under one arm. He only made it to the next intersection before a new form blocked his path. Lady Javinia Morrena, widow of the late Lord Eduard, stood in the hall, fanning herself with an Aelvin device. In Javinia, one could see where Alynna had received her beauty, but where the daughter was a stunning blossom, Lady Javinia was a flower in full bloom.

As soon as Mathis saw her, he stifled a groan and tried to duck around the corner. "King Mathis," Javinia called, curtsying. The motion exposed more than a small amount of bosom. "How nice to see you."

Though the war was far away, many of the nobility—those who had not returned to their own holdings—had asked for refuge in the castle. Against his better judgment, Mathis had granted their requests, mostly because he could not think of a good reason not to. 'It's harder to avoid you if you're in the castle,' was not the most political of responses.

"And you, Lady Javinia." Mathis said, taking her hand and touching the smooth skin to his lips. "I apologize that I have not been able to accept your invitation. With the war, and things as they are—"

"No need to make excuses, King Mathis," Javinia interrupted. "The demands on your time are great. Everyone knows that. I don't expect you to drop everything just because I requested a meal!" The slight quaver of her voice suggested that his neglect had wounded her, and she raised her fan to her forehead, swaying as if dizzy. Mathis moved to steady her, and Javinia fell into his arms. Her breathing was shallow, but at the King's touch, her eyes fluttered open. "My apologies, King Mathis. The heat…"

Mathis scanned the hall, but there was nowhere to sit. He either had to lower the noblewoman to the floor or hold her until she recovered. *This is ridiculous! I must tell Liseyl to line these corridors with benches.*

A light touch on his arm snapped Mathis out of his musing. "You sacrifice so much for Alrendria," Javinia whispered. "It must be lonely being king. I've been lonely too, since my Eduard… Perhaps… Perhaps we could take comfort in—"

A loud crash, immediately followed by the terrified scream of a child, resounded through the hall. "Dear Gods!" Mathis released Javinia, and the noblewoman, her strength miraculously returned, managed to stand on her own. Mathis ordered her to find a healer, and she left at a run.

Mathis ran in the direction of the sound, and turning a corner, he saw an ornamental suit of armor splayed across the floor. In the center of the mess sat a girl of four or five winters, tears streaming down her face. Her panicked screams pierced Mathis' heart. He dropped to his knees amidst the bits of armor and cradled the girl in his arms. "There, there," he said, looking the child over for injuries. "Everything will be all right."

The girl did not listen; her cries continued no matter how much comforting the King offered. Concerned that she had suffered some injury he could not see, Mathis was preparing to carry the child to a healer, when a small hand came to rest on the girl's shoulder. "That's enough, Ryanda," Mika said. "She's gone."

The cries immediately stopped, and Ryanda's teary eyes grew wide with wonder. A broad smile split her face. "Thank you, King Mafis," she said, regaining her feet. After smoothing out her dress and offering the King a curtsy, she sprinted down the hall.

Mathis stared slack-jawed at Mika. "I can protect you from more than assassins," Mika said solemnly.

Against his will, Mathis laughed. "Come along then," he said, standing. "I have reports to read."

* * * * * * * * * * * * * * * * * * * *

"Escaped!" Tylor roared, and the word thundered through the starless night. The soldiers nearest the Bull cringed and sought shelter among the horses. Only Halwer stood his ground, though a rivulet of sweat ran down his face. "What do you mean escaped?"

Salos, nearly invisible in black robes and hooded cape, answered calmly. "I warned you that Odara was not one to be trifled with, as did the Master. He is not pleased."

"*He* is not pleased," Tylor repeated, grinding his teeth together. "How could this have happened? When I left, the boy was locked in my Trophy Room!"

"At first," Salos explained, "your guards thought the Odaras dead." The Scorpion circled his brother slowly, his movement fluid. "Two corpses were found in the charred remains of your room. An alarm was only sounded when the bodies of our soldiers started appearing and your men decided they might have been wrong. By then, it was too late."

Tylor pivoted to keep Salos in view at all times. The ShadowMage's eyes, hidden deep within the cowl of his cloak, flashed unexpectedly, glowing with their own light, and Tylor shivered; the nearness of magic, even his brother's, sent chills down his spine.

"The tunnels!" the Bull exclaimed. His gaze shifted to Halwer. "Have the men search the tunnels. He must be hiding with the—"

"Jeran is not in the tunnels, Brother." A flare of torchlight caught Salos' face, exposing a smug grin and laughing eyes. "The sentries guarding the wall were murdered, and my dear, sweet Katya was attacked during the escape. Your men found tracks."

"Even better! The Odara brat couldn't have passed us without my scouts seeing him. He and the others must be between us and—" Tylor fell silent, his mouth working silently. "Katya?" he said weakly. "Is she...?"

"She was incapacitated, but left conveniently alive." There was no relief in the Scorpion's voice, no happiness. His tone carried no emotion; he was reporting a simple fact.

"What a relief—" Tylor looked at his brother suspiciously. "You think she's involved, don't you?" He shook his head, not wanting to believe. Katya had always been a favorite, as dear to him as his own children.

"Her time in Alrendria changed her," Salos whispered. "I have doubted her commitment to the Master for some time now. She is... corrupted." Again, the statement was a simple fact. Where Tylor would have raged or wept at such an admission, the Scorpion showed nothing. To Salos, Katya had been a failure from the moment he discovered that her Gift did not match his. Losing her was no more upsetting than losing any other tool. An unfortunate necessity. At times, Tylor pitied his brother.

"I don't believe it." Tylor balled his hand into a fist. "I *refuse* to believe it. She has followed my orders without question."

"Has she?" Salos made a tisking sound, chiding Tylor for his blind devotion. "Jeran changed so many of your rules; it's hard for me to tell. Perhaps if you'd kept tighter control of Dranakohr..."

A growl rose in Tylor's throat. "One of these days you will push me too far."

Salos nodded. "I dread that day, Brother. I truly do. But the fact remains: it's unlikely the Odaras could have escaped without help. Either Katya is responsible for that aid, or we have another traitor in our midst."

Tylor waved a hand dismissively. "This is a matter for another time! We still have a chance to catch them, if we act quickly. They couldn't have passed my army without someone noticing. Only a handful of passes exist; without knowledge of them, Jeran could wander these mountains forever. You said tracks were found." Tylor rubbed his hands together eagerly. "We can follow them. And when I find them... Who's to say what happened? Without the Master there to stay my hand, a sad accident could befall that troublesome—"

"You won't find them in the Boundary, Brother."

Salos' smug arrogance enraged the Bull. "Why not?"

"Because I found this not far from where we lost their trail." With a flick of his wrist, Salos threw something; it hit the ground with a thud. Tylor stooped to pick up the collar. "Without that," Salos said, "Jeran is free to use his Gift. I don't know where he's gone, Brother, but he's out of your reach."

The collar trembled in Tylor's hand, and a tense silence followed. With a roar that startled the horses, Tylor spun and threw the iron band. It tumbled down the mountain in a shower of loose stone. "Punish the slaves in the Barrows," he snarled at Halwer. "And in the *ghrat*! Make sure everyone knows it's because of Jeran that they suffer." Halwer hurried away to dispatch the orders.

With Halwer gone, only Salos remained to see Tylor's rage. "And what of Katya?" he asked in a sibilant whisper.

"*If*—and I say if, Salos, because I don't believe your accusations—you can prove she took part in the escape, she'll pay for it. Until then, she'll remain in command of Dranakohr."

"You're being sentimental, Tylor. It would be best—"

"I won't betray her based on suspicions. Prove that she helped Odara escape and she's yours. If you can't prove she did it, then find out who did." Tylor signaled, and in tight formation, the Bull's army continued its march under cover of night, moving out of the Boundary and into the open plains of Alrendria. "Either way, I'll have to deal with our traitor later. Right now, I have a war to fight."

* * * * * * * * * * * * * * * * * * * *

A streak of lightning arced across the sky, but the thick trees, their limbs locked in a tight embrace, prevented most of the light from reaching the ground. The crack of thunder shook the earth, startling birds from their nests and scaring the forest to silence. Winds whipped through the branches, howling like a creature out of a nightmare. The air, heavy with unshed rain, made the night oppressive. The cracked ground yearned for moisture; the withered trees begged for it. A trickle of water ran down the face of a rock, dripping into an empty stream bed three hands across. Between crashes of thunder, a wolf raised a mournful cry, and raptors occasionally shrieked in rage. Other creatures stalked the night, visible only when an errant flash reflected off their slitted eyes or white fangs.

The Mage walked calmly, unconcerned by the creatures around him. He wore stout black breeches and a matching shirt, but the heat did not bother him. A small sphere hovered over his shoulder, a ball of dull light barely a hand in diameter. From time to time, the light wavered or the sphere collapsed. When it did, the Mage cleared his mind and the light renewed.

Darkness did not concern him. With his Gift, he could make the sphere glow brighter; with concentration, bright enough to turn night to day. But there was no need. With the enhanced senses of one who held magic, the dull light more than suited his needs.

He walked purposefully, his footfalls making little noise on the hard-packed dirt. Nevertheless he felt eyes upon him; unseen watchers studied him from every direction. He ignored them, except when lightning caught one by surprise. In such instances, he shook his head and chastised the watcher with a tisking sound. Embarrassed, the animal slunk into the shadows, and each time, the hint of a smile touched the Mage's lips.

A dark mound appeared ahead, and the Mage approached. Once within the radius of his magical light, the mound took on substance, transforming into the body of a man. The face was unrecognizable, the armor scored with dents and cuts. A snake slithered out from beneath the corpse, running from the light.

Unphased by the specter of death, the Mage continued on until, without warning, a mountain cat emerged from the shadows to block his path. The Mage disregarded the growl and exposed fangs, and he moved to step around, but the beast intercepted him.

"Yes, you're very frightening," the Mage answered. "But you're not going to stop me." He stepped forward, and the cat growled again. "I don't want to hurt you. Or anyone else. But what I need to say must be said, and I won't let him stop me from saying it." They faced each other for a moment, but finally the cat bounded into the night, its passage marked by the rustle of branches. The Mage smiled. "I knew you'd be reasonable."

The Mage entered a clearing. Across the way two torches burned, their flames whipping back and forth in the gusts of wind that tore through the gap in the canopy. Piles of weapons and armor lay scattered about, some clean, some blood-crusted, and some covered in rust. Wagonloads of supplies littered the clearing. Some of the carts were overturned, their contents scattered through the grass; others stood untouched, as if waiting for their horses to return and cart them off to market. Armies of rats patrolled the stockpiles, keeping a vigilant watch.

A pack of hounds, their shaggy fur matted to their backs and their fangs bared, flowed from the shadows. On silent paws they took up positions around the Mage, two to either side. "An escort. How polite." With a casual gesture, he allowed the dogs to lead him forward.

Between the torches sat a throne, a monstrous seat carved into the trunk of a fallen tree. Another hound, larger than the others, lay at the base, and the Mage saw smaller dogs behind the massive chair. Perched atop the throne, on a crosspiece capped with a helmet, a golden eagle stared proudly, and in the throne sat a creature out of legend. A monster from a child's nightmare.

Twice the size of a man, it wore tattered rags and bits of hide. The garments might have once been fine—in their current state, it was impossible to tell—but now barely enough remained to call them clothes. Blood was smeared across arms and legs thick with knotted muscle, and an intricate pattern was drawn upon the creature's face in mud, except below the eyes, where twin tracks had washed the skin clean. Long hair, caked with mud, hung well below the creature's shoulders, and fiery almond-shaped eyes regarded the Mage. Rage, always close to the surface, beat within those eyes, and it could be heard in the growl that punctuated each of the creature's breaths. A golden medallion poked out from the remains of its shirt.

The Mage stopped several hands from the throne and looked around. His eyes drifted up to the eagle, down to the dogs. "It seems you've finally accepted your gift."

The creature gestured at the pulsing sphere. "It seems I'm not the only one."

The Mage's lips twisted up, and he glanced at the light hovering over his shoulder. "Our abilities don't make us evil. It's how we use them, and what we use them for, that matters. It took me a while to understand that."

Cold, humorless laughter drifted down from the throne. "You always did have a way with words, Jeran."

Jeran's smile grew sad. "How are you, Dahr?"

"No complaints," Dahr replied, slapping the arm of his throne with a palm. "My friends keep me company, and the Bull sends enough soldiers to feed my thirst." Somewhere in the forest, a cat roared. A pack of wolves picked up the cry and added their howl to it. Dahr leaned forward and eyed Jeran suspiciously. "How did you find me?"

For a time, Jeran did not speak. "A long time ago, a friend told me that if monsters existed, they'd live in the Darkwood. Once I heard the rumors in Dranakohr, I knew where to find you."

A tension existed between them where none had existed before. It pained Jeran. "I..." Dahr's voice caught. "I tried to save you. My friends and I... Once the Blood Rage passed, we tried to find you, but I was always one step behind Tylor. He had you in the Boundary before I could stop him. I... I'm sorry."

"It's not your fault." Jeran hoped he could make Dahr believe. "Why didn't you go back to Kaper? To Martyn?"

Dahr was asking his own question. "How did you escape?" He chuckled, and Jeran heard a hint of the man he remembered in the sound. "You first," Dahr said with a gracious wave.

"Tylor got sloppy. He thought I was finished, that Reanna's death and the death of my son had broken my spirit. He—"

Shock replaced anger. "Your... son?"

Jeran nodded, but the memory was too fresh, the wound too painful, for him to elaborate. "The Bull never imagined that their deaths would make me stronger, or that Katya—"

"Don't say her name!" Dahr yelled, and the pack growled in agreement. He took several slow breaths. "Never say her name."

"She helped me escape. Without her, I would have died."

"Without her, you wouldn't have been in Dranakohr! She betrayed me! She betrayed us!"

"You don't believe that any more than I do. She sacrificed herself—and her love for you!—to save Martyn. She couldn't have acted more nobly if—"

"I won't discuss this!" Dahr yelled. Jeran frowned, but eventually he ducked his head and let the matter drop.

"Now that we've dispensed with the pleasantries," Dahr said, his voice cold. "Why have you come?"

"To bring you back. It's time to rejoin the world of men."

Dahr's eyed flashed. "And if I don't want to go?"

Jeran cocked his head to the side. "I could make you. I have the power."

"You couldn't make me stay unless you watched me constantly." Dahr's hands gripped the arms of the throne so tightly the wood groaned. "Could you do that, Jeran? After all we've been through, after all you've suffered, could you make me your slave?"

"You know I couldn't."

"Then you'd best be on your way. I'm not going anywhere."

"Why?"

"There's nothing for me out there but pain. Here, I'm a king, and my subjects honor me. There are no oaths, no names, and no surprises. Here, there's only life and death, and enough of the Darklord's servants to quench my thirst for vengeance. Here, I'm happy."

"I don't believe you."

"I don't care what you believe. I don't need you anymore. I have a family."

Jeran looked at the dogs. "They don't believe you either, not if they know you. Anyone who does can see through your lies. The only person you've ever been able to fool is yourself."

Dahr stood, jerking out of the throne and reaching for his sword. He stood there for a long time, poised on the edge of attack, but with a supreme effort of will, he resumed his seat. "Don't press me, Jeran. I don't want to fight you."

"Ask them," Jeran said with a confidence that infuriated Dahr. "Ask them what you should do! I can't hear their thoughts, but I know their answer."

Dahr's lips pressed into a thin line, and his teeth ground together, but he relented. "As you wish. Fang! Shyrock!" The dog at Dahr's feet perked up her head, and above, the eagle fluffed its wings. "What do you think, should we stay here or go with Jeran?"

Nothing happened, and a smug grin spread across Dahr's face. "See, I—" With a shake, Fang stood and padded to Jeran's side. Dahr's eyes widened, and his mouth worked furiously, but no sound came out. When the eagle launched itself from the throne, made a circuit of the clearing, and landed on Jeran's shoulder, Dahr slumped back, defeated.

"Traitors," he mumbled, the strength gone from his voice. Jeran smiled knowingly, but Dahr saw something in his friend's eyes; he saw anger hot enough to match his own. "You hate too," he whispered, and the knowledge renewed his strength. "Perhaps not the same things, but you hate. How can you begrudge me my revenge?"

"I hate," Jeran admitted, though it pained him to do so. "But I am not a slave to my hate. Of all people, I'd think the possibility of that would frighten you the most." Jeran scratched Fang's head and met Dahr's angry gaze with a worried one. "Be careful, Dahr. The Darkwood has no monsters yet, but you walk a dangerous line. If you're not careful, you may become what you fear you are."

"GO!" Dahr thundered, waving his arms dramatically. "All of you, go! Leave me in peace!"

Jeran stepped forward, and though Dahr willed them to, none of the animals blocked his approach. "What of your duty to House Odara? Your duty to Alrendria? Are you truly ready to turn your back on all you've loved?"

"Where was Alrendria when all I love was lost to me?"

Jeran sighed heavily. He bowed his head and made to go, but with a lightning-fast movement, he drew the blade at his side and drove it into the arm of the throne. Dahr barely had time to flinch; he stared at the *dolchek*, its hand-carved hilt quivering from the force of Jeran's strike, its blade glittering in the light of the torches.

"I had a brother once," Jeran said, "to whom honor was the highest of virtues, a man of loyalty and undying compassion. The last time I saw him, he charged alone into an army of Tachans to rescue me from certain death." Dahr turned away, unable to stand Jeran's icy blue gaze. "In the mines of Dranakohr, when I saw my uncle tortured and watched Reanna murdered, memories of my brother kept me alive. I imagined him free, fighting for Alrendria, helping those unable to help themselves. Those images gave me the strength I needed to survive.

"Imagine my sadness when I learned my brother was dead." At this, Dahr turned back to face Jeran, and the tears on his friend's face cut to the core. Jeran gestured at the *dolchek*. "Bury that with him, if you ever find his grave." Jeran walked away, the magical sphere bobbing above his head.

"Jeran?" Dahr called, but Jeran did not respond. The pack followed him into the shadows. "Jeran!" Dahr called again, and when he still received no reply, his gut clenched. Standing, he drew his greatsword from beside the throne. "JERAN!" he bellowed at the top of his lungs.

With an animal cry, he swung his sword, shattering his throne with a single, well-placed blow and losing himself to the Blood Rage.

Chapter 22

Martyn wormed through the grass on his belly. He pushed aside the dry, yellowed blades, careful to make no noise, and signaled to the men behind him to follow. They moved quickly, too quickly for his liking, but timing was critical and the strong winds muffled the few sounds they made. When the ground began to slope downward, Martyn closed his hand in a fist, bringing the party to a stop. Edging forward, he pushed through the last few tufts of grass. A hungry smile spread across his face. "Right where they're supposed to be."

A small party, no more than five score in number, was setting up a camp in the valley below, toiling in the late afternoon heat. Archers patrolled the perimeter, but they walked with heads low and eyes squinted to ward off the stinging dust. A few held their bows ready, but most rested the weapons on the ground. The swirling winds buffeting the depression would make firing a shaft difficult and aiming all but impossible.

The Corsans not guarding the camp struggled to raise the tents, but every blast of summer wind ripped stakes from the ground and sent the men running to collect their belongings. One lone figure stood at the center of the chaos, shouting orders and gesticulating wildly. It was a wasted effort; the winds prevented the man's commands from being heard. Even when they could hear, the men paid their commander little heed. The Corsans, exhausted from a long march and the battle to set up camp, dropped to the ground at every opportunity, taking shelter behind half-buried rocks or wrapping themselves inside the thick canvas of the unpitched tents.

Only the very heart of the encampment remained orderly. A score of hard-eyed and grim-faced swordsmen lounged against a circle of wagons, sharpening their blades and watching their less fortunate companions run themselves ragged. Packed close together, the wagons offered some protection from the weather. They were so heavily laden they barely rocked, even when the winds howled through the depression with animal-like ferocity. *Fool*, Martyn thought. *Had he any sense, he'd have spaced those wagons out and pitched the tents inside.*

The Corsan commander's ignorance sat well with Martyn; the more inept he proved, the fewer Alrendrians would die today. Had the Corsans been entrenched, taking the wagons would prove far more difficult. The prince had few qualms about battle; killing Corsans ranked nearly as high with him as stealing Murdir's supplies, but he refused to risk his Guard unnecessarily. He knew he would need every soldier for the battles still ahead.

Martyn heard the quiet rustle behind him that meant his company was in position. Had he not known what to listen for, he would have mistaken the noise for the wind. They had been trained well, and the sloppy ones had been culled in the battles already fought. Martyn felt a presence at his side and smiled. "Take a look, Taymr. What do you think?"

The boy lunged forward carelessly, and Martyn stopped him from falling down the hillside. At just past sixteen winters, Taymr was barely old enough to join the Guard. Stringy brown hair, so caked with dust it looked gray, hung in front of dark eyes. Two long, spindly legs wrapped around a well-wrought, Alrendrian blade whose point dug a deep rent in the loose soil. Gashes ran the length of the boy's once-white uniform, and the seam at his left shoulder had split. Had his life hung in the balance, Martyn would have been hard-pressed to explain how a person could ruin clothes so quickly.

Taymr was one of the young men Martyn had recruited, one of many who hoped to find glory and honor in the war against the Corsans. He was also one of the most zealous, the most eager to risk himself. In previous skirmishes, he had thrown himself recklessly at the enemy, endangering himself and his companions. For that reason, Martyn had chosen him out, him and the others like him. He dared not send them home, but he hoped experience would temper these boys where words had not.

"They're disorganized," Taymr said loudly. His voice carried, and Martyn clamped a hand over the boy's mouth. He signaled for Taymr to speak softly. Eyes wide and cheeks red, Taymr nodded, and Martyn removed his hand. "The commander seems more concerned with the location of his tents than the welfare of his troops. He's hardly paying attention! Not like you, Prince Martyn! You're always keeping an eye on us."

"Take a closer look," Martyn sighed. "How many of the men aren't at their post? Where are the sentries? How many guard the wagons?" Taymr's brow furrowed, and he peered intently into the depression. "These are the things you need to look for!" Martyn chided. "The Corsan commander has made mistakes, but not watching his men isn't one of them! Those soldiers in the center are hardened veterans. They know what they're doing." Taymr nodded sagely, as if that was what he had meant the whole time.

"By the Gods, lad!" Kartoc whispered as he crawled up beside Taymr. Dark rings circled the Guardsman's eyes and black dirt smeared his cheeks. A long braid wound around his shoulders, its tip dragging across the ground. "With your legs wrapped around your blade like that, you're sure to kill yourself. Keep it at your side, like this!" Unceremoniously, and a little more roughly than necessary, the Guardsman untangled Taymr's legs and repositioning his sword.

The swordsman was frustrated, and with good reason. Kartoc had been assigned the worst duty possible: whipping the farmboys and shepherds into something resembling soldiers. It was an endless task, and a thankless one. Martyn wondered if the time had come to switch the Guardsman's duties. Lord Iban's voice echoed in his mind: 'Complacency and aggravation lead to mistakes, and mistakes to the grave. Keep your Guard happy, or you'll quickly regret it.'

"They all have bows!" Taymr said excitedly, jarring Martyn from his musings. "In a wind like this, bows will be useless. My da and I hunt all the time, but he'd turn us around if a storm half this strong sprang up." Martyn smiled, but Taymr wasn't finished. "They'd be safer in the wagons, too. Look where they're putting their tents." He pointed to the tight cluster of tents on the edge of the camp. "When we attack, they're going to be backed against the wagons with nowhere to go."

"It's good to see you listen occasionally," Martyn said, and Taymr's cheeks flushed dark red. Even Kartoc seemed impressed; with his free hand, he gave Taymr a friendly pat on the back. "Now," Martyn asked. "How should we attack?"

Taymr's eyes narrowed and he stretched forward, poking his head out farther. "Well, I—" His words choked off when a green snake slithered out of the grass and over his arm. Taymr's mouth dropped open, and he hissed in a breath.

Martyn's hand whipped out lightning fast, grabbing the snake behind the head and pulling it away from Taymr. He felt, rather than heard, the scream boiling up from the boy, but with the snake coiling around his arm, there was little he could do. Kartoc, with a speed that belied his stocky build, restrained Taymr; one hand clamped over the boy's mouth, the other pressed against his back, holding him down despite his frantic struggles.

"Stop movin', lad," Kartoc whispered. "It's not a viper, and it's less of a threat to you than I am at the moment." The words had no effect; Taymr continued thrashing. "Lie still," the Guardsman snarled, his patience gone, "or you'll sleep with a snake in your bedroll for the next ten-night."

Taymr froze immediately, and Martyn, once convinced the boy would not bolt, unwound the snake from his arm and set it in the grass, where it slithered away. "How should we attack?" he asked again as if nothing had happened.

Still trembling, Taymr outlined an intricate plan with numerous feints and ruses. Though hopelessly elaborate, the consideration Taymr gave to what many would have considered trivial matters impressed Martyn. "We'll make a Guardsman of you yet!" he laughed. Taymr beamed at the praise, and Martyn's expression grew grim. "Don't get too excited. Your plan is too complicated. The more maneuvers a Guardsman has to remember, the less he can focus on preserving his life and the lives of his countrymen. Simple plans are better."

"The prince is right," Kartoc grunted. "And sending a squad into the heart of the camp to kill the commander? That's folly, boy. Pure folly!"

Martyn nodded, though his tone was more comforting than the Guardsman's. "The Corsan commander looks raw, but his troops are seasoned. Why risk our men in an attack that might put someone with more experience in charge? Taking out a good commander is a sound tactic, but letting a terrible one live is a better one."

A rustling drew Martyn's eyes. "Ah, Cyrrus! Glad you could make it."

The Mage crawled out of the grass, his face contorted in disgust. Bits of grass and dried leaves clung to short black hair, dirt smeared his face, and his once-pristine robes were stained and torn. Frustrated gray eyes fastened on Martyn, and the prince fought to hide a smile. Watching the arrogant Magi crawling through the dirt brought Martyn no end of pleasure.

Martyn saw glimpses of his troops through the shifting grass. His soldiers were in position, lying along the edge of the ridge. A few gripped their swords, but most fingered their bows, ready for the attack. "You forgot one other thing," Martyn said, turning to Taymr. The boy looked up eagerly. "Use every weapon at your disposal."

The prince returned his attention to the Mage. "Is everyone ready?"

Cyrrus' eyes unfocused and his expression went blank. "Nielian and Josande have reached their positions. They await your command."

Martyn wrung his hands together, and his pulse quickened. It was a sensation he had experienced before, in the moments before other battles, and it was not one he relished. He had expected the feeling, the intense, nearly paralyzing spike of fear to lessen; but if anything, it had only grown worse. Steadying himself, he took one last look at the camp. "Now," he said, nodding curtly.

Cyrrus stood, exposing himself to the camp below. The winds caught his robes, sending them billowing behind him in waves. Across the depression, on the opposite hill, another form, silhouetted by the sun, stood up. Taymr moved to stand as well, but Martyn held him down. "Not yet. You'll know when."

The Magi raised their hands above their heads dramatically. Around them, the air crackled. The Alrendrians crouched behind them, poised for the attack. Even Kartoc was excited; Martyn knew by the way the Guardsman fingered the hilt of his blade.

One of the Corsan sentries noticed Cyrrus, and even from a distance, Martyn saw the soldier's eyes widen. Pointing at the hilltop, his arm moving wildly, the soldier raised the alarm. The delay had not been long, but Martyn hoped that if their positions had been reversed, his soldiers would have been more observant.

Someone spotted the other Mage and a second cry went up. All across the camp, Corsans stopped what they were doing and gathered to watch the intruders. The commander appeared, looking flustered. After conferring with his subcommanders, he turned and stared up the hill, shielding his eyes with a hand. He called out a series of orders to his men, and three parties quickly formed. One group moved toward each hill, and the third went toward the horses tied on the north side of the depression.

When the Corsans reached the foot of the hill, Cyrrus nodded, and Martyn leapt to his feet. "For Alrendria!" he shouted, drawing his bow. Around him, in a line nearly three hundred hands across, a score of Guardsman rose from concealment. Across the way, an equal number stood. Most had their bows drawn and ready to fire. Those who did not started down the hill at a jog, swords in hand.

Seeing the Alrendrians, the archers below fired a volley, but the swirling winds sent their arrows wide. The Corsans threw down their bows and drew their swords. As soon as they did, Martyn signaled to Cyrrus. The winds suddenly died, dwindling to little more than the barest breath of air. "Fire!" Martyn shouted, and two score arrows flew toward the Corsans.

The prince let his own arrow fly, and the shaft buried itself in the neck of a rough-looking swordsman. The man fell over, clutching at his throat. Quickly, before the Magi made the winds resume, Martyn fired a second shot. It went wide, missing its target by more than a hand.

The camp turned to chaos. Screams—agonized, terrified screams—echoed through the valley, and knowing that those screams came from the enemy brought little comfort to Martyn. The Corsans running toward the horses hesitated. Some turned and headed for the safety of the wagons, others hurried forward with even greater urgency. A jagged streak of lightning fell from the sky, changing their minds. Amid panicked, screaming horses, the Corsans fled.

The commander stood in the middle of the fray, shouting orders and trying to regroup his men. Few heard, and of those who did, fewer obeyed. When the rumbling started, low at first, but rapidly increasing in volume, the commander paused. A cloud of dust rose in the east. When he saw it, the commander gave up his position and raced for the wagons.

The Corsan commander had barely started moving when Dayfid and his riders galloped over the hill. They descended into the valley with swords drawn, shouting battlecries. "Guardsmen, charge!" Martyn shouted. As one, the Alrendrians threw down their bows and rushed forward, their swords flying free. As if on cue, the storm raged back to life, drowning out the screaming men and clanging swords. Martyn drew his own sword and started forward. Taymr followed a half step behind, brandishing his blade and shouting a lusty war cry.

Nearly half the Corsans had fallen in the initial assault, but the remaining men had regrouped and were heading toward the wagons. Dayfid was everywhere, his silver plate glittering in the afternoon sun, his white stallion rearing, its hooves kicking the air. The Guardsman's blade danced, cutting down any Corsan who happened across its path.

Martyn spotted a Corsan separated from his companions and moved to intercept him. The man saw the prince's approach and raised his blade in time to deflect the attack. His counterstroke was vicious; Martyn caught it with a parry, but the force of the blow sent a shock up his arm. They traded blows for some time, circling each other, and Martyn watched for an opening.

To Martyn's left, Taymr fought his own opponent. The boy was outmatched—the Corsan was more skilled and nearly twice his size—but quick wits and quicker reflexes kept him alive. Jhorval, blood streaming down his face, crashed into the Corsan from the side, and the man stumbled into Taymr's blade. Jhorval yelled something, and Taymr nodded. He wrenched his blade free and followed the Guardsmen into the fray.

Martyn slid around a wild swing and brought his sword in low. He felt the satisfying crunch as his blade hit armor, and the Corsan fell. Stunned, the man stared at Martyn and begged for mercy. With his sword gripped tightly in both hands, Martyn drove the blade into the Corsan's chest, and when he pulled it free, blood splattered his face. He heard a pitiful gasp escape his enemy's lips and watched as the Corsan's eyes dulled, watched as the soldier drew his last breath.

A wave of nausea stronger than any of the Corsan's blows struck Martyn. He dropped to his knees and retched. *That man was defeated. He asked for mercy. I shouldn't have...*

Martyn chided himself as he regained his footing. *Would he have shown you mercy? Debate the honor of your actions later! Right now, there are Corsans to kill.* He stumbled forward without bothering to wipe the blood from his face.

Dayfid and his men rode in circles around the encampment, making sure none of the Corsans fled. That was the way of their raids: no one escaped, and as little trace of battle was left as possible. The Corsans knew Martyn and the Alrendrians were out there somewhere, but every patrol, every supply wagon that disappeared without a trace made their fear grow. Reports had already arrived of desertions among Murdir's men, and every man who set down his sword and ran was one less to deal with.

A Corsan came screaming from the shadows of a half-erected tent. Martyn blocked the man's wild swing and pivoted to follow as he passed. He brought his sword around in an arc, but his feet shifted on the loose stone, and an ill-timed gust of wind caught the prince full on the chest. He staggered, and the Corsan—Martyn recognized the commander—skidded to a stop. With a cruel smile, the Corsan drew his sword back.

Martyn waited for his opponent to commit himself and then did something he had once seen Jeran do. He dove, not away from his attacker, but toward him. Tucking his shoulder, he rolled, and the Corsan's blade whistled over his head. Rising to a crouch, Martyn used his momentum to drive his sword up and into the commander's belly.

The blade hit point first but did not drive through. A dull thud reverberated in Martyn's ears, and his sword quivered violently. His entire arm went numb, and Martyn nearly lost his grip on the blade. He scrabbled backward, his eyes fixed on the Corsan's armor.

Not a mark, not the smallest scuff, marred the shining plate.

The commander smiled, baring slightly-pointed teeth. "Say hello to the Gods for me, Alrendrian pig!" His sword drew back hungrily.

Suddenly, the commander's eyes widened. Without warning, the Corsan's head exploded in flame, and the man fell to the ground screaming, his hands beating at his face. The smell of burning flesh reached Martyn's nose, and this time, he could not keep from vomiting. Before he turned away, Martyn noticed that the flames only burned the man's head; nothing below the neck was so much as singed.

"Stupid common," Cyrrus said, prodding the Corsan with his foot. "Wearing magical armor does little good if you don't wear the helmet too." He looked at Martyn, and his lips curled up in an amused smile. "Are you well, Prince Martyn? Uninjured, I hope."

"I'm fine," Martyn snapped, pushing himself to his feet. The Alrendrians controlled the valley, but a number of Corsans had taken refuge inside the ring of wagons. Even with such rudimentary defenses, casualties would be high if Martyn led an all out assault.

Martyn scanned the battlefield. Jasova was rallying the men, preparing to attack. "There!" Martyn called, pointing toward one of the wagons. "Can you move that wagon?"

The Mage arched an eyebrow. "Of course I can."

"Good. On my command, push it back as far as you can." Martyn turned away before the Mage could protest. Cyrrus did not like taking orders from a common, but Martyn had long since learned that the Mage would do what he was told so long as he was not given the chance to argue.

Martyn raced across the camp, shouting for Jasova. The Guard Commander saw the prince coming and signaled his men to hold their positions. Relieved, Martyn slowed, but he kept his eyes glued to the wagons and the Corsans trapped inside. He did not see the Mage hunched over on the ground until the last instant. He tried to keep from hitting her but lost his balance in the process. He winced as his shoulder and knees scraped against the rocky soil.

When Martyn saw who he had nearly fallen over, he sat bolt upright. "What are you doing here?"

"Tending the wounded," Sheriza replied, her voice cool, her eyes never leaving the bloody Guardsman before her. The Mage's hands danced over a deep gash that ran the length of the man's gut.

"This is a battle!"

"Ah," Sheriza said, fixing Martyn with an exasperated glare. "That explains all the injured men. I was wondering what had happened."

"But... But you're a Healer!" Martyn exclaimed. "You can't protect yourself! What's to stop a Corsan from sneaking up behind you—or walking right up to you for that matter!—and attacking?"

"Nothing." The reply was so simple, so calmly delivered, that for a moment Martyn could not believe he had heard her right. Sheriza closed her eyes, and the Guardsman hissed in a sharp breath. Martyn watched as the wound on the man's chest closed, the flesh knitting together, leaving no trace of injury. The Guardsman's eyes closed again, but this time, his breathing was slow and even.

Sheriza slumped over the Guardsman. She looked up at Martyn, and though the prince expected anger, he saw none; if anything, a measure of gratitude danced in the Healer's eyes. "Your concern is touching, Prince Martyn, but I won't hide when people need my Gift." She craned her neck around to assess the battle, and when she did, her lips compressed into a thin line. Tears glistened in her eyes. "Besides, this battle is over. Another splendid victory for Alrendria." Her tone lacked all joy; had she said defeat, the words would have carried no more sadness.

Martyn left Sheriza and hurried to where Jasova waited behind the protection of the half-raised tents. Though the winds blew the shafts well off mark, the Corsans used their bows liberally, doing everything in their power to hold the Alrendrians back.

Jasova looked exhausted. Scrapes and scratches ran the length of his mail, and blood ran freely down his left leg. A warm grin spread across his face at Martyn's arrival, and he nodded in the direction of the wagons. "We have them," he said, "but taking them will be costly."

"Get the men ready and wait for my signal!" Martyn said, and Jasova ran off, shielding his eyes from the wind. Far to his right, Martyn saw Cyrrus watching him. When Jasova signaled that all was ready, Martyn shouted. "Now!"

A moment of tense silence followed, but then a loud creaking came from the center of the Corsan's defenses. Slowly, one of the wagons turned, its wheels digging deep rents in the ground. It rolled backward, opening a gap in the Corsan's defenses and exposing the soldiers inside.

A second wagon began moving, and then a third. Across the camp, standing on the top of a hill, Martyn saw another Mage. More wagons moved, sliding inward, compressing together, until the Corsans huddled in a tight knot with nowhere to go. Martyn stepped forward. "Surrender now, and you'll be well treated."

The Corsans slumped, defeated. For one blissful moment, Martyn thought they would accept his offer. Then, with a wild cry, they launched themselves over the wagons in a last-ditch effort to escape. The Alrendrians surged forward to meet them, issuing their own battlecry.

Why don't they ever surrender? Raising his sword, Martyn ran to meet the charge.

Chapter 23

"Back to work! There's little enough light left to waste it!" The Guardsmen leaning against the side of a half-filled wagon jumped at Martyn's cry. With a weary salute, they resumed their onerous duty: hefting the bodies of the fallen into the captured wagons.

"Don't push them too hard," Jasova said as he limped toward Martyn. The Guard Commander had discarded his armor, but sweat still ran down his dirt-smeared face. Exhaustion painted his features and his shoulders sagged under an imagined weight, yet he studied the horizon alertly, almost as intently as he watched the worn faces of his men. Thick bandages bound his left leg, but blood had already seeped through the field dressing. "We still have the ride back."

"You should have the Healers fix that." Martyn gestured toward the commander's wounded leg.

"I tried!" Jasova laughed dryly. "Mage Sheriza took one look and told me to be on my way. 'We've men with real injuries, Commander,' she said to me. 'I'll see you tomorrow, when I've time to play with trifles.'"

The smile that spread upon Martyn's face was a genuine one. "The Five Gods know you don't want to get on her bad side! For a Mage sworn to cause no harm, her tongue can give a lashing I'd rather not live through again." They shared in a moment of laughter, then Martyn's expression grew serious. "Report."

"Most of the wagons carried weapons and food," Jasova said. "Supplies destined for the garrison at Ulanoc is our best guess. One carried gold and jewels, either from Murdir's coffers or plundered in raids."

"Gold?" Martyn repeated, pulling at his lip. "For Ulanoc?"

"Likely not. I think the payment was meant for Jule. Midlyn's been hurting; a bribe this large might be enough to buy Hasna's neutrality."

Frowning, Martyn scratched a hand across his two-day stubble. "For Hasna," he mused, "or another?"

"Mage Nielian confirmed that the Corsan commander's mail is Mage-wrought," Jasova continued. "I didn't witness all the tests, but I did see the armor engulfed in flame hot enough to scorch rock. It emerged without a blemish."

"And the other arms?" Martyn asked, making a note to discuss the armor with Nielian or Cyrrus. "Are they Mage-created?"

"Josande and Nielian are examining them now, but they suspect not. Only the commander wore Mage-created armor. Had they magical arms at their disposal, they would have used them. Wouldn't you have?"

Martyn shrugged, offering no answer. Around them, the Corsan encampment was being dismantled. Subcommanders bellowed orders to squad leaders, who shouted commands to their Guardsmen. The Guardsmen, in turn, found recruits and set them about the camp on various tasks. The men were not as lively as usual, the orders not carried out with the Guard's usual zeal, and those working the last row of wagons limped along even more slowly than their comrades. They had been on the move since well before dawn, and they had a long march ahead if they were to leave Corsan lands without being discovered.

The captured wagons had been arranged in three rows. Salvageable items went into the nearest, and the Guardsmen working them were the most lively. Light conversation belied their haggard appearance. They tossed sacks and crates haphazardly, and crammed loose items into whatever empty spaces could be found. Organization was not needed; everything would be sorted after they reached Darein.

Unsalvageable items went to the second row of wagons, a row half again as long as the first. The battle had been fierce, and many crates had not survived intact, but Martyn planned to take everything regardless of its state. Raids like today's had become routine for Martyn's troops, and one of the first lessons learned had been to never leave anything behind the enemy could use.

Not even the dead were spared scavenging, and the third row, nearly as long as the second, held the bodies of the slain. Once safely removed from Corsan-controlled lands, the dead would be stripped of arms and armor, clothes, and useable items. The bodies would be placed in a communal grave. Martyn had no desire to dishonor the dead, but every salvaged sword meant one less to forge, every reclaimed breastplate might one day save a living Guardsman. Whenever the morality of his decision troubled him, he dealt with it the only way he could: he ignored it. After the bodies were in the ground, he would pray for the souls of all the soldiers, Alrendrian and Corsan alike. It was the only thing he could do.

Only a few unclaimed bodies remained. Once they were recovered, it would be time to leave. A large party of recruits scoured the depression, looking for objects missed in the initial sweep and hiding all signs of the battle. Ikabhod's grim features and hard eyes ensured that the boys worked diligently.

When the supplies did not arrive and Murdir sent his scouts to investigate, they would find nothing. They would know what happened, but not where or when. Uncertainty would keep the Corsans on guard, and it might make the difference between victory and defeat. It was a strategy that had served Martyn well; twice now, his enemy had fled as soon as he appeared, screaming 'the Alrendrian Ghost!' as they ran.

Two Guardsmen carrying a body between them passed the prince, and Martyn winced when he saw the long, bloody gash running the length of the boy's side. Then he saw sightless, familiar eyes and he sighed. It was a boy from Taymr's village, and one of the young man's closest friends.

"Casualties?" Martyn asked, bringing his thoughts back to matters at hand. "As bad as they look?"

Jasova shook his head. "Two score dead, mostly recruits. Twice that in wounded. Things would have been worse if not for the Healers. Half the men walking would have died today, if not for their aid."

"Two score," Martyn repeated, and to himself, *Mostly recruits!* He hated himself for what he had to do; he hated the Durange and the Darklord for forcing him to do it. Though he knew it to be folly, he considered sending the boys home to their families, to their mothers, to their lives. He had no right to demand their sacrifice.

But he did have a need. *Alrendria* had a need. Every sword would count in the war to come; every man, woman and child would have to risk their lives for Alrendria's freedom. And it fell to him, Martyn Batai, Prince of Alrendria, to convince his people that their sacrifice was for the greater good, that their deaths were not only noble, but justifiable.

Rage built inside him, threatening to burst forth. *Another decision taken by duty! Another choice forced upon me!* The reality of his words hit him suddenly, and shame filled him. Duty might force him to send his people to their deaths, but it forced them to die. The demands of his rank—marriage to a beautiful woman, for instance—seemed trivial in comparison.

Martyn laughed, and the sound was discordant with the grisly pall of the battlefield. Jasova cocked an eyebrow, but the prince offered no explanation. "The Corsans?"

Jasova's eyes darkened, and the commander scrubbed a hand across his mouth. "Only a handful survived, and those who live do so only because their wounds prevented them from fighting to the last. We've tended the survivors as best we could." He pointed to a heavily-laden wagon trundling north. "They'll be taken to Sarin's Cross and held with the others."

A gust of wind brought the stench of blood to Martyn's nose. "Send one of the Healers with them. There's been enough death today." Jasova nodded. "Did anyone escape?"

If anything, the commander's eyes grew darker. "Dayfid and his men did well. Too well. Not a single soldier who ran survived."

"I'd rather a dead Corsan than a free one!" Martyn said fiercely, but even he heard his lack of conviction. "Dayfid can be overzealous," he added slowly, "but there are none among us more devoted to Alrendria. I'll talk to him." Jasova nodded but did not speak; his eyes remained distant. "Anything else?"

"No, my Prince. The supplies are loaded, and the recruits will be done shortly."

"Then signal the march. Tell Ikabhod to join us in Darein." Jasova saluted, fist-on-heart, and started forward. "And if you see Sheriza," Martyn called after him, "tell her I'd like to speak with her." Without waiting for the Guardsman's answering nod, Martyn went to his horse.

Taymr waited for him. At the prince's approach, the boy handed over the reins to Martyn's horse, and Martyn pulled himself into the saddle. The Guard formed rank around them, ready for the march home.

Quick is best, Martyn thought. He turned to Taymr. "Kristoph's dead."

The boy's mouth opened slightly, and he stared dumbly forward. A sheen of water filmed his eyes, and he turned away. When he raised his head, his eyes were dry. And angry. "Good," he said. "Better here, like a Guardsman, than cut down by a raider at home."

Taymr's cold sincerity sickened Martyn. He suddenly felt the need to escape, to remove himself from this valley and the memories of battle. Without waiting for Jasova's order, he heeled his horse to a trot. To his dismay, Taymr followed. Martyn had wanted to escape him, too.

Martyn galloped out of the valley, weaving deftly through the wagons and departing squads of Guardsmen. Out of the corner of his eye, Martyn saw movement, and he risked a glance. In one hand, Taymr held aloft the Alrendrian banner, and the Rising Sun, nestled on a field of white, shone down on the Guardsmen. Hawk-eyed Estaban, a blood-stained bandage wrapped around his arm, raised a hoarse cry. "Prince Martyn and Alrendria!" The cheer was taken up, first by a few, then in greater numbers, until the ground itself shook from the force of it.

Cyrrus and the Magi glared after the prince, not quite contemptuously, when the dust raised by his horse drifted over them. Stern and aloof, the Magi rode in a tight knot twenty hands from the nearest Guardsman. A short, balding Mage who appeared well into middle age rolled his eyes dramatically when Martyn rode past, as if watching the antics of an exasperating child.

Sheriza and the Healers rode separate, too, not only from the Guardsmen but from the other Magi. They looked drained. Dark rings circled their eyes and dirt smeared their usually pristine robes, but they held themselves straight-backed and proud. Like the other Magi, they did not cheer him, but they did not glare, either. In fact, they seemed more interested in his effect on the Guard, on the change in morale his passage caused, than on him. A number of conversations started in his wake.

Twisting around, Martyn stared at the long line of living soldiers, and behind them, the wagons carrying Alrendrian dead. The corners of his mouth drew down. *If not for them...*

Dayfid appeared on a distant hill, his unmistakable silver armor glittering in the sunlight. He waved, and Martyn returned the gesture, watching as the Guardsman spun his horse and disappeared from view, continuing his search for the enemy.

Once the valley and the marching army faded behind him, Martyn drew rein. He stopped atop a broad hill and looked out over the sweeping green plains. Gone were the smells of battle; now the scents of fresh grass and summer flowers assaulted him. A stiff, cool breeze blew from the north, and Martyn inhaled deeply, luxuriating in the fresh air and warm sunlight on his face. His muscles unknotted, and for a moment he forgot about the war.

Taymr stopped beside him, the Alrendrian banner still in hand, and shattered the illusion. "Why have we stopped?" the boy demanded.

"We're far enough ahead. Too far. Jasova will be furious."

Confusion spread across Taymr's face. "But you're the prince! What do you care if a Guard Commander is mad at you?"

"Being prince doesn't give me the right to do whatever I want," Martyn answered with a harsh laugh, remembering a time not too long ago when he thought it had meant just that. On the horizon, the first riders appeared, little more than black specks. "I've put myself—both of us!—in danger by riding so far ahead."

Taymr squinted to survey the countryside. "But there's nothing out here!"

"Listen to prince, little warrior," said a deep, booming voice. Taymr whirled around, and his hand reached reflexively for his sword. "He knows what he speaks."

Taymr's horse danced backward as the boy fumbled with his weapon, and Martyn snatched the reins to keep the animal from bolting. He waved for Taymr to stop, and the boy froze, but he kept a firm grip on the hilt of his blade. Martyn bowed deeply to the figure that rose out of the grass like an olive-skinned wraith. At less than twelve hands tall, the man could have passed for a Human, but the hairless face and piercing, almond-shaped eyes named him Garun'ah. Red-brown hair in wild curls framed an angular and pronounced jaw. The Tribesman wore tanned hides dyed to blend in with the dry grass. His jerkin was open in front, exposing a hairless chest and oiled muscles. A *dolchek* hung at his hip, and he held a short spear in one hand, its sharpened point covered in mud to keep the light from reflecting off it.

The Tribesman returned the bow. "Prince Martyn." His voice was a low rumble. "How went your hunt?"

"Well, Olin *uvan* Trayk," Martyn answered, straightening in his saddle. "We killed or captured over five score and lost less than half that."

Olin's eyes darkened when Martyn said 'captured,' but his words carried only admiration. "The Gods favor your sword, Prince Martyn. That is feat worthy of song." The Tribesman approached, circling wide to climb the steep hill. Taymr squirmed in his saddle, craning his neck around to keep Olin in view at all times, and his horse snorted and stepped about nervously.

A smile touched Olin's lips. "You must be the one my brothers call Prancing Pony. I hear of you." Taymr's expression grew angrier; he was not fond of the nickname.

"Are you alone, Olin?" Martyn asked, his eyes scanning the grass. He saw nothing, not the slightest movement, but that told him nothing. The Garun'ah would not be seen unless they wanted to be.

"My brothers are out there," Olin replied. "They track the enemy."

Martyn was instantly alert; his hand moved to his sword. "Corsans? How many? Where?"

A rumbling chuckle filled the air. "You truly are a Hunter, Prince Martyn." Olin pointed west, but a broad hill obscured the view. "Small bands. Ten at most in each. And inexperienced, even for Humans."

Taymr glowered, and his horse whinnied. Martyn tightened his grip on the boy's reins. "Inexperienced?"

"They make noise enough for a hundred, and scout only where they go. They could pass within hands of an enemy and never notice." The Tribesman's smile hinted that they had done just that.

"Are you sure they didn't spot you?" Taymr said coldly.

Martyn turned a dark gaze on the boy, but Olin only chuckled. "You are young, Prancing Pony, so I will not take offense."

The thunder of hooves drew Martyn's eyes. Dayfid crested the hill at a gallop, a cloud of dry dust trailing behind him. He adjusted his course and brought his mount to a skidding stop at the prince's side. "Corsans, my Prince." Dayfid's hair was tousled, his silver plate smeared with dirt and blood, but his eyes held an eager fervor.

Olin growled, muttering about the foolishness of Humans, but Taymr's face matched Dayfid's. This time, the boy drew his sword free in one smooth motion and turned west. The Tribesman cupped his hands around his mouth and whistled; it sounded like a birdcall, but no bird native to Alrendria. "Did they see you?" Martyn asked as his eyes rose toward the billowing cloud of dust that marked the Guardsman's passage.

"Of course!" Dayfid laughed, flashing a predatory smile. "They wouldn't have followed me otherwise."

The admission shocked Martyn, and he unleashed his temper on the Guardsman. "The battle was done and our presence unknown. Our mission was a success!" The smile faded from Dayfid's face, but his gaze grew more heated, not less. "Now, the Corsans know we're here! Everything we hoped to gain is lost! And for what?"

Dayfid's jaw clenched, and he trembled with the effort of holding his emotions in check. "Might I remind my prince that we are at war? Every living Corsan is another blade for our enemy, another sword to kill Guardsmen. These fools think I'm alone, and they're following me without precaution. Why not stop them now, when their numbers are few? Why wait for them to join a larger force?"

"The Guardsman speaks truth," Olin agreed. "If prey foolish enough to step into trap, there is no dishonor in springing it."

Martyn sighed. He had thought the killing done. For the day, at least. "How many, and how long?"

"Sixteen." Dayfid's smile returned. "I lured two groups together and killed three before leading them here." The Guardsman tilted his ear toward the wind. Martyn listened too; in the distance he heard a low rumble. "And not long, I think."

"Sixteen!" The Alrendrian army was still some distance away, too far away to be of assistance. "And you think we can defeat them with four?"

"Actually," Dayfid laughed boyishly, drawing his blade free. "Three. I didn't know about the Tribesman." Martyn's temper flared again, but he held his tongue. Dayfid caught the prince's mood. "Once these Corsans are defeated, my Prince, I will accept whatever punishment you deem fit. But for now, we should prepare for battle. I swear; I will let no harm come to you this day." The rumbling was louder. The Corsans would be upon them soon.

Martyn gained as much height as he could without bringing himself into sight of the enemy. Olin dropped to a crouch, disappearing in the grass, and put some distance between himself and the others. Martyn unsheathed his sword and surveyed the land. Dayfid faced the hill, leaning low over his horse's neck, ready to lead the charge. Taymr held his sword at the ready, but in his other hand he still held the Rising Sun banner, announcing to the world that he stood with Prince Martyn.

"Put that thing down!" Martyn hissed, and Taymr looked at him incredulously.

"But then they won't know who you are!"

"Exactly!" He snatched at the banner, tearing from the boy's grip, but before he could hurl it to the ground the first Corsans crested the hill to the west and came to a skidding stop. Seeing the banner snapping in the wind, one of them smiled. "A foolish move, Prince Martyn, riding so far ahead of your troops." To the south, a squad of mounted Guardsmen galloped toward them, but they were too far off. "If you surrender, I will guarantee your safety and the safety of your companions."

"A generous offer," Martyn replied, stalling for time. "But I decline. I will, however, accept your surrender on the same terms." He gripped his horse's flanks with his knees and readied for a charge.

"Don't be a fool!" the Corsan called. "Three against a score? You don't stand a chance!"

"Three?" Martyn repeated, looking confused. His eyes moved from left to right. "What do you mean, three?"

The Corsan glanced south again, gauging the distance between Prince Martyn and his army, and then he raised his sword. "Your men are too far away to help, and I am no fool. I have heard the rumors, but you don't expect me to believe that ghosts fight for Alrendria?"

"Not ghosts. Garun'ah." With that, Martyn dug in his heels, and his horse launched forward. Dayfid and Taymr rode at his side, bellowing 'For Alrendria!' as they drove toward the Corsans. The Corsan signaled the attack, but before his men could move, the grass around them exploded. Giant, shadowy forms appeared from nowhere, dragging men from saddles and silencing surprised screams with quick slashes.

Martyn saw Olin, snarling with the Blood Rage, wrap his arms around a horse's neck and pull horse and rider to the ground. The screaming beast landed with a crash, crushing its rider in the process. Martyn's mount leapt over the fallen horse, taking him past the Tribesman and into the fray. He saw a sword coming toward him, and his own blade rose to meet it. The ring of steel echoed in his ears, and his arm vibrated with the force of the blow.

It was the Corsan commander, eyes wide and jaw trembling. The sword came at Martyn again, flashing in the sun, and Martyn met the attack. His horse danced backward, giving him room to maneuver, and Martyn positioned himself with the sun at his back. The Corsan squinted but pressed his assault, lunging at Martyn and launching one reckless attack after another. *Is he truly this much a fool*, Martyn wondered, *or is killing me that important to Murdir?*

A lucky blow bounced off Martyn's sword, cutting a shallow line from wrist to elbow. Martyn hissed in a pained breath when he saw the blood blossom on his arm. *Who's the fool?* he asked himself.

With a scream, Martyn's opponent lunged again, his sword swinging in a broad arc. Guiding his horse with his knees, Martyn moved aside, slashing down hard. Swords connected in a bone-numbing crash, and the Corsan's blade fell.

Martyn grabbed the man and hauled him from the saddle. The Corsan landed with a grunt, and Martyn dropped down beside him. Holding his sword in both hands, his teeth pressed together with grim determination, Martyn stabbed down with all his might, wincing when he felt his blade pierce armor. He blocked out the Corsan's dying scream and wiped away the spray of blood that hit his face before turning to survey the battle.

The Corsans were trying to flee, but the Garun'ah—there were only three, Martyn noted—kept them penned. Dayfid stood at center of the battle, fighting three men simultaneously. He was on foot, his horse nowhere to be seen, and his opponents were all mounted, but there was no question as to who held the advantage. The Guardsman's blade was a whirlwind, and all three riders danced to keep out of his reach.

Taymr rushed past Martyn in a blur, galloping toward Dayfid. With a primal scream, he swung his sword, cleaving through the armor of one rider. He wrenched his blade free and rounded on the others. Dayfid used the confusion to step inside the guard of a second rider. He pulled the man from his saddle and leapt atop the horse.

Martyn cupped a hand to his mouth, but before he could call out, one Corsan broke free. He rode toward Martyn at a gallop, bearing down on the prince. Taymr moved to intercept, angling his horse to cut off the man's flight, but the Corsan saw him coming. Martyn saw the rider reach to his hip.

"NO!" Martyn flung himself forward, but he was too late. The Corsan's dagger drove into Taymr's chest, knocking the boy from the saddle. He landed with a thud and lay unmoving. The Corsan galloped past within hands of Martyn, but the prince let him go. He rushed to Taymr's side, dropping to his knees and tearing the boy's clothes away from the wound. Blood pooled around the dagger, and a dark circle was spreading across the boy's shirt. Martyn touched Taymr's neck; his pulse was weak, the skin cold and pale, but he was still alive.

The battle was over; the Corsans, save the one Martyn had let escape, were dead or captured. "Get Sheriza!" Martyn yelled. Dayfid winced at the accusation in the prince's tone, but he rode off immediately.

Martyn looked for the fleeing Corsan. He spotted the man to the west, silhouetted in the sun, too far away to catch. *After all my lectures, I let one get away. And for what? I could have stopped him easily, and there was nothing I could have done for Taymr!*

Suddenly, the Corsan's horse lurched, and the man fell. A Tribesman appeared out of the grass and hefted the body of the fallen soldier onto his shoulder before starting back toward the prince and his party. Martyn cast his eyes skyward. "I don't know which of you to thank, but your intervention is appreciated. I promise to be more careful in the future."

"Are you well?"

Martyn turned at the sound of Jasova's voice. "Just a scratch," he announced, raising his arm to show the wound.

"Martyn, what were you thinking? You—!"

"Not now!" Martyn snapped, but he saw the frustration dancing across Jasova's face. "I know. It won't happen again. I swear it. But we have more important concerns." At his feet, Taymr groaned, and the boy tried to rise. Martyn pressed him back to the ground. "Don't move!" he commanded. "Help is coming."

"Sheriza's on her way," Jasova said. "She's the one who told us about the Corsans, and that you were going to ambush them. She can't be more than a moment behind us." After Martyn's relieved nod, Jasova's gaze hardened. "Martyn, how could you—"

"I said not now!" Martyn regretted his tone instantly. He was angry with himself, not Jasova. In a calmer voice, he said, "Ambushing the Corsans wasn't my idea."

Jasova's eyes darted south. "Dayfid," he said through clenched teeth.

Martyn put a restraining hand on Jasova's arm. "We'll deal with him later."

They faced each other for a moment, but the Guard Commander eventually ducked his head in acknowledgement of the order. Before Martyn could say anything else, the grasses parted and Sheriza appeared. The Healer looked even worse than Martyn remembered, her face colorless and eyes hollow. She knelt beside Taymr and brushed a finger along the boy's wound. The gaze she shot at Martyn was sharp enough to slice leather, but the only thing she said was, "Hold him."

Martyn and Jasova pinned Taymr's arms and legs to the ground, and when they were ready, Sheriza yanked the dagger free. Taymr screamed and thrashed, but the two men held him steady. Closing her eyes, Sheriza pressed a hand over the wound. She sat there, unmoving, for some time, but finally, pale and heaving for breath, she removed her hand.

Only a smear of blood remained where the wound had been, and the boy slept soundly, his chest rising and falling evenly. Sheriza smiled, and then her eyes rolled upward and she pitched forward. Martyn caught her and cradled her in his arms. If she felt any gratitude for his aid, she did not show it. "Was this necessary?" she whispered. "Wasn't there enough killing today?"

"Why is this my fault?" Martyn's gaze shifted from Sheriza to Jasova and back again. "I didn't want this fight!"

"If not your fault," Sheriza asked, "then whose? You're the prince."

Martyn opened his mouth, a sharp retort on his tongue, but Sheriza sagged in his arms. Sighing, Martyn stood and carried the Mage toward the wagons. To Jasova, he said, "Add these bodies to the others. Leave no sign of the fight. And increase the number of scouts we have on patrol. I don't want anything like this to happen again."

Jasova saluted. "And Dayfid?"

Martyn frowned. "Leave Dayfid to me," he answered, an edge of ice in his voice.

Chapter 24

"Darein on the horizon, Prince Martyn." To the north, at the summit of a gentle rise, a small collection of buildings stood silhouetted in the afternoon sun. Ordered rows of sturdy tents surrounded the buildings, filling the open grasslands like the bazaars of Calan Durr. A dark line of hastily-erected timbers circled the base of the hill. The fortification was far from complete—the gates remained unfinished and long stretches of grass broke the wall into sections—but it was a start.

A frown darkened Martyn's features. No armed riders came to greet them, and the warning bells had not tolled. He had left strict orders that the alarm be sounded no matter what standard approaching riders flew. So long as the Corsans rode under Alrendrian banners, Martyn had no intention of being fooled again.

As if in answer to his thoughts, a bell sounded in the distance, a frantic gonging that brought all work to a stop and sent men and women alike in search of weapons. Those too young to fight ran toward the heart of the encampment; everyone else prepared for the worst. The blast of a horn joined the bell; three long notes filled the air with a pure sound. The horns had been Jasova's idea; he and Nykeal had devised a system to identify approaching riders and warn of threats. It had saved several border patrols already, and Martyn's only regret was that he had not come up with the idea first.

Martyn turned to Jac, a rough-looking, ebony-skinned Guardsman from the Family Ricci, on the Gilean border. The Guardsman rode his midnight-black stallion as if he had been born on horseback, and he watched Martyn expectantly. After the assault on the plains, Jac had never been more than a dozen steps from the prince's side. At Martyn's nod, he raised a horn to his lips and answered the call. Two short blasts followed by a long, a pause, and then another long note. *Prince Martyn returns victorious.*

The bell stopped immediately, and the distant figures resumed their work. When the clang of the first hammer blows reached Martyn's ears, he urged his horse forward.

Darein. Local lore claimed it had once been a mighty city, a center of trade and learning. Some said Darein had been destroyed during the MageWar; others insisted that Lord Peitr Arkam had razed it centuries earlier. Most did not believe the tales at all, or believed them to be fanciful exaggerations. Martyn knew the truth. Jasova had shown him the remains of a wall not far from where his men were building their own crude fortification. Broad foundation stones, ten hands across at their narrowest, ran parallel to the curvature of the hill. The stones were worn and all but buried in the dry soil, but they were there. Darein had once been a prosperous city, and Martyn intended to make it one again.

For now, all that remained of Darein was thatch-roofed huts and disintegrating buildings. It was barely large enough to be called a village, with its nearest neighbors a full day away and it more than a dozen leagues from the nearest trade route. The village appeared on no modern maps—Martyn had stumbled across the name while studying an ancient parchment detailing the border of the Arkam Imperium—it produced few goods, and it held even fewer people. Or it had, until Martyn chose it as his base of operations.

More than a few officers had argued, but Martyn had been adamant. Despite its obscurity, one thing made Darein very important: it sat on the edge of Harod's Trail, the ancient route between Vela and Souchar, the capital of Corsa. The trail had gone unused since before the MageWar, but the paving stones were still here, buried beneath a hand or two of dry dirt.

The grasses on the plains of southern Alrendria were thick and thorn covered, and some reached the height of a man, making passage through the plains slow and tedious. But the taller grasses put down deep roots, and they could find no purchase on Harod's Trail. An open swath nearly forty hands across cut through the rolling hills, with the carpet of grass and scrub never higher than a man's knees. The taller grasses to either side made hiding all but the largest of forces a simple matter.

This was how Murdir had sent his raiders into Alrendria undiscovered. Martyn was certain of it. To the west, the Guard patrolled the coastal towns; in the east, villages and Guardsmen were more common, and the trails well-manned and patrolled. But here, far from all eyes save those few in the village above, an army could cross into Alrendria without being seen. Though the villagers claimed to have seen nothing, all spoke of strange noises, and over the last few seasons, someone from nearly every household had disappeared. A few had been found torn apart by animals, but most had never been seen again.

Jasova rode up on Martyn's right with a sour-faced Dayfid at his side. "I told you I'd deal with him," Martyn muttered. He had postponed this discussion since the battle. He had hoped to spare himself of it for at least another day.

"The Guardsmen are under my command," Jasova answered. "It's my—"

"And you're under mine!" Frustration bubbled to the surface, and Jasova broke his stare with Dayfid to meet Martyn's gaze. He tried to convey something in that look, something important, but Martyn did not see it. After a moment, Jasova nodded apologetically. Martyn saw the Guard Commander's embarrassment, saw the look of smug satisfaction on Dayfid's face, and he groaned. He had left himself no choice; if he did not set things right, Dayfid would believe himself above his commander's orders.

"Your behavior was not worthy of a Guardsman," he said coldly, turning to face Dayfid, and the smirk on the Guardsman's face faded. "Not only did you risk your life and the life of your prince, you very nearly compromised our entire mission."

Dayfid opened his mouth, but Martyn did not let him speak. The man's heartfelt protestations and deep love for Alrendria were often enough to deflect all but the most direct reprimands. "No witnesses!" Martyn snarled. "Weren't those your orders, Guardsman? No signs of battle! Leave the Corsans guessing, wondering what's happening to their men, to their supplies." The memory of how close Dayfid's brash decision had brought them to ruin fueled Martyn's anger. "Villagers on both sides of the border speak of monsters roaming the plains, devouring the enemies of Alrendria. What better—?"

"Monsters!" Dayfid waved a hand dramatically. "You don't believe the Corsans think us monsters, do you? Murdir knows it's you."

"Murdir knows," Martyn agreed. His anger evaporated, turned by the well-timed question. "As for his soldiers…? Perhaps they don't believe us monsters, but they couldn't be more frightened if we were. They know we're out here, but not where or when our attacks will come. So long as we have the element of surprise, we have the advantage."

"Surprise," Dayfid growled with a hint of distaste. "Where's the honor in ambush? Why not march south in force? The Corsans have offered little resistance; we could drive them back to the Jinleyn Mountains!"

"We do not attack because we would lose," Martyn replied. He said it calmly, a statement of fact. "Murdir's forces outnumber ours five to one." Martyn saw the Guardsman's frustration, and he knew that, not long past, he would have felt the same way. "Why do you think we spread our attacks so far apart? Why do we never stage an ambush within a day's ride of Darein? We'd never survive a pitched battle. If what we've heard is true, Murdir could destroy us with a third of his army!"

"Then why hasn't he?"

"Only the Gods know!" Martyn answered. "In his place, I'd have attacked by now. I'd be scouring the plains for our encampment, doing everything in my power to stop us before we could dig in and put up a reasonable resistance." Martyn mimicked the deadly calm his father often used when scolding him. "But until Murdir does come after us, we offer our thanks to the Five Gods and continue to strike where he is not. When the Corsan army moves west, we attack east. When they march north, we slip around and pick at their flanks.

"Every time our position is reported, every time a rider is spotted, it makes it easier for Murdir to track us. And if he finds in Darein before we're ready for him…" Martyn let the word hang, giving the implication time to sink in. "Our troops are spread too thin. If we fall, Vela falls, and likely Alrendria behind it."

Dayfid trembled, though with rage or shame, Martyn could not guess. Finally, the Guardsman lowered his eyes. "I understand, my Prince, and I beg forgiveness."

The sincerity of the words, delivered with such emotion, tugged at Martyn's heartstrings. He placed a comforting hand on the Guardsman's shoulder. "Heed Jasova's words as if they were my own, if for no other reason than because he's your commander. I will leave you in his hands, and remember this: no matter what punishment he hands you, it's lighter than you deserve."

"You will remain in Darein for two ten-days to aid in the construction of the fortifications," Jasova said immediately. His eyes were not as forgiving as Martyn's. "Guardsman Laertes will assume your place on the raids." Dayfid stiffened—being kept from battle was the worst punishment he could face—but he nodded. "After that, I will consider this matter behind us. But the next time you put the prince's life at risk, I'll strip you of rank and have you scrubbing armor until you retire from the Guard."

Dayfid turned away, but Martyn stopped him. To Jasova, he said, "Ride ahead and inform them of our success. Have a detachment ready to escort the prisoners to Sarin's Cross. I don't want to parade them through the village again." Last time, it had taken a squad of Guardsmen to subdue the villagers. In Darein, the bad blood between Alrendria and Corsa ran deep.

Saluting fist-on-heart, Jasova galloped off, trailing a cloud of dust behind him and leaving Martyn and Dayfid alone. "You have fought bravely and well, Guardsman, risking your life in each and every engagement. I don't want you to think your service goes unnoticed. The armor we recovered from the Corsan Commander was crafted by Magi. When Mage Nielian has finished examining it, I'd like you to have it." Martyn glanced at his own narrow frame and chuckled. "I'd keep it for myself, but it's more your size."

Dayfid jerked upright, and his horse sidestepped. His eyes widened, and something akin to panic danced across them. He touched his breastplate and emphatically shook his head. "I cannot. This mail was given to me by my father. I could not set it aside."

"Don't let sentimentality override sense," Martyn told him. "I've not seen a battle yet where you're not at the heart of it. If anyone could use extra protection, it's you."

The panic returned, not as blatant but still noticeable. "I... I cannot..." Dayfid stammered. "I mean no disrespect, Prince Martyn, but... I... I am not comfortable with things of magic."

"Surely, you'd want—"

"NO!" The Guardsman's vehemence startled Martyn. "Please"—Dayfid pleaded for understanding—"Please give the armor to someone else. Someone who will appreciate it."

"Of course," Martyn said slowly. He knew that Magi were far from loved, but he had not known the fear ran so deep among his people. "I'd never force it on you."

"That you wished me to have it is gift enough." Dayfid's smile assured Martyn that no harm had been done. "If you'll excuse me, I should be about my duties." With a salute, Dayfid rode off to join the men. Martyn watched the Guardsman's retreating back for a moment before urging his horse forward.

He aimed for the gap that would one day be the southern gate to Darein. "Heave!" shouted a scarred veteran, and twoscore men strained to raise a log five hands across and set it in a hole. A second team stood ready to fasten the log to its neighbor with rope and bands of metal. A third group hauled another timber out of a wagon laden with hewn trees. Their draft horses snorted and stomped as the log dug a shallow rut through the soil.

Construction was proceeding faster than expected. With the nearest forest more than two days ride from Darein, Martyn's advisors had suggested that it could take several winters to gather the necessary resources. But in just over a season, more than half the wall stood unsupported, and with refugees flocking into Darein, the speed of construction would only increase. Squinting into the sun, Martyn saw the silhouettes of Guardsmen atop the palisade, meaning that work on the inside of the wall had begun as well.

As he passed through the gate, Martyn waved and called out encouragement. The villagers cheered and beamed at the compliments he offered. Once through the gate, the prince craned his neck around to yell greetings to the Guardsmen on patrol. What he saw stunned him. The helmeted sentries were no more than eight winters old.

"We need every able-bodied man and woman working if we're to set the defenses as quickly as you want," Nykeal said in response to Martyn's surprised expression. "From a distance, it's impossible to tell they're children, and they've sharp eyes. Twice now they've spotted riders before the Guardsmen." She laughed; it was a warm, rich sound. "They think it's a game!"

Martyn had not heard the Guardswoman's approach, but the sight of Nykeal's disheveled blonde hair and dirt-smeared cheeks brought a smile to his lips. He hopped from his saddle and gripped her arm in greeting. "As long as they don't lead the charge."

Nykeal studied the long line of wagons trundling toward the village. "Good hunting?"

"Fair enough," Martyn shrugged noncommittally—the last thing he wanted to talk about was battle—and made a gesture that took in the hillside. "How are things here?"

"We're ahead of schedule, for what it's worth. The first barracks will be ready in a day or two, and we'll have the smiths working inside before the rains come." With the exception of the fortifications, having real quarters for his men was Martyn's greatest priority. Though the ground was parched and cracked, and the grasses brown from lack of moisture, the Harvest rains turned these plains into a quagmire. Martyn wanted his Guardsmen safe and dry before that time came.

He looked at the tent-city springing up around his encampment. "Are there more tents up there?"

"More arrive daily from isolated villagers and ransacked farms." Exhaustion crept onto Nykeal's face. "A few refugees have even crossed the border, begging us to take them in. Inside a fortnight, Darein will hold more than a thousand commoners."

"A thousand!" Not many days past, Darein barely boasted a tenth that, and when he had first led his army here, the village held little more than two score. "Where do they sleep?"

"The villagers have taken in all they can, and we sent a good number of them south to help Hassan gather timber. The rest sleep unprotected or in whatever makeshift quarters they can build." Nykeal frowned, as if debating whether or not to say more. "Refugees are assigned work when they arrive. Anyone who refuses or discovered shirking their duty is put out. We have too much to do and not enough resources to house those who won't contribute."

Martyn tapped his lip thoughtfully. This was not something they had anticipated. "I agree. If they won't work, send them away. Forcefully, if necessary." The extra laborers would be welcome, but he already had more than enough people to protect. "Our food stocks won't last forever, so find out which refugees were farmers. Have them plow and plant the fields to the north of the wall with anything that will grow. Assign duties to the others as you see fit, but make sure to use some lumber from each shipment to construct shelters. I don't want anyone outside when the rains come." Martyn had never experienced it, but Jasova insisted that the one season of rain these plains received more than made up for the three dry ones.

They walked slowly up the hill, discussing other events and problems that had arisen in Martyn's absence. The ringing of hammer on anvil and the steady shout of commands grew increasingly loud, until it was all but impossible to carry on a conversation. An army of thickly-muscled smiths worked the forges, fashioning everything from arms and armor to nails and barrel staves. The sheer number of smiths was astounding; Martyn would not have been surprised to learn that every blacksmith within a hundred leagues had come to his call.

Loral and Torpin, two master smiths Martyn had brought from Vela, directed the others, but they were never far from a forge. Today, they worked side by side on a giant hinge for one of the gates. Torpin paused to raise his hand in greeting, but his hammer quickly resumed its rhythmic pounding.

Martyn watched the smiths with a passing curiosity. Their skills amazed him, and he wondered how they fashioned many of their wares, but he was wise enough to confine his curiosity to thoughts. Jeran had been curious about it too, so much so that he had worked for a couple of seasons in the armory at Kaper Castle. Sometimes, Martyn had trouble understanding the things Jeran and Dahr did.

Thoughts of his friends darkened Martyn's mood. "Have the others returned yet?" He had to repeat himself twice before the clanging had faded enough that the Guardswoman heard him.

"You're the first, though we spotted one of Rhodric's scouts this morning. He should be here by nightfall." Five riders appeared on the hill above, and when they spotted Nykeal, they rode toward her purposefully. Martyn recognized neither the horsemen nor the pendants flapping in the stiff breeze behind them. He gestured with his chin, and Nykeal's eyes followed. When she spotted the riders, she groaned.

"I forgot about them," she mumbled. Her stony glare intrigued Martyn; it was a rare to see Nykeal so upset. "The Gileans."

"Gileans?" Martyn repeated. He waited for the riders to approach. All five wore armor distinguishable only by the sigils stamped on the breastplates. They drew rein a few hands from Martyn and bowed their heads in greeting. Four were young, clean-shaven boys with close-cropped hair and haughty dispositions. The sun glinted off their armor, and the smell of well-oiled leather reached Martyn's nose. The young men looked around, and whenever their eyes fell on a commoner, their noses wrinkled. When a band of militia marched by in sloppy formation, they snickered and sneered. They kept their distance from Nykeal, though, and whenever their eyes drifted to the Guardswoman, they stared at her with a mixture of admiration and fear.

The fifth rider all but ignored Nykeal; he fastened his gaze on Martyn. A short brown beard, meticulously trimmed, framed narrow lips pressed tight. The man was only a handful of winters Martyn's senior, but his hawk-like eyes held seasons of experience. He moved his horse forward until he towered over Martyn. "You are Martyn Batai, Prince of Alrendria?"

Martyn ducked his head. "I am. You are well come to—"

"You're the one who parades your Aelvin whore in front of my cousin as if she were no more than another of your conquests?"

With a supreme effort of will, Martyn held his smile. "I consider neither Miriam nor Kaeille conquests. Both were forced upon me; I had no choice in the matter." It was only a half truth, but it was true enough for Martyn's purposes.

"Such an onerous duty," the Gilean said, making a tisking sound. "I'm sure it chafes your… honor… to have your affections divided thus."

"Ah, my manners!" Martyn said, feigning an abashed expression. "You must forgive me; I thought you were the Gilean allies my father promised. I didn't realize you were here to defend Miriam's stolen honor. Funny, though"—Martyn frowned thoughtfully—"*she* seemed tolerant enough of our circumstances when last we spoke." The Gilean had the decency to look embarrassed, but Martyn did not stop. "Would you like me to draw a dueling circle here, or can it wait until I wash the Corsan blood off my armor?"

His jest was not well taken. Nevertheless, the Gilean dropped from his horse and offered a bow. "I am Lord Jaem Douphan, nephew of Tarien, King of Gilead. My men and I were sent to aid Alrendria in its war with Corsa." His tone suggested that he did not relish the duty.

"Well met, Jaem," Martyn replied. He offered his arm, but Jaem did not take it. "This is our war, not Alrendria's. The Tachans and Corsans fight as one, and so do we—"

"I must protest our treatment," Jaem interrupted. "We had done little more than ride into sight of this… encampment, when that *woman*"—he glanced at Nykeal—"led a party to attack us."

Nykeal sighed wearily. "I tried to explain to Lord Douphan that we had no knowledge of his approach. I'm under orders to stop any unknown party."

Jaem opened his mouth to protest, but Martyn raised a hand. "You have my apologies, Jaem, but the Corsans have been masquerading as our allies, and I've been forced to take drastic steps to protect the lives of my people. We've established a series of signals to prevent such misunderstandings. Commander Jasova will assign one to your men. I suggest that you waste no time in learning it if you wish to avoid future misunderstandings."

The Gilean Prince glowered, but he appeared pacified. "If you'll excuse me," Martyn added, "I wish to clean away the dust of travel. A war council will be held at sundown." He pointed to the summit of the hill. "I'd be honored if you and your lieutenants would join us."

Jaem looked as if he had more to say, but he showed at least a modicum of restraint and simply nodded. "Very well, Prince Martyn." Hopping back into his saddle, the Gilean led his men up into the village.

"You know what to do with the wagons," Martyn told Nykeal. "Have the bodies stripped and buried. To the west, near the grove." It was a secluded place, with a few blossoming trees and brightly-colored wildflowers. It was no proper grave, but it would suffice.

"Nikki?"

Nykeal turned toward the sound, and when she saw Jasova hobbling comically on his injured leg, her face brightened. Martyn could not help but smile, himself. "The dead can wait a while longer, I suppose," he said, and Nykeal beamed her thanks. She jumped into Jasova's outstretched arms. *Hardly the kind of behavior you want to see from your Guard Commanders*, Martyn mused, yet he did not have the heart to stop them.

Martyn continued up the hill, ignoring the shouted cheers and urgent requests directed his way. He stared dumbly at the drastic changes that had taken place in his absence. When he had led the Guardsmen out, the area through which he walked had been empty grassland. Now, the grass had been cut away or trampled, and sections of the hill had been leveled. Clusters of mismatched tents formed a ring around the Guardsmen's ordered rows. Dozens of people thinned by hunger and dressed in ragged clothes scurried about, intent upon some task. Children played in the hollows between tents. Dueling with sticks. Singing.

Not everyone was laughing. Martyn saw Taymr, his left arm pinned to his side—Sheriza had not had strength enough to heal him fully—talking to a short, thin-faced woman and a man with shoulders so hunched he stood no taller than his companion. Taymr extended his hand, and the woman took a glittering object from it. She nearly collapsed when she touched it, and the man steadied her, but sobs as deep as hers wracked his shoulders. *Kristoph's parents.* Martyn allowed himself a moment to share their grief, but then he shook off his sorrow.

He had ordered the wall be built far from the center of the village to give Darein room to grow. In war, people always flocked to the safety, real or imagined, that an army offered, and Martyn had planned for that migration. Now he wondered if he had underestimated his needs, and if it was a wise decision to allow so many succor.

Regardless of the problems it was sure to cause, the influx of refugees suited him. Darein had once been a great city, and Martyn intended to restore it. For now it would be the staging area for Alrendria's southern forces, another link in the chain of guardposts along the border, but after the war, trade would begin again. With Midlyn. With New Arkam. Maybe even with Corsa. Martyn wanted Darein to be the center of that trade. He wanted to restore Harod's Trail and build something that would last the ages.

Martyn dismissed those thoughts as concerns for another day and left the tent-city. He entered a stretch of empty grassland, a gap between the refugees' tents and the ordered rows and regular arrangements that marked where the Guardsmen were quartered. The frames of three large buildings—the barracks Martyn had insisted be the first structures built—towered over the tents. One was nearly complete; the other two had roofs but no solid walls. Three more were being constructed on the far side of the hill, but now Martyn wondered if they would be enough. *If thousands come to Darein, we'll need more than the handful of Guardsmen we have to defend it.*

Beyond the barracks stood the remains of the village. Most of the huts had been gutted and converted to sleeping quarters for Martyn and his officers. The villagers who had lived in them had been given tents and promised better housing as soon as it could be arranged. Martyn had not wanted to do it, but at the time there had been no better option. Now, as he walked into the hut he had appropriated, he wondered how the family who had once lived here fared in the chaos of the tents below.

One step inside his hut, Martyn froze. A steaming tub waited for him. He had intended to simply remove his armor and rinse the blood from it, but the bath called to him, and he could not refuse. In moments Martyn's armor lay in a jumbled pile on the floor, and he settled into the tub with a relaxing sigh.

When he woke, the water was tepid and sun peeked through the baseboards of the western wall. "Gods! The council!" Martyn exclaimed, jumping up. His travel-worn clothes and bloody armor were gone; a neatly folded outfit had replaced them. Martyn dressed hurriedly and ran through the door. When he burst outside, a herd of hoofed beasts bigger than the largest bulls he had ever seen nearly trampled him. The creatures had broad, shaggy heads and hunched backs, and though they appeared docile, Martyn had no intention of stepping into their midst.

A villager rode up and urged the beasts away, and Martyn saw two more riders circling the herd, driving them toward an enclosure erected within the confines of the wall. The villager mumbled apologies to the prince and hurried off, but Martyn waited until the last of the beasts was well away before hurrying to the broad, two-story structure built on the remains of a stone foundation that stood upon the apex of the hill. Martyn often eyed the foundation with interest— most of the ruins remained buried, but what could be seen was easily the size of a small keep. *Someday... Someday, I'll learn Darein's secrets.*

He was one of the last to arrive. The others sat around a large table, and the buzz of conversation cut off with the prince's entrance. Charts and dispatches covered the table, and a large map of the Corsan border graced one wall. Jasova sat at the table's end with Nykeal on his left and an empty space on his right. Two of Jasova's subcommanders, Praetor and Kile, were also in attendance. Praetor sat beside Nykeal; Kile had the seat beside the empty one.

Jaem and two of his lieutenants sat directly in front of Martyn glaring distrustfully across the table. At Martyn's entrance, Jaem greeted him sourly. "Glad you could join us, Prince Martyn. I apologize for arriving so early." Martyn chose not to take the bait as he walked to his place at the head of the table.

Three Magi sat across the table from the Gileans: Nielian, Sheriza, and a stranger, an old man with white hair and a neatly-trimmed beard. He kept his eyes downcast, but Martyn noticed that neither of the other Magi so much as looked at him. Kal stood silently in the back of the room, arms folded across his chest. Across from him, Olin mirrored the *Kranach's* stoic glare. Two more Tribesmen, Rista and Darakth, kept to the shadowy corners and looked far less comfortable around the Humans than Kal and Olin.

Martyn took his seat, nodding to Pylias and Lacantha, who occupied the chairs to his left. "Report," he said simply, resting his elbow on the table and cupping his chin with a hand.

Lacantha, with his fiery red hair and hazel eyes, stood. "Good news from the north. The village militias have repelled three Corsan raids and located a half dozen bands before they caused any trouble." Jaem muttered something about villagers being forced to do soldiers' work, and Martyn shot a glare at the Gilean while waving for Lacantha to continue. "There's still trouble along the coast, but there've been no attacks inland for the last ten days."

The Guardsman's smile was well deserved, but Martyn did not want overconfidence to set in. "Good news indeed, but we can't allow small successes to lessen our vigilance. Increase the patrols and step up militia training. If a squad of Guardsmen can be spared, I'll assign them to the coast." Lacantha saluted, and Martyn turned to Pylias.

"Construction of the border forts is proceeding apace. As you commanded, each fortification is no more than half a day's ride from its nearest neighbors, and we are stationing a squad of Guardsmen at each site."

"A squad at each!" The outburst came from hook-nosed Praetor, of the Family Josan. He had commanded the border forces before Jasova. "You stretch our forces too thin, Prince Martyn!" Jaem nodded in silent agreement.

"What would you have me do?" Martyn asked. "Concentrate our forces here and leave the rest of the border undefended?" This was an old argument, and not one Martyn cared to rehash. "With the forts so close together, three squads can respond to any threat in less than a day."

"Three squads," Praetor scoffed. "If Murdir attacks in force—"

"Then only three squads die. Unless he attacks here, in which case, we all die. Don't forget how many men Murdir has, Commander." Martyn turned back to Pylias, leaving Praetor sputtering.

"We're building the fortifications near existing villages whenever possible," Pylias added. "The fortifications are little more than watch towers and earthen walls; with wood so scarce, anything more is impossible. The villagers have been helpful, though, likely because they believe having a squad of Guardsmen around will protect them."

"It might," Martyn said. "A little, at least."

"There are rock fields and old quarries in the hills northeast of Toursan," Jasova interjected. "Hauling stone is exhausting, but the Guardsmen might appreciate it if they have to face a Corsan attack, and we have more than enough hands milling about to spare a few."

"A good idea, Commander," Martyn said, tapping his lips thoughtfully. "I'll send a message to Lord Sorbael of House Menglor. His holdings are along the Anvil, and his House has been spared much of the fighting thus far; perhaps he'd be willing to part with some quarried stone. In the meantime, we'll send wagon teams and refugees to Toursan."

Martyn questioned Pylias about the condition of the forts, their strengths and weaknesses, and where the Corsans were most active along the border. Only one bit of news surprised him. "Attacks have almost stopped since we started building the forts. Most Corsans we see flee, and those who fight only hold for a charge or two."

The Tribesmen told similar stories. "The scouts I found make more noise than cubs on first hunt," Olin told them, "and walk within five paces of me without notice. Even for Humans, that is poor."

"Rista and I stalk heart of camp," Darakth added. "Two step from sentry. He not see till late. Cohr-saans easy prey." Rista's only contribution was a grunt; the gleam in his eye said he was ready to return to the hunt.

Commanders Praetor and Kile led small bands of Guardsmen and recruits like Martyn. At first, their raids had been to regain land taken by the Corsans, but now they were pushing deep into Corsan territory. Martyn had hoped the weak resistance he had faced was by chance, but the tales of the other Guardsmen troubled him.

"The Corsans fled like frightened children," Praetor boasted. He spoke of numerous encounters, and the way he told the tales made it sound as if he were the only Alrendrian to lift a blade. "One or two well-directed charges and the field was mine." Kile was not as prideful, but his recounting was similar. Successful ambushes and Corsans who fled at the first sign of attack. Undefended caravans and easily-overrun defenses.

When Kile finished, Praetor leaned forward with a hungry look in his eyes. "The Corsans are undisciplined, Prince Martyn. Give me the men I asked for, and I'll have Murdir pressed against the Arkamian border by winter!"

Martyn understood Praetor's obsession. The Corsans had made him look a fool and cost him his command. No one blamed him for it—no one could have held out with the meager forces he had had at his disposal—but the Guardsman had taken the loss to heart. Now that he was on the offensive, he wanted to regain his pride.

"Prince Martyn," Pylias said. "As you ordered, the border patrols have not pursued the Corsans, but the men think that letting them escape is foolish. Maybe Commander Praetor—"

"No," Martyn said, and Jasova nodded. They had discussed this issue at length and agreed that holding the border was more important than pushing the front south. "They may be trying to draw us into an ambush. As long as the Corsans keep away, leave them be."

Praetor looked angry, but he said nothing, and Martyn allowed his thoughts to drift while he listened to the rest of the reports. He jerked upright when Pylias called his name. "Yes, Guardsman?"

"There's one matter I forgot. I received word that the Rachannen are a tenday east of here. They should arrive—"

"Rachannen!" Jaem shouted, his chair creaking loudly as he stood. "I'll not fight alongside Rachannen dogs! I am Jaem Douphan, Marshall of the East, Cousin to—"

"Sit down!" Martyn yelled, and he slammed his palm on the table for emphasis. Jaem froze, and his face turned purple. "You press my patience," Martyn told him. "If you don't want to fight alongside Rachannen, then leave. We're all allies here. If you can't remember that, I don't want you at *my* side."

The silence was palpable, but Jaem finally backed down. "There's much history between Gilead and Rachannen," he said by way of apology. "A great deal of bad blood. But for the sake of our alliance, I'll restrain my temper."

"Good," Martyn said with a tight smile. "Now, I'm opening the floor to suggestions. Does anyone—"

Praetor cut him off. "I think we should move south in force." Martyn rolled his eyes. "With the Corsans disorganized—"

"Is killing all you think of?" Sheriza asked, casting a scathing look at the Guard Commander. "We've reclaimed what is ours, isn't that enough! How can—" At a gentle touch from the white-bearded Mage, she fell silent. Her eyes, however, did not stop smoldering.

"By moving south, we can...!"

"Strengthening our defenses along the coast will..."

"We should step up Guard training and fortify our position here..."

Martyn expected the bickering; it was standard for these councils. Only he and Jasova remained quiet. It gave them time to think, and gave the others time to air their grievances. This day, the arguments were worse than usual, and it was a relief when the door burst open and Lord Rhodric Carridin strode in.

"There is rioting in Ulanoc." A broad, barrel-chested man, Rhodric controlled vast estates in the southern regions of House Velan. A toothy smile showed from within his thick brown beard, and his triumphant gaze swept across the room, touching each member of the council. His armor was dented and dirt-smeared, and the sword swinging at his side still had smears of dried blood on it, but he stood as if he were a king addressing his subjects. His simple statement silenced the room.

Family Carridin was one of the largest in Alrendria, a Great House of its own until endless battles with Corsa forced it to join House Velan. A warrior at heart and a born commander, Rhodric Carridin would have been a Guardsman had fate not conspired to make him First of his Family. Despite his position, he had fought bravely in every Corsan engagement for the last quarter century, and from what little Martyn had learned of him, he was an ally worth having. Jasova, in particular, had a special bond with Rhodric, but the Guard Commander was tight-lipped about the details.

Martyn regained his voice first. "Rioting?"

Rhodric nodded. If anything, his smile grew broader. "The peasants have taken up arms against the Corsans. The garrison is fleeing. The men are scattered, the officers dead or imprisoned. The gates have been opened and the city begs for our aid!"

"A miracle!" Sheriza said. "The Gods be praised." Her words sounded sincere, but her eyes looked troubled. So, too, did those of the other Magi. The white-bearded one, in particular, seemed upset.

The bickering resumed, this time over the best course of action. "We should abandon this field and take Ulanoc," Praetor announced loudly. This time, even Pylias seemed to think the idea a good one. "We could hold Ulanoc against any army Murdir threw at us!"

"The fleeing Corsans..." Jaem mused. "Ulanoc's garrison must hold at least five hundred. If they're disorganized, now would be a good time to hunt them down. Every enemy dead makes our struggle that much easier."

Martyn raised his hand for silence. "Jasova?"

The Guard Commander looked up from the table, where his gaze had been fastened since Rhodric's arrival. "I don't like this. It's not like the Corsans to flee from peasants. They have no qualms about subduing resistance, and it's folly to abandon the only fortified city for leagues. It's as if they're asking us to move south."

Those words struck a cord with Martyn, and his mind began whirling. *Asking us to go south? Begging us, more like. Why?* He scowled, and around him, the argument resumed, louder than before. With sudden clarity, he understood, and panic filled him.

He stood abruptly, and the sudden movement shocked the room to silence. "Rhodric, take five squads of Guardsmen and the reserves. Go to Ulanoc. Secure the city, then strip it. Have everything that can be moved brought here. Have the—"

"Raze the city!" Jaem said. "Are you mad? Ulanoc is far more defensible than this playpen you're building. If you—"

"I said strip the city, not raze it!" Martyn snapped, his patience at an end. "If you won't be silent, I'll ask Olin to hold your mouth closed." Jaem glanced at the Tribesmen, who grinned, and Martyn continued, "Take everything, Rhodric. Every supply, every weapon, every man, woman and child should be brought here. Keep only enough to supply your forces. If this is a trap, we can abandon Ulanoc without loss, and leave the Corsans with an empty city to defend. If it's not, we can move the supplies and people back once the city is secure."

Praetor opened his mouth, but Martyn's stern glare warned him to hold his tongue. "Pylias, find the Rachannen. Tell them to ride to Vela as quickly as possible. When you return, stop at every village and have every man who can be spared sent here to defend Darein.

"Nykeal, I'm leaving you in command of the border. Forget housing; finish the fortifications. Lacantha. Kile. Round up every available Guardsman and recruit. Coordinate with the other commanders and leave only enough to maintain order here. Mage Sheriza, once again I must ask you for a favor—"

"What's this about?" Praetor demanded. Jaem was staring at Martyn as if he had gone mad, and so were most of the others in the room. "We can crush the Corsans, my Prince! Why pull back now?"

"Vela," Martyn said sourly. "Murdir's drawing us south on purpose. The Durange mean to attack Vela." Martyn swept his chair aside and stormed toward the door. "Jasova, march as soon as the men are assembled. Sheriza, I need you to take me and a few others to the city immediately."

Under his breath, he muttered, "I just hope we're not too late."

Chapter 25

The sun cast long shadows across grass-covered hills. A forest hugged the southeastern horizon, though the trees were uniform and too evenly spaced to be natural. Closer inspection revealed an apple orchard long left untended. A hard-packed dirt road curved with the land, wrapping around those hills too steep to climb. The hills to the south had a gentle grade and were covered with tall grasses and leafy shrubs. To the north, a steep hill paralleled the road, its slope a mass of tangled vegetation. A vine-choked fence ran the length of its flattened top, and a barn nestled against the base of the hill, its large double doors swinging in the stiff summer breeze. A small pen and chicken coop were built into the barn's weatherworn sides, but both were empty. Numerous creepers had snaked their way up the frame, and a large char mark covered the western wall.

East of the barn, a farmhouse faced the road, its shutters fluttering in the wind. The walls were faded and spotted, damaged by wind and rain. Some windows were broken; a thick film of dust covered the rest. The grass stood as high as the porch, and thick, thorny vines wrapped around the rails and crisscrossed the planks.

Silence reigned. If not for the thin plume of smoke rising from the chimney, Dahr would have thought he had arrived too late. He stared at the Odara farm in disbelief, and Fang nuzzled his leg, whimpering quietly. So much had changed. Once, this place had been alive, bursting with song and music and laughter. Once, happiness had lived here. Here, he had found a home, a family; he had thought his troubles over.

The happiness was gone, or if it remained it was buried too deep to sense. Now there was only pain, pain and loss and anger, and a feeling of hopelessness. A dark chuckle rumbled through Dahr's chest. *After all this time, the farm still suits my mood.*

Dahr took the porch's three stairs in a single step. At the door, he hesitated, his hand a finger's width from the stout oak. He knocked but heard nothing, not the approach of muted footfalls or a muffled greeting. After a moment, he raised his hand to knock again, but the door swung open, creaking loudly on its hinges, and Dahr stumbled backward.

That sandy blonde hair. Those unmistakable blue eyes. The broad smile, a smile warm enough to drive away the winter's chill or heat the coldest heart. "Aryn?" Dahr whispered, not believing his own eyes.

Aryn looked him up and down for a moment. "*Jokalla*, Hunter, and welcome. May you—"

"Aryn!" Dahr enveloped the man in a bear hug, pulling him through the threshold and lifting him from the ground. Fang crowded in, sniffing and panting, barking with excitement. "I thought I'd never see you again."

Aryn laughed loudly. "*Danko*, Hunter," he answered, clapping Dahr on the back. "You honor me. I've not received such warm greetings from one of your Race in many seasons. Not since before the Tachan War."

Dahr set Aryn down. "Don't you know who I am?"

After studying him again, Aryn said, "You're a Child of Garun, and a Hunter by the look of you." He gestured toward the door. "Please, join us. Food will be prepared, and drink. We will sing songs of the battles we've fought and the victories we've won."

Dahr grabbed Aryn by the shoulders roughly and turned him so they stared eye to eye. His rage, banished by the sight of Aryn, returned. It clawed at his heart, begging to be set free. "Aryn, it's me! It's Dahr!" He said the words desperately, as if Aryn's failure to recognize him was a sign, and that by forcing the elder Odara to admit his identity would prove something. Something important.

Aryn looked confused. "Dahr?" he repeated, shaking his head slowly. "No. No!" He wavered unsteadily, and for a moment, Dahr thought the older man might fall. "Are you here to claim him, Tribesman? I feared this day would come. It will break Jeran's heart, but I feared it might happen."

Dahr stared into Aryn's eyes, but there was not the slightest flicker of recognition. "I should warn you," Aryn added in a low voice, "Dahr doesn't know that he's Garun'ah, and I've not told him differently. He yearns to be the same as everyone else, and I thought the truth would break his spirit. He's suffered so much. I wanted to spare him what pain I could."

Aryn rubbed his head roughly, and he pursed his lips in thought. "I haven't seen him today, though. Nor my nephew. They're probably out in the forest. Come in, and while we wait, we can figure out how best to break the news."

For the first time, Dahr noticed the haunted look in the older man's eyes, and his heart sank. *The Durange! They're to blame.* The thought brought pain and a pang of guilt, which surprised Dahr. He had thought himself calloused to such things. Yet somehow, the Durange always found a way to hurt him. He looked up to find Jeran in the doorway, watching. "What's wrong with him?"

Jeran glanced at his uncle. Aryn no longer seemed aware of their presence. "The things he suffered in Dranakohr... Tylor..." Jeran waved his hand, but Dahr needed to hear no more. "Yassik thinks that, to escape the pain, Aryn retreated into his mind, forced himself to live in a happier time."

Aryn moved to the rail and stared out into the field, as if watching something. "You see that, Gideon!" he murmured. "And after only a few days of practice!" He sounded proud.

"Will he..." Dahr's lip twisted down as he stared at the husk of the man who had been like a father to him, "...recover?"

"It comes and goes. There are times..." Aryn began to weep; quiet sobs wracked his chest. "There are times when he's his old self, and times when he's worse than this. But he's improved compared to when I first found him." A tinge of hope entered Jeran's voice. "As to whether he'll fully recover, only the Gods know. Not even Yassik will venture a guess." Jeran laughed darkly at that, and sensing Dahr's confusion, he laughed even louder. "Once you know Yassik, you'll understand."

Dahr reached into his shirt and removed the *dolchek*. "You left this in the Darkwood." Jeran took the blade and slipped it into the waiting sheath on his belt. He took his uncle by the arm and turned toward the farmhouse, signaling for Dahr to follow.

The inside was much as Dahr remembered. A broad couch and two plush, hand-crafted chairs formed a semi-circle around the hearth. A circular rug, its once-bright colors faded, lay centered on the floor. A few paintings hung on the walls and small objects littered the mantle. Many seemed as out of place now as when Dahr had first seen them. A chunk of rock. A fragment of cloth with an unintelligible pattern. An ornate dagger. Try as they might, Dahr and Jeran had never been able to get Aryn to speak of his keepsakes. Now, Dahr understood why. He, too, had experiences he preferred to keep secret.

The door next to the hearth led to the kitchen. In front of the main entrance, a broad staircase climbed to the second floor. The archway beside the stairs opened into the dining room, and the narrow hall led to Aryn's library, a collection of several hundred volumes that had seemed like a treasure when Dahr had lived on the farm.

The familiar surroundings brought up a mixture of emotions. Joy, sadness, anger and regret all lumped together until Dahr no longer knew how he felt. He stood transfixed, mouth open and expression blank, until the kitchen door opened and shock drove all other thoughts from his mind.

A man—Dahr thought it was a man—entered the room holding a silver platter filled with sliced fruits and cheeses. He was at least five hands shorter than Dahr, but nearly as broad and thick with muscle. Dahr stared at the man's grey skin, broad nose, and slitted eyes.

The stranger made it only a step before he, too, froze. His eyes traveled upward slowly until they met Dahr's. His mouthed worked, but no sound came out. "Shael preserve me!" Grendor finally managed. "Jeran said you were big, but even after seeing Reanna, I never expected—" He shook himself, and his cheeks turned dark grey. Hastily setting the platter down, he closed the distance between them in a several short strides. "I am Grendor, *Choupik* of the Vassta." He extended his arm. "I am here to serve."

"No longer, Grendor. You serve no longer," Jeran said quietly. To Dahr, he added, "Grendor is an Orog."

"You are wrong, friend Jeran. I am no longer a slave, but I still serve. We all serve. Righteousness and honor, those are my masters now." Grendor smiled broadly, baring slightly-pointed teeth. "I am no longer a slave." He repeated the words, as if reveling in their feel.

"A thing to be proud of," Dahr said, gripping the Orog's arm. "Well met, Grendor. I'm Dahr."

"Yes, I knew you must be. Jeran's *chanda*. I have heard much about you." Grendor bowed. "It is an honor to meet you."

Dahr forced a smile and swallowed his anger. "The honor is—"

The door to the farmhouse burst open. "I saw that monster of a dog outside. Does that mean..." Wardel leapt across the room and wrapped his arms around Dahr, clapping his back forcefully. "Hah! I knew an army of Tachans wouldn't be enough to stop you! What were you thinking, charging them like that? You may be Garun's chosen one, but that's no reason to act like you're a God yourself."

Despite himself, Dahr smiled. He returned Wardel's hug, squeezing until the Guardsman gasped for air. "It's good to see you," Dahr said slowly, his voice low. They parted, and Wardel stepped back, eyeing Dahr concernedly. Even when he was happy, Dahr's voice carried undercurrents of anger, like the rumbling of distant thunder.

"You've changed," the Guardsman said. He did not sound happy about it.

"We've all changed," Dahr replied. For a moment, he even regretted those changes. But only for a moment. He needed his anger, needed it to do what he had to do.

"What's all this commotion?" Yassik asked from the stairs. Stifling a yawn with his fist, the old man fastened his gaze on Dahr. "Ah. You chose to join us, then? Good. From what Jeran's told us, you'll be a good one to have around."

Jeran made the introductions, and Dahr's eyes went even wider than when he saw Grendor. "Yassik? *The* Yassik? From the stories?"

"Not so many stories," Yassik admitted. "At least, not as anything more than anecdotes. But I'm flattered that you've heard of me. Jeran tells me you're *Tier'sorahn*. That's fascinating. I have a few questions I'd like to ask you, once you've had a chance to settle in."

Dahr glared at Jeran, who deflected it with a shrug. "It's not exactly a secret," Jeran replied. "And the nights in Dranakohr were long. We needed things to talk about."

Yassik tapped his lip thoughtfully. "You know, I haven't seen a *Tier'sorahn* since the MageWar, and back then I had far more important things to do. But I've always been curious. Do you hear words when you speak to them, or do they just send you thoughts? Can you hear all animals, or only some? How do you call them? What range do you have? Is there—"

The onslaught of questions was too much for Dahr. He stepped back, his eyes narrowing. Jeran put a hand on Yassik shoulder. "Yassik..."

"What?" the Mage said, startled. He looked at Dahr. "Sorry."

"I think Dahr might be a *Tier'sorahn*," Aryn said suddenly, stepping between Dahr and the Mage. His brow furrowed in confusion. "That's what you call them, right, Tribesman? I remember reading about them, and Aemon spoke of them often. I can't be sure, you understand, but I've seen him handle the animals. He has a gift, that's for certain, though I don't think he realizes it. Or, at least, he doesn't realize we can't do what he does."

Aryn scrubbed his face roughly, and he drew in a haggard breath. "Another secret. Do I tell him this one, or leave him be? He just wants to be like the rest of us." A single tear traced a path down Aryn's cheek. "How many secrets must I keep from them?"

Yassik looked at Aryn sympathetically. "Maybe we should talk of this another time," he said to Dahr, "if you don't mind."

"One should not be uncomfortable with what he is." Dahr wished the words sounded less hollow.

"Good," Yassik said, rubbing his hands together. "Then how about food? My stomach tells me it's time for supper."

"If we listened to your stomach," Wardel laughed, "we'd do nothing but eat and sleep, old man!"

Yassik stared down his nose at the Guardsman. "Jeran insists that we start for Portal tomorrow, and we've not been so long gone from Dranakohr that a hard ride won't be taxing. A good meal and a better night's sleep are not idle suggestions; they're sound advice. I have only our well being in mind." Dahr's stomach growled, and Yassik smiled. "You see, the Tribesman agrees with me."

"We've almost exhausted the supplies we bought in Keryn's Rest," Jeran said, "and I've little desire to return. They're not as tolerant of strangers as they used to be, and we told them we were passing through."

Dahr could see that Jeran was holding something back. "You didn't tell them who you were, did you?"

Jeran licked his lips, then shook his head. "Many of the villagers were captured when Tylor came for my uncle. When we left Dranakohr... We couldn't take them with us."

"Leave dinner to me," Yassik said, and he and Wardel headed toward the kitchen, dragging a docile Aryn between them and leaving Jeran and Dahr alone. For the first time, Dahr looked at his old friend, really looked at him, and the changes surprised him. Jeran had always been wiry, but now his skin stretched tight over iron-hard muscle. He looked thinner, too, and tired, and his shoulders slumped as if under a great weight. His face was hard, his features chiseled, and the dark circles around his eyes spoke of suffering and bone-numbing weariness.

The smile he fixed on Dahr was friendly and familiar though. "It seems like such a long time since we've been here."

The pain in Jeran's eyes called out to Dahr; it resonated with his own pain. "It was bad in Dranakohr?"

Jeran's smile faded. "It... I... I can't talk about it. Not most of it. But it was bad." He laughed a cold, humorless laugh. "Bad. That doesn't come close."

"At least you weren't alone," Dahr said, throwing himself onto the couch. "I thought... After Tylor took you away, I thought I'd lost everything."

"You were never alone, Dahr." Jeran fixed a piercing gaze on him until the larger man turned away. "Neither of us were." Jeran shivered and his mood brightened, as if he had shaken away the bad memories. "In any case, it's past, and we have other things to worry about."

Some time later, Yassik called them to eat. It was a simple meal, but to Dahr it seemed a feast. A rich venison stew fortified with potatoes scavenged from the remains of the garden was a welcome change from the fare he had eaten in the Darkwood, and the bread Wardel set on the table came fresh from the oven. Jeran even went down to the wine cellar and brought up a few dust-covered bottles.

At the head of the table, Aryn led the conversation. Though still lost in the past, he was much as Dahr remembered: laughing, joking and telling stories. If the blank stares hurt, they did not hurt much; if being called 'Tribesman' was a constant reminder of Aryn's condition, it was easy to forget when Aryn raised his glass and toasted to friends and family, to those long lost and those merely absent, just as he used to all those seasons ago.

Evening quickly turned to night, but the celebration continued. Jeran fetched more wine, and goblets were filled and filled again. Toasts were drunk to lost loves, to old friends, and to Alrendria. Grendor told Dahr of his people and their suffering north of the Boundary. In turn, Dahr told of his own life, his adoption into House Odara and his eventual return to the Tribal Lands.

Grendor listened, fascinated, and he followed each tale with a string of questions. That the Orog had never seen a Tribesman—or an Elf, for that matter—shocked Dahr at first, until he realized that until two winters ago, neither had he. When he said as much, the whole table burst into laughter. "By now," Jeran said to Wardel, "you'd think he'd remember that *he's* a Garun'ah!" Cheeks red, Dahr hid behind his wine and begged Grendor to tell another story.

Only Yassik remained quiet. He watched the table with thoughtful eyes, taking in every word, and he watched Dahr even more closely. At times, usually in the middle of Dahr's stories, he appeared on the verge of speaking, mouth half open, eyes intent. But each time he frowned, shook his head, and remained silent.

When the door to the farmhouse burst open, slamming against the wall with a resounding bang, it caught them all by surprise. Chairs slid back, grating across the floor, and everyone stood, tensed for action, hands reaching for weapons that were not there and eyes staring intently at the door, anticipating every kind of threat.

But it was not an army of Tachan soldiers and ShadowMagi that entered the room, it was an old woman, short and hunched, holding a gnarled stick about seven hands long in one bony, age-spotted fist. She took small steps, supporting her weight on the staff. Once inside, she turned to face them, glaring with vibrant, hawk-like eyes. "The lot of you make enough noise to wake the dead."

"Alwen!" Aryn said. "By the Gods, woman, I never thought to see you here! When did you arrive in Keryn's Rest?" He slipped around the others, almost at a run, and scooped the old woman up. Laughing, he spun her around, holding her tightly to his chest.

"Aryn Odara, you wool-headed rascal! Set me down!" He did as he was told, chuckling as Alwen straightened her dress. The glare she fixed on him was cold enough to freeze water, but the corners of her lips twisted up in a grin. Jeran and Dahr exchanged surprised looks; neither had ever seen Greise Alwen smile.

The old woman stared at Aryn for a long time. When she finally spoke, relief permeated her normally gruff voice. "I never thought I'd see you again, Aryn. It seems the Gods were with you, after all." Her eyes closed briefly, and her lips moved in a silent prayer. Then, without warning, her arms lashed out and grasped Aryn's head. She pulled him down until their faces were almost touching. "What did he do to you? You poor boy." She broke her grip and turned to Jeran. "He's not well. Not well at all."

Jeran nodded but said nothing. With a fond pat on Aryn's cheek, Alwen walked into the dining room, where her caustic gaze roved over the motley band. Her eyes widened in surprise—another first for the old woman, as far as Dahr was concerned—when they passed over Grendor. When she spoke, it was to Yassik. "I see you finally decided to crawl out of your hole."

"You make it sound like I've been hiding." Yassik rolled his eyes. "Or taking my ease while the rest of you've been hard at work."

"You might as well have been, for all the help you've been."

"All the help I've been!" Yassik shouted. "While you've been out here, patrolling the Boundary—a Boundary, I might add, in which you could not find Tylor's hideaway!—I've been deep inside Dranakohr, studying the inner workings of the Darklord's society. *And* keeping an eye on Lorthas, I might add."

"That's just like you. You've been the Darklord's slave for ten winters, and you expect me to believe that you *allowed* yourself to be captured? Salos probably stumbled upon you napping." The whip-like crackle of Alwen's voice was enough to make a grown man flinch, but Yassik stood unaffected. "Regardless, you should have been able to get word out at least once rather than leave us worrying about you. Did you forget about your Gift?"

Yassik harrumphed. "Lorthas collars the Gifted with a device that enhances the effects of the Boundary. I had to get a half dozen leagues away before I could remove the damn thing! Using the Gift is impossible in Dranakohr unless Lorthas trusts you, and he wouldn't trust me if I were his slave for a thousand winters.

For the second time that night, Alwen appeared shocked. "He… He *collars* Magi?"

"He collars the Gifted," Yassik corrected. "Any who refuse to join him, regardless of their strength or training."

Alwen's eyes hardened. "So, you allowed yourself to be captured, and then found yourself trapped." After a thoughtful pause, she nodded. "That does sound like one of your plans."

Face purple with rage, Yassik opened his mouth, a sharp retort on his tongue, but Dahr spoke first. "What do you want with us, Greise Alwen?" He tried to keep his tone polite, but the words came out harshly, and Alwen rounded on him. Her anger quickly transferred from the old man to the younger one.

"Has the cub finally grown some fangs? There was a time, not so long ago, when you'd run trembling at the thought that I was near."

Dahr laughed, at himself as much as her. "I was a child then, and foolish. I'm a man now."

"And twice as foolish, no doubt," Alwen snorted. "Better for you if you'd stayed frightened. Likely, you think your size gives you an advantage, eh? But what good is your strength if you can't move?"

Dahr found himself frozen in place, his arms pinned at his sides. Panic instantly set in, and he tensed, fighting against invisible bonds he could not break. Slowly, he rose off the floor, thrashing, his muscles bulging from the strain. He stopped rising when his head brushed against the ceiling.

"Is this what you've been reduced to, Alwen?" Yassik sighed. He took a deep drink of wine to hide a grin. "Frightening children? Ungifted children at that!" To Dahr, he said, "She's always been touchy about her size. Bullying others with her Gift was the only way she could make herself feel better."

"You'd know," Alwen snapped, "since you faced my ire more than anyone else, you old fool." They glared at each other, but their stares carried something more than hatred. "And I'm not bullying him, I'm teaching him. Teaching him to never let his guard down, that even the most harmless looking things can harbor great danger. If you'd remembered that, maybe you wouldn't have spent that last ten winters in—"

"Enough!" Jeran spoke with quiet authority, and Dahr dropped lightly to the ground. "You're either our ally or our enemy, Alwen. You can't be both. An ally would not bind a friend against his will; an enemy would not get a second chance to. Decide where you stand, then join us at the table or leave. These last few seasons have been trying, and I have neither the time nor the inclination to waste my freedom on foolishness like this."

"Well, well," Alwen said after a moment of strained silence. "It seems that you've learned a thing or two since last we met. I had not expected..." Her eyes bored into Jeran, measuring, calculating. "Very well, if you insist on seriousness, then serious I shall be. Tylor has marched south; his army passed to the west of here not many days ago. If he hasn't already learned that you're free, he'll learn it soon enough, and I'm almost certain he remembers the way here."

"You didn't follow them?" Yassik asked, his tone accusing.

"For a while, I did. Until one of those black-robe *Magi*"—she almost spat the word—"spotted me. He'll be a bit more cautious the next time he thinks he's found an easy target!" She grinned wickedly.

"You're getting sloppy, Alwen. Half a century ago, that Mage wouldn't have escaped with his skin intact. Why, I remember—"

"That you remember something you didn't scrawl into a book is impressive enough," Alwen shot back. "You don't have to bore us with what it is. My point is that Tylor knows about Keryn's Rest. If he decides to look for you, he'll probably start here. You may want to seek a better hiding place. Or better yet, you might want to come out of seclusion and get back to work."

"We're leaving for Portal in the morning," Jeran told her.

"Good," Alwen said, turning toward the door. "That gives me enough time to set my affairs in order."

"You're coming with us?" Jeran, Dahr, and Yassik all asked at the same time.

She shot a vexed look at them. "There's no point in staying here to watch the Boundary anymore, is there? I should have left winters ago, but Aemon asked me to keep my eye on things." She started hobbling toward the door. "It's about time that *Greise* Alwen left Keryn's Rest anyway." The word 'left' had a certain finality to it. "No one can live forever, eh? I think the village is starting to suspect that I'm something more than a crotchety old woman." Yassik started to say something, but Wardel hit him in the stomach hard enough to keep him silent.

Aryn stopped Alwen at the door. "Leaving so soon?" he asked, oblivious to the conversation that had just taken place. "Stay! I'll have Jeran bring some wine. It seems like so long since we've talked. Where is that boy?" He looked around, and finally turned to Jeran. "Have you seen my nephew?"

Alwen pulled Aryn down and kissed him lightly on the forehead. "I'll come back tomorrow, Aryn, and we can have a nice, long chat. Until then, get some sleep. You need the rest."

After she left, Aryn yawned. "I do feel tired," he told the others, starting for the stairs. "If you'll excuse me..." He climbed the stairs and disappeared down the hall. The others returned to the table, but with Aryn's and Alwen's departures, they could not recapture the mood they had shared before. One by one, they sought their bedrolls.

Dahr was the last to retire, and when he stepped inside his old room, he froze. Everything was as he remembered, covered with dust and much smaller, but otherwise untouched. He stood only a hand shy of the ceiling, and he would never fit on the small bed that sat against the room's back wall under a faded tapestry of a mountainscape. Dahr threw the blankets Jeran had given him on the floor and made a pallet for himself. In moments, he was asleep, and for the first time in a long while, his dreams were untroubled.

The next morning, the attitude in the farmhouse was subdued. Conversation was kept to a minimum, and each of them went about the preparations in his own way: stocking supplies, straightening the house, saddling the horses. The horses, three black mares, two stallions—one chestnut and the other white—and a large plow horse had been bought in Keryn's Rest. Dahr's warhorse, Jardelle, waited by the barn where Dahr had left him.

For the most part, Dahr kept to himself, but sitting alone in the farmhouse brought back memories, and he could not stand the bittersweet sadness that accompanied them. He fled outside, reveling in the sweet scent of the cool morning air. The day was not yet hot, but with the sun not fully clear of the horizon and not a cloud in the sky, it would be.

Something tugged at his mind, and Dahr's eyes were drawn skyward. Shyrock circled the cloudless sky, little more than a black speck at the edge of vision. The distance between them was great, yet Dahr could still feel the connection that bonded him to the golden eagle. He concentrated, sending out his thoughts. *Fly South. Seek the Durange.* He did not use words, exactly, but rather a mixture of thought and image, memory and emotion.

With a prideful screech, Shyrock wheeled about and flew south. Dahr watched the eagle disappear and hoped he had managed to impress the danger into which his friend flew. At his side, Fang whined, and Dahr patted the dog's head. "I wish I understood what I did. I wish I had someone to teach me." Fang nuzzled him, as if to say that Dahr was doing fine.

Dahr's eyes were drawn to the hillside, to the plateau that had once held Aryn's pasture. For a time, he debated climbing up there. After a while, he felt another presence behind him. "Everything's ready," Jeran said, following Dahr's gaze up the hill. "That's where it all started," he added. "For us, at any rate."

"Do you think…?" Dahr felt foolish for even asking. "Do you think he's still up there?"

"I doubt it," Jeran shrugged. "It's been a long time. Why would he stay with the whole world to roam?"

Dahr nodded, turning away. "It would have been nice to thank him. Now that I understand. Now that I could…"

Jeran laid a hand on Dahr's shoulder. "I know." That was all he said, but it was enough. "We should go." He turned to go, but Dahr did not follow.

"Do you ever miss it?" Dahr asked, and his gesture encompassed the whole of the farm.

"Sometimes," Jeran admitted, and after a long pause, he added, "Mostly, though, I just feel guilty."

"Guilty?" Of all the answers Jeran could have given, Dahr had not expected that one.

"I think how blessed my life—our lives!—have been. Growing up in Kaper… Raised by the King of Alrendria… Denied nothing. I think of all I've learned, all that I've done, and…" Jeran fell silent and Fang whimpered. "I think of those things and part of me is glad. Glad that things happened the way they did." He turned back to Dahr. "Then I think of what Uncle Aryn suffered for my happiness. It's almost more than I can bear." Moisture glistened in Jeran's eyes, but no tears fell.

Dahr grasped Jeran by the shoulders. "We will have our revenge," he promised. "We'll make the Durange pay for what they've done."

Jeran nodded. "I know. I just... I just want him to know that I'm sorry, but most of the time when he looks at me, all he sees is a stranger. That hurts the most."

It was not common for Jeran to let his pain show so plainly, and Dahr did not know how to comfort him. He turned Jeran away from the farm. From the past. "Come on," he said. "Aryn will recover. Until then, there are Durange to kill."

Alwen had arrived during their absence. She sat in the front of a broad wagon drawn by two giant horses. Wardel, Yassik, and Aryn were loading their meager supplies into the wagon beside Alwen's. The horses, saddled and ready, stood off to one side, grazing contentedly in the lush green grass.

For a moment, silence lingered, and Dahr saw Jeran battle for control of his emotions. "You're right," Jeran said. "He was almost his old self last night, wasn't he?" Dahr's nod was all the agreement Jeran needed. "Let's go!" he said, jogging toward the wagon. "We have a war to start." Fang took off after him, barking excitedly.

The abrupt change in mood surprised Dahr, but he recovered quickly. He ran to catch up, and his loping strides quickly put him far ahead. "The war started some time ago," he reminded Jeran. "If we don't hurry, we might miss it altogether!"

Chapter 26

"For the hundredth time, I don't know!" Dahr yelled. He glowered at Yassik, but the old man seemed not to notice. The Mage ran a hand through his beard and nodded thoughtfully, as if pondering how best to reword the question. Fuming, Dahr turned away. Since leaving the Odara farm, Yassik had been a constant irritation, watching Dahr like a hawk and asking questions constantly: questions about his heritage, about being *Tier'sorahn*, about *Cho Korahn Garun*, the Chosen One named in the Garun'ah's prophecies.

The questions about *Cho Korahn Garun* bothered Dahr the most. How the Mage had even learned of it remained a mystery. Jeran claimed he never mentioned it, and Wardel vehemently denied telling Yassik, but they were the only two here who knew. Somehow, his secret had escaped, or maybe he had escaped for a time, but now his secrets had caught up to him.

Cho Korahn Garun. The Heart of the Hunter. The one chosen by the God Garun to save the Garun'ah or lead them to destruction. Some Tribesmen believed Dahr was the Korahn, but Dahr did not; with all his heart he hoped he was not. He had no desire to lead the Tribesman and no right to do so. He was Garun'ah by birth, but his beliefs were Human. No Tribesman would be fool enough to follow him, nor did Dahr want them to. *Thousands of lives depending on me? I'm no Martyn, born to rule, nor a Jeran, destined to.*

He was caught between two Races, and he would gladly forfeit everything, his life included, if he could atone for his crimes and forget his past. But forgetting was not something he could do, nor could he forgive. Katya had been the traitor, but he had accepted her, brought her close, put her where she could harm Alrendria. His naivety, his willingness to love, had earned Jeran a four-season of slavery and nearly cost Martyn his life. That made him just as guilty as her. *More guilty. She, at least, remained true to her cause. I abandoned everything.*

Coppery curls framing a perfect face filled his vision. Piercing green eyes smiled at him, and warm laughter tickled his memory. His pulse quickened at the thought of her, and his lips began to curl upward in the beginning of a smile. Then, with sudden clarity, he remembered who she was and what she had done, and the sigh he had begun to utter deepened to a growl. His eyes snapped open, and a hazy red film covered the land. His hands tightened on the reins until the leather crackled.

Yassik ignored the growl and directed his next question to Fang, who loped at Dahr's side. "Is he always this disagreeable? I'm merely interested in furthering my knowledge."

Fang answered the Mage's query with a bark, and Dahr had the distinct impression that his four-footed companion thought he *was* being unreasonable. But before he could say anything, Alwen thumped Yassik in the arm with her cane. "Leave the boy alone," she said from her place in the front of the wagon. "It's obvious he isn't interested in talking to you." Dahr was not sure which upset him more: that he was grateful for Alwen's intervention or that she called him 'boy' so condescendingly.

He leaned down and told Jardelle to stay with the others, then dropped to the ground. He knew he could just as easily have reached out to the animal with his mind, but he felt more comfortable talking. "I'm going to hunt," he said, jogging toward a small forest to the northeast.

The Magi watched him go. Despite the fast pace Jeran had set, Dahr quickly put distance between himself and the wagon. Through Fang's eyes, he watched the Magi. "If that boy doesn't let go of his anger," Yassik said, "it will kill him."

"True, and provoking him like you do is probably the best way to help," Alwen replied snidely. "Honestly, the last thing we need is a rampaging Garun'ah on our hands."

"It's eating him from the inside, Alwen. You can see it just as well as I. If he *is* the Korahn, it might be wise if we kept him alive until *after* he saves the tribes. I don't know much about the prophecies of Garun, but I know enough to be worried!"

Alwen's lips pressed together firmly, and she fixed a dark glare on Yassik. She looked as if she had more to say, but Wardel let the reins fall slack and turned to face the Magi. "Maybe she's right. Dahr has a temper. I watched him tear apart a tavern once, and compared to now, he was just a little annoyed. Maybe you should let him figure things out on his own."

There was a drawn out silence. "I still think we should help him release his anger," Yassik said.

"Just make sure he releases it on you, old man," Wardel laughed. "I want no part of it."

"Why don't you go fetch Jeran," Alwen said crisply. "It's time he began his training."

"*Begin* his training?" Yassik sputtered, his eyes wide with indignation. "Why, I've taught him more in the last four seasons than most apprentices learn in ten winters! Twenty! I—"

"That's just like you!" Alwen snapped. "Taking credit for what the Boundary did. Do you truly believe you could have taught him a hundredth of what you did had he been able to do anything more than focus? You have many flaws, but arrogance was never one of them before."

Yassik refused to rise to the bait. Alwen had been goading him since she had arrived at the farm, but he avoided most of her traps. "I'll get Jeran," he said slowly. "Wait in the cart."

As the Mage wandered off, Dahr severed his bond with Fang and lost himself in the hunt.

* * * * * * * * * * * * * * * * * * * *

Jeran rode at the rear of the party, eyes closed and hands gently holding the reins. Yassik did not need to see the white halo to know that Jeran held magic; there was rarely a time since leaving *Dranakohr* that he had not. Grendor rode at Jeran's side, his broad body swaying awkwardly with the horse's every step, and held the lead line to Jeran's mount in one hand. In the other, he held a staff, the stout wood more than three fingers in diameter and half again as tall as the Orog. Without a curved blade fastened to its end or the notched grooves used to catch swords and axes, it was a far cry from the *va'dasheran* the *Choupik* in the MageWar had used, but Grendor had skill with it. Even without the blade, it would be a deadly weapon.

Without opening his eyes, Jeran turned to face Yassik. "One of these days, you're going to push him too far." Yassik's eyes sparkled, but he held his tongue. "Dahr doesn't like questions, and he doesn't like being reminded about what he is. Or rather, what the Garun'ah believe he is."

"You're using your Gift to spy on friends?" The words came out harsher than Yassik intended.

The smile slipped from Jeran's face. "Do you deny doing the same?"

Yassik puffed out his chest. "What an outrage! Why, I've never used my perceptions to spy... At least, not without—" He stopped when Jeran turned to Grendor. The Orog frowned, then shook his head.

"Another lie!" Jeran said, cold anger tingeing his voice. "Do you ever speak the truth?"

Jeran's vehemence shocked Yassik, who asked, "Do I get an explanation, or should I just start begging for forgiveness?"

"You've lied to me since the day we met!" Straightening in his saddle, Jeran stared down his nose haughtily and imitated Jes' voice. "Only a calm mind can seize magic. Only a Mage at ease with himself and the world around him can focus his Gift." Yassik fought to subdue a laugh; it was a fair impersonation.

"I don't need to be calm," Jeran said. "I've seized magic angry, sad, and frightened. Do I look calm now?" The aura around him flared, bright white tinged with streaks of red and gold. The look he directed at Yassik demanded an answer.

Yassik sighed heavily. "Do you think we train the way we do without cause?" This was a conversation Magi had with every apprentice. Usually, it came just before the apprentice was raised to full Mage, after seasons of intense study. He had hoped to have more time before discussing the matter with Jeran, but sometimes the apprentice discovered the truth too quickly.

"The Gift grants a Mage great power. We can create and destroy. Heal and harm. We can shatter mountains, move the winds, or create balls of fire to scourge our enemies all with our mind." A ball of fire twenty hands across appeared between Jeran and Yassik. The horses reared at the sight of it, nearly throwing Grendor from the saddle, and the heat was so intense that Jeran shied away.

The fireball disappeared as quickly as it formed, and Yassik frowned. "If we can shatter mountains, think of what we could do to flesh. We are capable of so much, miracles beyond belief and things so horrid even the Darklords refused to do them. Under most circumstances, conscience prevents a Mage from doing the unthinkable, but when a Mage is controlled by emotion, when rage, hatred or fear dictates our actions, who's to say what we might do. What would normally appall us may seem right and just when viewed through the heat of passion.

"Only by distancing ourselves from emotion can we Magi ensure that no harm is done without intent," Yassik continued. "What we tell our students is a lie, but one that serves a purpose. By the time most apprentices learn they can seize magic under any circumstance, doing it dispassionately is second nature. It's the only way to be sure that when they use the Gift, they use it with their heads and not their hearts."

"He speaks the truth, Jeran," Grendor said quietly. "He believes his words."

Yassik shot a look at the Orog, then beckoned to Jeran. "Come along. Alwen says it's time to continue your training." When Jeran looked perplexed, Yassik laughed. "You didn't think you were done, did you? That we'd leave you to puzzle out the rest on your own? You're like a blacksmith who knows every tool in his shop, but has no idea how to forge the simplest item. What good is having the Gift if you can't make it do what you want?"

Reluctantly, Jeran followed Yassik to the wagon. Alwen had cleared a space in the back large enough for the three of them to sit, and she had somehow managed to brew tea. The pot balanced precariously on the edge of a crate, but no matter how hard the wagon shook, it barely wobbled.

Jeran stepped down from his horse straight into the wagon, and he sat cross-legged in the open space Alwen had made for him. The old woman offered him a porcelain cup. "Is tea required?" Jeran asked. Jes had always brewed tea for her lessons too.

"It calms the nerves and helps you focus," Alwen said, forcing the cup into his hands.

Yassik sat beside them and Alwen offered him a cup, but the old man shook his head. He reached behind one of the crates and fumbled around for a moment. Finally, he pulled out a flask of red Feldarian wine. "I was never partial to tea," he winked. Alwen shot him a dark look, but Yassik only laughed. "What? This calms the nerves too!"

Alwen snorted, then turned and studied Jeran for a long moment. "Seize magic," she ordered. "As much as you can hold. Let me take a look at—" Her eyes widened when Jeran surrendered to his gift and his aura flared to near-blinding brilliance.

"That's enough!" she said quickly. "Let it go." The glow around Jeran faded.

"Impressive, eh?" Yassik asked smugly. "I told you, but you didn't believe me."

"Lot of good it does him, blazing like the sun, if he can't even snuff a candle." That she spoke calmly, without the slightest hint of acridity, was a sign of how flustered she was. "Now pay attention. These first few days will be frustrating. You *must* keep a rein on your temper. With your strength, there's no telling how much damage you might cause if you give in to your emotions. Why—"

"We've already discussed this, Alwen," Yassik said between sips of wine. "Jeran understands." To Jeran, he added, "This is the best phase of your training. As you learn to master your Gift, every day will bring new wonders. Don't let her spoil it for you!"

"It will be frustrating," Alwen repeated, "because there are no hard rules. How a Mage uses the Gift—and the way the magic manifests itself—is as unique as the Magi. No two Magi do things exactly the same way. There are patterns and consistencies, but no absolutes. I cannot show you how to make fire, for instance, only how I make fire. By watching other Magi and paying attention to what you do, you'll learn what patterns work for you. Now, seize your Gift. But just a bit of it, this time."

Jeran reached out to magic. Halos of gold and blue flared into being around Alwen, and a nimbus of brown streaked with purple surrounded Yassik. Waves of rainbow colored light came off both Magi in waves. Even Wardel had an aura of pale yellow tinged with streaks of blue that danced around his body in tight circles. Only Grendor seemed untouched. The air around the Orog remained colorless, lifeless. To Jeran, it seemed as if his friend were missing something. Grendor saw him looking and smiled, and Jeran felt a pang of regret that the Orog would never know the joy of magic.

A diffuse white light permeated everything, and when Jeran turned to face Alwen, some of that energy took on color. Strands of red, brown and burnished gold flowed together, weaving in a complex pattern, coiling and intertwining until, with a puff like a small explosion, a ball of fire appeared in the air between Jeran and the old woman.

Alwen held the flows for a moment, and then strands of blue extended from her body, wrapping around the fireball. With a hiss, it extinguished in a ball of steam. She turned to Yassik and nodded. Two thick tendrils of red stretched out from his aura, and when they collided, a ball of fire burst into being. After a moment, a thin green tendril reached out from the Mage, merging with the red, and the fireball took on a bluish hue.

"Stop showing off," Alwen snapped, and Yassik let the fireball disappear. It simply vanished, and without the hiss of steam like Alwen's.

"Do the colors mean anything?" Jeran asked.

Alwen opened her mouth, but Yassik beat her to the answer. "Over the centuries, there have been many discussions concerning the flows." His voice adopted the measured, lecturing tone Jeran had heard so often in Dranakohr. "At first, most Magi thought the flows represented the elements—Fire, Earth, Air, Water—but there are simply too many shades or, perhaps, more elements than we realize. Others thought that certain flows represented certain Gods. And still others—"

"There are a thousand theories," Alwen interrupted, "and no proof for any of them. The combination of flows a Mage uses remains the same throughout his life, but no two Magi use the same exact combination. What's important—"

"Then what's the point of this?" Jeran said in frustration. "You can't teach me how to use magic, because no two Magi use the Gift the same way. You can't explain how anything works, because despite millennia of study, you have no idea. I might as well ask Grendor to help me!"

Annoyed by the interruption, Alwen pressed her lips into a thin line. "We can't show you how to use your Gift," she admitted. "Not specifically, at least. But we *can* teach you the rules. Let you know what's impossible or—"

"Rules? Impossible?" Jeran turned to Yassik. "You said there were no rules and that nothing was impossible."

"They're guidelines more than rules," the old Mage admitted, though Alwen rolled her eyes at that, "and it's true that nothing is impossible, but some things are more difficult than—"

"Are you going to start this again, you old fool?" The exchange had the sound of an old argument, one often revisited. "Some things simply cannot be done. By now—"

"Will you let me finish a sentence, woman!" Yassik thundered. Thin streams of angry red shot off his aura. The yell caught Wardel by surprise, and the cart lurched;

its front wheel fell into a rut and the crates shifted dangerously. Even Alwen was caught off guard. She seemed stunned; her mouth worked, but no sound came out.

"That ought to keep her quiet for a while," Yassik said with a smile. Only then did Jeran notice the tiny knot of purple wrapped around the old woman's mouth. Other strands, even finer, entwined her body, holding her in place. "She'll pay me back for it ten times over, but if it gives me even a moment's peace, it'll be well worth it."

The throbbing vein at Alwen's temple was the only movement Jeran saw from the old woman, but the murderous stare she directed at Yassik spoke volumes. Yassik pretended not to notice. "As I was saying, nothing is impossible, but some things are easier. Most of it has to do with belief. If a Mage believes he can do something, it's far more likely he can. If, however, a Mage believes something absolutely impossible, then he might as well not waste his time. Our preconceptions of what can and cannot be done hold great sway over our abilities.

"Other factors affect the difficulty of any task too, strength being one of them. Just as some men are naturally stronger, some of the Gifted can do more than others." Yassik hooked his hands behind his head and leaned back against a crate. "Talent and technique are nearly as important. Every Mage has strengths and weaknesses. One might be better suited to working with stone, while another has a knack with fire. One a Diviner and another a Reader. Working with your strengths is always recommended, but the more winters you use magic, the better your technique will become and the more things you'll be able to do."

"It's just like swordplay!" Wardel said, sounding excited. "New recruits may be stronger than the aging veterans, but seasons of experience give the older men an advantage."

"That's right!" Yassik agreed, and he shot a warm smile at the Guardsman. "The differences between Magi led to the creation of Classes. Centuries ago, there were dozens of classes—groups of Magi dedicated to one aspect of the Gift—but now only the Healers remain. And the MageSmiths, I suppose, but only if you count the boy Lorthas has in Dranakohr. I saw him once, you know, working over his forge. If only I'd been able to talk to him. There are so many questions—"

Yassik stopped in midsentence. His eyes darted in Alwen's direction, and he smiled wistfully. "Strength and talent aside," he said, bringing himself back to the point, "some things are just more difficult. The why of it has never been fully explained, though I do have a number of theories on the..." He risked another quick glance at Alwen. "But I'll save them for another time. In general, working with solid things, like stones, carts or people, is easier than working with water, which is easier than working with air. A few Magi can whip up a powerful storm, but a light breeze will leave most weak-kneed for days.

"Fire, heat, and light are generally easy, though they grow more difficult with size. Practically any Mage can create a fist-sized fireball, but only the strongest can make one ten hands across." Yassik smiled smugly at the last, and Jeran thought briefly of the fireball, nearly twenty hands in diameter, that the old man had made.

"Creating things is relatively simple, with small things easier to create than large ones. It will tire you out, though, so most times it's easier to use what's on hand rather than fashioning something out of nothing. Uncreating things is a mistake"—Yassik wagged a warning finger in Jeran's face—"Not to say that it can't be done, but only a fool would try."

"You mean I can create something but not destroy it?"

"You can destroy to your heart's content, if that's what you want to do. Burn… Crush… Tear to pieces… Destroying's not difficult, but *uncreating* is. Not that you can't do it!" Muffled gurgles came from Alwen; the old woman shook and struggled against Yassik's magical bonds. "If you uncreate something, if you take it from something to nothing, there's a release of energy unlike anything you could imagine." He picked up a pebble rolling around the wagon's bed. "Uncreating something even this small would cause an explosion large enough to destroy all of Kaper. You—"

Yassik's eyes rolled up into his head and he fell over, asleep. "*Never* uncreate!" Alwen said sternly. "It's an abomination! Even the Gods are forbidden to send things to the Nothing. Those Magi who have done so—those few who survived!—were hunted down by the Assembly."

She picked up her cane and thumped Yassik in the stomach with it, hard. He grunted but did not stir. "I warned you centuries ago not to use your Gift on me!" She hit him again, and then a third time, before turning back to Jeran. "Enough talk. Seize magic, focus your Will, and try to create fire."

Jeran nodded and closed his eyes, but Alwen's vise-like grip delayed his first attempt. "Something small, Odara. I'd rather not see the entire cart go up in flames." Wardel spun around at the last, eyes wide, but a stern glare from Alwen sent the Guardsman's attention back to the road.

It seemed like Jeran sat there an eternity, trying to make the flows come together to form fire. Sweat beaded his forehead, then soaked his shirt. He mimicked Alwen's pattern, then Yassik's, but neither worked. More importantly, they did not seem right. He experimented with patterns of his own, allowed the flows to move as they wanted, kept the image of fire in his mind as he did so.

At some point, Dahr returned with a deer slung over his shoulder. He threw the animal over Jardelle's saddle and walked beside the wagon, his eyes on Jeran. Grendor rode opposite Dahr, his eyes curious and expression thoughtful. Jeran barely noticed; he was completed absorbed by magic. Each failure was a frustration, and every so often when something out of the ordinary happened, Alwen teased him about it. Though Jeran guessed she intended to lighten the mood, her comments only served to annoy him all the more.

On the verge of giving up, he wrapped two tan flows around a knot of red and smiled as an orange-red ball nearly two hands across crackled into being. His smile slipped when the fireball set one of the crates ablaze. Jeran released his hold on magic and the fireball disappeared, but the flames on the crate remained.

Alwen jumped to her feet and doused the fire by dumping the kettle over it. "Yet another reason we encourage the use of tea," Yassik said between yawns, stretching his arms above his head. Alwen shot him a scathing look.

Grendor hurried over to congratulate Jeran, but the victory was short-lived. Aryn galloped up to the wagon, his horse throwing up a cloud of dust. "Smoke on the horizon," he said, pointing west.

At the same time, Dahr stiffened, and he sniffed the air, as if testing it. At his feet, Fang growled, and in the distance, two hawks took to wing, darting west. "Tachans," he growled. He sounded hungry.

"Dahr," Jeran said warningly. He felt as if he'd gone five days without sleep, and the prospect of battle did not sit well with him.

"No more than a score," Dahr added, mostly to himself. He looked to the sky, to where the falcons circled. "You have my thanks." He pushed the deer carcass to the ground and vaulted into the saddle. Without galloped off without waiting to see if the others planned to join him. Fang ran after him.

Wardel stopped the cart and turned to Jeran, who sighed heavily. "You don't think I'd let him go by himself, do you?" He climbed into his own saddle and raced after Dahr.

Dahr was hidden by the rolling hills, but following his trail was not difficult. A line of trampled grass cut an arrow's path, diverting only around things too large to jump or too thick to crash through. As they neared the village, the path grew wider, far too wide to be made by a single horse and rider, and Jeran wondered what manner of creature Dahr had summoned to his hunt.

Jeran crested a rise and coughed on acrid-tasting smoke. Only a handful of buildings had been spared the torch, and the light from the burning village was almost bright enough to blind. A few terrified figures ran toward the safety of a nearby forest, and several beat against the sides of burning buildings or threw themselves bodily against doors engulfed in flame. Terrified screams and frantic pleas came from within.

On the south side of the village, a group of dark-armored soldiers stood in rigid formation, preparing to receive a charge. Dahr ran at full speed, his horse forgotten, and his loping strides carried him ten hands each. His greatsword, as tall as a man and honed to a razor's sharpness, was ready to taste blood. A pack of wolves ran at Dahr's side, growling and barking as they closed on their prey, and behind them a giant bear struggled to keep up.

The sight of the village's cruel treatment enraged Jeran, and he wished he were at Dahr's side. "Stop the Tachans," he yelled. "I'll help the villagers." With a nod, Grendor angled his horse toward the fray. Wardel followed the Orog, but Aryn kept his horse behind Jeran.

Dahr never slowed, not even when he reached the Tachans. He plowed through them like a bull, sending men flying in every direction. The wolves were at his heels, nipping and hamstringing, but they kept moving until they were past the soldiers and safe from their blades.

Those soldiers still standing turned with the pack, keeping their eyes on the wolves; they were unprepared for the bear. Its momentum alone knocked five men to the ground, and it trampled more as it clawed and mauled its way across the field. Dahr howled when the bear attacked, a sound that the wolves took up in concert.

As Jeran neared the village, the heat from the flames grew unbearable and the thick smoke made breathing difficult. *Water. I need water to put out the flames.* He surrendered to his Gift, gasping when a torrent of energy swept through him, and he fought to keep it under control as he considered which combination of flows to use. He wove bolts of blue and green and aimed them toward the nearest building, but when they gathered together, the air crackled with energy. "NO!" Jeran shouted.

A shaft of lightning arced out of the clear sky, hammering the farmhouse. Bits of the roof exploded, showering Jeran and Aryn with debris, and Jeran fell from his horse. On his knees he retched, thinking about the people in the building.

He risked a glance over his shoulder and saw Yassik and Alwen descending the hill behind him at a terrifying speed, their small forms bouncing around like rag dolls in the fast-moving wagon.

Jeran's gaze returned to the farmhouse, to the shattered bits of tile littering the ground, and he shuddered. "They were dead anyway," Aryn said, dropping to the ground at Jeran's side and laying a hand on his nephew's shoulder. "Given the option, they'd rather risk your magic over certain death."

Aryn's words had no effect; Jeran could do nothing but stare at the destruction he had wrought. Around him, the village burned. People were dying. Rough hands pulled him to his feet. "Enough!" Aryn said harshly. "These villagers need your help. Alwen and Yassik are too far away. Something must be done, and you're the only one who can do it."

It was the voice Jeran remembered, the one full of confidence and command. Nodding, he seized magic and started toward the next building, trying to figure out what to do differently.

The few remaining Tachans retreated toward the center of the village. Dahr and Grendor, flanked by the wolves and bear, advanced slowly. Wardel rode behind them, bow drawn, and he scanned the knot of enemies for a target.

A ragged villager, her clothes smoldering, scrabbled at the door of a building. She fled when she saw Jeran, half running and half crawling in her desperation to escape. He called after her, but she ignored him, and Jeran turned his attention on the farmhouse.

Time was short, but he did not want to make another mistake. Flames surrounded him; only one building—a large double-doored barn—had survived unscathed. Without warning, part of the building before him collapsed, and Aryn pulled him away from the falling debris. Low, piteous moans came from within the house.

There was no time to save the buildings one by one; Jeran needed to extinguish all the fires simultaneously. He allowed magic to suffuse him until his body tingled with life and energy. It was ecstasy, the pulsing feel of power, but Jeran had no time to enjoy it. He wove thick flows above the buildings, intertwining them in an intricate pattern. He allowed them to collapse in on themselves, and after they did, he added a thin strand of dark brown to the mix.

Lightning flashed again, but not toward the ground. Dark clouds, heavy with rain, bubbled out of the blue sky, and a heavy rain began to fall. It hissed as it met the flames. Exhausted, Jeran dropped to his knees, gasping for air. Aryn was at his side instantly, pulling him away from the fire.

Dahr had driven the Tachans into the village, toward the barn, its unburned frame standing in stark contrast to the rest of the village. "Ambush!" Aryn yelled suddenly, releasing Jeran and drawing his sword. His eyes were fastened on the barn. "Watch yourselves, men!"

Dahr, Grendor, and Wardel had their backs to the barn, and at Aryn's shout, the double-doors burst open and two score soldiers ran out. The pouring rain surprised them, but it slowed their assault by only an instant.

"Ambush!" Jeran yelled, taking up his uncle's cry. He drew his sword, and the Aelvin blade sang as it left its sheath. Fighting the thickening mud and his own fatigue, Jeran staggered toward the fray.

Aryn sprinted ahead of his nephew, his sword swinging wildly. "For House Odara and Alrendria!" His bold charge, one against twoscore, stunned the Tachans, and hesitation cost two their lives. Aryn's blade slashed, and the Tachans retreated. Before they could regroup, Jeran was at his uncle's side, his own sword slicing through armor and flesh with ease.

A ball of fire engulfed the soldier to Jeran's left and stones the size of his head hurtled by on his right. Jeran ducked the swing of his opponent, and his answering blow cleaved the man's sword arm above the elbow. Yassik and Alwen, soaked to the bone and covered in thick mud, stood off to the side, using their Gift to dispatch any Tachan foolish enough to get in their way.

Jeran met the attack of another attacker and dropped to his knees to duck the swing of a second. He drove his blade upward and felt a satisfying resistance. The soldier screamed, but Jeran wrenched his blade free and cut the sound short, then turned to face his other opponent. The man who had attacked him was gone, but Jeran saw another soldier running toward his uncle's exposed back. Without thinking, he seized his Gift. The magic hit him like a hammer blow, but he managed to hold on to it.

"Uncle Aryn! Watch out!" Jeran extended his hand and the Tachan flew backward, hitting the side of the barn with a resounding crash. The soldier dropped to the ground, his neck hanging at an odd angle.

Aryn and Jeran walked side by side through the deluge in their search for Tachans. The two Magi joined them, then Grendor and Wardel, but the only traces they found of Dahr were the ravaged bodies of his opponents and the howls echoing through the storm.

No one had survived the battle unscathed, but their wounds were mostly light. A gash on Grendor's side oozed dark blood, and Wardel winced with every other step, but Jeran and Aryn had only three small cuts between them and the Magi claimed that the wagon ride accounted for their bruises. The look Alwen directed at Jeran as she rummaged through the wagon for a bandage to bind Grendor's wound made him suspect that she blamed him for their injuries.

Some time later, when the rains had died and the sun once again peeked out from behind the clouds, Dahr appeared. He was covered in mud and blood, but his eyes shone triumphantly. "They're gone," he said with vicious finality.

Breaking through the doors took some time—Tylor's soldiers had gone to great lengths to seal them shut—but once clear, searching the wreckage was easy. Most of the houses were completely destroyed, the occupants dead. But in a few they found life: a crying babe cradled in the arms of its mother, her own breathing shallow but regular; three children, huddled in a root cellar with their father, his eyes sunken with fear. When all was done, nearly a score climbed from the wreckage of the village, and when those who fled returned, a third of the village was accounted for. They praised Jeran for his help, but to him this was no victory.

"To the southeast is the village of Keryn's Rest," he told the survivors. "Go there, and tell them... Tell them Jeran Odara sent you. They will take care of you, help you rebuild your lives."

The villagers did not go immediately, nor would they until they had saved what they could and cared for their dead. Jeran wanted to help them build a pyre, but Aryn stopped him. "We are needed in Portal," his uncle said. "Let the villagers do what they must. They need time to mourn before they move on." Dahr, his face tight with anger, and Wardel watched the villagers. Grendor looked on the verge of tears, but the Magi's expressions were hard to read. Their eyes were on Jeran.

"We ride for Portal!" Jeran said sourly, his eyes roving over the destruction. "Yassik! Wardel! Give the villagers what supplies we can spare. Alwen"—the old woman frowned at him, eyebrow raised—"You'll ride with me. I have much to learn."

Chapter 27

"It's not what I imagined," Dahr said as he and Jeran stared down from the crest of a tall, broad hill. The descent was unremarkable, the gentle slope opened into a green valley dotted with thin copses and isolated farms. But unlike any of a hundred other valleys on their journey north, this one did not give way to yet another featureless hill. A line of mountains cut from east to west across the horizon. Innumerable peaks, the tallest capped with snow despite the broiling heat, stretched into the summer sky. No small mountains heralded the range; no crevasses or fissures cut the land. The mountains simply began.

It was awe-inspiring, yet something seemed wrong to Dahr. The hills behind them rolled smoothly, and the small rocks and loose pebbles did not match the dark stone of the mountains. The jagged Boundary cut across the land like a scar, and Dahr felt the wound, the fading echoes of pain. The land itself had resisted the Raising, but it had been no match for the Magi and their Gift. Raising the Boundary had been necessary; it had likely saved Madryn from total destruction. *But at what cost?* The crime against nature the Magi had committed sickened Dahr. *Can't they feel what they've done?* His anger resurfaced, and a growl echoed across the plains.

The injury was an old one, though, and the land had begun to heal. Nature had started to reclaim the land, and it had instilled the Boundary with its own beauty. The mountains eclipsed the hills, taunting them with a majesty they would never know. Thick forests covered the once-lifeless slopes, and water fell from a thousand glistening falls. The damage caused by the Magi's decision might last for millennia, but in time nature would restore the balance.

In the back of his mind, Dahr heard the low hum that had become his constant companion over the last few seasons. When he had first heard it, what seemed an eternity ago, it had frightened him; once he learned what it was, what *they* were, it had terrified him. Now the *Tierenjah* had become his friends. When their thoughts were gone he felt alone, and when they returned, he felt elation he had only known once before, at the sight of Katya.

If only I knew how to control the voices. If only I had someone to teach me! Jeran was lucky to have the Magi, though Dahr doubted he would feel the same in Jeran's place. A few days huddled in the wagon beside that irascible woman and nosy old man would drive him mad. But they could not help him. No one could. The last *Tier'sorahn* died centuries ago.

Dahr had made some progress on his own. With effort he could separate the sounds in his mind, pull one voice from the crowd. With concentration, he could block them all out for a time. But he had so many questions and no one to turn to.

Fang sensed his mood and echoed his growl. She turned her head from side to side, scanning the horizon for threats. Her voice was the easiest for Dahr to identify. It was more than a voice, really; it had color, scent, texture, and a thousand other facets. Her presence. He reached out to it, not knowing how he did so, and sensed wariness and tension.

Dahr sent out a soothing thought, and Fang relaxed. He watched her calm, he felt it, and he reached down to pat her head. Frustration dug at him like a burr; his thoughts he could hide, but he had not yet learned how to shield his emotions. "It's not what I expected at all." He was not talking about the mountains. It was the city nestled in the Boundary's shadow that disappointed him.

Portal was not large; some of the villages they had passed on the journey north had more than matched it in size. A low wall thirty hands in height and less than ten wide formed a semicircle around the southern half of the city, the smooth, chiseled stone merging seamlessly with the featureless rock of the mountains. Three gates wide enough for two carts abreast stood open, each guarded by a small complement of Guardsmen. A narrow, hard-packed dirt road ran through the gates, weaving through farms and orchards that grew denser as they neared the city. The middle road was the widest and the most traveled, but even it faded to little more than a well-worn trail a league from Portal. Few travelers moved upon the roads, and those who did led laden carts toward the city.

Inside the walls, the wooden buildings gave way to stone, but the tallest structure was no more than three stories tall. Paving stones replaced the winding dirt roads, and the three avenues arrowed toward the castle, which stood hidden in shadow, eclipsed by the mountains around it. Though it seemed a daunting construction, with hard angles, turreted towers, and crenellated walls, Dahr's frown deepened.

All his life, Dahr had heard stories of Portal, the greatest fortification in all of Madryn. It was said that armies had battered against its wall for seasons with no effect, that not even Magi could breach its defenses. Dahr had expected more: walls to make Kaper's look small, with Guardsmen patrolling its length in squads and a fierce castle surrounded by layers of defenses. The city below seemed no different than any other, the castle no more unassailable than Kaper's. Cradled against the mountains, he saw no real need for the few precautions that had been taken. He turned to find five pairs of eyes staring at him. "It's small," he announced.

Warm laughter filled the afternoon air. "We should take him to Dranakohr," Wardel joked, mopping sweat from his head. "He'd be impressed by that!"

"You take him!" Jeran laughed too, but his voice had an edge to it. "I'm in no hurry to return."

"Are you going to stand up there all day?" Alwen yelled from her seat in the wagon. "I thought you wanted to *go* to Portal, not stare at it."

"Leave them be," Yassik chided. "You only get to see something for the first time once. Let them enjoy it."

Alwen sniffed, and looked at Portal disdainfully. "I don't know what all the fuss is about. It was a lot prettier before."

"Let them enjoy it!" Yassik insisted. "What's done is done, and few enough can remember a time when the mountains weren't here, even among the Magi. I—" He saw the blow coming just in time and managed to duck beneath the swinging cane. "What was that for?" he asked, his eyes wide with innocence.

"I'll thank you to stop bringing up my age, old man."

"Oh, Alwen!" For a wonder, not a hint of sarcasm entered into Yassik's apology; his words sounded sincere. "You know that's not what I meant! For most, these mountains have always been here. To them, they're *supposed* to be here. You can't expect people who don't understand what we did to hate what we had to do."

"I understand," Dahr muttered. He had not meant to speak out loud, but he must have, because both Magi turned toward him. Their gazes bored into him, seemed to peer into his very soul. The silence that followed was uncomfortable, and Dahr was relieved when Jeran broke it.

"Alwen's right." Jeran said, urging his horse forward. "Portal isn't the end of our journey; it's the beginning." They remounted and eased their horses down the hill. Jeran was eager to reach the city—he tried to hide it, but Dahr knew him too well—but he never allowed the horses to move faster than a walk.

The mines of Dranakohr had tempered Jeran's spirit as well as his body and added the fire of passion to his cold reason. Gone was the imperturbable young man with whom Dahr had grown up. Now, emotion broiled beneath the surface, struggling to be released. It was another bond between them, that barely-contained anger; it had helped smooth the edges from their reunion, and Dahr took comfort in the fact that he was not the only one filled with hate.

Jeran was harder than he used to be, more focused. His eyes took in everything, dissecting and appraising every bit of information. He had a piercing stare like Yassik's or Alwen's—the gaze of the Magi. The way Jeran seemed able to see to his heart made him uncomfortable, but he had never been able to hide anything from Jeran. Only Jeran's eyes had changed, not his ability.

Sensing eyes on his back, Jeran turned, and he smiled when he saw Dahr staring. It was his old smile, not the controlled grin he wore often of late. Dahr wondered if Jeran knew how quickly his personality could switch from strange to familiar.

He did not return the smile. For him, there was little joy left in the world, little enough left worth smiling about. The only time he felt at peace was on the hunt; the only times he smiled were when he forgot what he had done. *Martyn, the alliance with Illendrylla, all of Alrendria put at risk because of her. Because of me!*

In some ways, Jeran's no different than Aryn, switching personalities at a whim. The thought bubbled up from nowhere, surprising Dahr, and he looked around suspiciously. With so many voices in his head, he was never sure which thoughts were his own, and he often suspected his companions of distracting him when his thoughts turned dark. But none of the animals he traveled with had known Aryn before; this thought must have been his. Besides, he did not often hear words when the animals communicated with him. It was more a combination of images and feelings, sometimes mixed with sounds or scents. It was something hard to understand, and even harder to explain. *And the Gods know that old man has made me try to explain it!* Dahr felt another growl rolling up from his chest as his eyes fastened on Yassik.

He let his gaze slip past the Mage. Aryn looked at Portal, his expression thoughtful. Against his will, Dahr's anger surged. Anger at the Durange. At the Gods. At himself. It took all of his will to keep the Blood Rage at bay. *Everything Aryn suffered could be laid at the Durange's feet. If only Jeran and I... NO!*

He refused to blame himself for what happened. Jeran did, but they had been children. There was nothing they could have done.

Aryn turned toward him and smiled, and Dahr saw recognition in his eyes. That is the way it had been, of late: sometimes Aryn knew him, sometimes not. Today he was fine, but by tonight he could be blank-eyed, raving, or all but comatose. His affliction was as unpredictable as the winds. Dahr could endure Aryn not knowing him, but to see the man who had adopted him, the man who had been like a father to him, reduced to fits of weeping or cringing at every shadow's movement made the blood pound in his veins.

Jeran snaked down the hillside, weaving around scrub brush, to one of the three trails leading to Portal. They passed several farms on the way, and Dahr watched men and women in dust-covered clothes pulling weeds, running plows, mending fences, and feeding the livestock. The oppressive heat seemed to bother them no more than the dark shadows cast by the Boundary, and watching them evoked memories of his time on the Odara farm. *That could have been my life. I could have been at peace.*

The farmers lifted their heads to look as Jeran led his troupe past, but only long enough for a glance. Visitors were not as uncommon in Portal as in the smaller villages of House Odara, and seeing a group of weary travelers was nothing out of the ordinary. Even Dahr occasioned no comment; from a distance, he could easily be mistaken for a tall Human, and the mind had a way of not seeing what it did not want to see.

With his dome-shaped head, leathery grey skin, broad nose, and slightly-pointed ears, Grendor earned a few startled glares. More than one farmer stopped working at the sight of him and continued staring until they were long past. A girl of ten winters ran screaming for her mother when Grendor smiled at her, and an older boy shouted for his friends to come and see. By the time they neared Portal's walls, a small escort of children paralleled their course, their eyes fastened on the Orog.

A quarter league from the city, the farms stopped and a small town sprung up around the rapidly-widening path. The buildings, all solid timber, had an air of age to them. Portal grew as well, and even if it were still not as big or well protected as Kaper, the city seemed more impressive up close than it had from the hill.

The children attracted more attention than the riders, but once the villagers saw what the youngsters were looking at, they more often than not stopped what they were doing and joined the procession. By the time the party passed the last building and approached the gate, nearly a hundred people followed them.

Several thousand hands before Portal's wall the village abruptly ended. Not so much as a shrub grew on the broken, uneven approach to the city. Even grass was sparse, pushing up in small clumps through splits in the rocky soil. The trail made a beeline for the thick arch of stone protected by two portcullises and a gate of stout oak. The gate stood open, the portcullises raised, but the Guardsmen on duty did not welcome them.

At their approach, a squad of Guardsmen ran out to block the gate. A dark-eyed man with a fresh scar running the length of his face and the markings of a subcommander on his sleeve stepped in front of the others. His eyes had a haunted, harried look to them, and his uniform was spotted with dirt and torn in several places. He left his sword sheathed, but his fingers flexed unconsciously over the hilt as if he expected to draw at any moment.

"Peace to you," the man said in a deep, bass voice. His eyes swept over the party, pausing for a moment on Dahr and nearly popping out when they landed on Grendor, but his voice betrayed no surprise. "Portal is closed to visitors. You may take lodging in Sumarin. A representative of Family Talbot will be sent to inspect your goods."

Dahr looked to his left, to the far gate, where a wagon trundled through without trouble. "The guards at the other gates don't take their duties as seriously."

"The gates are barred to strangers, Tribesman," the Guardsman replied. His eyes roved over Dahr and his companions as if to say that he had never seen so strange a group. "Those we know well are free to pass. All others must wait in Sumarin."

"Has there been trouble?" Jeran asked, edging his horse between Dahr and the soldier. "We've been long on the road and would appreciate some news."

"No trouble that the Guard couldn't handle," the soldier answered. He fingered his blade but did not draw. "Now back away."

"If you're worried about attack," Wardel called out, his eyes scanning the battlements, "then why are the gates open? Why don't you have more men patrolling the walls?"

"And let the Durange think that we're afraid!" one Guardsman shouted. The subcommander silenced him with a glare, but another man shouted from the background. "A couple of raids aren't enough to frighten the Alrendrian Guard! The Bull may have supporters on this side of the Boundary, but he could never field an army large enough to threaten Portal."

Wardel frowned at the last, and Dahr thought of the army Jeran had told him the Bull led, but before anyone could ask another question, the subcommander drew his sword. "My patience runs thin. Back your wagon away from the gates. Find a room in Sumarin and someone will come to see you before nightfall."

Jeran stepped down from his horse and bowed his head politely. "Please inform Lord Talbot that Jeran Odara, the First Seat of House Odara, is at the gate. We have matters to discuss."

The Guardsman's face tightened as if he had been insulted. "Lord Odara is dead." He spat at Jeran's feet. "How dare you dishonor his memory?"

"I was captured by the Durange," Jeran replied calmly as he approached the Guardsmen, "but escaped. I come with news of—"

The backhanded blow sent Jeran reeling. Spitting blood, he struggled to maintain his balance. The Guardsman looked at him a moment, and then nodded, as if satisfied that justice had been done.

Dahr was off his horse in an instant. Greatsword in hand, he stalked forward. Wardel appeared on his right. The Guardsman's sword was still sheathed, but his hand hovered over the hilt, ready to draw. Grendor, staff held tightly in both hands, his face pale grey, ran up on Dahr's right. His lips pressed into a thin line, and he eyed the Guardsmen with grim determination. On a face that so often wore a broad smile, the expression seemed unnatural.

Several Guardsmen stepped forward, and another shouted out a warning. Inside the keep, an alarm began ringing. At the first gong, three shadowy forms appeared atop the wall, bows notched and drawn, and more Guardsmen sprinted down the battlements from east and west.

The two Magi remained in the wagon, seemingly unconcerned with the goings-on. Yassik's eyes shifted from place to place, and he wore the wide-eyed expression of a visitor gawking at the legendary city. Alwen looked far less happy. Brow furrowed, lips drawn down in a disapproving scowl, she glared at everyone with equal amounts of anger. "Boys," she muttered, rolling her eyes. "Always thinking with their swords."

Aryn was the only one who stayed in his saddle, and his horse stepped back and forth quickly. His eyes were on the wall above, shifting quickly from Guardsman to Guardsman and watching the soldiers racing toward them. He raised his bow but did not draw; he seemed torn between protecting his companions and not firing on the Guard.

With nerves as frayed as they were, another wrong move would provoke an attack, and if it came to a fight, Dahr knew they had little chance of victory. Even if by some miracle they did win, the Guardsmen were their allies, and no good could come from killing them. Nevertheless, he felt the Blood Rage coming on and found himself excited by the prospect of battle. His breathing quickened, his vision glazed over, and his heart pounded. A small voice in the back of his mind, one that sounded a lot like his own, reminded him that these men were friends. It screamed at him, begged him to stop, but it had no effect. The monster had returned, and the only way to satiate it was with blood. At his side, Fang barked a warning.

An instant before he rushed the guards, Jeran raised his hand, and Dahr froze. He struggled to run forward, to drive his blade into the heart of the Guardsman, but he could not move. His rage grew, and panic at being trapped too, but neither did him any good. He could not break Jeran's magic. He opened his mouth to scream, but no sound emerged.

Jeran straightened and wiped the blood from his mouth. He looked at Dahr and shook his head slightly, mouthing a silent, "Not now." For some reason, those two words did what Dahr's own frantic pleas to himself could not: the Blood Rage disappeared as if it had never been, and as it died, so did the magic holding him in place.

Raising his hands to show that he meant no harm, Jeran turned back to face the Guardsmen. "I am Jeran Odara, son of Alic Odara and the Lady Illendre. Find Lord Talbot. He will know me."

"The first blow was a warning," the Guardsman replied, his eyes narrowing. "I've had enough of you Durange and your coward's tricks! Lord Odara is dead!" The man seemed possessed; he quivered with unreleased anger, and though his eyes locked on Jeran, they did not appear to see anything. As the man drew back his fist for another blow, Dahr wondered if only Garun'ah experienced the Blood Rage.

The punch stopped a finger's width from Jeran's jaw. The man trembled, his eyes wide, and he struggled against unseen bonds. He looked terrified, and despite himself, Dahr felt sorry for the man. The other Guardsmen stepped back when their commander rose several hands off the ground. Those lining the wall notched arrows and prepared to fire.

Jeran closed his eyes and took a deep breath. He smiled, and balls of fire five hands in diameter flared into being on either side of him. He looked up at the men on the wall and said, "Enough!" At his words, a score of bows flew into the air amidst startled shouts. The Guardsmen were pushed back and pinned against the wall. "I don't have time for games. Bring me Lord Talbot!"

"What's the meaning of this?" a familiar voice demanded. "What's going on?" Of average height but powerfully muscled, Lord Gideon Talbot, Warden of the Portal, strode through the gate. Long black hair woven into a tight braid hung over one shoulder, framing a face chiseled from the Boundary, all hard lines and angles. His armor was black and emblazoned with a grey wolf. He looked exactly as Dahr remembered.

Talbot looked from left to right, and a frown pulled at his lips. "Paliver! Seric! Why are you standing against the wall? Ehvrit, you're in command here, why—" His speech broke off abruptly, and he stared slack-jawed. "Jeran?" The word was spoken softly, uncertainly. "Jeran, is it really you?"

"It's been a long time, Lord Talbot." The balls of fire disappeared with those words, and the Guardsmen stumbled as they found their bodies under their own control once again. Dahr heard the distant clatter of bows falling to the ground. Sweat beaded Jeran's face, and Dahr noted how quickly his friend breathed, but Jeran showed no sign of exhaustion as he fixed a warm smile on Lord Talbot.

"Too long," Talbot agreed, a broad grin spreading across his face. In three quick steps he was at Jeran's side, enveloping the younger man in a warm embrace and pounding him vigorously on the back. "By the Gods, boy, it's good to see you!"

When they parted, Talbot's eyes shifted to Dahr. "Can it be?" he asked, feigning disbelief. "Is this the little boy who pounded me into submission all those winters ago?" When he stepped forward to grip Dahr's arm, he had to crane his neck back to look him in the eye. Dahr took the arm, but then pulled Talbot into a bear hug. Just seeing the man brought back fond memories, and such things were too precious for a handshake.

Talbot studied Jeran's companions and laughed loudly. "You gather an odd group of followers, Jeran. I've not seen his like before"—he gestured toward Grendor—"but that skin names him Orog, though the Gods alone know where you found one of the Lost Race! A Tribesman, an Orog, at least one Mage in that ramshackle wagon of yours, and…"

For a second time, surprise left Talbot speechless, and his eyes widened. He ran forward and all but pulled Aryn from the saddle. "It can't be!" He clutched Aryn in a hug even tighter than the one he had given Jeran. After a long moment, Talbot stepped back and looked into Aryn's eyes. Worry spread across his face. "What is it, Aryn? What's wrong?"

For a long time, Aryn said nothing. Finally, he mouthed a single, tremulous word. "Gideon?" It was a question, something Aryn did not believe but wanted to.

"It's me," Talbot assured him, keeping a tight grip on Aryn's shoulders.

"Gideon!" Aryn repeated with more conviction. Recognition and a warm smile spread across his face, but just as suddenly, it was gone, and tears glittered in Aryn's eyes. "I couldn't save them, Gideon! I tried to, but he hunted them down. He killed them both. I couldn't stop him."

Talbot looked confused as he drew Aryn into a comforting embrace. Jeran swallowed, but could not bring himself to answer. Talbot seemed to understand. "Peace, my friend," he said, cupping an arm around Aryn's shoulder and leading him toward the gate. "The boys are fine. They escaped! They made it here, to Portal. I kept them safe."

"Safe?" For a moment, Aryn straightened, and a look of hope flashed across his face. But it only last a moment. "No," he said, sagging. "No. Tylor killed them. He told me so."

"The Bull is full of lies. You know that. I swear to you, Jeran and Dahr are alive and well, and closer than you think." This time, the words had no effect, and Aryn began to weep. Sympathy and anger warred across Talbot's face.

"Ehvrit, double the guard," Talbot ordered, his expression hardening. "No one enters the city that you don't know personally. No one! And wipe that grimace off your face. You did the right thing. How were you to know that this was really Lord Odara? He's never graced us with his presence before."

"Hestar, go to the keep. Tell Aleesa that Aryn and... No, better yet, just tell her we have guests. I want to surprise her!" The Guardsmen hurried about their tasks, and Lord Talbot waved for Jeran and the others to follow him. The smile he offered was inviting, but Dahr saw more than concern for Aryn in Talbot's gaze; he saw fear.

Chapter 28

Talbot led them down a broad avenue lined with dark paving stones. The road cut through the heart of the city, climbing in a gentle slope. In the distance, the castle stood silhouetted against the larger blackness of the Boundary. Featureless buildings with a handful of narrow windows and doors rose to either side of the street. Only a handful stood higher than three stories, and those had garrisoned watch towers atop them. No gaps existed between structures; each building stood flush against its neighbor. Cross-streets were rare and barely broad enough for a wagon. Wooden signs engraved with the owner's name and trade or sporting a faded picture hung above the central door on each building. Jewels and trinkets lay in a few dust-covered windows, but most shops stood boarded and barren. The bakeries and butcheries fared little better; only the armories exhibited any signs of life. Grizzled soldiers, eyes ringed with dark circles, entered bearing rust-spotted or nicked blades and exited examining new armaments. Few spoke or even noticed the passage of Lord Talbot, and those who did wore hopeless expressions.

The streets were all but silent. No craftsmen hawked their wares; no children played in t the alleys. The low rumble of life, a sound so overpowering in most cities, was absent, as if Portal itself were asleep. Or dying.

The few groups they passed consisted primarily of Guardsmen, and everyone walked in tight clusters regardless of whether or not they were soldiers. A pair of wagons escorted by a half score of heavily-armed men headed toward the gates. Though he peered down each cross street, Dahr saw no one, and to a man, those they passed headed south, away from the Boundary.

"What's happening here, Lord Talbot?" Yassik asked. "The last time I came to Portal, things were different."

"The war," Talbot answered grimly. He still had his arm around Aryn's shoulder, and he craned his neck back to look at the Mage. "In the southlands, this war might have just begun, but we've been fighting it since Aryn was captured. The Durange have been picking off my scouts for winters, and in the last few seasons they started attacking larger patrols.

"To make matter worse, the other Houses have demanded more soldiers, and with the Boundary to protect us, they wonder what need we have with Guardsmen?" Talbot's grimace plainly said what he thought of the other Houses and their complaints. "Twice now, the Durange have attacked the gates. Twice! What other city has weathered two assaults? The first time, the Bull's soldiers hid in a merchant caravan, the second in some hay wagons. The second attempt was pure folly, but the first... Had Malkov not by chance heard a cough, the whole city might have been taken."

To Dahr's left a door opened, and Fang's ears perked up. She growled, and Dahr peered into the dark, smoky tavern. A bleary-eyed Guardsman staggered outside, and seeing Dahr, he stiffened and reached reflexively for his sword. The man's eyes flicked to the side as he fumbled for his weapon, and when his gaze fell on Talbot, his manner instantly changed. He straightened, smoothed his wrinkled uniform, and waited until Talbot had passed before staggering away. Before the door swung shut, Dahr caught a glimpse of a half dozen other men bent low over their cups, reeking of fear.

"After the incidents," Talbot continued, "I ordered the Guardsmen to search every wagon that wanted entry to Portal. There were no more attacks, but our measures and Tylor's scourging of the countryside have driven away most of the merchants. My people expect an attack at any moment, and many have already fled. And now, with the…" Talbot shook his head. "You'll see for yourself soon enough. I'll not ruin it." Talbot refused to say any more as he led them through the silent streets.

They made an odd procession, Lord Talbot in front with an arm wrapped around Aryn, Jeran and Dahr with Fang between them a step behind, Wardel and Grendor riding behind them, and the two Magi in the rear, arguing heatedly atop the rickety wagon laden with goods. The castle loomed larger with every step, but for every hand it seemed to rise, the mountains rose a hundred. The dark, barren cliffs stole Dahr's breath, and he stared at them while relishing the feel of the cool mountain air on his face.

News of Jeran's arrival preceded them through Portal, and though the streets did not fill, Dahr felt eyes upon them. Looking up, he saw faces staring at them from the windows above. Quiet whispers reached his ears, hundreds of murmured questions, each spoken over one another. No one else noticed the watchers save Jeran, and he stubbornly refused to acknowledge them. In fact, the nearer they drew to the castle, the more his shoulders hunched and less he looked up, even to view the castle.

The buildings ended abruptly in a broad, open plaza. Stone walkways crisscrossed between thickly-treed gardens and ornate fountains. On the far side of the plaza, the road narrowed considerably but continued climbing until it met the portcullised gate guarding the castle's entrance. Two Guardsmen guarded the gate, and Dahr wondered if they were even necessary. Other than their party, not a single soul stood upon the plaza.

To either side of the castle the land descended with ever-increasing severity, so that Portal Keep stood on a promontory overlooking the Boundary. At the bottom of each slope, a wall a hundred hands high and twenty across stretched from the base of the castle to the mountains, forming a triangle with the rock wall to the north. But neither the castle nor the twin walls attracted Dahr's attention; the Boundary itself, towering over castle and city alike, held his gaze. To his left and right were rugged, snow-covered peaks; but to the north, for a span of more than two thousand hands, the rock was smooth and flat-topped, and it curved with a regularity that defied nature.

Suddenly, everything became clear to Dahr. Portal was not a well-defended keep tucked away in the mountains. The mountains were its walls, the smooth-faced cliff the barrier between Alrendria and *Ael Shataq*. The castle was a guardpost on the inside of that fortification, the final bastion if the unthinkable were to happen and the enemy breached the gates. The urge to stand atop the massive wall and look into the Darklord's domain nearly overcame him.

Dahr was not the only one awestruck by the sight. Wardel sat slack-jawed, his mouth working but no sound coming out, and Grendor's slitted eyes were as wide as saucers. Jeran's face betrayed no emotion, but his eyes swept from left to right, taking everything in, measuring and calculating. Aryn smiled at the sight of castle, a warm smile that gave the feeling of homecoming. Only the Magi remained unphased.

Talbot led them up the inclined road and stopped in front of the guards. "Lars. Carenthon," he called out in greeting. The soldiers saluted.

"There's word of trouble at the gates, Sir," one of them said, eyeing Jeran suspiciously. "But the castle remains unapproached. The Portal is secure."

"You've done well. The gates are secure. Just a couple of troublemakers up from one of the villages." Talbot laughed and pointed at the wagon. "See to our guests' belongings. I—"

"These are yours, young man," Alwen said absently. "We've no need of grain and seed. Not where we're going." Dahr turned at the sound. Yassik stood beside the wagon, busily patting dust and smoothing the wrinkles from his clothes. Alwen stared at him from her seat, and an angry frown deepened the creases in her heavily-lined face. She cleared her throat purposefully.

Yassik stopped what he was doing and glanced up. When he saw Alwen's expression, he flinched. With a sigh and rueful shake of his head, he offered his hand. She sniffed indignantly before accepting his arm and climbing down.

They left the wagon in the care of the Guardsmen and followed Talbot into the castle. The gate opened onto a broad, grass-covered courtyard. A number of small buildings nestled against the interior of the wall. The clang of hammer on anvil sounded from most, and a steady stream of people moved between the structures. Between the buildings were small gardens, many of them overgrown and filled with unharvested fare. Blue-liveried servants, far too few for the task, labored among the plants, drenched in sweat despite the cool breeze.

Portal Keep stood across the inner courtyard. Built from the same dark rock as the Boundary, its stones carved and strengthened by magic, it was an imposing sight. Arrow slits riddled the walls and a handful of Guardsmen patrolled the crenellations or stood watch atop the rounded towers. Atop the tallest tower, the Odaran Greatwolf snapped in the wind beside the Rising Sun of Alrendria.

A group of young men practiced half-heartedly in the middle of the courtyard without the supervision of a seasoned fighter. Their movements were sloppy and undisciplined, their stances wrong, and they hacked at each other with reckless abandon. When one poorly-aimed swing nearly took off the head of a spindly, hook-nosed boy no more than fifteen winters old, Aryn leapt forward.

"Hold!" he called, wrenching free of Talbot's grip. The boys froze as Aryn stormed toward them. "What's the matter with you? Haven't you held a sword before?" The children started to back away, but Aryn did not let them flee. He grabbed the young boy who had nearly lost his head and with barely-restrained anger, snapped out a series of orders. When he finished, he turned to the next boy, and then the next, giving each a series of drills to practice.

Most of the boys diligently complied, but the last, a young man several seasons older than his companions with dark brown eyes and shoulder-length black hair that mimicked Lord Talbot's style stood his ground. "Who are you to order me around?"

"He's Guard Commander Aryn Odara," Talbot announced, stepping forward, "and you'd be wise to listen to him, Kristaf."

The young man's eyes shifted to Talbot, then back to Aryn. "Commander Odara?" he repeated. Aryn, too, had stopped, and he stared at Kristaf, equally surprised. "I thought the Darklord had him, Father."

"He did until Jeran set him free. Aryn, you remember my son, don't you?"

"Kris?" Aryn said, shaking his head. "He was a babe the last time I saw him."

Kristaf no longer paid any attention to Aryn. He was studying the faces of his father's companions, and his eyes finally settled on Jeran. "Lord Odara," he said, dropping to one knee. "Welcome home."

An excited whisper sprang up among the other boys, and they quickly followed Kristaf's lead, dodging around Aryn and bowing formally, offering Jeran flowery praise and pledges of undying loyalty. Jeran waved away their compliments, urging them to rise.

"Are you here to assume command of Portal?" Kristaf asked. "To take control of House Odara?" He sounded eager, yet regret tinged his voice.

"Not yet," Jeran answered, and relief flashed across the boy's face. "Duty requires me to leave House Odara under your father's stewardship for a time longer. I have no qualms about doing so, especially with one such as you to keep an eye on him." Kristaf beamed at the praise, and even Talbot's lips twitched upward in a smile.

Jeran's companions were introduced, and with each introduction, the boys' excitement grew. The announcement of two Magi caused a gasp to ripple through the group, but when neither would demonstrate their Gift, the boys' attention quickly shifted. Dahr, towering over everyone, was the first Tribesman most had seen, and Grendor was even more of a sensation. Blushing dark grey, Grendor did his best to answer the stream of questions leveled at him, but the boys barely gave him a chance. They pressed in from all sides, examining him closely and reaching out to touch his rough skin.

"Enough!" Talbot snapped, and the boys fell back. "Grendor is no circus animal for you to paw. He's our guest and ally, and he should be treated as such. Kristaf, find your mother. Tell her to meet me in the Warden's Hall. And not a word about our guests! I want to surprise her."

With a formal salute and hastily-spoken, "Yes, Father," Kristaf took off at a run.

"He's not as difficult as his brothers," Talbot said with a fond laugh, "but he has an eye for danger and a bold streak the size of the Boundary!"

"I wonder where he gets that from," Aryn said with a twinkle in his eye. Ordering the boys around seemed to have broken Aryn out of his melancholy. The sudden change in Aryn's mood affected Talbot, in particular; he stared at Aryn with a mixture of hope and sadness.

When Talbot started toward the keep, Dahr looked at Fang. "That place is not for you." In response, he felt a twinge of indignation float through his consciousness. "Stay out of trouble." Fang walked in the direction of the stables.

They entered the keep through an archway with its massive wooden door thrown open and an iron portcullis raised high. A handful of servants hurried down the narrow passages without so much as noticing Lord Talbot. Despite their frantic pace, a layer of dust covered everything, and half the keep's lanterns flickered weakly or were altogether unlit.

Talbot took them to a large room deep within the keep. A round table covered with maps, dispatches, and hastily-scribbled notes dominated the center of the chamber. Swords and daggers hung on the walls between racks of polearms and ceremonial armor. The metal glistened and the wood gleamed, but many of the displays were incomplete and conspicuous gaps spotted the precisely-arranged armaments.

"Sit!" Talbot gestured toward the table. "I'll have food and drink brought! There's little enough to celebrate these—"

The door flew open and a plump woman with piercing brown eyes and a kind, motherly face strode in and cast her eyes about the chamber. When her gaze settled on Talbot, she frowned and angry wrinkles formed around her eyes. "What's the meaning of this, Gideon? No less than five men—my own son included!—told me to find you immediately but wouldn't tell me why. Why, I've half a mind to—" Her eyes slid past her husband and her tirade died.

Talbot laughed aloud. "I've not seen her that surprised in seasons! For that, Aryn, I owe you greatly."

"Is... Is it really...?" Aleesa Talbot stepped forward uncertainly, her arm half raised. Her mouth worked slowly, but she could not find words. When Aryn ran across the room and swept her into a tight embrace, a warm smile spread across her face. "Aryn!" she exclaimed, squeezing him tightly. "Dear Gods, I thought we'd never see you again!"

Aryn pulled back enough to meet her eyes, and a smile broader than hers lit up his own features. "It feels like I've come home, Leesa. After all this time..."

Reaching up to wipe the tear from Aryn's eye, Aleesa returned his smile. "I knew you were too stubborn to let that monster kill you."

"It was dark, Leesa," Aryn sobbed. His eyes glossed over and his body sagged. "So dark. He... He made me relive Jeran's death a thousand times. That was worse than the torture." Aryn trembled with barely-contained emotion. "I promised I'd take care of him!"

"There, there," Aleesa said soothingly. She wrapped an arm tightly around Aryn's shoulders and fixed a harsh glare on Talbot, as if he were at fault for Aryn condition. "Let's get you a hot bath and a warm meal. We'll talk all about it once you're refreshed." Without a word to the others, she led Aryn from the room.

The rest stood silently for a time; no one wanted to be the first to speak. "He'll get better," Talbot said suddenly. "There's no one tougher than Aryn Odara. He just needs time."

"Time's not something we have in abundance, Lord Talbot," Alwen snapped, hobbling toward the table. "We have much to discuss. Best we be about it."

"I'd thought to have a meal brought, Honored Mage," Talbot replied, "and give you and your companions a chance to refresh yourselves. My sons will want to take part in this council. They'll never forgive me if I—"

Alwen cut him off with a dismissive gesture. "Time waits for no man, Lord Talbot, and few Magi. The threat posed by Lorthas takes precedence over more trivial matters, like your sons' pride."

"Let them enjoy their reunion, Alwen," Yassik said, exasperated. "The Boundary's not going to fall tonight, and the Gods know there are few enough things worth celebrating these days!"

"Alwen's right," Jeran said somberly, taking a place at the table. "Lorthas has put his plan into motion. What little time we have can't be wasted on pleasantries. Send for your sons, Lord Talbot; they won't miss much. We can eat while we talk."

Talbot shouted for a servant while Jeran thumbed through the maps arrayed across the table. He selected three, and spread the first—a detailed map of the Boundary—in front of him. Yassik took the chair to Jeran's left and Talbot the one on Jeran's right. The three of them poured over the map.

Dahr sat across the table from the others. The high-backed chair pressed into the crease beneath his shoulder blades, and Dahr squirmed in an effort to make himself comfortable. With little knowledge of the Boundary and none of Dranakohr's location, he could not contribute to the conversation and quickly grew bored. As often happened when he had nothing to do, Dahr's thoughts turned to Katya, and his mood darkened.

After a time, Grendor sat beside him, and Dahr felt the Orog's slitted eyes on him. "How can you stand being alone?" the Orog asked.

Unconsciously, Dahr reached out to the babble in the back of his mind and it altered; some of the voices moved closer and others farther away. He sought Fang and found her, but she was indistinct, barely more than an impression, and he could not call to her. Shyrock was gone completely. A few voices leapt forward in a deluge of thought, images and impressions, but none addressed him or even seemed aware of his presence. He had found that to be the case in the places where Humans lived; it was harder to communicate with domesticated creatures than wild ones. That had to be important. Dahr just wished he knew how.

"I can always sense the animals," he said, letting out a slow breath, "though I'm not sure how. Those I form the strongest bonds with I miss as much as any friend, but for the most part, I relish the few moments of peace I'm given."

"You misunderstand, friend Dahr." Grendor's narrow eyes held a sadness Dahr had not noticed before. "I have never been separated from my people, and at times I long to be with them. Your world is so big, and those in it so untrusting. I long to return to the *ghrat*, to the comfort of my friends and family. I am afraid of being alone."

Resolve tightened the Orog's face. "This fear is my weakness, and I must defeat it if I am to free my people. Jeran tells me you willfully isolate yourself. You walk alone yet are never afraid. Do you not miss your family and friends? Your Race?" He gripped Dahr's arm tightly. "I ask you, friend Dahr, to help me conquer my fear."

Anger bubbled up inside Dahr. *How dare Jeran discuss my life with a stranger!* Grendor's words opened an old wound, and Dahr struggled not to take out his frustration on the innocent Orog. "I have no secrets," he answered coldly. "I'm alone because I'm meant to be. When Humans look at me they see a wild Tribesman. The Garun'ah see a weak, human-raised thing. I don't miss my people because I have no people."

Grendor's grip softened, and his gaze took on an edge of pity that drove spikes through Dahr's gut. His jaw tightened, but before he could speak, Grendor asked, "How do you stand it?" A tear slid down the Orog's cheek, and the sincerity of Grendor's concern diffused Dahr's anger.

"I... I..." Dahr was spared having to answer when Jeran suddenly stabbed his finger down on the map.

"Here!" Jeran announced triumphantly, glancing at Yassik. The Mage leaned in for a closer look.

"I think you're right, my boy." He scratched at his beard. "It's hard to be sure, but I think you're right." Jeran grabbed the quill and marked the spot on the map. Above the dot, he scrawled *Dranakohr.*

"My scouts have been over that area a thousand times," Talbot insisted.

"It's reasonable to assume that Tylor's been using ShadowMagi to hide the pass," Yassik said, and Talbot frowned uneasily. "It would require a Mage to be present at all times, but Tylor has enough Gifted that he can spare a few to hold an illusion."

"You Magi can do that?" Talbot asked.

Yassik's voice took on its lecturing tone. "With enough patience and practice, a Mage can do just about anything. The key is keeping the mind focused—"

"Yassik!" Alwen snapped. "I don't know if you intend to frighten the man or bore him, but in either case, hold your tongue. Now is not the time."

Yassik fell silent, but he glared at Alwen. Talbot studied the map for a moment and then pointed to a valley south of Dranakohr. "I'll recall the patrols and regroup them here. Once we find the pass, we'll start the siege."

"No," Jeran said sharply. "A direct assault would be folly. The entire Guard would break against Dranakohr's defenses."

"Then what do we do?" For the first time, Talbot looked defeated.

"Recall your patrols from the Boundary," Jeran told him. "Leave one to monitor travel to and from Dranakohr but make sure they do nothing to betray their position. Fortify your position here and increase patrols in the countryside. The Durange have been attacking villages in the guise of Guardsmen. The villagers no longer know who to trust. We must change that."

With the screech of wood on stone, Talbot stood. His chair flew back with enough force to crash into the wall behind him. He slammed a fist into the tabletop just as the chamber's door opened and Aleesa entered, flanked by two young men and a handful of servants carrying steaming platters and dark red wine. Kristaf came last, trailing a few steps behind the others, a look of excitement on his face.

"Villages have been attacked?" Talbot demanded, rounding on the newcomers. "Why have I heard nothing of this?"

"Because I know you, Father," one of the men, a younger image of Lord Talbot, said. "You'd have sent men to protect those people, and Portal can't afford to be stripped of its remaining defenders."

"*I* am the Warden of Portal, Alic," Talbot replied coldly. "I decide how best to serve House Odara."

"And I am Guard Commander in Shaolin's absence," the young man replied, standing his ground. "As commander of the garrison, my first duty is to Alrendria. Sending more men from our defense, especially considering what we face, would not be wise."

"Those are our people out there!" Talbot shouted. "Our people being slaughtered! Those farmers depend on us for protection!"

"And King Mathis depends on us to defend the Boundary." Alic's voice remained firm, but the sadness in his eyes mimicked his father's. "If Lorthas breaches the Portal, how well will those farmers fare? As a Guardsman, my duty lies first to Alrendria and then to House Odara. You taught me that."

"Alic's right, Father," the other boy added. He was of an age with his brother, but his features favored Aleesa's more than Talbot's. "The Portal must hold!"

Talbot looked to be on the verge of arguing, but Jeran interrupted. "It's not a matter worth fighting over," he said, easing Talbot back into his chair. "Once the patrols are recalled, you'll have enough men to protect the city and the farms." Talbot nodded, but the gaze he directed at his sons said the matter was not yet concluded.

At Aleesa's order, the servants cleared the table and set the plates and cups. While they worked, Jeran studied the new arrivals. "Alic," he said, nodding his head toward Talbot's eldest son. Alic returned the bow and Jeran turned to the younger of the twins. "And you must be Tourin. My uncle told me about you." He waved for them to join the table.

"And you must be Jeran," Alic said, taking the seat on Talbot's right. "The whole keep is abuzz with news of your escape." He eyed Jeran warily, not as an enemy, but as an unknown, someone who might put his family at risk.

"Didn't you have another son?" Jeran asked, turning toward Talbot. "Aelornic? And a daughter?"

Talbot nodded grimly. "Aelornic left winters ago to seek his own fortune. And Lendre... she's—"

"My daughter's not allowed to attend war councils." Aleesa interrupted. "I insist on raising at least one child who's not obsessed with guarding the Boundary. I had hoped that Kristaf..."—the boy blushed under his mother's pointed stare—"But it seems my words carry little weight with him."

"We can discuss family politics later, my love," Talbot said. He had regained much of his composure. "Our guests have had a trying journey. Let's get this council underway so they can rest."

After Talbot introduced his family to Dahr and the others, they began the council. Much of the day was spent discussing what Jeran had learned of Lorthas' plans. At Jeran's insistence, Dahr told them what he had done in the Darkwood. He marked on Talbot's maps the routes Tylor's troops preferred and shared everything he knew about their caravans.

Dahr's story amused Lord Talbot. "I'd heard rumors of monsters in the Darkwood. I assumed it was just talk, or at worst, a handful of Tylor's men causing trouble. If I'd known it was you...! You should have come here, lad. We could have used a fighter like you!" Dahr did his best to hide how good Talbot's compliment made him feel.

Once they finished with Dranakohr, Jeran asked about Portal. "Are things really as bad as you've hinted?"

"Worse," Talbot admitted. "Even worse than Alic let on. We've stripped the garrison. King Mathis all but demanded every Guardsman we had. The larger Families sent a few squads, but most insist they need their men to protect their own holdings. With Shaolin patrolling the Boundary, we've had all we could handle just keeping the city running."

"A dispatch came from Kaper some time back," Alic said, drinking deeply from his wine glass, "granting the Houses authority to raise levees and train Guardsmen in the King's name. It has eased the burden somewhat, but only so many men want to join, and I've no mind to impress men into service. Even if we train those we have day and night, it'll be a winter or two before they're truly battle ready."

"Considering what we face," Tourin added, "we may not have a winter or two. Morale is low, even among the Guard, and the attacks on the city haven't helped. The guards at the gates are there to keep the recruits in as much as to keep the Durange out. Even still, we lose a few more every ten-day." With that, the talk shifted to other parts of Madryn. Jeran wanted to know everything he could, and though Alwen had provided a few hints of news, she had not held a wealth of information. According to her, she had had more important things to do than keep informed of petty squabbles.

The council lasted until late in the night, with the tone changing from serious to light and back several times. Stories of Grendor's people, Jeran's adventures in Illendrylla, and Dahr's time among the Garun'ah were interspersed with more somber accounts of troop positions, army strengths, and Mathis' hastily-assembled alliance. Throughout it all, one question kept popping up.

"But *where* did Tylor take his army?" Tourin asked for the fifth time, exasperation tingeing his voice. "Don't get angry, Alic. I'm not saying Portal isn't a good target. Even if the Bull didn't know how weak our garrison was, a force his size and backed by Magi could take the city easily. But the facts are plain; he *didn't* attack here, and Dranakohr is not so far away that we shouldn't have at least heard of his approach by now. That means his army must be going somewhere else."

With a frustrated sigh, Alic shoved the maps, sending them flapping across the table. "But where, Tourin? With most of the Guard defending Gilead and the Corsan border, there's little enough to stop him."

"If he's gone to sea," Dahr said quietly, grabbing a map and tracing a finger from Dranakohr to Norport, "he could be halfway around Madryn by now. He could attack anywhere, with almost no warning."

"What can we do?" Kristaf asked, trying to sound as serious as his brothers. "Even if we knew where he was going to attack, we couldn't get word to them. And with an army of Magi at his disposal, what chance does the Guard have anyway?"

Talbot beamed at his youngest son, and Kristaf's cheeks reddened when he saw his father's smile. "Kristaf's right," Talbot said, "there's nothing we can do."

"Nothing *you* can do," Jeran amended. He stood and stretched his arms over his head dramatically, casting a pointed look at Yassik in the process. "You must continue to protect the Boundary. We'll worry about Tylor."

The others took Jeran's cue and rose. Yassik, wavering on his feet and fighting a yawn, reached for his wine glass and stumbled in the process. Only Wardel's quick intercession kept the Mage from falling flat on his face. The two left arm in arm, whispering quietly, and Alwen watched them go with a disapproving expressions. The others filed out behind them, leaving Jeran, Dahr, Lord Talbot and Alic alone.

Alic remained seated, and his eyes bored into Jeran. "What do you plan to do, Lord Odara?"

"Tonight, I plan to sleep. Tomorrow, I go to get some answers. And maybe the allies we need to defeat the Darklord."

Chapter 29

Dahr woke with a start. Large clouds drifted through a blue summer sky above, and a cool breeze blew against his cheek. Instantly alert, his hand swept out for the sword always kept at his side, but he felt nothing but grass. He rolled to his feet and surveyed his surroundings warily. He had fallen asleep in one of Portal Keep's towers, and the shift in setting worried him, but it was not what had him on edge. His mind was empty, devoid of voices, and Dahr found the silence unnerving. He reached out to Fang but felt nothing; he strained his mind to its limits but heard only the quiet ripple of the wind through the grass.

All his life, Dahr's connection to animals had given him strength. With them he had never truly been alone, and the constant reassurance of their presence had been a boon long before he knew they were there. Since accepting that he was *Tier'sorahn*, the connection had grown stronger, and the thoughts of the creatures closest to him were often so clear he swore they spoke aloud. Even in a strange place, with nothing but wild beasts around him, he always felt something: the hint of an image, a strong emotion, or just the vague impression of an unspoken thought. No matter how weak the connection, it was there, and Dahr had come to think of the voices as a part of him. Without them, he felt exposed.

At times having a thousand voices clamoring in the back of his mind was overwhelming, and knowing that the communication worked both ways, that the animals could contact him as easily as he contacted them, had frightened him at first. The last thing he wanted was to be unusual, and talking with the beasts of the field and birds of the sky certainly made him different. Whether the Garun'ah revered him or the Humans shunned him for that difference mattered little; all he wanted was to be left alone.

Now, with his wish granted and the only voice in his head his own, Dahr yearned for their return. Loneliness enveloped him, loneliness greater than what he felt after Katya betrayed him and handed Jeran over to the Bull of Ra Tachan. A hate-filled growl came unbidden at the mere thought of her.

Yet neither Katya nor the strange silence upset him as much as the knowledge that he dreamed. In all his life, he had only been aware of his dreams in one place, and he could only enter that place when the Darklord willed it.

"Good morning, little brother!" Lorthas' now-familiar voice called jovially. Dahr, cold sweat drenching his forehead and fear knotting his stomach, whirled to face the sound. The Darklord stood behind him, arms outstretched and eyes closed, as if luxuriating in the feel of the sun. "Your presence is strong," he said, exhaling slowly. "You must be close. Are you in Portal?" Fire red eyes opened and studied Dahr, and Lorthas made a tisking sound while wagging his finger in Dahr's face. "You should have told me you were coming! I could have arranged for us to meet in person."

Lorthas wore robes of pristine white, a near match for the locks of hair hanging in curls past his shoulders. His narrow, colorless lips drew down in a frown when he saw the look on Dahr's face, and he rolled his eyes. "Come now, brother! By now, you surely know I mean you no harm. Even if I did, I can't hurt you in this place." With a warm smile, Lorthas closed the distance between them, his graceful movements barely disturbing the thick grass, and put a friendly hand on Dahr's shoulder.

Dahr stepped back as if touched by a hot poker, and he raised himself until he towered head and shoulders above Lorthas. Somehow, he still felt as if he were the one being looked down upon. "Why have you brought me here, Darklord?"

"Always so formal," Lorthas chuckled. "I thought we were past calling each other 'Darklord' and 'Tribesman'." He gestured dramatically, and when Dahr looked, he saw two chairs facing each other on opposite sides of a small table. A bottle of red wine and two glasses sat atop the table. "We are here because I thought, with the beauty of summer upon us, you might prefer this setting to our usual one."

"Why are we meeting at all?" Dahr snarled. "I have nothing to say to you."

Lorthas looked affronted, and he sat heavily in his chair, his eyes wide with hurt. He raised his glass and took a long draught. "After all we've shared, after all we've discussed, you can so easily turn your back on me?"

"We share nothing. Nothing!"

"Such hostility! Such bestial rage! Today I see the wild Tribesman in you. You've never before allowed the monster to cloud your reason. I wonder what happened to poison you to me so."

The fire in Dahr's eyes matched the Darklord's cold glare. "I know what you did to Jeran."

For an instant, Lorthas' smile slipped. "Then he survived," Lorthas said, running the edge of the wineglass along the line of his jaw. "For a time, I worried that he had not. None of my agents have had word of him since he left Dranakohr."

Anger filled Dahr to the core of his being, and he stormed toward the Darklord without the slightest hint of fear. "You tortured him. You murdered his wife. His child!"

"I did no such thing," Lorthas replied, and something in the Darklord's voice froze Dahr in place. He could have sworn he had heard sorrow. Sorrow and regret. Lorthas leaned forward, and if Dahr's form looming over him disturbed him, he showed no sign of it. "I tell you truly, Dahr, I all but begged Tylor to be just in Jeran's treatment, and in the treatment of all my prisoners. What happened, especially to that poor Tribeswoman, was a tragedy. Were it in my power, I'd make Tylor pay for his transgressions."

With a weary sigh, Lorthas leaned back and spread his arms wide. "But my hands are tied. I am trapped behind the Boundary. I have no direct control over Tylor or his actions. Salos harbors some influence and obeys most of my commands, but the Scorpion has a... bond, of sorts, with his brother. I receive little aid from him where Tylor is concerned."

Lorthas gestured toward the other chair, but Dahr refused to sit. "You made Jeran a slave."

"A slave? No. Jeran was my prisoner, not a slave. All those in Dranakohr are prisoners of a war your side of the Boundary thought ended long ago, a war for control of Madryn. A war to protect those unfortunate souls different from the masses. Again I tell you truly: I treat those under my control no worse than I must, and once they demonstrate that they aren't a threat, they're free to choose their own path."

"A slave remains a slave no matter how well his master treats him."

Lorthas' lips quirked up in a wry smile. "Is that so?" The Darklord's eyes twinkled with amusement. "What about the Corsan soldiers captured by your prince? I hear he treats his slaves—I'm sorry, his prisoners—well, but they're worked hard and certainly can't come and go at will. Does that make them slaves like any other, or do you give special dispensation to your friends?"

Dahr refused to believe that Martyn would take slaves, but he knew the Darklord could not lie. Not here, in the Twilight World, where hearing the truth was as simple as asking for it. He tried to respond, but his mouth felt dry and wooden. "Martyn would never take slaves. If he holds prisoners, it's because—"

"—they're a threat to his cause," Lorthas finished, a satisfied look on his face. "Naturally. So are the prisoners I hold. The only difference is which side of the Boundary I stand on."

"Martyn would never mistreat a prisoner."

"Nor would I, but can you speak so certainly of all your prince's subordinates? Can you assure me that every Guardsman who's lost family or friends in this war would act as nobly as your prince?" Lorthas sipped his wine, pretending to hide a smile. "I tell you truly, I have not harmed a single one of my prisoners."

Anger surged through Dahr again, this time accompanied by confusion. He wanted to believe that Martyn was right to keep prisoners and Lorthas not, that the Alrendrian forces fought for the greater good and the Darklord's troops for ill, but he could not. The more he thought about it, the more he discussed it with Jeran, Fang or Shyrock, or even with Lorthas, the more it seemed that the only difference between the two sides of this war was what they perceived as right and what they believed was best. Each side had heroes, each side villains, and when all was said and done, war made everyone do things they would otherwise never have done. Desperately, Dahr said, "When the war is over, Martyn will free those he captures."

"When the war is over," Lorthas replied without missing a beat, "so will I."

"Enough!" Dahr roared, shoving his chair and sending it tumbling end over end through the grass. "I tire of this game!"

"The truth can hurt, brother," Lorthas said sympathetically, "and it doesn't always bring what we want to hear. But answer me this: if the Alrendrian armies fight for the equality of all man, and if those on your side of this conflict feel as you do in regard to slavery, then why has your king allied himself with the Rachannen? And why do my forces oppose that nation and their vile practices?"

"It's not true," Dahr said. He felt something inside him snap. His vision clouded over, and his heart raced. "King Mathis would never ally himself with those monsters."

Lorthas sipped his wine again. "My source is generally quite reliable."

"King Mathis would never ally with the Rachannen!" Dahr repeated, though it was more for his own benefit than Lorthas'.

"Hmmm." The Darklord nodded thoughtfully. "Well, you know him better than I. But I wonder… If Rachannon is not allied with Alrendria, why did they send an army to join your prince? This I *know* to be true; that army is hurrying toward the Corsan border as we speak. Meanwhile, my forces, or rather, those once under Tylor's command, are most certainly *not* allied with the Rachannen. In fact, Ryan Durange, the Tachan Emperor, even now leads a campaign against them."

"I don't believe you!" Dahr's hand clenched into fists, and his jaw clamped closed so tightly it hurt.

"You know I can't lie to you, Dahr. Not here." Lorthas' expression was sympathetic, and Dahr saw a reflection of his own pain in the Darklord's eyes. "The leader of the Rachannen force is a prominent nobleman and a slave owner of high regard. Why, I've heard he's even taken Garun'ah slaves from time to time. Poor Tribesmen…"

Lorthas trailed off, frowning thoughtfully, and when he looked at Dahr again, he shook his head sadly. "Have you ever seen a Tribesman enslaved, Dahr? Other than yourself, that is. One raised to the ways of the Blood? They don't survive long with their souls in the hands of another."

With a scream, Dahr brought his fist down upon the table, shattering it to pieces and sending splinters and shards of glass soaring through the air. The wine bottle upended, and its contents spilled to the ground, staining the grass the color of fresh blood. His hand bled from a thousand tiny cuts, but Dahr felt none of them. He stood there, his chest heaving with each hissing breath.

"Temper, little brother," Lorthas said, his voice dripping with condescension. "Do try to remember that you're a civilized being and not a wild animal. I know how difficult it must be with Garun's hot blood pumping in your veins, but I have such high hopes for you. I'd hate to see you turn into a mindless beast."

Even without a weapon Dahr felt unstoppable, and he lunged toward the Darklord, intent on the kill. Suddenly, he found himself hovering twenty hands above the ground. Lorthas stood below him, staring at him sadly. The shattered table was gone, and an identical one had replaced it. "I told you that I can't harm you here," Lorthas said with an edge to his voice, "but *you* most certainly cannot harm *me*. Don't presume upon our friendship too much, little brother. I may begin to think you don't like me."

Fear replaced anger, and Dahr thrashed, his arms and legs swinging wildly. "Let me go!" he demanded.

"As you wish," Lorthas said, and Dahr fell. His stomach leapt toward his throat as the ground drew closer. Arms flailing helplessly, he screamed and landed with a bone-numbing jar on the floor of his room in Portal Keep. His head smacked painfully against the stone.

Sitting up, one hand pressed against his pounding head, Dahr looked around. Bright morning sun shone through the chamber's window. His bed was a mess, the covers torn and twisted, and the small table beside his bed was a mass of broken splinters. Fighting dizziness, he stood and went to the window. The voices had returned, and their presence brought a tight smile to his face. One voice in particular drew his attention, and Dahr struggled to separate Shyrock's presence from the others.

The golden eagle landed on the sill with a graceful flapping of wings. Cocking his head to the side, he stared at Dahr with piercing, dark eyes. "No," Dahr laughed, "I'm fine. It's good to have you back. What did you learn?" Shyrock fluffed his wings, but Dahr could not read the bird's feelings. The animals could mask their thoughts from him when they wished to; it was a trick Dahr wished he could master.

Eventually Shyrock relented and told Dahr what he had seen. "No," Dahr whispered. "It can't be true!" Shyrock flapped his wings angrily, and Dahr looked chagrined. "That's not what I meant." With a screech, the golden eagle took to wing. He circled the tower twice before flying off to hunt.

For a time, Dahr stood at the sill and pondered Shyrock's message. Below, Portal Keep opened onto a broad, barren plateau four hundred hands across with steep sides forming rough triangles with the Boundary. The depressions were strewn with broken rock and scrubby vegetation. The depressions had no entrances to the Portal, but the keep's walls had matching, iron-clad gates on either side to allow access. A narrow stone walkway divided the depressions and connected the keep to the Wall. A dozen guard stations lined the span, but most were unmanned and all in poor condition. A broad archway, giant gates barred shut, allowed entrance to the cliff-like fortification, a length of featureless black rock spanning the distance from one mountain to the next and dwarfing everything around it save the Boundary. The Portal Wall rose more than five hundred hands above the tallest tower in the keep, and its magic-wrought stone was unmarked by assault or time. Tiny, indistinct figures patrolled the top, and more men sat rigidly at their posts, watching the portal to *Ael Shataq*.

Dahr donned fresh clothes and headed for the door, pausing only long enough to grab his sword and fasten the sheath over his shoulder. Walking purposefully, he once again noted the scarcity of servants, the uncommon silence. The feeling of emptiness, of abandonment, was echoed in the city outside. Lord Talbot and his sons had painted a grim picture of the situation in Portal, but Dahr began to wonder if the truth was even worse.

When he exited the keep's rear gate, he was half-surprised to find Aryn in the center of a hastily-drawn circle. Two dozen young men, most of them barely old enough to shave, stood around the circle, and Kristaf faced Aryn in the center. Kristaf attacked ferociously, his movements awkward but determined. Aryn held the boy at bay easily, calling out a continuous stream of suggestions.

"He's better when he's fighting," a voice said beside Dahr, and he spun around startled, his hand reaching reflexively for his sword. Aleesa Talbot stood in the shadow of the keep, her eyes fastened on Aryn. "He's almost his old self." Her frown deepened, and she wiped at her eyes. "What that monster must have done to him! He won't talk about it; the mere mention makes him look like someone dropped the entire Boundary on his shoulders. I—"

Aleesa broke off suddenly. With a sad shake of the head, she turned to Dahr. "Time will heal him if the Magi can't. I must believe that. How did you sleep, Hunter?"

Panic and rage fought for control when Dahr thought of his dream. "Well," he lied. "Your hospitality is appreciated, Lady Talbot."

"Leesa," she said absently, a motherly smile on her lips. "It's rare enough for us to have guests. I must make those I receive feel welcome." She studied Dahr for a long moment, her eyes calculating. "If you're looking for my husband, he's taken Jeran to the Wall. Gideon didn't want to, but Jeran insisted."

"Didn't want to take him? Why not?"

"Because..." Aleesa's eyes flicked toward the Portal. "If you really want to know, you should see if for yourself." Aleesa gave Dahr directions, and he started down the path. The Portal Wall towered over him, and Dahr imagined what it must have been like to build such a thing. Even with the aid of the Magi, it must have been a monumental task. He looked at the rusted gates and crumbling guardposts guarding the approach, and they appeared inadequate in the shadow of the great fortification.

The arched gate into the Wall stood four times Dahr's height. When he reached it, a rough-featured Guardsman of indeterminate age stopped him. The man studied him from behind the iron bars of his helmet. "Lobias told me I might see a Tribesman come this way." Dahr's jaw tightened, but before he could say anything, the man laughed. "Didn't believe him. Seems I was wrong. Lobias said you were to join the commander on the parapet. Take the left stair. If you see Lobias, tell him I owe him a tankard."

His anger receded to a dim throbbing, and Dahr nodded as the Guardsman fumbled with the latch to a smaller door cut through the gate. It opened with a squeal, and Dahr started through. As he passed, the man grabbed his arm. "There an Orog with your party?"

"An Orog and two Magi," Dahr replied, pulling his arm free.

Turning away, the Guardsman muttered. "I guess I owe him a cask."

Dahr hurried into the tunnel, a passage as wide as the gate cutting through the heart of the Wall. Lanterns hung at regular intervals along its sides, casting a dim light into the darkness. About a hundred hands distant, the tunnel ended in solid rock, but the shadows cast by the torches hinted at passages to the left and right.

"There's a mirror of this tunnel on the other side," a Guardsman said from the shadows, "that guards the way into *Ael Shataq*. The tunnel branches in the middle to force an attacker to fight in small groups. Even if the enemy broke through the far side, a handful of Guardsmen could hold them off in here forever." The Guardsman eyed Dahr up and down, and a smile spread across his face. "Bertram always was too eager to take a wager. Lord Talbot told me to expect you. This way."

Dahr followed Lobias to the side of the tunnel, where the Guardsman examined the wall. Dahr waited as patiently as he could, but the close confines wore at his nerves. Just as he was about to say something, Lobias touched the wall, and with a click the rock slid backward, exposing a staircase climbing into darkness.

"After six seasons, ya'd think I'd remember where the latch was," Lobias laughed. He handed a torch to Dahr. "Take the stairs straight to the top. The other doors lead to the barracks. Not too much in them now, so I wouldn't go exploring. A man could lose himself for days if he doesn't know his way."

Dahr eyed the tight passage warily, fighting down the nausea that rolled through him each time he thought of entering the small tunnel. "I'll keep to the stairs," he promised, taking them two at a time, his head ducked low so he would not hit it against the ceiling.

It took some time for Dahr to reach the sun again. Throwing open a simple door, he stepped out onto the parapet and into the fresh air. His heart raced and, his eyes firmly fastened on the open sky, Dahr drew several deep breaths to calm his nerves. When he was ready, he straightened and looked around in awe.

The Boundary surrounded him; rugged, snow-covered peaks glistened white in the sunlight. A stiff breeze blew south from the mountains, and Dahr turned his back to it and looked out over Portal. The city seemed insignificant from atop the Wall, a tiny collection of buildings eclipsed by the grandeur of the countryside. Even the keep, which had been imposing from below, had lost its power to inspire.

The Wall itself was nearly two hundred hands across, flat and smooth, and each side had raised crenellations that reached to Dahr's midriff. A series of stone buildings formed a neat row down the center walkway, and dozens of Guardsmen moved weapons and supplies in and out of them at a frenzied pace. More Guardsmen patrolled the parapet, but by and large the bulk of Talbot's forces stood along the northern wall.

Directly above the gate to *Ael Shataq*, a semicircular battlement protruded outward. Jeran and Lord Talbot stood at the edge, hunched over a piece of parchment and talking in hushed whispers. Dahr approached, ready to call out a greeting, but as he neared them, what he saw rendered him speechless.

The north face of the Wall stood even higher than the south; the drop was over two thousand hands and ended in a boulder-strewn field. Halfway to the ground, the gate from Alrendria opened onto a walled platform. The northern end of the platform formed a narrow ramp that descended at a steep angle, meeting the ground in the center of the field. Impassable mountains pressed in on either side, but to the north they ended abruptly. Cliffs as smooth as glass, as if cut by a knife and polished until perfectly smooth, framed a channel one hundred and fifty hands across.

In the pass camped an army the likes of which Dahr had never imagined. Thousands upon thousands of tents filled the horizon in orderly rows. Men sat horses in tight formation or practiced in rings drawn in the rocky soil. A narrow passage, just wide enough for carts to pass through, remained in the center of the portal, and a steady stream of supply wagons moved back and forth along its length. On the edge of the open hollow, teams of soldiers erected giant towers of wood and fastened them to the ground with thick ropes.

The sheer number of men was overwhelming. Tens of thousands camped at the mouth of the field, and the army disappeared in the distance. A low rumble reached Dahr's ears, a steady hum punctuated by sharper sounds, like thunder but coming from below. "Dear Gods!" Dahr exclaimed.

"I can understand why Lord Talbot wanted to keep this a secret," Jeran said.

"There's never been an army like that in the history of Madryn!" Dahr said. "Can the Portal stand against it?"

"Portal was designed to withstand attacks by forces a thousand times the size of its garrison," Talbot said. His hand swept from east to west "But against this…? If the Darklord's willing to risk this many men, who's to say if we can hold?"

"And those… things?" Dahr asked, pointing to the towers. "What are they?"

Jeran shook his head. "I've not seen their like before," Talbot admitted, looking equally confused. "Jeran suggested they might be siege towers, but they're staking them to the ground. I've a bad feeling that we'll learn what they're for soon enough."

Dahr took a deep breath. "Tylor's marching on Vela. Prince Martyn is leading the city's defense."

Talbot stared at Dahr in disbelief. "How could you possibly know that?"

"I just know," Dahr said. Talbot fixed a probing gaze on him. "I was told."

Jeran's gaze pierced into Dahr's soul. "By the... Mage?"

Dahr shook his head. "Shyrock saw them."

Jeran frowned thoughtfully, but a loud snap echoed from the north, drawing their attention. They turned just in time to see a boulder, just past the top of its arc, smash into the Wall two hundred hands above the ground. The rock shattered upon impact, and the battlement trembled, but as the debris fell away, the magic-wrought wall showed not so much as a blemish.

"Shael preserve us!" Talbot said as the second tower launched a boulder. This one flew higher, hitting more than halfway up the Wall. The ground vibrated again, but again, the Wall stood unphased.

"Well, we know what they're for now," Jeran said. "I need to take a closer look."

Dahr and Lord Talbot followed Jeran to the edge of the wall. Talbot drew a spyglass from his coat and offered it to Jeran. Jeran ignored him; his eyes unfocused and a look of concentration overcame his face. "Keep it. I'll see better with my Gift than with that."

Talbot shrugged and tried to hand the glass to Dahr, but Dahr waved it away. *Shyrock*, he thought, seeking out the bird's thoughts from the cacophony. *I need your eyes.* A moment later, the eagle flew overheard. He circled the battlement once and then winged toward the Darklord's army. With another shrug, Talbot raised the glass to his own eye.

Through Shyrock's eyes, Dahr watched a team of men struggling to reset the siege weapon's swinging arm. A second team hauled another boulder toward the construction and a third crawled around its base, inspecting it. A pile of lumber lay to the side of the three towers, and Dahr commanded Shyrock to fly closer. "They're building a fourth stone-thrower," he announced. Talbot grunted a reply.

"Fascinating," Jeran whispered. He blindly fumbled about for the quill on the stone in front of him. When his hand closed around it, he scrawled notes on the parchment.

A flash of white far to the north drew Dahr's attention. "Jeran!" he called, "Behind those horses. To the north. Is that... Is that Lorthas?"

Jeran's frown deepened, and his brow wrinkled in concentration. "I can't see anything!" he said. "There's a wall, and then... Nothing! It must be the Boundary!"

"In the white?" Talbot asked, squinting through his spyglass. "Dear Gods, I never thought I'd lay eyes on the Darklord. Is that him? How can you be sure?"

Dahr wondered if he were mistaken, if the man he thought he had seen was not the Darklord, and without warning, Shyrock dove to get a better look. "No!" Dahr shouted, panic gripping his chest like a vise. "Don't go any closer!" The eagle ignored him, sending back a single thought: the desire to find the man Dahr sought.

Bleached white robes appeared amidst the sea of armor. "It's him," Dahr said. "It's Lorthas."

"Gods!" Talbot breathed. "I hope none of the men see him."

"Shyrock!" Dahr yelled. "Fly! Go!" The eagle ignored him, swooping in for one final pass. Dahr saw the line of bowmen drawing before Shyrock did. "No!" he screamed, but it was too late. A volley of black-feathered shafts flew toward the golden eagle. "No!" Dahr screamed again, grief flowing through him. *It's my fault! All my fault.*

When the arrows exploded in flame, Dahr gasped and urged Shyrock to fly away. This time the eagle obeyed, but not until Dahr saw Lorthas staring at him. When those flame red eyes touched him, fear like he had never before experienced gripped him, and his mind went numb.

Lorthas smiled and raised a hand in greeting. Severing his connection with Shyrock, Dahr fell to his knees and trembled.

Chapter 30

"It's a *trebuchier*," Jeran said as he unrolled the yellowed parchment. "The Elves use it to hurl disks, but with some modifications I believe it could throw a spear."

Talbot took the sketch and studied it. "I can't say this makes much sense to me, but Charl might be able to make something of it. Kristaf, take this to the smithy. Now, boy!" Kristaf hopped down from his place on the far side of the table, ran to Talbot's side, took the sketch, and hurried from the chamber.

"You saw what the Darklord has set against us," Alic grumbled. "Do you truly believe a few spears will make a difference?"

Jeran shook his head. "You'll need every advantage if—"

"*We'll* need every advantage?" Tourin interrupted. "Are you leaving, Lord Odara?"

"I should already be gone," Jeran admitted. "King Mathis must be warned of this, and Martyn needs our help in Vela."

Alic mumbled under his breath, and Tourin hit his brother in the shoulder to quiet him. "We will hold Portal in your absence, Lord Odara," Tourin said, saluting fist-on-heart.

"Of that I have no doubt," Jeran said as he turned back to face Talbot.

"Where will you go?" Alic demanded, throwing Tourin's restraining hand off. "Norport is over ten days ride if you kill your horses, and reaching Vela, even by river, will take longer. Kaper's half a season away! By the time you warn anyone, Portal will be debris and House Odara will be the Darklord's domain!"

A tense silence filled the chamber. "The Wall will hold," Jeran said. "And if I succeed, help will arrive sooner than you think. I can't—" A fist pounding on the door silenced Jeran.

"Enter!" Talbot called roughly, and a young Guardsman stepped inside. In dull, dust-covered armor, he stared at them with haunted eyes, licking his lips nervously. Talbot waited, but when the soldier did not speak, his patience wore thin. "What is it?" Talbot snapped.

"A man approached the Portal Wall under a flag of truce," the Guardsman said, his voice cracking. "He requested an audience with you, Warden."

Talbot's face grew grim. "He was sent away unharmed?"

"Ahhh, well, Sir," the Guardsman stammered. His cheeks turned bright red, and he refused to meet Lord Talbot's stony gaze. "He was insistent, Lord Talbot, and as he came under a flag of truce, I—" Sensing the mood in the room shift, the Guardsman fell silent, and his shoulders crumpled under the weight of a half dozen angry glares. Aryn and Talbot exchanged exasperated looks. Tourin looked aghast; Alic enraged.

"You fool—!" Alic began, but Talbot cut him off with a gesture.

"It's done, Alic," he said sharply. "Where is this man?"

"He's waiting in the hall," the Guardsman answered hastily. "He's under guard."

"Oh, under guard, is he?" Alic waved his arms dramatically. "Well, we have nothing to worry about then!" Standing, Alic quickly closed the distance between himself and the nervous soldier. "I suppose, since he's under guard, he won't bother to tell Lorthas just how empty the city is, or how weakly defended the Wall?"

The young man trembled. "I... I was just doing what I thought right, Commander!"

"What *you* thought..." Alic slammed the boy against the wall, and the young Guardsman whimpered. "When Portal falls," Alic whispered, "remember who gave the Darklord his key."

"That's enough," Aryn said, and when Alic did not respond, he forcefully separated Alic from the Guardsman. "I said, enough!" Furious, Alic shrugged off Aryn's grip but did not resume his assault. "You are in command of the Wall! If you didn't anticipate this and issue orders to prevent it, the blame is as much yours as his."

"What's done is done," Talbot said, shooting a glance at his son that commanded the matter be dropped. "Best we see what information we can gather from Lorthas' messenger. If we work quickly, we might yet salvage something from this." He motioned for Dahr and Grendor to conceal themselves in the shadows. Jeran and Talbot, flanked by the twins, faced the door. Aryn and the Guardsman took places to either side of the doorway.

Aryn offered the Guardsman a smile. "It's all right, lad. Just bring the fellow in and help me keep an eye on him." The Guardsman nodded before opening the door and stepping into the hall. Aryn grabbed the hilt of his sword and bared several finger-widths of steel. An instant later, the door flew open and a dark-armored man strode inside.

A thick, curling mustache framed a hard mouth, and two dark eyes glared confidently down a broad, flat nose. The man's gaze roamed the room for a moment before fastening on Lord Talbot. He bowed formally. "Lord Gideon Talbot, Warden of Portal, Defender of the Boundary and First Seat of House Odara, I bring you greetings from the Mage Lorthas and his assurance that he means you and yours no harm."

"No harm?" Talbot replied icily. "Then how does the Darklord explain the boulders?"

A tight smile spread across the messenger's lips. "Just a means of getting your attention, my Lord. The Mage Lorthas knows, as do you, that it would take seasons to so much as chip the Portal Wall."

"In that case," Talbot grunted, "send my regards to the Darklord. Tell him I'm glad the army he massed isn't here to threaten my city. Tell him that summer in the Boundary is short and that he should send those men home before the snows come."

"I'm afraid things aren't that simple, Lord Talbot," the messenger chuckled. "The Mage Lorthas chases a fugitive of justice, a man named Tylor Durange. This man has broken a number of laws in my master's domain, and many in yours as well, I believe. We believe Tylor Durange fled *Ael Shataq* and seeks refuge on your side of the Boundary. The Mage Lorthas requests permission for his army to cross the Boundary so that we might bring this criminal to justice."

Alic barked a harsh laugh. "You must think us fools! We would never—"

Jeran silenced Talbot's son with a gesture and fixed the messenger with a piercing glare. "That's a large force for the capture of a single man," he said calmly.

"Tylor Durange has proven himself to be resourceful, and the Mage Lorthas does not take chances." The man's gaze shifted between Talbot and Jeran uncertainly for a moment, then shifted to Jeran. "I have been instructed to suggest that the entire force need not pass. I am happy to send across only what numbers you deem appropriate."

"How kind," Alic murmured. Tourin elbowed him discreetly.

Jeran frowned thoughtfully. "Tell Lorthas that we'll hunt down Tylor Durange on his behalf. When he's found, I will personally deliver the Bull's body to the Darklord." Jeran's tensed on the verge of surrendering to his Gift, and his eyes flared bright blue.

"A kind offer," the messenger replied, "but the Mage Lorthas prefers to have his own agents involved in the capture of the fugitive."

"So long as I live," Jeran said in a cold voice as he slowly stood, "no servant of Lorthas' will cross the Boundary and survive."

The messenger shook his head. "I told Mage Lorthas you would not see reason." He bowed formally to Jeran, and again to Lord Talbot. "I'm afraid you've left us no choice. If you will not let us pass, we will have to force a way through. I—"

Another knock cut off the messenger's threat. "What now?" Talbot growled. He signaled to Aryn, who drew his blade in an instant and leveled it at the messenger. He pulled the man aside and signaled the Guardsman to open the door.

A second Guardsman, younger than the first, bowed nervously. "A man at Midgate insisted on seeing you, Lord Talbot. He was quite insistent, and—"

"Dear Gods!" Alic shouted. "What purpose is there in having a guard if they refuse to guard anything? Did I not order that no one should pass the gates without explicit orders from me or Lord Talbot? If I so much as—"

"Alic." Talbot spoke quietly, but his words carried an authority that silenced the young commander. "I think you should return to your post and oversee the management of the troops. We can handle matters here." Alic's jaw snapped shut with an audible click, but he nodded and moved to leave. "And Alic," Talbot added as his son headed toward the door, "don't take your frustration out on the men."

A tense silence followed. "Yes, my Lord," Alic replied with a formal salute.

Talbot turned back to the Guardsman. "You were saying?"

The young man cleared his throat. "I did not disobey my orders, my Lord. The man was already inside the city. He was quite insistent, and I saw no harm in bringing him here."

Talbot nodded thoughtfully. "Very well. Once we've returned our guest to *Ael Shataq*, I'll attend to this man. Have him wait in the next room." The Guardsman left but was gone only an instant before the door swung open again and a man dressed in robes of midnight black that swallowed his body in shadow entered. Small eyes roamed the room contemptuously, softening only when they passed over Jeran. The ghost of a smile touched his lips when he looked on Jeran, and he inclined his head slightly.

At the stranger's entrance, Talbot jumped to his feet, shouting for the Guardsman to seize the intruder. Jeran stiffened, and his lips drew down in a frown. "ShadowMage," he snarled, and with that one word, hands reached for weapons.

Before anyone could react, Jeran saw bands of grey and silver flare into being around the Mage. A streak of bright red intertwined among the other flows, encircling everyone in the room, and a bolt of pure black stretched toward Jeran as he reached out to his Gift. Something tightened around him, and the pulse of magic slipped from his grasp. He reached out again, but the flows remained elusive, as hard to handle as during his first attempt to seize them.

The ShadowMage smiled smugly. "Salos warned us about you, Odara. You'll forgive me, I trust, but I can't risk you using your Gift against me." He waved an admonishing finger at Lord Talbot. "I did not come here to battle, yet you show such poor hospitality. I… What's this?" The ShadowMage turned to the shadows in one corner of the room. "Come out, come out!"

Dahr stepped into the light and moved slowly across the room. His eyes were wild, his muscles straining against every unwilling step, but not even his strength could match the Mage's power. The others—even the Darklord's messenger—struggled against similar bonds. Jeran remained unbound, but only at the ShadowMage's pleasure. Without access to his Gift, he could be held as easily as any other.

"I bring a message from Tylor Durange, the Bull of Ra Tachan," the ShadowMage said. "He offers a truce, an alliance of sorts. Emperor Durange tires of serving the Darklord, wasting his life away while Lorthas bides his time. He has severed all ties with *Ael Shataq* and even now leads his men toward Vela."

A smile twisted the Mage's lips. "I know what you're thinking, but your suspicions are unfounded. In Vela, Emperor Durange will secure passage home. Once he's safely at sea, he will provide Alrendria with his knowledge of the Darklord's plans. Once restored to his proper place in Ra Tachan, he will use his influence to end his brother's rebellion and bring peace to Madryn. At that time, he will order his men to abandon Dranakohr and hand the keep over to you. In return, all Emperor Durange wants is what has been denied him. His birthright."

His message delivered, the Mage stepped back and waited. Beside the door, mere hands from the ShadowMage, Aryn began to tremble. He shoved Lorthas' messenger aside and, teeth gritted, took a lurching step forward. His blade moved, slowly swinging up. "Tylor Durange has no honor. His promises are worthless. There will be no deal with the Durange. No mercy until the Bull is dead!"

Surprise touched the ShadowMage's face, but not fear. His eyes narrowed and Aryn stopped moving. "You no longer have the authority to make such decisions," the Mage said.

"My uncle may not speak for House Odara, but I do. Alrendria will make no pacts with monsters. If Tylor wishes peace, tell him to disband his army. Only when he no longer threatens Alrendrian soil will we discuss his future."

"Emperor Durange is no fool," the ShadowMage sneered. "Such a move would be suicide. The Bull of Ra Tachan no longer serves the Darklord. If he can't forge an alliance with you, he'll need every sword he can raise to defend himself. You must—Oh, do be still!" With an irritated gesture, the ShadowMage sent Aryn sliding across the floor. He hit the wall with a thud and went limp, though his body remained upright.

"How dare you!" Talbot bellowed. Dahr screamed his rage in concert with Lord Talbot, and he managed two shambling steps before the ShadowMage tightened his grip on them all. Tourin sat stone still, his fear-widened eyes desperately searching his body, as if, by looking hard enough, he could find and break the bonds holding him in place. Jeran noted all of these things absently as he slowed his breathing and cleared his mind, searching for the calm required to break the Mage's hold and seize his Gift.

The ShadowMage's lip curled up in disgust. "Commons," he said to Jeran. The word dripped acidly off his tongue. "Surely you understand by now. They aren't our equals. Not even Tylor, though he makes as useful a tool as any."

"Then why ally yourself with him?" Jeran asked, hoping to buy some time. "If he's no better than any other... common?"

"The Darklord is trapped behind the Boundary," the ShadowMage shrugged, as if that were answer enough. "Who knows how many millennia will pass before it finally collapses and he is free? I won't spend my life in Lorthas' shadow when there's a world ripe for the taking. And Tylor? The Bull has grand designs, but he's a common. How many winters does he have before he dies? Twenty? Forty? What is time to a Mage? When I decide to take power, no spawn of Tylor's will be able to stop me."

A dark look passed over the ShadowMage's face. "Emperor Durange does not want war, Odara. Let him reclaim what is rightfully his, what your family took from him, and the two of you can share Madryn. United, not even Lorthas could stand against you." Jeran did not answer, and the ShadowMage took it as a sign of uncertainty. "You require a token? Proof of my sincerity?" His eyes settled on Lorthas' messenger. "A foolish thing, allowing this man to see how weak you are, but no more foolish than the 'honor' which prevents you from killing him." A bony finger traced a path down the ShadowMage's jaw. "My gift to you, then."

Shafts of blue light swirled around the ShadowMage, and before Jeran could cry out, a bolt of lightning shot from the Mage's hand. The smell of roasted meat filled the room, and the messenger crumpled to the floor. A scorch mark five hands across marred the wall behind where he had stood.

As the man hit the ground, the door swung open and Alwen walked in. "What in the Gods' names is going on in here? You're using enough magic to—" Her eyes fastened on the ShadowMage and she was instantly ablaze with color. A pattern so intricate Jeran could not follow it formed around her; a second, less complicated one began to form around the ShadowMage.

The magic around Jeran weakened when the ShadowMage diverted his attention to Alwen. The flows were still there but less substantial; any disruption would give Jeran the opportunity he needed. Moving slowly, he sought to flank the ShadowMage while Alwen advanced on him. Thin beams of crackling blue energy flashing from her fingers. An invisible wall around the ShadowMage reflected Alwen's attack, and one bolt scorched a chair only fingers away from Lord Talbot's helpless form. Fear gave Talbot the motivation he needed to break the ShadowMage's hold, and he dove to the floor, pulling Tourin with him.

The ShadowMage returned Alwen's attack. Daggers and swords slipped from their places on the wall and hurtled toward old woman, cups flew from the table, and the table itself started sliding toward her. For the most part, Alwen ignored the assault. The few items that came close to hitting her jerked aside at the last instant and settled lightly to the ground. "Is that the best you can do?" she chided. "Why, I know children with better control of their gift. ShadowMage, indeed!"

In response to her jibe, a ball of white-hot flame materialized and arrowed toward her. The flames disappeared just as suddenly, and the old woman nodded. "Better, but not by much." A wicked grin spread across Alwen's face. "Now it's my turn." She stepped forward and vanished. The ShadowMage jumped, and he scanned the room desperately, flinging balls of fire in every direction. Seeking to protect his flank, he retreated toward the shadows.

"Now!" Jeran said, leaping forward. Grendor launched himself from the corner behind the Mage, wrapping his thick arms around the man and pulling him into a vise-like grip. At the Orog's touch, the barrier between Jeran and magic disappeared, and energy rushed into him in a torrent. The ShadowMage screamed a piercing wail that reverberated through the halls. He collapsed in Grendor's arms, crying piteously.

Jeran stopped, confused, as the ShadowMage fell to the floor, weeping bitterly. "Well, now," Alwen said, reappearing at Jeran's side and smoothing her skirts. "I'd forgotten they could do that."

"Do what?" Jeran asked.

"Block a Mage's Gift," Alwen answered. "An Orog's touch blocks the ability to use, or even sense, magic. Not a pleasant experience, I'd imagine, especially drawing as much as that poor fool was."

"What should I do with him, friend Jeran?" Grendor asked. He was holding the ShadowMage, but only weakly. The man showed no signs of resistance.

"Hold on to him," Jeran commanded. Around him, the room was chaos. Tourin and Lord Talbot helped a battered Aryn regain his feet. The door slammed open, and a handful of Guardsmen entered. Finding the chamber half-destroyed but no enemy to fight, a confused murmur spread among the soldiers. Talbot left Aryn with Tourin and went to brief his guards.

Jeran looked from Alwen to the ShadowMage. "Will he recover?"

"It's hard to say," Alwen replied with a brusque shake of her head. "An Orog's touch alone does no harm; it merely hides the Gift. But to have magic torn away in such a manner...? Where's Yassik? That old man may be a fool, but he knows far more of these matters than most. He'll have an answer to your question, or make one up if he doesn't."

"Yassik's gone," Jeran said. "He and Wardel left this morning."

"Left?" Alwen repeated, her eyes narrowing. "For where?"

"A number of places," Jeran answered. "On my orders."

"Hmmph," Alwen grunted. She hobbled to the ShadowMage and prodded him with her cane. "Clear the room," she ordered. "If he tries to seize his Gift again, we don't want anyone hurt."

Talbot ordered the Guardsmen to leave, and Tourin helped Aryn hobble to the door. "I'll escort him to the courtyard," he told Jeran. "If you still plan on leaving."

"Take Aryn to Northgate. Have him wait for us there." Tourin frowned, but dipped his head in acknowledgement and left. Once he was gone, Alwen dropped to her knees and studied the ShadowMage intently. After a while, she rapped on Jeran's leg with her cane. "Seize your Gift," she commanded, "but don't draw on magic unless he tries to."

A white aura flared up around Alwen, and Jeran opened himself to magic, gasping as the sweet rush of energy filled him. "Release him," Alwen said, and Grendor backed a half step off. Dahr moved forward, his eyes locked on the ShadowMage, waiting for the first sign of resistance.

The ShadowMage smiled as soon as Grendor released him, but the expression quickly turned to one of horror. "It's still there! I can sense it, but... But... NO!" The man's eyes rolled up until nothing but white showed, and he slumped to the floor, unconscious.

"We can't let him live," Alwen said.

"We could learn a lot from him," Jeran replied.

"He's a threat, and if you still plan on leaving, there'll be no one in Portal capable of guarding him."

"This man is a prisoner of war," Jeran snapped. "I won't kill him in cold blood."

"He's a ShadowMage," the old woman said sharply. "No greater threat exists, not to Madryn or to the Magi. Think of the devastation he could cause. Are the lives of thousands truly worth less than the murmuring of your conscience? Think of the greater good, boy!"

Jeran warred with himself. Alwen was right, and he knew that leaving the ShadowMage alive would be a foolish risk, but killing because of what a man might do brought him dangerously close to the Darklord's philosophy. "No man is incapable of redemption."

"Unbelievable!" Alwen said, casting her eyes toward the heavens. "This monster nearly kills us all, and all he can do is spout platitudes." Exasperated, she fixed her fiery gaze on Jeran once again. "We can't risk the fate of the Magi on the chances that this... man... will see the error of his ways. If you're too squeamish, boy, I'll do it."

"He's without his Gift." It was Jeran's last gambit, a stall for time while he worked up the courage to do what he knew he must.

"And what if it returns? Do we leave him here to destroy Portal when it does or keep him with us for the next thousand winters, just in case? You were always high-minded, but you were never a fool."

"Where's Yassik's collar? We're close enough—" Before Jeran could finish, a loud snap drew his eyes around. Dahr crouched over the ShadowMage, his hand around the man's throat and a smile on his face. The Mage's neck twisted at an unnatural angle. "What have you done?" Jeran yelled. He started toward Dahr, but surprisingly, Grendor blocked his way.

"The viper behind you, friend Jeran, is more dangerous than the one in front," the Orog said. Though shorter than Jeran by a couple of hands, Grendor had no trouble holding him back. "Dahr did what he had to do." Jeran backed away, and Grendor knelt beside the ShadowMage. "May Shael welcome you to the Afterworld," he murmured, reaching out and slowly closing the Mage's eyes, "and lead you peacefully to the Nothing."

Jeran faced Dahr for a long moment, but Dahr said nothing to defend himself or his actions. He matched Jeran's angry gaze with one of his own, and if his grin faltered, it was only for an instant. "We have to go," Jeran said, turning away.

He led them through the keep, past nervous Guardsmen asking about the ShadowMage and frightened servants trying to keep hidden. They emerged from the castle into bright morning light, and Jeran hurried to the courtyard where he had ordered Talbot to take their gear. Fang circled the legs of their, and Shyrock perched on the pommel of Jardelle's saddle.

The courtyard overflowed with people; nearly half of those still in Portal had come to see Jeran and his companions off. A roar filled the air, but it quieted when Jeran stepped into the light. Lord Talbot and Aleesa approached him, with Alic and Kristaf at their sides. "I wish I could stand at your side in the coming battle, Lord Talbot," Jeran announced in a voice that carried over the assembly. "But this war is greater than Portal, and the defense of Vela calls me south. Once Alrendria is safe, we will deal with the Darklord." He embraced Talbot, and the older man returned the gesture forcefully, slapping Jeran fondly on the back.

"I'll guard Portal until your return, lad."

"With you guarding the Boundary," Jeran replied, a broad smile splitting his face, "I need not hurry back." Jeran turned to Aleesa and bowed low. "I remembered you only vaguely, Lady Talbot, and though my memories were always of your kindly nature, they did not do you justice. I look forward to the day I can share your hospitality again."

Aleesa smiled politely. "Gideon and I look forward to your return."

"Where's Aryn?" Talbot asked. "You didn't send him ahead without saying goodbye, did you?"

"No," Jeran said. "Actually, I was hoping you'd care for my uncle while I... In his condition..."

"In my condition," Aryn answered, pushing through the crowd, "I'm still not dim-witted enough to wait at an empty gate while half the city walks in the opposite direction. You'll take me with you, Jeran, or I'll follow on my own. Not even Gideon knows Portal better than I do. He won't be able to keep me here against my will." Touring followed a half-step behind Aryn, and he offered Jeran an apologetic look.

"Then it's decided," Dahr said impatiently. "Let's hunt some Tachans." A cheer went up at his words, a roar of support that drowned out all other sound. "Where do we ride? To Vela?"

"No." Jeran turned to Alwen. "I need a Gate."

Alwen frowned suspiciously. "To where?"

"To wherever the Magi are hiding."

"Hmmph," she grunted, her frown deepening. "They're hiding for a reason, you know. They may not take it kindly if you just show up."

"I don't have time for games!" Jeran snapped, and Alwen jumped at the anger in his voice. "The Magi have wasted too much time already. Will you open the Gate or not?"

"Do you think it's that simple, then?" she asked. "Just order me to open a Gate and I can take you anywhere you want to go? There are factors to consider, young man, not the least of which are the distances involved and the amount of material that will pass through. The greater either—"

"You'll be transporting the five of us, our horses, and our gear," Jeran said, folding his arms across his chest. "If that's too much, the horses and gear can stay. The destination you know better than I do."

"As I said, there are many factors. Distance and size are only two variables. Without—"

"If I wanted a lecture on Gates, I'd have asked Yassik to do this," Jeran said, cutting Alwen off. "Can you do it or not?"

Alwen glowered as she sized up the party. "I can."

"Then open the Gate," Jeran replied, smiling politely. "We've already wasted too much time."

"Huddle in close," Alwen said, her voice cracking like a whip. "There's no need to make this any more difficult." A thin haze formed around them, emitting a light that quickly washed out Lord Talbot, the courtyard, and all of Portal. Fang barked, and Shyrock fluffed his wings until Dahr assured them that all was well. The horses danced nervously, stomping and turning in tight circles, and no amount of soothing calmed them. Grendor's mount reared, and the Orog's shoulder grazed the edge of Alwen's fog.

"Keep that Orog away from my magic!" Alwen yelled, hissing in a sharp breath. "Or do you want me to Gate us straight to the Nothing?"

Jeran reached for the reins of Grendor's flailing horse, but the animal danced out of reach. "Stop!" Dahr yelled, swinging his massive arm. The blow hit the horse with a thud, stunning it. Gripping the reins tightly, Dahr pulled the horse and Grendor to the center of the circle.

The light vanished in a bright flash, and the party found itself on a rocky, forested hill. Jeran looked down to find himself standing on the edge of a cliff. Waves crashed against the base, churning up the water and sending spray hundreds of hands into the air.

With the magical light gone, the horses quieted and silence descended. Dahr spun in slow circles, his eyes scanning the hills and trees. Aryn sat his saddle warily, one hand on his bow. Grendor lay low on his mount's neck, his skin uncommonly pale. "Where are we?" Dahr asked.

"Atoll Domiar," answered a strange voice. As one, they whirled to face the sound. A bear of a man, as broad as he was tall, stood before them. Thick rolls of fat hung over his belt, and two dull brown eyes stared blankly forward from a rotund face. Smiling, the man wiped the sweat from his bald brow. "Welcome. I've been expecting you, Jeran."

Chapter 31

Weapons were drawn in a flash. Dahr growled, and he tightened his grip on the hilt of his greatsword until his knuckles cracked. Grendor dropped to the ground the instant the man spoke, his staff swinging up into a defensive posture. Aryn circled wide. He raised his bow hesitantly and stared at the stranger. Jeran's hand went to his sword, but he did not draw it. His eyes flicked to Alwen. The old woman hunched over her cane, eyes closed, panting from exhaustion. "Who are you?" Jeran demanded "How did you know we were here?"

"I am Otello an'Entandale, Keeper of this Isle." The stranger bowed with a flourish, an odd motion with his bulk, and odder still that he somehow made it look graceful. His smile grew even broader. "But you may call me Oto. As to how I knew you'd be here... Well, let's call it a quirk of circumstance. I was patrolling this part of the island, and you Gated close enough for me to feel the magic."

"Then how—"

"Do I know who you are?" Oto laughed. "It's not like strangers arrive on Atol Domiar everyday. Though, recently..." He waved his hand dismissively. "In any case, you remind me of your father, and very few wear Alic's features. Besides," he added, offering Jeran an exaggerated wink, "a friend warned me to keep an eye out for you."

Oto laughed again, a warm sound that rolled up from his belly, and he daubed the sweat from his forehead with a kerchief. Convinced the Mage meant no harm, Jeran signaled for everyone to lower their weapons. "Now," Oto said, "let me take a look at your companions." He did not move, his expression remained fixed and his gaze an odd one: never changing, completely blank, yet at the same time deeply probing.

Suddenly, Oto sniffed the air, and a fond smile spread across his face. "Alwen!" he exclaimed, turning to face the old woman. "Have you finally decided to come out of hiding?"

The old woman's lips twisted upward. "Hiding!" she repeated, sniffing indignantly. "Aemon sent me into *hiding*, and when the High—"

"Careful, my dear," Oto said, wagging a cautionary finger. "Some on Atol Domiar are touchy about titles and such, and they take it to heart when people forget who the High Wizard is."

"Whether he acknowledges the title or not," Alwen retorted, "Aemon will always be High Wizard."

"Lelani might disagree," Oto laughed.

"Does that girl still have a burr up her skirt?" Alwen rolled her eyes dramatically. "I swear some people never grow up."

"Lelani is nearly a thousand winters old, Alwen."

"Exactly," Alwen said, hobbling toward the rotund Mage. "A thousand winters and she still needs to be reminded how powerful she is. Pride will be the downfall of the Magi."

"Pride is the downfall of all the Gods' creations, Mage Alwen," Grendor said quietly. "The arrogant cock commands the walk; the wise one stands where the fox can't find him."

Oto whirled around with a speed and dexterity that belied his size. His face contorted with concentration, and he leaned forward, a pudgy finger extended. When he touched Grendor's shoulder, Oto jerked his hand away, but his smile returned broader than ever. "I haven't seen one of you since I was a boy! I had almost forgotten how!" The Mage bowed low. "I am honored to meet you, friend Orog. May you always find peace and happiness on the shores of Atol Domiar."

"Your words lighten my heart, friend Mage," Grendor replied. "The blessing of the Mother be on you."

"And on you," Oto replied, extending his hand. When Grendor took it, the Mage shuddered for an instant, but then shook the Orog's arm fondly. "Well met!" he laughed. "Shael's blessing is indeed upon me, my friend. You have no idea how many wagers I just won."

Next Oto stepped toward Aryn. He ran his hands through the air around Aryn's body. "My friend," he said sadly, "you're different. Suffering has changed you, but there's no mistaking your presence. You still shine like the light of a thousand stars."

"Oto?" Aryn said dully, as if waking from a daze. He trembled, and looked unsteady in his saddle. Oto reached out a hand and when Aryn took it, the Mage helped him step down from his horse. "Oto?" Aryn repeated. "It's been so long. I haven't seen you since… since…"

"Laying them to rest was tough on us all," Oto said sadly. "You survived that challenge, my friend, as you will survive this one."

"Every day the Gods challenge us," Aryn said. The words sounded like a recitation. "Yet it is how we play their games, not whether we win, that concerns them most."

"You remember our lessons!" Oto exclaimed, clapping his hands together. "You were my best student. I—" In the distance, a horn blasted, and Oto's smile slipped. "Not again," the Mage groaned. "Will they never learn?"

Oto's expression grew blank, and Jeran saw a flash of color move away from the Mage's body. After a moment, the Mage said, "We have a little time, but we should not delay long. I should be on shore when they arrive." He turned to face Dahr and smiled. "Now, you I've heard much about, Dahr Odara. Freer of slaves. Tier'sorahn. Maybe even the Garun'ah's long-awaited savior? Let me have a look at you." Stepping in close, Oto ran a hand through the air around Dahr's torso and lightly brushed it against his face. The frown Dahr leveled at the Mage was cold enough to freeze water, but Oto paid it no heed.

"I sense doubt in you," Oto finally said, stepping back. "Doubt and fear, and a pain so deep it cuts to your very soul. But mostly, I sense rage. It bubbles so close to the surface even I can see it. You should be careful, Dahr Odara. Make sure you loose your anger only on those who deserve it."

Dahr bared his teeth, but before he could reply, Oto tapped a finger against Dahr's lips. "Time is short, my friend. You can yell at me about how happy you are later." With calm assurance, Oto took Jeran's arm at the elbow and squeezed it lightly. "I've been waiting to meet you for some time. I knew your parents well, and it has always pained me that circumstances prevented me from knowing you, too. You are welcome to my island, and I hope you find what you're seeking here."

Staring into Oto's eyes, Jeran had a revelation. "You're blind, aren't you?"

"My eyes don't work well," Oto admitted with a laugh, "but I see better than some. I—"

"You used to have better manners," Alwen interrupted. "Do you plan to leave us standing out here all day? And you"—she said, turning toward Jeran—"I thought I risked my life Gating us here for something a little grander than a chat in the forest."

"You'll never change, Alwen," Oto chuckled. "Come," he said, separating himself from Jeran and waving them forward. "Alwen is right. I've been an ungracious host to all my guests. We can discuss my infirmity later. Right now, we should be going. The men below will be expecting me."

Oto descended the narrow, twisting path at a fast pace, nimbly dodging the sharp rocks and thorny shrubs that tripped and tore at the others as they followed. Before long, Jeran panted with exertion, and he noticed that his companions fared no better, but Oto walked along gaily, his breathing no more labored than when he had addressed them on the hilltop, and he laughed and joked as he pointed out the interesting sights they passed.

Eventually, the sound of crashing surf reached Jeran's ears. To the north, a broad, flat-topped peak broke through the canopy of trees, dwarfing everything around it. "The Hall is up there," Oto told them, pointing to the distant summit and slowing so the others could catch their breath. "The island narrows in the center. When the tides are at their highest, the waves can cut Atol Domiar in two. Once, I was—" The horn blasted again, and Oto cut off suddenly. "Forgive me. Here I go, rambling on, when there are important matters to deal with. If you'll indulge me, we must hurry. The battles always fare worse for our men when I'm not present."

Dahr's eyes brightened at the mention of battle. "Battles?" Jeran repeated. "I thought Atol Domiar was abandoned."

"Skirmishes, really," Oto admitted. "The Black Fleet likes to provoke the men. Keeps them nervous, you know. Aemon told the Assembly… I mean, Aemon suggested to Lelani that we should keep the ships from coming near the island, and the High Wizard agreed, but the Assembly remains undecided. Until the Assembly makes a formal proclamation or the Black Fleet assaults us directly, very few Magi are willing to help repel them."

"Fools," Alwen glowered. "Can't they see what their endless debating is doing to Madryn?"

"They see only the past clearly," Oto replied, "and blind themselves to everything else."

"I do not understand, friend Mage," Grendor said, pulling his horse forward. "Why will the Magi not defend their home?"

"Oh, no!" Oto said, waving his arms dramatically. "The Magi aren't under attack. The Assembly's not even convinced the Darklord knows we're here, as foolish a notion as that is! That's part of the problem, you see, and something of a sore point between myself and the Assembly."

"If the Black Fleet isn't threatening the Magi," Jeran asked, "then who are they threatening?"

"Why, the Alrendrians, of course," Oto answered, his eyebrow raising. "The Alrendrian Fleet has been moored here for days, and the Black Fleet blockading Vela for seasons. Where have you been hiding?"

"Dranakohr," Jeran said sharply. "Tylor was not forthcoming with news."

Oto flushed, and he wiped his forehead vigorously with his kerchief. "Of course. Of course. My apologies." He urged them forward. "It will be easier to show you. We're almost there."

They crested a hill and the trees abruptly ended, giving way to fine white sand. A couple of black-hulled vessels, a ShadowMage standing in the prow of each, sailed parallel to the eastern shore. Off the western beach, an armada of Alrendrian ships drifted in the surf. Crewmen scurried about the decks, tightening lines and readying ships to sail, but nearly as many men lined the rails to watch the black ships.

Atol Domiar separated the fleets, protecting the Alrendrian ships, but the island offered no protection to the hundreds of Guardsmen loading supplies onto the longboats that bobbed just offshore. Rows of small tents lined the crests of the highest dunes, and small clusters of men ran for the safety of the forest as bolts of lightning flashed down upon their camp. Horses threw their lead lines and bolted, knocking men out of the way of their panicked flight. One tore past Jeran at a full gallop, nearly trampling Aryn.

The narrow stretch of land between the two beaches was a wasteland of scorched rock and blackened stumps. Pained screams echoed up the mountainside, drowning out the sound of crashing surf. The carnage disgusted Jeran, but not so much as the knowledge that the Magi were within sight of this and refused to help.

Grendor must have felt the same way, for he rounded on Oto. "How can you let this happen?" Anger contorted the Orog's kind face into a gruesome mask. "You are the Magi! You are all that is good in the world."

"My, my," Oto said. "Do all Orog think like that?" He shook his head ruefully, and his blank stare fastened on Grendor. "Being a Mage doesn't mean you always make the right decisions, my friend. If it did, Lorthas would never have become a Darklord and we'd not be in this mess." Smiling, Oto patted Grendor's shoulder. He shivered every time he touched the Orog, but his smile never slipped. "I used to think the same thing about the Magi, though, until I became a Mage."

"Why aren't the Magi doing anything?" Jeran asked. A jagged streak of lightning sent a group of Guardsmen flying in different directions.

"The Assembly is debating to what extent they wish to enter this war," Oto explained. His expression slackened, and Jeran guessed that he had extended his perceptions over the water. "Lelani angered a lot of Magi when she began dealing with King Mathis without the Assembly's approval. A number of influential Magi question her decision, and that is delaying the debate. Until the Assembly makes a decision, few are willing to openly aid Alrendria, in case the winning faction is one that disapproves."

"Fools," Alwen muttered. "Arrogant fools! When I finish with them, they'll wish they'd made their decision long ago."

"But this is their island," Grendor insisted. "How can they let this happen to their home?"

"The damage has been minor, so far," Oto replied, starting down the hillside. "And as I said before, few believe that the Darklord even knows this is where we're hiding. A foolish notion, since everyone knows Lorthas has agents in the Assembly, but—"

Oto cut off in midsentence and made an abrupt turn, jogging toward the shoreline. "Where are you going?" Jeran yelled, running to catch up. The others started to follow, but Jeran warned them back; exposed on the shore, they made easy targets for the ShadowMagi. "They'll see you down there!"

"I hope so," Oto called back. "Sometimes, my appearance is all that's needed to stop the attack. If it's not..." Oto's smile broadened. "They've gotten used to me attacking alone."

"Why are you helping the Alrendrians?" Jeran asked as he opened himself to his Gift. Magic filled him, and he gasped at the joy of it.

"As Keeper of the island, I am not constrained by the will of the Assembly. They don't like it, but they don't have the authority to stop me from defending our shores." Oto studied Jeran for a moment, then pointed to the farthest of the black ships. "Do whatever you want—fire and wind work well enough for me!— but do it to that one. I'll take the other."

Jeran surrendered to his Gift, and more magic entered him, until his body tingled with power. In the back of his mind, he heard Oto counting, and he desperately tried to think of something to do to stop the enemy ships. The memory of a small village came to him, and the destruction the Tachan soldiers had caused there. Hands clenched into fists, Jeran wove the flows in the pattern he remembered.

Oto shouted, "Now!" and Jeran released his magic. A bolt of lightning slammed into the hull of the farthest ship, shattering the mast and sending a spray of splinters into the air. The vessel listed, and a fount of water erupted where the blast had hit. The second ship burst into flame, a liquid fire that spread when the crew doused it with water. The burning liquid surrounded the ShadowMage, and when it touched the hem of his robes, the Mage began to shriek. If he thought to use his Gift to douse the flames, it did not work, and in a fit of panic, the ShadowMage threw himself over the rail and into the cold water. Without its Mage, the burning ship turned and limped away from Atol Domiar.

The sky above the Alrendrians quieted, and a cheer went up among the men. Jeran heard the cheers, but he heard the pained screams of the wounded even louder, and those shrieks echoed in his ears until he could not stand them. His eyes narrowed, and he allowed magic to consume him.

Bolt after bolt smashed into the sea and the fleeing ships. The hulls shattered and cracked under his assault, but more strikes missed than hit, hissing and crackling as they slammed into the sea. By the time Jeran fell exhausted to his knees, nothing but splinters and bobbing debris remained. Oto's grip on his shoulder was the only thing that kept him from pitching forward into the sand.

"That was impressive," Oto said, "but overdone. You need to learn finesse."

Jeran tried to reply, but he had yet to find his breath. His muscles felt like water. The sand between his fingers felt cool against his skin, and it was all he could do not to shake off Oto's grasp and curl up on the ground.

"A fine display, Mage Oto," a familiar voice said. "I donnae think they'll be comin' back for awhile. Once again, we're in yer debt."

"It wasn't me, Captain," Oto replied, pulling Jeran to his feet.

Jeran managed a weak smile, and he was instantly swept up in a bear hug. Hands like hammers pounded his back. "Kohr be praised! I never thought I'd see ya again, lad. Not after what happened."

"Captain Corrine," Jeran coughed. "It's good to see a friendly face."

"Aye," the captain agreed. He was much as Jeran remembered: hard, sinewy muscle covered by leathery skin; a wrinkled, weather-beaten face; and kind eyes drawn into a permanent squint. More grey graced his head, and his gaze was sadder than it used to be, but that sadness was not reflected in his toothy grin. "Friendly faces are rare these days. Now let me get a look at ya." The captain looked Jeran up and down, and nodded. "Not too bad, considerin'."

A sly smile spread across Corrine's face. "Where is he? I know ya two wouldna be far apart. Dahr, ya old rascal," the Captain yelled, cupping a hand around his mouth. "Get yerself down here, lad!"

The party broke from the trees with Dahr in the lead. He galloped down the slope and slid to a stop beside the grizzled old sailor. Leaping from his saddle, he gripped the captain's shoulders tightly. "Captain Corrine!" he said, his voice friendly. "What are you doing here?" His eyes jumped to the ships moored off the islands west coast. "Where's the *River Falcon*?"

"Gone, lad," the captain answered, a pang in his voice. "Scuttled by the cursed black-robes, Kohr gut 'em! I was lucky ta escape with me crew." The captain's jaw tightened. "That's why I'm here. Ta avenge me poor ship. King Mathis restored my rank and gave me the *Vengeance*, as fine a vessel as ya'll ever see."

Clapping Dahr's shoulders, Corrine stepped back and eyed the larger man with the same intense gaze he had fixed on Jeran a moment before. "Gods, but yer a big one. Ya look good, lad. Ya look good. But what brings ya—" The captain fell silent, and his narrow eyes opened wide. "Tis a miracle," he murmured. "Tis a blessed miracle."

The captain pushed past Dahr and nearly pulled Aryn off his horse. "Kohr be praised," Corrine said, beaming from ear to ear and hugging Aryn with enough force to make him wince.

"Bryn?" Aryn laughed. "Let go of me, you old seadog!" Aryn stepped away from the captain and pointed to the knot of rank hanging from Corrine's shoulder. "What's this? I thought you wanted out of the Guard."

"I did," Corrine agreed, "till those black-robes sank me ship. When I asked the King ta restore my rank, he gave me this command. Told me no one knew the waters around Vela better'n I." Corrine's gaze slipped past Aryn, and the creases on his forehead deepened. "You Odaras move in odd company," he said, eyeing Grendor. Jeran introduced the Orog to the captain, and Corrine seemed awestruck, but the happy reunion was short lived.

"Why's your fleet moored off the coast of this island?" Jeran asked.

"The Black Fleet's surrounded Vela, an' we cannae reach the harbor without passing through 'em. My men could take 'em, except for the black-robes. Near on fifty Magi out there ta my reckonin'." He winked at Jeran. "Two less today, though," he laughed, but his mood quickly grew somber. "We need to do somethin', though, what with that army bearin' down on Vela."

"The Bull?" Jeran asked, though he already knew the answer.

"Aye, lad. Thousands of men marchin' down from the north with the Bull at the helm. Vela's a ripe target, all but empty. The Guard was sent south ta fight the Corsans. I've ferried up as many men as we can hold, but if we cannae pass the blockade, little good it'll do the prince."

Jeran frowned. "I need to address the Assembly."

"I'll inform them of your arrival," Oto replied. "With luck, they'll welcome you tomorrow. In the meantime—"

"Now!" Jeran said, cutting Oto off. "Prince Martyn is in danger, and I mean to have this fleet to Vela before that army arrives."

"There are rules here, Jeran," Oto frowned, "and the Assembly does not take well to having them violated. Lelani, in particular, won't—"

"That chit could stand to be dropped a rung or two," Alwen snapped. "Stop trying to keep everyone happy, Oto. For a change, the boy's talking sense. Do as he says."

"You don't have to live with them, Alwen," Oto sighed. "Sometimes diplomacy is more effective than assault."

"Sometimes," Alwen agreed. "But not today. Take the boy to the Assembly."

"Very well," Oto sighed. "This way,"

"Ready the fleet," Jeran told Captain Corrine before following Oto toward the northern slope of the island. "We'll sail as soon as I address the Assembly."

"He's a good boy," Aryn said, his voice quivering. Everyone turned at the sound. Aryn's expression had slackened, and his eyes glistened with tears. "Jeran was a good boy, too. I miss him. Why did you take him from me, Tylor?" He shrieked the last, sinking to the ground, and Jeran looked at him sadly.

"Go on, lad," Captain Corrine said, waving Jeran away. "I'll take care of 'im." Corrine hauled Aryn to his feet and wrapped an arm around his shoulders for support. As he led Aryn toward the shore, he started yelling out a string of orders. "Ilim, get the horses to the *Vengeance*! Bril! Gather the men an' start ferrying supplies ta the fleet! Come along, lads, move yer mangy hides! We sail at nightfall! Lord Odara's takin' us ta Vela!" A cheer went up among the men, and before Oto led them into the forested tracks on the island's northern mountain, the entire beach was alive with activity.

The northern slope of Atol Domiar looked much like the southern: thickly-forested lands broken by jagged rock. Animals leapt and swung through the trees, and Jeran saw Dahr watching them from time to time, an odd expression on his face. No one spoke. Knowing that Tylor's army was days away from Vela weighed heavily on their minds.

Once the sounds of the men below faded, Jeran was able to lose himself in thought. His heart pounded in his chest, only in part due to his earlier display and their hasty ascent. In the heat of battle, with the magic pulsing through him, he had not been able to stop himself; his Gift had run unchecked. The loss of control terrified him. *This time, only the enemy suffered, but what if my magic ran wild on my own troops? Or on my friends?* With every step, Jeran's mood darkened.

After a while they passed a cabin, a modest home of stout logs with a thatch roof. After the first, others appeared, sporadically at first and then in small groups. Few were more than single-room structures, and only a handful could be considered proper houses. Many were in various states of disrepair. "The Magi live in those?" Dahr asked, eyeing the huts distastefully.

"A few," Oto nodded. "The hermits and grumpier Magi." He cast a sidelong glace at Alwen. "But most have been empty for winters. The majority of the Assembly lives close to the Hall." He dismissed Dahr's incredulity with a wave. "Many Magi have grown accustomed to living alone, my friend, and all of us have learned the value of living simply. In the past, those who called too much attention to their Gift paid the price for it."

The nearer they approached the peak, the better kept the buildings became. By the time the forest gave way to fields, many of the buildings were fashioned of seamless stone and roofed with tiles, yet even those structures were unimpressive, nothing like the grand palaces of Shandar or the castles in the great cities of Madryn. A simple stone obelisk stood in the center of a bubbling fountain. Jeran felt the tingle of a Reading, and he opened his mind to it.

Hundreds of terrified men and women dying from hunger and terrified of the rising water suddenly filled the field. One man, his eyes alight with madness, turned on his neighbor, mauling him with a sharpened cudgel. Another man drive a belt knife and stabbed at the first, and soon the whole field had erupted in violence.

Dahr's hand on his shoulder pulled Jeran out of the Reading. He shivered and tried to banish what he had seen to the recesses of his mind, where the tingle of the Reading still called to him. Across the field, a column of jagged rock jutted up from the ground. Thousands of hands at the base and twice as high as it was broad, the stone stretched toward the heavens. A giant door, oaken beams the size of trees and held together by banded iron, was fastened to the rock. "Like Shandar," Jeran whispered, and Dahr nodded.

"We Magi are sentimental, for the most part," Oto admitted. "When the decision was made to abandon Shandar, the Assembly recreated the Hall here."

"I still don't know what made the Assembly choose this place," Alwen muttered. "That most men are too afraid to venture here isn't reason enough." The old woman shivered, and her eyes glistened when she looked at the obelisk. "I hate this island."

"Many in the Assembly agree with you," Oto said, leading them toward the giant door. "Atol Domiar is a beautiful place, but most Magi cannot see beyond the past. If you go back far enough, there's no place in the world that has not suffered a tragedy. Jeran knows that, don't you?"

With the Reading he had viewed still fresh in his mind, Jeran grimaced. "Sometimes, it seems like there's little joy in the world." He studied Oto for a moment. "Are you a Reader, too?"

"No," Oto replied, "but I can sense the Talent in you. May I offer a suggestion? Delve deeper into your Readings. Pain floats to the surface of all things, but happiness buries itself deep, where it's safe."

Alwen rolled her eyes. "You sound more like Yassik every winter."

"Your husband's a wiser man than you credit him," Oto replied. He had gone a dozen steps before he realized that no one was following him anymore. Jeran, Dahr, and Grendor shared surprised looks; Alwen glared furiously at Oto's back.

"Yassik's your husband?" Jeran sputtered.

"You don't think she'd fight that much with anyone, do you?" Oto chuckled. Then he tapped his lip thoughtfully. "Then again…"

"That's enough out of you," Alwen snapped, but a measure of humor danced behind her gruff stare. "If you're going to take these boys to the Assembly, you'd best get it done with."

"Right you are," Oto replied, raising his hand. The giant doors swung open without making so much as a swishing sound as they drifted by, and Oto led them into a tunnel. As they moved into the darkness, globes on the walls sprung to life, glowing with a pulsing white light.

The tunnels were simple and undecorated, and they walked for some time down passages identical in all but slope. They passed a few people, mostly young men and women Jeran assumed were apprentices by the way they bowed as they passed Oto or Alwen. With each step, Dahr looked more nervous, and his shoulders hunched as if the weight of the entire mountain pressed down on him. His eyes kept flicking involuntarily toward the stone above.

In contrast, Grendor seemed at peace; the farther they went into the tunnels, the more alive he became, until he all but led the party, striding boldly ahead of Oto until he reached an intersection and was forced to wait for the Mage. He attracted a great deal of attention from those he passed, and a chorus of whispers followed the Orog through the halls.

Worries about his upcoming meeting with the Magi plagued Jeran's mind. He knew they would not like what he planned to say, and how they would react had him nervous. If he made a mistake today, it could cost Alrendria the war.

A familiar voice echoed out of a nearby chamber. "You must understand the importance of this. Alrendria needs our help! We have a duty—"

"You know that I want to help, Aemon, but I won't go against the will of the Assembly. Get the majority to agree, and I'll follow wherever you lead." Other muffled voices added their agreement.

Jeran grabbed Dahr by the arm and moved to the door. He pushed it open and stepped inside. The chamber was small and spartan, furnished with a plain table and matching chairs. Four Magi sat with their backs to the door and faced a fifth, a white-bearded man in dark grey robes. "Tanar!" Dahr exclaimed.

Aemon looked up, and when he saw Jeran and Dahr, his mouth fell open. A series of emotions flashed across his face, and he struggled to maintain his composure. "Hello, Grandfather," Jeran said coldly. "I wanted to thank you for arranging my stay in Dranakohr. I had a lovely time."

Chapter 32

The Magi turned and stared at Jeran with a mixture of confusion and disdain. One stood angrily, demanding to know who Jeran thought he was to interrupt a meeting of Magi. Jeran returned the Mage's glare, and the man fell silent. Dahr's mouth worked silently, and his eyes shifted back and forth from Aemon to Jeran. For his part, Aemon maintained his stoic expression by a thin margin. "Jeran," he whispered. Relief flooded his voice, and his eyes glistened. "It's so good..." The look Jeran cast on him made Aemon hesitate. "Is... Is Aryn with you?"

At the mention of his uncle, Jeran's anger faded. "He is, but—"

"I had hoped," Aemon interrupted, his voice cracking. "I only saw what would happen if you *weren't* captured by Tylor, and it was a fate I could not contemplate. But after I allowed you to be taken, I prayed you would return, and that you'd bring Aryn back."

"He... He's not well," Jeran stammered. "The things Tylor did... They affected his mind. I—" Jeran lowered his gaze, unable to continue.

A thin Mage with calm brown eyes and a commanding presence stood. "Where is this man?" he asked in a deep baritone.

Jeran's eyes snapped up suspiciously. "Why?"

"Dorthal is one of our finest Healers," Aemon hastily explained. "He's adept at conditions of the mind."

Jeran frowned consideringly. Finally, he nodded. "He's with the fleet. I'd be grateful for any help."

"Healing is its own reward," Dorthal replied. "I'm honored to serve as I may." He bowed curtly and hurried from the room.

"I'd like some time with my grandson," Aemon announced. For a moment, no one moved, then in a chorus of shifting chairs, the Magi stood, bowed politely to Aemon, and strode diffidently from the room, fixing Jeran with a cold stare as they passed. A waspish, cold-eyed woman of indeterminate age sniffed indignantly, and a stout man all but shouldered Jeran out of the way.

Once the Magi had gone, the door swung shut on its own. "Sit," Aemon said, gesturing toward the chairs. "You'll have to forgive them. They don't like being upstaged." Dahr started forward, but Jeran remained rooted in place. Aemon saw Jeran's pain, and his own eyes reflected it. "Do you hate me so much," he asked, his voice tinged with sadness, "that you won't even sit at the same table?"

"I don't want to hate you," Jeran said, scrutinizing Aemon's face. He saw similarities to his own face that he had never noticed before. "But why didn't you tell me?"

For a long time, Aemon said nothing, and when he did speak his voice carried the weariness of centuries. "Divining is a horrible Talent. It tells only part of a story, and the smaller part by far. But this one thing I've learned about it over the long winters of my life is this: If I remove choice, the Divining means little. I can poke and prod events, I can create the right circumstances, but every time I tell people what they *must* do, I pay the price. All of Madryn pays the price.

"Jule. Shandar. Macinae. Every time I had a Divining so frightening I told people what they *had* to do, the results were nearly as bad as the vision. But when I nudge people toward the path and leave the final choice to them, things usually aren't as bad."

"Not as bad?" Images of his time in the Barrows flitted through Jeran's mind, and the pain of Reanna's death resurfaced. "In that case, I'm glad you didn't tell me."

"I am sorry, Jeran. So very sorry. I did this because I saw no other option. Had I warned you, I know you would have surrendered yourself. It was not a matter of trust or honor; I only wanted to spare you what suffering I could." Aemon fixed his piercing blue eyes on Dahr. "I owe you an apology, too, my friend."

"Me?" Dahr said, startled to find himself drawn into the discussion. "I wasn't captured."

"No, but the blow I dealt you was a harsher one, I think," Aemon replied. "Had Katya not surrendered Jeran to Tylor, that monster would have killed him on sight. She gave herself up to save him, but I know how much her decision hurt you. Worse, I left you in the Darkwood, wallowing in pain, because I didn't know what to say, and it was easier to tell myself that I had more important matters to attend to than trying to make you understand. Katya—"

Dahr's eyes narrowed at the first mention of Katya's name, and as Aemon continued he tensed until his hands trembled on the arms of his chair and he looked half ready to launch himself across the room. "We will not speak of her!" Dahr said sharply, cutting Aemon off. "I should thank you for exposing her. Who knows what secrets I might have told our enemy!"

"Katya never—" Something in Dahr's eyes made Aemon stop. "I can't blame you for hating me," he said. "I hate myself. But what I did, I did for the good of Madryn. I have always put Madryn's needs above my own."

"It's of little consequence now," Jeran said, forcing himself to sit. "What's done is done, and not even the Gods can change the past. Those who suffered from your decision... from our decisions... are safe now. I—" Choking on his tears, Jeran turned away.

"Tylor murdered his bride," Dahr explained. "And his son."

Dahr's words hit Aemon like a hammer, and the old Mage slumped, his shoulders compressing. He caught his head in his hands and pressed his fingers against his temples. "Dear Gods!" he whispered. "A lifetime of mistakes—a Mage's lifetime!—and yet it's always the innocent who pay! Why are they the ones to suffer?"

Surprised to hear a reflection of his own thoughts echoed in Aemon's words, Jeran straightened. "Don't blame yourself. Not for their fate. You had no control over it."

"Lorthas. Jule. Shandar. Illendre." With each word, Aemon's frown grew deeper. "Now my own greatson! This time, the Gods demanded too much!"

"The Gods are not to blame for Reanna's death," Jeran snapped. "Tylor and I share that responsibility."

"If not for me—"

"NO!" Jeran yelled, and Aemon fell silent. He fixed Jeran with a probing gaze, and Dahr studied Jeran as diligently as Aemon did. Seeing the anger smoldering in Jeran's eyes, a mixture of anticipation and smug satisfaction contorted Dahr's features. "By your own admission," Jeran continued, "you didn't know what would happen once I entered Dranakohr. If you believe you did what was necessary, then mourn for the dead, but don't cheapen their loss by regretting your decision."

Another long silence filled the chamber. "Did it work, at least?" Aemon asked, the strength gone from his voice. "Did you learn in a four-season what takes most Magi a decade?"

In answer, Jeran opened himself to magic, filling himself with energy, drawing as much as he could hold. He watched as Aemon's expression changed from melancholy to awe. "By the Gods!" The hint of a smile twisted the corners of Aemon's lips. "Even after seeing you at *Cha'khun*, I never expected this!"

"The Boundary was a harsh mistress," Jeran said, "but Yassik's a good teacher. With him guiding me, I learned quickly."

"Yassik… is alive?" Aemon's smile grew. "After all these winters, I never thought to see him again! Is he with you?"

"He's attending to a few matters on my behalf," Jeran answered. "He should return soon." Mentioning the old Mage lightened the tension, and Jeran and Dahr soon found themselves answering a string of questions.

"One last thing," Aemon added when Jeran waved his questions away. "When did you figure out who I was? Dahr certainly had no idea!"

"I still don't believe it!" Dahr admitted. "A bumbling old man like you, the High Wizard Aemon?" With Aemon, as with Captain Corrine earlier, Dahr seemed a different person, more like the man he had been before Dranakohr. Jeran prayed the change would prove permanent, but he feared that once they left the confines of this hall, reality would return, bringing with it the anger Dahr cherished.

"I should have figured it out long ago," Jeran said. "You didn't go to great lengths to hide the fact. But it was your name that gave it away. When you first met Dahr, you told him you doubted anyone alive still knew what Tanar meant. It *means* grandfather."

"But how did you learn that?" Aemon laughed. "Did Yassik tell you?"

Jeran grinned. "*Miena larhnet ubal ost* Dranakohr, *Tanar.*"

Aemon's smile slipped. "Where… How… Did Yassik teach you that?"

As if on cue, the chamber door swung open and Grendor stepped inside. "Oto said I could not enter, friend Jeran," the Orog said with a smile, "but you have been in here so long. Have you changed your mind about speaking to the Assembly? Why did—"

Grendor's slitted eyes opened wide when they fell on Aemon, and he sank to his knees. Aemon's expression matched the Orog's. Hands shaking, the old man stood, then sank back into his chair again. His mouth worked silently. "Great One," Grendor stammered. "I… I am honored to be in your presence."

"An Orog?" Aemon whispered. "An Orog! Thank the Gods!" He leapt from the table and ran to Grendor, pulling him to his feet and gripping him in a tight embrace as Jeran introduced the two. Grendor's skin flushed dark grey, and he trembled nervously in Aemon's arms. "I never thought to see another of your Race again!" Aemon laughed, stepping back to get another look, as if he did not trust his eyes. "Are there more of you, lad?"

"Thousands, Great One," Grendor answered. "In Dranakohr and elsewhere. Our suffering has been great, but with Jeran's help we are preparing to resume our fight against the Dark One."

"Aemon! You can call me Aemon!" Aemon stumbled backward and half fell into a chair. The exuberance he showed was far different from the pain he had worn a moment ago, and when Aemon saw Jeran's eyes on him, he turned away, unable to meet his grandson's gaze.

"It's alright," Jeran told him. "The Emperor told me you blamed yourself for the Orog's fate."

"Did he? That old fool never could keep a secret." Aemon laughed again, but it lacked conviction. "Do you… Will you ever… I know it will be hard to forgive what I did, but…"

Silence consumed the chamber. "In time," Jeran answered, but the edge to his voice drained the joy from the moment. "When the pain is not as fresh."

"I hate to interrupt," Oto said, his round frame filling the doorway, "but if Jeran intends to address the Assembly, he had best be about it. You know how they get after midday."

"I should have known you didn't come here to say hello," Aemon said, smoothing his robes as he stood. "Come along. Let me introduce you. It'll give your words a little more weight with the Assembly."

They hurried through the spartan halls, this time with Aemon and Jeran in front and the others walking behind them. Alwen was gone, and when Jeran asked about her disappearance, Oto laughed. "You try to keep her where she doesn't want to be."

A murmur of excitement preceded them, and the sound of running feet echoed in the distance as apprentices and those too young for the Assembly Hall hurried to position themselves ahead of Aemon's procession. Aemon smiled and waved as he passed, all the while whispering to Jeran things that might help him in his speech to the Assembly. The apprentices returned Aemon's kindly waves with respectful ones, but for the most part, their eyes remained fastened on Dahr and Grendor.

As they passed, the crowd closed in behind them, following them to a black door nearly twenty hands across and twice as high. The older apprentices kept their distance, but the younger ones pressed in, vying for a better view of the strange visitors. Oto waved them back before extending a hand toward the door, which swung open silently, revealing a chamber unlike any Jeran had seen. He gaped at what he saw.

They stood at the end of a narrow platform that spanned one side of the chamber. To their right, narrow steps descended a dozen hands to the floor of a semicircular amphitheater several thousand hands across and many times as high. Rows of stone benches molded from the rock lined the floor. The floor itself sloped upward toward the back, giving each seat an unobstructed view of the platform.

Staircases wound up the sides of the Hall, opening onto balconies. The rails of the stairways and balconies were intricately carved, and the stone sparkled with iridescent color when it caught the light from any of a thousand magic-wrought globes hovering throughout the chamber. More staircases climbed from the first level of balconies to a second, and from those to a third, until at their highest, the balconies appeared as nothing more than rocky outcroppings, blemishes in the featureless stone.

The ceiling was open to the sky, though no breeze or sound entered. Large white clouds drifted across the opening, and several hawks wheeled in lazy circles above the Hall. It was a disconcerting sight, so captivating to the senses that it took a moment before Jeran even noticed the Magi. Thousands, from withered leathery-skinned men and women whose frail bodies could barely support their weight to bright-eyed youths full of their own power and importance, sat in clusters throughout the Hall. The groups had no pattern or placement, but each seemed a distinct unit, isolated from the others in more than just position. Some Magi glared angrily at the neighboring groups; others pretended to be the only ones present. Though more Magi than Jeran ever imagined were in attendance, the chamber was only a fraction full.

A lone figure, a thin woman with sharp features and elaborately-coiffed auburn hair, stood upon the stage. Her voice carried across the chamber so that even those in the farthest reaches of the Hall heard her without difficulty. Jeran knew she used magic, but he could not see it; as nervous as he was, he did not dare reach for his Gift. "In this time of crisis," she said in a calm and stately voice, "it falls upon the Assembly to do what is right, not just for the Magi, but for all of Madryn. What you accuse me of—"

A hawk-nosed Mage sitting in a large group not far from the stage interrupted. "What we accuse you of, Lelani, is making decisions outside your authority as High Wizard. The assistance you promised King Mathis is not binding without the support of the Assembly. Since you neglected to gain our approval prior to making your agreement, I see no reason to honor it until a full majority is reached."

Lelani turned to face her opponent. "In times of war, it is the duty of the High Wizard to determine where and how the Magi will fight. I was fully within my authority when—"

"The Magi aren't in a state of war," the hawk-eyed man interrupted again. "This is just another example of the liberties you take with your position." A chorus of voices rose throughout the Hall, some agreeing with the Mage, others coming to the High Wizard's defense.

Lelani raised her arms for silence, and when the din finally died, she said, "Those ships threaten our home, Valkov. This is our last sanctuary in Madryn. Our only refuge!"

"Please!" Valkov waved a dismissive hand. "Those ships and the half-trained children on them have threatened only the Alrendrians. If you had kept a tighter rein on Otello, Lorthas wouldn't know that a single Mage lived on Atol Domiar." The men and women around Valkov shouted their agreement. Other Magi, most in small groups seated in the rear of the Hall, shouted for silence or demanded that Valkov let the High Wizard speak. A few bold voices yelled that only a fool would believe Lorthas did not know the whereabouts of the Magi.

"It's the Keeper's right to defend the island," Lelani announced, and a number of Magi shouted agreement. "I don't have the authority to countermand Oto on matters of security."

"From arrogant tyrant to humble servant," Valkov said, chuckling. "You always were melodramatic, Lelani, and times such as these call for a level head. Perhaps you should consider stepping down... for the good of the Magi."

"You overstep yourself, Valkov!" Lelani said, her voice rising in volume. "I have served the Assembly well, and—"

"—led us from our homes to this quaint little island, where we hide from the commons like frightened children."

Lelani's face turned bright red. "How dare you!" she yelled, but the rest of what she said was drowned out by a wave of angry shouting.

"Valkov. Let the High Wizard speak!"

"You led the Alrendrians here, Lelani! Where are we to go now?"

"The High Wizard is the voice of the Magi! Where she leads, we go!"

"Straight to the Nothing, that's where!"

More and more voices added themselves to the din, until nothing could be heard but a thunderous roar. Behind Jeran, the young apprentices shrank back, frightened by the display of raw emotion from their teachers.

Two loud crashes suddenly reverberated through the Hall, and silence instantly ensued, though the mouths of more than a few Magi continued to work silently. Aemon held a black staff capped with a star-shaped amulet in his hand. Once certain that all eyes were on him, he stepped into the room. Oto walked at his right, the glare from his sightless eyes every bit as formidable as the angry expression Aemon wore. Alwen walked on Aemon's left, and Jeran did a double-take when he saw her. The old woman had discarded the faded hides; she stood before the Hall in a gown of shimmering blue. Her unkempt hair had been groomed, and it hung to her waist in flowing waves. She cast a gaze on the Assembly cold enough to make Aemon's look pleasant, and her lips drew down in a dark scowl.

"This behavior is an embarrassment," Aemon said, walking forward. "Especially with guests in attendance." As Aemon had instructed, Jeran and the others entered the hall one by one. Jeran's arrival drew little comment, but Dahr's appearance caused a stir, and when Grendor entered, a wave of excited chatter spread through the Hall. Aemon waited until they joined him at the center of the stage. Lelani looked annoyed at having to share her space, but one withering look from Aemon made her step aside. "Before you stands my grandson, Jeran Odara, son of Alic Odara and my beloved Illendre. Jeran was the Darklord's prisoner for several seasons. He wishes to address the Magi."

The massive doors started to swing shut, but they just as abruptly stopped. "Now, now, Lelani," Aemon admonished, "this is not an everyday matter, and Jeran wishes to address the Magi, not the Assembly. I think the students should be allowed to attend, don't you?"

A dissenting murmur rose, and Aemon turned his attention on the Assembly. "Do we now hide the truth from our apprentices?" he asked, his disappointment evident. "Do we now tell them only what we want them to know, molding their vision to match our own? In my day, we gave apprentices the facts and allowed them to reach their own opinions. Does the Assembly now shun that practice?"

Aemon waited, but no one raised a voice against him. He turned toward the door, and his stern grimace instantly changed to a warm smile. "Come in! Take a seat, children." The students, some barely more than toddlers, others several winters older than Jeran, entered the Hall. They hurried down the stairs and huddled in a tight cluster in the first few rows.

"He is no Mage!" a voice shouted from the back of the Hall. "Why should he be allowed to address the Assembly?"

Alwen sniffed, but Aemon addressed the question. "Are we Magi so much better than the rest of the Gods' creations that only our opinions are of consequence? Is our knowledge so absolute that the experiences of the untrained matter nothing? Jeran may be no Mage," Aemon's eyes betrayed a growing weariness with his fellow Magi, "but he has the Gift. He has stared into the Darklord's eyes. He defied Lorthas and lived to tell of it. How many of you can boast the same?

"Too few," he said when none dared answer. "Our numbers have dwindled since the MageWar, and far too few remember those dark times. Jeran has earned the right, through blood and suffering, to address this assembly. If he needs an advocate, I offer myself. Do any deny him the right to speak?" This time, the silence was absolute.

"Jeran," Aemon said with a polite nod, "The Hall is yours." He, Alwen, and Oto stepped back and the light around them dimmed, cloaking them in shadow. Jeran moved to the stage's center, and when Dahr and Grendor took positions at his side, he was grateful to them both. High Wizard Lelani held her ground for a moment, but when Aemon cleared his throat, she bowed her head and descended the nearest staircase, taking a seat beside the apprentices in the front of the Hall.

Staring out upon the faces of countless Magi, some of whom had survived thousands of winters, Jeran's confidence waned. Sweat beaded his brow, and his breath came in quick and panicked gasps. In Portal, his goal had seemed so clear, his path obvious, but here, with the eyes of millennia upon him, he could no longer understand why. He stammered but could not find the words he so desperately sought. The low murmur of conversation began to rise throughout the Hall.

"Remember Reanna and your child," Dahr whispered. "Anger will give you strength."

"Think of those who suffer in Dranakohr," Grendor added. "They are counting on you, friend Jeran."

Emboldened, Jeran spoke, hesitantly at first, but as the words began to flow, his confidence grew. "I come from the mines of Dranakohr," he said, and the Hall quieted, "where men and Orog toil under the yoke of slavery, forced to help Lorthas reshape Madryn to his vision. I have watched Salos' ShadowMagi torture and kill with magic, twisting the Gift you cherish and giving proof to the fears of the ungifted. I've seen an army trained by Tylor Durange to rival the Alrendrian Guard. Even now that army marches on Vela, where Prince Martyn, *your* prince, intends to make his stand. Outnumbered and ill-prepared, he stands little chance of victory."

As Jeran spoke, his anger lent his voice strength. His words thundered across the Hall without the aid of magic. "In the north, a handful of brave and loyal men defend the Portal against a host larger than any the world has seen. Corsans attack Alrendria's southern border daily, and in the east, the Tachan army presses deeper into Gilead and Rachannon with every passing. For the first time in centuries, the Drekka raid the Tribal Lands. With my own eyes I watched Lorthas' fleet attack this very island. Only one among you was willing to aid the men on your shores, men who stand no chance against the powers of the Gifted."

The murmuring returned, but Jeran ignored it. "You Magi debate what to do, what's in your best interest. Can there be any debate that Lorthas must be stopped? He's one of you, and you nearly destroyed Madryn to stop him before. Do you debate your oaths to Alrendria and question forsaking your honor for self-preservation? Prince Martyn may wonder that now. You profess to abhor those Magi who stand outside your Assembly, those who use their powers contrary to your dogma, yet you stand idly while Salos trains a force unbound by both rules and morality.

"Magic was a gift from the Gods. With it, the Gifted were to protect Madryn, not watch it wither." It took all of Jeran's will to keep from yelling. His heart pounded, but the pounding was no longer caused by nerves. In his mind, he relived the suffering he had witnessed and wondered how many wrongs could have been righted if the Magi had joined the fight from the beginning. "If you need a topic for debate, I suggest you discuss the hypocrisy of this Assembly!"

The Hall erupted in angry shouts. "Magi aided the Alrendrians in Corsa!" one voice called down from the balconies. Another yelled, "Magi have been counseling King Mathis for winters!"

"A handful of Healers and a few Magi defying the wishes of the Assembly do not count as aid!" Jeran scoffed. He flicked a quick glance over his shoulder and silently thanked Aemon for the information he had provided. "Advising the King to be cautious and hiding here while the world is torn apart does not count as aid!"

More voices rose in anger, but where at first, all had yelled at Jeran, now arguments broke out among the Magi. "We Magi are free to make our own decisions," one woman near the front of the Hall said. "Any who wish to help may do so."

"I've seen how this Assembly treats those who wish to do more. They are chastised for doing alone what you all should have done seasons ago! For what help they have given, those Magi should be honored, not ridiculed." Jeran inclined his head toward the High Wizard, and to his surprise, Lelani offered him a slight smile and returned his nod.

"These are the problems of men, not Magi!" cried a voice from the balconies. "We did not start this war. Why is it our duty to fight it?"

"You Magi raised the Boundary," Jeran answered. "You Magi hid the knowledge that it would fall from the people of Alrendria. This is not a new war; *you* started this war centuries ago and put it on hold when you realized you could never win. Defeating Lorthas is your responsibility far more than it's the responsibility of the ungifted."

"Why should we help the commons? For centuries they've hated us. Hunted us! After all we've suffered, we owe them nothing!"

"Suffering!" Jeran's harsh laughter cut through the Hall like a knife. More than a few Magi quieted at the sound. "What do you know of suffering? The tragedies you've survived are terrible, but they're no worse than the tragedies of any other. Do the villagers whose homes have been destroyed in this war not suffer? What of the mothers and wives who send their men off to fight your war; do they not suffer? What of the slaves held by our enemies?

"You Magi live for centuries, yet the *commons*"—Jeran nearly spat the word, and his lips curled distastefully as the use of the term—"suffer ten times more in their short lives, and without the Gift to help them rebuild what's lost! They are willing to fight. Why aren't you?"

The hawk-nosed man in the front of the Assembly, Valkov, stood to speak, and the Hall fell silent. "I know your words are heartfelt, young man, and all present can see that your intentions are honorable. But in the end, it was the commons who turned their backs on us, not the other way around. Their fate is no longer our concern."

The Magi around Valkov cheered, and a number of other groups shouted support. Jeran waited for the cheering to subside. "Not your concern," he said, nodding thoughtfully. "You Magi preach your superiority so well, I sometimes forget you're just as petty as other Humans. You claim enlightenment, you claim a duty to Alrendria, but you can't look beyond the fear of those who don't have centuries to learn tolerance or forgive those who see only the threat your Gift represents. Like most, you need a personal reason to fight." Jeran reached into his coat. "Perhaps this will help."

With a flick of his wrist, Jeran threw the collar at Valkov. The Mage did not flinch; the dark band of metal froze several hands from his face and hovered in the air, spinning slowly. "That amplifies the effects of the Boundary a hundredfold, making it impossible for a Mage to use his Gift. Lorthas puts them on anyone who refuses to swear allegiance to him. I wore one around my throat, as did the Mage Yassik before I freed him.

"Hundreds wear these collars. Many are untrained men and women born with a gift they did not know they had and too honorable to sell their souls to the Darklord. More than a few were Magi, raised and trained by this Assembly. And I say they *were* Magi, because as long as they wear those collars, they are no more gifted than any other common in the mines. Look at that collar—look at it!—and tell me again that this war is none of your concern."

A hundred conversations broke out at once, and the Hall filled with the babble of voices. Jeran hoped knowledge of the collars would prove the turning point for the Magi, the last bit of evidence they needed to devote themselves to the cause. He was sorely disappointed.

"This is grave news," a withered Mage with a permanent stoop to his shoulders said. "The Assembly has much to discuss." More Magi spoke out, demanding that Jeran leave so they could resume their talks. Only a small minority seemed affected by the collar, and most of them could do nothing but stare blankly.

Disgusted, Jeran lost his will to fight. "More discussion?" he asked, and his frustration radiated throughout the Hall. "When Lorthas told me you Magi were afraid of him, I argued. When he told me you were weak, and that you'd never dare oppose him, I argued. When he told me you were arrogant fools, and that your pride would be the destruction of Madryn..." Jeran started toward the door. "Sometimes, I guess even the Darklord is right."

The roar that followed him was deafening, but Jeran kept his back straight and his eyes focused on the door ahead. Without warning, the air solidified around him, holding him in place. Against his will, he was turned to face the wrath of the Assembly.

"We indulged your speech at Aemon's request," Valkov said, his narrow eyes fixed on Jeran, "but I will not allow an upstart like you to insult my family. Nor will I allow an untrained child to roam free, especially not in light of what you've just told us. You were lucky to escape Lorthas once; I don't think it wise to let you fall into his hands again. For your own good, you should stay with us." Valkov's eyes sparkled with power. "I insist."

Jeran opened himself to magic, surrendered to it, allowed the magic to flow into him. Already exhausted from his display on the beach, he hoped only to break Valkov's hold on him, but the flows rushed toward him, filling him with power as they never had before. The Hall blossomed with color; auras danced around all the Magi. A number of them, like Valkov, had seized their own Gift and were in the process of weaving the flows of energy.

With a thought, Jeran shattered the bonds holding him in place. Valkov staggered back a step as magic was torn from him, and several Magi dropped to their seats when Jeran drew even more magic into himself. He called to it, drawing energy from across the Hall, tearing flows away from any Mage trying to harness his power. Bands of light and power swirled around him in a vortex, filling him with light and life. Though the ungifted saw nothing odd, to the Magi, Jeran blazed like the sun.

Teetering on the edge of oblivion, each breath an agony of flame, Jeran fought to keep his voice even. "If anyone here uses their Gift on me or my companions again," Jeran announced in a voice as cold as the Boundary, "I will bring this mountain down around your heads. I am no child to be coddled for my own protection, and I am no man's prisoner. I did not bend knee to Lorthas. I will not submit myself to a collection of long-winded cowards."

A few Magi overcame their shock enough to voice their outrage, but Jeran used his Gift to silence the chamber. He was not quite sure what he did, nor was he sure he could do it again, but he knew no voice but his would be heard. He felt his control slipping and knew he had to finish quickly. "Hear this!" he said, and his words thundered through the Hall. "There is a chance, a small one, that Alrendria and its allies will survive this war without you; there is no chance that you will survive without us. Once we are gone, how long can you hold out against the legions of men and Magi that Lorthas will send against you?"

He looked across the Hall with unrestrained contempt. "The Magi were created to protect and guide the Races of Madryn, but you've turned your backs on them. You've chosen inaction, and so be it, for Alrendria is still a land of freedom. But there are no havens in this war, no neutrals. If you are not our ally from the start, you are never our ally. Should you choose inaction and then find the Darklord's army on your shores, I will do everything in my power to make sure you fight alone."

As his gaze traversed the Hall, Jeran saw a full spectrum of expression, from outrage to embarrassment, on the faces of the Magi. His gaze lingered for a moment on the children, and he offered them a weak smile. "For those unwilling to sit in endless debate, I offer an alternative. Leave this Assembly and join me. Together, we will face the Darklord. Together, we will defeat him!"

The giant doors swung open at his command and Jeran started toward them, walking briskly. Once outside, where the Magi could not see him, he released his Gift, and nearly collapsed when his strength followed the magic from his body. Dahr's quick reflexes were the only thing that kept him from falling over.

Aemon was at Jeran's side in an instant, and with Dahr's help, he dragged Jeran through the narrow corridors. "You made yourself a few enemies today," Aemon warned.

A wan smile touched Jeran's lips. "That didn't go as well as I intended."

"Funny," Aemon laughed, "It went far better than I thought it would." Concern entered the old man's eyes. "That was a dangerous thing you did, seizing so much magic, especially the way you tore the flows away from others. You need to rest. Let me find you a room."

"I'll rest aboard the ship," Jeran replied. "This place sickens me."

Aemon nodded and cast his eyes over his shoulder, in the direction of the Hall. "Perhaps it's for the best," he admitted, stopping in the middle of the hallway. A vertical streak formed in front of them, swirling outward in a shower of silver speckles. Captain Corrine stood on the far side of the Gate, waiting with a handful of men beside a longboat.

Jeran frowned thoughtfully. "Can you open a Gate from the deck of a ship?"

"If it's not moving."

"Will you come with us? I need to get that fleet to Vela, but I don't think I can do it alone."

"Jeran, my boy," Aemon said with a grin that stretched from ear to ear, "I thought you'd never ask!"

Chapter 33

Martyn leaned over the map, studying the land around Vela, looking for some place, any place, to stop Tylor's march. It had been eight days since Sheriza had Gated him, Dayfid and Kal to the city. They had crossed hundreds of leagues in an instant, an experience both exhilarating and terrifying. Jes had greeted him with vague reports of a force moving south. She had sent scouts out but none had returned.

Martyn knew that Tylor's attack would be substantial, and he had begged Sheriza to help him ferry men north. "Even well rested, I could Gate no more than five men a day," she told him bluntly, "and without the burden of horses or gear. After our little excursions into Corsa, you're lucky I got the four of us here without injury."

"But with the others—"

"With the others, you'd have maybe a hundred more men and Healers too exhausted to heal. I cannot do it, Prince Martyn. I *will* not do it."

Eight days! And still they had no plan, no hope. Behind him, Miriam squealed, and Martyn turned in time to see the princess duck Kaeille's kick and scramble across the floor, her hands covering her face protectively. She paused to catch her breath, and then circled the Aelvin woman for a moment before launching a clumsy attack that Kaeille dodged.

Martyn returned his attention to the map. He had ordered Jasova to march to Vela with all haste, but they would never arrive in time. Too late, Martyn had realized Murdir's foolishness for what it was: a ruse to draw him and his men south, leaving Vela exposed. The plan had worked too well; holding Vela now would take a miracle, but Martyn planned to hold even if it cost him all he had gained in the south. All the land captured along the border could be recaptured, but if Vela fell, it would strike a blow from which Alrendria might never recover.

The first refugees had appeared two days after his return. Bodies bent, eyes haunted, they carried a tale of broken dreams and lost lives. An army led by a man in black armor and a horned helm pursued them, leaving a trail of desolation in its wake. Few survived the army's passage, and those who did were ravaged, tortured, or packed into wagons and carted north.

As the days passed, the trickle of survivors became a flood. Those few who escaped fled south, spreading their tales throughout the countryside. Many abandoned their homes ahead of Tylor's advance, and all of them, entire villages, hastened to the imagined safety of Vela. They arrived alone or in small groups, mothers and fathers carrying weeping children on their backs, merchants with carts overburdened, strangers dragging each other forward, clinging to each other because they had no once else to cling to.

Vela filled to bursting, and so did the towns around it, and still the people came. The city could support no more, it could not support half the number packed inside. Yesterday, Martyn had closed the gates. He knew it was the right decision, but seeing his people camped along the banks of the Alren waiting for death rent his heart. He had also ordered the evacuation of the outlying villages. Towns were stripped of useful goods; fields picked clean and put to the torch. He hated doing it. Ordering the destruction of his own country was as hard as barring his people access to the city, but Martyn refused to let his conscience feed Tylor's army.

When news of the burning farms reached those in the city, it had touched off a panic. Fearing that Tylor had already arrived, thousands took to the streets, demanding entrance to the castle. Besieged by his own people, Martyn had spent a sleepless night pacing the parapets, watching as the Guard tried to restore order.

Fear of the Bull was not the only thing that had people on edge. The tight quarters and meager fare had frayed tempers, and old rivalries were rising to the surface. The last few nights had seen fighting throughout the city. Brawls had left no less than a dozen taverns in shambles and a riot—started by a rumor that the Magi in the city were ShadowMagi—left two score dead and four buildings charred to their foundations.

The violence drew Guardsmen away from their posts, leaving the defenses undermanned. Martyn needed the Guard alert and undistracted by internal matters, so he had ordered the taverns closed and the streets cleared. No one save the Guard could leave their homes after dark, and anyone found breaking the law was left outside the gates to fend for themselves. The decision had proved unpopular, but for the time being Martyn trusted that fear of Tylor would keep the people under control.

A frightened scream followed by a loud thud drew Martyn's eyes, and he looked up to find Miriam lying flat on the cushioned mat, breathing hard and rubbing the small of her back. Kaeille dropped to the mat beside the princess, pinned her arms to the floor with one hand, and made a slashing motion across Miriam's throat.

"Not bad," the Aelvin warrior said, "but this is the third time you were distracted by the same feint. You must learn from your mistakes, Princess. In battle, you only get one."

Miriam shoved the Elf's hand away and sat up, massaging her neck. Buds of rose red blossomed on her cheeks, and wisps of silken blonde hair stuck out at odd angles. She looked beautiful, and Martyn smiled, but when she saw him watching, she shot an angry glare in his direction. *Why's she mad at me? It wasn't my idea to teach her how to fight!*

"This is ridiculous," Miriam sniffed. "I am the Princess of Gilead, there—"

"All the more reason to know how to defend yourself," Kaeille interrupted. She offered her hand again, but Miriam refused it. With a groan, the princess stood. "Your trainers have been neglectful. You should have learned this seasons ago."

"*Princesses* do not learn how to fight," Miriam snapped, her nose held high. "We're taught finer methods of persuasion, and leave the brawling to street toughs and tavern hussies."

Kaeille showed no reaction to the thinly-veiled insult. "And what if you are accosted?" she asked, her green eyes fastened on the princess. "What then?"

"That is what my guards are for."

"Only a fool trusts another's blade over her own."

"A blade!" Miriam exclaimed, waving her arms dramatically. "If only you'd let me use a blade! What good will my hands and feet be against armed men?"

"My people have fought weaponless for millennia," Kaeille said, circling the princess slowly, studying her. "If trained properly, your hands can be as deadly as any sword."

"I'd still prefer the sword."

"A sword would encumber you," Kaeille warned. "Your greatest advantage comes from surprise. No one would suspect one such as you of being a threat."

"A dagger then," Miriam said. Her voice rose in volume; the red on her cheeks spread to encompass most of her face. "Something I can conceal."

"I would consider knife fighting," Kaeille laughed, "but only after you stop tripping over your feet. A drunken ox has better balance."

Miriam lunged across the mat. Kaeille easily sidestepped, and with a lightning-fast movement shoved the princess off balance. Miriam landed with a pained grunt. "If you have so much energy, then try again." Kaeille said, assuming a ready position. "This time, do not let anger dictate your attack."

Rubbing her tailbone, Miriam climbed to her feet. "I'm done with this game." She turned to leave.

"A wager then?" Kaeille goaded. "I am to dine with Martyn tonight. If you can knock me to the mat just once, you may take my place."

Miriam's eyes darkened, and she frowned. "And if you win?"

"Then you will not complain for ten days. You may have yet to beat me in the ring, but my ears burn from your 'finer' methods of persuasion." Miriam's frown turned to a snarl, and the princess dropped into a defensive crouch. Kaeille waited patiently for the princess' attack.

"One of these days," Martyn muttered, "they're going to kill each other."

Treloran laughed. "They only fight like this when you are around," the Aelvin Prince told him. "Any other time, you would think they were the best of friends. A few days past, I saw them laughing like a pair of old *amiende*."

Martyn sighed heavily as he watched the women spar. "When I'm alone with either of them, things couldn't be better, but as soon as the three of us are together, they fight like caged tigers. Worse, they give *me* as many cold glares as they give each other, as if this were my fault!"

Treloran closed the book he was studying. "You *were* the one who fell in love with them both."

Martyn's eyed widened. "I don't love Miriam! I—" A frown pulled at the sides of his mouth, and thoughts of the princess—her great beauty; the warm smiles that brightened her face when she thought he could not see them; the cunning way she manipulated people, twisting the scheming nobility into pledging their support for Alrendria—filled his mind. "Dear Gods," he whispered. "I do love them both. What a fool I am! Treloran, what am I to do?"

"Pray," the Aelvin Prince answered solemnly, though a merry light danced in his eyes. "At this point, there is little to do but pray."

Hiding another sigh, Martyn's eyes fell to the map and landed upon the spot he had been seeking. "Here," he said excitedly, pointing to a valley less than two days ride from Vela, a narrow passage between two rugged cliffs.

"An ambush?" Treloran mused, leaning in to study the map. "If this man is as great a commander as you claim, he will expect an ambush, especially in a place such as this."

"True," Martyn agreed, "but diverting his men around the chasm will cost him days, and if he knows how weak our garrison is, he won't dare risk it. Were I in his place, I'd send a party through to secure this valley"—Martyn pointed to the southern edge of the chasm, where the land opened into a broad bowl—"and move the rest of my men through in smaller groups. If we hide here and here, we can attack the advance force and be gone before the bulk of the army enters the field."

"Even if we succeed," Treloran said, "it will not stop the advance."

"No, but a victory will raise the morale of our troops, and in the end, that might make the difference. We don't have to destroy Tylor's army; we just have to hold on to Vela until reinforcements arrive."

Treloran frowned thoughtfully. "It might work. My uncle often used such tactics fighting the Tribesmen. We should find Commander Estande. We will have to leave soon if you intend to reach that valley before the Bull of Ra Tachan."

Martyn rolled up the map and stood to leave, turning just in time to see Miriam land a staggering blow on Kaeille's jaw. The Aelvin woman stumbled backward, and Miriam lurched forward for a second attack. Kaeille grabbed the princess' arm and used Miriam's momentum against her, tossing the princess over her shoulder. Miriam landed roughly, and the breath exploded from her body.

"Better," Kaeille said, rubbing her chin. "You surprised me that time."

"I still think this is a waste of time," Miriam sniffed, graciously accepting Kaeille's hand and climbing to her feet. "The Guardsmen do a fine job protecting me."

"The Guardsmen are not always around," Kaeille replied, looking pointedly around the empty room. "A wise attacker will wait until you are unprotected to make his move."

"You worry too much," Miriam mumbled. "Nothing has ever happened to me before." She saw Martyn smiling at her and blushed, forgetting herself long enough to return the gesture. She looked at the sweat-covered clothes that hung loosely on her body, and a hand rose to ineffectually smooth her unkempt hair. Mortified, she flashed Martyn a look cold enough to freeze water. "Enjoy your dinner," she said as she strode from the room.

Martyn turned a stunned gaze on Treloran, but the Aelvin Prince had no explanation. "She has a fire to match any *Ael Chatorra*," Kaeille said. "Valia be praised that she has no real interest in learning the blade, or I would find myself at the losing end of it one day."

Out in the hall, Miriam screamed, a terrified sound that tied a knot in Martyn's gut. A loud crash and clatter followed the scream, and then silence. In an instant, Martyn was running toward the door, wishing that he had brought his sword from his chambers. Treloran and Kaeille followed at his heels.

A rough-looking man dressed in dark clothes lay on the floor amidst the remains of a decorative suit of armor. Miriam stood over him, clutching a heavy gauntlet in her hands. When the man groaned and shifted, she squeaked and brought the gauntlet crashing down against his head. The attacker tried to roll over, his arms coming up defensively, and Miriam bludgeoned him repeatedly with her makeshift cudgel.

Martyn and Treloran rushed forward to help the princess, but everyone froze when Kaeille shouted out a commanding, "Hold!" The Aelvin woman walked past the princes and pulled Miriam away from the man. Kneeling beside the stranger, she took his head in her hands tenderly and examined his wounds. "Can you walk?"

The man nodded weakly. "Yes, m'lady."

"Then seek the Healer Sheriza, Guardsman. I thank you for your sacrifice, as does the princess. You will be compensated for your troubles." Kaeille helped the man to his feet and sent him stumbling down the hall before turning a smugly satisfied grin on the princess. "Will you take our lessons more seriously now?"

Miriam's first slap caught Kaeille by surprise, but the Elf caught the princess' arm on the backswing. They glared at each other for a long moment, but as Miriam's shock and outrage faded, her angry gaze softened. When the injured Guardsman tripped over his own feet and toppled to the floor with a veiled curse, Miriam giggled. "You should have seen the look on his face!"

"I remember my own training," Kaeille said. "The only person more surprised than my attacker was me."

"I didn't even think about what I was doing!" Miriam admitted. "He jumped out of the shadows and grabbed my shoulder, and all of a sudden he was on the ground."

"You now know your own power," Kaeille told her. "Fear will never paralyze you again." The two embraced and started down the hall, whispering to each other like old friends.

Martyn and Treloran stared after them in stunned disbelief, and Martyn turned to the Aelvin Prince. "In your training, did you ever—"

"Never."

"If I paid someone to attack you—"

"I would be furious."

"Then why—"

"I am only an Elf, Martyn. Only the Gods understand women." Treloran frowned and shook his head. "Sometimes I wonder if even the Gods understand. Let's find Commander Estande."

They found him standing along the seawall, his eyes on the distant black shapes that blocked entrance to the harbor. Short and unimposing, with wavy black hair and a long curling mustache, Gregor Estande did not seem the image of a Guardsman, let alone a Guard Commander. At barely ten hands tall, even Martyn towered over him, and his narrow frame was better suited to a child than a grown man, but Gregor had proved himself an able fighter and a clever strategist.

The Estande Family, a Family so small it no longer remembered when it had been a House, had holdings along the northern border of House Velan. Gregor's grandfather, Lord Dominic Estande, had seen the makings of a great man in Gregor. He had named the boy his heir at an early age, grooming him for politics in the hope that the charismatic young man would restore some measure of power to the Family.

Gregor surprised his family by joining the Guard, but no one had objected, least of all his grandfather. They saw military service as another means to their end, and when Gregor rose quickly to command, they saw in his success the restoration of Family Estande. Gregor received a number of half-hearted requests from his family to retire from the Guard, but the reputation he was building outweighed any true desire they had for his presence until Lord Dominic Estande took ill and rumors of an enemy army in the north surfaced.

Since Martyn first arrived in Vela, Gregor had received no fewer than a dozen letters demanding his immediate resignation. He refused to leave, and he had asked his grandfather to select another to lead the Family. His loyalty to Alrendria had earned him the hatred of his kin; now, none of the Estande Family would so much as acknowledge his presence.

Gregor greeted the two princes with a warm smile, then turned back to the ocean. "What is their purpose?" he mused, tugging at the end of his mustache. "Do they wait for the Bull, or are they simply meant to block our escape? For our sakes, I hope the latter. We would never survive an assault from east *and* west, even if the Bull had no Magi to aid his cause."

"Are you worried, Gregor?" Martyn asked. "Your voice is generally the loudest one proclaiming our inevitable victory."

"Bluff and bluster is good for morale, Prince Martyn, but those in command should share a more realistic assessment amongst themselves." Gregor's dark tone did not match his smile. "My apologies. Word arrived from the north: Lord Dominic is dead, our lands have been destroyed, and all but a handful of my Family has been enslaved."

Martyn sought the right words, but none were sufficient. "I'm sorry, Gregor."

"The loss of our lands is far from the worst. My sister was one of the few to escape. She has no idea what's become of my parents, my brother, or any of our family. We are alone, and she refuses to speak to me. She blames me!"

"There's nothing you could have done," Martyn said, though he knew his words would not relieve Gregor's guilt. "Your presence would have made no difference, except it would have robbed Vela of an able commander."

"Hard words," Gregor said, his smile slipping, "and no more pleasant because they're true. But my sister... Ah!"—he waved a hand dismissively—"She will come around. The pain of loss is still too fresh, that's all."

"I may have a way to soften the blow," Martyn said. "A way to bring your Family a small bit of revenge." Kneeling, Martyn unrolled the map on the ground, and Gregor stooped beside him as the prince outlined his plan.

"It's risky," Gregor said after a long silence. He tugged sharply on his mustache. "But in our situation, a little risk might be worthwhile if it gains us a small advantage." Energized by the thought of action, Gregor started toward the castle. "I'll gather our forces, Prince Martyn. I trust that you're going to insist on leading this ridiculous raid despite my strenuous and heartfelt protests?" He did not wait for Martyn's nod. "We must march by nightfall if we're to beat Tylor to the ambush."

"I'll meet you at the gates at dusk," Martyn called after the Guard Commander, who showed no sign of hearing. He watched the diminutive Guardsman stride purposefully toward the castle, outpacing men half again as tall as he. "Even alone, Gregor might be able to defeat the Tachans."

"Lord Estande is a spirited leader," Treloran agreed, his lips pursed thoughtfully. "All of your Guardsmen, down to the youngest recruit, has a spirit to rival *Ael Chatorra*. I look forward to seeing them in battle."

"You won't have long to wait," Martyn said. "Tylor will be at the gates in days." Treloran frowned, and Martyn caught something in the Elf's impassive stare. He shook his head violently. "I can't allow you to go. You're the Emperor's grandson and—"

"Not one of your subjects," Treloran interrupted, drawing himself up to full height. "Nor your responsibility."

"You're right," Martyn said, "but this isn't your fight."

"Perhaps it should be," the Aelvin Prince replied. "The Darklord has no respect for his own Race; what love will he show mine? Grandfather supports your cause, as does my mother. If they can see past the scheming of *Ael Alluya*, why should I blind myself?"

Martyn tried desperately to think of a reason for Treloran to remain behind. "I couldn't wish for a better ally," he said at last, though all he could see was the look on Charylla's face as he tried to explain why her son had died defending Alrendria.

"If only Aemon could see this," Jes said, stepping up behind them. "He never believed the Alliance of the Four Races could be rebuilt."

"He was right," Martyn replied, turning to face the Mage. "Only three Races remain."

A sad smile touched Jes' lips. "Then we had better pray three is enough." In the distance a bell began ringing. Guardsmen appeared from every direction, running toward the main courtyard. Jes leveled a stern glare at the prince. "Lord Estande claims you intend to attack Tylor's army."

"It's the truth," Martyn said, and Jes listened disapprovingly while the prince recapped his plan.

"What will this foolishness accomplish?" From the expression on her face, she was half a heartbeat from using her Gift on him.

"We're cut off here," Martyn explained, "with too few men to hold the city and reinforcements too far away to do any good. Vela is filled to bursting and thousands more clamor outside the gates for entry. The refugees are convinced that we'll be overrun, and the Guardsmen's morale is not much better.

"This raid may barely sting the Bull, but it will remind our people that he's just a man, and that his troops will die as easily as any other men. With luck, it will buy us the time we need. At the very least, it will prevent Vela from falling to rioters before Tylor clears the horizon."

Jes looked to be on the verge of arguing, but with a heavy sigh, her shoulders sank and the fire faded from her gaze. She suddenly looked older, much older, as if the weight of centuries hung on her shoulders. "I tire of war, of the endless justification for it. I hope you're right about this, Prince Martyn, and I wish you well."

She turned to go, but Martyn stopped her. "Have any more Magi answered your summons?"

"No." Her curt reply bubbled with frustration. "The Assembly refuses to take action, and those few who are already here, the Healers included, have earned themselves a great deal of trouble. You can expect no more help from the Magi than what you have."

"Can we spare..." Martyn ran through the list of Magi under his command. Their numbers were far too few for him to risk them unnecessarily, but his need was great. "I don't want to weaken Vela any more than necessary, but could you get word to the Mage Cyrrus? He should be in or near Darein. Tell him what we plan, and ask him if he knows two Magi suited to a raid of this type."

"I will do as you ask," Jes said, starting toward the castle.

"One more thing!" Martyn called. Jes stopped with her back to him. "Is Mage Sheriza still meditating?"

After a long pause, Jes answered. "She has not left her chambers in some time."

"I... I'd appreciate it if you kept news of this raid from her until we're gone. She pretends to be fine, but I believe she overexerted herself in Corsa, and again to bring me here. If she knew what we planned, she'd insist on going, and I don't think she's ready for another battle yet. She's stubborn and—" He stopped when Jes turned to face him.

"You never cease to amaze me, Prince Martyn," Jes said, her expression inscrutable. "I will keep her here by force, if necessary." With a bow of her head, she left the two princes standing in the courtyard.

"We do not have much time," Treloran said, looking skyward. The red-gold sun hung low in the west, silhouetting Atol Domiar and the Black Fleet, and casting long shadows across the courtyard.

"Gregor's not likely to wait," Martyn agreed, hurrying toward the castle. "Not even for his prince."

Chapter 34

"I don't like this," Gregor said, pulling at his mustache. He and Martyn crouched on the edge of a thick forest, buried behind a wall of loose scrub and overlapping branches. A broad valley opened before them, narrowing in the north into a chasm between two rugged cliffs. Dark grey clouds threatened rain, and thunder crackled ominously. "We should have done it my way."

The holes through which they peered were invisible from the valley, but they limited vision, and Martyn risked exposure by moving some branches out of his way. "This will work, Gregor. I know it will!" Gregor's small, dark stallion shuffled the leaves and snorted. Martyn ducked back into concealment and glared at the Guard Commander. "If your horse doesn't betray our position, that is."

Gregor chuckled quietly. "Horses are like women. The only time they're content to be quiet is when you want to know where they are. Any other time, they wonder why you're ignoring them." The statement, so casually delivered, caught Martyn by surprise, and he clapped a hand over his mouth to stifle a laugh. "One can't go into battle with a heavy heart," Gregor winked.

Out in the valley, the first of Tylor's soldiers emerged from the ravine. A few riders circled the depression, scouting the perimeter, but the bulk of the force remained in a tight cluster. As anticipated, only a small group arrived, and they watched the cliff's intently for ambush. Only a hundred men arrived with the first bunch, but more entered the valley with every passing moment. So far, there was no sign of the Bull.

Martyn had hoped Tylor's arrogance would force him to lead the march through the ravine, but the Bull had shown restraint. Deprived of the ultimate prize, Martyn waited for an amply sized force to gather. Too few and the ambush was pointless; too many, and they would never get back to Vela.

Hidden deep in the brush, rows of archers stood in calm and orderly formation, trying not to look nervous. A season ago, most had been farmers and craftsmen, but the threat of attack had forced them to join the militia, and Treloran's rigorous training had turned them into a modest fighting force. Martyn expected no miracles, but so long as they followed orders and held the line, he expected them to do fine.

In the center of the archers, three score Guardsmen crouched low to the ground, careful to keep their mounts between their shiny armor and the enemy. The cavalry would be the heart of the ambush, driving deep into the enemy before the Durange could respond. A similar company of Guardsmen and militia, under Dayfid's command, waited across the depression. When Martyn attacked, so would they, and the enemy would be forced to defend in both direction. With luck, there would be few Alrendrian casualties.

Atop the ravine, Treloran and the best of the Alrendrian archers waited. When the attack began, the Aelvin Prince would slow any reinforcements Tylor tried to send through the pass and prevent the men in the valley from retreating. Theirs was the most dangerous assignment, for it placed them firmly between Tylor's forces. To escape, the archers would have to break into small groups and flee through the backcountry, a twisting maze of forested hills and narrow canyons. If Tylor pursued them, it would buy Vela the time it needed for reinforcements to arrive. Martyn did not relish putting Treloran in such danger, but the Elf had ignored Martyn's protestations. "Fool Elf!" Martyn muttered. "If he gets himself killed, I'll—"

"If I get myself killed, you'll do what?" Treloran asked, stepping silently from the trees. A number of Guardsmen hissed in a surprised breath at the Elf's sudden appearance, and Gregor had his sword half unsheathed before Martyn's restraining hand stopped him.

"Is everything ready?" Martyn met the Elf's cool green eyes calmly.

The barest hint of a smile touched Treloran's lips. "Just as we planned."

"I don't like it," Gregor grumbled. When Martyn fixed an exasperated look on him, he scowled. "You have to trust your gut, Martyn, and mine tells me this battle is going to cost us."

"Every battle has costs," Martyn replied. "This one will cost the Durange more."

Gregor grunted unintelligibly and turned his back on the princes. Martyn climbed to his feet and signaled Treloran to follow. "I have concerns," he whispered.

"About the men?" Treloran asked, leaning in close. Martyn carefully avoided looking at his men; the last thing he needed was his troops knowing he lacked faith in them. "The archers?" Martyn ducked his head, and Treloran dismissed his fears with a gesture. "They are far from the greatest of marksmen, but they can hit a man-sized target from two hundred paces. These men, each and every one, have the spirit of *Ael Chatorra*. Had they not, I would not have trained them, let alone chosen them for this raid."

Some of the tension melted from Martyn's shoulders. "I knew I could count on you," he said, clapping the Elf's shoulder, and Treloran turned to hide his embarrassment. "Do you think our plan will really work?"

Treloran shrugged. "A strategy is only good until the battle is joined. After that, only skill and luck matter." Sensing his words had brought little comfort, he added, "Our plan is sound, and your men ready. Valia will smile on us, and we will strike a blow against the Darklord in her name." The Elf's eyes flicked toward the depression, and he started toward the trees. "I must go. Do not wait too long. What advantage we have will be lost if too many men cross the canyon." Two steps more and Treloran disappeared into the foliage. "Give me a count of two hundred, though," his light whisper drifted back to Martyn's ears, "or I might miss the battle."

Martyn turned to find Gregor signaling frantically. He dropped to the ground and wormed his way forward until he was fingers from the Guard Commander. "A rider," Gregor whispered, "no more than fifty hands off. He's past now, and none the wiser, I think, else we'd have Tylor's men all around us by now."

Settling into place, Martyn's tension returned. He eased his sword in its scabbard and felt comforted by the feel of the metal in his palm. He studied the field and was surprised to discover that the number of enemy soldiers had nearly doubled. "A large group appeared not long ago," Gregor explained, as if reading Martyn's thoughts. "And riders are coming through the pass faster than ever. We should not delay."

"When the Magi arrive," Martyn said, "we will attack." Gregor's pressed for haste, but Martyn ignored him. He faced the field as if studying his opponents' position, but in truth, he let his mind wander. As often happened of late, his thoughts drifted to Kaeille and Miriam.

Those two confused him to no end. Their competition, the wagers for his time, the jibes and jokes exchanged when one would be alone with him or when he complimented one and not the other made no sense to Martyn, but their odd friendship perplexed him even more. Since leaving Kaper, the two women had formed a bond, though a transient one. Sometimes they appeared life-long friends, sharing secrets over a cup of tea; at other times, their animosity resurfaced in full fury, making the journey from Kaper seem a pleasant outing.

That they were friends of sorts lightened Martyn's heart, but he did not understand how it was possible. Had he been forced to share the one he loved, he never could befriend the man he had to share with. He often wondered if their friendship were an act; neither liked to draw undue attention. But propriety could not explain why they spent so much time together. *And what do they talk about? Me?*

Martyn's own anxiety amused him; whatever friendship they had or secrets they shared was his fault. Kaeille had taken his order to protect Miriam seriously. As *advoutre* and *Ael Chatorra*, she felt it was her duty to protect not only Martyn but his family as well. Though Miriam had yet to officially announce her intention to marry Martyn, Kaeille had decided it was a certainty, and the Aelvin woman had become one of the loudest voices in support of the union.

It was Miriam who truly astounded Martyn. Other than their love for him, which should put them at odds, the princess and Kaeille had little in common, and what few words she exchanged with the Elf in Kaper had been heated barbs or barely-concealed insults. That she had so willingly accepted Kaeille's protection had been a pleasant surprise; discovering that Miriam was allowing Kaeille to teach her self defense had been a shock, and learning that the princess was teaching Kaeille about Human customs had struck Martyn dumb. The Gods had either smiled on him or were playing him for a fool; Martyn only wished he knew which.

He closed his eyes and images of a blonde princess and a green-eyed warrior filled his mind. He loved them both; he could no longer deny it, and he hated himself for it. He almost regretted his decision, or rather, he regretted the decision Emperor Alwellyn had taken from him. Life would have been easier had he left Kaeille in Illendrylla. And had duty not forced Miriam on him, he could have had a lifetime of happiness with Kaeille. Regardless, he had decided to bear the burdens duty placed on him. Others had sacrificed far more.

Had he hated one and loved the other, he could have lived with both, but by loving both, he could not help but feel guilty. He wondered if he could ever look at one without thinking about how his treacherous heart hurt the other. He wished Jeran or Dahr were with him; they might not understand, but they would have made him feel better. They had always protected him, even from himself.

Martyn's expression darkened when he thought of his friends. He wondered if Jeran were still alive and if Dahr had escaped capture. He wondered what had happened to them during the intervening seasons, and if he would ever see them again. *One last time, that's all I want. One chance to thank them for what they did.* The image of a red-headed warrior made his hand tighten painfully on the hilt of his sword. *She's to blame for this, and someday I'll make her pay!*

"Martyn!" Gregor called out urgently. The Guard Commander shook him roughly, waking Martyn from his daydream. "We must move now!"

"I said when the Magi returned!" Martyn snapped, his eyes flying open. The field below held over a thousand men, and small parties were fanning out from the central body, setting up a perimeter. A group of lightly-armored men stood in a line, taking orders from a soldier in dark plate. To the north, another score of mounted troops galloped into the valley, yelling that they had been ambushed in the pass.

"We are here," Cyrrus said, casually brushing dust from his robes. "My Magi are ready, though I tell you again that this plan is folly. What do you expect to gain by killing a pittance of the army arrayed against you? You should fortify your position in Vela, and—"

"Time, Cyrrus," Martyn interrupted. The Mage had been against this raid from the start, and he had not been afraid to voice his opinion. "Time and confidence. Look at the men! You can see the hopelessness in their eyes. If we can make them believe we have a chance of victory, if we can prove to them that the Darklord's soldiers are men like any other, then whatever losses we suffer here will be worth ten thousand fresh swords."

Cyrrus sighed heavily, and Martyn waved him away. "If you don't want to fight, then leave. I want no one beside me who doesn't want to be here."

"I've pledged my aid to you, Prince Martyn, and I'll fight as you say. Even when your battles are poorly chosen."

"As long as we understand each other," Martyn replied, forcing a smile. He went to where his horse stood tethered, moving carefully so as to not make any noise. "Ready the men," he whispered to Gregor, and the Guard Commander rolled to a crouch and starting issuing commands. The subcommanders moved down their lines, whispering orders, cavalrymen mounted and moved closer to the tree line, and archers formed into small groups.

Martyn nodded to Cyrrus. In front of each squad, a tiny puff of red smoke flashed into being and hovered. Across the valley, Dayfid would be doing the same, readying his men for the charge and waiting for the signal to attack. Pointing at a group of archers, Martyn made a circular motion with his hand and pointed at Cyrrus. The Mage sniffed disdainfully as the archers took up positions around him. He looked as if their presence would do him more harm than good.

Climbing into his saddle, Martyn moved his horse to join the line of cavalry. "What is this?" Gregor asked, running to Martyn's side.

Fixing an expression on his face that Martyn hoped would brook no argument, he said, "I plan to lead the charge."

"That's not what we agreed on," Gregor snapped, positioning himself between Martyn and the field.

Images of Jeran and Dahr, of Iban, of all the men who had died at his side flashed through Martyn's mind, and the scowl that drew down his lips made Gregor draw back. "I will not ask men to die while I hide in the shadows." Cyrrus rolled his eyes. "Seeing their prince will give them courage."

"You commons think you're so clever." Exasperation tinged Cyrrus voice. "But glass is not as transparent as your motives. Revenge radiates from you like the fire of the sun, Prince Martyn. If you must act the fool, you should at the very least not deceive yourself over the reasons."

Gregor laughed quietly, but in the end he shook his head and stepped aside. "I knew you'd never stay behind." He called to one of the Guardsmen. "Malikai! Protect the prince."

A dark-skinned bear of a man with a cruel smile and an eager gleam in his eye ran forward, saluting fist-on-heart. "I'll be ground to dust 'fore even a scratch mars his pretty hide."

"He's no poet," Gregor said, choking back another laugh, "but you'll not find a better Guardsman in all of House Velan." Gregor leapt into his own saddle and signaled the troops to make ready. "At your command, Mage."

Cyrrus closed his eyes, and Martyn knew the Mage was projecting his thoughts across the field. "They are most organized on the southern line," he whispered. "Aim your first charge there to break the seasoned soldiers and stop them from rallying their men." Martyn nodded, listening intently while Cyrrus dispassionately described the enemy's formation. When he finished, Cyrrus raised his hand to signal the charge, and Martyn had a sudden realization. Despite his cold manner and disrespect for those without the Gift, Cyrrus had devoted himself wholeheartedly to the Corsan campaign, defying the Mage Assembly and following Martyn's orders even when he did not agree with them.

Martyn caught the Mage's sleeve, and Cyrrus' eyes snapped open. He fixed a stern glare on the prince. "I..." Martyn cleared his throat. "I just wanted to thank you. Your aid here and in Corsa has been invaluable. Alrendria owes you a great debt."

Cyrrus said nothing, but Martyn saw the shock in his eyes. He had never expected gratitude and did not know how to react to it. Finally, he ducked his head in silent acknowledgement and raised his arm above his head. When he dropped it, the red smoke disappeared, and the Alrendrian host launched its attack.

Martyn was the first to break through the trees. Across the valley, he saw Dayfid burst into view, his silver armor flashing despite the gray pall above. Two hundred heavily armed horsemen galloped into the valley behind him. Small clusters of mounted archers followed the cavalry, bows drawn and at the ready. As soon as the horsemen broke off the charge, the archers would ride in to cover their retreat.

Before he knew it, Martyn was closing on the first enemy soldiers and all thought was ripped from his mind. Screaming a battlecry, he swung his sword in a wide arc, ignoring the spray of blood that hit his face. His opponent, a wide-eyed boy who had not so much as drawn his weapon, fell to the ground in a heap, and Martyn's horse jumped over him, trampling another soldier in the process. The man's curse changed to a scream as the riders following the prince crushed him under their hooves.

Martyn plowed through the enemy, swinging his sword back and forth. A second soldier, even younger than the first, fell to his blade, and then a third. Another boy turned to flee but was run through by his own men. To Martyn's right, Gregor leaned sideways in his saddle. Almost horizontal, he stabbed, catching a Tachan soldier just beneath the shoulder. Gregor pulled himself back up, ducking an awkward attack. His answering blow felled a second enemy soldier.

Malikai fought like a demon, swinging his short-hafted, double-bladed axe faster than the eye could follow. Five men fell to his hacking blows before Martyn's second opponent hit the ground, and he grabbed a sixth man by the throat and lifted him with tree-like arms. Flashing a wicked, gap-toothed grin, he smashed his head against the enemy's. The Tachan landed with a bone-jarring crunch and lay unmoving. The sight brought a wave of nausea to Martyn's gut, but he forced it away and sought another opponent.

Two soldiers, one of them mounted, charged Gregor. The Guard Commander dodged one attack and tried to position his horse to face both attackers, and they fanned out, trying to flank him. Martyn started toward them, but without warning the ground before him erupted, sending enemy soldiers flying and dust billowing into the air. Martyn's horse reared, and when he finally got the beast settled, the way to Gregor was blocked.

"For Alrendria!" Martyn yelled, and those nearest him took up the cry. The Guardsmen surged forward, and Martyn led them toward the heart of the valley, cutting down anyone foolish enough to cross his path. All around him, explosions of dirt and fire appeared wherever more than a handful of Tachans gathered, and arrows rained down upon anyone who sought to flee from the cavalry.

In moments, Martyn found himself staring at Dayfid. The Guardsman's eyes were alight with fervor; blood painted his armor red. Seeing his prince, Dayfid smiled triumphantly. "Victory!" he shouted, holding his sword aloft. Martyn could not help but share the Guardsman's joy. "These Tachans fight like children!"

"They *are* children!" Gregor spat, pulling up beside Martyn. "I've not seen a one who can boast more than twenty winters!"

Gregor was right; Martyn had seen few seasoned fighters among the Tachans. The older soldiers were as often as not crippled with age or hobbled by injuries. He spun around slowly, his eyes scanning the field, and he saw his men spread out, hundreds of tiny groups pursuing the remnants of Tylor's advance guard. "Signal the retreat," he said urgently, a knot tightening in his gut. "Where's Cyrrus? We must signal the retreat!"

"Retreat?" Dayfid repeated. "Why? The field is ours!"

"It's a trap!" Martyn hissed. He spotted Cyrrus in the distance and kneed his horse, shoving Dayfid out of his way. "Rally the men! It's a trap!"

"A trap?" Dayfid repeated incredulously, wiping the blood from his sword and staring at Martyn as if he had gone insane. "How could it be—" A loud explosion to the north cut him off. The trees on both sides of the canyon exploded in flame, and a dark cloud of smoke boiled up into the cloudy, late summer sky.

"Our Magi didn't do that!" Martyn yelled. More explosions rocked the cliffs to the north, sending debris tumbling down the sides. "Treloran," Martyn whispered, wincing with every blast. He started to turn his horse north but checked himself. There was nothing he could do for the Aelvin Prince; he had to save the Guardsmen.

"Cyrrus!" Martyn shouted, reining in beside the Mage. "There are ShadowMagi to the north." Close behind Martyn, Malikai scanned every face as if expecting betrayal. Even Cyrrus seemed frightened by the man; after a quick glance, he refused to meet Malikai's gaze.

"Ciomae tells me there are at least three Gifted in the northern hills," the Mage said curtly. "What would you have me do about it?"

"Signal the retreat!" Martyn said, almost pleading. "We've done all we can."

Whatever sharp retort Cyrrus had ready died on his lips, and he nodded. "At last, a sensible suggestion." Martyn ignored the Mage's muttering; he had more important matters to deal with than arrogance and condescension.

"To the north!" Malikai called, his voice booming. Hundreds of soldiers poured into the valley, spreading out as they hit the plains, forming into well-ordered ranks and bearing down on the scattered Alrendrians. Cries of "For the Bull!" and "Long live the Darklord!" thundered across the valley.

"Martyn!" Gregor shouted from somewhere behind the prince. "To the south!" Martyn whirled around again and blinked in stunned surprise as groups of enemy soldiers suddenly appeared. Most groups numbered barely a score of men, but a few held close to a hundred, and each had a dark-robed figure in its center. As one, they moved to block Martyn's retreat.

The trill of a horn reverberated through the air, coming from both nowhere and everywhere. The sharp note drowned out all other sound. All across the field, Alrendrian soldiers broke off their attacks and fell back. "To me!" Martyn shouted, trotting south. "Rally to me!" He craned his neck around to watch the riders closing on them.

"Gregor, get word to the archers! Tell them to fire on the ShadowMagi. A dead Mage is worth a thousand dead soldiers!" Cyrrus' face tightened at the comment, but he said nothing, and as Gregor galloped away, Martyn waved for Dayfid. "Rally your men and lead them south. We need to break through the enemy before Tylor's host reaches us." The sound of the approaching riders was like distant thunder, a low rumble steadily growing in volume.

Dayfid sat unmoving, a stupefied grin on his face. "Guardsman!" Martyn shouted, and Dayfid snapped to action as if awaking from a dream. He raced north, bellowing at the top of his lungs. The farthest Guardsman heard Dayfid's rallying cry and turned to rejoin the host; the most frightened gained confidence from his words and hurried to rejoin his companions. Dayfid galloped back and forth across the field, herding his soldiers like cattle, forcing them away from the approaching cavalry.

The enemy to the south had blocked the path out of the valley. ShadowMagi stood every four to six hundred hands, their black robes billowing in the wind. "How many men will it take to break that line?" Martyn asked.

Malikai frowned. "Hard to say. Never fought Magi before."

"Can you do it?" Martyn demanded. With every passing moment, he felt hope wane.

The Guardsman's frown turned into an eager grin. "Tell me where you want the hole, my Prince, and it will be there before you are."

"There!" Martyn shouted, pointing southwest, where the line was thinnest and the Magi fewest. "I want you—" The rest of what he had to say died on his tongue when, in the distance, he saw a volley of arrows stop in mid-flight. They hovered hands away from a black-robed figure.

By the time Martyn regained his voice, Malikai and a third of the men who had rallied to Martyn's call were racing ahead in a tight wedge, dodging fireballs and explosions. Cyrrus remained at Martyn's side, but the Mage's gaze was distant. "Dozens!" he said, incredulity and anger warring in his voice. "There are dozens of them! Even the Assembly won't be able to stand aside once they hear of this. How could—!" With a cry of pain, Cyrrus fell from his horse, his arm a mass of flames. He landed with a thud and rolled back and forth frantically, trying to douse the fire.

Martyn wheeled around, waving for his men to continue on. "Follow Malikai!" he shouted, vaulting from the saddle and landing at the Mage's side. "Follow him to safety!" Dropping to his knees, Martyn shoveled loose dirt onto Cyrrus' arm and ripped shreds of smoldering fabric from his robes.

"Thank you," Cyrrus said weakly once they had put out the fire. What remained of his arm hung uselessly at his side, a blackened husk of dead flesh with charred bone visible at wrist and elbow. Martyn marveled at the Mage. Cyrrus calmly examined a wound that would have the toughest of Guardsmen weeping like a child, and he stood without so much as a groan. "We've lost a great deal of time, Prince Martyn. We should not tarry."

Martyn glanced around. On a field that moments before had harbored a defeated enemy lay the bodies of his men. The screams of the wounded pierced his ears, and each lifeless, unmoving body stabbed at his heart. He watched the Bull's army bearing down on his scattered forces, slowing only to dispatch the wounded they passed. Fires raged through the northern forests, and Martyn muttered a quick prayer, asking the Gods to protect Treloran.

"We must move!" Cyrrus insisted, grabbing Martyn by the shoulder and dragging him forward. Jolted into action, Martyn hoisted the Mage onto his horse and climbed onto his own. He slapped Cyrrus' mount to get it moving and followed at a gallop. Cyrrus rode awkwardly, his eyes unfocused, his skin wan and sweat-soaked. Somehow, he kept from falling.

Ahead of them, Malikai hit the Tachan line at a dead run. The men following him plowed into the enemy with swords swinging and blood-curdling cries on their lips. The line stretched and thinned, but it did not break. Malikai's charged halted hands from victory, and the Bull's soldiers surged in on the Alrendrians from three sides.

He couldn't do it, Martyn thought. He tightened his grip on the hilt of his sword. He no longer believed he would survive the battle, but he planned to make a strong accounting of himself before he fell. He turned to face the approaching riders, hundreds of armored soldiers racing across the valley at a full gallop.

The sound of pounding hooves grew louder, until Martyn thought the very ground beneath him trembled from the force of charge. His horse screamed, rearing and stomping nervously as the ground began to shift. A ripple of earth moved away from the Alrendrians, gaining strength, rising and falling like a wave on the ocean. It hit the enemy with enough force to throw horses into the air. When the dust cleared, Martyn let out a breath he had not realized he held. The charge was broken. The bulk of Tylor's forces struggled to regain their feet; those who still stood approached slowly, wary of another attack.

"Sinjhit," Cyrrus said weakly, and Martyn heard the worry in the Mage's voice. He turned in time to see a young Mage collapse. "He's overextended himself," Cyrrus told Martyn. "We must help him."

A triumphant cry drew Martyn's eye south. Malikai's men had broken through the Tachan line, and a trickle of Alrendrians crossed through the gap. Malikai had been dragged from his mount, but he carved his own path through the Tachans, grinning wickedly with each swing of his bloody axe. Other soldiers took up positions around him, holding open the gap and driving the Tachans even farther back.

A Guardsman approached the fallen Mage, but as he knelt to help, a half dozen arrows sprouted from his back and he pitched forward. Lightning crashed not far from Martyn, sending men and horses flying. The enemy fought like demons to close the breach in their line, and the Tachans to the north were regrouping. A dozen ShadowMagi closed in on Martyn's position, raining lightning and fire down from the sky. For the first time, Martyn truly understood what threat a group of Gifted posed, even to a city the size of Vela.

"Protect our Magi!" he shouted, hoping some of his men could hear over the howling winds that suddenly whipped across his face. "Get the Magi to safety!" They had only six Magi with them, three stripped from Vela's defenses and the two apprentices who had accompanied Cyrrus. If even one survived the day, Martyn would count it a victory.

He and Cyrrus raced toward Sinjhit, but Gregor beat them there. The Guard Commander dropped to the ground beside the injured apprentice and placed a hand on the young man's throat. Then, with a strength that belied his small frame, he hefted the young man onto his shoulder and threw him across the back of his horse. He knelt again and checked the Guardsman, but stood empty handed.

"Get him out of here!" Gregor shouted, tossing the reins to a Guardsman riding behind Martyn. The young man took off at a run, leading the horse and its unconscious rider toward safety. "You shouldn't be here," Gregor said to Martyn. "You should have fled at the first sign of trouble."

"What do you think I've been doing?" Martyn laughed harshly, offering a hand to Gregor. With a curt nod, Gregor took Martyn's hand and placed his foot in the stirrup, but when Martyn went to pull him up, Gregor stiffened, and his grip went slack. He pitched forward with a groan, and his face slammed against Martyn's leg before he slid to the ground. Two black-shafted arrows quivered in his back.

"Gods!" Martyn yelled, climbing down from the saddle. He stared dumbly, not sure what to do, as bright blood ran from Gregor's armor and stained the grass red. A Guardsman to his right screamed, and to his left a second scream cut off suddenly. Black shafts filled the air, and Martyn ducked behind his horse, dragging Gregor with him. Between his mount's legs, he saw a party of archers moving toward him with two black-robed Magi at its front.

Cyrrus tried to dismount, but he lost his footing and fell to the ground, landing with a bone-jarring crash. The Mage groaned weakly, and blood poured from his mouth as he crawled toward the prince. One of the ShadowMagi spotted Martyn, and a cruel smile spread across his face. A ball of orange flame appeared in front of him, and the Mage drew back his hand as if to throw.

A large form exploded from the tall grass, knocking the ShadowMage to the ground. The Tribesman unsheathed his *dolchek* and buried it into the ShadowMage's body repeatedly, snarling like an animal with each blow. The fireball exploded, engulfing the enemy archers, and they fell screaming to the ground.

The Tribesman arced backward with enough force that his spine snapped. He rose slowly into the air, and the other ShadowMage studied him for a moment before flinging him aside and returning his attention to Martyn. He approached slowly, his sneer turning into a smug smile. The few Guardsmen remaining attacked, but their shafts bounced off thin air. The ShadowMage paid the arrows no more heed than he did the men firing them.

A hand grasped Martyn's knee, and the prince jumped. Cyrrus' flesh had turned a sickly shade, and his eyes were barely open. "I am no Healer," the Mage croaked, "but I did what I could." Beside Martyn, Gregor breathed easier, though his wounds remained.

Cyrrus pushed himself to his feet, heaving with each breath, but his eyes flashed with the power of the Gift as he stood. He focused on the ShadowMage, disgust radiating across his face. "Protect my apprentices, Prince Martyn," he said, lurching forward. The ShadowMage laughed when he saw the broken and burned form running toward him, and his eyes narrowed dangerously. When whatever feat of magic he planned never materialized, fear entered the black-robed Mage's eyes. "For Alrendria and the Assembly!" Cyrrus screamed as he unleashed his Gift.

The air itself exploded, and the ShadowMage's frightened scream cut off abruptly. The blast knocked Martyn to the ground, and he threw his body over Gregor's. Hot wind buffeted them, and something solid smashed against the back of Martyn's head, making the world spin.

When he regained his senses, he found Dayfid standing over him, fighting off a handful of enemy soldiers. "Can you stand, my Prince?" the Guardsman shouted, driving his blade deep into an opponent's gut. "They're right on top of us!"

With a pounding in his head that Martyn thought would never stop, the prince climbed to his feet. He hefted Gregor onto his shoulder and threw the Guard Commander across the back of his horse. Gregor grunted at the rough treatment, but Martyn paid it no heed. He vaulted into the saddle and urged his mount to run. The enemy was almost upon them, the riders closing the distance at breakneck speed, but Malikai and his men had completely broken the Tachan line. The surviving Alrendrians fled up the valley's southern slope.

Martyn passed Malikai at a gallop, and before his horse carried him out of earshot, he heard Malikai bellow for his men to fall back. Arrows followed them up the slope, and he winced at every shaft that buzzed past. *It would be my luck to survive the battle only to fall steps from freedom!*

A strong wind rose, gusting erratically and blowing the enemy's arrows off target. Two Magi stood atop the hill, not far from the treeline. Squads of Guardsmen surrounded each Mage, and several men looked ready to drag the Magi away, should the enemy draw much nearer.

When he crested the hill, Martyn skidded to a stop and turned his horse to view the valley. The Tachans continued their charge, and their numbers far exceeded what remained of Martyn's forces. His men were wounded and exhausted; they would never survive a fight, and they would never be able to outrun the Bull's horsemen.

Martyn smiled. "Now!" he shouted, and hundreds of archers sprang from the trees, where they had hidden since the start of the battle. They ran forward, dodging the stunned Guardsmen who had ridden with Martyn into battle, and formed a line along the hillside. "Fire!" Martyn shouted, and arrows rained down upon the Tachans.

The first volley caught the enemy completely by surprise. Scores of men fell screaming, and those who were not killed instantly were trampled by the men behind them. A second volley flew before the Tachans knew what was happening, and a third before they could react. Hundreds fell before the Tachans turned to flee, and scores more in the panicked rout that followed. Martyn watched with grim satisfaction as a ShadowMage disappeared under the press of soldiers, hauled from his horse and crushed by his own men. Near the base of the valley, two more ShadowMagi stood close together, using their powers to keep the panicked men away. They lashed out with their Gift, striking down any man who drew too close.

Once the last of the enemy left bowshot, a cheer rose among the Alrendrians. "Alrendria!" the Guardsmen shouted. "Alrendria and Prince Martyn!"

Dayfid approached. Sweat slicked his hair, and blood ran from a shallow gash along his cheek. Gore and blood covered his armor. He looked stunned. "An ambush?" he said incredulously. "You never told me!"

"I never told anyone," Martyn said, fighting exhaustion. Now that the fighting was done, the exertion of battle weighed heavily on him. "I suspected a trap and thought to even the odds. Of all those in our initial assault, only Lord Estande, Prince Treloran, and I knew the truth."

Dayfid surveyed the field. "It seems to have worked."

"Not as well as I would have liked," Martyn admitted. "Tylor guessed our plan perfectly. Almost perfectly." Another round of cheers rose from the Guardsmen. Dayfid started to say something else, but Martyn cut him off. "Gather the men and ready them to march. We bloodied Tylor, but we didn't defeat him, and I'd rather be well on our way to Vela before the rest of his army gets through the pass." Dayfid saluted and hurried to carry out his orders.

Weak laughter came from behind Martyn. "I never thought that ridiculous plan would work," Gregor said. Blood dribbled from the Guard Commander's lips, and he coughed, a wracking, wheezing cough that spewed blood on the ground below. "Gods! This hurts."

"We'll get you to Sheriza," Martyn promised. "She'll be able to heal you." Martyn looked at the triumphant faces of his men, listened to their cheers and laughter. Only a fraction of the men he led into the valley had returned, and most of those who lived would bear the scars of this day for the rest of their lives. "They think this is a victory!" He looked into the valley, at all the unmoving shadows dotting it. "A third of Vela's defenses dead, and they think this is a victory!"

"Let them think it," Gregor wheezed. "That's why we came here, remember?" Gregor's eyes fluttered and closed, and his breathing slowed. Martyn stared into the valley for a moment more, then glanced to the northern ridge. He uttered one last prayer for Treloran's safety and ordered his men to return to Vela.

Chapter 35

Jeran's knees buckled when he stepped onto the sand. Dahr caught him as he slumped, steadying him, and Jeran smiled weakly as he struggled to hold his own weight. His skin was ashen and his eyes sunken. For a moment, Dahr thought Jeran might lose consciousness, but he pulled free of Dahr's grasp and took a shambling step forward. "What you did back there..." Dahr said, keeping close in case Jeran fell again. "You're a braver man than I." Jeran smiled weakly, but a bright flash of light stopped them in their tracks and made them shield their eyes.

"Brave is the polite way of saying foolish," Alwen said sternly, brushing dust from her dress. She glared at Jeran for a moment, then shifted her gaze to Dahr, who shivered unconsciously when the Mage's eyes leveled on him. "The last person to address the Assembly so cavalierly was Lorthas, and some of those fools are old enough to remember. From now on, you had best tread carefully around the Magi."

Jeran laughed coldly. "If I have my way, I won't be treading near any of them for quite some time. I meant what I said. If the Magi are unwilling to deal with Lorthas, they can go to the Nothing. I won't save anyone who won't try to save himself." Dahr growled his agreement, and Alwen's eyes narrowed to angry slits. Grendor, who had just stepped through Aemon's Gate, froze at Jeran's words. His eyes widened, and he glanced nervously at Alwen.

"Jeran!" Captain Corrine called. The old sailor ran toward them, moving awkwardly through the sand. "Jeran! A Mage appeared not long ago and demanded ta see yer uncle. I tried ta stop him, but—"

"It's alright, Captain," Jeran assured him. "Dorthal is a Healer. Aemon sent him." As if summoned by the words, Aemon appeared. Behind him, the Gate rotated closed, the silver specks collapsing in upon themselves. "Captain Corrine, this is my grandfather, Aemon. I—"

"Aye," Corrine said, bowing low. "We met before, Great One. Long ago."

"Not so long for all of us," Aemon replied, returning the captain's smile. "At my daughter's wedding, if I recall correctly. You were a friend of Aryn's, a brash young man eager to join the navy." Aemon looked the grizzled sailor up and down. "You've done well for yourself, it seems."

"If I knew we were planning to picnic on the beach all afternoon," Alwen grumbled, "I'd have finished my tea before rushing down here." She fixed a hard gaze on Jeran. "I thought you were in a hurry."

"Alwen's right." Jeran's quick agreement caught the old woman off guard. For once, Alwen had nothing to say. "We can talk aboard ship. Where's Aryn?"

"Aboard the *Vengeance*, lad," Corrine answered, pointing to a three-masted Raker bobbing in the waves several thousand hands from shore. "Yer mounts an' yer gear's been loaded too. The Fleet's ready ta sail."

Jeran started forward purposefully. He stumbled again but caught himself and shrugged off Dahr's and Grendor's helping hands. "I'll be fine," he said roughly, moving forward at a more measured pace.

"Do you want me to open another Gate?" Aemon asked.

"No." Jeran fixed his eyes on the shore. A longboat waited in the shallows. It was no more than two thousand hands away, but Dahr wondered if Jeran could make the distance. He tested his weight with every step and moved more slowly with every passing moment. "The longboat needs to be returned; we might as well take it."

Dahr knew the truth. The Magi were sure to be watching after Jeran's performance in front of the Assembly, and Jeran would not show them any weakness, no matter how exhausted he was. Aemon suspected Jeran's true motive too. "There's no need to prove yourself to them. What you did in there was—"

"Ill advised." Alwen finished. "You risk losing control of your Gift every time you seize so much magic. You don't have the training necessary to—"

"I'm aware of my limitations," Jeran snapped, and that his emotions floated so close to the surface was a greater sign of exhaustion than the way he fought for every breath. Jeran quickened his pace, leaving the two Magi behind. He waved the others away too, but Grendor and Dahr took up positions to either side of him despite his dark scowl.

Grendor looked at the waves crashing on the shore and swallowed nervously. "Friend Jeran," he called, but when Jeran's expression remained fixed on the horizon, he turned to Dahr. "Friend Dahr, how big is the ocean?"

"I don't know," Dahr admitted. Silently, he applauded the Orog's performance. Grendor had proven himself brave, but from his behavior Dahr could almost believe the Orog feared the water. It was just the thing to draw Jeran from his malaise; he could not stand to see his friends in pain. "Large enough that you can't see from one side to the other. Large enough that ships can sail for days without spotting land."

Grendor's face turned as pale as Jeran's, and he dropped his eyes to the sand at his feet. Jeran turned to say something and stumbled again; when Grendor took his arm, Jeran did not pull away. Dahr ducked his head in approval of the tactic and followed them to the longboat.

It was a tight fit, and the surf was rough. The longboat rose with every wave only to crash down into the next trough, sending walls of water cascading over the bow. Grendor kept up his act until they reached the *Vengeance*, cringing every time the boat rose and wincing when it fell. The Orog's terror kept Jeran occupied until the longboat bounced against the *Vengeance*'s hull.

A rope ladder rolled down the side of the vessel, and Captain Corrine waved for Jeran to take the lead. "After you, Lord Odara," Corrine said with a broad smile. The short rest had done wonders for Jeran; he sprang to his feet with renewed vigor and climbed the ladder. Dahr followed close behind.

Thunderous cheers greeted Jeran when he reached the deck. Listening to shouts of 'Long Live Lord Odara!' made Dahr's jaw clench, and he leaned in close. "How does it feel to be a hero?"

"I wish I were back on the farm," Jeran replied as he smiled and waved to the cheering men. "A hero?" he repeated, dismissing the word with a shake of his head. "What have I done to deserve it?"

Dahr laughed coldly. Jeran's humility, feigned or not, grated on his nerves. "You escaped from Tylor Durange and the Darklord, saved these men from ShadowMagi, and without pause stormed up the mountain to chastise the entire Mage Assembly. Now you plan to lead them against the Black Fleet and an army of Tachans. And you wonder why they think you're a hero?"

Jeran turned to face the mountain where the Assembly hid and his expression grew blank. "I did nothing up there but cost Alrendria allies, and death followed my flight from Dranakohr. You don't think Tylor let my escape go unpunished, do you?" His eyes roamed the *Vengeance* again; this time, as his gaze passed over the cheering crew and excited Guardsmen, Jeran's good humor faded. "More likely than not, I'm leading these men to deaths, too."

Caring hurts, Dahr thought as his eyes swept across the deck. Images of Katya flashed through his mind, and his hands clenched into fists. "Focus on your goal, not on those who might die. It will make it easier."

Something in the way Dahr spoke made Jeran wary. "You say that as if you don't care about them."

"About the Guard? About Alrendria?" Dahr knew how he should answer; he knew what Jeran wanted to hear, but Jeran had always been able to peel away the layers around his words and get to the truth hidden beneath. He shook his head. "I once cared about a lot of things, but caring nearly cost you your life and Alrendria its prince. Now, all I care about is you and Aryn. And revenge." He gestured at the men. "I don't want these men to die, but if they must die to ensure Tylor's fall and the defeat of the Durange, then so be it."

It sounded heartless; Dahr knew that. But it was how he felt, and he could change it no more than he could change the tides. He waited for Jeran to rail at him, to tell him how disappointed he was. Instead, Jeran turned away. "I hope someday you understand that what happened wasn't your fault."

Those simple words cut more deeply than any argument would have. *It was my fault!* Dahr felt the first stirrings of the Blood Rage. He reached out to grab Jeran's shoulder and force him back around, but before he could, Captain Corrine leapt over the rail.

"That's enough!" the captain shouted. "Back ta yer posts, ya lazy fools! This is war, not a victory parade. Save the cheerin' fer the harbor!" He stopped between Jeran and Dahr, and once certain the crew could not see his face, he smiled. "Fine bunch a boys I got here. An' not a one of 'em that doesna love ya, Jeran." He watched with pride as the crew bustled about the ship. "You get us ta Vela, lad," he added, clapping Jeran on the shoulder, "an' they'll follow ya ta the ends of the world."

"Captain," Jeran asked, "how important is this ship to you?"

Corrine frowned, and he scrubbed a hand through his grey-flecked beard. "She's a fine vessel, lad, the finest I've ever sailed, but if gets these boys where they need ta be and costs the Bull a few black-robes, I'd consider her loss a fair trade."

Jeran frowned thoughtfully. "If I only had a few more Magi."

"Will four be enough?" Oto asked. Dahr whirled around to find a stout oak door standing upright on the deck behind him. The door opened and the rotund Mage stepped through, a cluster of nervous, wide-eyed children at his heels. Three Magi followed the apprentices. "The apprentices can't do much," Oto added, "but they want to help too."

When the last Mage closed the door, it faded from sight. "Oto, what are you doing here?" Jeran asked. Though he seemed excited, Dahr noted the wary eye Jeran kept on the Magi, and he backed away, easing his greatsword in its scabbard. Against Magi, the blade would do him little good, but if it came to blows, he would rather die with a weapon in his hand.

"We're accepting your offer," Oto replied. "The Assembly will debate until Lorthas knocks on their door, and I've no more patience for fools who refuse to even believe our enemy knows where—!" Oto's rant cut off when he tripped over a coil of rope. He fell heavily to the deck, and two of the apprentices helped him regain his feet.

"Thank you, children," Oto said, patting one apprentice's head fondly. "If you could find me a place to sit, somewhere out of the way, it would be appreciated." One of the boys took Oto's hand and navigated the Mage across the deck. Jeran walked beside them, but Dahr stayed back a few steps and kept an eye on the other Magi.

"Valkov thinks the Black Fleet is here to watch the Alrendrians," Oto scoffed, "but those ships are here to keep the Magi bottled up, I'd bet my life on it! Lorthas must have agents among the Assembly. He must! How easy it must be for him to play one faction against another." Oto became agitated as he spoke, his skin turned bright red, his unblinking eyes bugged out, and the vein at his temple throbbed. Dahr sensed the Mage's anger and fed off of it. "Not even Lelani believes me! No one will consider the possibility that not all Magi can be trusted, that ShadowMagi walk among us."

One of the three Magi following Dahr whispered something, and Jeran cast a suspicious glance in their direction. "Now, Jeran," Oto admonished, "do you really think I'd bring people with me you couldn't trust? I thought…" He paused for a moment, and then warm laughter echoed across the deck. "Then again, you've known me less than a day, so maybe you *should* be suspicious."

The apprentice led Oto to a bench nestled in the shadow of one of the *Vengeance*'s three masts. Jeran sat beside Oto, but Dahr kept his distance. "Why do you think I'm suspicious of the Magi?" Jeran asked.

"I can't see," Oto chuckled, "but that doesn't mean I'm blind. You suspect almost everyone, and with good reason! Even without the Gift, I'd be a fool not to know that." He pointed to the nearest Mage, a hard-faced man with a crooked nose and a scar running the length of his jaw. "Nashime is the closest thing we still have to a BattleMage. The two shorter men are Falco and Adias. They have a talent I thought you might find useful."

A loud crash drew their attention. Grendor stood in the center of a throng of sailors. The men pressed in, whispering to each other and reaching out to prod the Orog, as if to make sure he were real. Grendor shied away, his skin dark grey. In the process, he tripped a passing crewman, knocking the crate in his arms to the ground and scattering its contents across the deck.

The crash drew the Magi's attention, and they seemed interested in Grendor, too. Falco and Adias, flanked by the apprentices, hurried toward the Orog, and the sailors parted around the Magi to let them pass. Nashime held his place, stone-faced and cross-armed, but his eyes remained on Grendor, his expression thoughtful. "Someone should talk to them about that," Oto said, clearing his throat. "There's no need to make the poor boy feel like an exhibit in a menagerie."

"You said those two Magi had a talent?" Jeran prompted.

"What? Oh yes! Both are adept at manipulating the weather, especially the wind."

A broad smile spread across Jeran's face, and he gripped Oto's shoulder fondly. "Thank you. You've solved my final problem." Standing, Jeran told the apprentice at Oto's side to find Aemon and the captain. Then he hurried off. Dahr followed.

They met Dorthal at the door to the captain's cabin. The Healer looked haggard, his eyes sunken and his expression grim. "What happened?" Jeran demanded, grabbing the Mage roughly. "What's wrong?"

"Nothing," Dorthal said wearily. "Nothing that magic can cure." Disgust flitted across the Mage's face. "What they did to him... Layer upon layer of hurt, taken over the course of winters and never properly healed. Tylor Durange is a monster; Madryn will be a far better place when he's gone."

"And his mind?" Jeran prompted. "Will he—"

"There's nothing wrong with him," Dorthal said curtly. "Nothing that magic can heal. He's built walls to protect himself, and only he has the power to bring those walls down." The Healer drew a slow breath, and when he next looked at Jeran, a measure of his calm had returned. "I apologize, Lord Odara. Needless suffering frustrates me, and encountering something I can't heal frustrates me more. Your uncle has improved since you found him?"

At Jeran's nod, Dorthal tapped his upper lip with a measured rhythm. "With time, I believe he will heal. Familiar places and familiar people will speed his recovery, and as the memories of his confinement fade, he will improve." The Healer went to leave, but after taking a handful of steps, he stopped. "I was only a child when the MageWar ended, and I thought the tales of Lorthas exaggerated, but Aemon claims the Bull is just a tool of the Darklord, another weapon in Lorthas' hand." Dorthal's expression contorted angrily. "After seeing what they did to your uncle, for no reason other than revenge, I can't ignore the truth any longer. You have my support, even if it means defying the Assembly."

Dorthal left, and Jeran ducked into the captain's cabin with Dahr a step behind. The room was spartan, even more barren than Corrine's cabin aboard the River Falcon. Charts of varying size hung from the walls, and several maps were clamped to a table that itself was bolted to the deck. Two small chests lay secured in one corner and a hammock swung across the other. A large window filled the rear wall. The open ocean stretched from horizon to horizon.

Aryn sat beneath the hammock, huddled in the corner with his arms wrapped around his knees. He looked up when they entered, squinting at the bright light pouring through the doorway. "Tylor?" he called out, unconsciously pushing back against the wall. "Back so soon?"

"I'm not Tylor," Jeran quickly said. "It's me, Uncle Aryn. It's Jeran."

"Jeran," Aryn repeated. The word carried an aching sadness with it. "I failed him, you know. Tylor caught him. I failed them both."

Seeing Aryn reduced to such a state enraged Dahr. Aryn's sobs knifed at his heart, and seeing the moisture glistening in Jeran's eyes made him wish that he, too, could still weep. He felt the Blood Rage coming upon him, the quickened breathing and inability to think about anything other than vengeance.

Suddenly, Aryn pushed away from Jeran. "You have to take me with you. Tylor must pay!"

"Peace, Uncle," Jeran said. "There'll be time enough for revenge tomorrow." Jeran went to the table and hefted a pitcher from the hole in which it was secured. He poured a cup half full and mixed in a small amount of powder from a tin Alwen had given to him. "Here," Jeran said, offering the cup to Aryn. "It will help you sleep." Aryn lifted the cup slowly, suspiciously. Jeran sighed. "I'll drink some myself, if it will convince you."

After a long pause, Aryn shook his head. "No. I trust you. I want to." In one swift motion, he gulped the contents of the cup.

The effect was almost instantaneous. As Aryn's head drooped, Jeran and Dahr pulled him from the floor and settled him in the hammock. "What about you?" Dahr asked. "After what you did today, you need rest more than he does."

"I have to talk to Aemon. But I'll sleep after that." Jeran's eyes flicked toward Aryn. "Will you stay with him?" Dahr nodded, and Jeran left. He sat on the floor across from Aryn and stared at his one-time protector, imagining ways to make Tylor pay.

* * * * * * * * * * * * * * * * * * * *

A mast creaked loudly, and the groaning wood startled Dahr from his dark musings. He shifted, stretching muscles long since stiffened and took comfort in the press of his sword against his back. He reached over his shoulder and gently caressed the hilt. *Soon*, he thought grimly, but with more than a hint of anticipation. *Soon.*

Dahr stood alone at the bow of the *Vengeance*, eyes alert. Clouds blanketed the sky and few stars pierced the canopy, their weak flickering doing little more than accentuating the darkness. Water lapped against the hull as the *Vengeance* raced south around Atol Domiar, but the sound of the spray was the only noise; at the captain's orders, no man was to speak above a whisper until they engaged the enemy.

Lookouts stood atop the masts and more men clung to the rigging, watching the horizon for any sign of life. Dahr knew he should be up there, too—his eyes and ears were keener than any of Corrine's sailor's—but he had no wish to share the company of men. They were not his people; theirs was not his cause.

Fang growled, and the sound rumbled through the night air. "I know," Dahr whispered. His lips twitched up in the semblance of a smile as he absently stroked the hound's head. "I hate waiting, too."

Another growl echoed across the deck, and Dahr's scowl returned. "They are *not* my people," he insisted, "or I'm not theirs. I betrayed them every bit as much as she did, and they know it." Disagreement flowed through the bond he shared with Fang. They were not words, exactly, the thoughts received, nor images. It was more complex, a combination of things jumbled together. He was not even sure how he knew the thoughts were Fang's; he just knew.

Dahr growled in response, but Fang showed no reaction to the threat. The two of them faced off for a time, but Dahr turned away first. *The truth is, I don't stay away from them because they think I'm a traitor. I stay away because they think I'm a hero.*

He had gloated at Jeran's reaction to the crew's praise. Seeing the smug confidence wiped from his face and watching his embarrassment as he tried to deny what he was had brought Dahr a measure of joy. That Jeran had survived his trials unscathed, that he had emerged from Dranakohr unscarred, clawed at Dahr's innards. To see even a hint of uncertainty, of anxiety, of *humanity* in Jeran's eyes made him feel better, though it shamed him to admit it, even to himself.

When the crew had started cheering him, though, his amusement quickly faded. The tales they told were exaggerated and embellished. They attributed Alrendria's alliance with the Tribesmen to him and claimed he had forced the Garun'ah and Elves to set aside their differences. In whispers, they spoke of his wild charge against the Bull, his suicidal attempt to save Jeran. They talked of him as if he were as much a hero as Jeran, and he was too much of a coward to tell them the truth.

A wave of shame threatened to quench the white-hot rage consuming him. He could forgive himself for opening his heart to the enemy—she had deceived him at least as much as he had deceived himself!—but for the rest, there could be no forgiveness. When the lives of his friends had hung in the balance, he had acted, not to save his prince or rescue his brother, but to satiate his own need for revenge. At the crucial moment when Katya's betrayal was realized, Dahr's only thought had been to kill her. To kill Tylor. To kill everyone with a drop of Durange blood in their veins. That was his secret; that was his disgrace.

Another image came to him, this time from Shyrock. The eagle's eyes were not meant for night, but Dahr had insisted that he look for the Black Fleet and Shyrock had been willing. Danger and threat permeated the eagle's warning, but the images were garbled, distorted, and hard to separate. Dahr could not tell if Shyrock had seen a ship or something else entirely, but whatever it was that had frightened him, it was headed their way. Dahr strained his eyes and peered into the gloom.

A break in the clouds let through a glimmer of starlight, and a dark silhouette appeared no more than two hundred hands away. The shape was odd, not like that of a Raker, but it paralleled their course and Corrine's fleet had several Royan and Arkamian vessels with it, so Dahr was not sure if it was an enemy vessel. He called to Shyrock, asking the eagle to move in closer, but before he could, a light flared, a ball of pale luminescence hovering over the shoulder of a black-robed man. The light was weak and well-hidden, but Dahr knew that none of the Magi would have raised a light. Aemon's orders had been explicit.

Dahr sucked in a breath to shout warning to the Magi standing ready on the *Vengeance*'s deck, but then he saw her, and the words froze in his mouth. Dressed in armor that highlighted the curves of her lithe figure, Katya strode onto the deck of the enemy vessel. The ShadowMage's light illuminated her flame red hair, hair that fell in tight curls past her shoulders. Green eyes swept over the waves, passing over Dahr. As they did, Dahr felt a chill, part bitter anger and part deep longing. He wanted to cry out, to scream for the Magi to incapacitate the vessel, but he could not.

Katya's gaze moved back, and this time she saw him. Her eyes widened slightly, but when Dahr made no move, her lips pulled up in a smile. She signaled, and the ShadowMage's light faded. Before blackness enveloped her completely, she ducked her head in thanks, her eyes never leaving Dahr's, and touched her fingers to her lips in parting.

"You must love her very much," Lorthas said, stepping from the shadows.

Dahr whirled around to face the Darklord. "You! What are you—" Realization quickly dawned. "A dream! I've asked you to stay away from my dreams."

"I could not help myself, little brother," Lorthas apologized. Fiery red eyes regarded Dahr with sympathy. "I've always had a weakness for tales of love."

"I don't love her," Dahr insisted, the lie grating against his teeth. "She betrayed me. She betrayed everything I cared about. I hate her."

"The two often go together," Lorthas said, almost sadly, as he took a seat on a narrow wooden bench. He waved for Dahr to join him, but Dahr refused. With a resigned shrug, the Darklord settled back and sipped from a glass of wine.

Dahr looked for Fang, but the dog was no longer there. He reached out in his mind, but sensed nothing, neither bird nor beast answered his summons. *A dream*, he reminded himself. *This is all a dream.*

"You're better off without her, you know." The Darklord's words struck a nerve, and Lorthas did not fail to notice Dahr's reaction. He shook his head. "She's just like her uncle, and we all know the kind of man Tylor Durange is. Just ask Jeran."

"I don't want to hear this from you!" Dahr snapped, his anger returning. "I don't want anything to do with you!" He started to run away, but a wall of air held him in place.

"If not from me, then who?" Lorthas asked. "No one else has the courage to tell you the truth. Jeran sees it, but even he lacks the will to face you." Dahr winced at the last and squeezed his eyes shut, praying to wake. "Ah, you've seen it then," Lorthas said with a smile. "The disappointment in his eyes. The pity. The fear... No one knows how you feel more than I do, little brother. I saw the same look in Aemon's eyes once, long ago. They don't understand your pain, because they haven't experienced it. They never will. But I have. I know what you've suffered, and I sympathize."

Dahr struggled against the bonds holding him in place. He glared at the Darklord, but Lorthas showed no reaction. Gently setting his glass upon the bench, Lorthas walked toward him, circling him slowly. His gaze burned into Dahr's soul. "Shame grates within you," he whispered, and Dahr's mouth went dry. "You feel as if you've failed everyone, everything. You feel as if the Gods have tested you and found you wanting. You struggled to the best of your abilities, did everything you could, and it wasn't enough."

Lorthas leaned in until their faces were only a finger's width apart. "You tire of seeing the guilty thrive and the innocent punished. You tire of failing, of watching evil triumph despite your best efforts to stop it. Your frustration turns to anger, and that anger becomes a hate you must struggle to control. You tire of fighting—only a God would not!—and you want to strike out against those who caused your pain. You want to—"

"I am not you!" Dahr shouted. The Blood Rage consumed him; rational thought began to fade. He thrashed against Lorthas' magic until his body ached from the effort.

"No," the Darklord agreed. "You're not like me. In fact, you're in danger of becoming something far worse."

The Darklord's words hit Dahr like a thunderbolt. The Blood Rage fled, and a cold dread replaced it. "What... What do you mean?"

"I harness my anger, using it against whatever threatens me and to protect those I care about. You, however, fear your anger. You flee from it. You deny its existence. It builds inside you like a volcano until you have no choice but to lash out. You have no control; you rage at everything, even those things closest to you. That will be your undoing, little brother. To save yourself, you must take control. Either that, or you risk losing yourself entirely."

"No!" Dahr refused to believe, but this was the Twilight World. He knew Lorthas could not lie here, but the implications of the Darklord's words stung him to the core of his being. "I don't believe you."

"Then ask Jeran. Or even Aemon!" Lorthas replied. He smiled at the last. "How it will gall him to agree with me, but he'll have no choice. He cares about you too much to deny the truth just to spite me."

"I don't believe you!" Dahr yelled, but his words lacked conviction.

"I don't have time for these games," Lorthas sighed. "Believe what you will; that is your prerogative. But believe this: Tylor will reach Vela in two days time. If you want to save the city—and your prince—you had best make sure you reach the harbor by sunset."

A tense silence spanned the distance between Dahr and the Darklord. "Why should I believe you?"

"Because I have nothing to gain by misleading you," Lorthas said. "And because, in the Twilight World, I cannot." When the explanation did not sway Dahr, Lorthas frowned. "Tylor is a despicable creature. I've watched him brutalize people for winters and said nothing. I tried to convince myself that the ends, *my* ends, would justify his means, that the death of a hundred innocents would be a small price to pay for a Madryn where everyone, even Magi, could live without fear of persecution.

"Inaction has proven to be a poor choice. By turning a blind eye on his acts, I've only made Tylor bolder. He takes greater liberties, and his list of atrocities grows. What he did to Jeran, for no reason other than vengeance..." Lorthas' lips pressed into a thin, bloodless line, and he turned away so Dahr could not see his face. "I can no longer in good conscience ally myself with such a man. Tylor Durange is everything I hate about our world; he represents everything I spent my life fighting. He thinks he's safe, that the Boundary protects him from me. He thinks he can use my men and Magi to make Madryn his."

Lorthas' lips drew back in a sneer, and Dahr's own anger flared up in response. His pulse quickened, and as he stared at Lorthas, he shared something with the Darklord, something that both repulsed and excited him. "This I tell you truly, Dahr. Even were it to cost me my own life, I would do anything to hasten Tylor's journey to the grave. That man is without compassion. Without love."

The bond between them broke, and the connection Dahr had momentarily felt fled. Harsh laughter bubbled up from deep inside. "Love? What do you know of love?"

"Far more than you, little brother," Lorthas answered, smiling sadly. Dahr heard the ache in the Darklord's voice, saw the longing in his eyes. "And the story is not a happy one, though, in truth, it is not so different from your own. I once loved a Mage of great beauty and wisdom, a woman of interminable spirit.

She was one of the few who saw beyond my frail, withered body and loved the man inside. We were so similar, she and I, and we shared so much, including a vision of the future, a future where Magi no longer lived in fear of commons.

"I thought we were united in purpose, that our souls were one. But when I told her that the Assembly's endless vacillation would lead to our destruction and insisted that we take the fight to the commons, she betrayed me. She warned Aemon and turned the Assembly against me."

Lorthas met Dahr's eyes, and his pain matched the pain in Dahr's heart. "Over the centuries, I've tried to forgive her, but the wound she left was deep."

As suddenly as it appeared, the wall of air was gone, and Dahr was free to move again. Instead of fleeing, he turned toward Lorthas. "What you said about Tylor... It was the truth?"

Lorthas nodded, and Dahr opened his mouth to ask another question, but a new voice beat him to it. "I had not thought you so foolish as to come this close to me, Lorthas. Not even in the Twilight World." Dahr moved involuntarily toward the shadows, frightened to be discovered in the presence of the Darklord.

A young woman stormed toward them across the empty deck. Short—her head barely reached Dahr's chest—and slight of frame, she stalked toward them with a power that belied her stature. Curls the color of cornsilk framed a pretty face, and lips of cherry red drew up in a cool, confident grin. Twin orbs the color of the sky glared daggers at Lorthas. She spared a brief, disappointed glance at Dahr. "And you! I knew you had secrets, but this...!" Anger flushed her cheeks, and Dahr stepped away, even though his motion took him closer to the Darklord.

Lorthas' eyebrow rose, and he smiled appreciatively. "A stunning image," he said, eyeing the woman from head to toe. "But one should not live in the past." He waved his hand casually, and the beautiful woman withered into a far more familiar form.

"You made a grave mistake coming here," Alwen snarled, hobbling forward on her cane.

"You are no threat to me," Lorthas said absently. His smile was gone; regret now tinged his voice. "Ah, Alwen, the winters have not been kind."

"Kind enough," she replied. "Kinder than you were."

"Do you hear death approaching, Alwen? Do you feel his breath upon your neck? As the twilight of life settles upon your stooped shoulders, do you finally realize the simple truth I tried to explain to you so long ago?" Alwen stopped a few strides from Lorthas, and the Darklord's smirk returned. "Yassik never understood. While he was my... guest... I tried to explain it to him, but I could never make him see. But you... I always had faith in you."

Alwen's jaw clenched. "For what you did to him... I've tried not to hate you, Lorthas, but I can't forgive you for what you did to him." As if just remembering that they were not alone, Alwen spun toward Dahr. "This does not concern you," she said brusquely. With a snap of her fingers, Dahr jerked awake.

He was in Corrine's cabin; across from him, Aryn slept fitfully in the hammock. Dahr fled the room, drawing deep breaths of the cool sea air and trying to calm his pounding heart. He saw Jeran standing with Aemon and the captain, and he hurried to join them. "Then you can do it?" Jeran asked as Dahr approached. After a pause, Aemon nodded.

"It's dangerous, but I think so. I certainly don't have a better idea."

"Dangerous?" Captain Corrine guffawed. "Dangerous is nae the word. What the lad plans is suicide." Seeing Dahr, the captain roared a laugh and waved him over. "Are ya in on this too, lad?" Before Dahr could say that he had no idea what they were talking about, the captain clapped him on the shoulder. "I shoulda known as much. Well, Kohr damn me if I have a better plan. Give me two days ta ready the men and—"

"We have to leave now," Dahr interrupted. "Tylor attacks in two days."

Aemon arched an eyebrow and stroked his beard thoughtfully. The captain laughed even harder. "How could ya possibly know that, lad?"

Dahr fixed his eyes on Jeran. "I know."

After a moment, Jeran nodded. "Captain, Mage Adias will help you visit the other ships. We sail at nightfall. Aemon, find Oto and figure out how best to deploy the Magi we have." The captain and Aemon disappeared, leaving Jeran alone on the deck with Dahr. "Let's go back to the cabin. I want to hear everything he told you." The look he fixed on Dahr was every bit as powerful as Lorthas'. "Everything."

Chapter 36

Dahr staggered from the cabin and was surprised to find the sun low in the western sky. The discussion had seemed brief, with Jeran probing relentlessly for details of his conversation with Lorthas. Dahr quickly went on the defensive, and although he volunteered most information willingly, he prided himself on the few secrets he kept, like Katya's presence in the dream and the bond he had felt with the Darklord. The interrogation left them exhausted, and Jeran now slept fitfully, wrapped in a coarse blanket on the deck of the captain's cabin. Dahr, too, yearned for sleep, but he dared not risk a return to the Twilight World or his dreams. Both were haunted.

He wandered the deck of the *Vengeance*, surprised by the changes that had taken place. Gone were the piles of weapons and goods destined for Vela. The few remaining crates were in ordered formations stacked two high. The sailors moved about frantically, tying off lines and readying the ship to sail. Soldiers gathered in the stern, taking commands from a gruff-looking Guardswoman named Dharva whom Dahr had once met in Kaper. She had a rough tongue, a short temper, and little patience for those who did not follow orders.

In the bow, a smaller group of Guardsmen waited. Each wore full armor and carried a near-bursting sack slung over one shoulder. All but a few looked terrified. Captain Corrine stood in front of them arguing with a gaunt Mage with close-cropped hair and black eyes. The Mage leaned wearily against the rail with one hand wrapped around the polished wood. It looked like that grip was the only thing keeping him upright.

The Mage listened to the captain, and when Corrine pointed to a vessel anchored less than two hundred hands away, the Mage followed the finger with his eyes. After a long pause, he nodded, and a Gate opened on the *Vengeance*'s deck, a wavering blur that slowly steadied itself. "Six," the Mage croaked. "Only six."

Not a man moved; even the eager ones looked frightened now. It took an order barked by the captain to get six Guardsmen to step forward. From the terrified glances they shared, they half expected the Gate to close on them. "If ya are nae through that Gate afore I reach ya," Corrine yelled, "I'll shove the lot of ya over the deck." The captain's angry stance made anywhere, even the Nothing, seem a better place to be than the deck of the *Vengeance*, and the Guardsmen leapt forward, eyes closed. As soon as the last man passed, the Gate collapsed, and with it, the Mage.

"No more," he said, waving away the captain's hand. "Not for a time."

"We sail now, Mage," Corrine replied. "And I'll not have these boys crowdin' me deck. Lord Odara said everyone not needed must be sent ta other ships."

"I can do no more," the Mage snapped. "There are limits to every man's Gift!" He cut off abruptly and drew slow, deep breaths. When he spoke again, his tone was calmer. "My apologies, Captain, but I can not help. I have a part to play in the battle, too; if I overextend myself, I won't be able to do what I must. Over there," he gestured with his chin. "See the man in the dark robes. That's Nashime. He may be able to help you."

For a moment, Dahr thought the Captain meant to argue, but instead he turned his back on the Mage. "Leave four," the Mage said weakly. "I can take four."

Corrine nodded brusquely and selected out four Guardsmen, the four smallest, to stay. The rest he ordered to follow him, and he started toward the dark-robed man with short, purposeful strides. He squinted at the sun as he walked, gauging the time, and mumbled something as he passed Dahr that sounded a lot like a prayer.

Dahr turned to follow the captain and nearly ran over a child. The boy, who could not have been more than eight winters old, stumbled back, his eyes widening as he stared up at Dahr's towering form. Seeing the child's terror, Dahr fought down a surge of anger. Instead of lashing out, he mumbled an apology and made to walk around.

"Wait!" the boy said nervously, and when Dahr turned to face him, he licked his lips. "*Jo'kalla. Oto miessta Hunssa da noch.*" He pointed to one of the ships and smiled proudly.

"What?" Dahr asked, his expression blank.

"Did... Did I say it wrong?" the boy asked in a squeaky voice. "I studied Garu at the Academy."

"The only language I speak is this one," Dahr growled, and the boy backed up another two steps. Beads of sweat sprouted on his brow. "Peace, boy! Haven't you heard that Tribesmen are little more than trained animals? I'm no more dangerous to you than a caged bear." He smiled to show he meant no harm, but if anything, the apprentice looked more frightened than ever. "What did you want to tell me?" Dahr asked, his patience wearing thin.

"Mage Oto sent me." He started hesitantly, but by the time he finished his words came out in a rush. "He wanted you to know that your dog and horse were moved to one of the other boats, where they would be safe."

"Fang? Jardelle?" Dahr whirled around, searching the deck, and he stretched out his thoughts. He could not sense them; they were too far away for him to contact. "Where?" he snapped, fastening angry eyes on the boy. "Where was she sent?"

"I... I don't... There," the boy stammered, pointing to a distant ship. "Mage Oto told me to tell you."

Embarrassed, Dahr lowered himself to a crouch. He still had several fingers on the boy, but their heights were more of a match. He thought it would put the child at ease. "Thank Oto for me," Dahr said, "and I should—" He had hoped to apologize, but tempering his voice proved difficult; he was angry at himself, at his lack of control, and some of that anger seeped out.

The boy did not wait for Dahr to finish. "I... I have to go," he said, backing away. "Mage Oto said we'd be going to our ship soon."

"Wait!" Dahr called, grabbing for the boy. With a squeak, the child ran, nearly knocking two sailors overboard in the process. "Wait," Dahr called again, lowering his eyes to the deck.

When he looked up, Alwen stood before him, and Dahr fell back startled. He grunted when his tailbone slammed into the deck. Alwen snorted, and the disapproving look she directed at him did little to quench his boiling blood. "Any fool knew you'd grow to be a giant," she told him, "but even I thought you'd end up with more than half a wit."

Dahr quickly regained his feet. He towered over Alwen, but somehow, he still felt as if she were looking down at him. "I didn't mean to frighten the boy," he said reluctantly. "It was just—"

"If you think I'm talking about the poor apprentice you just sent leaping across the deck like a frightened rabbit, then you're even more of a fool than I thought." She thumped her cane against Dahr's chest for emphasis.

His jaw clenched, and Dahr braced himself for what he knew was to come. "I don't want to talk about it."

"I should imagine not," Alwen sniffed. "Chatting with the Darklord like he was your childhood friend. Standing face to face with the most hateful man in Madryn's history and not so much as batting an eye or stammering in fear. I'm half surprised I didn't come across you sipping wine or enjoying a hot cup of tea." Dahr turned away at the last, hoping Alwen mistook the red in his cheeks for anger. He *had* shared wine with Lorthas on many of his visits.

Alwen rolled her eyes toward the heavens. "Why must I always surround myself with idiots?" she asked before returning her gaze to Dahr. "Did you forget who he was? The Darklord is not a man for casual conversation. How long has this been going on?" Dahr did not answer. "Why are you protecting him? What do you have to hide?"

"ME!?" Dahr thundered, drawing the eyes of everyone in earshot. He cast a dark glare across the deck, and those who turned toward the sound quickly found themselves more interested in their work than in whatever Dahr had to say to the Mage. "You never shared your relationship to the Darklord, why should I share mine?"

"My relationship with Lorthas is common knowledge to anyone old enough for it to matter. But you," she said, thumping his chest again, "thought you could keep yours secret. Did you think Lorthas was the only Mage who could enter the Twilight World?"

Suddenly, Dahr realized what Alwen was intimating, and the anger he had tried to bottle up boiled to the surface. "You think I'm a traitor?" He spoke quietly, but his words carried a menace that made Alwen's eyebrows rise despite his calm tone. "I never sought Lorthas! He found me and dragged me into the Twilight World against my will. I had no choice but to listen; where else was I to go?"

Alwen opened her mouth, but before she could speak, Dahr grabbed her by the waist and lifted her so they stared at each other eye to eye. He trembled with the effort of holding her gently; every instinct he had begged him to squeeze. She fastened her hawkish glare on him, and he laughed. "There was a time when that frown would have had me cowering beneath my bedrolls for days, but I'm a child no longer. You think I'd betray Alrendria? You think I'd betray Jeran? You may be a great Mage, but you're as blind as Oto."

Her piercing gaze delved into his soul, but Dahr stood unphased. He had thought his words a bluff; now he realized he had spoken truly. He was not afraid of Alwen anymore. He was not afraid of anything. "Look as much as you want," he told her, setting her gently on the deck. "Stare to my very core if you must. You will find no traitor."

Alwen straightened her skirt, smoothing the wrinkles from the fine material. Then, without warning, her hand jerked back and she swung her staff. Dahr caught the swing easily, and a smug, self-satisfied grin spread across his face. "The next time you want to hit me," he told her, "you had best use your Gift, else you might find—"

The blow made Dahr's head jerk back, and his eyes watered from the sting of it. He dropped Alwen and rubbed his jaw, and the old woman smirked as she wrested her cane away from him. "We will talk about this later," she told him in no uncertain terms. "After we've given our blood a chance to cool."

She started to walk away, but paused. "A word of warning, if you're wise enough to take it from a blind old woman." She waited for Dahr's nod. "For all his faults, Lorthas wants the same thing as Aemon: Peace between the Four Races. The only difference between them is the means by which they try to reach that goal. It's his path that makes Lorthas evil, not his destination. Truth is only an abstraction of perception." Dahr frowned in confusion, and Alwen explained. "If Lorthas believes he's a misunderstood savior, then it's true, at least to him. It's all a matter of perception. The Twilight World can't distinguish between what a person believes and what is actually true."

"Truth is truth," Dahr replied stubbornly. "If you told me this ship could fly, even if you believed it, that doesn't mean it would. It's a ship, nothing more."

"Just because a thing does not fly doesn't mean it can't. And if I believed... Well, Yassik is fond of saying that anything's possible." Dahr started to speak, but Alwen cut him short. "This conversation grows too philosophical for my taste, and I'm too tired to argue semantics. If you need proof, you need look only at yourself. Some might call you Garun'ah. You have the look, the bearing, your emotions run close to the surface. But some might call you Human. You act Human. You speak Human. You say 'please' and 'thank you' and eat your meals with a knife and fork. Most of the time, at least. What's the truth? Are you one or the other? Both? Neither? Ask a hundred people, like as not you'll get a hundred answers, and each one just as true."

Dahr shook his head, and Alwen walked away. "Think on what I've said," she told him. "And remember, this conversation is far from finished." She slid smoothly across the deck and disappeared in the commotion.

"Ready the sails!" Captain Corrine boomed down from the wheel tower. With a great flapping sound, the canvas rose. The sails billowed out as the wind caught them, and the *Vengeance* lurched forward. Dahr cast his eyes out to the water, where hundreds of other sails rose in unison. He turned his gaze up to the wheel tower and saw Captain Corrine standing proudly at the helm, a broad grin on his face.

Dahr raced to the bow to watch the fleet. He relished the feel of the salty air on his face, and grinned as the *Vengeance* pulled to the front of the armada. The other vessels took position behind them, forming a wedge that cut across the Western Sea. The shores of Atol Domiar raced by, and the *Vengeance* skipped across the surface, jumping from wave to wave.

She's flying, Dahr thought as he felt the mighty vessel gliding across the water, but the thought struck him as ironic, and they quenched the joy he felt at sailing. Scowling, he stared west, where the sun hovered over the horizon. The last golden rays fell over him, bathing the Alrendrian fleet in a warm glow, but thick clouds were forming in the south, a long line of blackness that threatened to swallow the light.

Tomorrow might decide this war, Dahr thought grimly. *If we lose, Vela falls, and Martyn with her. If we win... we buy ourselves another day.* A cold chuckle rumbled up from his belly. For seasons he had prayed for battle, for a chance to redeem himself, and now that it was upon him, he wished he were somewhere else. Anywhere else. *How different would things be if I had done my duty in that valley? With Tylor dead and Jeran free, this war might have gone very differently. I—*

"Friend Dahr?" Grendor stepped up beside him, interrupting his thoughts. The Orog's skin was paler than normal, and he swallowed nervously when he looked over the rail. After a quick glance he stepped back, swaying unsteadily, and he fastened his eyes on the deck. "Is all well with you? You seem troubled."

Dahr glanced at the Orog from the corner of his eye. Though he stood more than four hands taller than Grendor, they were of equal breadth, and solid muscle bulged from beneath the Orog's sleeves. Concern painted Grendor's face, though Dahr could not fathom a reason for it. The two of them had little in common besides their friendship with Jeran, and Dahr could count on his fingers the number of conversations they had shared. "I'm fine," he said gruffly, turning his gaze back to the water.

Grendor started to say something, then changed his mind. He forced his gaze out over the water, his slit eyes widening as he looked upon the sea. The silence that fell between them was palpable. Dahr sensed the Orog's uneasiness, but he had no interest in conversation. "What are you afraid of, friend Dahr?" Grendor asked suddenly.

"Afraid!" Dahr exclaimed. Grendor jumped, and he wrapped his arms tightly around the rail. Only then did Dahr sense the Orog's fear. Sweat beaded Grendor's brow, he trembled uncontrollably, and his eyes had a distant, haunted look to them. Dahr knew he could not be the reason—Grendor had seen far worse behavior from him than an angry shout—and he realized that Grendor's qualms about the water had been no act. The smug smile that pulled at his lips at seeing the stalwart Orog terrified shamed him, and he turned away, struggling to even his tone. "What do you mean?"

"I lived in the *ghrat* all my life," Grendor said, his voice weak, "far beneath the Boundary. Even on those few occasions when I was allowed outside, the mountains surrounded me, protected me. But here"—he made a sweeping gesture from horizon to horizon—"there is nothing but open skies and more water than I ever imagined. I know there is nothing to fear, not here at least, but the strangeness of your world terrifies me.

"There are times when all I can think of is home, and I wonder if I made the right decision. Tana would tell me no. She said I was a fool for following Jeran. But my people have suffered enough, and I want to help free them! I know this is a great thing we do, a great purpose we fight for, but fear threatens to drown me, and I do not know how long I can fight it.

"I have watched you since we met, friend Dahr. You, who have suffered far more than I, face each day bravely. I often wonder if there is anything you fear, and how you fight that fear when it tries to claim you." Grendor looked sheepishly at the deck. "I would make myself more like you, if you will help me do so."

"You're afraid? You?" Despite his best effort, Dahr barked a disbelieving laugh. Grendor looked confused, but Dahr dismissed him with a wave. "I have fears, Grendor, but what I fear is the very thing that would give you peace. I, too, lived as a slave, and I can't stand the thought of being in a cage again, even if that cage were my home. You wonder if you made the right choice? Think of your friends, your family, and all the others trapped in those mines. Think of their suffering and then tell me if you'd rather be back there or here fighting with Jeran."

"Here, without question!" Grendor said, and Dahr heard the Orog's conviction. "But how do you fight something that numbs your soul? How do you face your fear and—"

"Anger," Dahr interrupted. "Anger drives me to do what I must." He pursed his lips and studied Grendor for a long moment. "But I can be of little help to you. You already face your fears far better than I could." The admission stung, but Grendor had taken a risk asking for Dahr's help; he felt he owed the Orog something in return. "Were I put in a cage again, I'd rage until I bloodied myself against the walls, yet you stand here calmly discussing your fears while staring at the very thing you fear the most. This Tana of yours may be right, and you may be a fool, but you are no coward."

Admitting his fear soured Dahr's mood, and receiving proof that the Orog was braver than he was only made it worse. His scowl deepened, and his jaw clenched so tight his cheeks hurt. Anger and self loathing filled him, and Dahr stared blankly at the water, lost in dark thoughts.

The sea had half swallowed the sun when Grendor's hand on his shoulder brought Dahr back to reality. "What are those?" the Orog asked, one hand pointing over the rail. Shaking himself from his stupor, Dahr followed Grendor's finger.

Two forms rode alongside the bow, gliding effortlessly on the waves created by the *Vengeance*'s passage. The two creatures moved with grace and precision, jumping and dodging, diving out of sight only to reappear on the other side of the bow. They looked to be fish, but were unlike any fish Dahr had ever seen. Their skin was smooth, not scaly, and every so often, one sent a spray of water jetting from a hole atop its head. "I've never seen their like before," Dahr admitted.

"There are many strange creatures in this world," the Orog said. "Once, in the caves below the *ghrat*, I found a lizard whose skin glowed blue, and it—"

The rest of Grendor's words were lost on Dahr. He reached out, seeking contact with the creatures. He still understood little of what he did, but he had learned a few things. A collection of images formed in his mind, pictures of himself and his life. Around those images he wrapped feelings of friendship. The last seemed necessary; more than a few animals had bolted at the first touch of his mind, sensing the predator in him. He cast out the image, focusing his eyes and thoughts on the creatures.

What came back shocked him to the core. He felt an intense, overwhelming happiness and serenity, feelings of welcome and acceptance. The two fish leaped from the water in unison, somersaulting in midair and clicking out a greeting before diving below the surface. In spite of himself, a broad smile spread across

Dahr's lips, and he laughed aloud. The laughter drew a sailor's attention, and he paused to look over the rail. "Angelfish," he grinned.

"Angelfish?" Grendor repeated, and the sailor nodded.

"Aye. They've been known ta rescue drownin' sailors and haul 'em back ta shore. 'Tis a good omen ta see one afore a battle."

In all his experience, Dahr had never encountered an animal with such a joyful outlook. The angelfish had needs and fears like any other creature, but they only worried about such things when it was important; the rest of their time they devoted to enjoying life. Dahr questioned them relentlessly, and his questions piqued their curiosity; soon they began to ask their own. Dahr struggled to explain who and what he was, and what he and his friends hoped to accomplish, but he was never sure if his answers made sense. He was too inexperienced, and he had no one to guide him. Often he wished he were not the only one who could hear the Lesser Voices; if he had someone to talk to, he might be able to puzzle things out faster. "They're beautiful," he said, closing his eyes and basking in the angelfish's thoughts.

"Aye," the sailor agreed, "they're beautiful. An' they make a fine stew." Dahr's expression turned cold, and the sailor swallowed nervously. "We donnae try ta catch 'em," he added hastily, backing away. "But they sometimes come up in the nets hurt or dead. What would you have us do, toss 'em overboard anyway? Meat is meat to a hungry man."

Dahr's fists clenched, and he started forward, but he caught a thought from the angelfish that froze him in his tracks. "It's the way of things," he said, saying aloud what he felt coming to him from below. "All things must die. The only tragic death is a wasted one."

"Aye!" the sailor nodded eagerly. "That's what I'm sayin'! Ya'd not want us ta waste good meat!" Sensing his opportunity, the sailor hurried away.

"You speak wisely, friend Dahr." Grendor said, bowing his head respectfully. "I have often heard the Elders say such things."

Leaning over the rail, Dahr sent his thoughts out to the angelfish one last time, and what they sent back filled him with a peace that washed away his anger. For a moment, he thought of his life before leaving Kaper, before everything had changed, and a genuine smile touched his lips even as a tear traced a path down his cheek. "Go," he told them. "We sail into danger, my friends. You don't deserve to suffer for our foolishness."

The angelfish disappeared beneath the waves, but before Dahr could turn away, they sprang from the water, leaping high enough that he could have touched them had he been leaning over. Behind him, several sailors called out.

"Angelfish! Two of 'em off the bow!"

"I told ya, Byr, the Gods favor us!"

"Victory for Alrendria!"

Grendor turned to Dahr. "Did you see—" Dahr silenced the Orog by placing a finger to his lips. He nodded once and turned to face the water. They stood in silence until the sun set and darkness enveloped them, then Grendor left to find his pallet. For a time, Dahr tried to sleep as well, but uneasy dreams and thoughts of the Darklord kept him from a proper rest. It did not take him long to find his way back to the deck, where he stared out into a blackness deep enough to match his heart's.

Chapter 37

"You know what's at stake," Jeran said to the two dozen Guardsmen huddled around a magical sphere casting just enough light to illumine their faces. "The chances that any of us will survive are small, but our actions here will ensure that the fleet reaches Vela." A chorus of muttered agreement followed, but fear tinged every voice. "You are all essential," Jeran added. "If I thought fewer could do what was needed, I'd have sent more of you to other ships. I know you're afraid; so am I. But even knowing what you face, every one of you chose this path, and for that, Alrendria thanks you. I thank you. I know you'll make me proud."

It was not much encouragement, but Jeran hoped it would be enough. "Any questions?" No one spoke, and several Guardsmen shook their heads. "Return to your posts and get ready for battle. No lights, and no noise until we engage. When Aemon gives the signal, go to the Magi immediately. Dismissed."

Jeran waved one man back. "Assante, a moment." The wiry sailor approached as the ball of light faded into nothingness. Jeran extended his perceptions, but even with the aid of magic the night remained dark. The sailor swallowed nervously. Spikes of red and blue shot through his aura. "You're sure you'll know them when you see them?" Jeran asked. "Everything hinges on you, and from what I saw, all those ships look alike."

"That's because ya look on 'em with a shoreman's eyes," Assante answered. Jeran sensed confidence from the man. "Three ships, black like the others, aye, but with a different bearin'. They smell of command, those three, and at least one of 'em is present at every encounter. Aye, m'Lord, I'll know those ships."

"Assante has eyes like a hawk," Captain Corrine said from the shadows. Jeran turned and saw the captain approaching on his left, his body enveloped by a strong golden glow. How the man could see in the pitch black of predawn Jeran did not know, but the captain navigated around several obstacles before stopping beside Jeran. "If he says he'll know those ships, ya can trust him."

"He speaks the truth," Grendor said from behind Jeran. "Both of them do."

"Then get to your post, man," Jeran said, affecting a jovial tone, "and let us know when you spot the enemy."

"Aye, m'Lord." Assante left, and Jeran watched him feel his way amidships. Once he was out of earshot, he turned to the captain. "Is everyone ready?"

"As ready as they're gonna be, lad," Corrine replied. He sucked in a breath and blew it out in a rush. "Kohr blind me, I donnae know how Ries can steer through this. I've never seen a night so black, and there are shoals and shallows aplenty 'tween here and Vela."

"Alwen will be his eyes," Jeran assured him. "Come dawn, we will be where we need to be."

"I hope yer right, lad. I hope yer right." The captain sniffed the air and turned east. "The light'll be upon us soon. I'd best be gettin' to me post. May the Five Gods favor you today."

"May Shael protect you and Balan guide you," Jeran answered.

"And Kohr ignore you," Dahr added, finishing the prayer the captain had taught them.

Corrine chuckled. "I'll make sailors of ya yet."

With Captain Corrine gone, Dahr and Grendor stepped forward. "Are you two ready?" Jeran asked. "You know what you're supposed to do?"

"You've only told us a dozen times," Dahr growled, but Jeran thought that, for once, Dahr was faking his anger. "Maybe you should go over it again."

"Friend Jeran, you worry about others when you should worry about yourself. Keep Dahr with you; I can fend for myself."

Jeran shook his head. "I'll be fine."

"If not Dahr, then a Guardsman or two. You—"

"I'd take everyone with me if I knew how!" Jeran laughed. "But to be honest, I'm not sure what I want to do will even work. Magic isn't a simple thing." Worried expressions greeted his words, so Jeran sought to reassure his friends. "I tell you, I'll be fine."

Dahr barked a low laugh, and Grendor shook his head. "I do not need truthsense to know you do not believe that," Grendor said, holding out his arm. "Be careful, my friend."

Jeran gripped Grendor's arm at the elbow, then Dahr's. "You, too."

"Come on," Dahr said to Grendor. "We need to get ready." Grendor followed Dahr toward the bow, leaving Jeran alone. He stood in silence as the dawn approached, going over his plan time and again, looking for flaws, wondering if it would work. It was a gamble, one with the odds in the Darklord's favor, and many would die even if all went well. But it was the best he could come up with. It was their only hope.

When the first hint of gray tinged the horizon, Jeran felt a presence at his back. "You're risking a lot," Aemon said, his voice a low whisper. "If you fall—"

"Is that a Divining," Jeran asked brusquely, "or an opinion?"

"My vision revealed that you had to go to Dranakohr or all would be lost. I can't believe that meant—"

"I *did* go to Dranakohr," Jeran reminded him. "Maybe that's all that was required. Maybe rescuing Yassik or confronting the Magi was the key." He drew a deep breath and tried to keep his temper in check. "If you can tell me that what I plan will lead to the Darklord's victory, I won't do it, but I won't risk everything just because you're worried about me."

The silence between them was cold and awkward. Jeran hated the feel of it. "I... I just don't want to lose you again. You should let me—"

"No!" Jeran voice echoed, and a number of heads turned toward him. Scowling at his own foolishness, he continued, "We've discussed this. You must protect the *Vengeance* from the ShadowMagi. And when the time is right, you must leave, no matter how fierce the fighting, no matter how few respond to your call. You must survive."

"Why me?" Aemon demanded. "You have far more life ahead of you than I. Why should I hide in the corner, afraid to show my face? I've been fighting battles for millennia, young man, and I—" The look of stony resolve on Jeran's face stopped Aemon's tirade. His shoulders slumped, and defeated, he tried a different tactic. "Do you remember what you told me of the Emperor? How sad his life has become? Is that the life you wish for me?"

"No," Jeran answered after a time. "I wish his sadness on no one. But what the Emperor refuses to see is that the purpose he serves by being is greater than the purpose he serves by doing. You ask why you? You're a symbol, one of the greatest in Madryn. Aemon the Wise. Savior of Alrendria. For five thousand winters, men have sung about your valor and slept sound with the knowledge that so long as you fight, all would be well.

"But me? I'm unknown to most, and dead to most who know me. Whether I died here or in Dranakohr makes little difference. If I survive, my future is unwritten, but if you fall, your legend falls too. Your death would crush our morale and strengthen our enemy's. Like it or not, you serve a far greater purpose alive, even if that forces you away from the fight."

"I am not a God," Aemon replied, his cheeks flushed with anger. "No matter what you or the rest of Alrendria might want to make me!"

"A God?" Jeran shook his head. "But a legend? Yes, and one of your own making. Accept it, deal with it, or you *will* end your life as lonely as the Emperor."

They faced each other for a time. Finally, Aemon smiled. "You're a lot like your mother, you know."

Jeran returned the smile, but it was forced. He had yet to reconcile his feelings for Aemon. He wanted to love the man as he had, but he could not forget what had happened. "Yassik tells me she was a lot like you."

Aemon's smile broadened, and he clapped Jeran on the shoulder proudly. "The worries of an old man aside, this will work. I know it will. Good luck, my boy." Aemon's presence faded as quickly as it had appeared, and Jeran turned his attention to the horizon. The sky was brightening, but thick clouds muted the light and a mist clung to the sea. A stiff wind blew from the south, where the sky remained dark. Distant thunder rumbled over the deck.

Behind him, Guardsmen and sailors lined the deck, crouching behind ordered rows of crates, bows notched or swords held ready. A handful of sailors scurried about, silent and sure-footed now that a glimmer of light reached their eyes. Atop the wheel tower, Alwen stood with Captain Corrine, using her Gift to guide the steersman. Subcommander Dahrva signaled that all was ready. Jeran returned the signal and looked up to where Assante hung from the rigging. The sailor's eyes were fastened on the horizon.

A glimmer of motion caught Jeran's eye, and he whirled around in time to see a hulking form ghost by not three hundred hands distant, the dark black hull shrouded in mist. In that instant of shock, he almost gave the order to attack. Others spotted the ship as well, but to their credit, not so much as a gasp escaped the crew, and the black ship disappeared behind them.

Jeran raised a fist above his head, the signal to make ready. Seizing his Gift, he extended his perceptions over the waters, gliding high above the waves to get a better view. What he saw numbed him. "Hard to port!" he shouted. "They're waiting for us! Turn now!"

With his words, the mist disappeared completely and nearly three dozen vessels lined bow to stern with archers popped into view. The Black Fleet formed a loose semi-circle around the *Vengeance*, blocking their passage from east to west. The ship that had passed them moved to cut off their escape, and several others positioned themselves along their flank, tightening the noose.

"Ambush!" Jeran yelled as the *Vengeance* lurched. The sudden motion sent sailors and soldiers toppling, and pained shouts echoed in Jeran's ears. "Everyone hold your position! Fire on my command!"

"Jeran!" Corrine's voice boomed down from above. "Look starboard, lad!" Jeran followed the captain's wild gestures and saw a dozen ships break away from the ambush. Beyond them, another group of black-hulled vessel sailed southeast toward the Alrendrian ships making a beeline for Vela. The wind blew against the black vessels, but their sails were full and they glided effortlessly over the waves.

Jeran muttered a quick prayer, asking the Gods to give his Magi better control of the winds than the ShadowMagi. After that, he dismissed them from his thoughts. There was nothing more he could do for them; they were on their own now.

The enemy's first volley was in the air, but the shafts clattered harmlessly off the shield Aemon hastily raised. Lightning arced across the sky, but no bolts crashed into the *Vengeance*'s hull. Jeran looked up, but Assante still scanned the ships, his eyes roving from one to the next. They had little time, even with Aemon and Alwen protecting them. With the element of surprise gone, so was their greatest advantage. But if he made a mistake now, if he ordered the attack a moment too early, the results would be just as disastrous.

"There!" Assante yelled, and Jeran followed the sailor's finger to a two-masted vessel near one end of the arc of ships. The captain's course brought the *Vengeance* broadside to the ship, and when Jeran dropped his fist, the Guardsmen sprang to action. They tore the covers from five small catapults fastened to the deck and concealed from view. Though crudely-made, the weapons had been crafted by Guardsman Yashiki, a stern-faced Guardswoman from House Morrena and one of the finest engineers in the Guard. Jeran trusted that they were up to the task. *They had better be. Everything hinges on them.*

"Snap to it, men!" Yashiki called out, her black braid whipping around as she spun to survey her teams. "Fire at will, but miss more than once and I'll have your hides!"

"Archers ready," yelled subcommander Xanthar, an aging veteran from House Aurelle. A ball of fire appeared out of nowhere, headed straight for his head, but Xanthar barely reacted. He seemed more surprised when it disappeared. "Wait for my order!"

The first catapult let fly with a loud snap. Men on the enemy ship scattered, and when the barrel hit the deck it shattered with a crash, sending splinters flying in every direction. The rest of the catapults released. Three missed; the fourth slammed into the hull of the command ship. "Fire!" Xanthar shouted, and a volley of arrows, their ends aflame, arced into the morning sky. Flames engulfed the ship, and a cheer went up among the Guardsmen.

"Don't stand there like fools," Yashiki shouted. "Get the next volley ready. You think they're going to stand there and let us burn them down one by one? Move it!" Sailors on the black ship scrambled to raise their sails and get out of range.

"Second squad, fire!" Xanthar called out. "Shoot at anything that moves, and twice at anything in black. We're not taking any of these arrows home with us, boys!" A dark blur streaked through the air, and Xanthar fell. Several men moved to help him, but the old Guardsman was back on his feet in an instant. The head of an arrow jutted from the back of his shoulder, a feathered shaft from his chest, but if the wound pained him, he showed no sign of it. "Who told you to stop shooting!" he yelled at the Guardsmen coming to help him. "Back to your posts, and the next man who so much as looks sideways gets tossed overboard!"

The *Vengeance* moved into range of more enemy ships, and arrows fell upon the deck like rain. A second volley flew from the catapults; this time, three barrels hit their targets and a fourth shattered harmlessly in the air, spilling its oily contents across a magical dome. Fire arrows followed, and two more ships went up in flames. An instant later, the sky itself seemed to catch fire when an arrow ignited the oil spilling down the ShadowMage's shield.

Yashiki grabbed a man by the scruff of the neck and shook him roughly. "Miss again," she growled, "and you'll ride the next barrel."

"Lord Odara!" Assante's called, drawing Jeran eyes. The sailor still clung to the rigging, though a number of arrows feathered the sails behind him. "There, m'Lord!" Assante pointed to a vessel well behind the line of enemy ships. Jeran extended his perceptions, but could only see a few men in the rigging and a solitary, black-robed figure standing at the bow. The ship was stationary, though, and that was all he needed to know.

He drew on magic, and when a vertical line appeared and widened, he exhaled sharply. He had not lied when he had told Dahr and Grendor this might not have worked; he had never made a Gate before and had not been sure he could. His Aelvin sword sang as it came free of its scabbard, and Jeran launched himself through the Gate toward a surprised ShadowMage.

* * * * * * * * * * * * * * * * * * * *

"This is folly," Alwen grumbled. "Pure and utter folly! I can't believe I allowed the boy to talk me into this." Three more fireballs arced toward the *Vengeance*. Gathering her will, Alwen extinguished them. She sighed wearily and thumped her cane against the deck in frustration. *The fight's just begun, and I'm already tired.*

"If you had a better idea," Aemon grunted, "I'm sure Jeran would have listened."

The two Magi sat back to back on the foredeck of the wheel tower. Around them, the battle raged, but Alwen had yet to decide who had entered the fray with the element of surprise. Surely, the Darklord's soldiers had expected them—the sheer size of the enemy fleet attested to that fact—but the *Vengeance* and her crew had scored the first blow, and a major one at that. Of the ships arrayed against them, five burned and flames surrounded a sixth. Only the Gift of the ShadowMage on board had saved it from destruction. *If they knew we were coming, why didn't they go after the fleet?*

"Because of us," Aemon answered, startling Alwen. *If I'm talking out loud, I must be more tired than I thought.* "Jeran knew that if we were aboard, it would make the *Vengeance* too tempting a target. Lorthas would do just about anything to get his hands on us."

"You mean we're bait!" The very idea galled Alwen. "Lorthas wouldn't risk losing Vela just to get us."

"True, but Jeran's clever. He also—" An arrow shot past Aemon, not three hands away from his head, and took a passing sailor in the neck. The sailor fell, clutching at his throat and gurgling. "There's too many! I can't stop them all." He started to climb to his feet.

"Keep calm, you old fool," Alwen cautioned. "You won't do anyone any good if you go flying off the handle. You know how you get." Alwen felt some of Aemon's tension ease as he drew on his Gift and concentrated on blocking the enemy arrows.

If the battle had started in the Alrendrians' favor, the tide was quickly turning. The catapults had been their greatest advantage, but the confusion caused by the first few volleys had subsided and the enemy captains were spreading out. Only three catapults still worked; one had been smashed by lightning and a second broke under stress, sending a cask of oil spilling across the deck. A contingent of soldiers was even now shoveling sand over the spill, hoping to dry it up before a stray bolt from a ShadowMage set the *Vengeance* aflame.

The ShadowMagi had been hesitant at first, but as soon as they realized she and Aemon were not attacking, they had grown bolder. Outnumbered, the two Magi could do little more than stop most of what the enemy threw at them. Worse, if the captain kept to his current course, the *Vengeance* would soon lose the wind. "Folly," Alwen mumbled, readying herself for the next attack, "Pure and utter folly."

* * * * * * * * * * * * * * * * * * *

"Blast!" Corrine shouted. The enemy vessels were in disarray, hurriedly raising sails to avoid the catapults, but there was no pattern to their flight. Ships took whatever bearing gave them the best wind, and the oncoming storm had gusts blowing every direction. "I need a gap! Morey, do ya see anything, lad?"

"No, Sir!" Morey cried. Blood streaked the sailor's pale face. "We're surrounded. There's nowhere to go!" He looked ready to pitch himself overboard.

"Stand fast, sailor!" Corrine yelled. "I need yer eyes!" Again, the captain swept the enemy line, looking for a hole big enough to squeeze the *Vengeance* through. "Sami?"

"Nothing, Captain."

"It's no use," Corrine muttered. "Gods preserve us." He tightened his hands on the wheel. "Preparing to come about! Brace for—"

"Captain!" came a cry from high above, where Assante clung desperately to the rigging. "There—!" A flash of light half-blinded the captain, and the thunder that followed knocked several men to the deck. Only his grip on the wheel kept Corrine standing. Part of the mast slammed down against the wheel tower, leaving a hole five hands across in the deck and sending splinters everywhere.

The captain looked up anxiously; the lightning had taken the top off the main mast and a long tear ran twenty hands down the sail, but the damage could have been worse. The *Vengeance* was still sea-worthy. Groans and screams reached the captain's ears, but Corrine blocked them out. "Captain…" Assante, broken and bloody, crawled toward Corrine. When the sailor lifted his head, the captain winced. Only one eye remained; the other orb oozed blood.

"Peace, lad. I'll find help."

"No!" Assante said. He looked around, gasping for air, and a smile broke across his face. "There!" he said, shoving out his left arm. "Black sail. Third command."

Corrine followed the sailor's finger. A ship, not far from the *Vengeance*, with sails the color of darkest night, bobbed in the waves while the other ships moved around it. "Aye, there she is! Good work, lad!" He glanced down, but the life had faded from Assante's eye. "Kohr's blessing be on ya, lad," Corrine muttered. He called to Morey and pointed out the ship. "Donnae let that thing out of your sight!" he ordered, turning the wheel. The *Vengeance* shifted, listing as the massive Raker came about. Corrine aimed her straight for the enemy vessel.

"Captain!" Morey called out anxiously.

Corrine saw them, too. Two ships were heading toward them, one ablaze and drifting, the other moving to intercept them. "We can make it!" he said, hoping he sounded like he believed it. "Tell those Guardsmen ta get ready. We'll only get one chance."

* * * * * * * * * * * * * * * * * * * *

Dahr crouched behind a crate, the hilt of his greatsword clutched in one hand. Grendor knelt beside him, and three squads of Guardsmen huddled around them both, waiting for the captain's signal. Arrows flew overhead in ever-increasing numbers, and the elements themselves, wielded by the ShadowMagi, rose up against the Alrendrians.

The *Vengeance* lurched, and Dahr reached out to steady himself. As the Raker turned, he risked a quick glance over the crate. Before a flight of arrows forced him back under cover, he saw a dark sail off the bow drawing closer. To his surprise, his hand shook nervously, and he chuckled; he had thought himself beyond such things. He wished for Fang or Shyrock, or even Jardelle; the Lesser Voices were all quiet, though, and the silence weighed heavily on him. He looked at Grendor, sitting beside him with eyes closed and a look of calm on his face. "You aren't nervous?"

"Terrified," Grendor replied, but his voice betrayed no hint of it. "More of the water than the battle. But the peace of Shael will see me through both."

Dahr barked a laugh. "You must teach me this peace of Shael."

"Shael's teachings and Garun's blood do not match easily," Grendor replied, and his cheeks turned dark gray. "My apologies, friend Dahr, I meant no insult. If you wish to learn the ways of the Mother, I will gladly teach you."

Dahr clapped the Orog on the shoulder. "After the battle. For the moment, I think Garun's Blood will serve me better." A series of whistle blasts echoed down from the tower. "That's the signal," Dahr called out. "Guardsmen, ready!" The squad commanders called back, each in turn, and Dahr turned to Grendor. "And you? Are you ready?"

"As ready as I will ever be," Grendor replied.

Dahr raised himself up for a look. The *Vengeance* skipped across the waves, quickly closing the distance to the enemy ship. "We're coming in too fast," Dahr said. A glance to his left told him why. A fiery ship, its crew diving overboard to spare themselves from the flames, bore down on them. Grendor tugged on his arm and pointed right; a second ship, its deck lined with archers, approached at full speed.

"Corrine won't be slowing down!" Dahr yelled. "When I give the signal, run, and run fast. You make that jump or you'll be swimming to Vela!" He tensed, and raised himself up on the balls of his feet.

"One thing puzzles me, friend Dahr," Grendor said. The Orog, too, had raised himself to a crouch and tucked his staff under one arm. "Once we accomplish our mission, how are we to return to the *Vengeance*? How are we to get to Vela?" Dahr did not answer.

Once they drew within a hundred hands of the enemy vessel, the *Vengeance* turned so they would pass broadside. The enemy sailors ducked for cover, expecting a volley from the catapults, and Dahr gave the order to attack. Leaping over the crate, he sprinted toward the railing. The ships were twenty hands apart when he jumped, but he cleared the distance with little trouble. When he landed, he pulled his greatsword free of its sheath and swung at the nearest sailor. The man had barely registered Dahr's presence before he dropped lifeless to the deck.

Dahr looked around, and when he did not see Grendor, the first real sorrow he had felt in a long time tugged at his heart. But when the Orog pulled himself over the rail, Dahr smiled. Grendor had lost his staff, but he had made the jump; a full third of the boarding party had not. Dahr heard them splashing in the water below, calling for help, begging for someone to toss them a line. Dahr ignored them; he could not waste time on the dead.

"For Alrendria!" he cried. "Guardsmen, take the ship!" The squad leaders took up the cry, rallying their men and leading them away. Their surprise would only last a moment. If they were to win control of the vessel, they had to use that moment to the fullest.

Dahr pulled a shortsword from the belt of a dead sailor and tossed it to Grendor. "Can you use that?" Grendor shook his head. "Well, try to look like you can." He started forward, searching the deck for prey. "Come on. We have a job to do."

* * * * * * * * * * * * * * * * * * * *

Jeran landed with a thud. His Gate hovered several hands above the deck and the unexpected drop made him stumble, giving the ShadowMage time to recover. "Fool," the Mage said, drawing on the magic around him, "you cannot fight magic with steel."

As he had done at the Mage Assembly, Jeran surrendered to his Gift. Magic filled him, and he ripped the flows away from the ShadowMage. Denied his Gift, the Mage stumbled back, eyes wide, and Jeran advanced. For the moment, the two of them were alone, but if someone saw him, things would go from difficult to impossible. "You deserve a slow death for what you and the others have done," Jeran said, his voice cold. "But I'm pressed for time, so—"

Something crashed behind him, and Jeran whirled around. A soldier stumbled away, open-mouthed. Jeran recognized him, a guard from the mines of Dranakohr. "You...!" the soldier gasped. The man drew in a breath, but Jeran was faster. He reached to his hip, drew his *dolchek*, and threw the blade. It took the man in the throat, pinning him to the post behind him. A quiet gurgling was the only warning he called out.

In the time it took Jeran to deal with the soldier, the ShadowMage recovered enough to take hold of a trickle of magic. He used it to weave a shield around himself. "I may not have enough strength to kill you, but you are no longer a threat to me either." He laughed cruelly, a measure of his confidence restored. "The magic you hold could tear this ship apart, true, but if you use even a fraction of it, every Mage in the fleet will know you're here, and I think you wish to avoid that kind of attention. You risk detection even holding that much magic.

"As for your blade, without my Gift I feared it as any man would, but the strongest steel in Dranakohr could not pierce my shield." He inclined his head respectfully, but his sneer held only contempt. "If you'll excuse me, Lord Odara, I must inform the captain of your arrival." He started to walk away.

Defeated, Jeran's shoulders slumped and he let go his hold on magic. As soon as he did, the ShadowMage reached for the flows, and in that instant of distraction, Jeran stabbed. The Aelvin blade pierced the Mage's shield without slowing, cutting deep into the man's midriff. The ShadowMage grunted in surprise and dropped to his knees. "This is an Aelvin Blade," Jeran said, "forged by the greatest of their MageSmiths. And you're a fool to think I'd come to battle unprepared."

Jeran sheathed his sword and removed the ShadowMage's cloak. He wrapped the black fabric around his own shoulders and pulled the hood up to hide his face. Dressed like this, Jeran knew he could pass for one of the Darklord's servants, and the disdain ShadowMagi had for commons ensured that only a handful on board would recognize him as an imposter. Jeran retrieved his *dolchek* and threw the corpses overboard. Then, drawing upon seasons in the royal court at Kaper, he affected the most arrogant demeanor he could muster and went to meet his crew.

* *

Fires burned all across the *Vengeance*. Aemon extinguished them when he could, but when the ShadowMagi received no counterattacks to their magic, their attacks grew in frequency, and Aemon could spare little of his Gift to fight fires. Only one catapult still worked, but the oil had run out some time ago. Yashiki had the crew loading anything they could find onto the weapon. Xanthar had fallen, his body riddled with arrows, and dozens of others had died with him. Aemon cursed whenever he saw the dead. *Five hundred winters ago, not a single shaft would have hit this boat.*

The remaining archers held their posts, firing at any target that came into range, but it was a hopeless fight. A child commanded them, a boy no more than seventeen winters old. The boy already had an arrow in his thigh, and as Aemon watched, another missed him by less than a hand. The boy barely flinched, and he pulled the shaft from where it quivered in the wood behind him and notched it to his bow.

Aemon protected the men as best he could, but his strength was fading. The ship listed, and two of the three sails flapped uselessly. The Black Fleet was in disarray, but enough of the remaining ships pressed the attack to make victory hopeless.

"It's time," Alwen said. Sweat drenched her face and she all but lay prone, staring blankly at the sky, using her Gift to see. "If we wait any longer, I won't even be able to *open* a Gate, let alone pass through it."

"We can hold out," Aemon assured her. "Dahr and Grendor will be back any time now, and Jeran—" Alwen's cane caught him in the temple, and he staggered. His hold on magic wavered, and he struggled to keep control. "Fool woman! Do you want us all to die?"

"I don't have time to talk sense into you," Alwen snapped as she hoisted herself to a seated position. "Beating sense into you works faster." With the groan of strained wood, the foremast toppled. It crashed to the deck in a tangle of rope, sail, and wood. The whole ship vibrated from the shock. "Give the signal, Aemon."

Aemon sighed. With a defeated nod, he signaled the retreat.

* * * * * * * * * * * * * * * * * * *

The attack had turned into a bloody mess. Within moments of their arrival, the enemy had sounded an alarm. After that, the Alrendrian advantage disappeared. The Guardsmen were driven back and split apart, forced to fight in small clusters and kept away from the important areas of the ship. And if the strong, gusting winds lessened the effectiveness of the enemy archers, the sheer number of them cancelled any advantage derived from it. Soldiers boiled up from below in an endless torrent; the enemy more than doubled Dahr's squads of Guardsmen.

At some point Dahr and Grendor had been separated, and Dahr searched for the gray-skinned Orog nearly as much as he searched for the enemy. He jumped back as a tangled knot of rope hit the deck in front of him. Another step would have seen him crushed by the heavy line. A glance upward showed an enemy sailor taking aim with a cask, but Dahr easily dodged it and watched as a sword pierced the sailor's chest. The man toppled forward, splashing into the ocean below. A Guardsman peeked over the rail above, grinning triumphantly.

Before Dahr could wave his thanks, the Guardsman's body exploded in flame, and he followed the sailor into the cold water. *I have to find that Mage!* Dahr thought as he ran forward. Near the stern, he found himself caught in a bloody struggle between a handful of Guardsmen and a larger enemy force. The Alrendrians guarded a hatch to the hold, and the sailors were trying to push the Alrendrians back to free the soldiers trying to force the hatch open from beneath.

Dahr leapt into the fray, howling his anger. The first stroke of his greatsword cleaved clean through one soldier and dug into the side of a second. Both men fell, and Dahr jumped over them, swinging his blade at another sailor. He landed in a pool of blood and lost his balance, but his fall took down two more men. A sharp pain stabbed at his gut when he crashed into the deck, and the flailing soldiers landed several solid blows on his head and shoulders before a Guardsman rushed over and dispatched them.

The Alrendrians used the confusion of Dahr's attack to cut down the remaining sailors. Two Guardsmen Dahr knew from Kaper, Olric and Iselidor, pulled him free of the tangled limbs and helped him to his feet. The rest stood on the hatch, which jumped and jerked as the men trapped below beat upon it.

A spike of pain shot through Dahr's side when he took a step, and the hand he put to his stomach came away bloody. More blood dribbled down his face, and the ache in his head and back almost blotted out the pain in his gut. "The wound is deep," Olric said, pulling aside the tear in Dahr's shirt, "but you'll live. Let me bind—"

"Later," Dahr growled, shoving the Guardsman away. The pain made his head spin, but Dahr ignored it. His eyes roved the deck, and when he found what he sought, he uttered a prayer to whichever God might be listening. "Does anyone have flint and steel?"

"No, my Lord," Iselidor answered, and the other Guardsmen echoed him.

"Then find a lantern or something that's burning and get back here quickly!" Olric turned to run, but the Guardsman suddenly burst into flame and fell to the deck screaming. Iselidor and a second Guardsmen hurried to quench the flames, but Dahr stopped them. "He's dead already!" Dahr snarled. "And unless you want to follow him to the Twilight World, find that Mage!"

Each step was an agony, but Dahr ran to a heap of cloth bunched up on the deck. The barrel had hit the sail squarely, cutting a huge rent in the canvas, but the heavy material had cushioned the fall and the cask had not shattered. Oil leaked from several cracks, but the barrel was still mostly full when Dahr hoisted it over his head. He ran toward the hatch. "Open it!"

The Guardsmen obeyed, but when they realized what Dahr intended, something entered their eyes, a mixture of terror and disgust. Dahr ignored it; he needed neither their approval nor their acceptance. He would do what was necessary to win this battle.

As soon as the hatch opened, a sailor popped into view, striking out blindly with his dagger. Dahr threw the barrel with all his strength, and the cask took the man in the head, sending him crashing down the ladder. The barrel broke, spilling oil everywhere, and shouts of surprise drifted up from below.

"Throw him in," Dahr said, pointing to Olric.

The Guardsmen hesitated. "But—"

"Throw him in!" Dahr yelled. The Blood Rage was upon him, and for once, he made no effort to control it. "Or I'll throw you in."

Iselidor grabbed one of Olric's boots, and dragged the man toward the hatch. When he did not move fast enough, Dahr shoved him out of the way. He pulled the body toward the hatch, ignoring the flames and the stench of burning flesh. The oil ignited as soon as Olric's body dropped into the hold, and flames rose several hands above the hatch. Panicked screams followed the fire up from below. "The whole ship will burn!" Iselidor shouted.

"You didn't think we were going to sail this thing back to Vela, did you?" Dahr replied as he slammed shut the hatch. He hurried to a large crate and, bracing himself against the deck, pushed. The crate moved a finger's width before pain exploded up his side. White spots flashed before Dahr's eyes, and he had to struggle for breath. "Help me!" he gasped, and the Guardsmen rushed to his side. Together, they slid the crate over the hatch.

"Block the other hatches," Dahr ordered, "and find that Mage before we're all killed!" Dahr saw fear in the Guardsmen's eyes, but whether they feared death or him, he did not know. Or care.

Another Guardsman exploded in flame, and Dahr screamed in rage. *Where is that Mage?* Suddenly, the image of a black-robed man crouching atop the wheel tower came to him. He saw the man crawl toward the rail and peek over, then smile and close his eyes. A ball of fire erupted from the man's hands, dropping toward the deck below. Before it hit, the Mage dropped out of sight and crawled toward the other side of the tower.

I told you to stay away, Dahr said to Shyrock. The eagle circled high above the ship, and when Dahr told him to leave, he shrieked his answer. Pride and defiance filled Dahr's mind.

Dahr ran toward the wheel tower, ignoring the pain lancing his side and the burning in his chest. When he found the stairs guarded by a half dozen soldiers, he ignored them too. They raised their bows when Dahr appeared and drew as his great, loping strides carried him toward them. He made no attempt to dodge when the archers fired.

Fire burned across Dahr's right arm when an arrow sliced through flesh, and a second shaft embedded in his shoulder. A third buried itself in his thigh, but the arrows hardly slowed him. Lost in the Blood Rage, he felt no pain. He took the stairs three at a time, and a single swing with the flat of his greatsword sent all six archers tumbling over the side of the staircase.

Dahr vaulted the last few steps and landed on the tower. An instant later, he was running forward, his eyes sweeping the deck. The black-robed Mage crawled toward him, head tucked down and eyes fastened on the deck. Another man ran back and forth, shouting orders with the fervor of a man who knew death called for him but refused to answer. Dahr named him captain, and by the number and size of the insignia he wore, a man of some influence in the Darklord's Fleet. He sidestepped, bringing his greatsword around in a sweeping arc. The captain's body crumpled to the deck, and his head soared over the nearest rail.

The brief delay deprived Dahr of his surprise and gave the ShadowMage time to seize his Gift. Dahr slammed into a wall of air harder than any stone, and the force of the sudden stop knocked the breath from his lungs and splintered the arrow in his leg. He howled, and would have fallen except that the air enveloped him. With each breath, it tightened, crushing him where he stood.

"Foolish dog," the ShadowMage said, regaining his feet. "You should have struck at me first. Now, you'll suffer a pain greater than any you could imagine. You'll scream the air from your lungs, and that very air will crush you where you stand." Dahr gritted his teeth against the pain. Spots flashed before his eyes and each breath became more difficult to draw. Shyrock shrieked in frustration, but the golden eagle could do nothing to help.

Color leached from Dahr vision, and darkness loomed. A streak of grey fell from the sky, and Dahr's invisible prison vanished. He dropped to his hands and knees, gasping for air. A scream boiled up from within, but the ShadowMage's panicked howl drowned out Dahr's cry.

Dahr looked up to find Grendor behind the Mage, one arm wrapped around the man's throat, the other gripping his middle, holding him immobile. The Mage looked terrified; his eyes rolled up in his head and he thrashed pathetically. "Kill him," Dahr croaked, struggling to rise.

Grendor tensed, but uncertainty marred his features. "I... I—"

"Kill him!" Dahr repeated, louder. He pushed himself forward but lost his balance. His face hit the deck with a thud, and the impact dizzied him. He toppled sideways, pushing the arrow deeper into his shoulder, and screamed as his flesh tore and fresh blood leaked from the wound. "Do it, Orog!"

Grendor closed his eyes, and the muscles of his arms bulged. A loud snap echoed across the deck, and the Mage went limp. Dahr's lips curled up in a satisfied smile when he saw the ShadowMage's body fall lifelessly to the ground.

Tears stained Grendor's cheeks as he hurried to Dahr's side and helped him to rise. "Don't cry for me," Dahr said, spitting blood. "I'm not dead yet."

Grendor blinked as if surprised. "My tears were for the ShadowMage. Could you not feel his terror, friend Dahr? Such a death must be a terrible thing."

The Orog's sympathy for an enemy shocked Dahr, and he recoiled from Grendor's touch. He wished he had not, as the motion sent another wave of nauseating pain through him. It was an effort to stand, even to breathe. Blood stung his eyes and his clothes were soaked red. He could not remember how much of the blood was his, and how much his enemies'. *It's almost over*, he thought. *But I can still do a little more.*

"Get me to the wheel," he said when his first shambling step almost sent him back to the deck. Grendor took his arm and half dragged him to the wheel. The steersman watched them approach, and when they came within twenty hands, he shrieked and threw himself over the railing.

With no one guiding it, the wheel spun on its own, and the ship lurched. Dahr pushed free of Grendor's grasp and stumbled forward, grabbing the wheel in one hand and stopping it from spinning. It took most of his strength to hold the ship steady.

"We must go," Grendor urged, tugging on Dahr's uninjured shoulder. Flames raged across the deck, and the battle for control of the vessel had turned into a fight for the longboats. A column of bright blue light erupted in the distance, beaming up into the cloudy sky. "There is Aemon's signal. We must go!"

Dahr scanned the horizon. Not far off, three enemy ships sailed close together, but they had lost the wind and struggled to turn. Dahr aimed for the center of the formation. With the wind at their back, their ship leapt forward, and the spray that blasted across the deck as they crested each wave hissed as it met the flames. The storm had nearly reached them; dark clouds hovered ominously overhead, and thunder rumbled continuously.

"The *Vengeance* is the other way," Grendor said.

"We'd never make it," Dahr replied. He looked at Grendor, and saw fear in the Orog's eyes. "But when we arrive in the Twilight World, we'll know that we served Alrendria till the last."

Dizzy, Dahr dropped to one knee. Blood seeped from a dozen wounds, but the pain had all but disappeared. Awkwardly, he reached for the rope at the base of the wheel. The sturdy line was hard to hold and it kept slipping from his grasp, but he waved off Grendor's attempt to help. With great effort, he looped the coils over the wheel spokes, holding the ship on course. "If I could have spared you this," he said apologetically, "I would have. This is the price I have to pay for my mistakes, but you deserve better. Know this, Orog; you're a great warrior, and a far braver man than I. I'm honored to count you among my friends." With that, the world went black, and Dahr fell broken and bloody to the deck.

＊ ＊ ＊ ＊ ＊ ＊ ＊ ＊ ＊ ＊ ＊ ＊ ＊ ＊ ＊ ＊ ＊ ＊ ＊ ＊

Morey lay at Corrine's feet. Blood oozed from the sailor's scalp, but his eyes stared unblinkingly skyward. The column of light Aemon had conjured nearly blinded the captain, but he was not yet ready to leave. The *Vengeance* tilted from the water she had taken on, and flames ravaged her decks. "I donna like losin' two of me ships ta ya black sails," Corrine muttered. "But at least I took a few of ya with me this time."

He aimed the *Vengeance* toward the nearest enemy vessel and tied off the wheel. After patting the massive wheel one last time he sprinted to where the Magi had gathered what little remained of his crew. As he approached, two tiny holes appeared in the air, showing green grass and a white castle beyond.

＊ ＊ ＊ ＊ ＊ ＊ ＊ ＊ ＊ ＊ ＊ ＊ ＊ ＊ ＊ ＊ ＊ ＊ ＊ ＊

Jeran found the captain atop the tower, kneeling upon a chart of the Western Sea. A wild look entered his eyes when he heard someone approaching, and he reached instinctively for one of the daggers that weighted the corners of the chart. He calmed when he saw Jeran's black-cloaked form. "Where have you been, Mage? I sent men to find you long ago."

"I've been busy," Jeran replied, speaking in a raspy croak, doing his best to approximate the ShadowMage's voice. The captain waved for Jeran to join him, and he started forward slowly, his head tucked down to hide his features.

"There's a battle going on," the captain reminded him harshly. "An important one, in case you've forgotten. You're supposed to be relaying messages for me. What have you been doing?"

"Serving the Master," Jeran said. The ship had changed course; it now sailed toward the fray. Fires burned on the horizon, and black ships scattered in every direction. Of the *Vengeance*, there was no sign.

Only one other man occupied the tower, and he stood behind the wheel, his back to Jeran and the captain. "One ship!" the captain yelled suddenly, slamming his fist into the deck. "We wasted our fleet to destroy one ship! Why?"

"They have Magi," Jeran answered. The captain's burning glare spoke volumes, and Jeran chuckled at the unspoken question. "Even we can't see in the dark. We knew they were coming, but their Magi hid their numbers. But did they hide how many they were, or how few?"

The captain snorted derisively. "We were ready for them, at any rate," the captain said. "Captain Dyson will make sure no ships reach Vela."

"Perhaps," Jeran replied. "The Magi on the Alrendrian ships control the winds. They might beat our fleet to the harbor."

"What! Why—" The captain glared at Jeran. "You Magi keep too many secrets. If those reinforcements reach Vela, the city may hold."

"There is always risk in war."

"We could have stopped them if you had… Aaahh!" The captain pounded his fist into the deck. "And this ship!" He thrust his finger at a dark spot on the map. "It's one ship! Why can't we sink a single ship?"

"It will sink," Jeran promised.

"But at what cost? Half a dozen ships on fire, at least three lost, and half my fleet routed." Swiping the daggers from the map, the captain tore the parchment in two. "All for one worthless ship!"

"Perhaps the Gods aren't on your side today," Jeran said, drawing his sword and letting his voice return to normal. With his free hand, he swept the hood from his head. "Perhaps the Darklord underestimated our determination."

The captain scuttled backward, and he opened his mouth to call for help, but something held his tongue. "Where's my crew?"

"About half a league back," Jeran smirked.

"You killed over two hundred men? Left them to the cold mercy of the sea?" The captain looked for his weapons, but they were out of reach. "What kind of monster are you?"

"I am what Lorthas made me," Jeran replied, his expression tightening. "I killed my enemy. You would have done the same."

"You're a Mage. You could have killed them quickly instead of making them suffer!" The captain's eyes shifted wildly from side to side, and Jeran thought he detected a hint of madness. "But you forgot one thing. You think you're clever, but you forgot."

Jeran drew his sword back to strike. "What did I forget?"

"That drawing so much magic might draw undesired attention," the man at the wheel said. Jeran felt the man reach for magic, and he threw himself to the side just as lightning scorched the deck where he stood. The stench of charred wood filled the air.

Six more ShadowMagi appeared on the stairs to the tower and dropped the shields they have woven to hide themselves from Jeran's Gift. They spread out, circling Jeran, and the captain, cackling madly, climbed to his feet. He recovered one of his daggers and pointed it at Jeran's chest. "You'll never leave this ship alive."

"Who said I intended to?" Jeran asked, smiling wryly. He opened himself to magic, surrendering to his Gift. He allowed the energy to flow into him unchecked, until it pulsed within him to the point that he could not draw breath. The ShadowMagi unleashed their magic, but Jeran blocked their attacks without quite knowing how he did it, and while they readied their next assault, Jeran funneled his magic into the chaos of the storm above.

Winds buffeted the ship with enough force to make the masts groan. Lightning exploded around them, slamming into the hull, leaving gaping holes and charred streaks in the seasoned wood. Fires sprang up without warning; items tore away from their fastenings and pummeled the captain and his ShadowMagi.

Jeran laughed aloud when he saw the damage he wrought upon his enemy, but when he tried to lessen his assault, he found the magic beyond his control. Fear replaced satisfaction, and panic quickly followed. He struggled through the exercises Yassik had taught him, but none were effective. The magic raged through him, and he could no longer direct its outlet. The storm grew worse; waves forty hands high slammed the ship. One crested above the deck, sweeping Jeran overboard. He hit the water with a bone-jarring slap and blackness closed in around him.

* * * * * * * * * * * * * * * * * * * *

Strong hands drew him upward, pulling him out of the water. "Friend Jeran," Grendor said. "Thank the Gods!"

"Grendor?" Jeran said weakly. He smiled when he saw the Orog in the front of a battered longboat, but when he saw Dahr, all the color left his face.

"He lives," Grendor said, "but only barely." Dahr sprawled across the bottom of the boat, lying in several fingers of bloody water. He bled from numerous wounds, and no less than four arrows were lodged in his flesh. The worst had pierced his shoulder from front to back, just fingers above his heart. His skin was pale and cold, his lips blue.

Grendor grabbed the oars that he had set aside to pull Jeran aboard. "I will do my best, friend Jeran, but I fear I won't be able to reach Vela in time."

The thought of using magic again terrified Jeran, but he had no other option. If he did not, Dahr would die. "I can open a Gate, but I don't know for how long." He focused his Gift—just opening himself to magic made his head spin—and fastened his eyes on the far distant cliff that Aemon had told him was Vela.

A vertical line appeared at the end of the longboat. It widened some, but when it stopped, it was barely wide enough for a man to fit through. An open courtyard was visible on the other side. "Can you make it?" Jeran asked. Grendor nodded and dropped the oars. He hefted Dahr over his shoulder and stood in a crouch. The longboat wobbled under the sudden movement. "Remember not to touch it!" Jeran called out. "If you do—"

"I will do my best, friend Jeran," Grendor said, gasping for air. With that, the Orog ran forward. Jeran realized that the Gate was too small, and he opened himself to magic. The Gate widened a half hand more in each direction, and Grendor dove through, missing the edge by less than a finger's width. Their passage hit Jeran like a thunderbolt, and the Gate began to close even though he had not released the flows. He tried to stand, but his legs buckled. When he rose again, sputtering water, the Gate was half its size and shrinking rapidly.

Jeran readied himself to dive through, but motion to his right drew his attention. The enemy ship, burning and blackened, sailed toward him at full speed. The captain stood at the wheel, a wild light in his eyes, and Jeran did not need his Gift to see the hate radiating from the man. Paralyzed, Jeran watched as the ship drew near, and it was only at the last instant that he remembered his Gate.

He threw himself forward just as the black ship rammed the rear of the longboat.

Chapter 38

"Move!" Martyn yelled from atop the broad archway spanning Vela's main road, but his voice barely carried over the din. "We close the gates at dawn, and I don't intend to leave anyone out there!" Behind him, Guardsmen patrolled the interlocking buildings and dead-ended allies that served as Vela's defenses. Torches lined the walkway, and from Martyn's vantage point it appeared as if the city were on fire. A train of slow-moving wagons snaked along the approach to the city and trundled through the gates.

Squads of Guardsmen struggled to keep the river of refugees moving. The only safe place in a hundred leagues was Vela, and many believed the city offered the only chance for survival. "My Prince?" A Guardsman—a child, really, but he wore the uniform—stood nervously behind Martyn. "There's been another incident."

"And there will be more," Martyn told him. "Just keep them moving, and deny entry to anyone who breaks the peace." Once the Guardsman left, Martyn sighed. As dawn approached and Tylor's army drew closer, fights were becoming more frequent. The lightless night had provided a measure of peace, but the approaching dawn renewed the peasants fear.

Thousands had entered Vela in the last few days; thousands more still lined the approach. The number of people seeking refuge defied all expectations. Food would soon be in short supply as it was, without the extra mouth still awaiting entry. Only a fraction of the harvest had been ready to reap, and Martyn had ordered the remaining fields destroyed. He would rather risk starvation than willingly feed the Bull's army.

Standing on its lonely promontory, Vela was ripe for siege, but its architects had taken its weakness into consideration. Fields had been incorporated into the city, and access to the harbor stood behind the first two lines of defense. But with the Black Fleet stopping all but a trickle of supplies from the sea and most of the fields long since turned to parks or leveled to create more housing, it was shaping up to be a long winter. Jes had taken steps to make the city self-sufficient, but it would be a four-season before her newly-dug gardens produced any yield.

Despite these setbacks the Velani remained confident. Vela had survived the MageWar intact, and many believed it would stand against the Bull. Martyn wished he shared his people's optimism, but to him things looked bleak. Less than a thousand trained Guardsmen remained; the bulk of the garrison consisted of newly-recruited boys and conscripted militiamen. The best of his archers were with Treloran—*if he's still alive!*—lost in the forests north of the city.

Vela's fortifications were strong, but unlike in Kaper, no magic strengthened these stones. The Corsan skirmishes had given Martyn an idea of the Magi's capabilities, and the battle three days past had dispelled any remaining illusions of their limitations. Even a handful of Magi could reduce the walls of Vela to rubble, and unlike during the MageWar, the might of the Assembly was no longer on Alrendria's side. Of the few Magi at his disposal, most could not lift a finger to defend themselves without falling ill.

"This siege will be over in a day," Martyn muttered.

"That's the spirit!" Gregor laughed, hobbling toward the prince. A sturdy staff supported the bulk of the commander's weight, but even walking brought a stream of sweat to his brow.

"I mean we have no chance of winning," Martyn added in a whisper.

"With war and women, you never admit defeat." Gregor smiled. "Just thinking it gives your adversary an unhealthy advantage."

Martyn pointed south, where a line of inky blackness defied the first glimmer of sunlight. "Do you think the storm will slow the assault?" As if on cue, lightning flashed.

"Those clouds move fast, and they won't stop Tylor. The Bull will arrive before nightfall, and the battle will start before dawn. I'd stake my life on it."

Martyn studied Gregor, his lips pursed together thoughtfully. "You shouldn't be here," he said. "You should—"

"I need to lead my men. I may be of little use on the battlefield"—Gregor thumped his near-paralyzed leg for emphasis—"but I can still tell others when and how to fight. You're the one who should keep from the walls. One stray arrow and Alrendria will be without an heir."

Martyn opened his mouth to retort, but at the last instant, he changed his mind. "I'm not sure which of us is the more stubborn, but I'll let the matter drop if you will. This is where we need to be, for the men, if not for ourselves. Besides, whether I fight here or hide in the castle, once the walls are breached, I'm dead. There's no escape this time." In some ways, Martyn felt he deserved what was to come. He had cheated fate one time too many. This time, the Gods had given him no options.

Pounding hooves echoed up from below, and Martyn turned to see what was happening. Two horses galloped recklessly toward the gate, narrowly dodging the throngs of people clogging the street. Half a dozen Guardsmen pursued the horsemen, calling for them to stop. "Thieves?" Martyn asked. "Spies?"

Gregor squinted, and a wry smile spread across his face. "Even more dangerous," he laughed. "Women. And one of them a princess."

Martyn saw Miriam's flowing blonde hair and slender frame bouncing atop one of the horses. "What's she doing here?" he demanded, starting toward the stairs.

"Remind her that today's not the best day to tour the countryside!" Gregor yelled, and his laughter followed Martyn to the street.

Martyn emerged on the street just as Miriam reined in her mount. Seeing him, the princess dismounted gracefully and started toward him, her hands reflexively smoothing clothes and hair. Behind her, Kaeille skidded to a stop and jumped awkwardly from the saddle, but she had her shortsword in hand before she hit the ground and was never more than three paces from Miriam.

"You shouldn't be here," Martyn said. He turned to Kaeille. "How could you let—?"

"You must come to the castle," Miriam interrupted.

"Your concern is appreciated." Martyn forced a smile. "But I won't cower in the castle while these men are forced to die in my name."

"This isn't about your pride or your duty." Miriam's voice was cold, but Martyn detected fear as well. "You must come to the castle now!"

The princess' words carried an urgency Martyn could not deny. "Why? What's happening?"

"Any description of mine would not do the sight justice. You must see for yourself, but you must hurry!"

Martyn hesitated. Part of him believed this to be a trick, a clever ruse to pull him from the battlements. Once in the castle, he wondered if they would ever let him leave. In the end, Miriam's fear decided him; he would do anything to quiet the trembling of her lips. "I'll go," he promised, caressing her shoulder. "Ready a horse. I need but a moment."

Martyn met Gregor halfway up the stairs. Away from the eyes of his men, Gregor allowed his pain to show plainly. "I must go to the castle," Martyn said. "Send a rider when the Bull's army is spotted. Until then, the gates remain open."

"Martyn," Gregor frowned, "we discussed this. In order to prepare—"

"I won't leave them out there to die!" Martyn snapped. "I won't! The gates remain open as long as they can."

"Tylor's sure to have men among these refugees," Gregor said, his breath hissing out between clenched teeth. "We could already have a thousand traitors in our midst, and you want to risk adding a thousand more?"

"Disarm them, or lock them in cages if you must. Take whatever steps you deem necessary, but don't close those gates until Tylor is standing in front of them."

Defeated, Gregor sighed, "I'll send a messenger when we spot the enemy." Martyn hurried to where Miriam waited on her horse. A tall gelding stood beside her, and Martyn took the reins. As soon as he was in the saddle, the princess heeled her mount to a fast trot. She would have galloped if Martyn had not restrained her.

Miriam said nothing when Martyn slowed the horse to a fast walk, but her eyes argued with him. Martyn took her hand, relishing the feel of her soft skin. "Everything will be fine," he assured her, wishing he believed the words. She smiled, and he moved his horse closer to Kaeille. "She should not have left the castle."

"Lord Estande says the same of you," the Elf sniffed, "but you come and go as you please. I am Miriam's protector, not her nursemaid. She decides where to go; I make sure she arrives safely."

"This is my home, not hers," Martyn countered. "Miriam's a guest here. She must be—"

"Alrendria will never be her home if you keep her from becoming part of it. How do you expect her to learn anything locked inside that castle, sheltered from anything that could upset her? Your princess is no warrior, but she is not weak. Coddle her, and you will make an enemy of her."

"If anything were to happen..." The mere thought sent a chill down Martyn's spine.

Sensing his pain, Kaeille turned away, but not before Martyn saw tears glistening in her eyes. When she spoke, her voice was firm. "She loves you too, though she denies it, but if you continue to treat her like a child, she will resent it. And you." Martyn reached out to Kaeille, and she jerked away from his touch. She looked at him, and a tight smile replaced her tears. "She is nearly the most stubborn Human I have ever met."

"I love you, too," Martyn said, caressing the Aelvin woman's cheek. Kaeille said nothing, and in the silence, Martyn's thoughts drifted to the coming battle. When he next looked up, they stood before the castle.

Dismounting, Martyn started toward the barred double-doors, but Miriam waved for him to stop and led him to the seawall, where a group of Guardsmen stood staring out over the Western Ocean. A Mage stood in their midst, his eyes unfocused and distant. His grim expression was enough to make Martyn glad he had heeded the princess' plea. "What's going on!" he demanded. "No more secrets."

"Ask Mage Czan," Miriam replied. "He can explain better."

Martyn stormed toward the Mage, but the old man gave no indication that he saw the prince. That troubled Martyn. The Magi were usually aware of what happened around them even when their minds were elsewhere. "Mage Czan?" Martyn called, and when the old man did not respond, Martyn grabbed him by the shoulders and shook him. "What's happening?"

The withered Mage with large, sunken eyes shook himself as if waking from a dream. Even that movement seemed enough to break him in two. Of all the Magi who had answered Martyn's call, Czan was among the oldest, and despite the longevity granted by the Gift, his age showed plainly. His movements were slow, his thinking slower, but when his eyes fastened on Martyn, the prince saw a measure of power.

"That's a good girl," Czan said, patting Miriam absently on the head. "I didn't think you'd find him so fast."

"What do you want, Mage Czan?" Martyn asked, his patience wearing thin.

"This way." Crooking a finger toward Martyn, Czan hobbled to the wall. "Move, children," he said to the Guardsmen with only a hint of condescension. "Let the prince see."

Frustration and amusement warred within Martyn. Like all Magi, Czan expected obedience, and he seemed oblivious to the fact that some of the 'children' he ordered around had seen more than fifty winters. But Martyn found it difficult to hate Czan for the way he treated the ungifted. His manner was more that of a doting grandfather than an arrogant Mage.

The Guardsmen obeyed without hesitation. Young or old, they smiled when Czan thanked them for being 'good little boys and girls'. "Look, Prince Martyn," Czan said, pointing a finger to the west, "and tell me what you see."

Martyn peered into the gloom. The first rays of morning light had appeared in the east, pushing back the curtain of night, but the distant horizon remained hazy and indistinct. Black clouds spanned the southern sky, dark and foreboding, and lightning flashed with rhythmic ferocity. In one of those flashes, Martyn caught sight of a grey wall, a hazy, swirling mass that obscured everything beyond. "Fog?" the prince said, his irritation peaking. "You brought me here to see fog?"

"Not just fog," Czan replied, and he shook his head sadly, as if Martyn had disappointed him. "A fog of distinct shape, and one that does not move despite a strong wind. It has sat there since well before dawn. I cannot see inside it."

"The ships?" Martyn bit down on his upper lip. "But why? We know the Black Fleet is there. They've been there for seasons! Why hide now?"

"Perhaps they seek to draw our attention away from Tylor the Bull," the old man answered. "Or perhaps they are not hiding from us." Czan shrugged. "As I said, I cannot see inside."

"Sails!" a Guardsman cried frantically. "I see sails!" Martyn scanned the horizon, but saw nothing. He demanded to see the speaker, yelling for the others to clear a path. In a few moments, a stick of a boy stood before him, his cheeks a dark shade of red. The Guardsman could barely bring himself to meet Martyn's eyes.

The boy was afraid, but Martyn had no time to coddle him. "What did you see?" he demanded. "Where?" The boy stuttered, and Martyn grabbed him by the shoulders. "What did you see, Guardsman!"

Soft hands separated Martyn from the boy. "Gods! Can't you see he's frightened?" Miriam stepped between them and gently raised the young man's chin so he looked into her eyes. Her smile made him blush all the more, and he tried to pull away, but Miriam's grip remained firm. "Tell us what you saw," Miriam ordered, her words a soft whisper. "Please?"

"I... I saw sails to the south. Toward Atol Domiar. I know you can't see them now, but I saw them. I swear it!" A few Guardsmen laughed, and a few called out jokes about Rheganol and his ghosts, but a stern glare from Miriam silenced them all.

"I believe you... Rheganol. Show me where you saw the ships." The boy, still trembling, went to the wall and pointed southwest, well away from the stationary fog. Martyn stared into the darkness for a long time but saw nothing. The laughter returned, and Martyn was just about to dismiss the boy when a streak of lightning arced across the southern sky, illuminating scores of tiny, black specks. *Ships—they could be nothing else—and headed this way!*

Martyn sucked in a quick breath. "Gods, boy, you have eyes like a hawk! There," he called, pointing. "Wait until the lightning flashes." Martyn did not wait for the others. He ordered one Guardsman to advise Lord Estande of this development; a second rider he dispatched to the harbor to ready the fleet. If the Black Fleet was attacking Vela, his captains had orders to run the blockade. The Rakers were captained by the best men in the fleet, but everyone knew they would stand no chance against Magi. Martyn refused to risk a full third of Alrendria's navy on a hopeless cause.

"Prince Martyn," Czan said in his calm and steady voice. "The fog is gone." At the same time, another Guardsman shouted. "Fire! The ships are on fire!"

"Our ships?" Martyn cried, spinning around and squinting into the rising sun to peer into the harbor. "How—!"

"No, the black ships! Look!" Martyn turned back to the sea. The grey haze had disappeared, revealing the Black Fleet. But the vessels no longer hovered around the harbor like silent predators. Chaos enveloped the fleet; the ships moved in every direction, with no regard to the other vessels in the flotilla. Flames coated the decks of at least two, and black smoke cut a swath across the sky. As Martyn looked on, another ship began to burn, and the very air around a fourth burst into flame, covering the vessel in a dome of fire.

"What's going on?" one Guardswoman demanded, and others echoed her confusion. "Who are they fighting?" Other voices called out, each more panicked than the last. "Has the attack begun?" Confusion began to give way to fear. "I see only black sails! Why do they fight each other?"

"Martyn!" Miriam tugged at his sleeve. "Look! Those ships are headed toward us!"

A full third of the enemy fleet was nowhere near the fray. They made a beeline for the mouth of the harbor, clawing their way forward despite a strong headwind. A smaller group, just over a dozen ships, had veered away from the firefight, and the course they took sent them even farther south. "Two fleets," said a grizzled old Guardsman, his head shaking sadly. "One comin' from the south and one from the north, and a handful more to pick off any enough to escape. Our boys'll never make it out alive."

"We're doomed!" one young man cried, dropping to his knees. The others fed off his panic. "We can't stand against the ShadowMagi!"

"You think those fires are just a distraction?" Czan's voice boomed over the courtyard, drowning out the frightened cries. The Mage no longer appeared the addled old man. His words conveyed power and authority; his tone, confidence. "To what end? They neither stopped us from seeing the attack nor preparing for it. Lorthas may be cold-hearted, but he's no fool. Why waste ships and why attack today when the ShadowMagi must exhaust themselves to sail against the wind? Open your eyes, Alrendrians, and see your salvation!"

Czan winked at Martyn, then started toward the castle. When Martyn called him back, the Mage replied, "I must tell the others that company is coming. You had best prepare to greet them yourself." Despite his small steps and shambling gait, the old man moved quickly. If he heard Martyn's repeated attempts to recall him, he ignored them.

Fear resurged in the Mage's absence, and Martyn stared at the closer of the two fleets. *If I can find a way to stop them, or even slow them, I can—*

"They're Alrendrian!" he shouted. He had to shout it several more times before anyone heard, and no one truly believed until the white sails and Rising Sun banners were clearly visible. Only then did panic give way to cheers.

"Those ships move against the wind," Miriam noted. "They must have Magi on board."

"Magi?" Martyn repeated, and despite himself he smiled. A few more Magi might mean the difference between victory and defeat. "Oh, Gods!" Martyn cursed, and a quick glance confirmed his fears. The enemy vessels were moving fast; they would reach the harbor before the Alrendrians. "We have to slow the black ships! We have to make sure our fleet reaches the harbor!"

Martyn's words were lost in the tumult, but a nearby Guardsman, a great bear of a man with arms the size of small trees and a thick black beard nearly three hands long, heard him and reacted. "Quiet!" he bellowed, and his words echoed across the courtyard. Silence instantly descended over the Guardsmen. "Do you think this is a summer festival? This is a war, and we have an enemy to fight. Get to your posts, and make sure our boats get here before those black ones do." Stunned silence followed the orders, and the man frowned, an expression so severe it made the nearest soldiers back away.

"Move!" the Guardsman shouted, and one menacing step sent the others scurrying for the catapults. The giant siege engines had been constructed and secured along the horseshoe of the upper courtyard. Tall mounds of loose stone, the largest no bigger than a man's fist, lay to either side of the great machines. "It'll take forever to sink a ship with those little stones," Miriam said.

"We don't have to sink them," Martyn told her. "We just have to slow them down." The princess did not look convinced, but Martyn had no time to explain. He turned to the giant Guardsman. "You," he called, waving the man over. "What's your name, soldier?"

"Einar, of the Family Bhere." Einar saluted, his hand thumping forcefully against his chest.

"Keep that black fleet from overtaking our ships," Martyn said, "and you'll end this day a subcommander."

A glint entered the giant's eye. "What do I get if I sink 'em?"

"Do that," Martyn laughed, "and you can name your reward."

A crooked smile drew up the Guardsman's lips, but if anything, the gesture only made him look more frightening. He paced behind the catapults. "Eight men to each," he shouted, "four on the shovels, three on the winch, and one to aim. Get those rocks flying, or I'll be puttin' you in the buckets and throwing you at the Black!"

"Rheganol!" Martyn spotted the boy pressed against the sea wall, trying his best to stay out of the way. When he saw the prince approaching, he swallowed nervously. "Go to the harbor and tell the captains that help is on the way. Have them clear the docks. I'm not sure how many ships are coming, but we'll need to unload them quickly. Tell Captain Eli that if the Black Fleet enters the harbor, he's to do everything in his power to stop them. Understood?" Rheganol nodded, and Martyn waved him away. "Then move, boy!"

Martyn turned to tell Miriam to go to the castle, where she would be safer, but before he could, the air across the courtyard shimmered. Silver sparkles swirled for a moment, then rotated outward. Suddenly, Martyn found himself looking at the deck of a ship. Flames roared across the corpse-littered planks, and pained screams echoed across the courtyard. When the first soldier, his face a bloody mess, came through, Miriam gasped and nearly fainted.

Drawing his sword, Martyn halved the distance between Miriam and the stranger before he realized he faced a battered and broken Guardsman. Skidding to a stop, Martyn watched stunned while more sailors and soldiers hobbled through the Gate. He went to help, but a flash of light blinded him. When Martyn could again see, a familiar face stood in front of him. "Captain Corrine?" The captain turned, but there was no recognition in the gaze he leveled on Martyn. "I haven't seen you since Grenz."

"Prince Martyn?" It was half a question. "Aye! Kohr blind me, yer not the same boy who left me ship, but it's you. I'd bet me life on it." The captain's words were friendly, but his eyes were haunted. He saluted wearily; Martyn saw exhaustion in the man's eyes.

Understanding dawned. The flames. The fog. It all made sense. "You attacked them?" Corrine nodded. "How many ships did we lose?"

"One. Just one." Corrine spat on the ground, as if the one were too many. "But a finer vessel I ne'er sailed." The captain shook his head roughly, as if trying to dispel an image from his mind. "I've seen things today..." He broke off, and Martyn was suddenly glad the captain had not explained. "Did it work, at least?" Corrine asked. "Did they make it?"

"They've a good lead, and my men are doing what they can to lengthen it." Martyn glanced at Einar. The Guardsman paced the line, his voice booming louder than the thunder roaring up from the south. Volleys of loose stone lofted over the wall, splattering the water with deadly force.

A sharp pain exploded in Martyn's shoulder, and he turned to find a small woman beside him. Gray hair lay disheveled across her face, and her dress was tattered and scorched. She held an oaken cane in one hand, and she smacked it against his shoulder a second time. Martyn winced, but he hid his pain and fastened an imperious gaze on the stranger. "I am Martyn Batai, and—"

"I know who you are," the old woman snapped, poking him in the chest. "Stop daydreaming and find me a Healer. He's overextended himself again, and at his age..."

"Who?" Only then did Martyn notice the old man unconscious at his feet. Soot stained the Mage's hair and beard dark, and a bloody gash ran the length of his brow. His breathing was shallow and irregular.

"Who?" the old woman repeated. "What does that matter? If I told you this was Muttonhead the Dung Carrier, he needs no less help." Martyn stared slack-jawed, and the woman drew back her cane. "I said fetch a Healer!"

Martyn backed away, more to take himself outside the old woman's reach than out of any desire to obey. He mustered as much courtesy as he could manage. "I'll send for Sheriza."

"When you find her, tell her not to dally. Aemon needs her immediately."

Aemon. "Gods! Why didn't you say it was Aemon?" The old woman rolled her eyes, but Martyn had no time to waste. He turned, already running, and nearly knocked over Miriam. The princess stood behind him, eyes wide and mouth hanging open. If she noticed that he had almost trampled her, she gave no indication.

"That's... Aemon?" Miriam asked breathlessly. "The Great Mage?"

Martyn grabbed her shoulders. "We have to find Sheriza. We have to—" On the far side of the courtyard, Martyn saw another Gate open. A stocky figure carrying a huge burden emerged, but before he made it two steps, the figure collapsed and lay unmoving in the grass. "Find a Healer," Martyn yelled, no longer able to hide his anxiety. "Find them all!"

Pushing past Miriam, Martyn raced across the courtyard, ignoring the Guardsmen who urged him not to approach the strangers. He slid the last few hands and came to a stop beside the prone figures. One was a man the likes of which Martyn had never seen, gray-skinned and bald, short but with arms half again as big as Einar's; the other was a giant, covered from head to foot in bloody wounds. What seemed like a quiver's worth of arrows protruded from the giant's torso.

The gray-skinned man opened his eyes, and Martyn fumbled for his sword, remembering too late that he had dropped it after the old woman mentioned Aemon's name. "Please, friend," the stranger said, "I need help. We must get him to the Magi."

Somewhat reassured, Martyn helped pull the stranger free from his companion's tangled limbs. Together, they lifted the giant, but as soon as they turned him over, Dahr's body slipped from Martyn's numb hands. He hit the ground with a thud, but not so much as a grunt escaped Dahr's lips.

Martyn scrambled forward on hands and knees. "Dahr?" He touched Dahr's cheek, recoiling at the cold and clammy feel of his flesh. He shook Dahr, lightly at first and then with more urgency, but his efforts provoked no response. Panicked, Martyn pressed his thumb against Dahr's throat, and when he felt no pulse, tears welled in his eyes.

A loud crash drew the prince's eyes. He barely had time to see a shadowy form hurtling toward him before it knocked him to the ground. A shower of water and splintered wood followed the man through the closing Gate, and Martyn shielded his eyes from the debris.

Drenched, sore, and dazed, Martyn sat up slowly, groaning at the ache in his ribs. His jaw dropped when he saw Jeran sitting beside him. "It's good to see you," Jeran said before collapsing.

Chapter 39

Jeran woke to the sound of distant cheering. He found himself on a cot in a small, sparsely-furnished room with Martyn sitting beside him. When he saw Jeran move, a broad smile spread across the prince's face. "How often are you and Dahr going to save me?"

"You don't make it easy," Jeran replied, groaning dramatically. "Convincing Brell Morrena that you never touched his saddle, let alone loosened the straps, was far less challenging." Memories of the nobleman lying on his back in the dust with the entire court of Kaper watching brought a laugh to both of them.

Martyn grasped Jeran's shoulder fondly. "I've been praying to all five Gods for a miracle, and they not only brought you back, they sent me Aemon and several thousand Guardsmen. I'm starting to think we might actually win."

"I'd have hoped you'd be a little more cautious by now. You should have left Vela a long time ago."

Martyn set his jaw defiantly. "If Vela falls, so does Alrendria. Portal is already under siege; if Tylor attacks them from the south, the city will be overrun and all the might of *Ael Shataq* would be leveled against us. Vela is the gate to the Alren, and with the river we could field an army at Portal in a matter of days. Tylor knows that; that's why he's attacking here first."

"You might not have learned caution," Jeran said, "but you've learned a few things these last few seasons. Still, what chance did you have here?"

"None," Martyn admitted. "We might have held out a ten-day, but with the ShadowMagi at his disposal, Vela would have fallen. Now, though—?"

"You have to stop trusting to fate," Jeran interrupted. "One day, Dahr and I might not be around to save your skin." Martyn's face fell at that, and a hollow feeling filled Jeran. "Dahr! Is he...? Did he...?"

"The best of the Healers are with him," Martyn answered, but all the joy had left his voice. "If he can be saved, they will save him."

Thinking of Dahr sobered Jeran's mood, and a silence fell between him and Martyn. "Lord Estande and I are holding a council shortly," Martyn said. "The troops you brought may save this city." Jeran levered himself up to a seated position, and Martyn shoved him back down. "Sheriza said you needed rest!"

"You don't think I came all this way just to sleep through the battle, do you?" Jeran shrugged off Martyn's hands and struggled to his feet. The room lurched when he stood, but he did his best to hide his dizziness. Fresh clothes had been set out, and he hurriedly dressed. His head throbbed every time he bent over, but he kept a smile glued to his face. "I feel fine." Martyn's skepticism frustrated him, and he forestalled the prince's attempt to protest with a wave of his hand. "I know Tylor better than anyone here."

They squared off for a moment, but Martyn finally raised his hands in surrender. "Fine. You know best. You always did." Martyn preceded Jeran from the room and led the way through the castle. While they walked, he briefed Jeran on troop deployment and Gregor's plan for the city's defense. Jeran did his best to listen but was constantly distracted. Servants froze when he appeared and stared at him as he walked by. If he turned to meet their gaze, they quickly looked away; if he called out a friendly greeting, all but the bravest blushed furiously and fled. A handful of Guardsmen saw them and took up positions as an escort. To Jeran, it seemed as if they were far more interested in him than in their prince.

Even the Magi acted oddly. When Jeran tried to focus his Gift and nearly toppled to the floor when the magic rushed into him, a young woman came to his aid. She could have easily passed for a common if not for the bright aura that flashed about her as she grabbed for the flows and directed them away from him. "You have pushed yourself too hard," she whispered. "It would not be wise to draw upon magic until you are rested."

"You have my thanks," Jeran said. His eyes met the woman's, and her cheeks flushed red. She hid a smile with her hand and hurried down the hall. Jeran watched her go, baffled. "Why...?"

Loud laughter filled the hall. "Stop acting so modest!" Martyn exclaimed, and when Jeran turned a confused gaze on him, the prince rolled his eyes. "You defied the Darklord and escaped from Tylor's hidden prison. You scattered the Black Fleet and quite possibly saved Vela from destruction. You arrive here out of thin air with an Orog—an Orog, Jeran!—and... What was the other thing...? Oh, right. You called the Mage Assembly cowards and fools. To their faces!" Martyn's grin widened. "It's hard to imagine why everyone thinks you're something of a hero."

"I only did what I had to do." Jeran mumbled, quickening his steps. He felt uncomfortable under all the admiring eyes.

"What you had to do," a new voice asked, "or what you thought you should do? You make it sound as if you had no choice."

"Oto!" Jeran turned to find the rotund Mage hurrying after them, dragged along by two young apprentices. Jeran introduced Martyn to the Mage while Oto patted his brow with a lace handkerchief pulled from a hidden pocket.

"I've been looking for you, Highness. Here." Oto held out a cloth-wrapped bundle tied with a golden cord.

Martyn turned the bundle over in his hands. "What is it?"

"Something for your highest tower, I think," Oto replied. "Aemon's banner. The Golden Eagle. I took it from the Hall. Thought it might do us more good here than collecting dust inside that mountain. Fly it where Tylor's men can see and it might give them second thoughts."

"I'll have it raised immediately." Martyn handed the package to one of the Guardsmen. "Lower the Rising Sun if you have to. I want everyone in the city to know that Aemon is with us. And you!" Martyn pointed to a second soldier. "Find an Odaran standard. Fly the Greatwolf beside the Velani stallion. I want the Bull to know that Jeran beat him here!"

"Great," Jeran sniffed. "When he sees that, Tylor will likely storm the city without his army, and the Gods protect anyone who gets in his way."

"Your presence might enrage the Bull," Oto said as they resumed walking, "but it will also spread fear through his army. The sight of you pacing the battlements with your mighty Aelvin sword will inspire faith in the righteous and strike fear in the hearts of our enemies. Ah, if only I had the eyes to see such a magnificent sight..." A broad grin painted the Mage's face, and despite himself, Jeran laughed. "That's a sound I love to hear," Oto quietly added. "There's far too little laughter these days."

The two guards outside the war room moved aside at Martyn's approach, opening the way into a spartan chamber dominated by a circular table. A number of the attendees, most wearing the insignia of subcommanders, Jeran did not know, but Kal and Grendor sat close together and as far from the Humans as they could. Jes sat apart from everyone. A young Guardsman Martyn introduced as Dayfid stood face to face with Gregor, and the two of them alternated their stares between a map of Vela and each other.

"I tell you, we must attack now!" Dayfid said, his face flushed with anger. He pounded a fist against the table for emphasis. "The Bull thinks us weak. He doesn't know about our reinforcements! If we launch an attack—"

"An attack will waste lives." Gregor interrupted. "Even with the new troops, our forces are no match for Tylor's. It's foolish to think the Bull has no eyes in Vela. My orders stand. We—"

"Your orders will see us killed!" Dayfid threw his hands up in frustration. "The walls won't protect us from that host. Tylor has time and numbers on his side; he'll whittle us away man by man."

"I think Dayfid's right," one subcommander added, a slight quaver to his voice. Dayfid grinned triumphantly. "The Bull has scores of ShadowMagi. What chance do we have against them without surprise on our side?"

"Your men speak wisely," Kal said, standing. "I see no point in waiting for death behind these walls. If we must die, then so be it, but I would rather my death be beneath the stars."

"Hah! Even the Tribesman agrees with me." Dayfid said, rounding on Gregor. "Open your eyes, Estande!"

"You forget yourself," Gregor roared, his temper flaring, "and I tire of your arrogance. I am commander of the Guard, not you, Guardsman. You will fight when and where I tell you. Is that clear?" Dayfid trembled with the effort of keeping his temper in check, but he finally managed a curt nod. "Good. Then sit." Gregor dismissed him with a gesture, and Dayfid reluctantly resumed his seat. After a moment, so did Gregor. "If we attack, we die," the commander continued. "And while an honorable death beneath the stars might appeal to some,"—he shot a glance at Kal—"I, for one, would prefer to live." Gregor noticed them in the doorway and inclined his head. "Prince Martyn. Lord Odara, welcome. Honored Mage, please join us."

"I see that we're all getting along splendidly," Martyn said as he took his place at the table. Jeran sat beside the prince, and the two apprentices led Oto to a chair next to Grendor. Once seated, the Mage reminded the children that what they had heard was never to be repeated and shooed them away. They needed little urging; both apprentices left at a run.

"A simple misunderstanding, my Prince," Gregor told Martyn. "The young Guardsman seems to enjoy opposing my every suggestion."

"It's wise to consider all options," Martyn replied, and Jeran heard the lies of a trained diplomat. "The additional troops and Magi may have created new opportunities. Dayfid can be overzealous, but I'm sure he meant no offense. Did you?" The gaze Martyn fixed on the Guardsman was cold.

"No, I did not," Dayfid said sullenly. "My apologies, Lord Estande. I want only what's best for Alrendria."

"You're not the only one here with a temper," Gregor answered, waving off the apology.

"Well, then," Jes said in a calm and measured voice. She had sat through the exchange with a stony expression, and Jeran knew from experience that her patience was wearing thin. "Maybe we can continue in a more civil manner?"

Gregor and Dayfid mumbled apologies to the First of Velan, and Jes turned to Jeran. "It's good to see you again, Lord Odara," she told him before addressing the group. "The arrival of supplies and troops *has* changed our situation. While I agree with Lord Estande that a frontal assault is not the wisest option, I do believe our current strategy is no longer the most effective. We have less than half a day before our enemy arrives. The odds are against an attack tonight—he's more likely to attack in the morning, when the sun is in our eyes and he had a full night to refresh his troops—but Tylor was never one to do the expected. We must have a plan ready before he arrives."

"The Bull will win any siege," Dayfid repeated. "No amount of troops or supplies will change that. He must be defeated quickly and decisively."

"I agree," Kal said. "My Hunters—" A broad smile spread across the *Kranach's* face when the door swung open. "Little Brother!" he called out, rising. All eyes swiveled toward the doorway.

"They insisted on coming," Sheriza said, preceding her two wards. "I've never met two more stubborn patients in my entire life."

"Magic isn't medicine," Aemon said gruffly, shouldering his way past the Healer. "How many times must I tell you, Sheri, that once you heal someone, they're healed? You don't have to coddle them like an infant." Aemon's flesh was pale, his steps slow and deliberate, but his eyes sparkled as he settled into a chair. Jes frowned when she saw him, her lips compressing into a line. Jeran thought she might be on the verge of ordering him back to bed.

"You pretend to know a great deal about magic," Sheriza replied, "yet you overextended yourself like an apprentice barely out of swaddling. Don't lecture me about my Gift until you've learned control of your own." With an angry sniff, Sheriza stormed from the room.

Kal and Martyn rushed toward Dahr, fighting over who would be the first to greet him. Kal won, and gripped Dahr tightly by the shoulders. The prince was only an instant slower, and he forcefully pulled Dahr away from the *Kranach*. The wounds which had criss-crossed Dahr's body had been healed, with only a few dark circles to mark where the arrows had pierced his flesh, but his eyes were empty, almost lifeless. Once he freed himself from Martyn and Kal, he took a seat beside Jeran without a word for the others.

"Try not to look so happy to be here," Jeran whispered, leaning in close. He meant it as a joke, but the look Dahr gave him drove all thoughts of humor from his mind.

Martyn stared at Dahr for a moment, then returned to his chair. "We have an opportunity here, and we must find a way to exploit it. The Bull likely knows of our reinforcements, but it's less likely that he knows about the Magi who defected to our cause. Thanks to Lord Odara's intercession with the Mage Assembly, nearly two score Magi and three times that number in apprentices have come to Vela. They've been appearing in small groups for the last day, and it's doubtful that even the Assembly knows they're gone yet. Adding their strength to the Magi we already have gives us a powerful advantage."

"The Bull has Magi," Dayfid reminded him, and the Guardsman's lip curled up in a sneer when he said the word. "His are trained to kill. Half the ones we have can't defend themselves, let alone others."

"Not all of the new Magi are Healers," Martyn explained. "Those who aren't may not have trained their powers for war, true, but they have far greater experience than the ShadowMagi. Aemon himself will lead our Magi, and his name alone should be enough to give Tylor pause."

Aemon opened his mouth to speak, but a loud crash outside kept him from offering his advice. "I will not be coddled like a child!" A second crash resounded against the door, which opened to admit Aryn. The guards lay on the floor, struggling to rise. One reached for his sword. Jeran signaled for them to hold, and Martyn leapt to his feet.

"What's the meaning of this?" he demanded. "Who are you to—?"

"Prince Martyn," Aryn interrupted, saluting fist-on-heart. "I apologize for my late arrival. My nephew must have forgotten to pass along your invitation."

"Uncle," Jeran said, "you should rest."

"This is my fight more than yours!" Aryn shouted. "I've been fighting Tylor Durange since before your birth, and I've a score to settle with him." Aryn glowered, and the power of his gaze made Jeran back down. "I weary of this. I raised you, Jeran, not the other way around, and I'll not have you telling me where I can go or what I can do." He turned back to Martyn and bowed low. "I am Aryn Odara, my Prince, a friend to your father and once a Commander in the Alrendrian Guard. I beg you to restore my rank so that I may fulfill the oath I took many winters ago."

"Aryn Odara," Martyn whispered, his eyes shifting between Jeran and his uncle. "It's an honor. My father will be overjoyed to hear of your return." He stared at Aryn for a long moment, and then shook himself as if waking from a dream. "I grant your request, Lord Odara. This is Lord Gregor Estande, Commander of the Guard in Vela. You will be his second."

"My Prince," Gregor said, inclining his head toward Aryn. "I would not take offense if you handed the care of the city to Lord Odara. He has—"

"—been rotting in a cave for over eight winters," Aryn finished. "Keep your command, Gregor. It will be an honor to serve with you again." Gregor bowed again, and with another withering glare at Jeran, Aryn took a seat.

Martyn cleared his throat. For those who had just arrived, he outlined Vela's defenses and described how they intended to deal with Tylor's army. "We only need to hold out for a few days," he announced, though Jeran saw through his façade of bravery. "If Treloran survived, he will have gathered his men together and will be leading them here. Jasova marches north from Darein with all the men we can spare, and a Rachannen force approaches from the east. Each of these groups must be within days of Vela."

Aemon's expression blanked, and his eyes drifted toward the ceiling. "I see nothing, Prince Martyn, but even I can't see a full day's ride away. They may be out there."

"If we could find them..." Martyn said. "If we could coordinate an attack..."

"That's a lot of 'ifs'," Jes said, sighing wearily. "Perhaps we should concentrate only on what we know to be true."

"Truth?" Martyn countered, his frustration surfacing. "The truth, Lady Jessandra, is that the enemy can overwhelm us at any time. The truth is, even without his Magi, Tylor could probably raze Vela to the ground. The truth is, if Vela falls, so does Alrendria." A chorus of dark mutters filled the chamber. "This is what Tylor believes," Martyn added, raising his hand for silence, "and it *is* true, but only to a certain extent. As we stand now, the odds are weighted against us, but if even one of the three forces were to join us, the truth might be different. If all three could be brought to our aid...?"

"I can find them," Jeran said. As exhausted as he was, the mere thought of using magic made his gut churn, but he saw no alternative. Martyn was right; without reinforcements, Vela would fall. "I can Gate outside the city and search for them."

"Others have tried," Jes said, and her condescension grated in Jeran's ears. "None have returned. We believe Tylor has scouts and ShadowMagi spread around Vela to intercept any scouts."

"I don't fear ShadowMagi," Jeran replied. "And the risk must be taken if we're to win." He turned away from Jes. "Jasova knows me; it's unlikely he'll mistake me for an enemy."

Martyn frowned. "Very well. But take Dayfid with you. If the Bull has any surprises waiting, you'll need an extra sword, and after you find Jasova, one of you can go in search of the Rachannen. If only we had a way to reach Treloran—"

"My Prince!" Dayfid interrupted. "My place is here! I want to fight the Tachans."

"There will be fighting enough for everyone," Martyn replied. "Jeran needs someone he can trust, and you've proven yourself time and again." For a moment, it looked like Dayfid meant to argue, but in the end he acquiesced. "With a little luck, we'll take Tylor completely by surprise. If the Gods are with us, we'll strike a blow to the Darklord's forces that he won't soon forget."

"Good," Dahr said, his voice rumbling over the table. "I'd hate to deprive you of too many slaves."

Silence reigned. All eyes turned toward Dahr, and no one looked more surprised than Martyn. "What did you say?" the prince asked.

"That's what you do with your prisoners, isn't it?" Dahr's gaze was blank, his lips turned down in a dark scowl. "Make slaves of them? Lock them in pens and make them plow your fields and build your walls?"

"The Corsan prisoners were made to build our fortifications," Martyn admitted, "but they were not mistreated. I promise you that, Dahr. They were fed and housed as well as our own soldiers."

"Then it's true," Dahr said, and what little light remained in his eyes died. "You've made them slaves."

"Prince Martyn speaks the truth, little brother," Kal said quietly. "The men captured are treated with honor. These Corsans are not of the Blood, nor are they even *Aelva*, who in their way are just as honorable as our Hunters. They cannot be held to their word. They can not be trusted to run free."

If Dahr heard Kal, he showed no sign of it; his eyes remained fastened on Martyn. Jeran reached out to calm him, but Dahr shoved his hand away. "They should not be enslaved."

"That's ridiculous," Martyn laughed, but Dahr did not share in the humor. "What would you have me do with them?" the prince asked, his temper flaring. "Wag a finger in their faces and tell them not to attack us again, then give them back their swords and see them on their way?"

"Anything is better than the cage." Dahr's dark tone left no room for misinterpretation. "Anything is better than being a slave."

"Kill them?" Martyn choked on the words. "You think I should kill them? Hundreds of men? Just line them up and execute them? What kind of monster do you think I am?"

"Free them," Dahr shrugged, "or kill them if you must. At the very least, admit your hypocrisy. You and your father pretend to love freedom—Alrendria claims to honor freedom!—yet you take slaves and don't even have the decency to show remorse about it."

The Guardsmen looked shocked, and those who had overcome their surprise were growing angry. Even Aryn shook his head angrily. Again, Jeran tried to intervene. "Dahr—"

"I saw your eyes," Dahr growled, cutting Jeran off. "There's no sympathy in them for the lives you've stolen. If your father was the man he claimed to be, he'd have found another way. He styles himself a noble man, but in the end, he's little better than the Corsans. Little better than the Bull himself."

"How dare you!" Martyn said, rising to his feet. He glared at Dahr, but Dahr showed no reaction. "After all he did for you, how dare you liken your King to that monster?" Martyn's white-knuckled grip on the table was the only think that kept him from launching himself at Dahr. "Let them go or kill them, do you really think those the only options? They are the enemy, but they're still human!" A cold sneer spread across the prince's face. "Maybe I should have just taken them to my bed, like you did."

In his haste to rise, Dahr nearly fell from his chair. He bared his teeth, and a low growl rumbled through the room. Martyn held his ground, matching Dahr glare for glare. Kal, Aryn and Grendor eased themselves from their seats and started toward the two young men, ready to intercede should it come to blows.

The subcommanders reached for their swords; the grating hiss of steel on leather rang through the room. Bright auras flared up around Aemon and Oto, and though Jes looked down in disappointment, Jeran knew from his long days of training with her that she was ready to seize magic in an instant.

"Enough!" Jeran shouted, his voice cracking like a whip. "Is this what it's come to: the two of you at each other's throats? This is what Tylor wants." He shifted his gaze to Dahr, and then back to Martyn. "This is what the Darklord wants. If we no longer trust each other, then Lorthas has already won. We might as well open the gates and welcome Tylor to Vela."

"You," he said, jabbing a finger into Dahr's shoulder. "Leave now! And be glad I know you didn't really mean the things you said." When Dahr, trembling with rage, turned to face him, Jeran thought for sure he planned to attack. "I'm warning you for the last time. Walk away before it's too late."

Dahr stared at him for a long moment, then he whirled and crossed the distance to the door in two long strides. He threw the door open hard enough to snap a hinge and plowed through the two guards, sending them to the ground for a second time.

With Dahr gone, all eyes returned to Martyn. "Go," he whispered. "Everyone go. You know what needs to be done." One by one, the others filed out, until only Jeran and the prince remained.

"What's wrong with him," Martyn demanded. "How dare he—?"

"He didn't mean it. You know he didn't."

"He's changed, Jeran. He's not the same man."

"We've all changed."

"But he… I don't like what he's become."

Jeran laughed coldly. "I don't think Dahr likes what you've become either." Martyn tried to say something, but Jeran waved him to silence. "Truth has many facets, Martyn. Give Dahr time, and he'll see that you did the best thing. Think about it long enough and you might even understand his point of view." He gave his words a moment to sink in, and then he said, "What you said to him was cruel, and undeserved. Dahr's suffered a lot."

Martyn struck a defiant stance. "We've all suffered, Jeran. This war has left no one untouched."

"Untouched? No." Jeran drew a slow breath. "But do you really believe you've suffered as much as any other? You've lost some men, maybe even some friends, and you've led men to their deaths, but have you felt the Darklord's touch or Tylor's justice? Have you lost the one thing you loved the most or believed yourself a traitor because you didn't see what no one else saw? You have your princess and your mistress both; you didn't have to choose between them. You lead Guardsmen in battle like you always wanted. You have your father, your Kingdom, and everything that really matters. Tell me, Martyn, do you really think your suffering matches Dahr's?"

"He should have known!" Martyn insisted, slamming his fist down hard enough to make the markers on the map jump. "She was a Durange! How could he not have known?"

"How didn't *you* know?" Jeran countered. "Or Iban? What if I told you I *did* know and said nothing. Who's the traitor now?"

"You... knew?"

"Since before we entered Illendrylla, and I suspected even longer."

"Then why—?"

"Katya did nothing wrong, even though she had ample opportunity, and I won't condemn someone because they might betray me. If you would, then Dahr's right: you're no different than Tylor Durange."

"She betrayed you! She handed you over to the Bull."

"My idea," Jeran said. "My decision. You had to be saved."

Martyn set his jaw. "She's a Durange." Jeran shook his head and drew a deep breath, but Martyn fell back into his seat before Jeran could speak. "It will never be the same again," he sighed. "Between the three of us. Will it?"

Jeran closed his eyes. "I have to go. If Jasova's out there, I'll find him, and bring him as quickly as I can. Good luck, Martyn. May the Gods smile on us all tomorrow."

Chapter 40

Martyn stormed toward the gate trailed by a handful of Guardsmen. "You're sure no one's seen him?" the prince asked, irritated. The streets were deserted save for those who would fight in the coming battle. If Dahr were around, he would be hard to miss. "He should be here!"

The darkness pressed in around them, and the heavy air hung like a wet shroud, making breathing difficult. The storms had passed, but clouds obscured the stars and a thick mist clung to the ground. The torchlight barely penetrated the gloom, and the torches flared and hissed as if the air itself fought to extinguish them. "No one's seen him," one guard said. "We sent a runner to the castle as you requested." Martyn detected a hint of frustration in the Guardsman's voice. *I haven't asked that often. Have I?*

The gate to Vela stood closed and barred, and several bodies sprawled on the ground around it. The first riders had appeared just before sunset the previous day, hundreds of men in heavy black plate with a bronze bull embossed on the breast. They had kept their distance, but their arrival caused a panic, and the terrified refugees had rushed the gates, overwhelming the Guardsmen.

The fighting had been fierce, and for a time it looked like the city would be lost before Tylor arrived. In the end, Malikai and his Guardsmen rallied the defenders and restored order, but not before dozens had died and many more were wounded. Martyn could not help but feel that the Bull had won the first battle, turning Alrendrian against Alrendrian.

A handful of men barely old enough to shave were removing the dead, loading them onto wagons and carting them to large pyres built within the city walls. There would be no time to properly dispose of the dead, just as there had not been time to remove them until now, or time enough to save them in the first place.

Martyn took the stairs two at a time, eager to escape the grisly scene in the courtyard. Clusters of archers lined the battlement, never more than twenty together and each group separated by a good distance. Aemon had suggested the deployment; he claimed it was more difficult for Magi to target small groups. The old man had made a number of suggestions, some of which Martyn thought foolish, but it had been impossible to disagree. Aemon was a legend, and Martyn did not know how to argue with a legend.

His escort in tow, Martyn moved to the edge of the wall and peered into the darkness. Tylor's army was out there somewhere, and that knowledge wore at his men's resolve. The darkness obscured everything, even the buildings directly below were little more than dim outlines. The fields beyond the city, and the enemy upon those fields, remained completely hidden.

Gregor had ordered the gates closed after the riot, a decision which had sent Martyn into a rage. Too many stories had preceded the Bull for him to feel comfortable abandoning his people to Tylor's mercy. Their argument had been heated but brief, and in the end Martyn had relented. The gates remained closed, but every seaworthy vessel was ordered to transport refugees across the Alren. Any captain who refused had his ship commandeered, and Martyn had recalled the fleet to aid in the evacuation. A handful of young Magi were left to monitor the mouth of the harbor, but if the Black Fleet regrouped, there was little anyone could do to stop it.

Captain Eli was charged with the task of evacuating those trapped outside the walls. Captain Corrine was burdened with the more difficult assignment of convincing those inside Vela to flee. Even if Jeran found help, their chance of victory was slim, and Martyn wanted to move as many people as possible to the southern side of the harbor. If Vela fell, his people could flee to Darein or Kaper to make a last stand. It might not save them, but it would buy them time, and time might be all Martyn could give them.

Gregor and Jes had supported his decision. Fewer people in the city increased their chances of surviving a siege and reduced casualties if they did not. But the Velani were a proud people, and persuading them to abandon their homes was not easy. Martyn did not envy Captain Corrine his task. Squinting, he peered into the darkness, looking for any sign of movement. "Dawn should be upon us soon."

"Dawn should be upon us now!" Gregor snarled, limping out of the shadows. The Guard Commander leaned heavily on his cane, grimacing with every other step. Dark rings circled his eyes, and when he stopped next to Martyn, he looked to be on the verge of collapse. "We should be able to see something, or *hear* something, at least."

The implication sent a chill down Martyn's spine. He adjusted his sword in its sheath and looked to where his bow lay against the rampart. "Magic?"

"What else? Damn those ShadowMagi and their Gift!" Gregor slammed his cane down for emphasis, but it slid on a smooth stone and he lost his balance. He hit the wall with a grunt, and instead of pushing himself back to his feet, he sprawled out exhausted and waved away Martyn's attempt to help him up. "They could be a hundred hands away and we'd never know it."

"Darkness is darkness," Martyn replied. "If we can't see them, I'll wager they can't see us." Gregor did not look convinced, so Martyn tried to steer the conversation away from the battle. "Any word of Dahr?"

"Gods!" Gregor exhaled sharply. "How many times—"

"Prince Martyn?" Martyn turned toward the speaker, a boy of no more than fifteen winters. He wore a Guardsman's uniform, but from his clumsy salute and awkward stance, Martyn guessed he had not worn it long. "I come from the castle. Lord Odara is gone."

"I know," Martyn said, dismissing the boy with a wave. "He left yesterday."

"No, my Prince. The other one. Lord Dahr Odara. I was told you'd want to know."

"Dahr, gone?" Martyn frowned, and the messenger grew more nervous.

"His dog and horse too. His room was not slept in."

"Gone," Martyn repeated. "Why? Where would he go?" Remnants of his anger resurfaced, and with no other target, Martyn focused on the boy. Gregor reached out a restraining hand, but Martyn pushed it away.

The young Guardsman trembled. "I... I don't know. I—"

"It doesn't matter." Martyn's frown deepened. What little good humor he had mustered vanished, and he waved the messenger away. "Resume your post. Prepare for the battle."

"Yes, Sir," the boy said, nearly tripping over his own feet in his haste to escape.

"Why would he leave?" Martyn asked, staring into the darkness. He did not expect an answer.

"Young Dahr has lost his path," Oto said, tapping out a path with his cane. "He straddles the line between good and evil, and he's no longer certain which is which. Or which he is." The Mage stopped on Martyn's left, opposite Gregor. He, too, looked over the wall, his head turning from side to side as if he could see more than darkness. Aryn, wearing the uniform and armor of a Guard Commander, stood behind Oto. A deep frown furrowed the elder Odara's face, and his hand absently caressed his sword. He nodded to Gregor, then took up a somber watch.

"That's absurd," Martyn said, dismissing the notion. "Dahr's an honorable man. He knows the difference between right and wrong."

"Is it that easy then?" Oto faced Martyn, and his sightless eyes bored into the prince. Martyn felt uncomfortable beneath that probing, empty stare. "To know right from wrong?"

Martyn opened his mouth to answer, but Oto raised a hand. "No answer is required, Prince Martyn, for no answer is correct. To some, perhaps knowing good from evil is a simple matter, but for others, seeing the distinction is difficult, especially when unjust steps must be taken to reach a just goal."

"I... I don't understand."

"As well you shouldn't. I barely understand the matter myself, and I've been pondering it for centuries." Oto tapped his lip thoughtfully. "I hear you forced those outside the walls onto ships against their will. At swordpoint, even." Martyn tried to speak, and again Oto waved him to silence. "I also hear that you're not forcing those within the city to leave, even though you believe Vela will fall and all within will become the Darklord's slaves. How can both be the right thing to do?"

The prince started to stammer a reply, and Oto chuckled. He patted Martyn on the shoulder. "I want to discuss this with you more, but perhaps we should wait. In my experience, philosophy and warfare don't mix well. Both tend to require one's undivided attention." Oto returned his gaze to the horizon.

Martyn stared after the Mage for a moment before turning to Aryn. "Is everyone ready?"

Jeran's uncle nodded. "The Guardsmen are in position and waiting for your signal."

"And the Magi?"

"Aemon's preparing them. Very few have used their Gift in battle before..." Aryn shook his head as if warding off dark memories. "Trust me when I say that a Mage who doesn't know what he's doing can be more of a threat than the enemy."

"Does Aemon know what *he's* doing?" Martyn asked, stroking his chin. The question earned him a laugh.

"Aemon may not look like much of a warrior, but no one alive has more experience in battle than he does. He knows—"

"Dear Gods!" Oto exclaimed, and all eyes swung toward the Mage. He still stared at nothing, but now his brow was furrowed in concentration and he shook his head.

"What do you see?" Gregor demanded, levering himself up to peek over the wall. The absurdity of the question hit Martyn, but he, too, scanned the horizon desperately. If anything, the darkness had only grown deeper.

"You don't want to know, Lord Estande, but I fear you'll see it all too soon. The enemy approaches." As if cued by Oto's words, a series of notes filled the morning air with ominous intent, shrill sounds that reverberated off the walls and sent a murmur of apprehension down the line. A low, bass booming began to beat a rhythm, growing in volume until it seemed to come from every direction. The darkness pressed in, and a cold wind gusted from the north. A nervous murmur went up among the Guardsmen.

"A simple trick," Aryn said loudly, "meant to unnerve us." He turned to a group of runners—boys too young to join the Guard but eager to help—standing behind them. In normal times, children so young would have been kept far from the battle, but today every willing body was needed for the defense of the city. "Inform the subcommanders that Tylor approaches, and remind them that drums and darkness can't hurt us."

The runners disappeared into the gloom, and a piercing shriek, the tortured cry of a woman, marked their departure. A second scream followed, and then more, one upon another, women and children, begging the Guardsmen for help. After a few moments, even the hardest hearts began to ache. "This is unbearable!" Gregor snarled. He turned to Oto. "Can't you do something?"

"And expose our strength to the enemy?" Oto made a tisking sound with his tongue. "The peasants were evacuated days ago, Commander. There's nothing out there but ShadowMagi. And even if those screams were real, there's nothing my people could do except die trying to save them. At the moment, we still hold the advantage; I think it unwise to risk that advantage just to ease our guilt."

Even though Oto spoke quietly, Martyn heard his words clearly; he suspected that Guardsmen all along the line could hear them just as well. "It takes a significant amount of the Gift to sustain an illusion on such a grand scale," the Mage said. "Every passing moment weakens the ShadowMagi more, and for little gain. Let them play their games; it takes more than shadows and screams to frighten the Alrendrian Guard."

If Oto's words had an effect, Martyn did not see it. The Guardsmen huddled close around the torches, cringing at every scream and scanning the skies as if expecting death to descend on them at any moment. *At this rate, the battle will be over before we see the enemy.*

"Lord Estande," Oto said suddenly, "Ready your archers."

Confusion flitted across Gregor's face, and he waved at the darkness. "For what? Tylor himself could be fifty hands away and we'd never know it!"

"Don't worry, Commander. I will be their eyes." Throwing up his arms, Gregor barked out a string of orders. The archers moved quickly, seasons of intense training overcoming their fear, and took up positions atop the gatehouse, notching arrows to their bows. Oto waited for them to get into position. "One volley and then back under cover. Ready? Draw... Aim lower... A little lower... Now!"

Pained screams rose up from below as the Alrendrian archers dove for cover. Several balls of murky, orange flame drifted over the wall and a number of arrows clattered against the stone, fired from below. "Ha!" Oto laughed. "That got their attention!"

Gregor paced nervously, pausing now and then to lean over the wall and squint into the darkness. "How many men are down there?"

"A handful, Lord Estande, hoping to reach the gate before we noticed them. But the rest are coming now. Foolish. They're bound to kill themselves marching in the dark. Perhaps we had better light the way for them." Oto took a deep breath and rose, levitating easily to the top of the wall despite his bulk. The movement startled Martyn, who wished, not for the first time, that he had the Gift of magic. It seemed to make life much simpler.

Oto stretched out his arms and the air around him swirled. The screams cut off suddenly, the drums faded to a low thumping, and the darkness receded. Blue skies appeared above the Mage, and a bright ray of golden sunlight fell upon him. The light spread quickly, moving to encompass the Alrendrians, and the unnatural night boiled away from the walls in a rolling wave.

A dozen bodies appeared at the base of the wall beside a discarded battering ram and a handful of grappling hooks. A moment later, a cheer went up when the fleeing backs of a few score soldiers and two black-robed Magi materialized from the ether. But the cheers subsided when the darkness abruptly disappeared, the illusion discarded, and the full might of Tylor's army came into view.

Cramped wooden buildings extended several thousand hands beyond Vela's first defensive wall, the narrow avenues and low overhangs making the approach to the city difficult despite the shoddy construction. The homes were empty, that part of the city barren. The stubborn residents and skulking refugees hiding in abandoned homes had been gathered up and forced aboard the last of Captain Eli's transports.

Beyond the buildings stood Tylor's army, thousands upon thousands of men in armor the color of night, an army larger than any Martyn had seen or even heard of. They advanced slowly, a line of soldiers that spanned the horizon, and Martyn realized that what he thought to be the measured beat of drums was actually the thunder of his enemy's steps, the elegant synchrony of precision marching.

The sun's sudden appearance had no effect on the Bull's forces. The enemy neither slowed nor stumbled; they advanced at the same stately pace, showing discipline enough to rival the Alrendrian Guard. ShadowMagi dotted the ranks, their black robes standing out even in the sea of dark armor. A few walked among the soldiers but most stood apart, and a gap opened for them wherever they passed. With the darkness gone there was no hint of magic in the air, but from the predatory way in which they approached the city, one could not doubt that they were ready to use their Gift.

Squads of black riders flanked the infantry. They halted some distance from the city, forming several column. Horses were of little use on Vela's twisting streets, but the cavalry's presence made escape all but impossible and allowed Tylor to protect his flank. Five towers of wood and steel as tall as the walls trundled past the cavalry, followed by dozens of catapults and ballistae. Lines of men and women, dressed in rags and bound by chains, drew the siege engines. Masked men walked among them, using lashes to drive their charges forward.

In the midst of it all, Tylor Durange rode upon his armored horse, a powerful beast that stomped the ground with every other step. Dressed in the spiked black armor and horned helmet that gave him his name, the Bull held aloft a sword so black it drew the light from the air around it, leaving a swirling shadow in its wake.

"Dear Gods," Gregor whispered, and the color drained from his face. His expression hardened, and he affected a commanding stance before marching down the line, shouting orders. Aryn started in the other direction, his orders mirroring Gregor's. Wherever they passed, Guardsmen straightened, and a measure of confidence returned. It was a transient strength, though; once the commanders were gone, terror returned, and with it the pall of despair.

"We don't have a chance," Martyn whispered, unable to take his eyes off Tylor's army. "We can never hold the city."

"We must hold, Prince Martyn," Grendor said. The Orog wore a leather jerkin hastily tailored to fit his broad frame and studded with bits of metal. In his hand he held a staff fitted at one end with a curved blade. "If we do not, all of Alrendria will fall, and your people will suffer the same fate as mine."

Martyn had not expected to see the Orog on the wall, and he bowed his head formally. "Your presence is welcome, but this is not your fight. If you would prefer to stay in the castle—"

"Over ten centuries ago," Grendor interrupted, "the Elders vowed to help Aemon defeat the Darklord. I will do my part to fulfill that vow." A broad grin spread across his face. "Besides, this is Jeran's fight, and I've sworn myself to him. Before he left, he asked me to protect you, and the best way to do that is to protect this city."

Martyn eyed the grey-skinned man warily. They were virtually strangers, the two of them, but Jeran trusted Grendor. That should have been enough. "You seem confident enough. Don't you fear death?"

"All things die, Prince Martyn, but as the Elders say, 'A coward dies a thousand deaths, the brave man dies but once.' " The Orog frowned, and he suddenly looked troubled. "Of course, they also say 'Fools fight when they can, heroes when they must, but the wise man never.' "

"Well, then," Martyn laughed, hiding his suspicions and waving for Grendor to join him. "Let's hope you're a hero and not all that wise."

The blast of a horn drew their gazes back to the enemy, who had reached the edge of the city. A path had opened through the infantry, and the siege towers were brought forward. "Fools!" Gregor laughed as he marched back down the line. "Those towers are too big. They'll never get them through."

The siege towers were as wide as Vela's twisting streets, and they would never navigate the sharp curves. The towers stopped in front of the first buildings, and another trumpet blast signaled their arrival. Then an eerie silence descended on the city. Several ShadowMagi drew together, and one pointed to the castle, where Aemon's banner flapped in the wind. They showed no fear, but Martyn hoped Aemon's presence would make them cautious.

Tylor rode to the front line, his troops gracefully stepping aside to create a path for him. The ShadowMagi followed, forming a line of black robes and hate-filled glares in front of the towers. "I've been here before," Gregor said. "This is where Tylor demands surrender and talks about the glory of joining the Tachan Empire."

"There will be no surrender today," Aryn said grimly. "No mercy. Not even the Bull's twisted variety. He's here to kill." Tylor rode from one end of the ShadowMagi to the other, his eyes on the city. When he reached the end of the line, he raised his sword, but nothing happened.

"Everyone down!" Oto shouted, his voice thundering from one end of the wall to the other. Without thinking, Martyn threw himself to the stones.

A terrible sound filled the air, and the wall trembled. Winds tore across the battlements, buffeting those too foolish to follow Oto's advice. One Guardsman sailed over the rampart, knocked from his feet despite the heavy armor he wore. Something thudded into the gate, and the stout wood shuddered. A second blow followed, and a third, an unrelenting onslaught that sent men running to brace the gateway. All around them objects smashed into the wall. Screams filled the air, and something worse, a sound like falling rock, as if a mountain descended upon the city.

Martyn risked a glance over the wall. Dark funnels descended from a suddenly cloudy sky, criss-crossing the battlefield and kicking up clouds of dust that obscured the city. When a stone the size of his fist flashed by his head, Martyn dropped behind the wall for protection, but Oto stood calmly upon the battlement throughout it all, his robes blown by the gusting winds. Untouched by debris, his head swept from side to side, and his blank eyes studied the horizon. Occasionally, he pointed at something and his lips moved in a silent chant.

The wind stopped as quickly as it began, and calm returned. Martyn stood cautiously, and his mouth fell open. "Dear Gods," he whispered. After all his exposure to Magi, the extent of their power still amazed him. "If they can do that, there's nothing to stop them from tearing the walls down. Or all of Vela!"

The destruction was total. The carts and other obstacles placed in the streets to slow Tylor's advance were gone. The streets themselves were gone, as were the buildings. The ShadowMagi had swept the approach to Vela clean. Small piles of debris and the occasional broken beam, looking like grave markers on the desolate landscape, were all that remained. The buildings had been shattered against the wall or thrown into the harbor, only the smooth black stone of the promontory remained.

The siege towers were advancing; the guards drove the slaves forward with their whips. "If they could level the whole city," Oto asked, descending from the rampart, "then why didn't they? You have Magi, too, remember? Lorthas' Magi could destroy this city with their Gift, but we would never allow such a catastrophe to happen."

"Then why didn't you stop that?" Martyn demanded, pointing to the barren land and the approaching army.

Oto shrugged. "To what end? Those buildings were empty, their owners gone."

"The men are already convinced we will lose," Martyn replied. "When they see things like that, how will we ever restore their confidence?"

"Magic is not a limitless gift, Prince Martyn. A Mage can only do so much before exhaustion overwhelms him. The darkness... The drums... Everything the enemy has done takes effort. The ShadowMagi have great power, yes, but they haven't been using magic long enough to understand it. Let them exhaust themselves with these foolish theatrics. You'll be glad you did when the battle truly begins."

With every thunderous step, Tylor's army drew closer. Ranks of soldiers marched behind the siege engines, ready to rush forward once the towers reached the wall. Tension rose along the battlement, and Martyn struggled to keep his men focused. He was not the only one to struggle; in the distance he heard shouting, and before he could investigate, several dark blurs streaked down from the wall. Two slaves fell, their bodies riddled with arrows, and the towers rolled to a stop as the other slaves tried to flee.

Martyn raced toward the shouting voices. His bodyguards and Grendor ran after him. "I said stand down!" Gregor yelled as Martyn moved into earshot. A handful of militiamen protected a dozen archers from an equal number of Guardsmen. Gregor stood out front, his sword drawn and his face flushed with anger. "What are you doing, man? Those are our people down there!"

"My people are behind this wall," one archer replied, "and if those towers reach us, they'll all be dead." The towers had started forward again, the slaves urged onward by their overseers' whips. "Hold a moment, lads. Let 'em get closer."

"Stand down," Gregor repeated, his voice a growl. "I won't warn you again."

"I don't know much about soldierin'," the man said, taking aim with his bow, "but it seems to me like you need every man you can get, and fightin' us isn't gonna make winnin' this battle any easier." The man sighed heavily when he saw Gregor's glare. "Listen, swordsman, I can't say as I like shootin' another Alrendrian, but if stoppin' them keeps my family safe, I'm willin' to live with the guilt."

Gregor's lips narrowed to a thin line, but before he could speak, Grendor shot past in a grey blur, his staff swinging faster than the eye could follow. The Orog ducked a clumsy swing from one militiaman, and with a series of well-placed blows knocked the man aside. Using the blade fastened to the end of his staff, he sliced the archer's bowstring.

The others moved to attack Grendor, and Malikai ordered the Guardsmen in. They quickly subdued the poorly-trained militia. "Get them off the wall," Martyn ordered. "I want no man here who refuses to obey orders." With a gruff nod, Malikai herded the prisoners toward the stairs, and Martyn turned to Gregor. "He's right about one thing. If those towers reach the walls, this battle's over."

"Then maybe we should do something about that," Aemon said, stepping into view. The Mage wore dark robes and carried a black staff capped at one end with a golden eagle. His white beard and hair had been neatly trimmed, and power radiated from his bright blue eyes. Awed whispers followed him as he strode confidently down the battlement.

"Great One," Grendor said, bowing low.

"I thought you promised not call me that." Aemon smiled as he went to the wall and surveyed the enemy army. "You were a fool to come here, Tylor," he said, his voice thundering over the city. Even Tylor's well-disciplined troops froze at the sound. "A fool to face me again. Twice I let you live, but my patience wears thin. Turn back now. Return to *Ael Shataq*. You have no future in Alrendria."

"For the Darklord!" Tylor shouted, and the Bull's army took up the cry. The roar matched Aemon's voice in power; it made the very walls tremble.

"That decides it then," Aemon said sadly. He aimed his staff toward the first tower, and it erupted in flames. At the same time, the chains holding the Alrendrians snapped. Aemon moved his staff, pointing to each tower in turn, and then the catapults behind them. Each jab of the eagle totem brought a new flash of flame and another cheer from the Alrendrians.

The slaves, freed of their bonds, stared hopelessly at the army behind them. "Come along now," Oto called, waving them forward. "This way!" He stood outside the gate, though how he had gotten there, Martyn had no idea. Oto craned his head around, and his blank stare sought out Gregor. "Lord Estande, the gates, if you will."

Gregor hobbled off, shouting for the gates to be opened. The freed Alrendrians surged forward, but not before Tylor's archers drew and fired. Martyn tensed, but he refused to turn away from the massacre. When the shafts bounced harmlessly off a wall of air, the prince found himself cheering every bit as loudly as his men. "That is why we call him the Great One," Grendor laughed.

Tylor could do nothing but watch his siege engines burn and his slaves escape. When his archers readied a second volley, he waved for them to hold. The slaves reached the gates without incident, and when the last man was inside, another cheer went up among the defenders.

"I thought that old woman said Aemon was weak," Martyn whispered to Grendor. "If this is him weak—"

"He *is* weak," Sheriza said, and Martyn jumped at the whip-like crack of the Healer's voice. She stood a few steps behind the prince, her eyes fastened on Aemon and a deep scowl across her face. "Far weaker than he'd ever admit. He won't be using magic today, and shouldn't use it for some days to come."

Martyn glanced at the burning towers. "Then how…?"

"Vela's saviors stand behind you, Prince Martyn," Sheriza answered, pointing over Martyn's shoulder to where three Magi guarded a group of children ranging from eight to sixteen winters old. The apprentices, some standing on stools so they could see over the wall, stood immobile, their faces contorted with concentration. "The first thing a Mage is taught is how to protect himself," Sheriza explained. "Once the prisoners are safe, the apprentices will return to the castle where it's safe."

"Alrendrian owes them a debt," Martyn said, and he vowed to pay it. *Somehow, I'll pay them back.* His gaze returned to Aemon, who stood unprotected on the wall. "If he can't defend himself, then he should go with them. And you—"

"Aemon won't leave," Sheriza said with finality. "As for me, the wounded will be down here, not at the castle. They will need me."

A horn's trill reverberated through the air, and with a scream of defiance, Tylor's army charged. They surged around the ShadowMagi, past the burning hulks of the siege engines, and came toward Vela at a run. Martyn barely had time to retrieve his bow before Gregor ordered the archers to fire. Shafts rained down upon the attacking host, the archers firing as quickly as they could notch and draw. In the courtyard and alleys behind them, swordsmen rushed forward to repel the attackers.

Explosions ripped through the advancing army, sending men flying in showers of flames and stone. But the Magi weren't the only ones bringing their Gift to bear; black-robed figures took aim at the defenders, too. Lightning arced out of the clear sky and balls of flame drifted over the wall, lighting whatever they touched afire. After a few moments, Martyn realized that Aemon had advised him well; the small pockets of defenders took far fewer casualties to magic than the Bull's tightly-packed army.

Tylor's troops reached the wall with a shout of victory. Many leaped over the low barricades and ran down the narrow alleys between buildings only to find themselves blocked by walls of solid stone. Guardsmen poured burning oil on them from above, and archers fired at point blank range through murder holes. The screams of the dying filled the morning air.

The defenders fought well, but the tide of Tylor's army proved too strong to turn back. Before long, grappling hooks scraped the battlements and ladders clattered against the rooftops. For every ladder toppled and every rope cut, three more appeared in its place.

Martyn fired his last arrow and scanned the wall. To his left, Aryn and a squad of Guardsmen battled a group of black-armored warriors; to his right, Malikai and Einar fought beside Gregor. The Guard Commander stood in the thick of the fray, his cane discarded and his sword cutting through any enemy in reach. He shouted orders continuously, pointing out targets to his men even while seeking his own opponents.

A ladder with two soldiers clinging to it thudded into the wall in front of Martyn, and the prince barely had time to duck before one of them swung an axe at his head. He returned the attack reflexively, and one man fell, his strangled cry cutting off abruptly when he hit the ground. The second man vaulted from the ladder, landing a few steps from Martyn. He fell instantly, the point of Grendor's blade piercing his chest. The Orog looked shaken, his gray skin tinted yellow, as he wrested the blade free. Without so much as a grunt, he picked the enemy soldier up and tossed him over the ladder. Martyn smiled when he heard the shouts of the men who could not avoid the falling body.

Grendor shoved the ladder with the end of his staff, and it teetered vertically for a moment before falling backward. Another ladder slammed against the wall several dozens hands away, and Martyn ran toward it. They fought like that for some time, trying to keep the ladders from the wall, but the press of enemies was too great and it became impossible to hold them back. "Prince Martyn," Einar called. The grim-visaged Guardsman sported a new bloody scar on his cheek. "Lord Estande suggests we fall back to the next line."

"If we lose this wall, we lose the harbor," Martyn answered, "and any hope of escape. Tell Gregor to hold here as long as possible." An arrow whizzed by Martyn's head, but he barely registered it. "As long as possible!"

"Yes, my Prince!" Einar slammed a fist against his heart and left at a run. He stopped several paces away to hack through a grappling hook. The fireball hit him at the same time the arrow pierced his chest. The Guardsman turned a blackened and still smoking face toward Martyn before he toppled from the wall. *What a waste*, Martyn thought, starting out in search of Gregor. *He'd have made a fine commander.*

Tylor's soldiers were everywhere, and the Guardsmen were hard pressed. Order was gone and discipline failing; Guardsmen moved along the parapets in packs, like wolves hunting prey, and they fought enemies as they found them. They fell upon the Tachans like beasts, howling and screaming, and even the strict discipline of the Bull's army could not protect them from the Guardsmen's fury. The militiamen fared far worse. Most ran about aimlessly, hacking at anything that approached, including each other. The seasoned enemy soldiers had little trouble with the conscripted townsfolk, and many went out of their way to hunt down the untrained Velani.

Terror painted most faces, and Martyn half expected the militia to flee. He shouted encouragement as he ran by, reminding them that they fought for their homes and families. When he could, he paired them up with Guardsmen. Working together, they would have a better chance of survival. He hoped it was enough; in truth, he had little time to waste on them.

Martyn spotted Gregor and hurried toward the Guard Commander, but an explosion lifted a dozen hands above the rooftop. He landed with a crash that sent a jarring pain through his shoulder and slid along the coarse stone, his arms afire with the pain of a thousand shallow cuts. When he finally stopped, he rolled onto his back and felt for his sword.

A jagged hole cut through the wall where the gatehouse had once stood. Dark-armored soldiers poured through the breach, shouting triumphantly, and more than one defender cast away his weapons and ran. Another explosion rocked the wall, and Martyn saw a second gap open to the north, where Aryn was trying desperately to rally his men. Climbing to his feet, Martyn saw Tylor's army pouring into Vela, hacking and slashing at anything that moved.

"Fall back!" Martyn shouted, knowing it was too late. "Fall back to the next line!" The buildings shuddered again, and the prince lost his balance. He dropped to his knees, wincing as another jolt of pain shot through his body, and forced himself to stand. He reached for the man next to him—one of his guards—but when he saw the bloodied face and blank stare, he turned away. A second Guardsman still lived, and the prince helped the man up. His other guards and Grendor were gone.

A trumpet blasted over the tumult, calling for the retreat. Black-armored warriors raced through the streets, shouting out their victory and calling for Alrendrian blood. Behind the soldiers, a tight formation of ShadowMagi formed, a small knot of black-robed destruction. One Mage directed the others; a simple gesture from his bone white finger crumbled walls and toppled buildings. *If those Magi can't be stopped, we're doomed.*

Unguarded and isolated, focused as they were on their task, the ShadowMagi made an easy target, but Martyn had no troops with which to mount an assault nor any way to pass through the army separating him from the ShadowMagi. Then he noticed a tight wedge of soldiers running away from the city and a familiar gray-skinned figure at the point, his bladed staff cutting down every enemy in reach. A squad of Guardsmen spread out behind Grendor, and Martyn saw Malikai's broad form hacking away at the enemy. Huddled close together in the center of the wedge were a group of unarmed Magi.

"That's suicide!" Martyn muttered, and he silently asked the Five Gods to grant them luck. "They'll get themselves killed out there."

"They'd probably do a decent job of that in here, too," Oto said, approaching Martyn. The Mage stumbled over the dead Guardsman's body and barely managed to catch himself. Martyn offered a hand, but Oto waved it away. "It's not safe for you here, Prince Martyn. I've come to take you away."

"I'm not going anywhere," Martyn said sternly. "I won't abandon Vela. My people are here. Miriam and Kaeille are here!"

"You misunderstand. I meant only to evacuate you to the next line of defense. It would do the troops good to see a familiar face. Conditions there are not... What's that?"

Oto never moved. His eyes still stared straight at Martyn, so the prince had no idea of what the Mage spoke. "What is what?" he demanded, whirling in circles. He scanned the defenses, the ground, and the battlefield. Aryn and his men were being pushed back. The defenders were breaking. The Bull's army was moving deeper into the city, cutting off any chance for retreat. Nothing had changed. He was about to dismiss Oto's question when a party of mounted warriors crested a hill to the north and filled the sky with arrows. The attack caught the enemy by surprise, and a half dozen volleys cut through their flank before the Bull's troops turned to defend themselves.

"Is that Lord Odara?" Gregor asked, limping toward Martyn. Two score Guardsmen followed the crippled commander. When he reached them, Gregor glanced at Martyn then at the city behind them. *No doubt he wants to escort me to safety, too.*

"From the north?" Martyn replied, shaking his head. Just then, a large eagle swooped past the prince, screeching defiantly, and Martyn laughed aloud. "It's Dahr!" He squinted and shielded his eyes from the sun with a hand. He soon recognized another familiar form. "And Treloran!"

Dahr rode at the front of the charge, his greatsword flashing in the morning sun. Atop his giant warhorse he towered over everyone on the field. Fang ran at his side, and Martyn half-expected an army of beasts to burst from the forest and come to Vela's defense. No other animals appeared, but Dahr needed no help; he cut through the first rank of enemy like a farmer through wheat, and those few who dodged his blade were trampled by Jardelle or mauled by Fang. A bestial roar, audible even over the din of battle, echoed over the wall, sending a chill down Martyn's spine.

The effect it had on the enemy was even greater. The charge faltered, and the stream of men passing through the holes in the defenses slowed. Dahr and his riders drove into the enemy lines, then pulled back and attacked again. Treloran's archers rained death upon the Bull's soldiers from above.

Meanwhile, Grendor had circled wide around the ShadowMagi, and they did not notice his approach until it was too late. Discarding his staff, the Orog launched himself bodily into the enemy, bowling over half a dozen black-robed figures and struggling to keep himself atop as many as possible. The Guardsmen ran in at his heels, cutting and slashing, and the Magi who traveled with them unleashed their Gift on the remaining ShadowMagi. *Celebrate the small victories*—Martyn heard Lord Iban's voice clearly—*in battle, small victories are often the only victories.*

A horn sounded, and Tylor's cavalry charged. Martyn scowled. The Alrendrian archers would be no match for the dark-armored horsemen, and not even Dahr could hope to stand against such odds. Martyn cursed as the riders raced toward the Aelvin Prince's unprotected flank; he had no way to warn Treloran and no time to call for reinforcements. All he could do was watch as the enemy bore down on his people, his friends.

The ground in front of the enemy cavalry exploded. Horses reared and screamed, throwing riders and stalling the charge. Treloran heard the sound and turned to face the new threat. For a moment, Martyn held out hope, but Tylor's commanders rallied the disorganized riders and resumed their charge.

When it seemed that nothing could save the Aelvin Prince, a group of riders burst from concealment atop a thinly-forested hill. Hundreds of wild men in mismatched armor screamed war cries and hollered taunts as they raced to cut off the enemy. Jeran rode in front of them, his Aelvin-wrought blade flashing in the sunlight.

The riders hit the Tachan line with neither formation nor discipline, but what they lacked in order they made up for with tenacity. Only Dahr matched their ferocity, and he wheeled his own riders around to pin the enemy between his men and Jeran's. Trapped between two forces, the enemy commander slowed his charge, and Treloran's archers open fire.

A series of trumpet blasts drew Martyn's gaze south, where a number of Rakers sailed toward the northern bank of the Alren. The lead ship ran aground, grinding to a stop in the sandy soil, and the sailors threw a ramp over the side. Dayfid, unmistakable in his silver armor, leapt upon the gangplank and ran toward the enemy. Scores of Guardsmen followed him into the fray. More ships ran aground to unload their cargo of soldiers, and still others stayed farther out, ferrying men to shore in longboats. Jasova stood in the prow of one boat and Miriam's cousin, Jaem, in another. A tight smile worked its way onto Martyn's face. "Signal the charge."

"They'll never know what hit them," Gregor laughed. At his command, a trumpeter blew the signal to attack, and Martyn could not remember hearing a sweeter note. A strange silence descended over the city in the note's wake, but it lasted only an instant before the gates to Vela's second wall burst open and the defenders rushed out screaming, "For Prince Martyn and Alrendria!"

"We'd better hurry," Martyn laughed, "or we might miss all the fun." He started for the stairs, but the Guardsmen beat him there. He turned to face Gregor, and saw the battle raging behind the commander's eyes.

"I wouldn't want to hide up here either," Gregor admitted. "But at least let someone else *lead* the charge."

"Lord Estande," Martyn said, offering a formal bow. "I'm not a complete fool." He let the Guardsmen lead the way, and left Oto and Gregor hobbling behind.

Chapter 41

Martyn waved from atop his mount, and a cheer preceded the prince through the streets. Lord Gregor Estande, his left arm wrapped in a blood-soaked bandage, rode on the prince's right; Aemon, his eyes distant and introspective but his smile bright, on his left. Thousands lined the streets, more to see the ancient Mage than to cheer their prince, but for a wonder, Martyn did not seem to mind that the attention was not focused on him.

Jeran rode in the second rank, with Aryn and Dahr flanking him, and he hoped the expression he wore appeared more genuine than it felt. Behind him, Kal and Grendor walked alongside Treloran and Dayfid. The *Kranach* leaned in close to Treloran's horse and whispered something to the Aelvin Prince, who laughed. Dayfid flashed a grin at every pretty girl who caught his eye, and Grendor did his best to remain unnoticed. Each time someone pointed him out and shouted 'Orog', his skin turned darker, until he nearly matched the dark stone of the streets.

Rank upon rank of Guardsmen and militia followed them. Most barely had the time to wipe the blood and grime from their bodies before being relieved of duty and forced into this procession, but if the heroes of Vela were ashamed of their dented armor and soot-streaked hair, they gave no sign of it. The Guardsmen marched in precise formation, treating this parade like any other duty, but Jeran saw the pride in their eyes, the joy that each cheer brought. The militiamen were less organized; many broke rank to run to loved ones or grab a girl from the crowds and spin her around in a tight embrace. No one cared. The inns and taverns had thrown open their doors for feasting, and the sounds of revelry echoed over the clamor of trumpets and pipes. The people of Vela would long remember this victory.

Victory! Jeran thought wryly. *Victory in name only.* Nearly half the city lay in ruins, the buildings smashed by magic or burned in fires set by Tylor's men, fires which still burned in some parts of the city. With winter looming on the horizon, thousands were without a roof over their heads or a hearth to warm themselves by. Finding food would be an even greater problem. Tonight, the people feasted, but with the fields destroyed, hunger would be a well-known visitor to Vela this winter.

The dead lay everywhere except along the route upon which Martyn had planned his procession. Over a thousand Guardsmen and many times that number in militia had lost their lives, and thousands more were missing. The injured outnumbered the living, and despite the Healers' best efforts, many more would succumb to their wounds in the days to come.

Too many dead, far too many lives cut short by Lorthas' twisted vision. The knot in Jeran's gut tightened, and he fought the urge to vomit. He felt their pain, the pain of all those who had died, the pain of all those who lay dying. If he had done more, tried harder, he could have saved them. These people had counted on him to protect them, and he had failed them. The distant wails drowned out the cheers, and the huddled forms kneeling in the shadows drew his attention far more than the squads of happy Guardsmen or the people calling out his name.

He looked down one avenue and saw two children, no more than twelve winters in age, tugging at a motionless shadow. Jeran wanted to go to them, to help. He would have preferred doing anything to being here—clearing away bodies, salvaging what remained of the city, or repairing the defenses—everything seemed more worthwhile than pretending this victory meant something more than it did. Yet Martyn had been adamant. As soon as the debris had been cleared from the main roads, he insisted upon the parade. "These people have lived in fear for seasons," he said to counter Jeran's objections. "They need to celebrate, if only for one night. The dead will be here tomorrow, Jeran. Let tonight be for the living."

Martyn was right, and Jeran knew it, but admitting it did not make him enjoy the parade.

"What's wrong with you, lad?" Aryn whispered. "You look like you just swallowed a lemon."

"There are more important things to do than this. I'm in no mood for celebration."

"You'd rather be digging ditches or burning bodies?" When Jeran nodded, his uncle frowned. "Well, too bad. Tonight's not about you, or even about Alrendria. It's about them." He gestured at the cheering crowd. "They neither asked for war nor desire it. They've lost family, friends, their homes, their lives. Many have nothing to go back to but scorched fields and bad memories." Aryn must have seen something in Jeran's cold gaze he did not like, because his arm shot out and caught Jeran's arm. "Every now and then, living's no longer enough, and a man needs to remember *why* he wants to live. A night of happiness will fortify this city better than any shoring of the defenses."

He let go, and patted Jeran's shoulder fondly. "I know it's hard to let your guard down, to set duty aside, but it's necessary to do it from time to time. If you don't enjoy life, you can lose sight of what makes living great. If that happens… Well, let's just make sure it doesn't. Enjoy yourself, lad. Our problems will still be here tomorrow."

Despite Aryn's urgings, the slow procession through Vela remained more bitter than sweet. Jeran could not shake the hollow feeling from his gut, nor completely ignore the sense of foreboding that lingered in the air. The more the people cheered him, the greater he felt his failure. At times, he heard the voices of the fallen crying out his name and saw the pallid faces of lost friends staring at him from among the crowd. It was not a Reading, though Jeran felt the tingle that told him he could view one if he wished; this was something new, something unwelcome.

"Are you going to sit up there all day?" Aemon asked, offering his hand. Startled, Jeran blinked and looked around. They had left the crowds behind; the white edifices of the castle loomed above them, and the setting sun hung over the waters of the Western Sea. Jeran reached out slowly and took Aemon's hand. As he stepped down from the saddle, the old Mage eyed him curiously. "What's wrong?"

"What?" Jeran asked, and then he shrugged. "It's just… It's nothing. It doesn't seem right, celebrating like this."

Aemon pursed his lips thoughtfully, then clapped an arm around Jeran's shoulders. "Those men and women died so that we might live, my boy. Don't cheapen their sacrifice by wallowing in misery. I've lived through a number of battles, so trust me when I say that you'll have time enough to mourn later."

"You're right," Jeran said, forcing a smile. He felt no better, but he made an effort to hide his misgivings. "Everyone's right! Come on! Let's drink a toast to the heroes of Vela."

A trio of pipers stood before the castle's entrance, playing a lively tune. Guardsmen, already deep in their cups, danced and sang to the song, and they called for Jeran to join them. Jeran refused, and he led Aemon to a row of casks arranged along the castle wall. They tapped one, a dark Feldarian wine, and raised their glasses to the fallen.

Some time later, a lanky Mage called to Aemon, and the old man begged Jeran's leave, promising to meet up with him later in the night. Jeran found his way to the nearest barrel and filled a mug with ale. He downed the drink and filled the mug a second time before wandering the courtyard.

Revelers filled the grounds to bursting. Musicians had taken up places around the castle, and the sound of their playing drifted in and out over the roar of conversation. Wagonloads of food were distributed freely, and drink flowed in abundance. Tall piles of timber were set alight to ward off the darkening sky. Familiar voices called out for Jeran's company, but the press of bodies was too great, and Jeran stayed away from the throng. His depression remained, though it was dulled by drink, and he sought a place of peace, somewhere where he could watch the festivities without participating.

Jasova, his hands cupped behind his head, reclined against the seawall, telling tales of the Corsan skirmishes to a group of wide-eyed recruits. The boys leaned in close, hanging on his every word, and Jasova reveled in the attention. He barely acknowledged Jeran's passing, pausing only long enough to raise his mug in salute. Jeran waved back, but hurried on before the Guardsman asked him over to tell a tale or two.

Lord Estande had dispensed with his cane. He walked by Jeran with the aid of a flaxen-haired beauty, and a second young woman—buxom, dark-haired, and half the commander's age—wiggled her way under his other arm. Gregor laughed loudly, planted a kiss on the woman's cheek, and let his two charges lead him away.

At the point of the promontory, a group of Magi surrounded Grendor, harassing him with questions. Grendor looked more terrified among them than he had on the battlefield, and he cast furtive glances over the wall as if contemplating a leap into the ocean. Jeran started to go to the Orog's rescue, but then he hesitated. He had no desire to offer himself as a sacrifice, and no doubt the Magi had questions for him as well. His indecision saved him; Oto appeared, demanding that Grendor follow him immediately. He spirited the Orog away, urging him for haste, but before they disappeared into the crowd, Jeran saw the blind Mage laugh and hand Grendor a tall glass of wine, which the Orog gulped.

Chuckling, Jeran started toward them, but he saw Dahr silhouetted in the setting sun, sitting alone beside a catapult atop a pile of rocks. With the hilt of his greatsword protruding over his shoulder and the scowl on his face, he made a menacing sight. The revelers gave him a wide berth; even Malikai kept his Guardsmen away. Jeran reached for a mug from a passing servant, but took the entire tray instead.

"You timed your attack perfectly," he said as he approached Dahr. "Was it Shyrock?" Dahr nodded, and Jeran forced a mug into his hand. "I thought I saw your eagle lurking about. Here, drink this." Dahr tried to protest, but Jeran raised his tankard. "To the dead." Dahr sipped, but after catching Jeran's expression, he drained the mug in two large gulps. Jeran handed him a full mug. "To the living."

This time, Dahr downed the drink without argument. When Jeran handed him a third, he sighed. "How long do you intend to keep this up?"

"If I have to enjoy myself, then so do you." Jeran took a fresh mug for himself. "Your turn. What should we drink to?" Before he could answer, Dahr's eyes flicked up at a passing shadow, and he stiffened. He scowled, and his teeth ground together. A low, angry growl rumbled from his throat. He gripped his mug hard enough to dent the thick metal.

Someone reached over Jeran's shoulder and pulled a tankard from the tray. "Let's drink to friends, lad. And to giving that whoreson Durange a taste of defeat."

Dahr stood slowly. He towered menacingly over Jeran, who hastily interposed himself between his friend and the newcomer. "Harol, this is my friend, my brother, Dahr. Dahr, this is our ally from Rachannon,"—Jeran made sure to put great emphasis on the word 'ally'—"the man who helped me break Tylor's cavalry and saved Prince Treloran from the Bull. Dahr, meet Lord Harol Grondellan."

Barrel-chested and well muscled, Harol Grondellan remained a daunting sight despite his advancing winters. Unkempt black hair fell like a mane around his head, and a thick beard turned mostly grey obscured the bottom half of his face. A jagged scar cut across his forehead, and others crossed his massive arms. Piercing, near-black eyes studied Dahr. "I saw you on the field, Hunter. I've never seen fighting like that, not even from a Tribesman, and I've fought with and against your people in days past." He raised his mug and looked deep into Dahr's haunted eyes. "To you, and to the heroes like you who will save our world from the likes of Lorthas and Tylor Durange."

"To friends and allies," Jeran added, fixing Dahr with a pointed glare, "and to setting aside past differences." He drank deeply, as did Lord Grondellan. After a long pause, Dahr sipped his ale. Jeran preyed that Dahr could keep a rein on his temper, though he knew it would be a daunting task. Harol Grondellan had once been Dahr's master; he had bought the young Garun'ah from a Slaver named Gral. In the best of times, Dahr had trouble keeping control of his anger when faced with Slavers and slave-owners, and these were far from the best of times. But the last thing they needed was a fight with the Rachannen.

After draining his mug, Harol wiped the ale from his beard and stepped close to Dahr. "Come with me," he said, clapping an arm around Dahr's back. "Let's find something with a little more kick—maybe one of you Tribesmen has a skin of *baqhat!*—and you can tell me how a Garun'ah ended up an Odaran Wolf."

"I'm not sure it's a story you'd like to hear," Dahr replied, and Jeran could only imagine the effort it took for Dahr to restrain himself. The last time Dahr had seen Harol Grondellan, he had nearly killed him in his escape, and it was that flight which had brought halfway across Madryn and to the Odara farm.

Booming laughter filled the night. "Just tell me the parts I'll like then!" Lord Grondellan called for his men to come meet the Alrendrian Giant and pulled Dahr toward the crowd. Before he disappeared, Dahr glared at Jeran. His lips pulled up in the semblance of a smile, but the expression carried little joy.

"Just try not to kill him," Jeran whispered. Alone again, the desire to celebrate faded, and Jeran set the tray down. Moving slowly, with one hand on the wall for balance—the drink had done little to lessen the hollowness in his chest, but it had impaired his mobility—Jeran walked to the edge of the promontory and looked out over the ocean. Somewhere out there, the Black Fleet was regrouping. *Will they return, or will they seek a different target?*

With a cold laugh, Jeran realized he did not care, and that it did not matter. If the Black Fleet returned, the Alrendrians could not defeat them on the water, not even with the Magi who abandoned Atol Domiar; but those same Magi would be more than enough to protect the city from an attack. If the fleet went somewhere else, nothing could be done until it reached its new destination. Either way, for the time being the Darklord's ships were not a threat.

Music, cheering, and laughter beckoned, but to Jeran, the music sounded flat, the celebration forced. Today had been a tiny victory in a long war. The first MageWar had lasted three and a half centuries and ended little better than a draw. This war had begun a decade ago, when Tylor escaped the Boundary, and the first real battles were only now being fought. For eight centuries, the lands and races of Madryn had bickered while Lorthas prepared. Most people still believed the Boundary whole, the Darklord defeated. Jeran wondered what they would do if they knew the truth.

Thoughts like those did little to improve his mood, and he suddenly wished he had brought the ale. He turned to retrieve it, but a group of Guardsmen surrounded the catapult, and Jeran's desire for privacy outweighed his need to drink. He stood in the dark for a long time, until the moon had crossed half the sky. Eventually, he felt her presence behind him.

"You look well, considering." Jes wore a gown of light blue, and her black hair hung in tight curls to the middle of her back. She smiled weakly, and her eyes caught a glint of firelight and amplified it, blazing with the fire of the Gifted. Her gaze was impassive, but Jeran knew her too well. Her indifference hid concern. "As First Seat of House Velan, I should be offended that you didn't greet me upon your return. Under the circumstances, I'm willing to forgive the discourtesy."

Jeran looked at Jes and his pulse quickened. She was as beautiful as he remembered. "My apologies, Lady Jessandra. Tylor's approach left little time for pleasantries." He struggled to keep his voice even, the depth of his feelings hidden, and his eyes firmly fastened on Jes' face. Inebriation did not aid him, and Jeran's cheeks burned. *How can I love her? She lived before the Boundary!*

"Jes, I…" Jeran turned away. An image of Reanna formed in his mind and guilt washed over him so strongly he thought he would never find his voice again. "I never thanked you… For training me. I know you didn't want to, but without your help, I'd have never survived Dranakohr."

Jes closed the distance between them and took Jeran's chin in her hand, turning his face so their eyes met. With her other hand, she brushed the tear from his cheek. Her touch sent a chill down his spine, but he thought again of Reanna, and his excitement disgusted him. "You should not have had to suffer that," Jes whispered. "Aemon should not have—"

"Aemon did what he had to do to protect Alrendria, to protect all of Madryn," Jeran's tone hardened with each word. "You would have done the same. Don't deny it! You and he have manipulated events for centuries, led man and Mage alike down the paths you chose without bothering to ask anyone if it was the path they *wanted*. I don't fault you for it, but you can't dance a thousand puppets around a fire without burning a few."

Ashamed, Jeran tried to pull away, but Jes' grip tightened and she held him steady. She peered into his eyes, and Jeran felt her seize magic, but he had no energy to study the flows or try to guess what she was doing.

Without warning, the tingling of a Reading came upon him, not from around but from within. He had no time to suppress it; his memories enveloped him and Jes. Together, they relived his captivity, from the days spent bound and drugged in the back of a wagon to the night of his escape. The seasons of hunger and torture, of watching Tylor punish others to hurt him. Nothing remained secret, not his anger, not his despair, not the truth about what had kept him alive when he had all but lost hope: dreams of a raven-haired Mage with a waspish temper. Everything was laid bare, but worst of all were his memories of Reanna: what Jeran had truly felt for her, and what had happened to her because of him.

It lasted only a moment, but for Jeran, it was as if it had all happened again, and it took all of his strength to remain standing. Jes jerked away as if her hand had been burned. "Jeran…! I…" She raised her hand to her mouth; her lips trembled behind her fingers. She tried to speak again but could not find the words. In her haste to escape Jeran's memories, she all but ran away from him.

Some time later, Martyn found Jeran leaning heavily against the wall. "There you are! I've been looking all over for you. Where've you been?"

"Here and there," Jeran said, forcing a smile. "Enjoying the party."

"Come with me!" Martyn urged, grabbing Jeran's arm. "Hurry!" The prince pulled Jeran across the courtyard, past dying bonfires and drunken soldiers. Kal and Olin, skins of *baqhat* in hand, sang a lively song, their voices loud and slurred. A group of young Guardsmen sat around them and joined in whenever they reached the chorus. Lord Grondellan snored drunkenly against the castle wall, his men sprawled around him. Though dawn threatened to brighten the horizon, no end to the festivities was in sight.

Jeran wondered where Martyn was taking him. He asked, but Martyn offered no explanation; he simply urged Jeran for greater speed. When they stopped before a group of familiar faces, Jeran tried to hide his relief. "*Teshou e Honoure,*" Kaeille said reverently. "I am pleased you escaped the Dark One. May Valia continue to give you Her blessing."

Dahr was there as well, as well as Grendor, Aryn and Treloran, and another woman, a beautiful blonde-haired woman with fiery blue eyes and a commanding presence. She studied Jeran as he studied her, and in her gaze he saw little of the awe which seemed to greet him of late. The lack of reverence was refreshing. "This is Princess Miriam of Gilead," Martyn said, flourishing his hand. "She's agreed to become my wife. My Queen!"

The news drove Jeran's melancholy away, and a broad smile split his lips. "What wonderful news!" he said, clapping Martyn's shoulder before bowing respectfully to the princess. "By marrying Martyn, you do Alrendria an honor and me a great favor. As the winters pass, it becomes more difficult to keep the prince out of trouble. Your calming influence and wise counsel will no doubt aid me immeasurably. For that, I'm grateful."

Martyn faked an angry glare, and Miriam laughed. "It's you who honor me, Lord Odara, but you give me more credit than I deserve. So far, I've had little success in controlling your prince." She touched her fingertips to Martyn's cheek. "In my time here, I've come to realize how deeply Martyn loves Alrendria, and how noble you Alrendrians are. We face a terrible enemy, but united, Alrendria and Gilead, man and Tribesman, Elf and Orog, we will win. In the face of that realization, how could I let petty jealousy and girlish dreams stand in the way of victory?"

"Tomorrow, we'll leave for Kaper," Martyn said. "We won't reach the city before winter, and travel will be difficult, but there's much to do, and the sooner we're married, the better."

"I can have you in Kaper tomorrow." As soon as he said it, Jeran wished he had not made the offer.

Martyn's brow drew up in confusion, but then understanding dawned. "A Gate! I keep forgetting that you're a Mage! But why wait until tomorrow? Why not now?"

"Because these things are difficult," Jeran replied, "and it's been a long day. Grant me some sleep or my Gate might take us to the Nothing instead of to Kaper." Martyn reluctantly agreed, and as if mention of sleep had summoned it, fatigue fell upon him like a hammer blow. Jeran excused himself and started toward the castle. By the time he reached his room he was weak-kneed and bleary-eyed, but no sooner had he lay upon his mattress then the door opened, and Martyn peeked in.

"Don't get up," the prince said hastily. "I've a message for you, and I wanted to tell you before I forgot again. Before I left Lynnaei, the Elf twins, they said you should seek them in Aemon's Tomb. I don't know what they meant, but they—"

"It's alright," Jeran told him. "I understand." Martyn left him to sleep, but for a long time, Jeran just lay there, staring into the darkness.

* * * * * * * * * * * * * * * * * * * *

"I can't take anyone else!" Jeran insisted. He had intended to take only a handful to Kaper, but with every passing moment, Martyn and Miriam thought of someone else who had to make the journey. "There are limits to what any Mage can do, and I'm still not recovered from the battle."

"Then we should ask the other Magi to help," Miriam said imperiously. "My cousin and his horsemen must accompany us. He refuses to be left behind."

"Princess, you're talking about several hundred men. It would take every Mage in Vela to move that many, and it would leave them exhausted for days." Miriam pouted angrily, and Jeran sighed. "I can take your cousin, but no one else. If you wish to, you may seek other Magi, but I doubt many have the strength to Gate more than one or two. The others can be brought to Kaper later, but we waste time arguing, and I thought you were in a hurry to formally announce your betrothal."

For a moment, it looked as if Miriam intended to argue, but she finally relented. "Very well, Lord Odara, you know far more about the Gift than I. If Jaem can come, that will be suitable."

With a whispered prayer to the Five Gods, Jeran surrendered himself to magic. It filled him with life and power, and he wove the flows, creating a bridge between Vela and Kaper. The Gate opened onto the highest tower in the castle. The city spread out below, the Great Bridge visible in the distance. A solitary figure stood at the wall with his back to the Gate, lost deep in thought and unaware of what was going on behind him.

Martyn hissed in a sharp breath. "With powers like this, no one is safe."

"A Gate can only be opened accurately from a well-known place to a well-known place," Jeran said reassuringly. "Had I tried to open a Gate to Roya, it might have appeared anywhere on the island, or even over the ocean. Keep the enemy out of the palace and you'll be safe enough." He motioned toward the Gate. "After you,"

"No." Martyn turned to Aryn. "Commander Odara, I believe there's someone who would very much like to see you."

Aryn smiled gratefully and stepped through to Kaper. "Mathis?" he called out, and the King whirled around, startled by the sound. Seeing the Gate, his eyes widened, and his hand reached for the sword at his side, but then recognition dawned.

"Aryn? Aryn!" The King hurried forward to embrace his old friend. Mathis' eyes went toward the Gate, and when he saw Jeran and the others, tears ran unashamedly down his face.

With an exaggerated flourish, Martyn waved the women forward. Giggling, Miriam crossed through the Gate, followed by Kaeille. Without waiting for permission, Jaem strode past Martyn as if he were a prince. Treloran went next, and then Dayfid, whom Martyn had insisted be included. The Guardsman had served well in the Battle of Vela, and Jeran suspected that a command awaited Dayfid in Kaper.

As each person passed through the Gate, maintaining it grew more difficult. Sweat beaded Jeran's brow and his knees felt like they were about to buckle. He doubted he could hold the Gate for four more people. "You next," he said to

Martyn, and the prince, after one look into Jeran's strained eyes, hurried through. Jeran winced when the price crossed through the gateway, but before he could tell Grendor to go, a hand grasped his shoulder.

"It's time," Yassik said. The Mage looked haggard, his robes dirty and ripped, his shoulders slumped. "Everything's ready."

"Now?" Jeran asked, and Yassik nodded. Jeran turned to the Gate, to call for Martyn, to explain, but the prince was already watching and no explanation was necessary. Somehow, Martyn knew.

"Good luck," Martyn said, waving goodbye. Jeran was surprised; a four-season ago, nothing short of brute force would have kept the prince from something like what Jeran planned. Smiling sadly, Jeran let his hold on magic slip.

At that moment, Aryn looked up and saw Yassik, and when he saw the Gate closing, he went into a rage. "You can't do this," he screamed, running toward Jeran. "This is my fight! I have a right to be there! This is *my* fight!" Aryn leapt for the Gate, but Martyn intercepted him. He fought so fiercely that it took Martyn, Treloran, and Mathis to hold him still until the Gate closed completely, sealing him in Kaper.

"Goodbye, Uncle Aryn," Jeran whispered. "May the Gods bring you peace."

He turned to find Dahr staring at him. "Where are you going?" Dahr demanded.

"To free some slaves. Want to come?"

Chapter 42

"I should rest," Jeran told Yassik. "When does the attack begin?" Dahr and Grendor trailed a few steps behind. For once, the Orog seemed more excited by the prospect of battle than Dahr. He leaned forward so as to not miss Yassik's response.

"Wardel will wait until he hears from me," Yassik answered, scrubbing at his eyes. "Truth be told, I could use some sleep myself. Not to mention a bath. It's best if we wait until after sunset anyway. Too many would notice our disappearance otherwise."

Yassik stifled a yawn while Jeran gave the Mage directions to his chambers. "Try to keep hidden. The fewer people who know you're here, the better."

"I'll be as quiet as a mouse," Yassik promised. "Alwen's not one to take kindly to me disappearing like I did. If she finds out I'm in Vela, she'll have my hide."

Yassik turned to walk away, but Jeran stopped him. "When the time comes, how many men will you be able to Gate?"

"I've been pushing myself pretty hard these last few days, but once we get to Dranakohr, the Gift will be useless." A thoughtful frown spread across the Mage's face. "Five, maybe six men. No more than that."

"I'll be lucky if I can manage that many," Jeran admitted. "I'd hoped to take a few score with us, but we'll have to make do."

"You'll think of something, boy. You always do." Yassik drew up the hood of his cloak and strode off with the imperious stare of the Magi. A few Guardsmen eyed him curiously, but no one stopped him. The Magi policed their own, and they did not take kindly to interruption, so only a fool would stop one just for wearing filthy clothes.

Jeran turned to Dahr and Grendor. "Who should we take with us?"

Grendor offered Subcommander Malikai and his Guardsmen; Dahr suggested Jasova and some of the troops from Darein. Jeran rejected both. "Martyn ordered Malikai to help maintain order while the defenses are repaired, and Jasova must return to the border before King Murdir realizes we've left it undefended." Jeran tapped his lips thoughtfully; of all the soldiers he knew and trusted, none seemed suitable.

"Why not take me?" Harol Grondellan asked as he rolled out from beneath a cart. Dark rings circled the Rachannan's eyes, and his unkempt hair fanned out from his head like a mane. He stood slowly, groaning with the effort, and brushed dirt from clothes stained dark with ale and wine. "I can have as many men as you need at your disposal immediately, and their absence won't be noticed by many." He laughed loudly. "And welcomed by most, I'd bet."

Dahr's jaw tightened, and his teeth ground together so loudly that Jeran thought they might break. "Lord Grondellan, you don't even know where we're going."

432

Another laugh rolled up from the Rachannan's belly. "What does that matter? I've seen that look on the faces of many Tribesmen." He gestured toward Dahr with his chin. "Wherever you're going, you go to do battle. I've a score to settle with the Durange, and I'd be a fool to pass up a chance to kick him while he's down."

Jeran frowned. "I'll expect your men to follow my orders without question." Dahr turned his glare on Jeran.

"My boys may be rough around the edges, but they know how to fight. The first one who disobeys will wish the Bull had gotten a hold of him. I guarantee you that."

"Pick out twenty of your best," Jeran said, his decision made. "Meet us at the stables after sunset."

"They'll be there, lad," Harol grinned. "Might I ask where we're going?"

"No. And no one's to know about this mission. No one. The first man to breathe a word of it will wish that *you* had gotten a hold of him. Understood?"

"Perfectly, lad. Perfectly. I'll see you at sunset." Before he left, he clapped Dahr roughly on the shoulder. "I look forward to fighting at your side, Hunter!"

As soon as Lord Grondellan was out of earshot, Dahr rounded on Jeran. "How could you invite him? You know who he is!"

"He's our ally," Jeran snapped. Exhaustion clawed at what remained of his patience. He knew Dahr deserved a better explanation, but he had no time to soothe Dahr's temper or mediate his mood swings. "And I chose him because there's no one better. He hates the Durange as much as you do, and his men have experience fighting in mountains."

Dahr bared his teeth, but before he could speak, Jeran stopped him. "I want you at my side, Dahr, but I won't be forced to justify every decision. If you want to help me, then you must obey me. You'll follow my orders no matter how much you disagree with them." Jeran stepped in close. Though forced to look up to meet Dahr's gaze, he knew he held the advantage. For the moment, at least. "No arguments. No debate. You agree to follow my orders or I'll leave you standing at the Gate while the rest of us go to fight Tylor. Swear it, Dahr. Swear it on your honor, and on the honor of the House that adopted you when no one else would."

For a tense moment, Jeran thought Dahr would balk, that the Blood Rage or the anger he bottled up within would prevent him from making the promise. "I swear it," he said through clenched teeth. "I swear on my life and on House Odara that I'll follow your orders, Jeran, even if they go against my better judgment. I will make Harol Grondellan believe himself my lifelong friend before I betray your trust. Just don't deny me my chance at redemption."

Jeran gripped Dahr's shoulders. "I wouldn't dream of it." He looked at Grendor, who had watched their exchange with a curious expression on his face. "Get some rest," Jeran told them. "Tonight will be a long night."

* *

The last hint of daylight cast long shadows on the ground when Jeran entered the stable. A handful of stableboys bustled about their chores, but the cavernous chamber was otherwise empty. In his most imperious tone, Jeran dismissed the stableboys. They left at a run, and Jeran took up a position in the center of the stable. He drew slow, deep breaths, calming his nerves and preparing to seize magic. The Gate he had opened that morning had drained him, and despite a day of unbroken sleep, he did not yet feel himself.

Yassik arrived some time later, with Grendor and Dahr not far behind. Fang trotted at Dahr's side, and Shyrock stood on his shoulder. "They won't be much use in the mines," Jeran told him.

"They go with me," Dahr said flatly. His expression carried no warmth, and for a moment, Jeran felt as if he were looking at a stranger.

"Very well," Jeran conceded. "But Jardelle's too big. We can come back for him later." Dahr's lips drew down in a frown, but he nodded once and took his place at Jeran's side.

"It will be nice to go home, friend Jeran," Grendor said. He carried his bladed staff at his side, and the weapon looked at home there. Jeran could not decide whether that made him happy or sad.

"In all of history, you're probably the only person ever to be excited to learn he's going to Dranakohr," Jeran joked, and the Orog blushed dark grey.

A few moments later, the Rachannen began to filter in. They were a rough lot, scarred and grim-faced, with dirty uniforms and mismatched armor scavenged from the dead, but they moved with a steadiness that belied their appearance. Each man carried an assortment of weapons and most had a large sack of provisions slung over one shoulder. They eyed the horses, and the boldest started toward some of the better mounts, but Jeran stopped them.

"No horses," he said, "and drop the sacks. We take only the clothes on our backs and the weapons at our sides."

"We track the Durange, eh?" one man asked, stepping forward. "How d'ya expect to catch that army without horses?"

"And how are we supposed to live without food?" demanded another. Several others started grumbling, and for a moment, Jeran wondered if he had made the right decision.

"Quit your whining, dogs!" Lord Grondellan bellowed as he stormed into the stable. The Rachannan nobleman had changed clothes and groomed himself since their last meeting, and he was a far more imposing sight. He still wore his dark leathers, but the blood and grime from yesterday's battle had been washed away and the armor had been painstakingly oiled. A shortsword swung at his right hip and an axe at his left. Two long daggers hung from his belt and a series of shorter ones were sheathed on a strap that looped over one shoulder. "You go where Lord Odara tells you and how he tells you. The first one who thinks of questioning him gets my axe through his head. Understood?" He bared his teeth in a smile that only looked cruel because it seemed so sincere.

The Rachannen soldiers fell silent. Sacks were hastily discarded, and the men fell into rank. Another man, skinny and tall, with angular features and a hooked nose, appeared at Lord Grondellan's side. He surveyed the group—his gaze lingered a moment on Dahr—and he jotted down a few notes in a small ledger. "Pardon me, Lord Odara," he asked, bowing low, "but if you don't intend to chase Tylor's army, might I ask where we're going?"

Dahr's eyes narrowed dangerously, and Jeran frowned at the newcomer. "And you are?"

"Yurs," Lord Grondellan said, tisking his tongue against the roof of his mouth, "how rude of you. Jeran, this is Yurs, my chief steward and long time friend."

"This mission is for warriors," Jeran said. "We can't afford—"

"The final decision is yours, of course," Harol interrupted, "but Yurs can take care of himself, and if we win this battle, you may have need of someone with his skills. No one can run a household, or a captured castle, as efficiently."

"You know where we're going?" Jeran asked suspiciously.

"I was hungover under that cart," Harol laughed, "but I'm not a fool. Tylor has only one stronghold this side of the Boundary worth taking. It's a bold plan, but win or lose, someone's bound to make a song about it. 'The Assault on Dranakohr!' The only question remaining is whether it will be an epic or a dirge?"

Jeran quickly described the castle's defenses and outlined his plan of attack. "Yassik, Grendor, and I will join with Wardel in the tunnels. Our forces will secure the caverns across the Boundary, cutting Dranakohr's connection to *Ael Shataq*. Dahr, you and Lord Grondellan will attack the wall to prevent—"

"The wall!" Dahr snarled. "I—"

"Tylor has his best men guarding the wall," Jeran shot back, and his glare silenced Dahr. "If you can keep them occupied while we secure the tunnels, Dranakohr's supply lines will be cut. Even if we fail to take the castle in the assault, the Darklord's forces will not be able to hold out indefinitely without supplies from *Ael Shataq*." Dahr's disappointment tore at Jeran's heart, and he struggled to soften his tone. "There will be blood enough for everyone, Dahr, I promise you. You'll get your revenge."

"It's time," Yassik said, glancing toward the stable door. "Full night will have fallen over Dranakohr."

"You first," Jeran said. "Take as many as you can. I'll bring the rest."

An aura of magic sprung up around Yassik, and the air in front of the Mage pressed in upon itself and then exploded outward. A blast of frigid air blew across the stable, and a dusting of snow toppled through the Gate. The Rachannen stepped back warily, but Grendor drew a deep breath and exhaled slowly, a broad smile on his face. He waited for Yassik's nod before jumping through.

One by one, the Rachannen followed. After the seventh, Yassik raised his hand. Sweat beaded the Mage's brow, and he trembled visibly. "I'll barely get myself through. Can you bring the rest?"

Jeran looked around. Eighteen men. *Never*, Jeran thought, but he forced a smile. "I guess I'll have to. I'll see you on the other side." Yassik crossed through the Gate before Jeran finished speaking, and the magical portal collapsed in on itself as soon as he was on the other side.

"With powers like that," Lord Grondellan said, "it's a wonder that Magi haven't taken over the world."

"They did," Jeran said. "Long ago. But not with Gates. Even the most powerful Magi would have difficulty moving a dozen men, and if a Mage moved too much he wouldn't be able to use his Gift for days. Besides, it's almost impossible to open a Gate in an exact place, and if another Mage knows what to look for, Gates can be detected pretty easily. All in all, they're not the advantage they appear to be."

A frown darkened the Rachannan's face. "And if the ShadowMagi know how to spot these Gates?"

"Then we're going to have problems."

Lord Grondellan turned to Dahr with a toothy smile. "You hear that, Hunter? This will be a battle for the ages!"

The door to the stable opened, and Aemon strolled in. "Jeran! I've been looking all over—" When Aemon caught sight of the Rachannen—Lord Grondellan and Yurs both bowed formally; the others pretended not to notice his arrival—he frowned. "Did somebody just Gate from here? What's going on?"

"We're going to Dranakohr," Jeran explained. "Yassik and I have a plan to free the slaves and take control of the castle." Aemon opened his mouth, and Jeran quickly said, "Don't try to talk me out of it. My mind's made up. This is right thing to do."

Aemon's eyes widened in feigned outrage. "I only wanted to know how I could help!"

"Help? But Alwen said you wouldn't be able to use your Gift for a long time."

"Alwen's always been melodramatic, and she's not half as bad as that Sheriza. Healers!" Aemon said the last word like a curse, but he smiled as he said it. "I'll not lie to you, lad, I'm not at my best, but I've still a few tricks ready for the Durange."

Jeran frowned. "I guess I have no choice. How could I tell you no?"

"A wise decision. Now what can I do?"

"We need to move these men to Dranakohr. I can't Gate them all myself, and you aren't familiar enough with the area, but together—"

"You want to use what the Tsha'ma taught us?" Aemon finished, and when Jeran nodded, he said, "I think we can do it. I wish Rannarik were here, but..." Aemon closed his eyes, and the old man's aura flared brightly. "I'll open myself to you. When you feel the connection, draw on the magic through me. It will add my Gift to yours, but you'll remain in control of the flows."

Jeran opened himself to magic and waited until he felt something, a slight tug coming from Aemon's direction. He surrendered to his Gift, and felt energy pour into him through Aemon. He wove a Gate, and a vertical line twenty hands high appeared, opening so fast Jeran barely had time to stop it before it spanned the breadth of the stable. Concentrating, he reduced the Gate's size to something more manageable.

The Rachannen went through two by two, and Jeran felt little more than a twinge at each passing. Aemon bore the brunt of the burden, and through the bond they shared, Jeran could sense how much the passage of the soldiers drained his grandfather's Gift. If not for Jeran's rein on the magic, Aemon would have long since lost control of the flows.

When only he, Dahr and Aemon remained, Jeran severed his connection to the older Mage. The Gate wavered and shrank, but Jeran caught it before it closed completely and sustained it with his own Gift. "Amazing," Aemon panted. Sweat poured down his brow. "The Tsha'ma should never have kept this from us."

"They had their reasons," Jeran reminded. "Good ones."

"I know," Aemon replied. "And I'll keep my promise to them. I'll cross over next, and then Dahr. Once you're through, we—" Aemon staggered, and his instructions cut off in a yawn.

"Catch him," Jeran said.

Dahr grabbed Aemon just as the old man collapsed. He lowered him gently, settling him on a pile of loose straw. "What happened?" he asked, a tinge of concern in his voice.

"Just a trick I learned from Alwen," Jeran answered. "Ready?"

After one final look at Aemon, Dahr started for the Gate. Jeran grabbed his arm as he passed. "You can't hurt her."

"What!"

"She's not to be harmed. In fact, if it's in your power, I'm counting on you to protect her."

"Rrraahhh!" Dahr lifted Jeran by the shoulders and slammed him against the wall. With the jarring impact, Jeran's hold on magic wavered, but he kept his focus. "You ask too much." Dahr's voice was cold and hard, full of hate. "She betrayed me. She betrayed all of us! I'll kill her for that."

Dahr's grip tightened painfully, and his fingers crept toward Jeran's throat, but Jeran vowed not to fight back. "She saved Martyn." He forced his voice to remain calm and even. "She helped me escape Dranakohr. I owe her my life several times, and you will... not... hurt... her. I have your oath; I expect you to keep it."

Jeran saw the tears Dahr refused to acknowledge threatening to fall. "You tricked me," Dahr whispered, letting go. "I won't forget this."

"Forget?" Jeran shook his head. "I never thought you would. But someday, I hope you'll forgive. Now, through the Gate." Dahr dove through, Fang a step behind, and Jeran felt their passage like a blow to the stomach. *Thank the Gods for Aemon. I'd have barely gotten three men through without him.*

"Jeran? Is that you?" Jes stood in the doorway, peering into the dim light. Jeran sighed heavily; when he chose the stables, they had seemed an ideal place to meet, quiet and somewhat isolated from the castle. "Jeran? I thought I felt something, and... What happened here?"

Jes ran toward Aemon, dropping to her knees in the straw and cradling his head in her lap. "What happened to him?" she asked, her voice breaking.

"He's fine," Jeran assured her. "He's just sleeping."

Jes looked up, and she saw Dahr staring back from between jagged, snow-covered rocks, his face illuminated by the light drifting through the Gate. "Where does that go?" Jes demanded. "And what happened to Aemon?"

"That goes to Dranakohr," Jeran said, and Jes' eyes widened, but before she could say anything else, Jeran struck out with his Gift. "And this is what happened to Aemon." Jes slumped, and her head landed gently on Aemon's chest. Jeran smiled as he turned toward the Gate. "Alwen, that may have been the most important thing you ever taught me."

* * * * * * * * * * * * * * * * * * * *

Jeran pushed through waist-deep snow, wishing he had remembered the bitter cold outside the mines. Shivering, he drew his cloak close about his shoulders and tried to get his bearings. His Gate had not opened near the tunnels, and though he was loathe to admit it, he had no idea where Yassik and the others were. He had been hugging the wall of the valley for some time, moving closer to Dranakohr and hoping to find his companions before he was discovered.

A stiff breeze gusted across the snow-covered fields, driving fresh powder and frozen rain into Jeran's eyes. At his side, Dahr showed no sign of discomfort. He stared unblinkingly forward, and he did not shiver despite his bare arms and thin shirt.

They rounded a crag and Jeran crouched, signaling for his men to halt. Dranakohr loomed over them, its covered walkways and ominous towers illuminated by the light of a thousand torches. "Gods," Lord Grondellan said, crawling to Jeran's side. "It would take an army winters to break this place."

"Then I'm glad we didn't bring an army," Jeran replied, but his jest fell flat. He pointed to a deep crevasse across three hundred hands of open field. "That's where we need to go. We'll have to risk exposing ourselves, but the distance isn't great. We should be able to pass—"

"Who's there?" a voice called out. Jeran pressed himself deep into the snow, mindless of the cold trickle that worked its way down his neck. A guard stepped out of the shadows, his sword at the ready and a crude torch waving back and forth. "I heard you," he yelled. "Best come out now. If you make me hunt you down in this accursed snow, you'll regret it."

The man moved closer and stopped hands away from one Rachannan. The man all but buried himself to escape detection. The guard waited a moment, then sighed heavily. "You'll regret this," he repeated, reaching for a horn at his belt.

Before he could sound the alarm, the snow around the solider erupted, and the man disappeared. His attempt to cry out was drowned in a bloody gurgle. When the snow settled, a Tribesman covered head to foot in white furs stood in the soldier's place. "Come," he called, his voice muted as he wiped his *dolchek* clean. "You move slower, you miss battle."   .

"Cat's Claw!" Jeran called out. He climbed to his feet and went to greet Sadarak Cat's Claw, *Kranor* of the Afelda.

"I weep when Mage Yassik tell me you live," Cat's Claw said, gripping Jeran in a bear hug so tight he could hardly breathe. "I glad Gods not call you to them." The *Kranor* looked at Jeran's companions. "*Cho Koran Garun,*" he said to Dahr, bowing with his hands wide apart. "I honored to fight at your side." Dahr said nothing; he barely acknowledged the Tribesman's presence, but Cat's Claw did not appear offended by the insult.

Squinting into the snow, Cat's Claw focused on Lord Grondellan. "You, I know too! We meet in battle."

Lord Grondellan swept back his cloak and shook the snow from his shoulders. "You are Sadarak, Warrior-king of the Afelda?" Cat's Claw dipped his head, and Lord Grondellan nodded. "We fought at Suyn's Crossing and Loughlin's Mill. I've never met a more formidable opponent. You bloodied my men at both encounters."

Cat's Claw grunted. "But you send my Hunters home with nothing." The Tribesman laughed suddenly, a low, guttural sound muted by the wind. "And today we fight enemy who makes our differences look like fussing of children. I welcome your blade, Black Bear."

"Cat's Claw..." When the Tribesman turned to face him, Jeran could not find the right words. "Reanna... I..."

"Today we avenge Snow Rabbit," Cat's Claw promised, "and the Hunter who might have been." He clapped Jeran's shoulder again and pointed to a distant outcropping in the shadow of the wall. "My Hunters wait. You hurry to cave. Mage Yassik grows impatient."

Jeran sprinted across the snowfield, keeping to the shadows whenever possible. Cat's Claw led Dahr and the Rachannen into the darkness, toward the waiting Afelda Hunters. Jeran had no time to waste; once the *Kranor* rejoined his men, the battle would begin.

* * * * * * * * * * * * * * * * * *

"He should be here by now!" Yassik said, pacing the chamber. Grendor stood against the wall, his eyes following the Mage back and forth. Outwardly, the Orog appeared calm, but sweat beaded his scalp and his hands slid absently up and down the bladed staff. The Mage sighed heavily. "I should go look for him."

Ehvan blocked Yassik's passage. "I can't allow that. If Lord Odara is out there, he'll come here. If he's been captured... There's nothing to be done then but carry on." The young man had changed in the days since Jeran had left. The recklessness, the eagerness to fight overwhelming odds in the name of justice was gone; the grim face of reality had replaced it. He had grown his hair out and sported a ten-day's growth of beard.

To make himself look older, Jeran thought as he stepped out of the shadows. *To make the men respect him.* "Peace, Yassik," he called. "I've not been gone from Dranakohr so long I don't know where the Barrows are. My Gate opened farther away than anticipated, and crossing the fields was difficult."

"Lord Odara," Ehvan said, bowing low. "The men are ready. We've done everything exactly as you ordered." Jeran saw the idolization in his eyes, the need for praise.

"I never doubted you," Jeran said, forcing a smile. Relief flooded Ehvan's face, and for some strange reason, seeing the young man's pride improved Jeran's mood as well. "Yassik told you what we plan, but you know the situation here far better than I. Is there anything I've missed?" Hesitation flashed across Ehvan's face. "If you know something, tell me! Lives are at stake, Ehvan!"

Ehvan dropped to a crouch and unrolled a map. It had numerous scrawlings upon it: red for the Darklord's soldiers, blue for the rebels. "Here," Ehvan said, pointed to an unmarked cavern. "And here. None of our men have been able to get close, but a lot of guards have been going in and out of these caverns."

"Has Tylor moved his armories?" Yassik asked.

"No," Ehvan answered. "We don't know what they've been doing in there, except... I think they're barracks, hidden underground to flank us if we attack. Grissam and the others think I'm a fool, but the Durange know what we're doing even though we've tried to keep our presence secret."

Jeran tapped a finger against his lips while he studied the map. "What do you think we should do?"

"Two cells should be sent to block the cavern entrances. Collapse them, if possible, and guard them if not. If I'm wrong, we'll be short two score men when the fighting starts, but if I'm right, it could make the difference between winning and losing."

"See to it," Jeran said. "Yassik tells me you single-handedly held the resistance together." Ehvan's cheeks turned red, and he glanced at Yassik. The Mage winked. "I'm putting you in command of the Barrows assault. After the cells capture their targets, you're to secure the forge and armories, then free the prisoners. Move slowly, and make sure you don't leave any Durange behind. Whatever ground we take tonight, I want to make sure we can hold it."

"I won't fail you, Lord Odara," Ehvan said. He rolled up the map, stuffed it into his shirt, and stood. A stone clattered, and Ehvan threw a cover over the lantern, plunging them into darkness. They waited, afraid to move, straining with both eyes and ears. Even with his senses enhanced by magic, Jeran saw nothing. After a tense moment, Ehvan uncovered the light.

"Grendor," Jeran continued, "you'll lead the attack on the *ghrat*. I'm counting on you to convince your people to fight. Without them, we won't be able to win."

"My people have suffered long enough," Grendor replied. "It is time to face the truth. It is time to set them free." The Orog's slitted eyes narrowed even more than normal, and he looked at Jeran suspiciously. "Where will you be, friend Jeran?"

"Where I'm needed," Jeran answered, waving away further questions. He turned to Ehvan. "How many subcommanders do you have?"

"Subcommanders? Umm… Two score cells wait for my signal, and each cell has a leader."

"Two score," Jeran repeated. "Grendor, did you bring enough firesticks?"

The Orog removed two bundles of hand-long rods from his pack. Jeran took the bundles and struck them against the wall. A series of hisses filled the chamber, and a puff of smoke rose. When the smoke cleared, dim blue flames burned at the end of each stick. "Do you have runners ready?" Jeran asked.

"One cavern over." Ehvan replied. "One runner for each cell. Just as Mage Yassik requested."

"Give a stick to each," Jeran said, handing the bundles to Ehvan, "and tell them to go. When the fire burns out, begin the assault."

Ehvan glanced at the sticks nervously. "That doesn't give them much time."

Jeran smiled. "Then they had better hurry."

* * * * * * * * * * * * * * * * * * * *

Dahr crept through the snow, his greatsword held ready, and stared into the night as if expecting an ambush at any moment. Cat's Claw walked on his left, the *Kranor* all but invisible in his white hides, and Lord Grondellan on his right. The others spread out behind them, Hunter and Human side by side, men who, not too many seasons past had been at each other's throats over a stretch of land smaller than the city of Kaper.

Jeran would be happy to see this, Dahr thought, eyeing the odd procession. One Rachannan tripped when Dahr's dark gaze passed over him. To the man's credit, he made no sound as he sprawled in the snow, not so much as a grunt, and he quickly regained his footing with the help of a passing Tribesman.

The Garun'ah seemed at home; they moved through knee-deep drifts as if strolling through open fields. Fang had not been so fortunate, and Dahr had been forced to order the hound to wait in the caves. The Rachannen had a hard time of the march, too; their heavy leather constrained their movements and weighed them down. Only Lord Grondellan seemed unphased. He walked as silently as any Tribesman, so quietly that when he grabbed Dahr's arm, it surprised him. Instantly tense, pulse racing, Dahr barely kept from striking his one-time master.

Lord Grondellan gave no indication of knowing that he stood half a heartbeat from death. He tapped two fingers to his eyes and pointed into the darkness. Dahr raised his hand to signal a halt and crouched. Using his free arm, he swept snow over his exposed skin. The bitter cold was welcome; it helped quench his Blood Rage and kept him from thinking about the man next to him, the man who had once owned him.

Not twenty paces away, a soldier appeared, tying the laces to his breeches and shivering. Batting his arms about his shoulders, the man hurried to the wall, where he fumbled around confused, tapping at the stones. Eventually, a cleverly-concealed door opened, and the soldier disappeared. The door swung shut behind him.

The column started forward as soon as the man was gone, and Dahr led them to the place where the soldier had vanished. He studied the wall, looking for the mechanism that triggered the catch. "It probably leads to a guardroom," Lord Grondellan whispered, tapping at an oddly-sized stone. "I'd guess there are several of these along the wall."

Dahr agreed but did not say so. Instead, he bared his teeth. "Cat's Claw, can your Hunters find these doors?"

"Do you offer insult? If doors exist, my Hunters find them."

"How long will it take for you to run the length of the wall?"

The *Kranor* squinted into the darkness. "It long run, and snow deep. Twenty counts of ten."

It was faster than Dahr could have made the distance. "Then go. Leave ten men at each door you find. We'll count to three hundred, thirty counts of ten, before we attack." Dahr separated out eight Rachannen. "You'll stay with me. The rest of you, follow Cat's Claw." In a whisper only the *Kranor* could hear, Dahr added, "Leave the Rachannen at the nearest doors. They won't be able to keep up."

Cat's Claw chuckled as he gripped Dahr's arm. "May Garun guide your blade." With that, he disappeared, whispering his count; the Hunters and Rachannen trailed behind.

"Keep quiet, lads," Lord Grondellan whispered to his men as they passed. "Keep to the shadows and try to save a few Durange for me."

Dahr counted silently as the men around him tensed for the attack. His heart pounded, and his breath came in short, powerful bursts. He longed to feel his blade bite into the flesh of an enemy, to hear the music of battle, to finally find an outlet for his anger. His entire life had become a war, a struggle to maintain control despite the Gods' efforts to turn him into an animal. Only in battle could he find the release for all that threatened to overwhelm him. He savored these moments, the few moments where duty allowed him to be the monster he was.

He had just reached two hundred when the door flung open and Dahr found himself face to face with two black-armored soldiers. Both froze when they saw him standing in the snow, his hair blowing in the wind like the mane of a lion, and in that instant of hesitation, Dahr struck. His blade skewered the first man, and the second fell back sputtering, trying to raise an alarm. Lord Grondellan got to him before Dahr did; a dagger thrown from the hip turned the man's mewling into a gurgle.

Dahr pulled the men off the stairway and threw the men into the snow. "Bury them," he said, kicking powder at the bodies.

"It'll do no good, lad," Lord Grondellan said.

"We need to give Cat's Claw more time," Dahr growled, rounding on the Rachannan.

"True, but I don't think he'll be willing to wait." Dahr followed Lord Grondellan's finger and saw a third man on the stairs. The soldier was out of reach, and before Dahr could move, he fled, taking the stairs two at a time and screaming at the top of his lungs. Lord Grondellan sheathed his dagger and drew both sword and axe. "So much for plans," he said, sprinting through the door and up the steps. Despite his girth, he moved quickly, and the look of excitement on his face matched Dahr's. "Come along, lads! Let's let them know who's come to visit!"

The Rachannen surged forward, pushing Dahr in front of them. Their lust for battle matched his own, and he could not help but be caught up in their excitement. By the time Lord Grondellan reached the top of the staircase, Dahr stood at his side, and when they burst through the door and found a room full of guards hastily donning armor, he howled with delight.

* * * * * * * * * * * * * * * * * * * *

The stick in Yassik's hand had burnt halfway down by the time Grendor and the Mage reached the *ghrat*. "Home," Grendor whispered, though the word felt wrong. The walls were the same, the halls and caves identical, but the *ghrat* felt different, strange and inhospitable. The caverns which once offered comfort pressed down on him in a way they never had before. The silent halls were more oppressive than peaceful, the air stale and heavy. "The Elders say that once you leave, you can never go home again."

"The Elders say a lot of things," Yassik replied. "Sometimes, they're right. What's important is what you think." He offered the Orog a smile. "Well?"

"I think..." Grendor frowned. "I think this place was never home, not to me or any Orog. I think the Elders are wrong. I think if we want the Gods' forgiveness, we will have to earn it."

"And I think," Yassik said, clapping Grendor on the shoulder, "that there's hope for you yet. Come along, now. I'm not the one you need to convince."

They continued through the *ghrat*, but the halls remained silent, the *lientou* empty. Most lay barren, a few had threadbare bedrolls but no one slept on them.

"It is not time for the Telling," Grendor said anxiously, "but perhaps my people have gathered for another reason."

The dim light of the firestick provided ample illumination as Grendor wove through the halls of the *ghrat*. He feared the worst, that Tylor had punished his people in his place, that all the Orog had been killed because he had escaped. When he heard the first voice echoing in the distance, a tear filled his eye. "Praise to the Mother," he whispered. "Guide me with Your wisdom."

Grendor entered the hall proudly, with the intention of proclaiming his return and demanding that the people join him in his quest for freedom, but what he saw drove away his grand plan. Thousands huddled on the floor of the cavern, more Orog than he had ever seen together at one time. The cries of the wounded filled the air. Emaciated men and women writhed on the floor, hunger gnawing at their frail forms. Hardly an Orog stood who did not have a blood-soaked bandage wrapped around an arm or leg, and many bore more gruesome wounds—missing ears, sightless eyes, lashes by the score.

Yassik sucked in a breath. "Dear, Gods!"

"I did this," Grendor said. "Jeran and I. We did this."

"No!" Yassik rounded on the Orog. "This is Tylor's doing, not yours. He's the monster. You can't blame yourself for this. You can't—"

"No, friend Yassik. I am a *Choupik*. I, and those who came before me, were supposed to protect the Orog from the Durange. And from ourselves. I failed, and when the opportunity came, I fled." Grendor's expression hardened, and he sought the Elders. He saw his mother, blessedly uninjured, standing across the chamber beside Craj, the Eldest. "I can run no more. I must be like Dahr, and face my people without fear."

He stepped forward, the butt of his staff clicking against the stone. His appearance drew little notice until a child, his head wrapped in soiled bandages, saw him and backed away fearfully, crying out, "He carries a weapon!" The Orog had sworn to set aside their weapons long ago.   The child's cries drew attention, and soon the hum of conversation filled the hall. All eyes fell on Grendor and Yassik. Grendor ignored the eyes and whispers; he focused on the Elders and did not stop until he stood before them.

His mother saw him and ran to him. He could see she wanted to hold him, to clutch him to her chest and welcome him home. Something stopped her, though, and she simply reached out and caressed his cheek. "It pleases me that the Mother returned you to us. You are uninjured?"

"In flesh," Grendor answered. His response did not suit her, but he waived off her questions and addressed Craj. "It is time to end our service to the Darklord, Eldest."

Craj edged closer, leaning heavily on his staff. His white eyes stared blankly, but he stopped when only a hand's length separated him from Grendor. "Long ago, we pledged ourselves to the Darklord to save our people."

"And before that," Grendor replied, "we pledged ourselves to Aemon, to fight Lorthas to the last." Grendor faced his people, but the sight of them sickened him. They had deceived themselves—*he* had deceived himself along with them!—into believing that because they were slaves of evil, they could not help the evil they created. His people had forgotten who they were; now was the time to remind them.

"I met the Great One," Grendor announced, his voice carrying across the cavern. "I walked at his side. He wept when he saw me, wept that the Orog lived. I am glad he's not with me now. It would shame me for him to look upon you, to realize that we Orog have become cowards and servants of evil!"

The Eldest was unmoved. "All Orog know of our sins. That's why the Goddess sent us to the *ghrat*, to punish us."

"Lorthas sent us to the *ghrat*, not Shael! But the Orog who chose to serve Lorthas are long dead, and the sin of their decision died with them. The Mother loves us. She would never deprive us of our lives, our freedom. *We* forged this prison, not the Gods. We carved it from the stone with our own hands, and only we can free ourselves from it."

"That Human has corrupted you!" Zehna cried, shoving her way to the front of the crowd. Tears trailed down her cheeks, but hatred filled the gaze she cast on her grandson. "He has blinded you to the truth! Now you will spend eternity in the Nothing and… and… And that's what you deserve!"

Zehna wailed, and her cry knifed through the chamber, but it could not pierce Grendor's armor. *I am brave. I am a warrior.* He repeated those words like a mantra, drawing strength from them. "No, Tana," he said, surprised by the calm sound of his voice. "It is you who have blinded yourself. All Orog have. Jeran opened my eyes. He helped me see that by ignoring evil, we serve evil. We may not have aided the Darklord willingly, but we did aid him, and it is for that sin which we must pay."

"Hmmm," the Eldest thumped his staff against Grendor's chest with enough force to make him wince, but Grendor refused to give ground. "Who are you to tell the Orog what to think? What do you know that your Elders do not?"

"I know that I am a *Choupik* of the Vassta, protector of my people. I know I have breathed free and returned unpunished by the Gods. I know that a promise made under threat of death is no promise to be honored. I know that we pledged to help the Humans fight the Darklord, to end the MageWar. And I know that if my people will not fight for me, then I will fight for them, and if Shael demands my blood in return, I offer it gladly. I will not die a slave."

The silence throughout the cavern was complete. Grendor braced himself for the Eldest's wrath, but instead of yelling, a grin split Craj's wrinkled face. "He is ready. The time is at hand." Lorana sobbed, but pride filled the gaze she fastened on her son.

The firestick in Yassik's hand sputtered and died. "The attack begins," Grendor announced. "I go to honor my pledge to Aemon. Who will follow me?"

Zehna turned her back on him, and she was not the only one. Many turned away, unable to face the implications of Grendor's revelation. Some, mostly younger Orog, kept staring at him, but no one spoke. After a moment, Grendor knew he had failed. "Come, Yassik. Jeran will need us." Head hanging, he started toward the cavern mouth.

"The *Choupik* stand with you, friend Grendor." A powerfully-built Orog stepped out of the crowd holding a stout cudgel fashioned from a table leg. Others followed, from little more than boys to withered elders. All carried crudely-fashioned weapons. "We have thought on your words, and the words of the Human. Today, we fight in the name of the Goddess. We fight for our redemption."

A broad smile split Grendor's lips. Before he could speak, a scream cut through the cavern. More screams followed, and the distant sound of battle came with them. "We must find the ShadowMagi. Our touch removes their Gift. If we do not stop them, the Humans will fail." He turned to Lorana. "Gather those who will not fight here, Mother, and block the entrance. I will leave enough *Choupik* to protect you."

"The *Choupik* belong in battle," Lorana answered. "Go, my son, and win back our freedom. We will fend for ourselves."

Grendor raised his bladed staff. "For freedom and salvation!" The answering roar thundered through the *ghrat*.

* *

Jeran rounded the corner, ducking reflexively when he saw the blade swing toward his throat. The sword clattered against stone, and Jeran pivoted, ready to strike. "Peace, Dralin!" he said, checking his return swing and stepping away from the smith.

"Jeran?" Dralin's eyes were sunken from exhaustion and scars crisscrossed his arms and back. Fresh blood flowed from a cut across his forehead, and he wiped it away absently as he looked Jeran up and down. "I should have known this was your doing. You brought an army, did you?"

"Not quite five score all told," Jeran said, "and most of them are still outside." Clashing swords and battlecries came from every direction, and Dralin cocked his head to the side, confused. "The rebellion has begun," Jeran explained. "Once we win control of the Barrows and *ghrat*, we plan to push into the castle. My men outside will take the wall and prevent reinforcements from coming. Even if we fail to take Dranakohr, we may be able to block the passage through the Boundary."

"Risky, but—" The sounds of battle drew closer, and Dralin glanced nervously down a side passage. "The Commander has been moving men into the caves for the last few ten-days. They've been hiding in caverns off the main tunnels."

"Ehvan was right," Jeran murmured, but he ignored the dread gnawing at his gut. "What's done is done. The battle is joined. Will the slaves fight?"

"Not all of them," Dralin replied, "but most. Tylor wasn't pleased when he learned you escaped. The Orog bore the brunt of his rage, if you ask me, but you'll not hear that from most. Their spirit's almost broken, but if they think there's a chance, they might have just enough fight left in them."

"Gather anyone willing to fight and take them to the armory. Find Ehvan. He will know how best to use the help."

Dralin started down the tunnel toward the Barrows. "What about you? Where are you going?"

Jeran did not answer, and he continued down the tunnel at a run. The Barrows were dark, but not the pitch black of the deeper caves; the ShadowMagi had used their Gift to provide the slaves with a meager light. It was not much, but with his magic-enhanced senses, it was enough.

The hall widened in front of him, and Jeran heard voices. He exploded into the room, seizing magic and squeezing his eyes shut. Bright light flashed, and the Bull's soldiers cried out. The room lurched unexpectedly, and a noxious odor filled the air. *The Boundary did that. I must be careful.* The distraction was all the advantage Jeran needed; he bore down upon the guards like a tempest, his Aelvin blade slicing through armor. He struck and pivoted and struck again. When he finally stopped, gasping for air, a dozen men lay dead.

"Not the most honorable way to fight," a man said from one of the small tunnels that converged on the guardpost. Jeran recognized him. Grissam, one of Ehvan's rebels, spat on the nearest guard and strode into the room. In one hand he held a blade covered in dark blood. "Not honorable at all. But effective."

"How long were you there?" Jeran demanded.

"Long enough."

"Then why—?"

Grissam laughed. The throaty sound sent a chill down Jeran's spine. "Are you kiddin'? If I'd stepped into the room, you'd have cut me down before I could shout out 'friend'. Besides, doesn't look like you needed my help."

"Why are you here?" Jeran detested the man, and part of him wished he did not need men like Grissam. But when you had to fight, you used whatever weapons were available.

"Ehvan told me to find you. We hold the armories, but the Durange still control the smithy. There's been no sign of the Orog, and the rest of the Humans are cowering in their barrows. There are more soldiers down here than we guessed. Ehvan thinks we're going to have a hard time holding. I think we're lucky to have survived this long."

"The Orog will come," Jeran said, "and the Humans too. Hold out as long as you have to, as long as you can. If we fail now, we fail utterly." The clatter of armor and the sound of marching feet reached their ears: more soldiers on the way down from the castle. "I'm going to the castle entrance. Gather as many men as you can and follow me. If we can stop the Bull's men there, it doesn't matter what else we hold."

"The castle?" Grissam spat again. "Do you know how many men the Commander has guarding the entrance?"

"It doesn't matter," Jeran said, surrendering to magic. The flows wavered; he was close enough to the Boundary to feel its effects, but far enough away that he was not worried. Much. "None of them will be alive by the time you get there."

The enemy burst into the room, but the first soldier stopped short when he saw the bodies littering the floor. He was little more than a boy, freckled and wide-eyed. He blanched at the sight of all the blood and bent over to retch. The soldiers behind him did not stop, and they pushed him into Jeran's waiting blade.

* * * * * * * * * * * * * * * * * * * *

Blood splattered Dahr's cheek as he wrenched his blade free. His opponent fell to the hard stone of the corridor. "These small halls give you an unfair advantage," Lord Grondellan grumbled. "We haven't met a soldier who could reach you."

"I'd prefer to be outside," Dahr replied, sniffing the air. More Durange waited ahead; he could almost taste them. He straightened, and his head hit the ceiling. With a pained grunt, he rubbed his skull. "Or at least able to stand." Lord Grondellan laughed aloud at that. Bent at the knees, Dahr shuffled forward.

Dahr and Lord Grondellan explored the corridors honeycombing the wall, seeking a way to the parapets. They encountered resistance, but nothing compared to the initial skirmish, and nowhere near the number of men expected. They were alone; the others had broken off to explore cross passages or gotten separated in one of a dozen skirmishes. The halls were so narrow that having a large group made little difference. Two could defend a corridor as easily as two hundred.

Dahr welcomed the solitude. He had tried to lose Lord Grondellan as well, but the man refused to be left behind. Despite himself, Dahr could not help but remember hunting with his former master. Once, they had pursued a wild boar for nearly a ten-day, and when they eventually came upon it, Lord Grondellan had allowed him to take part in the kill. It was the first time he had been allowed to participate in a hunt, and the feeling when his spear pierced the beast's flesh had been exhilarating.

Dahr grinned at the memory, and then he remembered who Lord Grondellan was, what he had been, and the urge to strike the man down returned. *No one would know*, a voice whispered in the back of his mind. *Kill him now, and you can say the Durange did it.* His hand tightened on the hilt of his greatsword, but another voice, one that sounded like Grendor's, begged him to stop. *You promised Jeran. Do you take your oaths so lightly? Seek peace, Dahr! Seek the peace that comes so easily to the Orog.*

"You alright, Hunter?" Lord Grondellan asked. "That last swordsman didn't reach you, did he? You look like you're about to fall over."

"I'm fine," Dahr snarled, pushing ahead. The close confines wore on his nerves, and he yearned to breathe free air. A door appeared on his right, and he hesitated before easing it open. Two soldiers lay in their beds, sound asleep. Somehow, the screaming and fierce skirmishes had not awakened them.

Lord Grondellan stepped forward, careful to step around the three overturned bottles on the floor, and his hand reached for one of the daggers on his chest. "What are you doing?" Dahr whispered, grabbing the Rachannan's arm. "They're asleep."

"I'm making sure they stay that way," Lord Grondellan replied, pulling his arm free. "It may not be honorable, Hunter, but I'd rather not turn to find them at my back."

"Like this?" Dahr spun, but it was too late. A man stood in the doorway with a loaded crossbow. When Dahr tensed, the man hefted the weapon a little higher. "I wouldn't," he warned, and Dahr lowered his sword. "I don't know what you expected to gain with this. There's no way you could—"

A blade sliced through the soldier's throat and cut off his speech with the gurgle of blood. As the body fell, Yurs stepped into view. He looked at his dagger distastefully, and then bent down to carefully wipe the blade on the soldier's shirt. "I've found the way to the top, my Lord. If you would follow me?"

"Good work, Yurs. You have my— Watch out, lad!" Lord Grondellan leapt toward Dahr, shoving him against the wall. Dahr hit with a thud, and turned to attack, but he stopped short when he saw one of the drunken soldiers plant his dagger in the Rachannan's shoulder. Lord Grondellan howled, and he punched at the man, who fell against his companion. Before the enemy soldiers could regain their footing, Dahr fell upon them, hacking with his greatsword. By the time he finished, Yurs had removed the dagger from Lord Grondellan's shoulder and was tying thread to a needle to stitch the wound.

"You have my thanks, Hunter. After that blow, I don't know that I could have taken them both." Lord Grondellan winced when Yurs applied the dressing, and again when he tested his shoulder. "Won't be using my axe for a while, but I'll survive."

"I owe you thanks, too," Dahr said, though he hated to admit it. "He'd have killed me. You… You saved my life."

"That's what allies do, eh?" Lord Grondellan smacked Dahr on the shoulder with his good arm. "And friends, too? I like you, Hunter. You have spirit." After fastening his axe to the loop on his belt, he turned to Yurs. "You said something about outside? I think the Tribesman might like a breath of fresh air."

When Yurs opened the door to the parapet, Dahr was surprised to find himself on the far end of the wall. A few hand off, a narrow path twisted up the mountain, ending in a sheer cliff. Across that chasm stood Dranakohr, but the bridge was raised and the gates barred. A Tribesman spotted them and ran over. "Cat's Claw say find you. He say wall taken. He say Garun'ah cubs put up better fight."

Dahr nodded, but before he could answer, a bell began ringing in the castle. A horn sounded, and the bridge began to lower. "What are they doing?" Lord Grondellan asked.

"They're calling for help," Dahr replied, his hand tightening on the hilt of his sword. Dahr grinned wildly, and above, Shyrock shrieked a challenge. "The rebellion has begun, and they want the guards down here to help secure the castle. Find Cat's Claw," he told the Tribesman, "and gather cloaks from the dead, enough for all our men." He turned to Lord Grondellan. "They want help. Why not give them some?"

* * * * * * * * * * * * * * * * * * * *

"He went where?" Ehvan demanded, and the young man standing in front of him blanched. A shout and the sound of clashing swords echoed through the cavern, but Ehvan had lived in the Barrows long enough to know they were distant. The children in front of him were not as experienced, or fear had gotten the better of them. With every new sound, they tensed as if expecting an attack at any time and from every direction.

Maybe they've reason to think that. The Darklord has more men down here than any of us guessed! Bands of soldiers still roamed the tunnels, and the enemy was better trained than his ragtag band, but Ehvan's men knew the caves better. At last report, the rebels held all of their targets and all but two of the choke points, but it had been some time since the last report. The advantage had shifted several times already, and for all he knew, the Darklord's troops could be bearing down on his position right now.

"Lord Odara entered the castle as soon we arrived," the boy stammered. "He told us not to follow, not until the mines were secure, and that we were to hold this tunnel at any cost, even if the Bull himself led a charge against us."

Someone stepped from the shadows, and Ehvan launched himself toward the movement, his blade swinging. He checked his attack at the last instant. Sorvan, one of his lieutenants, flicked his eyes toward the sword hovering fingers from his throat. He had not even flinched. "You should announce yourself," Ehvan snarled.

"What good would it have done?" Sorvan replied. "I announced myself at the last checkpoint and still had to fight my way past."

"You attacked our own men?" Ehvan asked, mortified.

"They attacked me," Sorvan replied with a casual shrug. "But that was the only time. Most of our troops look like them"—he pointed to the boys huddled in the center of the cave—"They soil their breeches every time a torch flickers." Ehvan believed him, he had nearly been forced to fight his way past his own men twice, but that did not make him like Sorvan any more.

"Someone's coming," called a child near the tunnel to the Barrows, and the others rushed to his side. Each young man held a torch in one hand and a weapon in the other. They tensed, ready to pounce at the first sign of an attack.

"We're friends," a voice called. "We mean no harm."

"Step into the light," Ehvan called, muscling past the guards. He did not lower his sword, but he wanted to make sure no one attacked unless there was need to. "Keep your weapons down."

A grey-skinned figure stepped from the shadows. Wounds, many fresh and oozing dark blood, covered his body, but he carried himself as if he felt no pain. He held a cudgel in one hand, its end splintered and stained red. Other Orog followed, two of them dragging a black-robed figure. The ShadowMage look terrified; he thrashed against his captors, but they held him in iron grips. "We fought his brothers in the caves," the Orog told Ehvan. "He cannot touch his Gift while we hold him. I am Drogon, *Choupik* of the Narise."

"Ehvan, leader of the resistance." Ehvan stepped forward to look at the ShadowMage, but Sorvan pushed past him and plunged a dagger into the man's chest. The ShadowMage arched his back, his eyes wide, and then slumped.

An Orog grabbed Sorvan, and the Humans raised their weapons and surged forward. "Stop!" Ehvan yelled, hurling himself between his men and the Orog. "Hold your places." The guards stopped, several even look relieved, but they all watched the Orog warily as Ehvan gave them access to the chamber.

"There was no need to kill," Drogon told Sorvan, his deep voice booming through the cave. "He posed no threat."

"He's a Mage," Sorvan answered, spitting on the body. "He got better than he deserved."

"Enough!" Ehvan turned a harsh glare on Sorvan. "Find Yassik. Tell him Jeran's gone into the castle alone and I'm leading a cell after him."

"Tell him yourself," Sorvan replied. "I'm not your message boy. Send one of them." He gestured at the children resuming the posts around the chamber.

Ehvan gave no warning; his fist connected solidly with Sorvan's jaw. The man crumpled, but he was back on his feet in an instant, his hand reaching for his dagger. Drogon restrained him. "Follow my orders," Ehvan snapped, "or you'll get what *you* deserve."

Sorvan glared, but he finally sheathed his blade. "We'll settle this later, boy," he said, wrenching himself away from Drogon and starting down a tunnel.

"Can you spare some men," Ehvan asked Drogon. "There may be more Magi in the castle."

Drogon separated five Orog from the ten who followed him. "I will join you as well," he said. Ehvan murmured his thanks while he selected men from his own command. He took the best and most experienced and prayed to the Five Gods that he was doing the right thing. He left Tyrel in charge, a boy of only eighteen winters, but the only one present who had been a member of the resistance. The only one who did not look like he wanted to sick up.

"Come along," Ehvan called. "We have to find Lord Odara!"

* * * * * * * * * * * * * * * * * * * *

"He went *where*?" Yassik yelled. It was the first time Grendor had ever heard the Mage sound angry. "Alone?"

"To… To the castle," the woman repeated. Grendor reached out to comfort her, but the woman shied away from his touch, and the look she gave him made him wonder if the wound he had taken had disfigured him in some way.

"That fool!" Yassik said. He began to pace the hall. "He's not ready for this."

"Begging your pardon, Mage Yassik," the woman interrupted. "Lord Odara killed two score men at the gate to the castle single-handedly. With his magic, he's unstoppable."

"With his magic, he's in danger!" Yassik beat his fist against the wall. "Fool! Fool boy!"

"I do not understand, friend Yassik," Grendor interjected. "I have seen Jeran use magic in battle before and little harm was done."

"No. You've seen Jeran use magic before, and you've seen him in battle before. Sometimes the two events were close together, but they were never at the same time. It takes great concentration to control the Gift, just like it takes great concentration to keep from getting your head chopped off. Very few Magi are able to do both simultaneously, and even then, only after seasons of intense training. If Jeran tries to use magic while fighting, he could find himself distracted long enough to be killed. Or he could be wounded, and his magic might run wild. Or, he might not pay enough attention and the magic will run wild regardless."

Yassik paced the cavern more, then grabbed Grendor by the shoulders. "We have to find him. We have to warn him. I don't care what the plan was; Jeran must be stopped." He turned to the woman. "Find Guardsman Wardel. Tell him Jeran went to the castle and that we need every available man. We must take Dranakohr tonight or all may be lost."

The woman looked to Grendor for confirmation, and after a moment, he nodded. "If we lose the *ghrat*, Jeran will never forgive us. But I swore an oath to protect him, and I will do so. From the Bull of Ra Tachan. From the Darklord. Even from himself."

* * * * * * * * * * * * * * * * * * *

"Stay back, lad. I'll handle this." Lord Grondellan, uncomfortable in the tight-fitting cloak, walked beside Dahr. The other Rachannen, along with Cat's Claw and all the Tribesmen who could be found, marched behind them in ranks of two, moving as quickly as possible up the treacherous slope. One soldier sent a loose stone skittering off the edge of the path, and it clattered as it tumbled down the long descent.

"I'd rather stay in front," Dahr said, "in case something goes wrong."

"No offense, lad, but not too many Humans grow to be your size. Yurs and I can handle the guards. You and the other Tribesmen stay back until we're inside."

Dahr reluctantly fell back beside Cat's Claw. Gusting winds drove across the trail, limiting visibility and driving bits of ice and stone against the flesh hard enough to sting. Dahr pulled the hood of his cloak close to shield his face.

A man cried out, and Dahr turned in time to see a Rachannen fall, his ankle turning on an icy patch. He scrabbling helplessly as he slid toward the edge, but just before he went over, a Tribesman threw himself to the ground and grabbed the man's hand. With the help of two other soldiers, they hauled him back onto the road, where he lay panting.

"Thank Garun no one fall," Sadarak said once the column had resumed marching. "I never see trail like this."

"The Bull must use the caves to enter Dranakohr," Dahr said, testing each step before transferring his weight. "It's not even winter yet!"

The column approached the bridge, an oaken arch suspended by chains as thick as Dahr's arm that disappeared into the darkness above. The wooden monstrosity creaked and groaned in the wind. Lord Grondellan and Yurs crossed confidently, but Cat's Claw hesitated. "I not like these things," he admitted, glancing over the side. Dahr looked too, but darkness swallowed the ground and he had no way to gauge their height. "I never like them, but none chill my heart like this."

"The Gods wouldn't have brought us here just to watch us tumble from a bridge," Dahr said. He stepped forward, and the bridge lurched under his weight. The chains were not long enough to set the bridge upon the stone; the walkway hovered half a hand above the ground, swaying in the wind. Pretending not to care, Dahr continued onward.

Cat's Claw followed, and the Tribesman fastened his eyes on the heavens. "Garun better mention this night when I meet him in Twilight World."

When Dahr stepped off the bridge, Lord Grondellan signaled for him to wait. A moment later, the gate swung open and a soldier approached. "Any trouble at the wall?"

"Bah!" Lord Grondellan waved dismissively. "Nothin' we couldn't handle. A few peasants jumping through the snow like jackrabbits. My men made quick work of them. The situation here?"

"I've had reports of an uprising. We've received no word for some time, but the Commander sent extra squads down to the Barrows. I figured you could spare a few men to help guard the castle."

Lord Grondellan laughed loudly. "It's not like an army'll be attackin' from the south, eh? Truth be told, I'm glad ya called. You know how cold it gets down there at night?" He turned and waved for the column to advance. "I'll gladly put a few slaves in their place if it means a hot meal and warm bed." Preceding the guard into the castle, Lord Grondellan asked, "Tell me, soldier, how many men are stationed with you?"

"It's just the five of us," the soldier replied, brushing the snow from his shoulders. "Everyone else was called away."

"A pity." Lord Grondellan spun around and drove a dagger through the man's chest. The soldier gasped, but Lord Grondellan cupped a hand over his mouth to stifle his gasp. Yurs moved as quickly as his master, throwing himself at two of the guards. The first fell with blood blossoming from his throat; the second tumbled off the edge of the cliff, his scream cutting off abruptly. The other two soldiers drew their weapons before Dahr and Cat's Claw were upon them, but the two Tribesmen made quick work of them. They hid the bodies outside and pulled the gates closed.

Dahr divided the men into groups of five. "The enemy expects the attack to come from below. Surprise is on our side."

"These'll help too," Lord Grondellan chuckled, tugging at his cloak. "Just make sure you know who you're killing before you kill 'em!"

Each group took a different passage with orders to search the castle and flush out the enemy. To Dahr's dismay, Lord Grondellan refused to leave his side. "Those boys know what they're doing," he laughed when Dahr tried to give him his own command. "Besides, you have a nose for battle. I'm not letting you out of my sight."

They searched room after room, crisscrossed a dozen different halls, but found nothing. No sound save their footfalls reached their ears. Most chambers were barren and dust covered, as if unlived in for some time. "It's like the castle's abandoned."

"They're around somewhere," Lord Grondellan said. "It's a big place, and there's a fight going on below. But I'd prefer that we eliminate any enemies up here before we go down looking for a fight. Let's try this door."

Dahr heard voices behind the door Lord Grondellan pointed to. He waved for silence. "The rebels hold the mines, but we have them trapped in the entry hall," a man's voice announced. "A few small groups may have slipped past before we reclaimed control of the lower levels, but access to the castle is secure."

"What is this I hear of Magi attacking our men?" a second voice demanded.

"Rumors! The ShadowMagi are intolerable, but they aren't fools. A few soldiers were probably killed by mistake. The men are on edge. They're exaggerating."

"This rebellion must end now. Gather the reserve squads and lead them down to the Barrows. Tell Eschi to bring the full might of the ShadowMagi to bear against the slaves. Order the men up from the wall. The slaves must be taught a lesson. One that they won't forget again."

"Yes, Commander," the soldier said, and a door slammed closed. "Alright, you have your orders. Gather your troops and head to the mines. Show no mercy! Make the slaves beg for the sweetness of the lash before they die!"

With a roar that built up from deep within, Dahr kicked in the door and leapt inside, his greatsword swinging. A dozen soldiers sat around a long table covered in maps of the caves. Dahr's strike severed one soldier's arm and drove most of the way through the table. Dahr wrenched the blade free, but not before the other enemy soldiers had drawn their weapons and attacked.

Lord Grondellan pushed past Dahr, bowling over two men and sending a third jumping back from his wildly swinging sword. The rest of Dahr's squad, a Tribesman and two Rachannen, joined the fray, bellowing at the top of their lungs.

The one-armed soldier struggled to raise his weapon, but could not take his eyes off the bloody remains of his left arm. Dahr grabbed the man by the throat and crushed his windpipe with a squeeze of his hand. Then he jumped onto the table. Two men saw the look in his eyes and bolted for the door; Dahr dove after them. His sword drove through the midriff of one, but Dahr could not pull it free again. Letting go, he turned toward the second soldier, who brought his sword to bear.

Dahr dodged the awkward swing and tackled his opponent. The Blood Rage overcame him as he grappled with his foe; the pounding of his heart was the only sound he heard. He barely felt the pain when a third man scored a blow across his back and did not notice when a Rachannan spitted the man on his dagger. All he saw was the fear in his enemy's eyes; all he felt was the thrill of the hunt.

A loud crack reverberated through Dahr's body, and his opponent's back bent at an unnatural angle. The man's eyes rolled up, showing only white, and Dahr rolled off the man and reclaimed his sword. The Tribesman was down, a bloody gash running the length of his torso, and one of the Rachannen as well. Only three of the enemy still stood. Lord Grondellan, pinned in a corner, fought two; the remaining Rachannan fought the third.

Dahr stepped toward Lord Grondellan, then hesitated. If he let the man die here, his conscience would be clean. He would not have betrayed his oath, and his master's blood would not be on his hands. *Leave him*, the sibilant voice whispered in his head. *He doesn't deserve to live!*

One of Lord Grondellan's opponents landed a solid blow, and the large man crumpled, his sword clattering to the stone floor. Defenseless, he looked into the faces of his attackers and waited to die. Dahr saw no fear in the Lord Grondellan's eyes, only acceptance and a touch of regret.

"NO!" Dahr launched himself across the room. His swing cleaved through the first soldier, shaved a lock of hair off Lord Grondellan's head, and buried itself deep in the second man. Both men fell, and the second pulled Dahr down with him. By the time Dahr regained his feet and pulled his sword free, the fight was over. The last enemy soldier and the Rachannan had fallen to each other's blades.

"At this rate," Lord Grondellan said as he ripped a strip of cloth from his cloak and tied it around his leg, "I'll not have any limbs left by the end of the battle."

"We should go," Dahr said, offering his hand. "Anyone nearby was sure to hear the shouting, and I'd rather not be here when they arrived." He helped Lord Grondellan to his feet and wrapped one arm around the man's shoulders for support. They limped toward the door.

"What happened here," a new voice called, and Dahr froze. "Soldier," the voice demanded, the sound crisp and commanding, "What happened?"

Dahr turned. She was as beautiful as he remembered. Dark red curls framed a perfect face; red lips pursed together angrily as she surveyed the carnage. Black leather armor clung to her body, but she moved in it gracefully. "Soldier, I won't ask—" She turned her eyes on him, green eyes the color of emeralds, eyes that bored into his soul.

"Dahr," Katya gasped, her voice a hoarse whisper. She slumped back, unable to speak. "I thought... I feared..."

Dahr saw motion out of the corner of his eye, and he caught Lord Grondellan's wrist before the older man could throw his dagger. "No," he said, and in that moment of indecision, Katya ran, her footfalls quickly fading in the distance. Dahr turned a hard gaze on Lord Grondellan. "She's mine."

* *

Jeran dredged his memory for the correct path through Dranakohr. The halls were empty, too empty, and the implications worried him, but he had no time to deal with that right now. He was needed here, distracting the guards and giving the rebels the time they needed to secure the caves. About a hundreds hands away, five soldiers stood at an intersection of halls. Jeran opened himself to magic, but before he could attack, a squad of soldiers appeared and set upon the five men, shouting, "For Tylor the Bull!" The five men fought fiercely, but the squad made short work of them.

They're fighting their own? Confused, Jeran decided not to give the enemy the chance to strike first. He sprinted forward, sword at the ready, and released his Gift. A ball of fire appeared and preceded him down the hall, the bright red flames gaining speed with his every step. The Tachans dove for cover, and when the flames exploded, only one soldier was caught in the conflagration.

One less man to fight was more than Jeran had hoped for; the fireball had only been meant as a distraction. He vaulted over the smoking corpse and attacked the nearest soldier. Blue sparks flashed when Jeran's blade met his enemies'. Pivoting, Jeran cut a deep gash across the soldier behind him, and then spun again, trading blows with his original opponent. The others were regrouping, but Jeran had a moment before they were upon him.

He ducked a swing and stepped inside his opponent's guard, stabbing upward. He felt the resistance of steel driving through armor. The soldier blanched and let out a raspy gasp before crumpling. "It's not a fair fight," Jeran said to the seven remaining men, stalling for time while he seized magic. Little flashes of lightning danced around his body, though they were only meant to frighten. "But I'll take it easy on you."

Jeran charged, but as he did, a measure of confidence returned to his enemies' eyes. A flash of black caught his eye, and Jeran threw himself to the side, drawing on magic even as he fended off an attack from the nearest soldier. His fireball missed the ShadowMage by more than a hand, and the woman paid it little more attention than she would have an insect. She stepped around the bodies and drew upon her Gift; her aura came to life with streaks of silver and black.

Ducking another blow, Jeran swung his sword at the nearest soldier while preparing another attack for the Mage. A glancing blow caught Jeran's arm when he released his Gift, and the jolt of pain made his hold on magic slip. Energy surged through him, building until it had nowhere to go but out.

An explosion ripped through the hall, knocking Jeran to the floor. Stone fell from the ceiling, and the walls blackened and crumbled. Covering his eyes, Jeran felt blindly along the floor for his sword. His hand closed on the tree-trunk hilt and he sat up. When he vision cleared, he found the soldiers down, some dead, others writhing on the floor. The ShadowMage was gone. Whether she had run or had been destroyed in the explosion, Jeran did not know, but he did not want to wait around to find out. Soldiers he could deal with, and maybe even Magi, but he would rather not face both again.

He ran, and he heard the sounds of battle all around him. Two Orog crossed the hall in pursuit of a fleeing ShadowMage. To his left, a Tribesman battled three soldiers, the great sweeps of his waraxe driving the Tachans back step by step. Jeran ignored them; he had one target, and he knew where to find her.

He burst inside, dropping to a crouch, but no guards waited. He had only been to the Commander's Hall once before, but he remembered it well: nearly a hundred hands from side to side and twice as long, with a large fireplace dominating one end and ornate tapestries hanging from the walls. When Tylor commanded Dranakohr, the chamber had held many treasures; now it stood all but barren. Brass containers filled with oil lined the sides of the hall. Flames danced across the surface of the containers, flickering and hissing. An Aelvin rug lay on the floor, but most of the treasures Tylor had stolen were gone. A single, cushioned chair remained, its back to the door.

The chair moved slightly, and Jeran smiled. "I knew you couldn't do it," he said confidently. "I knew you wouldn't fight against us, Katya."

A familiar sigh echoed through the room, and the sound of it froze Jeran in his tracks. "I should have known it would be you, Odara," Tylor said, standing. The Bull's shining black plate shimmered in the lamplight. The chair's cushions tore as the spikes and barbs adorning the Bull's armor pulled free. "Will you never give me a moment's peace?"

"How...?" Jeran stammered. "You must have Gated here!"

"Gated?" Tylor sounded confused at first, and then his eyes narrowed. "Magic? You think I would subject my body to magic?" The Bull dismissed the notion. "I was never in Vela. In fact, Vela was just a distraction. Lorthas has more important targets in mind."

"I saw you there!" Jeran insisted. "Leading the assault."

"You saw Halwer." Tylor shook his head ruefully. "He said he could do it, but I doubted him. He said he could convince everyone he was me, that he had served me so long he could guess my every thought. He was a good man."

Stunned, Jeran could do little more than watch as Tylor drew his sword and examined its edge. "Where were you, then?"

"Here and there," the Bull replied. "Let's just say I was tying up a few loose ends." Tylor swung his sword, testing the blade, and a cold smile spread across his face. "I think we've played this game long enough. I tire of our feud. What say you we end it now, once and for all?" He leveled his sword at Jeran's chest.

Jeran raised his own blade and reached out to magic. The flows came to him easily, but once he held them, something changed. They felt locked, rigid, different than they had ever felt before. He tried to release the magic, but it would not go. Tylor saw his fear and laughed. "The Boundary runs right behind that wall," he said, pointing to the hearth. "You won't be able to use your wizard's tricks on me today. It will have to be a fair fight."

Jeran gripped the hilt of his sword so tight it hurt, but his face remained calm. "I don't need magic to kill you, Durange."

"I've waited a long time for this, Odara. Finally, my sons will be avenged!" Tylor ran forward, his sword swinging. Jeran met the attack and spun, bringing his own blade around to strike at the Bull's flank.

Tylor anticipated the attack and dodged; Jeran's swing went wide, pulling him off balance. Rather than fight the fall he rolled with it. Tylor's answering blow missed by a finger's breadth, and Jeran rolled to his feet, sword raised defensively. "My only regret is that I killed the Tribeswoman so quickly," Tylor mused as he stepped sideways to circle Jeran.

"She's at peace," Jeran said, his eyes locked on Tylor. Hate and rage railed against him, struggled to take over, and a part of him clawed at his Gift, fighting to unleash his magic even if he destroyed himself in the process. He drew on his training to keep emotion at bay.

Jeran lunged, and Tylor parried; sparks flashed when their blades met. They exchanged blows, dancing around each other, the clang of steel counting the beat. Before long, Jeran fell into a rhythm. He found the peace that often filled him when he worked the sword, and it changed the feel of the battle. His reactions became automatic; he barely had to think. He knew the Bull's thoughts, could anticipate his attacks. Before long he had Tylor on the defensive, driving him back one slow step at a time.

The strange balance he found, the balance between combat and magic, extended beyond the room. As if he had extended his perceptions, he knew things. Ehvan and Wardel led an army of slaves and Orog in an assault on Dranakohr. The Tachan positions had been overrun and the remaining soldiers were falling back, but Lord Grondellan and Cat's Claw already held most of the castle. He felt other things too: the injured, the dying, the pain of those he had known during his time in the mines. Their suffering echoed in the back of his mind, and the tears they shed made his heart ache.

"Katya serves Lorthas," Tylor said, shattering Jeran's peace. When the Bull saw that his words had had an effect, he launched a vicious attack, driving Jeran back and scoring a hit with the flat of his blade. "She commanded Dranakohr in my absence. She ordered the punishment of the slaves, the starvation of the Orog."

"I don't believe you," Jeran said, but the Bull had planted the thorn. *What if I'm wrong about her?* Teeth gritted, he took the hilt of his sword in both hands and swung. Tylor parried, and the jolt sent a shock up Jeran's arm.

"You'll never be certain, though, will you? If you let her live, she might betray you later. You won't know the truth until it's too late." Tylor stabbed, and Jeran miscalculated. He dodged the attack, but the movement brought him within Tylor's reach. The Bull lashed out with his fist, and the blow made spots of light dance before Jeran's eyes and sent him reeling backward.

"Uncle?" Katya stood at the door, her sword drawn, her eyes conflicted. Tylor saw her and smiled.

"Katya, how nice of you to join us. I believe you know my guest." The Bull attacked again, but Jeran was ready for him. His answering swing glanced off Tylor's armor. Tylor looked surprised. "You're not that bad a swordsman, Odara. Almost as good as your father was. But he couldn't beat me, either."

For a moment, Jeran faltered, but he felt the tingling of a Reading coming from Tylor, and without thinking, he opened himself to it. What he saw snapped something within him, and he beat Tylor back with a series of lightning-fast blows. "My father did defeat you! I know the truth! You're a coward, Tylor, and your brother's a treacherous monster!"

Tylor retreated, and Jeran pressed his advantage relentlessly. First one blow slipped past Tylor's guard, and then another. Most of Jeran's attacks glanced harmlessly off the Bull's armor, but a few struck solidly, and the Aelvin blade gouged deep rents in Tylor's magic-wrought mail.

A blow from behind knocked Jeran from his feet and sent him skidding across the floor, fighting to remain conscious. "I don't appreciate being called treacherous," Salos hissed, stepping into the light. "*I* made no promises to your father, and I make no promises to you."

Tylor looked at his brother, and then at Jeran. Salos sighed. "Please, spare me your lectures. He is not without skill. Had I let this fight continue to its conclusion, the boy might have killed you, or you him. This way, the outcome is secure. Just kill him and be done with it."

"No," Tylor said, "it's not that. How did you...?"

Salos' jaw tightened. "Do you think I spent this much time in Dranakohr without honing my Gift? The Boundary is a distraction to me now, nothing more. After all this time, and especially under these circumstances, I'd appreciate some trust. And a little gratitude."

Tylor hesitated, but his need for vengeance overpowered his distrust of magic, and he strode forward boldly. Jeran struggled against Salos' Gift, but he could not break the Scorpion's hold. "This isn't how I imagined it," Tylor admitted, raising his sword, "but it will suffice."

A gray form darted across the room, and the magic holding Jeran disappeared. Jeran rolled away as a scream cut across the chamber. Tylor's sword clanged against the stone where Jeran's head had been an instant before.

Grendor pulled Salos to his feet, his iron-like grip keeping the Scorpion from using magic. "He will bother you no more, friend Jeran."

Back on his feet, Jeran moved to attack, and Tylor beckoned to his niece. "Katya, join me! Together, we can defeat him easily."

Katya hesitated, and her eyes slid from her uncle to Jeran and back again. "I can't. This is a matter for the two of you to settle. I'll take no part in it."

The betrayal cut Tylor deep. "This is the greatest insult you have done me yet," the Bull said, and for a moment, Jeran pitied him. "To kill my sons in battle, I can understand. But this...? I loved her like a daughter, and you stole her from me!"

"I didn't steal her," Jeran told Tylor. "You lost her. Just like you lost your throne and everything else that was important to you." Enraged, the Bull attacked, but Jeran easily dodged the awkward charge and his answering swing sent Tylor reeling. "For my mother!" Swords met, and blue sparks flashed. "For my father!" Aelvin steel pierced Mage-wrought armor, and the Bull howled. "For Uncle Aryn!" A well-placed kick sent Tylor stumbling backward and gasping for air. "For Reanna!" The blow severed Tylor's hamstring, and he fell to his knees. "For my son!" Jeran's final swing cleaved Tylor's gauntlet. Hand and sword clattered to the floor.

The Bull cried out and clutched the stump of his arm tightly. He turned to Katya, begging her for help. "Katya! Please!"

Lips trembling, Katya turned her back on him. Her whisper floated through the chamber. "I love you, Uncle."

Defeated, Tylor faced Jeran and saw death looming over him. He chuckled, and a trickle of blood ran from his nose. "Finish it, Odara, but know this: We are not so different, you and I. Kill me now, and you prove it."

"We are very different, Tylor." Jeran stepped in close, lowering himself so they faced each other eye to eye. "I forgive you," he whispered, and Tylor's eyes widened. "You believed that what you did was right, that your motives were pure. That you were wrong no longer matters. Die knowing your enemy holds no grudge against you. You didn't understand, and for that, I forgive you."

Jeran plunged his sword into Tylor's chest. The Aelvin blade screeched as it drove through the Bull's armor. Katya winced at the sound, but she turned toward the wall to spare herself the sight of it. Salos struggled against Grendor's hold, and his lips drew down in a sneer. Silently, Jeran asked the Gods to provide Tylor with a peaceful journey to the Nothing. Then he looked up. "Dahr, No!"

Dahr stood behind Katya, his face a mask of rage. His sword was raised, and his arm trembled with the effort of not swinging. Katya turned to face him, and as she stared into his eyes, a tear traced a path down her cheek. "I did this to you," she whispered, reaching up to caress his cheek. He flinched from her touch, and her eyes moved to his sword. "Do it. Please, Dahr, set me free."

"There's been enough killing today!" Jeran yelled. "Dahr, remember your promise! Don't become the monster you think you are!"

Dahr's blade edged closer to Katya's throat. Suddenly, Grendor screamed, and a loud clatter followed his agonized shriek. Blue flames engulfed Grendor's body. The oil from the toppled lamp hissed as it spread across the stones, soaking into Grendor's clothes and blocking the path to his rescue. Of Salos there was no sign; the Scorpion had disappeared into the shadows.

Dahr dropped his sword and ran across the chamber, sprinting through the burning oil, heedless of his own smoldering clothes and the small balls of flames he kicked up with each step. Without stopping, he scooped Grendor up and carried him to the hearth. Depositing him roughly on the stones, he shoveled handfuls of ash onto the Orog to soak up the oil. Then, ripping the cloak from his own shoulders, Dahr smothered the remaining flames. Every touch brought a fresh cry of agony to Grendor's lips, but Dahr ignored them. He worked single-mindedly and did not stop until the last hint of fire was gone.

Jeran approached, afraid of what he would find. Burns covered Grendor's face and body, and his left hand was a lump of ruined flesh and exposed bone. His breathing was shallow, his pulse erratic, and he shivered as if lying on a bank of snow. But when he opened his eyes and saw Dahr, he smiled. *After all of this, he can smile! How can he smile?*

"Friend Dahr," Grendor said weakly. "The Mage pushed me into the flames. I tried to hold on, but I could not. I could not. Tell Jeran... Tell him I am sorry I failed."

"You didn't fail," Dahr said, his voice breaking. "Jeran's alive. You saved him."

Jeran stepped in close, kneeling in the ash so Grendor could see him. "Dranakohr is ours," he said, reaching out to touch the Orog's unburnt shoulder. "We have won, and we have you to thank for it. You did a great thing today, Grendor. Your people are free!"

"Free," Grendor repeated, and his smile broadened. "It was all worth it. Thank you, Jeran." His eyes closed, and he slumped. With a final sigh, his chest went still.

Dahr put his head to Grendor's chest. "We need a Healer."

Jeran shook his head. "We don't have one."

"Then open a Gate, and I will find one."

"The Boundary is there," Jeran said, pointing to the hearth. "I couldn't use my Gift if—"

"Then find someplace where you can!" Dahr yelled, grabbing Jeran's shirt and pulling him close. "He wouldn't let me die when I wanted to; may the Gods damn me if I let him die now. Make me a Gate." Dahr lifted Grendor gently and cradled him in his arms.

Their eyes locked, and Jeran saw something in Dahr's pained expression that he had feared lost forever. He saw compassion. "This way." He started for the door, waving for Dahr to follow. To Katya, he said, "You, stay here."

Jeran ran through the halls, Dahr a half step behind him, until he felt the block on his magic slip away. Energy surged through him unexpectedly, and he almost lost his focus. He opened a Gate; the line of silver speckles opened outward to reveal the castle at Vela. "Hurry," Jeran said, panting. Flows of energy danced around him, pounding against his control. "I can't hold it."

"If he can be saved," Dahr said, sprinting toward the Gate, "I will save him." He leapt through, and his passage hit Jeran like a thunderbolt. His hold on magic evaporated, the Gate folded in upon itself, and Jeran collapsed on the cold stones of Dranakohr.

Afterthoughts

"That fool!" Lorthas raged. His red eyes burned, and for the first time in decades he felt the bounds of his prison pushing upon him.

"It is not as bad as it seems, Master," Salos replied. The Scorpion sat across the chamber. It was a simple, unadorned cave, one of many discovered along the Boundary, neither as familiar nor as comfortable as Lorthas' chamber in Dranakohr.

"We lost Dranakohr *and* Vela," Lorthas sneered, "the fleet is scattered, and that fool you called a brother is dead. He had more faults than I can name, but for some strange reason, he inspired something in people. Who shall replace him? You? That one-eyed freak in Ra Tachan? I had thought to use your daughter, but she appears to have joined the enemy."

Salos' jaw tightened, but other than that tiny concession, he showed no reaction to Lorthas' jibe. "Vela was never our target," the Scorpion said. "If the Alrendrians think they've won a victory, it only furthers our plans. The damage to the fleet is not as severe as first believed. The ships are regrouping and will soon be ready to launch their next attack."

"But Dranakohr—"

"Dranakohr is inconsequential." Salos' interruption infuriated Lorthas, but he could do nothing about it. The Boundary separated them, and for now it protected the Scorpion. "Let Jeran believe he's severed our tie to Madryn," Salos added. "If he is really that naive, we'll win this war more quickly than anticipated."

Lorthas frowned. "Then you think it's time?"

"Yes, Master. Allow me to give the order."

Lorthas pressed the palms of his hands together and tapped his index fingers against his lips. "Very well. Unleash the maelstrom."

* * * * * * * * * * * * * * * * * * * *

The door opened and Sheriza stepped out. A wiry man and an ancient, stoop-shouldered woman followed, and a second Mage appeared in the doorway behind them. Of the four, only Sheriza dared look Dahr in the eye. He still wore the outfit he had worn into battle, stained with blood and dirt; the only thing he had cleaned was his sword. "You healed him?" The way he asked, it did not sound like a question.

Sheriza shook her head. "There was nothing I could do."

"You're a Healer!" Dahr snarled. The wiry man flinched, and the unknown Mage interposed himself between Dahr and Sheriza.

"I'm a Mage," Sheriza replied, shooing her companion away.

They faced off for a moment, glare for glare, but Dahr turned away first and dropped his eyes to the floor. "I brought him as fast as I could."

"You did nothing wrong," Sheriza said, agitation giving way to sympathy. "Your friend is an Orog. My Gift can't touch him. I swear to you, if I could have helped him, I would have."

Dahr nodded sullenly. "He's dead then?"

Sheriza's eyes widened. "Heavens, no! Your friend is close to death, but he still lives."

"But you said—"

"I said *I* could do nothing for him. Master Fel"—the man bowed nervously— "is an alchemist of great renown. Lady Resita makes a poultice that eases the pain of burns. Their help has been invaluable. If the Orog survives the night, he should recover."

The other Mage snorted derisively. "Charlatans," he muttered.

Sheriza's slap staggered the Mage, though the blow had a greater effect on her than him. Dahr grabbed the Healer to keep her from falling. "Master Fel is a healer," Sheriza scolded, "and he will be shown respect."

Abashed, the Mage flushed. "I only meant—"

"You meant that since he doesn't have the Gift, his skill is a mockery of ours. But remember this: if not for him, that poor young man would have died while you watched helplessly. Now go!" The young Mage hung his head and slunk away. Sheriza turned to Master Fel. "You must forgive my apprentice. He's young and still enamored of his powers."

"No offense, Mistress," Master Fel said hastily. "I must get back to my shop. We will check on the Orog tomorrow." With another nervous bow, he led the old woman away.

"You should rest," Sheriza told Dahr. "There's nothing more you can do for him."

Dahr scowled. "I'll wait until he wakes."

"It could be days. And you have your own wounds—"

"I said I'd wait!" Dahr yelled. Sheriza studied him for a moment more before bobbing her head and walking away.

Once she was gone, Dahr entered the room. Grendor lay on the bed, his body swaddled in clean white rags. The Orog's chest rose and fell at a steady pace. *If he survives the night...* Dahr took up a position in front of the door. "You can't die, Grendor. I won't let you."

* * * * * * * * * * * * * * * * * * * *

"Bring him in!" Jeran sat at his desk—at Tylor's desk—in the upper levels of Dranakohr. Papers lay scattered about, so many he had lost track of them all. A fire burned in the hearth, but the window behind him was open and a cold breeze gusted across the chamber. Katya stood motionless in one corner, watching the doorway. Since the battle for Dranakohr, she had never been far from Jeran's side.

The clamor of movement echoed up from the courtyard below. Many of the Darklord's former prisoners raced to leave before snow clogged the pass and delayed their escape. Ehvan and the remnants of the resistance guarded the wall, but they had orders to allow anyone they knew to leave unmolested. Many of them wanted to go too, but Jeran hoped he could convince them to stay. He needed good men in Dranakohr.

The door opened, and two Orog guards entered with their prisoner between them. Quellas' eyes darted around the room frantically, but he could not meet Jeran's imperious stare. Sweat drenched his brow, and he flinched when Jeran asked, "You have something to say to me?"

"Yes... Yes, Lord Odara."

Jeran signaled, and the guards let go. Quellas shuffled forward slowly, his eyes fastened to the floor. He stopped on the far side of the desk and dropped to his knees. "I beg you to take pity on me. Show mercy."

"Mercy." The word fell from Jeran's tongue like a headsman's axe. "The same mercy you showed Reanna, or did you have another kind of mercy in mind?"

"He swore she wouldn't be harmed!" Quellas moaned. "He told me he wanted to stop the rebellion before his men were killed. I only—"

"You convinced yourself you were saving lives to justify betraying your oath as a Guardsman."

"Yes... No! I... I just couldn't stand the dark anymore. I had to get free."

Jeran drew a slow breath. "I would have preferred the first explanation." He picked up his sword from its place beside his chair. The Aelvin steel rasped as he drew it from its scabbard. "You betrayed your oath as a Guardsman." He circled the desk, spinning the sword in his hands. The blade whistled as it cut through the air.

"You betrayed your oath to Alrendria." Quellas squeezed his eyes shut and mumbled an incoherent prayer.

"You betrayed me." Like lightning, Jeran stabbed the point of his sword into the stones a finger's width from Quellas' knees. "You deserve no mercy, but I won't kill you."

Jeran resheathed the sword, and Quellas heaved a sigh. "Thank you, Lord Odara. You won't regret this. You—"

"Since you cast your lot with the Darklord, I'll let Lorthas decide your fate." He turned to the Orog. "Leave him in the tunnel to *Ael Shataq* with a three day supply of rations. If he returns, execute him."

The Orog bowed. "How many firesticks should he be given?" one asked.

Jeran blinked as if caught off guard. "None. Let Lorthas provide him with light. It's the least the Darklord can do." The two Orog nodded again and restrained Quellas.

"No!" Quellas screamed as they dragged him toward the doorway. "You know how I am in the tunnels, Jeran. You know I can't stand the dark! Please! I beg of you. Anything but this. You call this mercy?"

"No." Jeran's smile was icy. "I call it justice."

* * * * * * * * * * * * * * * * * * * *

"Grandfather?"

The Emperor raised his head at Astalian's call. As was the custom, the *Hohe Chatorra* bowed deeply when the Emperor acknowledged his presence, and a beam of sunlight illuminated his haggard face and sunken eyes. *What news does he bring,* Emperor wondered, *that even the magic of the Vale is not enough to ease his mind.*

He motioned for Astalian to join him, and while the Aelvin warrior approached, the Emperor struggled to rise without revealing how difficult it was for him to do so unaided. "What troubles you, my son? Has there been no word of Treloran?"

Astalian's cheeks reddened. "Lady Hahna sent a runner yesterday, Grandfather. Treloran is well and back in Kaper. He and Prince Martyn defeated the Darklord's forces in Vela. I thought someone—"

"And no doubt they thought someone else would tell me as well. I am used to being forgotten, my friend. No, don't apologize! I ran the Empire for millennia; I know how distracted one can get during the exciting times."

"But Treloran is your kin. You should have been told."

"I am not without resources, Astalian. I have kept a closer eye on my grandson than you might expect. Now, tell me what brought you to my garden with that horrible expression on your face."

Astalian turned away. "Luran is coming."

"He's returned!" The Emperor beamed at the prospect. "I knew he just needed time alone. Ready—"

"No, Grandfather," Astalian interrupted. "Luran leads an army against Lynnaei. He preaches a return to glory. He has demanded that all loyal Elves join his cause. The northern districts are behind him, and the rest of the Empire is divided. Our people are at war."

The Emperor's chest tightened; he pressed a hand against his heart and struggled to draw breath. "Luran... My blood..." The Emperor closed his eyes and stood motionless so long that Astalian came forward to take his arm.

At the warrior's touch, the Emperor's eyes shot open. The power of the Gift made them glow a brilliant green. "Bring Charylla here, and send a runner to request Lady Hahna's presence. You have mobilized the army?" Astalian nodded. "Gather our forces here. Luran will try to draw us out, but Lynnaei is the Empire's heart. He cannot hope to take power if he does not hold it."

Astalian turned to carry out the Emperor's orders. "Send a messenger to the Garun'ah," the Emperor called after him. "They need to be on guard. Luran will not abide by the agreements we have reached. And ask them... Ask if, in the spirit of our new friendship, they can offer any assistance. The *Kranora* are wise men. They will understand that my continued presence on the throne is preferable to Luran's."

As soon as Astalian was gone, the Emperor sank into the soft grass of the Vale. *Luran*, he wept, *what have you done?*

* * * * * * * * * * * * * * * * * * * *

The man looked young, barely thirty winters, and did not carry himself with the arrogance of a slowed Mage. He was the first ShadowMage brought before Jeran who had not been branded with the Darklord's sigil. He was the only one to shy away from Jeran's gaze. He was the first to look ashamed. "What's your name?"

The man reached up to brush a lock of brown hair from his face. His hand grazed the iron collar fastened around his throat. "Albion, my Lord."

"You are the one who created the collars? You are a MageSmith?"

Albion swallowed nervously. "I created the collars, my Lord. I would not presume to call myself a MageSmith."

Jeran drummed his fingers against the desk. "Why?"

"My Lord?"

"Why did you create them?"

"I was ordered to, my Lord."

Jeran sighed. It was not the answer he had wanted. "And now that you wear one?"

"It is not something I would wish on anyone, my Lord."

"Yet you created them nonetheless." Jeran opened himself to magic; it filled him, but his proximity to the Boundary prevented him from using his Gift. It still heightened his senses, though. Sped up his reflexes. He reached for his sword.

"But—" Something in Albion's eyes made Jeran pause, and he signaled for the man to speak. "But I have seen ShadowMagi wearing these collars, and I myself was given one. If you use my creations the same way your enemy did, can they be evil? Is it the device you hate, or how it was used?"

Jeran paused to consider Albion's words. "I am a simple man, my Lord, a blacksmith by training. When my home was destroyed and I was brought here, I expected my life to be a short one. The High Inquisitor discovered my Gift and told me that I had an ability thought lost, that I could attain a measure of freedom if I learned how to harness that Gift. I was in no position to argue. Given the choice between death and the forge, I would choose the forge any day.

"Have you ever worked magic into an object, my Lord?" Albion's eyes swam with the memory of it. "It's a feeling unlike anything you could imagine, far more intense than merely holding magic. And to know that something I created will endure, that my creations will be coveted across Madryn... Yes, I regret the use to which some of my works have been put, but one cannot blame the weapon for the kill. Do you think the Mage who forged your blade stopped to consider the number of lives it might end? Would you condemn a common blacksmith for making a sword, or a fletcher for his arrows? I ask only to serve, my Lord. Trust me to use my Gift the way the Gods intended, and I will trust you to use my work in the proper manner."

Jeran stared at Albion for a long time before he spoke. "If you so much as think of using your Gift against my people—"

Albion bowed. "I have no doubt you will give me but one chance to prove myself. I will not disappoint you."

Jeran turned to Drogon, the Orog in charge of watching the ShadowMagi. Drogon studied Albion's face for a moment before nodding. "He speaks the truth. He wishes to serve."

"Remove Master Albion's collar," Jeran said, encouraged by the outcome of the meeting. "Assign two *choupik* to guard him. If they suspect he's using his Gift improperly, they are to kill him immediately."

Albion bowed, and when Drogon unlocked his collar and the cold metal clanged against the stones, he smiled. "I will not disappoint you," he repeated before leaving.

* * * * * * * * * * * * * * * * * * *

"Take me closer."

The bearers set the palanquin down in front of the bodies: one woman and several dozen cubs, gutted and left to die. Yarchik studied the scene for some time. "This is not the work of the Drekka. They have lost their way, but even they would not do this."

"You suspect the *Kohr'adjin*?" Sohrta, the Channa's *Kranach*, asked.

Yarchik closed his eyes tightly. For the first time in seasons, he felt his age. "I suspect my son." The *Kranor* looked upward, and three stars fell from the Heavens, leaving red trails through the night sky.

"When blood drips from a clean sky and the future lies dead on a sea of green, the servants of the Chaos God will reap their finest harvest. Death will descend from the north, turning Tribe against Tribe and Hunter against Hunter. Only *Cho Koran Garun* can heal the wounds of ages and save Garun's Blood from the Nothing. Where is our Savior? His trial has passed but His war continues. Where is our Destroyer? His heart is cold and His soul dying. Garun's chosen stands on the precipice; only the scorpion's sting can save Him. And His fate shall be the Blood's."

Yarchik raised a trembling hand to brush the moisture from his cheek. "Burn the bodies," he ordered, "and send a Hunter to their tribe. Sohrta, you must warn the Elves that the Drekka are moving south and may cross the river. Ask Nebari if the Empire will join us once again in fighting our common enemy."

Sohrta bowed his head. "I will leave before sunrise." He disappeared into the night.

"Take me back," Yarchik ordered. As the bearers lifted him, he sighed. *Dahr, where are you?*

* * * * * * * * * * * * * * * * * * *

"You made this?" Jeran asked, turning the locket over in his hands. He opened it, and a blue glow emanated from the stone inside.

"Yes, Lord Odara," the boy said nervously, and Yassik patted his shoulder reassuringly.

Smiling, Jeran closed the locket and handed it back to the apprentice. "That's a rare talent you have." The boy smiled. "Would you like to work with Master Albion? He knows more about working magic into objects than any Mage alive."

The boy nodded eagerly, but Yassik frowned. "Are you sure that's wise?"

"Do we have a choice?" Jeran replied. "Can you teach him what he needs to learn?"

"But Albion is—"

"Under constant supervision. I have given him a chance, more because I need him than because I want him, but I won't promise him freedom and treat him like a slave. Albion still needs to earn my trust, but I refuse to condemn him for the crimes others committed. Supervise their sessions if you want, but unless you have a better idea, I suggest we let Albion train anyone with this talent."

After a moment, Yassik nodded. He turned the boy toward the door and started to leave. "A moment, Yassik?" Jeran called, and the Mage sent the boy on ahead. "How many of the apprentices have left Atol Domiar?"

"Oto has spirited away all those too young to choose for themselves, and most of the older apprentices are not content to sit in the shadows while the world is destroyed around them. They haven't had centuries to forget about their homes and families. Almost all the apprentices have joined you, several hundred at least, maybe closer to a thousand. A few stragglers trickle in every couple days."

"Their training must continue," Jeran announced. "It must be hastened. Albion's working on something that might help, but in the meantime, the apprentices need to resume their practice. I want you, Oto, and Alwen to oversee the construction of an Academy here in Dranakohr."

"Jeran, I know what you're thinking, but it'll take seasons to prepare those—"

"I don't have seasons, Yassik, and neither do they! Lorthas sees any Gifted who don't share his views as tainted by the Assembly. He won't wait until the children are trained before making them a target."

Yassik snorted. "You make it sound as if you're doing this for their benefit."

"You want the truth? Fine! Without the Assembly behind us, we need a weapon to balance the power of the ShadowMagi. Those children are that weapon. Train them. Train them however you feel best, but do it. And quickly, Yassik. It may already be too late."

* * * * * * * * * * * * * * * * * * * *

Martyn stood atop the tower, his arm wrapped firmly around Miriam's shoulders. Winter was coming, but the long days of Harvest were still upon them and the sun bathed Kaper with its golden light. The prince smiled. For the first time in a long while, he felt content.

"I think we should marry in the spring," Martyn announced. "It will be a short betrothal, but under the circumstances, I feel we might be waiting too long." Miriam turned to look at him, and something in her gaze took his breath away.

"Spring is acceptable," she said coldly, but Martyn knew her arrogance was affected. This time. "It will give your friends in the north a chance to finish their business and return for the ceremony. I... What's that?"

Martyn followed the princess' finger northwest. A dark, oily cloud rose to obscure the evening sky, and as they watched, the shadow drew closer.

"I must find my father," Martyn said, and he left Miriam alone on the tower. The guards inside moved to follow him, but he ordered them to watch the princess as he ran through the castle.

The King was in his council chamber with Commander Bystral and a Guardsman Martyn did not recognize. Mika stood behind the King's chair; since

Martyn's return, the boy had been bound to the King as tightly as to his own shadow. "Martyn, I was just about to—"

"There's an army approaching."

"You know?" The King rounded on the Guardsman. "You said you spoke to no one!"

"I did not, my Liege! I haven't said a word since leaving Aurach!"

Mathis waved his hand dismissively. "No matter. Tachan loyalists have thrown Rachannon into civil war, and when Joam and King Tarien shifted their troops to protect Aurach, Ryan Durange launched his attack. Our forces are pinned along the River Selange, and the Tachans have overrun the border. It will take some time to—"

"Father," Martyn interrupted. "The army I saw was to the west, and it's on the horizon."

Bystral's chair screeched across the floor, and the Guardsman stood. Silence reigned throughout the chamber. "Gods," King Mathis whispered. Then, in a stronger voice, he said, "Rally the guard, Commander. Prepare the city for a siege."

* * * * * * * * * * * * * * * * * * * *

"We need better maps," Jeran said to the small group of men and Orog gathered around his desk. Frustration and fatigue wore at his composure; it was an effort not to shout. Katya stood like a statue behind him, glaring at anyone who dared protest. "Tylor cared little about the tunnels, but maybe we can find a use for them."

Jeran turned to each person in turn. "Iyrene, what about food? Our stores won't last until midwinter. We need more supplies. Use the Magi if you must. Junden, I don't care if they're collared, I want the ShadowMagi under constant Orog guard. Your people put the fear of the Gods into them. Ehvan—"

"Lord Odara," a voice called from the doorway. "He's here. Just like you said."

Jeran frowned, but he stood, smoothed his clothes, and belted on his sword. "You know what needs to be done. We'll meet again in three days." He left without another word, and when Katya tried to follow he waved her back. Once outside, he did his best not to run.

He found Lorthas sitting in his usual place by the fire, sipping a glass of wine. "Jeran, Jeran, Jeran," the Darklord said, a slight grin on his face. "You stole my castle."

"You're no longer welcome here," Jeran said. The Boundary cut across the room, pulsing with energy, and Jeran seized magic to prevent his Gift from running wild. He wiped all expression from his face and drew upon his training, hoping he appeared more controlled than he felt. Lorthas radiated confidence and assurance, qualities Jeran had hoped to find lacking in the Darklord at this meeting.

"And after all the hospitality I showed you," Lorthas replied, shaking his head sadly. "I won't stay long. I just wanted to thank you for killing Tylor. Putting him in command of Dranakohr was a bad decision, and I'm deeply saddened by the steps he took in my name. It's my own fault, really. I try to use the tools the

Gods give me as best I can, but I often lack the resolve needed to dispose of a man who has done *me* no wrong."

"You may be glad to see Tylor dead," Jeran said, "but not because of the things he did. You wanted him dead because he defied you. He killed without waiting for your blessing."

"You presume a great deal," Lorthas sneered, his hand tightening on the arm of his chair. "I neither relish the deaths of the innocent nor condone them. I don't want to destroy Madryn, nor do I want to rule it. I just want to be a part of it again. I want to be free! I want a world where peace presides over war, where all the Gods' creations stand equal. I want the Gifted to walk without fear of prejudice or death. I want the commons to know that no Mage will harm them without facing justice. I want the Four Races to stand side by side, working together as they did in the old days, without ideological or political differences pulling them apart. I want to erase the borders that have divided our land.

"The Gods charged the Gifted with the duty of guiding and protecting the peoples of Madryn. The Assembly has forgotten that duty. I have not." Lorthas stood, and he closed the distance between them, stopping only when blue sparks jumped from the Boundary, arcing through the air. "It's not too late, Jeran. Together, we can end the bloodshed. Together, we can forge the perfect world."

"You can't make people to believe what you want them to. You can't create a mold and force the world through it. Aemon says—"

"Aemon and I want the same things!" Lorthas yelled, storming away from the Boundary. "We have always wanted the same things. I'm just willing to acknowledge that not everyone wants what we want, and that sometimes a few innocents must suffer for the greater good."

"Leave," Jeran said, and at his signal, two Orog stepped from the shadows and leveled crossbows at the Darklord's chest. Part of Jeran wanted to give the order to fire while Lorthas was defenseless; part of him knew he could not do it. "If you return, it had better be to surrender."

The bolts aimed at his heart had no effect on Lorthas. "I'll leave. But remember this, my young friend: You could have ended the war today, one way or the other. I was willing to talk; you refused to listen. I, the bane of the Magi, the terror of Madryn, stood defenseless before you, deprived of my Gift"—he spread his arms wide—"but you lacked the resolve to murder me. What happens next hangs on your conscience."

Walking backward, Lorthas disappeared into a shadowy tunnel hidden beside the hearth. The last thing Jeran saw was his blood red eyes staring out from the darkness. "This is not over, Jeran. One day, the Boundary will come down. Then, you and I will have a chance to talk face to face."

Author's Note

First of all, I'd like to thank everyone reading my books, with a special thanks to anyone who took the time to read this little note tucked away at the back of *Jewel of Truth*. As a reader myself, I know how frustrating it can be waiting for an author to put out the next installment in a series, and your patience has been appreciated.

Now that I've spent a few years on the other side of the book, I'm a bit more sympathetic to the plight of the author. Of all the writers I've met these last few years, only three wrote full time. The rest of us have to balance our writing on top of a regular job and all the rest of life's little distractions. For my part, I promise to keep writing as fast as my schedule allows, and all I ask of you in return is that you continue to read what I write, and that you help me in my quest to support quality speculative fiction and the people who create it wherever you may find them.

As many of you may already know, this past year was a tough one on both Tyrannosaurus Press and myself. Both of us were located in New Orleans prior to Hurricane Katrina and the storm did quite a bit of damage to my home and to T-Press' inventory. For a while it was unclear whether the publishing house would survive the storm at all, and I was worried that I'd never get the chance to finish the Boundary's Fall series.

With the support of family and a vast number of friends and acquaintances who donated their time, abilities and effort, I am happy to say that Tyrannosaurus Press was able to release both *Jewel of Truth* and its short fiction anthology, *Beacons of Tomorrow*, with only the slightest of delays. And with the outpouring of concern from readers like you regarding not only the well-being of me and my family but also the fate of Jeran, Dahr, and Prince Martyn, my faith in this endeavor has been greatly restored.

Again, thank you all for your support, and rest assured that I am already hard at work on *Forge of Faith*, the penultimate volume of the Boundary's Fall series. I hope my work continues to please.

— Bret Funk
Bret_Funk@TyrannosaurusPress.com

Dear Patron: You are invited to make a brief comment or two, signed or unsigned, after reading this novel. Your comments may help other readers in their book selection. (Positive as well as negative comments are requested.) Thank you.

Easter